By Bryan McLachlan

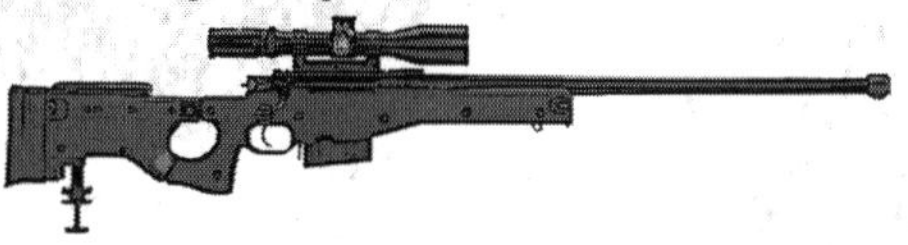

ISBN: 1463726910
ISBN-13: 9781463726911

THE BEAR HUNTER

By Bryan McLachlan

PROLOGUE

Outside Kandahar, Afghanistan, Friday, September 13, 1985

Though the night was relatively quiet from the usual small arms fire, the occasional crack of mortar and artillery rounds being hurled and exploding into some poor bastard's hide site acutely reminded Captain Marcus A. Kaderri, United States Army Special Forces, that he was in the midst of a shooting war. Kaderri glanced at the green luminous dots on his watch. The morning's mission was to begin at 0500 hours, exactly in one hour and twenty-two minutes. He pulled at his four week old beard then wiped a strong, calloused hand over his rugged face. He tossed the heavy Afghan blanket aside, rose from the unforgiving rocky ground ten feet in from the mouth of the cave and stretched his lean muscular six foot, one hundred seventy pound frame.

He pulled the black knit cap off his head, scratched his short brown hair and quietly stepped to the cave opening. During daylight hours when he was visible to Russian and loyal Afghan forces, he wore the traditional pakol hat. Kaderri's steel gray eyes easily adjusted to the darkness and it took a few moments to spot the two teams of AK-47 armed Afghan mujahadeen sentries thirty meters down the slope. Dispersed in the caves and surrounding terrain were the eleven members of his Special Forces Operational Detachment-Alpha 524, commonly known as an A-Team.

"Have a good sleep, Boss?" Staff Sergeant Leonard Puckett appeared at Kaderri's side with a steaming canteen cup of coffee held in an outstretched hand. Deeper in the cave, Puckett manned the radios for any incoming traffic and had a can of Sterno lit to boil water.

Kaderri put the cap back on his head and eyed the outline of the young sergeant and grasped the warm cup. "I haven't had a good night's sleep since I stepped foot in this country eight months ago and I lost at least fifteen pounds. I'd kill for a patch of grass to sleep on instead of this rocky crap." He scraped his foot along the ground, sending stones and pebbles tumbling down the slope. "But considering, yeah, I slept well. Thank you," he said then raised the aluminum cup to his lips. The instant coffee, with powdered cream and sugar, immediately warmed his insides against the cold mountain air.

"You're welcome, sir."

"Anything come in last night?" Kaderri asked the team's junior radio operator after taking another swallow.

"No, nothing." Puckett answered.

Kaderri nodded in the darkness, pursed his lips and breathed a sigh of relief. He had hoped for what exactly Puckett had told him. After all the time and effort that was put into planning the mission, he feared the commanders higher up might get cold feet and pull the plug. His mission was still a go. With tempered excitement, he tapped Puckett on the back and ordered, "Have Master Sergeant Ireland get everyone over here."

A flash of white appeared on Puckett's face between the ever thickening facial hair, giving away a toothy smile. "Right, Boss!"

Ten minutes later, Kaderri, along with his A-Team and the four Mujahadeen commanders, gathered around the battery operated light in the cave for the morning briefing. The Green Berets dressed in the Afghan wool payraan tumbaan shirts and pants and some also wore the wool chakman coat for added warmth. From a distance, it was impossible to tell the Americans apart from their Afghan allies. Even though he could speak fairly well in Pashto and Dari, the two official languages of Afghanistan, Kaderri was grateful the Afghan commanders spoke better English because the dialect these tribesman were using in Pashto was different than the one he learned in the US Army's language school at Presidio of Monterey. Kaderri looked at each of the gathered men in the eye before he spoke. "Ok, gentlemen, we're still a go," he stated in a business tone as he shifted the falling blanket over his shoulders.

His comment was answered with broad smiles from the Afghans and curt nods from some of the Americans. This was an important mission and as far as the team knew, it was one of the most important missions the small teams of American special operations forces had since the Soviets invaded this barren wasteland of a country in 1979.

Kaderri's team, along with the other special ops teams in country, were there primarily to gain intelligence on the Soviet military machine. Specifically how well the soldiers would fight, how well their equipment worked and how well they would hold up in sustained combat operations. The A-Teams were also there to provide training, logistics and weapons to the Afghan rebels, the Mujahadeen and to be a pain in the ass for the Soviet invaders. On frequent occasions, the special ops forces would lead and engage in violent ambushes and knock down fights along side the Mujahadeen against the Soviet and loyal Afghan forces.

Their last engagement was a good example of one of those occasional skirmishes. Kaderri, with five of his men and fifteen Afghans, tangled with and wiped out a thirty man Soviet infantry unit in a spectacular ambush that was pure textbook. The victory came at a high price, though. Four Afghans were killed and four wounded.

The new mission was psychological as well as tactical. If all went well, it was hoped it would hasten the erosion of the morale of the Soviet Army and the support of the people in the USSR. It may even cause some political unrest among the Politburo.

"Ah, Captain!" Mohammad "Mike" Karmal, the Afghan commander of the resistance fighters Kaderri and his team attached themselves to, called out as he clapped his hands together when he entered the cave. His weathered face beamed with anticipation. "It's going to be a good day!"

"Salam," Kaderri greeted in Pashto. He looked approvingly over Karmal's shoulder and studied a small group of his men sitting on the stepped rock ledges that were used as seats inside the wide part of the tunnel dubbed the 'sitting room'. They were cradling their mixed assortment of stolen and captured Soviet weaponry. The band of fierce, disciplined fighters were armed with RPG-7 and -16 anti-tank weapons, AK-47 automatic rifles, RPK-74 light machine guns, Makarov pistols and American supplied Stinger anti-aircraft missiles. Kaderri and his men carried brand new AKS-74's that they brought in with them when they infiltrated the country, along with other specialized weapons and equipment.

Karmal turned. "You see, Captain, this morning my men outside have learned well. They are hiding just like you taught them."

Prior to the briefing, Kaderri studied the surrounding area as he had done every morning, trying to pick out any irregularities in the landscape that would betray the outline of a man. He admitted to himself that he had a tough time locating the fighters. "Well done, Mike. Where are the rest?" he asked. Occasionally, men would disappear, either by capture or desertion.

"Sleeping in the cave," Karmal answered with a sweep of his hand.

Mohammad "Mike" Karmal was born on the outskirts of Kabul, Afghanistan, and graduated from Penn State University with a bachelors degree in political science and a law degree from Harvard. When he came to America to pursue his education, his curiosity in the social aspects of the American college scene got the better of him and he attended his first fraternity party. Greeted at the door of the frat house during pledge week, one of the drunk brothers had difficulty pronouncing Mohammad, so the brother decided his name was "Mike." Since that moment, Mohammad Karmal has gone by the name of Mike, at least when it came to dealing with Americans. When the Soviets invaded his country, his love of country and the prospect of continued living under an iron fist propelled him to take up arms in resistance.

"Once again, Mike," Kaderri asked Karmal, "your people are sure Borushko is going to be in the convoy?"

"Yes," Karmal nodded swiftly, almost shaking the pakol off his head. "My sources said they can guarantee that Major General Vasily Ivanovich Borushko will be there. He is making the 'milk run' to Qalat to prove that the war is going well for the godless Soviet Army." He spat his disgust and then began waving his arms in excitement. "A television crew will even be along to film their propaganda!"

Kaderri couldn't help but smile. Eliminating the commanding general of the Soviet 65th Motorized Infantry Division would put a damper on the Soviet propaganda and the citizens support for their fighting units in Afghanistan. The death of a general may also wreck the morale of the front line Soviet troops. That was an affect the higher ups were hoping for if he pulled this off. There was one major element of concern for this op. "Any changes in who's guarding the convoy, Mike?"

Karmal's face beamed like a spotlight in the night. "It's still Kabul's own Twelfth Infantry!"

Kaderri raised his eyebrows at that fortunate stroke of luck. *Holy shit! Could this still be true?* The commanding general of a Soviet infantry division was being protected by the worst unit in Afghanistan! Clearly that wasn't a military decision, Kaderri thought, but a political one. Kaderri shook his head and wondered how Borushko felt about being left on a broken limb that was dangling over a cliff. Support in Russia must be extremely low to put a general's head on the chopping block. Karmal's information confirmed that this was purely a propaganda move to show the legitimacy of the puppet Afghan government and military and let the world see they were capable of protecting a high profile target.

And the world was going to see the Soviets fail.

There was no way, Kaderri thought, a Soviet general was going to allow himself to be protected by one of the most inept infantry divisions on the face of the earth. Somewhere, he knew, lurking in the background like a hungry lion would be elements of a Soviet motorized rifle brigade with all their firepower, waiting to pounce and destroy anyone who attempted to take out the division commander.

No matter. Captain Marcus A. Kaderri had prepared this mission as if he and his small, combined team of Americans and Afghanis were going up against a larger, well trained force.

Kandahar Airport, Kandahar, Afghanistan, Friday, September 13, 1985

The scowl had been imbedded on Major General Vasily Ivanovich Borushko's pocked leathery face since he received orders from the Politburo two weeks ago to put himself on display on the weekly convoy headed to Qalat to deliver the scheduled supplies and rations. In his mind, he was being ordered to commit suicide for the good of the Soviet Union! Hell, they would probably make him Hero of the Soviet Union, a nice honorable designation to go on his headstone! Fat chance he was going to allow that to happen.

At the moment, the airport was the only piece of real estate in a thousand square kilometers that the Soviets owned and controlled. The city of Kandahar itself was in enemy hands, as was a majority of the countryside. Despite blowing the city to bits with superior fire power, the stubborn rebel inhabitants refused to surrender and continually harassed and killed Soviet soldiers on a regular basis. Instead of beating their heads against the wall in fighting a war they were not prepared for, the Soviets abandoned the thought of capturing and occupying the city and settled on controlling the airport, in effect managing through air power most of the traffic that came in and out of the city. It was an ancient siege warfare method of starving the inhabitants out and then pound the shit out of them at a later date when they would be weaker and without the strength to fight back.

Tuned out of the staff's morning routine activity in the large, bullet ridden metal aircraft hangar that doubled as the command post, Borushko rose from the dented metal folding chair holding the cup of scalding coffee and strode through a thick cloud of cigarette smoke over to the easel mounted map of the airport and surrounding countryside. Folded thick, hairy arms across a barrel chest that stretched his camouflaged uniform, Borushko studied the mountainous terrain, looking for the spot on the convoy route that was the most likely site for an ambush, and his potential death.

"Comrade General?"

Borushko immediately recognized the deep voice of Colonel Ivan Voloshin, commander of the 34th Motorized Rifle Brigade, one of the four brigades attached to the 65th. "Yes, Colonel?" he responded without taking his eyes off the map.

"Sir, Tiger Flight just checked in."

Tiger Flight was two heavily armed Mi-24 attack helicopters assigned to sweep the convoy's route to spot and, if possible, clear any enemy forces from the area. Those two helicopters were also tasked with shadowing the vehicle that Borushko would be traveling on, acting as a personal escort and bodyguard. He finally turned and bore down on the colonel. "What do they have to report?" he asked unpleasantly.

Voloshin gave a weak smile. "They have spotted nothing, General."

Borushko nodded once and allowed himself a faint sliver of hope, but that quickly faded. He sent out Spetsnaz units to patrol the most likely ambush spots, and if the helicopter pilots couldn't spot groups of twenty men on a mountainside with infrared sensors, that meant either the pilots were blithering idiots or the few Spetsnaz teams and small infantry units weren't in place. Maybe the teams were in fact in place, but were so well hidden the sensors couldn't identify them? He shook his head dejectedly. The most likely answer was the infrared sensors on the helos weren't working again.

"Suicide, Ivan!" He slammed a balled fist into an open palm. "This is nothing but suicide!"

"Sir?" Voloshin was caught off guard.

Borushko drained the bitter coffee and dropped the tin cup on the table with a loud clang. Drops of the brown liquid splashed out. "This mission they are sending me on." He could feel the anger well up inside and suddenly he knew he could no longer keep it contained. "I lost a lot of good men fighting these rebels and securing the airfield," he thrust his finger toward a dirty window and the city beyond and clenched his teeth as he continued to seethe. "And the thanks I get from those fools in Moscow is to go out on that convoy and commit suicide!"

Voloshin involuntarily took a step back and glanced around at the now silent staff, searching for the political officer who would immediately report the outburst to the Kremlin. "But-"

Borushko cut off the colonel. "Make sure your brigade is ready, Colonel," he hissed through clenched teeth. "I don't trust our Afghan allies from the Twelfth. I would bet on them turning over our operations plan to the rebels."

"Yes, Comrade General."

Ambush site, highway AO1, twelve miles northeast of Kandahar, Afghanistan

As the sun's predawn orange and purple light grew on the horizon, the reaction force of combined American Special Forces A-Team and twenty Mujahadeen Afghan fighters had been settled for the past couple of hours next to their hide sites just a few hundred meters away from the ambush site. The unit was only to be used in case Kaderri ran into trouble and he needed assistance in exfiltrating from the area. If they had to be called in, that would mean the mission went into the shitter.

At the moment, they were out of hiding and listening to Captain Kaderri give the final briefing. Amid scrub brush and tall green grass, Kaderri kneeled near the edge of ridge on the rocky soil next to a boulder half his size. One hundred fifty meters down from the crest of the ridge, the AO1 road that lead from Kandahar Airport wound its way like a brown serpent through the rugged mountains, coiled around large and small rock croppings and gnarled trees, and littered on its back were wrecked and burned out hulks of Soviet BMP-1 infantry fighting vehicles. He pointed to the bend in the road seven hundred meters away from their position and addressed his men for the second and final time. "As we scouted earlier, when Borushko's vehicle comes out of that turn, that is when I will fire." Kaderri repeated his instructions in Dari.

"Captain," Mike Karmal smiled, "if you need help in this important mission, my men will be ready to assist you! We want to kill as many of the godless communists as we can and get them out of our country!"

Kaderri nodded but doubted Karmal's men would be needed in this mission. This wasn't a straight ambush where destroying as many of the enemy as possible with overwhelming firepower was the objective. This ambush would be one man pulling the trigger one time seven hundred meters from another man in a moving vehicle. It would be a mission that would take all of his sniper training and concentration to successfully pull off the shot.

Kaderri hefted the tailor made M-14 rifle with a 10X Leupold scope and twenty round magazine and read the hands on his watch. Standing next to him was his spotter,

Sergeant First Class Robert Wolff. Both men had shed the Afghan payraan tumbaan long shirt and chifrali chugha coat for American military Battle Dress Uniforms and state-of-the-art Ghillie suits. The torn strips of burlap and camouflaged netting secured to an old flight suit that comprised their Ghillie suit would break up the outline of their human shape. It was virtually impossible to spot a man in the field when he was wearing one. "Ok, Bob, we've got two hours until the convoy arrives. Let's get into position."

"Right, Boss."

"Gentlemen, let's get this show on the road." To the Mujahadeen he said, "Bazmi binim," see you soon.

The men dispersed, melting back into the countryside to await their prey.

Kandahar Airport, Kandahar, Afghanistan

The uneasy feeling that had wrapped itself around Major General Vasily Borushko since he received orders for his new mission had grown stronger the closer he got to the time of departure. For one last item, he sat down at his battered desk and wrote a final letter to his wife professing his love for her and their seventeen year old son, Mikhail. Taking the time to fold the paper neatly, he put it in an envelope, sealed it and left it with his aide to deliver it in the event he did not return.

Outside the hangar with his hands on his hips, he surveyed the final loading of material on the trucks under a red rising sun. All seemed to be going as scheduled.

"Comrade General!" came a shout from behind.

Borushko's blood pressure skyrocketed when he heard the nasally voice of the idiot charged with filming his suicide and the destruction of the convoy. "What is it now, Boris?" he grunted while turning to stare down the man.

"Comrade, your men have mounted the lights on the truck for me and my crew to film you. I will make you look like a movie star!"

A dead one, was the first thought that came to mind. "Very good, Boris. Now get out of my way," he barked. "We are leaving in ten minutes."

Ambush site, Kandahar Province, Afghanistan

The roar of a Soviet Su-27 splitting the air gave Captain Marcus Kaderri a bit of a worry. He stole a glance through some dangling strips of burlap on his Ghillie suit and watched the deadly fighter bank to the north and fly away. Just as soon as the jet engine sounds faded away, it was replaced by a more ominous and threatening one. The slapping sound of helicopter blades bouncing off the mountains at low level signaled the approaching convoy. Nimble and deadly low level attack helicopters were something Kaderri didn't want to deal with but had a nasty surprise planned if necessary.

His eyes begun their methodical search, looking for movement against the mountain background. There! He spotted a menacing pair of Hind-D attack helicopters as they rounded a mountain and straddled the road. They were swaying back and forth like annoying insects but these ones carried a nasty, deadly sting.

"Convoy," Wolff stated quietly from his prone position next to Kaderri. He had the spotting scope up to his eye and the radio handset in his hand alerting the rest of the hidden team.

"Right." Kaderri turned his attention away from the helicopters and fixed his sight on the line of vehicles kicking up a light cloud of dust from the dirt road. A squadron of BMP-1 armored personnel carriers led the column, their low turret mounted 73mm cannons dared anyone to test their firepower and accuracy. Kaderri noticed the first BMP was equipped with a mine plow, slowly clearing the way for the rest of the column against any anti-tank mines planted in the dirt. Kaderri concentrated on the commander sitting high in the hatch and confirmed his suspicions: Soviets. Following the BMP's were three, eight wheeled BTR-60PB's, most likely filled to capacity with heavily armed infantry. After them were the trucks filled with supplies and the Afghan troops of the Twelfth Infantry Division.

"This could take awhile, Boss," quipped Wolff.

Kaderri chuckled as he fit the sniper rifle into his shoulder. He rested his cheek against the wooden stock and followed the vehicles through the scope. "I think the general is a little worried about being ambushed," Kaderri said while he watched the steady parade of armored vehicles. "Jesus, he has a lot of firepower."

"I would be too if my ass was hung out to get shot off."

Ten vehicles had gone past when the sight through Kaderri's scope changed dramatically. A dented white pick-up truck with a pair of spotlights and a television crew focused their attention on the BTR behind them. High in the hatch was the commander, a large man standing tall and proud.

And exposed.

Wolff let out muffled laugh. "They couldn't make it any easier for you, Boss." He went silent and concentrated on peering through the spotting scope. "Target identified. That's him," he confirmed in an ice cold tone. "That's Borushko."

"Confirmed." Kaderri immediately responded and put the cross hairs on Borushko's chest. A head shot at this distance and on a moving and bouncing vehicle would be just about impossible to make. For the third time, he reached out and felt the bipod, making sure the arms were locked. As he peered through the scope, Kaderri made some adjustments to the scope for elevation and wind.

Despite the fact that he was going for a body shot, Kaderri, like all snipers, noticed the man's eyes. Borushko's were bright and shiny and full of life. At the same time they were intense and dangerous. Like the professional he was, Kaderri put any thoughts aside that he was going to target and kill another human being.

"One hundred meters," Wolff called out the distance to where the shot was supposed to take place.

The adrenaline immediately coursed through Kaderri's veins and he took shallow breaths to calm his movements and heart rate. With a flick of his thumb he released the safety and moved his finger onto the trigger. Ignoring Borushko's eyes, Kaderri concentrated on keeping the crosshairs on the center of his chest. He followed every roll and pitch of the pick-up truck in front of Borushko's armored vehicle as well as Borushko himself as he stood in the commanders hatch of the personnel carrier.

"Fifty meters."

Then the pitch and roll of the pick-up ceased as they rode across a level piece of hard packed dirt. Kaderri timed his breaths and heartbeats. He regulated his breathing, took a breath, let it half way out and waited for the next heartbeat. The instant his heart was between beats, he squeezed the trigger.

"Enough!" Borushko spat out the airborne dust that collected in his mouth and shouted the order over the roar of the engine with an impatient wave of his hand to the film crew in front of him. "Shut those lights off!" He was willing to go along with being filmed for the propaganda, but placing spot lights on him was tantamount to hanging a target on his chest.

"But Comrade!" Boris cupped his hands around his mouth and shouted back in protest from the rear of the pick-up truck.

Borushko would not hear it. "No! You-"

A single hammer blow slammed into Borushko's chest, sucking the air out of his lungs and ending the litany of harsh words that was being directed at Boris. He had just enough time to see the front of his shirt turn red before the world went black and he dropped through the hatch and fell dead on the armored floor.

The report of the gunshot began to fade away. "That's a kill," Wolff declared unemotionally, professionally, as he observed through the spotting scope.

Kaderri made a perceptible nod as he watched the single round penetrate the Soviet general's chest. After the target fell, Kaderri took his finger off the trigger and engaged the safety. There was no need for a second shot. "Ok, Bob, let's get out of here," he said and turned his attention to escape and evasion. "Keep an eye on the sky for those fucking helos and fast movers."

"Roger that." Wolff got on the radio and alerted the rest of unit. "This is Sierra Two, We're coming in." Both men rose from their prone positions.

Suddenly from below there was a shout and then all hell broke loose with the ripple of heavy AK rounds being fired. Bullets suddenly whizzed past Kaderri's and Wolff's heads. Fountains of dirt kicked up as the bullets slammed into the ground inches from their limbs. More bullets chipped off rock splinters near their heads.

"Holy, shit!" Kaderri yelled and dove behind the rocks as another wave of bullets moved closer to their mark. "Where the fuck did they come from?"

"Who are they?" Wolff asked as he peered around the rocks and emptied the entire thirty round magazine from his own AK, causing the enemy to dive for cover.

Kaderri took advantage of Wolff's action to do a quick search. One hundred meters below he spotted the enemy, slowly emerging from their hide sites behind rocks and scrub brush. Kaderri realized General Borushko had the right mind to set up a reaction force at the likely ambush spot. Kaderri brought the sniper rifle up to his shoulder, disengaged the safety and placed the crosshairs on the head of a kneeling camouflaged soldier and squeezed the trigger. The rifle kicked against his shoulder. The large 7.62mm bullet pierced the bridge of the soldiers nose, blowing out the back of his head and caused his lifeless body to tumble backwards and roll downhill. He quickly acquired another target and pulled the trigger.

A furious hail of bullets responded.

Kaderri pulled his head behind the rock like a turtle pulling its head into its shell just as the rounds impacted all around. As he tried to make himself smaller than the boulder, the gravel underneath him gave way. Quickly he began to slide down the hill. He dug his feet and hands in the dirt, desperately trying to stop his momentum from carrying him past the cover of the boulder. Frantically he clawed at the dirt and was able to stop, but not before exposing his legs.

Just as he was scurrying to get back behind the boulder another volley of fire came his way. A round tore through his Ghillie suit near his hip and another slammed into his knee cap. "Ahhh!" he screamed and took the white hot pain, pulling himself back into cover. He looked down to find the material on his pant leg turning red with blood. Clenching his jaw to absorb the pain, he pulled his legs behind the rock. Not out of the fight, he turned around, brought the rifle up and sighted it on the chest of an advancing enemy soldier. One more shot and kill.

Wolff let go another ten shot salvo, dropping one more enemy soldier. Instead of seeking cover, this time the enemy kept on advancing towards their position and firing while another group would lay down covering fire. These men were well trained. "We're in deep shit, Boss. These guys aren't Afghan infantry."

"Russians!" He stated and fired again. "They must have set in last night!" Without a further thought, he gave the order. "Call for help!"

"Just fucking great!" Wolff thumbed the button on the handset. "This is Sierra Two! Mayday! Mayday!"

The return fire picked up in tempo as the Soviets moved closer, coordinating their fire as they advanced uphill to within fifty meters. Kaderri put the cross hairs on another soldier when a volley of bullets nearly found their mark. *Crack!* A round whizzed past his ear, but the next two rounds tore the rifle from his hands. He rolled for cover and reached for his holstered sidearm. More bullets slammed into the ground, sending stinging fountains of rock and dirt into his face and eyes. "I can't see!" he yelled to Wolff and scratched at the debris in his eyes. His hands fumbled to get the canteen off his web belt.

"Hang on!" Wolff called out and emptied another magazine at the advancing enemy.

All of a sudden from behind them, a scream reminiscent of a rebel yell followed by a roar of automatic weapons filled the air. The reaction force of Kaderri's team and Mike Karmal's fighters rushed down the hill and engaged the attacking Soviets.

"Boss is down! Boss is down!" Wolff shouted, loaded another magazine and fired to keep the enemy at bay.

"Boss! Where are you hit?" The medic, Sergeant First Class Jesse Hughes asked calmly as his hands ran over Kaderri's body, searching for anything out of the ordinary.

Kaderri was curled on his side, pouring water over his eyes and his hands furiously tried to clear away the dirt. "Can't see, got dirt in my eyes," he answered with a grimace. "I also took a round to my knee." He winced as a stab of pain shot up his leg and the blood continued to stream down his calf and pool in his boot.

Hughes grabbed the canteen out of Kaderri's hand and flushed the eyes. "Take this," Hughes ordered Sergeant First Class Len Puckett. "Hold open his eyes and pour it in."

"Right," Puckett responded and did as instructed.

"Let me see your knee," Hughes said above the deafening gunfire and cut away the bloodied pant leg.

Kaderri forced a few blinks and shook his head to clear the water and dirt. When he was able to open his eyes on his own, he ordered. "Stop, I can see," he told Puckett.

"Sure, Boss?" Puckett asked, looking into Kaderri's eyes.

"Yeah, thanks." He wiped the water off his cheeks with his hand and when he pulled it away, it was smeared with blood.

"You have a small cut on your cheek. It doesn't look too bad," Puckett reassured him. "Shit!" He spied a enemy soldier sneaking up, grabbed the AK and fired a burst. "Ok, we're good." He announced then reached into Hughes' first aid kit, tore open a gauze pad and placed it on the cut to stem the flow of blood.

Kaderri propped himself up on his elbows to see the damage to his knee. "Leave it, get back into this fight." There were still enemy out there.

"Right." Puckett dropped the gauze pad, leaned around the boulder and resumed firing.

Kaderri was about to issue new orders when the dreaded sound of helicopter blades coming up the valley signaled the arrival of the grim reaper. All eyes turned towards the direction of where the sound was coming from.

"Shit!" Hughes cursed and grabbed Kaderri under the shoulders and began to lift. "Think you can walk?"

"Get me up and I can run." He at least thought he could. Effortlessly, Kaderri was hauled up and cringed as the pain shot through his body. Suddenly, Kaderri wasn't so sure about his mobility. He took a trial step and collapsed behind the boulder.

"Stay down!" Hughes ordered and removed a splint from the bag. In matter of seconds, he had it secured to Kaderri's leg. "That should help."

Kaderri reached out and picked up the damaged sniper rifle to use as a crutch. On his second try to stand he had success. "What's going on?" he asked once the pain became tolerable and looked down the slope at the suddenly dwindling battle. The Soviet force was being eliminated.

Less than six minutes had passed since the general was hit by Kaderri's shot. "We gotta to get out of here. Those goddamn helos will cut us to ribbons," Kaderri stated what everybody already knew. He took his binoculars off his web gear and held them to his eyes, focusing on the activity on the road. The Afghan soldiers from the convoy had finished dismounting from the trucks and the armored fighting vehicles were slewing their menacing turrets in their direction. "We gotta fucking move, now!"

Silence momentarily enshrouded the battlefield, giving way to the ominous phrase 'the calm before the storm.' Kaderri's unit was hurriedly regrouping to get the hell out of the area before the Soviet and Afghan onslaught was upon them. The approaching attack helicopters grew louder and an Afghan shouted and pointed at their position in the sky. Everyone's head turned just as the big armored Hind's flew past, circled slowly in search of their target, and slowed to a hover.

"Down!"

"Cover!"

The men scattered in all directions, attempting to evade the impending attack.

The rippling salvo of the 57mm rockets leaving their under wing tubes split the air. The helos disappeared in a cloud of smoke as the rockets motors ignited. With a roaring *whoosh*, the deadly fingers reached out for the scattering men and exploded with teeth rattling force, slamming nearly everyone into the ground. Geysers of dirt, rock and smoke sailed high into the air, creating a wall of dust while the hot, razor sharp shrapnel sliced through the air and soft flesh.

Just as the sound of the exploding rockets dissipated, the chatter of the Hind's 23mm cannons signaled the big choppers were coming in for a strafing run.

"Cover!" someone yelled, causing the men still alive to find better protection behind a rock or into a shallow crater caused by the exploding rockets.

The cannon shells tore through the freshly churned dirt, sending up more chunks of earth and stone.

A few brave men returned fire with the AK's, doing no damage but revealed their positions.

With their strafing runs ended, the Hind pilots gunned their engines as they banked away to come in again from another direction.

It was on the turn they exposed their hot engines.

From hidden locations higher up on the mountain, about a hundred meters above the ambush site, four men armed with Stinger anti-aircraft missiles crouched like stalking lions on the hunt waiting to spring on their prey. A group of Karmal's men and a Green Beret were waiting for such an opportunity and sprang the anti-aircraft ambush.

"Fire when ready!" Staff Sergeant Steven Caron, the leader of the group ordered. Tracking the exhaust through the sites on the Stinger anti-aircraft missiles that Kaderri's team had supplied, the Mujahadeen waited until they heard the tone that the missile had locked on the target. Almost simultaneously they launched their deadly shoulder fired missiles. Four white smoke tentacles raced out from hidden locations and sought the helicopters hot exhaust. Immediately they armed the next set of missiles for another volley.

The helicopter pilots immediately took evasive maneuvers as the missiles closed. They split their tight formation and began spewing white hot flares to fool the heat seekers on the nose of the missiles.

It didn't work.

Two missiles tracked each of the wildly maneuvering helicopters and quickly closed the distance. The closest helicopter discharged more flares and nosed into a steep dive while turning to the right to hide the engines exhaust and get around mountain top. The first missile ignored the burning flares and exploded like a thunderclap ten feet from the fuselage, sending hot fragments into the engine and tail rotor. The second missile detonated a split second later, blowing the tail boom completely off and turning the helicopter into a huge spinning twisted metal fireball that plummeted to the ground.

Cheers went up as the burning hulk hit the ground and exploded.

For a moment the second helicopter appeared to get lucky. Just as one missile got close enough to detonate, the pilot put the aircraft into a violent maneuver and fired off flares, confusing the missile and causing it to sail harmlessly through the air. But the maneuver didn't fool the second missile. Just as the pilot leveled off, the second missile flew up the tail pipe. In another thunderous explosion, the broken helicopter was engulfed in a magnificent huge red black ball of flame and fell like a meteor trailing thick black smoke until it plunged into the earth.

"That should buy us some time," Wolff commented as another round of cheers could be heard at the death of the last helicopter.

Karmal appeared at Kaderri's side with a grin that spread from ear to ear. "We've done well. Got two choppers and a Spetsnaz unit! And you Captain, a Soviet general!"

Kaderri clapped Karmal on the back and matched his smile despite the pain in his knee. He didn't know if it was a Spetsnaz unit they fought, but he wasn't going to debate Karmal at the moment. "Well done, Mike." The dismounted enemy infantry was getting closer. "Now, let's get the dead and wounded and get out of here."

CHAPTER ONE

Sunday, October 5, Keene, New York. Present day

The rising sun in the east illuminated the horizon with strips of red and gold and cast it's long dazzling tentacles across the colorful autumn landscape, setting the mountains ablaze in brilliant patches of red, yellow and green. Tiny warblers and blue jays chattered as they flitted and darted through the trees. The forty five hundred plus foot peak of Mt. Colden loomed in the near distance and nestled in the High Peaks Region of the Adirondack Mountains on one hundred forty five private acres was the rebuilt three bedroom log house, which was the second home; that belonged to Marcus A. Kaderri. A few years back the original house was blown up and burned to the ground by an Israeli commando team in their vain effort to kill him.

Kaderri sat on the wide wrap-around deck suspended off the second floor of the house in a comfortable wooden Adirondack chair with fallen leaves swirling at his feet. He wore his favorite navy blue fleece pullover and sweatpants to guard against the mountain chill and sipped at the steaming mug of coffee. The crisp smell of the mountains and the burning birch wood curling out of the chimney filled his nostrils and gave him a sense of peace and belonging.

While his senses were filled with the outdoors, his mind was filled with the memory of the battle that took place there. It was an unimaginable fight that left a dozen Israeli commandos dead along with the man Kaderri had hunted, Moshe Koretsky, an officer in the Mossad, the Israeli spy agency. Also killed in the fight was one CIA officer with two more wounded. But the bloodshed didn't stop there. Kaderri's best friend, Bob Wolff, was severely wounded, as was Albany detective Gary Trainor. Kaderri himself didn't emerge from the fight unscathed as he was the unlucky recipient of three bullets. If it wasn't for the heroic effort of his former team medic, Jesse Hughes, there was a very good chance that Wolff or himself may not have survived.

Those thoughts of that terrible day were quickly cast aside when he heard the light pounding on the sliding glass door that opened from the kitchen. A smile immediately spread on his handsome, weathered face as he turned to the source of the noise. On the other side of the glass door holding a stuffed football and wearing footed fleece pajamas, a sweatshirt and knit cap was Sean, the two-year-old future linebacker for the NFL football Giants. Obviously excited to see his dad, Sean began to run in place and his small hands pounded on the glass. Kaderri laughed at the display of excitement, put his mug on the table and effortlessly rose from the chair. Striding over to open the door and scoop up his son, the door suddenly slid open and Sean sprinted out into the powerful opened arms of his dad.

"Daddy!"

"Now how did you open the door?" Kaderri asked and gave his son a kiss as he easily held him in one arm.

Sean turned and pointed over his shoulder. "Mommy."

"Oh, mommy did," he answered, not knowing if Sean actually understood the question or if he was just proudly pointing out his mommy was there.

"He couldn't wait to come down," Sara said. She wore a maroon fleece pullover and gray leggings and stepped out onto the deck holding onto Samantha, Sean's twin sister. Her head was resting comfortably on Sara's shoulder and tucked under her long wavy black hair. "She, on the other hand, doesn't want to wake up."

Kaderri placed his rough hand on Sara's cheek and kissed her full, delicious lips. Her beauty took his breath away like diving into a cold mountain lake. "Good morning, Babe. Why didn't you leave her in bed?" He asked and then kissed his bundled daughter on the cheek.

"I tried. You know these two. Where one goes, the other must follow. Sam didn't want to miss out on what her brother was up to."

Kaderri chuckled when Sam wriggled her nose but kept her eyes closed. "It looks like she doesn't want to miss out on her sleep either. Difficult decision for a two year old at this time in the morning. Play or sleep." He then put Sean down, who chased a red maple leaf across the deck, then pinched Sara on her tight butt. "Coffee?"

"Frisky devil. Yes, please."

Kaderri gave a mischievous smile as he crossed his arms and tilted his head. "There was a time when you would walk out here wearing that skimpy bikini you modeled for the poster. By the way, you could still wear that, or nothing at all–"

"And have hot passionate sex for all the wild animals to watch and hear us scream in delight." Sara finished the sentence with her own smile. Her almond shaped brown eyes twinkled with remembrance. She then pointed to the kids and raised an eyebrow. "That was before these two. Someday," she gave a soft seductive kiss, "we'll do it again."

When Kaderri emerged from the kitchen with a steaming mug of coffee for Sara, and his own mug refilled, he also had two cups of milk for the kids in sippy cups and a heavy wool blanket draped over his shoulder. Sara was sitting in one of the Adirondack chairs with Sam still sleeping on her shoulder while Sean, holding onto the spindles of the wooden railing, curiously stared at a hawk circling nearby. Kaderri placed the coffee on the table and threw the blanket over his two most favorite females.

"Thank you. Marc," Sara began after taking a sip, "it doesn't get any better than this, does it?"

Kaderri couldn't agree more. He was married to one of the most beautiful women in the world who also owned the most successful fitness club in the Capital District of New York State and with him, produced two beautiful children.

Kaderri's life, both in the military and the financial world, was nothing but success that was born out of hard work. After a highly successful and decorative, though shortened, career in the U.S. Army, Kaderri became an insurance agent and financial planner. After a few years of working for an agency and using the same tenacious work ethic that earned him his Green Beret, he ventured out and opened his own financial services company. In his employ were four full time agents and four support staff. Though he still sold individual policies across the kitchen table, his business evolved into primarily dealing with retirement and pension programs for corporations and financial planning for wealthy individuals.

When their joint incomes, rental property income and investments were added up, the Kaderris had a net worth of over seven million dollars.

"You're right, honey. You are absolutely right. It doesn't get any better than this," he completely agreed with her statement. Though he never had any difficulty in talking to Sara before, he was a bit apprehensive in bringing up the subject of his contract employment with the Central Intelligence Agency. "Babe, since we're on the sentimental family stuff, I called Paul Mc Knight and told him to take my name out of the hat."

The look of disbelief quickly covered Sara's face as she moved a strand of hair behind her ear. Even the birds seemed to have gone quiet. "What? Why?" She bared her perfect set of white teeth. "And you did that without talking to me?"

Kaderri eased himself into the chair, ready to take on this discussion. "What if something happens to me on a mission?" he asked reasonably.

She narrowed her eyes into slits and fired off an icy stare. Her pleasant features became hard and her voice took on an edge. She leaned over the armrest and pointed a French tip manicured finger at his nose. "What happens if you the cross the road at the wrong time?"

He underestimated the severity of her reaction and wasn't so sure to continue with the pre-planned responses he had mapped out in his head. He spread his hands at an attempt to ease her anger. "C'mon, Sara, you can't-"

She cut him off, her finger getting closer to his nose. "Don't give me any line of BS, Marcus. It won't work." She softened somewhat and sat back in the chair. "Look, Marc, that line of work is who you are, remember? We've gone over this before. If you didn't get your knee shot out, you'd still be in Special Forces, right?" She didn't let him answer. "And most likely you would be in Afghanistan, Iran, Iraq or some other part of the world hunting these goddamn terrorists. Besides, with the threat of more terrorist attacks against us, don't you think people with your talents might be needed?"

Kaderri shook his head in tepid disagreement. These were the same points his CIA boss, Paul McKnight, had brought up. "You're right, about my knee, but Babe, I'm an old guy. There are plenty of guys out there today who are as good if not better than me." He stole a glance at Sean to make sure he wasn't getting into trouble.

Sara gave a hard stare, clearly unconvinced. "I doubt it."

Kaderri shrugged. He was a legend in the Special Operations community and some of the missions he pulled off, the ones that weren't classified, were being taught in classrooms and written in history books. He took a sip from his mug and swished the coffee in his mouth before he swallowed. The thought of leaving Sara and the kids without a father was unthinkable, especially when he purposely put himself in jeopardy on a mission. Twenty years ago the thought process would have been much different. There was a lot to be said about being older and wiser compared to having youthful indiscretion. He had left the military and CIA life behind and hoped that life had left him.

"What time do you want to head home?" Sara asked, changing the subject.

"We either get home before the Giants game, or we leave after it."

"Ugh!" Sara rolled her eyes and cradled Sam's head. "I forgot, it's Sunday in the fall. Life revolves around what time the football game is on."

He gave her a funny look. "Duh."

Sara had received yearly renewable season tickets as part of her payment package for modeling a bathing suit and Kaderri had missed very few games since receiving them.

"Thank God you sold the tickets for today! I'm beginning to think season tickets were a mistake!"

Monday, October 6, Northeast of Dervezekem, Turkmenistan

Things were going well for the good guys. Al-Qaeda forces world wide were being eliminated and the top leaders were being hunted down one by one. If at all possible, it was preferred to capture the murdering sons-of-bitches for obvious intelligence reasons, but most of the time they met their demise in a violent fashion.

Harold Weston's job was to hunt down and kill the enemy that aided, murdered, or sought to commit terrorist acts on his fellow citizens. The thin, fit, sandy colored haired man with blue eyes first spent time in the 80's in Afghanistan with a Special Forces A-Team helping the Mujahadeen frustrate and defeat the Soviet army. After the fall of the Soviet Union, Special Forces missions dropped off considerably and Weston jumped ship to the CIA where he has been working for the past ten years as a Specialized Skills Officer, aka field officer, and most recently in the Special Activities Division. That was the paramilitary wing of the CIA which drew most of its personnel from the Special Operations community in the American Armed Forces, which included, Army Green Berets, Delta Force, Rangers, Navy SEALs, Force Recon Marines and Air Force Para Rescue.

Tough challenges were nothing new to Weston and attempting to capture or kill Ahmed Rashid Halabi, a Saudi national who made millions of dollars from selling weapons to al-Qaeda, Chechen rebels, or any other terrorist group in the world proved to be one of the tougher ones. The Saudi government turned a blind eye to all requests for help.

His search took him over the border from Afghanistan into southeastern Turkmenistan, another arid, mostly desert country with very sparse areas of vegetation. Apart from the Kopetdag Mountains, where he was, the country was swallowed up by the huge Garagum desert. It didn't take a rocket scientist to figure out the bad guys running weapons from Afghanistan hid in the only mountainous and green area in the country.

With the morning sun to his back, Weston brought the binoculars to his tired and strained eyes. He was hidden among the rolling hills covered with oak and pistachio trees and scrutinized the movement in the small clearing one hundred fifty meters away from his slightly elevated position. A partially obscured dirt road led into the clearing from the north where the main dirt road was located a full kilometer away.

There were seven men in the clearing clothed in various dress. Three were clean shaven and wearing winter uniforms that appeared to be Russian Red Army. One was wearing jeans and a down jacket while the others sported beards and wore traditional Muslim dress, turbans and kaffiyea's. They were sitting around and on top of stacked piles of wooden crates smoking cigarettes and not paying attention to their surroundings. Weston smiled at their complacency but couldn't determine which one was Halabi. Apparently they felt secure because they did not put out any security, at least any that was spotted by Weston or the assault team. That made seizing this particular weapons cache much easier.

He nodded in satisfaction. So far his intelligence network was good. Damn good. Weston whispered into the microphone of the Cobra Modular Infantry Radio RA3185 at his lips. "Injun Six, this is Comanche, over."

"Injun Six, go," whispered the commander of the US Army Special Forces Operational Detachment A-317.

"Confirm seven enemy soldiers, copy?"

The reply came back immediately. "Confirm, seven. I don't see any transportation or security, do you? Over."

"Negative. Should work to our advantage. Tomahawk, I say again, Tomahawk. Copy?" Weston excitedly gave the execute order.

"Roger, Tomahawk." The reply was crisp and dry. Over the MIR, Injun Six then instructed each shooter who they were to hit, guaranteeing simultaneous hits. "All Braves, fire on my call."

Ten seconds later, a rippling cacophony of small arms fire broke the silence. Weston watched in professional admiration as the Special Forces team, hiding a short distance away, fired from their concealed positions and sprayed the enemy with accurate and deadly fire. First to die were the two men sitting on top of the tallest pile of crates. Multiple rounds slammed into their torsos, knocking them off their perch and sending the crates tumbling. The other five never had a chance to react as a hail of bullets rained down upon them. In an instant all seven men were dead.

In one fluid motion, the camouflaged Special Forces troopers rose from the ground like apparitions, their M-4 carbines held securely to their shoulders and rapidly advanced upon the bodies.

"We're clear," a trooper announced over the communications set.

"Fresh meat, guys," another trooper said in serious voice. "Keep an eye out for hungry leopards, cheetahs or other critters with sharp fangs." Big cats were indigenous to the region and a free meal was hard to pass up.

Easing from his hide spot with his senses still on a heightened state, Weston sure handedly gripped the M-4 and made his way to the ambush site. Small branches and tall grass broke and fell flat with every footfall. He paused to survey the carnage and found exactly what he expected. Bloodied and torn bodies of the enemy lay where they fell and the Special Forces team was already at work, searching the bodies for intelligence and the crates for booby traps.

"Nice shooting, Captain," Weston congratulated the commander of the Special Forces team as he strode up to him. "Didn't damage a single crate."

"All in a day's work," Captain David Tully stated flatly. His face was smeared in camouflage paint and his hard eyes were still assessing the scene. "Of course you spooks like things nice and tidy, right? No loose ends?" A glint of white poked through his lips.

"Ah, young captain," Weston took the jab in stride, "remember I was one of you guys while you were still sucking on your mother's nipple."

That earned a broad smile from the captain.

Before Tully could respond, Sergeant First Class Webb called out. "Sir, Mr. Weston, you've got to see this."

The two men walked over to the soldier who was kneeling next to a body with three holes in the center of his chest. His face had a day old growth of beard, blond hair cut short and was one of the men wearing Russian uniforms. "What have you got, Sergeant?" Weston asked.

"Look at these," the sergeant looped his finger under the shoulder boards of the dead man's field jacket and held up a small bottle of Russian vodka removed from one of the pockets.

Weston and Tully simultaneously let out a whistle. "Do you think that's a coincidence?" Tully asked Weston.

"I don't think so. In my line of work, coincidences are rare. At any rate, I'd sure like to know why a Russian colonel is out here with these weapons and al-Qaeda and Taliban ragheads." Weston slung his weapon. "I wonder if he's really a Russian?" Focusing on the primary aspect of the mission, Weston called out, "What about Halabi? He's supposed to be here. Is he?"

"Doesn't look like it, sir," came the disappointing reply.

"Shit," Weston cursed aloud. Maybe his intelligence wasn't that good after all.

Webb was rifling through the last pocket of the dead man and pulled out a wallet. He opened it, found a picture ID and compared it to the face of dead man. "He's a Russian," Webb tossed up the wallet to Weston.

This was quite the turn of events. Weston, fluent in Russian, read the name on the military ID. "Colonel Anatoly Yezhov. This complicates things."

Monday, October 6, Paktika Province, Afghanistan

In the rugged landscape of dust covered rocky mountains and scrub brush, Leonard Puckett, Central Intelligence Agency, Special Activities Division, former Sergeant First Class, United States Army Special Forces, sat on his forty-plus year old haunches and observed the sixteen soldiers, two squads of eight, of the newly formed Afghan Army. They were led by three American Special Forces troopers that advanced slowly in a wedge formation towards the trio of brown painted, sheet metal roofed buildings in the process of being camouflaged to look like dirt and rock piles. Mixed in with the unit were two local tribesmen and Mike Karmal, the same man Puckett fought alongside more than two decades earlier against the invading Soviets. The tribesmen were used as scouts, and Puckett had his concerns about them. Mainly, he didn't know where their loyalty lay.

Despite the expulsion of the Taliban from power, their brutal ways still held some sway in this area. Money still talked in this country and was a primary motivator for many things– fear, loyalty and information. Often times, the decision on where a person put his allegiance was solely depended upon how much cash was offered. To the east of their current location was the lawless Federally Administered Tribal Area on the border with Pakistan, meaning, for the most part, that the creed of 'anything goes' was paramount. Also still in existence was the practice of an eye for an eye retribution over personal gripes and still unsettled territorial disputes among warring tribes.

All these factors came into consideration when an operation was planned and how much information was disseminated. Puckett always kept a wary eye on the scouts and always had one of Karmal's most trusted men hovering around them.

The larger, corrugated tin building was the size of a three car garage. The windows were boarded up and it was flanked by two smaller wooden sheds, which also had sheet metal roofs covered with dirt to prevent the reflection of the suns rays. The three structures in the middle of nowhere immediately made them suspect as being part of the Taliban or al- Qaeda terrorist network. According to Puckett's intelligence, these buildings were used as a light weapons storage facility and a large delivery had arrived a couple of days ago.

He stood and let out a breath which crystallized into a cloud. He took one more look around, searching for signs of the enemy. Suddenly a chill engulfed his hard weathered body as his senses went on a heightened state of alert. Danger was lurking in the scrub and rock and he instinctively hunched his shoulders.

Gripping the M-4 carbine tighter that was slung across his chest, Puckett cautiously followed the team as they advanced towards the buildings.

Crack! Crack!

Then came a prolonged burst of automatic weapons fire. A pair of enemy fighters sprinted from behind the shed on the right.

"Down!" Sergeant First Class Anthony Michaelson, walking on Puckett's left, yelled as the incoming small arms fire snapped around them.

Before the shout was out of Michaelson's mouth, the men in the combined Afghan-American unit hit the ground for cover, brought their weapons up and returned fire.

The two enemy fighters were down, their bodies dropped next to the shed.

The incoming fire ceased.

A few minutes had passed without incident, causing Sergeant Michaelson to issue new orders. "On your feet!" He pointed towards the buildings and maneuvered the fire teams on a steady advance towards the threat. "Move out, and watch your ass. More fuckers might still be around."

Puckett rose to a knee and scanned the ground before him. He let the fire team move first, then rose to both feet and moved one sure footed step at a time. His cheek rested comfortably on the stock of the rifle, while sharp, predatory eyes searched through the M-68 scope for a target.

There! He spotted an enemy soldier popping out from behind the corner of the left shed, an AK held to his hip and pointed his way. Puckett took a bead on the man's head, placed the scope's small red dot in the center of the enemy's face, thumbed the selector to single shot and squeezed the trigger. The M-4 popped in his hands and he dropped the enemy in a heap. A mist of red hung suspended in the air where his head had been.

"Move on the right flank!" Master Sergeant Chris Knapp, the tall, thin, and leathery faced commander of the detail yelled in English and Dari to the Second Squad to get a flanking movement.

Like a choreographed play, the men moved in sequence. Four soldiers, one fire team, lay on the ground and gave a base of supporting fire while another moved in for the attack. They were careful not to fire into the building for fear of detonating what may be in it.

Puckett watched anxiously as the flanking troops disappeared around the shed. There was little concern that the good guys would prevail because this group of Afghans were trained well, but one never knew what was going to happen in combat.

Suddenly from behind the buildings, a brief firefight erupted. A short burst from a single weapon was immediately answered by at least three weapons in return.

Puckett, like everyone else, turned their attention in the direction, watching, waiting, ready to help out.

Then just as fast as it started, it ended. An eerie silence filled the air, along with the smell of cordite stinging Puckett's nostrils.

"Clear!" Karmal announced when he emerged from behind the building, his AK-47 still gripped in his hands.

Puckett rose from the ground. "What did you shoot?" he asked.

Karmal managed a smile and held up a crooked leathery finger. "One more bad guy."

The two other men emerged from behind the center building dragging the dead enemy fighter by his feet. A small dust cloud rose from the ground and a trail of blood oozed out from the holes in his chest and forehead.

"Grab the rest and search 'em," Knapp ordered Karmal. "Tony! Get security set up"

"Right." Michaelson answered and issued orders to the squads.

"Shall we go inside?" Knapp turned to Puckett and asked matter-of-factly as he slung the M-4 across his chest. "I believe the guards for the building no longer pose a threat."

The smallest organized unit the U.S. Army Special Forces is the twelve man unit know as an Operational Detachment-Alpha, ODA, or A-Team, A captain is in command of the detachment with his XO, executive officer, being a Warrant Officer. The remainder of the detachment consists of non-commissioned officers ranging from master sergeants on down to sergeant. Each ODA is comprised of a team sergeant, two NCOs for heavy and light weapons, communications, engineering, and two medics. With this configuration, the ODAs can split into two separate units with the same effective ability, or mix and match personnel for specific missions.

In the case of Special Forces Operational Detachment A-301, commanded by Captain Ian MacDonald with Warrant Officer 3 Rodney Couch, things were a little different. MacDonald would have normally assigned Couch this mission, but he was recovering from injuries sustained two weeks prior in a fall that resulted in strained knee ligaments that left him on crutches. Because of that, MacDonald put the very capable team sergeant, Master Sergeant Chris Knapp, in command.

"Lead the way," Puckett gestured with the rifle towards the center building.

The door was locked with a shiny new padlock, giving confirmation to the intelligence that the building was used for something important and wanted others to stay outside.

"Dorsey!" Knapp called over his shoulder. "I need the bolt cutters." He checked the door to make sure it wasn't rigged with explosives.

A moment later, Sergeant First Class Pete Dorsey, a wiry man with dark hair, matching beard and hard brown eyes prepared to cut the lock.

Knapp and Puckett stood on either side of the door and brought their weapons to their shoulders in case they were ambushed from inside by some die hard believer.

"Go," Knapp ordered the lock cut.

After a quick snip and the lock was removed and Dorsey pushed the door open on creaky hinges. A thorough search with a trained eye and a Surefire flashlight mounted on the hand guards of the rifle around the inside of the doorframe yielded no booby traps.

"Jackpot," Puckett called out after illuminating a solid wall of olive green crates with his mounted flashlight.

"Holy shit," Karmal blurted one of his favorite American phrases after appearing in the door.

Weapons at the ready, the men entered the building and paused a moment to let their eyes adjust to the light differential. Using their flashlights, they began to wander among the crates, being ever so careful not to trip any explosive devices. "Knock out those windows," Puckett said to no one in particular as he carefully stepped over to where the light was seeping through the boards. "We need some light in here."

"We really hit it this time, Master Sergeant," Dorsey stated excitedly.

Suddenly a lone shrill whistle from outside the building ended their brief jubilation.

"Incoming!" came the warning call from outside.

Whump! The spotting round landed fifty meters to the north of the building.

Immediately more whistles screamed in the air as the deadly mortar rounds made their descent.

The men raced out the door and scattered, diving to the ground before the shells impacted.

Whump! Whump! Whump!

Puckett bounced on the hard ground and covered his head as the white hot razor sharp shrapnel whizzed past him and dirt and rock pelted his exposed body. Dust made its way into his mouth and nostrils, causing him to cough and gag. It had been awhile since he was exposed to mortar fire and realized quickly that he didn't miss it one bit.

Knapp belly flopped next to him. "I hate those things."

Puckett reached for the mouthpiece on the Camelbak water bladder to rinse out his mouth when the cry went up again. "Incoming!"

"Ah, shit!" Puckett braced himself for the next salvo and curled into a ball.

Whump! Whump! Whump! The ground shook again. This time it was closer and his teeth rattled with every impacting round.

Another volley followed moments later, this time a round hit one of the smaller sheds, blowing it pieces and setting it on fire.

"Anybody see where they're coming from?" Knapp screamed above the echoing report, peering through the smoke and dust.

"That way!" One of the Afghans had binoculars to his eyes and pointed northwards to a small rock and scrub brush covered hill on a low ridge line about five hundred meters away.

All of a sudden, secondary explosions thundered from the burning shed. Whatever ammo was inside began to cook off.

"Fuck! Stay clear of that fire!"

Men began scrambling further away from the shed searching for cover.

"Movement!" Michaelson announced above the exploding ordnance. His comment was immediately followed by a short burst of gunfire. Fortunately, the rounds sailed harmlessly overhead.

Looking through his own binoculars, Puckett saw a head duck behind a rock approximately two hundred meters away. "I'm on it," he spat out more dust and rose to his feet. Ignoring the burning shed, he started for the area where he saw the lone enemy soldier. It was an opportunity to get a prisoner. "Mike!" he called to Karmal and thumbed the safety on his weapon. "Get two men, the scouts and come with me."

"Ok," Karmal blurted and went to carry out his orders.

"Hold on there, Puckett," Knapp ordered getting to his own feet.

Puckett stopped. He knew what Knapp was going to say and wasn't going to listen to him. "We've got to stop those mortars!"

"No shit," Knapp gave a dirty look. He didn't need someone to state the obvious.

Another large explosion detonated from the burning shed.

A shrill whistle announced the arrival of another barrage. The rounds impacted near the remaining smaller shed, knocked a hole in one of the sides and sent Knapp and Puckett back down to the ground.

"We got to move out of here!" Knapp said, searching for a place that had better cover.

Some of the troops responded with small arms fire, shooting in the direction where they saw the enemy and hoped for a lucky shot.

Puckett turned to face Knapp, his face was still in the dirt. "Listen, I also have standing orders to take prisoners if at all possible and I believe it's possible."

"That's SOP," Knapp propped himself on his elbows and informed Puckett of something he already knew. "My orders are to take the weapons in that building and protect your ass."

Puckett's tone made it clear he was not to be denied. "I'm going, Master Sergeant. You seem to forget I know how to do this."

"That was along time ago, Len," Knapp said reasonably. "You're older now and not as sharp. I can't stop you because you are not under my command, but I don't want to carry your body out of here–or anyone else's–because you're rusty. Also," Knapp lowered his voice and put an edge into it, "being a spook, I don't think it would be wise to venture out there. What happens if you get captured? Puckett, I don't know what info you have inside your head, but I bet the enemy would love to know and it would be harmful to the missions in country."

Puckett paused for a moment. His once light brown hair was now half gray and he no longer had the physical strength he once had. He knew the risk, but intelligence was needed. "I'll be fine. None of the Afghans know what I do."

"Not even your friend, Karmal?"

Puckett shook his head. "No. He still thinks I'm SF. You take care of what needs to be–"

"Incoming!" More whistles of raining mortar rounds pierced the air.

"Not again!" Puckett drove his face into the rocky ground and braced himself once again for the incoming mortars.

Whump! Whump! Boom!

The first two rounds were walked towards the unit's position, exploding forty then thirty meters away. The third round fell short and blew the shed apart and caught fire. Sharp wood and metal splinters sliced through the air with a menacing *zing!*

Suddenly the mortars had stopped. Silent seconds ticked away into minutes.

A thought came to Puckett while his face was still in the dirt. "I don't think they want to destroy the main building with the weapons. That's why they stopped."

Knapp disagreed. "They can't shoot straight, that's why. I'm going to call in air support to take out the mortars." Knapp crawled away to find the radio.

"Hey don't forget," Puckett called to the scampering Knapp, "my call sign is 'Poltergeist." Working for the CIA, he thought it would be funny referring himself as something ghostly. "See you when I get back." He readjusted his knit cap and marched off as Knapp shook his head.

Puckett glanced at his watch. Six minutes had elapsed from the time the first round hit. He rose to his feet, gathered Karmal's group and led them into the rocks to find the sons-of-bitches who lobbed the mortar rounds on top of their heads.

The mortar fire the enemy directed was determined, not the usual harassing fire that had been seen throughout Afghanistan since the ouster of the Taliban. Usually one or two rounds would be fired and then the attackers would run and hide to lob a few more rounds another day.

But that wasn't the case this time, Puckett mused. The last attack indicated the people in the hills were determined to keep the weapons, which was uncharacteristic. Were the bad guys running low on weapons and needed to hold these? He would extract that information if someone was captured.

He glanced towards the sky. He had to get it done before the air support arrived and blew the enemy to bits.

In single file, the five men followed one of the scouts up the rocky slope and were prepared to pounce on anything that moved. The scout, twenty meters ahead of the rest of the group, suddenly froze. Puckett, third in line, dropped to a knee and brought the M-4 rifle up to his shoulder. Immediately adrenaline pumped through his veins and his heart rate increased with the terrifying excitement of combat. His eyes began to search for the reason why the scout halted.

Instinct told him he was in a world of trouble.

All of a sudden a hurricane force of small arms fire rained down on them from the higher ground fifty meters to the right.

"Ambush!" Puckett yelled above the incoming fire. Immediately he dropped to the ground as bullets bored holes in the dirt, splintered rock and cracked in the air around his head. He spotted dust and smoke from a half dozen positions, betraying the shooters locations.

He quickly squeezed off short bursts to make the ambushers duck and looked across the line of prone men to see who else in his team was shooting back. He was relieved to see all the men engaged but one. The lead scout was dead.

Damn! Puckett turned his attention back to the ambush and peered through the scope to acquire another target when dark round objects were suddenly hurled towards him. "Shit, grenades!" He closed his eyes and curled into a tight ball to protect himself from the impending detonation.

He held his breath as the metal objects grated on the rocks as they rolled and bounced past him.

BOOM! BOOM! The grenades exploded and showered the area with razor sharp shrapnel. Puckett cried out and felt as if he were being stung by a wasp. "Shit, that burns!" He looked at the wound on his hip to see a small spot of blood form on his army combat uniform. More grenades exploded along the line of men. Ear piercing screams told him men were being hit.

Puckett realized he made a mistake by trying to take a prisoner and should have listened to Master Sergeant Knapp. He gazed skyward to see where the damn air support was to help him get out of there. He reached for the walkie talkie buckled to his wounded hip to call Knapp for help, but found a jagged hole in the center of it, making it unusable.

Mortar rounds began dropping behind his position. He quickly turned to watch the blossoming fountains of dirt create a wall, cutting him off from his escape route.

The loss of the communications gear meant Puckett was on his own. He was left with two options, try to flee through the mortar barrage or break the ambush. Weighing each option, he knew fleeing would be suicidal. The enemy had them boxed in. If he told his unit to turn and run, they would be cut to ribbons by small arms fire and the mortars. The only viable option was to break the ambush with his pitiful sized unit and hope that Knapp would arrive with a force after hearing the firefight.

Knowing the only way to break an ambush was to directly assault it, Puckett rose to his feet, raised his rifle to his shoulder and let loose with a long burst. "Follow me!" he waved the men forward hoping they would follow. He fired another burst and charged, intent to get into the rocks and among the ambushers.

He changed magazines as his strong legs propelled his lean body forward, his hard soled combat boots dug into the rocky ground. He stole a glance to see who was following and didn't break stride as the other men formed a line and charged uphill with him.

The intensity of both the outgoing and incoming fire increased. An enemy soldier fell forward, riddled by a burst of fire. Puckett closed the distance. His heart practically pounded out of his chest and his breathing was heavy. He could see the individual enemy soldiers pop out from cover. He was thirty feet from one ambusher, trained his weapon on the fighter and squeezed the trigger. The bullets impacted on the torso, killing him instantly. Confident that they were about to break the ambush, he slewed his weapon to search for another target. "Keep going! Don't stop!" he encouraged the men.

Hammer blows suddenly crashed into his thighs, followed by excruciating pain that took his breath away and knocked him to the ground.

It took a moment for him to realize he was shot. "I'm hit!" Puckett screamed above the fire and clenched his teeth against the white hot pain.

Another high pitched scream was off to his right and he turned to see one of the Afghans on his team hold his stomach and sink to his knees. A final burst to his chest and head finished him off.

Puckett rolled over as more white hot pain shot through his body. He reached out for his weapon to continue the assault but the sudden reduction of outgoing fire grabbed his immediate attention.

"Hold on, Mister Puckett!" Mike Karmal yelled. "We're coming to help!"

"No! No!" Puckett waved him off. "Keep going! Break the ambush!" He frantically waived in the direction of the ambushers.

Puckett turned to see Karmal and another Afghan crawling towards him, small fountains of dirt and rock bracketed them, inching closer and closer as the marksman zeroed in on their targets. The Afghan rose to one knee and squeezed off a few rounds. When he paused to change magazines, bullets tore into him. Without a sound, he fell forward and didn't move.

"Ahh!" Karmal screamed. Bullets knocked the weapon from his grasp and smashed into his hand.

"Mike! Stay down!" Puckett screamed, reached out for his weapon and swung it in the direction of the attackers.

Loud shouts in Dari from his front caught his attention and he turned to see three angry enemy fighters with their dirty turbans askew head his way. Their deadly bayonet– tipped AKs pointed directly at his forehead.

"Khuda hafiz," goodbye, they snarled.

Shit. Puckett froze, his breath came in labored pants as a smiling enemy fighter put the bayonet tip on his throat. He didn't have time to shoot. He said a quick prayer to make his death quick and be allowed into heaven.

It was over.

"Nyet!" A deeper voice commanded, halting the enemy from sticking him.

"What the hell?" Puckett said aloud before an unseen rifle butt to his temple made the world go dark.

Fifteen minutes after Puckett and his small unit left, the sudden eruption of gunfire turned everyone's attention from the warehouse towards the direction of the hills. Master Sergeant Chris Knapp looked up from inventorying a crate of machine guns and ran out the door of the remaining building. "What's going on?" he asked to anyone who was listening. "Who's doing the shooting and where is the goddamn air support?"

"Firefight," Dorsey answered quickly, binoculars held to his eyes and a walkie talkie clutched in the other hand. The dull echoing sound of exploding grenades punctuated his answer. "Poltergeist, this is Minuteman, come in, over." He waited for an answer before he repeated the call. When there was no answer, Dorsey dropped the binoculars, turned to Knapp and gave the unwelcomed news. "Puckett doesn't answer."

"What do you see?" Concern crept into Knapp's voice. Exploding mortar rounds added to his unease.

"Nothing but smoke. Too many hills." Dorsey kept the binoculars to his eyes.

Snatching the radio handset from it's cradle, Knapp called to find out where the air support was. "Valley Forge, this is Minuteman Three, over."

"Minuteman Three, this is Valley Forge, go." Captain MacDonald had studied American history in college and always referred to historical figures or events for call signs. As the unit commander, he was Minuteman Six and the base operations was Valley Forge. Warrant Officer Couch was Minuteman Two and Knapp was Minuteman Three.

"Where the hell is Hatchet!?" Knapp shouted angrily, wanting to know where the Apache gunships were. "We're in a goddamn fight here! Over."

There was a three second pause that seemed to take forever. "Minuteman Three, Hatchet RTB'd. Mechanical problems. Saber is ten minutes out, over."

"Fuck!" Knapp clenched his jaw and squeezed the mic in anger without keying it. Great time for a gunship to return to base! "Fuck, again! I knew the spook would run into trouble!" Then he pushed the button to respond and brought the mic to his mouth. "Roger, Valley Forge. Out."

Knapp angrily shook his head and found the Afghan commander. "Keep four men here to work on the cache." He barely heard the man's affirmative response and immediately issued new instructions. "Listen up, we're going up there to help Puckett. The first gunship RTB'd and its backup is ten minutes out." He waited for the Afghan commander to relay the information then took a deep breath and bellowed, "Lock and load! Lets go!"

Ten minutes later when they arrived at the ambush site, their fears were realized. The bodies of the four Afghans were discovered, but neither Puckett's or Karmal's were to be seen. The only encouraging signs were the blood trails that led into a previously unknown cave complex. If Puckett or Karmal were dead, they'd have found the bodies.

"What have you got?" Knapp asked Michaelson just as the sound of helicopter blades slapping the air signaled their arrival. He looked up to see two deadly AH-64 Apache gunships, armed with a full compliment of rockets on their stubby wings, approaching fast.

"Puckett's radio," Michaelson answered and held up the shattered device.

Reaching for the satellite radio on Michaelson's back, Knapp switched frequencies and contacted Saber before they shot up his unit by mistake. "Saber, this is Minuteman Three, over."

"This is Saber Leader, Minuteman, what have you got?"

"Saber, sweep the area, enemy has dispersed, I say again, enemy has dispersed. I'm marking my position with yellow smoke, copy."

Michaelson grabbed a soup can sized canister off his MOLLE gear and pulled the pin. A cloud of yellow smoke immediately poured out from the top and he tossed it a few yards away.

"Roger Minuteman, confirm enemy has dispersed. I see yellow smoke. Commencing sweep."

"Affirmative, yellow smoke. Minuteman out." Knapp watched the sleek Apaches fly directly overhead and then go into a left hand turn and begin their hunt in ever widening circles. Switching frequencies again he pressed the transmit button and spoke into the handset. "Valley Forge, this is Minuteman Three, over."

"This is Valley Forge, what have you got? Over."

Knapp thought of the irony he was about to relay and hoped the operator at the end took him seriously. "Valley

Forge, Poltergeist is MIA. Say again, Poltergeist is MIA. Need additional personnel for a search in a cave complex. We also have four friendly KIA and one additional MIA. Saber is on station, copy?"

There was a longer than usual pause before Valley Forge got back on line. "Roger, Minuteman, Poltergeist is MIA. Help is on the way."

Monday, October 6, Forward Operating Base (FOB) Warrior, Kashah, Paktika Province, Afghanistan

Two miles east of the village of Kashah on a high plain in the southeast mountainous region of Afghanistan was the United States Army's Forward Operating Base Warrior. It was strategically located less then thirty miles from the Pakistan border and the notorious Federally Administered Tribal Area. It was a vast and rugged territory where warlords reigned and die hard Taliban and al-Qaeda hid and regrouped.

The primary inhabitants of FOB Warrior was Bravo Company, 1st Battalion of the 75th Ranger Regiment. Their job was to take the fight to the enemy in its safe haven and destroy him.

Bravo Company was made up of three platoons and twenty three year old Second Lieutenant Jack Dover, on his first combat deployment, was the leader of First Platoon. Two weeks prior, he had his first taste of combat in an unnamed valley a few kilometers from the base and led his unit on a successful ambush where four Taliban fighters were killed. From that moment, he knew his deployment would be full of action.

Dover, dressed comfortably in the new digitally camouflaged Army Combat Uniform, or ACU, checked the kerosene level in the heater that was in the center of the tent then eased his wiry one hundred seventy pound frame into a folding beach chair. The plywood floor of the tent was cramped with cots, military equipment of all shapes and sizes and personal items that filled every available space. He shared the tent with his two counterparts, Second Lieutenants Phil Chase and Ramone Hernandez. Container Housing Units or CHUs, pronounced 'choos,' were promised to replace the tents before the frigid weather set in but had yet to arrive.

He opened a bottle of Gatorade pulled from the ever stocked cooler, compliments of care packages sent from concerned groups and loved ones back home, and put his tired feet on top of a discarded ammo box. He dropped his Kevlar helmet, referred to as a 'K-pot,' in his lap and ran a calloused hand over the patch of black hair on top of his head and across his stubbled beard. He took a long pull from the bottle, closed his hazel eyes and let out a sigh. He savored the moment's rest before he opened them again. When he did, he stared at the picture of his fiancée, Renee, taped to the inside webbing of the K-pot and longed for her touch. His mind began to drift back to the night before his deployment where she emerged from the bathroom in the hotel room wearing a hot pink stretch lace thong teddy that highlighted her ample cleavage and tiny waist. Thin hips and long shapely legs stood on three inch black pumps. Dark wavy hair framed her pretty face and fell past her shoulders. Her passionate brown eyes always made his heart flutter and another appendage stir.

"Lieutenant Dover?" a voice suddenly called and stole him from his memory.

"In here," he answered and faced the tent opening to see who was coming in. It sounded like Sergeant Wheeler.

"Mission, sir," Sergeant Andy Wheeler announced with a concerned look as he stood in the opening. "You're needed ASAP."

Rest, as he had learned quickly in a combat zone, was going to have to wait. "Right behind you." Dover capped the Gatorade and blew Renee a kiss before he placed the K-pot back on his head. "Love you," he whispered to her.

Wheeler didn't bother waiting and in four long strides, Dover caught up with the lanky sergeant. "Ok, Sarge, what's the scoop?" He slung the M-4 over his shoulder and watched a crew dart over to one of the big CH-47 Chinook helicopter's.

"Don't know for sure, sir, but my guess it's a search and rescue op."

Immediately he thought of what he had to do. First on the list was to find his platoon sergeant, Sergeant First Class James Isles.

Monday, November 6, Paktika Province, Afghanistan

Master Sergeant Chris Knapp looked at his watch and then into the sky. Twenty five minutes had passed since he'd made the call about Puckett missing. He was pissed and could feel his blood pressure rise.

"Master Sergeant Knapp," Dorsey came up to his side and pointed to the radio handset. "Helo inbound with a platoon of Rangers."

"About fucking time." He immediately looked towards the sky, searching for the helicopter.

The distinct slapping of the twin rotors from big Ch-47 Chinook helicopter reverberated through the hills when suddenly as if out of nowhere the first olive drab painted helo raced in at a hundred feet off the ground and settled down on the rocky terrain, kicking up a gale force spray of swirling debris. Sitting in the side door with his head masked by a flight helmet and dark visor, a door gunner kept his gloved hands on the mounted mini-gun, ready to spew up to six thousands rounds a minute on any enemy soldier he could see. Without shutting down their rotors, the back ramps opened and disgorged the platoon of heavily armed infantry.

As the Rangers emptied out of the CH-47s, the Apaches of Saber flight circled overhead, keeping a constant vigil covering the bigger birds.

Two infantrymen approached Knapp. A wiry figure, his face smeared with camouflage paint and his Outer Tactical Vest worn over Interceptor body armor, was brimming with pouches of ammunition, grenades and other gear. An M-4 carbine was held in his hands low across his hips. By his side was a similarly dressed shorter man, with a radio strapped to his back.

"You Master Sergeant Knapp?" the taller man with the single subdued Lieutenant bar on the chest tab asked in a business like tone. Intense hazel eyes shone from under the K-pot, and his jaw was clenched with determination. The elastic strap on his helmet and the Velcro name tag had the name 'Dover' stenciled on it.

"Yes, sir." Knapp, older by a dozen years, liked what he saw in the young kid. He didn't salute, not because he disrespected the young Lieutenant, but he didn't want to draw any unnecessary attention and mark the officer as a target.

"Lieutenant Jack Dover, Rangers," he offered his strong hand.

Knapp shook it and stared into the young man's eyes, measuring him. He quickly believed he would not have any doubts about this Ranger. "Lieutenant. What'd they tell ya?"

"I got a short briefing before we headed in. Two men MIA, probably captured during a firefight. We're here to find and rescue them, correct? What have you got for me?"

Knapp nodded. "Blood trails leading up into the hills and caves," he pointed with his weapon. "Caves around here are like trees in a forest."

Dover looked in the direction Knapp was pointing and set his jaw. "Ok Master Sergeant, how do you want to do this?"

Knapp liked the Lieutenant even more. He had a head on his shoulders. "We'll start by briefing your men, sir."

"You got it." Dover turned and called out. "Rangers, we move out in five! Squad leaders on me!"

CHAPTER TWO

Tuesday, October 7, The Cave, Afghanistan

Puckett woke with a headache like he'd never felt before and felt as if his body were run over by an automobile. Including all the years of hard partying and drinking himself into many stupors over the course of his life, none of those hangovers compared to the steady hard throbbing that beat inside his head like a pile driver. In addition, the constant pain was like a vise being cruelly tightened. Christ, he thought, even his eyelashes hurt!

He sat up on the rock floor and forced one eye open. Immediately his world began to spin and his stomach churned. Instantly he closed the eye to halt the sensations and took deep breaths to regain control. "Shit."

There was an awful taste of dried blood and dirt in his mouth and as his breath hit his nose, he winced at the foul smell. His jaw hurt as much as his head and when he ran his tongue across his teeth, he discovered a couple of them had been knocked loose.

Puckett steadied himself by taking deep breaths and tried again to open his swollen eyes. There was no spinning this time and he was able to see through the puffy slits. A ghostly dim light emanated from the lone bulb hung over his head and everywhere he looked, gray-brown rock surrounded him. He involuntarily shuddered.

He was in a cave.

When he exhaled, his breath formed a cloud that momentarily suspended in front of his face before it disintegrated. From what he could gather, the cave was about eight feet in diameter and continued on from either side of him. A string of dim lights suspended from the ceiling cast an eerie glow until they disappeared around a turn. Where was he? Afghanistan, Pakistan? He could only imagine. He reached up to touch his eye and discovered his hands were in irons. He let out a groan and searched his memory for how he got into this predicament and more importantly, how to get out of it?

As he continued to take stock of his situation, Puckett shifted his weight. A sudden white hot pain shot through his thighs that quickly spread throughout his body. "Fuck, that hurts!" he cursed and clenched his eyes and teeth and balled his fists to absorb the pain. When the pain subsided, he looked down at his blood soaked pants and remembered the bullets he took during the firefight. The wounds were neatly bandaged with spots of blood that seeped through the sterile gauze. That piqued his curiosity. The Taliban and al-Qaeda usually weren't human enough to bandage their wounded enemy.

He steeled himself in an attempt to move his legs. If they could bend, then there was a chance he could walk on them and make an effort to escape. Staring down at his knees and gritting his teeth, he made his first attempt.

Nothing.

Leaning his head against the wall, he tried again, this time focusing all of his drained energy on his legs. Taking a deep breath, he balled his hands and let out a groan as he called on his fit muscles to move. Sweat beaded on his forehead and dripped down his temples as he put more energy into his attempt.

Come on! He willed his muscles to move.

He breathed deeper and pushed harder. Sweat poured out of his skin and strained against the shackles as he ignored the increasing pain. The groan he emitted came from the pit of his stomach.

There! He did it! Ever so slightly his knees moved inward but the effort sapped all of his energy. He collapsed against the wall, taking deep heavy breaths. He was only able to savor the victory for a brief period because of the realization that trying to escape wasn't going to happen in his condition.

Harsh shouting echoed from somewhere in the cave. From around a dimly lit corner came two mean looking sons of bitches with dirty turbans and even dirtier clothes. Between them they were dragging a bloodied man by his arm pits and dropped him across from Puckett like a sack of rice where he lay in an immovable heap. One fighter turned and leveled an AK at Puckett while the other shackled the prisoner to the opposite wall.

Puckett got the message not to offer any help and instinctively knew that his turn was next.

Tuesday, October, 7, Langley, Virginia

Since the terrorist attacks on America on September 11, 2001, Paul McKnight, the man in charge of the National Clandestine Service, formerly called Operations, in the Central Intelligence Agency, had aged. When the CIA got the go ahead to commence operations in Afghanistan and Iraq long before Operation Iraqi Freedom began, he aged even more. The lines on his face were etched deeper and his mouth was forming a perpetual scowl. His closely cropped salt and pepper hair lost most of its pepper. Despite the aging and political turmoil within the Agency, McKnight hadn't lost any of his command authority or focus on the mission. At times he actually allowed himself to relish in many of the successes the war on terror had accomplished, even though the public would never find out about them.

In his spacious and richly decorated office, McKnight sat back in the high leather chair behind his mammoth gleaming mahogany desk with his favorite sized Arturo Fuente cigar clenched between his teeth. A manila folder with a single sheet of paper held in his calloused hands caused him to become angry and concerned at the same time.

"Damnit!" he spat and rubbed his forehead with his thumb and index finger. The report listed the name of the second intelligence officer he lost in Afghanistan in as many months. The first one, Greg Zelnick, was killed when the Humvee he was riding in hit an IED. The second officer, Leonard Puckett, was missing in action. For Puckett's sake, McKnight hoped that he was killed in combat or died immediately after receiving his wounds. If not, genuine torture would be used on him and it would be painful and hideous beyond description.

He also didn't need Puckett creating a disaster by spilling any of the intelligence he gathered or the names of agents he had working for him.

He shuddered at what they would do to him. Cutting off toes and fingers were a forerunner to the beheadings and or disembowelment which were some methods the bastards liked to use.

Dropping the folder, McKnight leaned forward, picked up the telephone and punched a series of digits he knew by memory.

"Major Albrecht," the voice on the other end said immediately.

"This is Paul McKnight, I need to speak to General Garrett."

"One minute, sir." When the director of the National Clandestine Service called, he was put right through.

As expected, it didn't take long for the commander of the Special Operations Command to get on the line. It also helped that General Garrett used to be a major and worked for Paul McKnight when he was a colonel in the U.S. Army Special Forces.

"Hi, Paul, I believe you're calling for a status report on your man?" He never bothered with small talk and fighting a war against terrorists in dozens of countries made his conversations even shorter.

"Got any good news for me, Hank?"

"No, I'm afraid I don't. We haven't found him yet, or the Afghan who was with him. The Rangers and Team 301 are still on it."

Damn. "Keep me posted. I'd like to tell his wife something."

"I hear you. Will do."

"Thanks." The line went dead. Frustrated, McKnight chomped on the end of the cigar.

Wednesday, October 8, Albany, New York

Marcus A. Kaderri sat behind his highly polished cherry desk and rubbed his tired eyes. His spacious 80 State Street corner office sat on the seventeenth floor right in the heart of downtown Albany. The papered walls held a flat panel television and various framed pictures and prints. The most important pictures, which sat on the corners of his desk, were the ones of Sara in her wedding dress and of the twins on their second birthday. There was also a book shelf filled with manuals and binders and a new compact stereo system. Well-watered plants and trees were tucked in the corners and rested on plates so the water wouldn't damage the deep burgundy carpet. Besides his desk, there was a round table, just as highly polished as his desk, with four leather chairs.

The large glass windows behind his desk gave him a panoramic view of the small city and the Capital of New York State. When he looked to the left, the Capitol building commanded from the top of the hill. The beautiful ornate gray stone building where, he liked to say, the self-centered, better-than-thou, live-your-life-the-way-we-tell you politicians conducted the state's business did their dirty deeds. He had a tendency to look at the building and then shake his head in amazement and disgust.

To the right was the Hudson River, a ribbon of greenish brown in the near distance that gave him the peaceful solace when he needed to think, and many times he had taken a walk down the hill to the Corning Preserve, a serene strip of land that stretched along the west bank of the river. It was also the place where on a mission, he shot and killed a drug dealer with a crossbow, impaling his body to car with the bolt.

Kaderri leaned his head back and let out a huge yawn that almost locked his jaw in place. Sam was up all night with a cold, coughing sneezing and feeling down right miserable, which in turn kept him up all night. Still, he was able to get his daily five mile run in the morning before heading to his office.

"Marc!"

Louise Faith's energetic squeal from outside the open door shot him out of his chair and sent his heart into warp speed. She bounded through the door and came to a sudden stop in front of his desk. Her energy kept her bouncing on her toes. Kaderri stood behind his desk and glared at her. "Jesus Christ! Louise, are you trying to give me heart attack?" He asked his shoulder length auburn haired assistant who had been with him from the day he opened his financial services company.

Louise's shapely legs were moving back and forth under a brown skirt like they were being shocked with electricity. Her pretty face beamed like a searchlight in the night and her green eyes had a glint to them. "Look!" she squealed again and thrust her left hand out. This time her whole body shook, her ample breasts jiggling under a tight fitting red turtleneck.

Kaderri immediately spotted the diamond engagement ring on her finger as the sunlight from the windows caught the cuts in the stone. "Congratulations!" he moved from behind his desk to give her a hug and a kiss.

"Thank you! Thank you!" She wrapped her arms around his broad chest and shoulders and squeezed. "I can't believe it! I'm going to get married!"

"Good for you, Louise. Jim couldn't be any luckier," he said meaning every word.

Louise pulled away, her smile still stretched from ear to ear. "I know."

Kaderri let out a laugh. "Tell me," he sat on the edge of the desk, "how did he propose?"

More energy seemed to take hold of her as she began to tell of the event. As she talked, her hands flapped in the excitement and paced in front of the desk. "I invited him over for dinner Saturday night and as usual when we were done, he began to help me clean up. I told him to sit down because I made chocolate mousse for dessert." She halted her pacing. "So like a good gentlemen, he did as instructed."

Kaderri rolled his eyes and said, "Smart man."

With a smile, she thrust a pointed finger at him. "Right!" Then she continued with her episode. "When I brought the parfait glasses out there was a box on the table in front of my chair." She resumed pacing and her hands covered her cheeks. "I froze when I saw it and nearly dropped the mousse. I put the mousse down and opened the box. I was shaking so much I didn't think I could open it! As soon as

I opened it he asked me to marry him." She finally stopped pacing. Once again she shrieked. "I said yes!"

"That's great!"

"He got one knee and put the ring on my finger. It was perfect!" She paused, smiled and added, "Then I jumped him right there on the table."

Kaderri chuckled and wasn't surprised by her openness. Sexual comments and innuendos from Louise was something he had grown used to and expected, almost on a daily basis. It had been that way from the beginning and he wouldn't have it any other way. "Good for you. What happened to the mousse?" He asked with a wry smile.

A smug look spread across her face. "We um…used it." Finished with her story, Louise turned to walk out the door then paused. She looked over her shoulder, wiggled her buttocks and added, "Now you lost your chance to take me to bed."

Kaderri chuckled. "My loss, most definitely."

"That's right. It is." She quickly changed subjects and pointed to his chest. "Sara didn't pick out your tie, right?"

Before he could respond, she walked out the door. He looked down suspiciously and held out his red and blue paisley tie. What was wrong with his tie? He thought it went well with his custom made navy blue and chalk pinstripe suit and white French cuffed shirt.

Chuckling again and shaking his head at the giddiness of his assistant, Kaderri moved back to behind his desk to continue with the retirement plan a client wanted him to set up for a fifty-five employee company.

The secure line on his phone rang. Only two people knew the direct number.

He picked it up before the second ring. "Yes?" he said hesitantly.

"Marc, it's Paul."

Another mission was something he wasn't interested in and was going to say so if asked. "What's up?" he asked his former boss at the Central Intelligence Agency.

As usual, Paul McKnight got right to the point. "Leonard Puckett, remember him?"

Kaderri took a quick breath of air at the mention of a fellow soldier. "He was my RTO, which I assume you already knew."

"Of course. He works for me now and he's MIA."

Kaderri felt a twinge of pain for his comrade. "Where and how long?"

"Afghanistan for a couple of days," McKnight acknowledged. "Haven't heard a thing either. No ransom, no gloating, not even a whisper for a trade."

Without any claim to the missing CIA officer, Kaderri knew that was bad news. "Doesn't sound good," he offered.

"No, it doesn't," McKnight agreed.

Kaderri thought of an idea which he was sure others had as well. "Do you think he went into hiding?"

"No. I'm assuming the worst. Listen, I got to run. I just wanted to let you know about one of your team. Marc, this is top secret."

"Right." Kaderri automatically understood he was not to mention this to anyone who did not have top secret clearance. "Thanks, Paul. Keep me posted?"

"Will do." Then the line went dead.

To Kaderri's surprise, talking to McKnight didn't cause him to get a strange unexplainable sensation that usually meant he was getting involved in something dangerous. Still holding onto the phone, he immediately punched the speed dial button that put him through to the private office of his former teammate, CIA partner and best friend, Robert Wolff.

"Crawford Enterprises, Optics Division," A pleasant young female voice stated.

Kaderri was surprised to get the main operator. The number programmed into his phone was a direct line to Wolff's office. Kaderri quickly searched his memory for Wolff's extension. "Extension 114, please."

"Hold on, I'll connect you."

Kaderri waited a short moment until another female voice came on line. This one was more mature than the main operator. "Director's office," she announced.

Kaderri let out a sigh. It was never this difficult to get to Wolff. "Bob, please."

"May I tell Dr. Wolff who's calling?"

Kaderri raised an eyebrow. Wolff must have gotten a new secretary who addressed him by his academic title. He was never that formal. "Marc," Kaderri answered casually to her question.

There was a moment of silence before she spoke again. "Marc-?" Clearly she was looking for his last name.

Kaderri smiled to himself and answered, "-us."

Another pause before she answered bruskly, "Hold on please."

A moment later Wolff came on line. "Mr. Marc Us?" Wolff's voice asked with a chuckle. "That's a new one."

"I thought I was being clever, Doctor," he paused, then added, "hell, everyone calls me Marc except for Sara when she's mad."

Wolff chuckled again. "Smart ass."

"New secretary? Why was she answering your phone? New scope or thermal sight not working right and having to screen your calls?" Crawford Enterprises designed optics for the military, ranging from rifle scopes to laser range finders.

Wolff laughed. "Phone problems, actually. Technology upgrade that doesn't work and yeah, she's new. Jackie moved away. Listen," Wolff sounded as if he was pleading, "Amy's good at what she does, so let her warm up to you before you have any fun with her."

"Hmm," Kaderri teased. The normally quiet man in social situations who was as interesting as a potted plant had a mischievous side that few had known. There were many ways Kaderri knew how to have fun, and few outside the Special Forces community knew exactly how.

"Marc," Wolff threatened. "Play nice! No gag gifts of dead snakes and explosives are out! Anyway, what's up?"

Kaderri cast all kidding aside. "I just hung up with Paul," Kaderri explained. "Len Puckett is MIA in Afghanistan." Wolff had security clearances as high as Kaderri, so he knew it would be permissible to tell Wolff the news. Besides, they all served together.

"No, shit? When?" Wolff asked with a shocked, concerned voice. He was closer to Puckett in the team than

Kaderri was. Both Wolff and Puckett were NCOs while Kaderri was an officer, so automatically there was a barrier, even in a close, tight knit unit such as an A-Team.

"A couple of days ago and there's no sign of him."

"Fuck, that's not good." Wolff stated what seemed to be the thought of the day. "This is the first of us who's had something like this happen, isn't it?"

Kaderri searched his memory for any bad news that had befallen anyone on the team. The only name that came to mind was Steven Caron, another teammate and friend who died in his arms on a stoop in Albany as a result of an errant bullet in a drive by shooting. "Besides Steven, nobody as far as I know."

"Hmm." There was a brief moment of silence before Wolff spoke again. "Seems strange that Paul would just call out of the blue and let you know what's happened to Len."

"Those are my thoughts too. I had no idea Len was working for him. Did you?"

Wolff's answer was a quick, "No."

"Something doesn't feel right," Kaderri suggested in regard to the conversation with McKnight.

"You get *that* feeling again?" Wolff questioned.

Kaderri always got this strange, unexplainable feeling throughout his body when he was going to be thrust into a dangerous situation. It was akin to other people's 'little voices' or the mysterious sixth sense. He laughed half-heartedly, "No, not yet."

"That's encouraging," Wolff said thankfully. "Hold on." After a pause he spoke again. "Marc, I gotta run, keep me up to date?"

"Right." Kaderri hung up the phone, but tucked away in his mind remained the question of why McKnight would call. Could it be as simple as what he said?

Wednesday, October 8, Rangers, Paktika Province, Afghanistan

There were many signs of human activity in the area. Foot slides, scraped rocks and footprints, but nothing solid that led Lt. Jack Dover to the two missing men. Many of the cave openings lead to dead ends or were too small for a man to move through but every possibility had to be investigated. Even the orbiting helos had reported nothing. It seemed as if the Earth had swallowed Len Puckett and Mike Karmal.

Dover's patience was wearing thin and frustration was building as time ticked on. He stared at the dark four foot opening to the latest cave, almost willing one of his men to appear, guiding Puckett and Karmal from the bowels of the mountain. His hands tightened around the pistol grip and hand guards of his rifle, turning his knuckles white.

"Easy, Lieutenant," Master Sergeant Chris Knapp cautioned as he approached from behind. "Getting pissed isn't gonna help find them any faster."

Dover turned to the leather faced Green Beret. A calm ease was on his face. "We got more than forty men combing this fucking hill and birds in the air and nothing! How do you do it, Master Sergeant?"

Knapp shrugged. "Experience. You'll learn. If not, you'll be an ineffective commander."

"You got any tricks I should know about? I'm always willing to listen and learn." Dover waited for some keen insight from the Master Sergeant.

"No, sir. You're doing everything right. They're in there," he pointed with his head. "We'll find 'em."

Wednesday, October 8, The Cave, Afghanistan

Time was no longer a measuring instrument for Leonard Puckett. His watch was taken away from him, along with the rest of his equipment and knit hat, but he tried his damnest to keep track of how long he was in captivity. As of now, he guessed it was somewhere in the neighborhood of thirty-six hours. The only time he counted was the number of trips he made to the interrogation room he called the dungeon. Before every trip, he was blindfolded until he was strapped into the chair and the harsh white light was shone into his eyes.

He didn't know how long it had gone on for, but he was thankful the latest beating in the dungeon was over and welcomed being shackled to the stone wall. The cold stone was the closest thing to an ice pack he was going to get and he pressed his beaten face to it to take out some of the sting.

He took a shallow breath and winced. A stab a pain felt like fire as his lungs expanded and his rib cage moved. By feel he knew that at least two if not three ribs on his left side were broken. His left eye had swollen shut and the cuts inside his mouth were never going to heal with all the blows he kept taking. Three of his front teeth were now missing, two on the bottom and one on the top. When the blood filled his mouth and had to spit it out, he had to lean his head down and let the blood drain. The swelling and numbness of his lips prevented him from pursing his lips to spit, so the blood simply ran down his chin and cheek. His blood-stained clothing made it appear he was wearing a red bib. The ironic thing that kept him baffled was his shot up legs had received rudimentary medical attention. Bandage his leg wounds but beat the crap out of him? Maybe his captors didn't want him to bleed to death before they extracted all that they could out of him? Humor, he said to himself, would help keep his sanity. At least for a little while. He surmised that if he looked in the mirror, he would be the poster boy for a hockey team.

Puckett put the humor aside and concentrated on his fabricated story, making the fictitious life and unit he was supposedly a member of come to life. He also concentrated on what lies and deceptions he told his brutal interrogators to keep from straying off the path.

The interrogators were something else, he noted. They were brutal, but efficient. Not the type he expected in the third world country that was run by thugs. The interrogations were designed and executed with precision which led him to believe there were other people involved. There were two men who always hid in the shadows and during the last interrogation he swore they spoke Russian. Puckett acted as if he was knocked unconscious after a brutal hit to his temple and let his chin slump to his chest. It was then he heard one man speak to the other, but their whispers were just a little too low for him to discern any clear words or dialects but it was enough for the language to be identified as Russian. If they were indeed Russians, that would explain their interrogation method.

Though he held out a sliver of hope, he knew that it was just a matter of time before he would break, then die. Every man had his breaking point, he just didn't know where his was and relying on his training and thinking about getting back to his wife gave him the strength to carry on. Because of his wounds, escaping from this hell hole seemed pretty remote. Puckett was sure that a search and rescue mission was underway, he just didn't know if they would be able to find him before it was too late.

A shout in Dari signaled that the shit was about to start again.

Wednesday, October 8, Kiri, Chechnya

The early snow had been falling all day in and around the outskirts of the small town of Kiri in the southeastern region of Chechnya, on the northern slopes of the Caucasus Mountains. They were small flakes that floated on the wind, accumulating to just a few inches, but it blanketed the ground nonetheless and nestled in the crooks of the branches of the birch, beech and massive oak trees that filled the thick forest and the undisturbed undergrowth that weaved into a tangled mess. For the hard men in the war fighting business, weather was a non factor.

Major Mikhail Vasilyevich Borushko, the executive officer of the 1st Battalion 70th Motorized Rifle Regiment of the Russian Army savored the rabbit stew in the tin bowl sitting in the back of the cramped command BMP armored personnel carrier enjoying the brief moment alone, away from the daily grind and stress of a combat unit. As he put each flavorful spoonful into his mouth, he thanked the soldiers who shot the furry little creatures and the cook for making a flavorful hot meal that went well on this cold day. It sure as hell beat the borscht that was still a common staple in the army.

The battalion's primary mission was to interdict Muslim terrorists infiltrating from Chechnya's eastern neighbor, Dagestan. The mission, for the most part, had been successful in the three months they have been out there, ambushing a dozen groups of terrorists, killing all of them for a total that approached sixty. The 1/70 also fought off a determined attack, while they were in a laager, that netted another hundred killed and thirty captured Chechen rebels. The close-in fighting had hardened Borushko, where he learned that death was an instant away and every minute he lived he was going to get the most out of it. The battalion hadn't come through the fight unscathed. They had forty-seven casualties with twenty-one killed and three BMP's lost to RPG fire.

There was sure to be more fighting in the foreseeable future as more enemy fighters infiltrated across the border. There were just too many ways to get through the mountains to completely shut off the flow of rebels and suicidal zealots.

The population in the town of Kiri was mixed in either support for the Russians, the Chechen rebels or a complete indifference to both, just as long as they were left alone by all parties. Because of this, a foray into the town could be dangerous not only to the Russian soldiers, but the innocent civilians as well. Constructing a base within the town could have invited deadly confrontations on a daily basis. With the constant threat of clashes, the five-hundred-plus men of 1/70 set up its base two kilometers from the town limits, erecting and supplying everything they needed to sustain themselves. Fields of fire were cleared up to a klick away from the base perimeter and suspected infiltration routes were constantly under watch. Land mines, concertina wire and machine gun emplacements were deployed as an added deterrent.

Putting another mouthful of food into his mouth as his brown eyes scanned the open field through the open rear ramp and falling snow, Borushko contemplated what twists had occurred in his country ever since the collapse of the Soviet Union and the infusion of capitalism. Life was completely different from his childhood, even in old traditional enclaves such as the army. Some of the changes were good while others were downright harmful, at least in his opinion. Fighting these fucking Muslims in this mountain hideaway this way was one of the harmful changes. The old Soviet Red Army would have come into Kiri with a division or two and annihilated the place, killing and destroying everything that stood against them. End of story.

But not anymore. Warfare had evolved into low intensity conflicts where armies no longer faced each other and slugged it out. And the twenty-four hour news media that covered such events kept them under a microscope and reported everything they saw and with their own spin. Annihilating a village would cause a world uproar and bad PR.

Because of this, commanders and politicians had to worry about collateral damage and non-combatant battle deaths, at least to some extent. Those precautions made it harder to kill the enemy and allowed the men in his unit to be at the receiving end of the first shot, meaning they would die before they had a chance to shoot back.

Other improvements in life in Russia were becoming apparent. Food was now in more abundance than ever before and many different styles and quality of clothing was more readily available. More importantly, Western technology was now available on the open market. American know how, Borushko had to admit, was second to none in the world, and when it came to their military equipment, it was obvious why Iraqi forces were decimated in the 1991 Persian Gulf War and met the same fate in the second Persian Gulf War, known to the Americans as Operation Iraqi Freedom. The Russian generals who had preached over the years that Soviet equipment was superior to their American foe had either retired or disappeared. In hindsight, it was a good thing Russian and American forces never met in battle. Despite the numerical superiority of the Red Army, it was clear who the victor would have been.

Another positive in the new capitalistic society were less obstacles to encounter in getting things done or going places. There was no more checking of papers at impromptu roadblocks, which sometimes led to being detained for hours if some smart ass KBG/FSB or GRU officer decided he didn't like you. Or having your possessions taken, or, which happened on countless occasions, just being shot on the spot for whatever reason.

The controlling fear used by the Communist Party no longer existed.

Borushko smiled to himself, thankful for those changes. Gone was that everyday fear of being harmed or disappearing into a Gulag and capitalism allowed him to get involved in a lucrative criminal organization. Early in his military career he made contacts with the Russian mafia, a ruthless group from Moscow known as Solntsevskaya. Because of this affiliation, Borushko was lining his pockets with more money a month then he would have ever made in a lifetime in the army. The material rewards in his possession and that he had available to him were items he only dreamed about as a child. The brand new Mercedes-Benz E500 to go along with a spacious two story Dacha in Romanovo, seventy kilometers north of Moscow with the latest in audio and video home entertainment equipment and security system were just the beginning.

With luxuries like those and the open ended opportunity for them to continue, he thought, as he wiped the bottom of the bowl with a thick slice of bread, was the way it should be. That is why at the end of two months time, his tenure in the army would come to an end. At the end of this month he would be rotated out of his current assignment with the remainder of his time sitting behind a desk and out processing.

"Comrade Major?" a young voice called urgently from outside the armored vehicle. "Are you still in there?"

"Yes, Corporal," Borushko answered immediately, recognizing the voice of Corporal Pletnev. He dropped the bread in the bowl, wiped the corners of his wide mouth with his thumb and forefinger and waited for the corporal to appear at the rear ramp.

"Sir, you're needed over at communications right a way."

A hundred thoughts raced through Borushko's mind. Everything from getting orders to move out to attack the Muslim rebels in another stronghold or listen to the bad news of fellow soldiers getting blown apart in an ambush to another disheartening message that the supply convoy will not be arriving again. He rose from the hard seat in the armored vehicle and placed the bowl on the cold steel floor. Dropping the fur lined ushanka hat on his close cropped blond head and grabbing the AK-47, he walked down the ramp to where the fully armed corporal was standing.

Armored vehicles weren't designed for comfort, so when Borushko reached the bottom of the ramp, he halted and stretched to his full six foot-one height and swung his hips back and forth a few times to work out the muscle cramps. "What's the problem?" he asked as he stepped towards the communications tent.

"I don't know, sir," Pletnev answered and dutifully fell in on Borushko. "Captain Agranov sent me to find you."

"Hmm," Borushko grunted. Captain Pyotr Agranov, the officer on watch, must be nervous about something, he thought to himself. He's got a good head on his shoulders and can handle most anything.

Pulling the zipper of his coat up a little higher and crunching the winter cap further down on his head to protect himself from the sudden icy breeze, Borushko trudged through the snow in silence to the large communications tent a hundred meters away.

Without pausing, Borushko pushed aside the series of overlapping tent flaps, stepped onto the plywood floor and stomped his feet, knocking the snow and muck off his boots. The corporal was doing the same. Inside the tent was much warmer and crowded. With a skeptical eye Borushko surveyed the men and wondered how many were in here because it was their job or just for the warmth. He turned to Pletnev. "Thank you Corporal."

"Yes, sir." Pletnev understood the dismissal and returned to his post.

Tables and desks, topped with radios, computers and other types of equipment needed to run a battalion in combat, lined the perimeter of the forty by twenty tent. From outside the tent, a steady hum from the gasoline generators that powered the heaters and electrical equipment droned through the fabric wall. Though the set up was typical for a mobile field unit, in a couple of days the battalion was going to move into the more permanent quarters being erected. Regular heat, running water and more civil amenities were going to be welcomed.

Borushko removed his ushanka and scanned the cigarette smoke filled tent. It didn't take more than a few seconds to find Captain Agranov with a cigarette dangling from his lips hovering over a group of radio operators. Borushko began to make his way through the maze of equipment and wires towards the captain when Agranov looked up from a clipboard and made eye contact.

"What is it, Pyotr?" Borushko asked once he got at his side.

Agranov placed the clipboard down in front of the closest radio operator. In a hushed voice he said, "Colonel Yezhov has missed the last two check in times."

A shiver ran down Borushko's spine. This conversation wasn't just about the colonel and his relation with the battalion. This was about their link to the Solntsevskaya. He remembered Yezhov was headed to Turkmenistan and was going to be out of communication for awhile, but missing two prearranged times with Agranov meant something had gone wrong.

"His first scheduled time was supposed to be Tuesday morning and the second was supposed to be an hour ago," Agranov reminded in an alarmed whisper.

Borushko grabbed the captain by the shoulder and silently led him outside the tent to the generators where the humming would mask their conversation. "I know when he was supposed to check in!" Borushko snapped at his childhood friend and criminal colleague. He took a breath and blew it out between pursed lips. "I'm sorry, Pyotr," he said quietly and placed his hand on Agranov's shoulder. He regained his composure so they wouldn't raise any suspicion of their extracurricular activities.

Agranov nodded acceptance then offered, "When he didn't call in Tuesday morning, I assumed he had a reason. But when he missed today-"

Borushko nodded his understanding. He glanced around to make sure they weren't being watched before he continued. "Something must have gone wrong. First we have to find out where he is." He shook his head when he realized he just stated the obvious.

A look of concern etched into Agranov's face. He took one last drag on the cigarette and flicked the butt. "What are we going to tell brigade headquarters when they come looking for him or when we have to go back into combat? He's due back from leave in two days?"

Another icy chill ran down Borushko's spine, freezing him to the core. This posed a major problem, and one he wasn't sure how to deal with. The battalion was in the middle of a war fighting Chechens and the commanding officer was missing. What would he tell the brigade commander if they issue new orders and Yezhov hasn't returned? It was one thing if Yezhov was killed or wounded in action, but not returning from a scheduled leave was an entirely different matter. There is no way he could go out to search for Yezhov and leave the battalion, which, as the executive officer, would be in his hands. He could cover for the colonel for a few days, especially if they didn't receive orders to move out. What bothered him most was the effect of Yezhov's disappearance on his scheduled departure from the army if he had to take over of the battalion.

"Then we have to work fast. We better make some calls." Borushko referred to the connections in the Solntsevskaya.

Agranov bounced on the balls of his feet in an effort to stay warm. "There is something else," he whispered almost conspiratorially.

"What?" Borushko hissed through clenched teeth. He didn't need anymore bad news.

Agranov gave the hint of smile. "This is better news, my friend."

Borushko lightened his demeanor somewhat. Good news was always welcomed.

Captain Pyotr Agranov contained his excitement. He looked around again so no one could overhear their conversation.

"Eduard and Aleksander sent a message they have captured an Afghan and an American Green Beret."

Borushko's eyes narrowed into slits. Eduard Tomsky and Aleksander Karsavin were conducting Solntsevskaya business in Afghanistan. "That's risky, capturing an American. What's so good about that? Anyway," he became perplexed, "why is Eduard sending information to us? They have nothing to do with our operation."

"Listen, would you?" Agranov let out a frustrated sigh before his face beamed with excitement. "Of course they didn't give much details, but they say both the American and the Afghan have knowledge about who killed your father! They sent a text message and an e-mail to both of us with the list of names of those who were involved! Didn't you check your cell phone?"

Borushko slowly shook his head. He shut his phone off while he ate lunch in the BMP. He clamped his jaw and his eyes bored a hole into Agranov. A thousand childhood memories of him and his father hunting and fishing together in the Ural Mountains and enjoying the extra benefits bestowed a general in the Soviet Army came flooding back. Suddenly the thoughts of their missing commander seemed less important. A promise that Borushko made had been locked away and forgotten about since that fateful day in 1985 came rushing to the front of his memory.

Wednesday, October, 8, The Cave, Afghanistan

Whack! The stinging clap on Puckett's only good ear rung his bell. The top half of the other ear had already been sliced off. He clenched his teeth and balled his restrained fists in an attempt to absorb the pain. This beating had to have gone on for at least an hour, and it was as brutal as ever. Another tooth was knocked loose, his jaw popped when he opened it and his abdomen felt as if it were a heavy bag for a heavyweight boxing champion. The bulb from the spotlight aimed into his eyes wasn't that bright as far as spotlights go, but it did have the desired effect. He was unable to see who was in the room with him and the light hurt his eyes, with the pain spreading to the back of his head. Every time he closed his eyes to get some relief, he was rewarded with a more vicious smack to open them again. Instead of looking directly into the light, he tried to manipulate his focus and avoid the bulb itself by looking just off to the side. It didn't help much.

"What unit you with!" The interrogator asked in broken English.

"Sergeant Leonard Puckett." He spit out a mouthful of blood that dribbled down his chin. He hung his head to hide the fact that he had closed his eyes to keep them from getting damaged further, then continued giving the only information required by the Geneva convention. Not that it mattered. "United States Army, one three-"

"Infidel!"

Puckett steeled himself for the next blow. The punch came fast and hard and slammed into his abdomen, knocking the air out of his lungs and causing his eyes to burst wide open. He doubled over as far as the restraints on his arms that held him to the wooden chair would allow and gasped for air like a fish out of water.

Then immediately from behind, someone grabbed his forehead and jerked it back, exposing his throat. A cold blade pressed on his vulnerable Adams apple signaled his approaching death. His body went rigid as fear he had never known gripped him.

"No," commanded a stern accented voice from one of the two men Puckett believed to be Russian.

There was a slight hesitation, then the flat side of the blade was slowly drawn across his throat as it was removed. Puckett's trained ear did not hear the knife being returned to its sheath.

Once his head was released, he fell forward again to alleviate the pain from the blow to his stomach and muttered a prayer that his demise would be quick and pain free, or have the cavalry arrive in time to get him out of this place alive.

"Leonard Puckett, United States Army Special Forces," the Russian stated in accented English. "From what I gather, you like Afghanistan. You were fighting here once before, correct?"

How the fuck did he know that? Puckett asked himself as the pain in his stomach began to subside and his breathing almost returned to normal. It then became clear, Mike Karmal broke under the strain of the interrogation, otherwise the Russian would not have known about his prior visit.

Puckett shook his head in defiance. "No."

"Come now," the interrogator said in a calm, conversational tone. "Your friend told us all about you and your special forces team fighting with the rebels."

Bingo! The man just confirmed he was Russian, whether he did so intentionally or not. Only the Soviets called the mujahadeen rebels. Puckett detected movement and the light was removed from in front of his eyes. He seized the opportunity and immediately shut his eyes tight, attempting to force out the white spot that may be permanently burned into his retina.

The respite was short. A few moments later he was told to open them with a slap to the head. Fuzzy shadows appeared at first, then slowly ghost like images materialized and he was able to make out his surroundings. He was still in the cave and this room was approximately twelve foot square and appeared to be a natural formation but was reinforced with wooden beams. The only other feature he could make out was the open wooden door off to the side.

Two big dirty men in stained robes appeared in the opening dragging the listless body of Mike Karmal. They took two steps in and dropped him on the floor with a thud.

"Here is your comrade," the Russian said.

"Mike!" Puckett called in alarm for his friend. He turned his head and pulled against the restraints as far a he could go to get closer. "Mike! Wake up!"

No response.

"Mike!" Puckett yelled louder, hoping his raised voice would elicit some response.

"Now, Puckett," the Russian patronized and placed himself between Puckett and Karmal, blocking the motionless man from view.

"Ivan," Puckett called out, catching the Russian off guard. "What are you doing here? I remember hearing your comrades got their asses kicked a few years back in this country and your army ran away with its tail between its legs. Looking for a little revenge or learn how to fight and win a war?"

There was a noticeable pause before the Russian responded.

"My business here has no concern of yours," he snapped. Easily switching back to a conversational tone, the Russian continued with the interrogation. "Tell me about *your* time here, Puckett, particularly in 1985 and the shooting of General Borushko."

"I am very interested in that also," the other Russian asked in heavily accented English.

Wednesday, October 8, Rangers, Paktika Province, Afghanistan

"Sir," Sergeant First Class Roger Isles, the five-foot-ten-inch 1st Platoon sergeant and veteran of both Gulf War 1 and Operation Iraqi Freedom approached from Lt. Jack Dover's left just as he stuck his head out from the opening of a small cave. He resembled a chipmunk emerging from its home. "I've got a status report."

Dover pushed his rifle out then finished crawling on his belly out of the hole and took the offered hand from Isles to help him up. "I hope you have good news, Sergeant, because that damn cave was worthless," he said sourly. He picked up his rifle, stood and dusted himself off. He stepped out of the way as Corporal Ross' rifle then his head popped out of the same hole. He offered a hand to his fire team leader.

The platoon sergeant shook his head. "We've searched seventeen caves and holes so far," Isles said with distaste. "Except for some intel, we have come up empty. I take it you came up empty as well?"

"Nothing," Dover spat and readjusted the plastic knee pads that fell to his shins.

"This sucks," Ross simply stated and walked away.

Dover was firmly disgusted that they couldn't find the two missing men. Two fucking days of scouring the rocks looking for an opening to a larger cave where the men could be. They had to be somewhere in the mountain! The intelligence they recovered from some of the caves was extremely valuable and the Intel guys back at headquarters were going to have a field day with what they found. Some of the information they recovered, Dover knew, would end up with him leading his Rangers on strike missions and raids.

But what was going to happen in the future was not his concern.

Of the three blood trails the Rangers were following, two ended with the discovery of dead fighters. One body was left hidden in the shadows of a boulder and the other in a small gully. The third just simply disappeared, presumably because someone was able to stem the flow of blood. The whole situation was pissing him off because he knew the longer that time ticked away without his team finding Puckett and Karmal, the closer they were to death.

"How many more caves do we have to go? Got any idea?" asked Dover. He was hoping Isles would say very few. Crawling around like a mole got old real quick.

Isles shrugged and shook his head. "It's hard to say, sir. This place is honeycombed. We could be here awhile."

Dover let out a sigh and was about to issue new orders when he glanced at PFC Tony Montana sitting against a rock thirty meters away down slope. Dover's blood began to boil. Twenty minutes earlier when he went into the cave, Montana was in the same spot, which led Dover to assume Montana was pausing a moment for a drink. It was clear now Montana was slacking in his search and rescue responsibilities.

"With me," Dover angrily ordered Isles and stormed towards Montana. "He's been sitting there for too fucking long."

As he approached the private, he became more angry that a Ranger would pull such a stunt in shirking his duties. He stopped next to Montana and prepared to tear the soldier a new one.

"Sir," Montana spoke first and pointed his rifle to a small opening in the side of the hill next to a cluster of rocks. "I think our guys are in there." He remained seated against the rock. "Or under there," he corrected himself.

"What?" Dover blurted, being caught unawares. "How do you know that?"

"I'm curious to know that, too," stated Isles a bit more skeptical than his commander. There was an icy edge to his voice.

"I've been watching that spot for some time, sir. At first I thought this was just another small cluster of rocks on the ground, but do you see that bird over there? Above the bigger rocks?" He pointed to a small black bird ten feet away that had its eyes trained on the same spot Montana was pointing to.

"Yeah?" Dover answered with a little more patience. His Ranger was on to something. He quickly ran over Montana's bio in his mind and remembered he was an avid hunter from Colorado. Most likely he knew something about animal behavior.

"Well, sir, he doesn't want to get too close to it. He flies or hops over to it then moves away, but he never leaves the area."

"Meaning?"

"Meaning, sir, there's something there that the bird wants to check out, but has second thoughts."

Dover remained silent and focused his attention on what Montana had said and observed the bird. Sure enough, the bird did its little dance around the small cluster of rocks and then backed away. "Have you gone over and checked it out yet?" He looked down at Montana.

"Not yet, sir. Don't want to spook it."

Dover patted his gear, searching for his standard issue USNV PVS-7D night vision goggles. The next generation of light weight goggles combined night vision along with a thermal imager.

"Nice work, Montana. Let's see if this turns out to be the place where these ragheads are keeping our guys."

"What have you got, Lieutenant?" MSgt. Chris Knapp asked just as Dover brought the goggles to his eyes. A spot of red-orange immediately blossomed in the center of the screen, right where the bird was. "I got a heat source," Dover stated excitedly as the fuzzy plume of red filled the view in his screen. "Looks like an exhaust vent."

Dover then relayed what Montana had told him and handed him the imager, but Knapp already had his top of the line USNV-14B night vision goggles, Noggs for short, up to his eyes.

"That's gotta be it," Knapp stated in agreement. "Let's get a fucking back hoe in here and dig it out."

There was a renewed sense of urgency and hope.

"Sir!" a ranger called out from next to the side of the hill. "Footprints!"

They were in business.

Wednesday, October 8, The Cave, Afghanistan

The smell of terror suddenly filled the cold, damp cave chamber as Puckett nervously watched the fighters within move with a determined purpose. Sweat began to leak from his pores as the fear grew deep. There were four men in here beside himself and Karmal-two Taliban fighters and the two Russians.

Karmal sat listlessly on the rock floor a few feet away from Puckett, his hands bound behind his back with frayed rope and his beaten, bloody head hung with his chin resting on his blood stained chest. He appeared to be drifting in and out of consciousness. He would lift his head, utter a low moan, the swollen right eye lid would flutter for a moment and his head would drop again. Puckett couldn't tell if Karmal's actions were caused by the brutal beatings or if they were drug induced. He assumed it was the former.

"You've been taught well to resist, Mr. Puckett," acknowledged the Russian he dubbed Ivan as he squatted in front of Puckett. The other Russian he dubbed Igor.

Puckett grunted trying to read Ivan's pale face through swollen, painful eyes. What he saw was a cold, calculated professional face with hard, dark, uncaring eyes.

"There are many ways to break a man, as you well know," Ivan gestured nonchalantly with a wave of his hand. "One thing I have learned about you American soldiers is your absolute devotion to not leaving any man behind, and protecting others. Admirable, but sometimes not practical."

Ivan rose and slowly retreated to a corner of the cramped stone room. Puckett spied out of the corner of his eye one of the ugly Taliban fighters moved to a position next to Karmal and point a Makarov pistol at the back of his head.

Puckett's heart began to race and he tried to break free of the restraints to save his friend, but he knew there was nothing he could do to prevent what was going to happen.

"No! No! Don't do it!" he pleaded in a loud angry voice. His muscles pulled against the restraints.

"Too late, Mr. Puckett," said Igor. "You should have told us what we wanted to know when we asked."

Puckett knew the comments were a ruse. They had no intention of letting Karmal and himself out of the cave alive. He was going to take to his grave his affiliation with the CIA.

"You see, Puckett," Ivan spoke conversationally, "these Taliban fighters don't put the value on human life like you or me."

"Right. You're a real charitable son-of-a-bitch," Puckett stated coldly. His heart raced and he clenched his fists to keep them from shaking. The vacant uncaring look in Ivan's eyes told him the end for Karmal was at hand.

Ivan turned to the Afghan and nodded.

In less than a heart beat, the thunderous sound of the pistol report echoed off the stone walls. The bullet passed through Karmal's head and blew out his forehead and left eye in a spray of bright red blood and shards of bone. The bullet then passed through Karmal's foot where it ricocheted off the floor and struck the wall.

In slow motion, like an object beginning its roll down a long slope, Karmal's body slumped forward. When he landed, what was left of his face had turned towards Puckett. The jagged hole in his forehead and eye socket oozed blood and gray goo that ran like a river and pooled on the uneven stone floor.

Ivan stood in front of Puckett with his arms folded. "We have some questions we want you to answer. Particularly who shot General Borushko." He motioned towards Karmal's body. "Or..."

CHAPTER THREE

Wednesday October 8, Rangers, Paktika Province, Afghanistan

Fifteen minutes after the discovery of the footprints, a Ranger discovered the hidden entrance to the cave where they believed Karmal and Puckett to be. It was large enough for a man to walk through in a slight crouch and was concealed behind a large boulder that stood three feet in front of the entrance. A few drops of dried blood and scuffed footprints found on the ground near the entrance confirmed their suspicions, and gave the platoon hope of finding the two missing men.

Ten feet inside the mouth of the cave, the passageway expanded to where two men could easily stand shoulder to shoulder. It was apparent this section of the cave was widened by human hands. Tell tale scars where sledgehammers and chisels struck the walls had left jagged edges.

Dover held to his word and allowed the special forces operators to take the lead in rescuing their man. The point element consisted of Knapp, Michaelson and one Afghan translator, Hamid. They moved in silently and cautiously, ready to deal with any event decisively and violently. Michaelson and Knapp were both armed with M-4 carbines outfitted with USNV-441 COM-SPEC weapons sights and a combat Surefire light under the barrel. Silenced 9mm Berettas were secured in holsters strapped to their thighs. Hamid, as most of the Afghan's were, was armed with an AK. Grenades, both fragmentation and smoke, hung from their web gear. The view through their Noggs cast everything in a ghostly yet clear green light.

With their right shoulders against the cave wall and weapons up in firing positions, the three man team moved further into the cold, inky blackness. Silently they moved down the throat of the mountain, the stone walls closing in on them. Fifty feet in, they rounded a corner and Knapp came to a sudden halt. Not more then ten feet in front huddled together with a glowing candle between them were two enemy guards, talking among themselves and facing away from the cave entrance and sharing a smoke. Rookies. They would pay a price for not being at the mouth of the cave.

Without looking, Knapp quietly handed the M-4 back to Michaelson and withdrew his silenced pistol from the holster strapped to his right thigh. Taking aim on the man on the right, Knapp placed the sights on the man's head and squeezed the trigger twice in rapid succession. Just as quickly, he flicked his wrist to the left and put two shots into the head of the second enemy before he knew his companion was dead. Both bodies fell on each side of the lit candle.

The two Green Berets immediately pounced on the dead bodies, checking for a pulse or any signs of life. As expected, there were none. They waited a moment to see if their action had drawn attention.

When no bad guys arrived, Knapp spoke quietly into the boom arm microphone on his voice activated RA3185 Cobra Modular Infantry Radio communications gear. He made the call to Dover, who like all the other Rangers, had their own MIR sets. "Bravo One Six, this is Minuteman. We're clear. Two enemy dead. Out." He then turned to Hamid, the Afghan who tagged along. "Stay here with these two."

The soldier acknowledged with a nod.

Knapp and Michaelson then moved in deeper, checking out what lay ahead.

Standing outside the entrance of the cave under a cloudless blue sky, Dover paced back and forth like a nervous father waiting to hear from the doctor about his pregnant wife. He came to an immediate halt and nodded when Knapp's voice came into his ear. "Contact." A shiver shook down his spine.

They found the enemy.

The PW team, Privates First Class Eric Fletcher and Keith Doyle, were waiting outside the cave when Dover pointed to the black opening. "Go," he ordered the two men assigned searching prisoners or dead bodies for information.

"Yes, sir," the two Rangers responded and darted into the cave.

"Minuteman," Dover called into the mic to warn them friendlies were coming in and not to shoot them. "PW team is on it's way in. Don't shoot 'em, copy?"

"Roger, Bravo One Six, out."

Dover then wheeled on his heel and found his competent platoon sergeant. "Sergeant Isles, have First and Third Squads set up a perimeter out here. Second Squad," he looked directly at the tall lanky young leader of Second Squad, Sergeant Bill Parks, "with me."

Isles was already moving. "Yes, sir. First and Third Squad leaders, get moving! You heard the man, set up a perimeter."

The squad leaders immediately relayed the order to their prospective commands, the highly trained Rangers who overheard Dover were already moving to comply.

"Sergeant Dorsey?" Dover turned in the opposite direction and spotted the Green Beret kneeling on the ground staring at the topographical map he had spread on the dirt and was comparing it with the GPS. Staff Sergeant Wicker, the other Green Beret, was peering over his shoulder.

"Over here, Lieutenant," Dorsey answered without looking up from the map.

Wicker gave a wave.

"We're going in." Dover's lips suddenly went dry at the prospect of engaging in close quarters combat. It was a nasty business where death was always inches away.

"Right, sir. My men are ready." Dorsey folded the map and put it back in it's plastic, waterproof case that was secured to the Pouch Attachment Ladder System, or PALS, webbing on his assault vest. "Fall in!" He then ordered the Afghans to fall in behind Second Squad.

While First and Third Squads went about the task of setting up their circular defensive positions twenty meters from the opening of the cave, Second Squad formed in a single file outside the cave entrance. Wide, alert eyes from the nine man squad were in constant motion, searching the landscape for any signs of danger. Warm breath cooled into a cloudy mist in front of the men's camouflaged faces, then dissipated like the enemy they had been searching.

Sergeant Isles came up to Dover to report. "Perimeter's set."

"Good. Stay alert and don't let anyone trap us in there," Dover gave a wry smile, knowing Isles wouldn't let that happen. Dover then turned towards Second Squad. "Fire Team A, you take the lead. Move and hold position when you get to the PW team." As expected, he received curt nods from the determined Rangers. "Move out."

Dover slid into the third spot in line. The squad moved forward and without hesitation, brought their rifles up and entered the cave. Their hard soled boots quietly stepped on the worn floor as they moved confidently into the abyss.

The sunlight illuminating the entrance of the cave quickly faded; causing the squad to don their Noggs. When they rounded the first corner they came upon the PW team searching the bodies of the Taliban guards with the aid of their flashlights.

Dover knelt next to Fletcher who was unraveling a beige, bloody turban. "Anything?" he whispered, not knowing if enemy forces were nearby.

"Yes, sir. Hamid," he nodded in the direction of the Afghan and spoke in a normal voice, "has a hand drawn map of what looks like this cave complex that we found on this dead guy here."

Dover felt a wave of elation. If it was true they wouldn't be stumbling around in the dark anymore. He laughed inwardly at his choice of words. "Let's take a look." He stood, placed the Noggs on his forehead and took the map from Hamid's outstretched hand. He clicked the flashlight on and pointed the beam on the worn and dirty sheet of creased paper. The crude map showed the cave complex was shaped like a tuning fork. The two parallel tunnels were lined with chambers on the inside walls.

"What's this say?" Dover pointed to a chamber off to the left of their position.

"Machine," Hamid answered immediately.

"How far up is Master Sergeant Knapp?"

"'Bout a dozen meters, sir," the Afghan answered pointing to the handle part of the tuning fork. "Right here at this connection."

"Come with me," Dover wheeled and headed towards Knapp's position. "Minuteman," Dover spoke into the comm set, "this is Bravo One Six, I'm coming down, out."

A few steps later he came upon Michaelson and Knapp, who just happened to be pointing his weapon at Dover for security reasons. "What have we got?" Dover asked the two senior NCO's. His ears perked up to a quiet, rapid humming.

"All's quiet, Lieutenant," Knapp answered in a hushed voice and dropped his rifle. "We're at the junction of two tunnels. It's basically a 'T'. While we were waiting for your squad, we did a little snooping." Knapp removed his night vision goggles and directed the flashlight to the ceiling that was attached to the barrel of his weapon. "Look." The beam illuminated a string of work lights suspended from the damp ceiling. Before Dover could ask the obvious, Knapp continued. "They lead into a chamber over here on the left just around the corner."

Dover recalled the layout of the map. "The machine room."

"You can say that, sir," Michaelson agreed. "How'd you know?"

"We found a floor plan on one of the dead ragheads. What's in there?" Without waiting for an answer, he shut off his goggles, clicked on his flashlight and followed the beam of light to a wood door. Michaelson and Knapp were right behind him.

The humming noise came from the other side and when Dover placed his hand on the coarse door, he could feel a slight vibration.

"Give it a push, Lieutenant," Knapp said when he saw Dover feeling for a knob. "We've already checked it out."

"What's that noise?"

"Machinery." Michaelson answered, checking their backside to make sure no bad guys snuck up on them.

Dover paused for a moment, suddenly realizing what a fool he'd been. Usually machinery, the kind that runs on electricity, would be in the machine room. He rolled his eyes and thanked God it was dark enough to hide his sheepish grin. He did as the Master Sergeant suggested and pushed the door open.

The louder humming hit him first, immediately followed by the smell of gasoline exhaust that filled his nostrils.

He stood in the door and let out a soft whistle when his light beam illuminated three generators on wooden pallets with leads that snaked their way to individual circuit breaker boxes. Two generators were working.

That was definitely not a typical cave formation.

The walls of the room were squared off and coated with soundproofing material. Snaking their way out of the breaker boxes were more wire leads that exited the room through the rock walls, presumably to provide power to other parts of the cave. There was also an exhaust fan and ventilation duct that poked through the ceiling. Dover checked his location with the GPS and the coordinates matched the spot where he stood outside at with Montana.

"Lieutenant?" Michaelson called as if he was about to give a young child a lesson.

"Yeah?"

"Let's close the door and take a look at that floor plan." Michaelson spoke in an authoritative, even tone, letting the young Lieutenant know he still had a lot to learn.

Shit! He couldn't believe his stupidity! By keeping the door open, the sounds of the running generators echoed down the tunnels. He hoped he just didn't jeopardize the mission by alerting the ragheads in their underground home that intruders had entered. "Right," he answered as confidently as he could.

Dover placed the hand drawn map on the ground between them and studied it in silence under the beam of the flashlight. It was easy to determine the location of where they were in the cave, but it was quickly evident that the floor plan was nowhere near to scale. They were at a 'T' as Knapp had mentioned moments before and with a dirty finger, Dover traced the tunnels that were the upright ends of the tuning fork.

Just how long they were was anybody's guess.

According to the map, Dover counted eight chambers, four in each tunnel that did not appear connected. The layout resembled hallways in an apartment building with the apartments on the interior. If the layout was true, this should be a simple, straight forward clearing operation. A plan quickly formed in Dover's head and he turned to Knapp and Michaelson. "Let's go outside. Second Squad, Sergeant Dorsey," Dover called into the microphone touching his lips, "we're coming out."

Once outside, Dover gathered the leaders and laid the hand drawn map on the ground for everyone to see. The plan to search and clear the cave complex was simple. Master Sergeant Knapp would take his shooters and the Afghans and clear the left tunnel, while Dover would lead his Rangers clearing the right. Shoot first orders were given. Dover wasn't interested in taking prisoners.

Five minutes later, Dover completed his briefing. "Any questions? Suggestions?"

"No, sir." They replied in unison.

Dover waited a moment longer for a concern to pop up. Just because he was the commander, it didn't mean he knew everything. He was waiting for a flaw to be brought to light. When nothing materialized he ordered with confidence, "Move out."

The juncture of the main tunnel became crowded with both squads. In the blackness and wearing their Noggs, the men stealthily moved into a formation called a train or stack. They assembled in single file with their shoulders near the cave wall and weapons held tight into their shoulders. Eyes peered over the M68 gun sights and disciplined fingers rested on the trigger guards. Each soldier was assigned a specific sector, whether it was high, low, left or right, front or back or a combination of two. With this formation, the entire train was protected and it limited the chance of blue on blue–friendly fire–casualties.

Knapp's team aligned in the same formation and disappeared to the left to begin their room clearing operation.

Dover placed himself between the squads two fire teams, aptly tabbed A and B, so he could control both units. Fire Team A was tapped to clear the chambers while Fire Team B was tasked with security.

Despite the chill in the cave, beads of sweat formed on Dover's forehead and his heart began to beat faster as they approached the first chamber. He wiggled his finger around the trigger in nervous anticipation. He took a breath, gave the hand signal and whispered the order, "Go."

With weapons up the Rangers swiftly and silently entered through the stone archway chamber. Heads and weapons moving as one as the team members moved in concert, sweeping their assigned sectors, ready to shoot on sight.

The chamber was roughly twelve by twelve in size and packed with a file cabinet, a small card table with scattered papers covering the top, personal computers and a loaded AK-47. There was no sign of Puckett or Karmal.

"Clear," one of the Rangers spoke softly into the comm set.

Undeterred at the absence of the two missing men, Dover ordered the team out and down the tunnel to the next chamber.

Again, the squad repeated their maneuver and once again they came up empty.

Exiting the second chamber and heading towards the third, a firm hand to Dover's chest halted him in place.

In the parallel tunnel, Master Sergeant Chris Knapp was leading his team, their right shoulders were scraping against the stone wall. As his team approached the first chamber, he paused for a moment, held a clenched fist above his head, signaling the team to halt. In unison they sank to one knee. A soft steady light from a low wattage bulb gave away the faint outline of the doorway. Quietly he inched closer. Three feet from the doorway, he heard hard soled shoes shuffling on the rock.

The enemy was there.

A robed figure suddenly walked through the stone opening studying a piece of paper he held in one hand illuminated by a flashlight. He took one more step then stopped.

The cone of light halted inches from Knapp's boot tip. His heart jumped in his throat as he was caught unawares and froze. His heart pounded like a drum in his ear and held his breath. High octane adrenaline coursed through his veins.

He loosed the safety on his M-4, peered through the scope and sighted the weapon's red aiming reference, also know as the 'small red dot,' on the center of the man's head and applied pressure to the trigger. Just as he was ready to pull the trigger, the figure turned the opposite way and headed further into the dark cave. Only the sweeping beam of the flashlight was visible until it disappeared into another chamber.

Knapp's heart rate suddenly slowed and he let out his breath. "Hold fire," he whispered. He would have to move fast to clear the area. "We're going in," he whispered again, "Wicker, watch for that raghead coming back."

"Right."

Taking a quick glance over his shoulder, the team was alert and ready to follow.

Stealthily, Knapp, in a crouch, crept through the stone opening, his finger poised on the trigger. Suddenly off to his right there was a flare of light as a fighter standing next to a table lit a can of Sterno under a teapot. He took his finger off the trigger and decided on a silent kill. Gripping the rifle tightly in his hands, he crouched low and snuck up on the unsuspecting enemy. With a hard sharp swing, Knapp struck the man in the back of his head with the butt of his weapon. There was a shallow grunt, and the enemy soldier slumped to the ground. Instantly, an Afghan soldier withdrew his knife and slit the enemy's throat.

After a quick scan of the chamber revealed no sign of Puckett or Karmal, Knapp moved on to the next one.

"I got something up here, L-T," whispered Second Squad leader Sergeant Bill Parks. He removed his hand from Dover's chest then crouched on one knee.

"What is it?" Dover asked quietly in Parks' ear as he looked over his shoulder.

"There's a slight bend up here and light and voices coming from that chamber. There's also a curtain pulled back just a bit."

Every Ranger heard Park's information through the MIR.

"This could be it," Dover said as a surge of adrenaline rushed through his veins. His heart began beating at a rapid pace, so fast he thought the enemy might be able to hear it.

"Rangers," Dover whispered into the microphone, "let's take 'em down."

Dover took the lead in front of the train. Clutched in strong hands, he brought his weapon up to his shoulder and took a determined step to free who he hoped were the captured men.

The slight bend in the corner blocked most of the dim light that escaped the opening, but there was still enough light to see with the naked eye, allowing the Rangers to remove their night vision goggles. Too much light would actually hinder their sight with the goggles on. "Take your Noggs off," he whispered and let his eyes adjust to the light.

Suddenly there was a sudden harsh yelling and the disturbing sounds of a man being beaten. Then confirmation of who it was.

"Answer the question!" yelled Ivan. Spittle flew from his lips and his pale face had turned crimson as Puckett repeatedly answered every question with the same response–name, rank and serial number.

"Puckett, Leonard, United States Army-"

Crack!

The blow to the back of his head came as no surprise but this one hurt more than the others. His vision began to fade to gray, beginning with the loss of his peripheral vision, and his eyes rolled back into his head. His empty stomach quickly churned with a wave of nausea and bile shot up his throat. Control of his bodily functions began to slip and he did everything in his power to contract the muscles in his battered body.

"Last time, Puckett," Ivan sneered. "I'm tired and don't have time for your little games."

Puckett's vision slowly returned and the nausea diminished. He breathed heavily through his nose to calm his body down and prepare for the rest of the beating that was sure to get worse.

Click.

The loosening of a weapons safety sounded like a sonic boom in Puckett's ear. This was it, he thought, as he looked down at the cold lifeless body of his friend, Mike Karmal.

His time on Earth was up.

Dover paused outside the opening, his tough lean body was as hard as the cave's rock wall and listened to the beating of Puckett. With clenched teeth and a set jaw, he turned back to his men and gave hand signals that they were going in. The camouflaged faces stared back at him, wide dark pupils in seas of whites reflected the gritty determination he was feeling.

He tapped Fire Team A leader, Corporal James Ross, on the shoulder then gave the signal to move in.

"On three." He gave a quick countdown and with lightning speed, Dover crashed through the curtain with his weapon up. He turned left to cover that sector, his eyes and mind working like a computer, sorting and cataloging everything that lay before him. A dead body was on the floor, a Caucasian restrained on a chair in the middle of the room with a burly raghead pointing a pistol to the back of his head. Two more Caucasians were standing off to the side and another raghead was in the near corner to the left. It was a stage performance set up for an execution.

The surprise was complete. The first threat was to the man sitting on the chair with an enemy pointing a weapon at the back of Puckett's head. Dover sighted the small red dot from his weapon on the center of ragheads face and squeezed off a three round burst. The pakol was knocked off the enemy's head, along with the top half of his skull. Without missing a step, Dover swung his weapon around and took out the enemy in the corner with another three round burst.

Simultaneously, the other Rangers who rushed through the door took care of business in their sectors. The gunfire echoed off the stone, magnifying the sound. Sgt. Ross moved in and killed the two Caucasians with perfectly aimed headshots. He dropped them before they had a chance to react.

Just as fast as it started, it was over.

"Rangers!" another soldier announced as he pointed his weapon at the man on the chair.

"Puckett, U.S. Army," the battered man said in a hoarse voice, relief displayed on his bloody and battered face. "Thank you."

Dover needed to make sure. "Poltergeist?"

Puckett nodded.

"Clear!" another Ranger called out letting everyone know the room was secure of enemy soldiers.

The small chamber was filled with the smell of gunpowder and death. The Rangers had to move quickly in the event enemy reinforcements arrived.

"Cut him loose," Dover ordered to no one in particular. "Medic!" he called for Reynolds. "Puckett's yours," he ordered the steely eyed twenty year old once he entered the chamber. "You guys know what to do. We're out of here when Doc's ready. Sergeant Parks," Dover called to the fire team leader outside the door, "stay alert."

"Yes, sir," came the reply.

As Dover stood in the center of the room, he focused on two tasks. While his eyes saw the events folding out in front of him, his ears were listening to the short clipped phrases from Knapp's team as they too engaged and killed enemy fighters.

"Oh, man," one Ranger spouted as he leaned down to search one of the bodies, "these guys are messed up. We did them good."

Immediately two men began searching the dead and broken bodies for identification and intelligence, while others secured weapons and began collecting documents. As they went about their business, they all sent curious glances to the two dead Caucasians.

"Need help, Doc?" Dover asked as he stared at the beaten face of Leonard Puckett. The man's face was swollen and dirty and speckled with blood. One eye was so puffy it was almost closed. Fresh blood dripped from a cut somewhere in his mouth and half of one ear was missing. Dover winced.

"Not yet," Reynolds answered without looking away from his patient and tapped a vein on Puckett's right arm in preparation for an IV.

"Do you know who these guys are?" Dover kneeled next to Puckett after Reynolds eased him onto the ground and inserted the needle into his arm. He pointed to the dead bodies that covered the floor.

Puckett nodded and answered in a voice that signaled some of his strength and determination was not exhausted. "The guy on the ground next to the chair is Mohammad Karmal. We called him Mike. Fuckers shot him not long before you got here. The raghead is a raghead motherfucker who shot Mike and did most of the face rearranging on me. But the other two, I called Ivan and Igor."

Dover narrowed his eyes and cocked his head as he watched a fire ignite in Puckett's good eye. He took out a pad of paper and a pen from his breast pocket to write down what Puckett was going to say. Surprised, he asked, "They're Russians?"

"Yeah," Puckett said through cracked lips. He held up a dirty hand, searching for the Lieutenant's.

Dover grabbed the calloused hand and got a firm grasp.

"Thank you," Puckett said again, looking directly into Dover's eyes.

"You're welcome." Dover patted Puckett on the shoulder. "Hang in there, we'll get you home." Dover then decided that the questions he wanted to ask would have to wait. Puckett was in no condition for a debriefing under these conditions.

Static chirped in his ear. "Lieutenant?" Knapp's voice came over the communication gear.

"What have you got, Master Sergeant?"

"We're clear. Eight enemy KIA, but no Poltergeist. You've got to come take a look at this, sir."

"On my way. We found Poltergeist, I say again we found Poltergeist. He's alive."

Thursday, October 9, Kelif, Turkmenistan

The small town of Kelif sat quietly north of the Amu Darya River on the border with Afghanistan. Some of the inhabitants, the actual number not known to the locals, were members of the U.S. Army 3rd Special Forces Group.

Stationed in the newly freed country with the complete backing of the elected government in support of the global war on terrorism, Harold Weston sat on the cushioned chair in the somewhat spacious office on the first floor of the three story concrete building that was home to the only river shipping broker in the city. He tried his hardest to stifle a yawn.

Although he was in great physical shape, his overworked body was sore, despite the fourteen hours of sleep he had.

His two week mission that took him through four different mountain valleys, an unknown number of unnamed valleys and passes, and at least a dozen mountain peaks in the thin air had worn him out.

That mission was accomplished three days ago and was considered a tremendous success in that he found a large weapons cache that was destined for al-Qaeda. Two dozen Russian SA-7 anti-aircraft missiles, one hundred Kalishnikov rifles, a dozen RPK machine guns, five hundred fifteen pounds of Semtex plastic explosives, dynamite and thousands of rounds of ammunition. All of which was now in the hands of the US Army.

Shortly after the weapons were removed from the site, two members of ODA-317 set up a two man listening post a klick away. They radioed that they spotted three tarp covered trucks, the lead one a pick-up truck, heading to the cache site. Going on the assumption that they were connected with the weapons, Weston called in an air strike from a pair of A-10 Warthogs that were on call. It took less than five seconds for the A-10's tank busting 30mm chain guns to shred the trucks and the occupants in them.

When the team moved into examine the contents of what was destroyed, the pick-up truck was still burning and the remnants of the driver and passenger were splattered in the wrecked cab. The other two trucks were smoldering and inside the middle truck, the team was surprised to find a dollar packed suitcase between the two destroyed bodies in the cab. The driver and passenger of the third vehicle were shot to pieces just like the others.

Another result of the mission was the elimination of the hierarchy of one group of smugglers and their suppliers. But the failure to capture or kill his elusive prey, Ahmed Rashid Halabi, left a sour taste in Weston's mouth. With the absence of Halabi, that meant one of the main suppliers of weapons to the enemy was still in business, and would continue selling weapons to the highest bidder or to any Taliban or Al-Qaeda sympathizer. Because of not getting Halabi, Weston considered the mission only a partial success. It wouldn't be long before he was back on Halabi's trail.

"Taking anything for the aches?" Colonel Lou Cavallo, the five foot five inch second generation Italian-American Special Forces commander, teased as he rose from the chair behind the desk and moved over to the worn, second hand couch. Though Cavallo was small in height, he sported an athletes body with broad shoulders and a thin waist. Because of the nature of his profession, his thick black hair was well beyond regulation length, ending halfway down his ear and extending past the top of his collar. He wore blue jeans and a hooded gray sweatshirt under a green goose down vest. Cavallo looked more like a civilian hunter than an elite soldier. But looking at his intense brown eyes revealed the type of hunter he was. "Need any more help?" he asked Weston.

Weston shook his head. "Nah. I have a gorgeous long legged, busty blonde that takes care of everything. She masssages away the pain to the point where I fall asleep." A smile spread to his eyes. "The way she wakes me up is even better!" His smile grew wider as he recalled the feel of her mouth on him.

Cavallo laughed heartily, a disarming smile displayed crooked teeth. "You've done well, Weston. Ever think of coming back into the teams?"

"No, sir," he shook his head. "Been there, done that. I like being able to come back into a nice soft bed, hot showers, good chow, use an expense account and of course my nurse. This OGA stuff," military personnel referred to CIA employees as OGAs or Other Government Agency, "is to my liking. But thanks for asking."

Sitting in an armless chair across from Cavallo's desk was Weston's boss, Russ Hannigan. He was frowning. A tall, balding bureaucrat with no sense of humor, Hannigan believed bantering served no purpose except to waste time.

"Easy Hannigan," Cavallo instructed with a push of his hand. "Lighten up."

"We have important material to cover, Colonel," Hannigan stated tersely. "In case you forgot, we are in a war."

Cavallo bristled at the remark and shot Hannigan an icy glare. He was in command of all Special Operations Forces operating out of Turkmenistan and was well aware of being in a war. He leaned forward and snarled. "No shit? I didn't realize that. I thought I was here on a fucking vacation and the joint operations I send my teams on with your guys is just for sightseeing." His eyes bore into Hannigan. "And my three wounded troopers I sent home with holes in their bodies were doing what?"

Weston cringed at the idiocy of his boss. Many times his habit of opening his mouth and inserting his foot was overlooked because he was effective at his job as a CIA case officer or the new term, Collection Management Officer. But it was embarrassing at times and he had the personality of a toad.

"Is there any new information on the Russians we killed at the site?" Weston asked aloud, easing the sudden tension in the room.

Hannigan spoke first, his face no longer twisted in displeasure. "No."

"Did your people call the Russians and ask if they have a," Cavallo paused, reached over to his desk, grabbed a sheet of paper and read the name, "Colonel Anatoly Yezhov missing from a motorized rifle battalion?"

"I wanted to," Weston answered under his breath then caught a quick silencing glance from Hannigan.

"Out with it," Cavallo ordered sharply after seeing the exchange. "And don't give me any 'need to know' bullshit." He leveled a steady gaze at Hannigan. "I need to know if I'm fighting Russians."

Hannigan came clean. "We wanted to, but it's out of our hands."

"There's more to this, isn't there?" Cavallo asked.

"It appears so. We're sort of on shaky ground. We, Central Intelligence, concur with Weston's assessment that *those* Russians were supplying the terrorists. What's surprising was the finding of the Russian colonel, a lieutenant and a sergeant along with the ragheads."

Cavallo interrupted. "You didn't tell the Russians we have their dead people, did you?"

Hannigan shook his head. "No. We didn't tell the Russians anything."

"Why?" Cavallo challenged.

"I was getting to that," Hannigan shot back. "We always knew the Russians were never going to be a true ally in Operation Enduring Freedom. I also believe they want us to fail in Afghanistan, just as they did."

"That ain't gonna fucking happen," Cavallo stated steadfastly.

"Anyway, they have never stopped selling weapons to our enemies and they have always done it using the same method, through other hostile governments. What's surprising is the direct selling of weapons in the field to the terrorists."

Cavallo bit his bottom lip and narrowed his eyes into slits. "Call the fucking Russians on the carpet. We got the proof."

Weston interjected, getting into the conversation and stating his piece. "There's another theory I have. There's a possibility that this is all black market transactions and the Russian government has no clue as to what is going on. The other dead Russians, Bedny and Novikov, I don't think they're soldiers, unlike the colonel."

"Why's that?" Cavallo asked a bit softer.

Weston leaned forward, resting his elbows on his knees. "First, their physique was no where near anything resembling a soldier, especially in a line unit. Too flabby and absolutely no muscle tone."

"So what, " Cavallo insisted, "call the fucking Russians on it. Let them know they have impersonators. Either way the weapons shipments will be halted. The Kremlin gets the bad apples in their army and we save American lives. It's a win-win situation for all."

"I agree," Hannigan hesitated in his comment. "CIA wants to see how far up the chain of command this goes. See if there are any more links with the Chechens, al-Qaeda, and other foreign nationals."

Cavallo thought for a moment and steepled his fingers under his chin. "Makes sense. Weston, are you still going to need my men to get Halabi?"

Weston set his jaw and his nostrils flared. He banged his fist on the table. "Absolutely, Colonel. I'm gonna get the son-of-a-bitch!"

Thursday, October 9, The Cave, Afghanistan

Lt. Jack Dover knew Master Sergeant Knapp was in the last chamber at the end of the tunnel. His morbid curiosity almost caused him to look in each chamber as he walked past, but decided against it as Knapp's request for him seemed urgent.

When Dover arrived at the last chamber, he pushed aside the heavy canvas drape covering the opening and stopped like he hit a wall. "Whoa, holy shit," Dover exclaimed. "What's all this?"

"C'mon in, Lieutenant," Knapp invited. He was rifling through a sheaf of papers.

Photographic spot lights illuminated a wooden chair near a wall. Both dried and fresh blood streaks stained the wood as well as the large piece of gray canvas hanging behind it. The canvas, looking like a piece of abstract art, was also perforated with bullet holes. Halfway across the chamber, a video camera perched on a tripod had its lens focused on the chair. Two dead Taliban fighters were on the floor, red rimed holes punctured their foreheads.

The wall on the far side was lined with rickety bookcases filled with video tapes. The adjacent wall had dented file cabinets that some of the soldiers were rifling through.

"I reckon it's a shooting gallery," Michaelson stated, trying not to sound flippant. He pointed to the chair with his rifle. "I'd call this the punishment chair. What does this say?" He handed a video cassette to one of the Afghans who translated the label.

"August meeting and Omar," the translator said in passable English and handed the tape back to Michaelson.

"Whatever the hell that means." Michaelson put the tape back on the shelf.

"We hit the jackpot, Lieutenant." Knapp shifted his weapon and flung his hand in a sweeping motion. It looks like some of these tapes are interrogations, ops planning and training videos. At least that's what the labels say."

Dover scratched the back of his neck. "Intelligence is going to have a field day in this place."

"That means we're going to be busy, sir," Dorsey added.

Thursday, October 9, Kiri, Chechnya

"Comrade Major!" the night watch officer banged on the door frame of Major Mikhail Borushko's tent.

"Yes?" Borushko was lying on his cot, drifting in and out of sleep when he recognized the voice of Lt. Savinkov.

"Lieutenants Martov and Grigorenko are here to see you, sir."

Borushko bolted upright from his cot, his heart raced and he had a difficult few seconds processing what the watch officer had just told him. Could it be? Could Lieutenants Osip Martov and Feliks Grigorenko be alive? They were on Colonel Yezhov's personal staff and this was the first good news he had regarding Yezhov, Novikov and Bedny. Novikov and Bedny were not in the military, but members of the Solntsevskaya who also accompanied the Colonel on the arms sale in Turkmenistan.

Borushko rubbed a tired hand over a wary, stubbled face and hurried over to the door. He yanked it open and found the two lieutenants standing there looking worn and tired. Lt. Savinkov was blocking the view of his partners.

"Come in! Come in!" Borushko waved his hand and stepped aside. Facing the confused Lieutenant who was clearly trying to figure out why a major would be excited to see two junior officers, he sternly stated, "That will be all, dismissed."

"Yes, sir." Savinknov saluted, pivoted and walked away.

Borushko closed the door, anxious for news to find out what happened to the weapons, cash, Yezhov, and his two colleagues. Behind the closed door, all military formality, including rank were non-existent with these two men. He pulled a liter of Stolichnaya vodka from under his bed and handed it to Martov.

Osip Martov was a short, powerfully built man with a barrel chest, thick, light brown hair and dark, dangerous eyes. His forearms and biceps were large and solid.

Feliks Grigorenko, on the other hand, stood a head taller than Martov with dark hair and one continuous eyebrow. He wasn't as powerfully built as Martov, but it was clear his athletic body had strength and his cold brown eyes were just as dangerous.

"It's good to see you!" Borushko said quietly and shook hands with both men. They had to speak softly because of the possibility that someone was eavesdropping outside the tent. He then got right to the point, "What happened?" He sat on the edge of the cot, leaned forward and rested his elbows on his knees. His eyes narrowed into slits waiting for the answer. There was a lot at stake here.

"Ambush," Martov said flatly and took a long pull from the bottle. "They are all dead. Yezhov is dead, Bedny is dead, Novikov is dead." He then sat on the edge of Borushko's small desk while Grigorenko sat on the folding chair.

"Shit," Borushko blurted and slammed his fist onto his thigh. "How? Where are the weapons now? Who conducted the ambush? How did you survive?"

Grigorenko answered. "We were waiting for the truck to return-"

Borushko held up his hand, cutting Grigorenko off in mid sentence. "What do you mean waiting for the truck to return? Where did it go? Where did they both go?" Something didn't make sense here and the strong odor of a set up burned into his nostrils. Yezhov packed the weapons in two trucks. Why did one go one way and one go the other?

"When we got to the delivery site, the buyers only had a pick-up truck and asked if they could borrow our truck.

Something about having to haul vegetables because the truck that they were supposed to use had a dead battery or other nonsense, I'm not sure. They said they would bring it back. The other truck left as planned because the colonel didn't want two trucks traveling together to draw any suspicion. Anyway, as planned, we unloaded the weapons and waited for the Muslims to pick them up and bring back our other truck so we could get home."

Borushko sat in silence for a minute, his mind spinning like a flywheel. What the hell was Yezhov thinking? Did he really trust the warlord that much to give him his only transportation out of there in case they ran into trouble? My God, that was a really stupid thing to do! And he asked the very question. "What was Yezhov thinking?"

Grigorenko spread his hands. "I don't know why he did that, Mikhail. Maybe he was drunk or something, he was hitting the vodka pretty hard, as usual."

Alcoholism was still rampant in the Russian army, so hearing about someone being drunk didn't raise too many eyebrows. Yezhov was one of the hard drinkers, and Borushko always thought that someday it would come back to bite him and the organization in the ass. In the regiment he could cover for the drunk colonel, but in the Solntsevskaya, where money was at stake, covering for someone was much harder to do, and sometimes not worth it.

Grigorenko continued. "Yezhov talked to the Muslim in charge before the trucks pulled into the clearing. I don't know if he was an Afghan, Chechen, or Turkmen or what. Anyway, once we pulled in, we unloaded the weapons and his men took the trucks. We," he pointed to Martov and then to himself, "moved up the road and set up the OP," an Observation Post, "just as we planned. Novikov and Bedny remained with Yezhov."

"Nothing seemed out of the ordinary?" Borushko challenged harshly.

"No," Martov answered shaking his head, unrattled by the harsh tone. "Everything seemed ok."

Borushko stared hard, but knew in his gut that Martov and Grigorenko had nothing to do with Yezhov's apparent screw-up. He softened his tone. "What happened next, Osip?"

Martov took a healthy swallow of the vodka and then a deep breath before he began. "It was just after sunrise, we were sitting at the OP, keeping our eyes to the road as that would be the biggest threat, when we heard a short burst of gunfire coming from Yezhov's position."

"We didn't hear any return fire. Everything was over in less than ten seconds," Grigorenko interjected then continued. "We headed back to the clearing, and once we made it to the tree line, we saw armed soldiers."

"Not typical hired thugs, criminals, or other warlords?" Borushko asked, his curiosity going up an extra notch.

"No, these men were trained, disciplined. When we saw that, we went to ground and stayed put for a few hours. The two of us were in no position to take on the force that was there."

Borushko let that settle in. A trained force meant professionals. "Who did the hit?"

"Can't say for sure. The security element that we saw were Turkmen, so I'd bet they were all with the Turkmen Army."

Martov jumped back into the conversation. "They took out the weapons and bodies by helicopter."

"Shit!" The evidence pointed to a military unit that carried out the ambush. No warlord or gun runner would be able to fly a helicopter in the Afghanistan theatre of operations without the American's knowledge, unless they, the Americans, were part of the operation. "Who's helo? American or Turkmen?"

"I don't know, but the helo's were CH-47s."

"There were also two Apaches orbiting."

Borushko sighed heavily. "Then it's safe to say to the Americans were involved, yes? I don't think they would allow the Turkmen to pilot their top-of-the-line attack helicopters."

Grigorenko continued with the explanation. "We went back to the clearing and checked things out, hoping we would find someone alive. There was nothing, no bodies, no weapons. We only found blood stains."

"The trucks," Borushko remembered they had left prior to the firefight, "where did they go?" More and more this appeared to be set up. "Did they ever come back? With the money?"

Grigorenko shook his head. "No."

"There's something else," Martov said worriedly. "Yezhov had his field jacket on, with insignia, and he probably had his military ID with him. Bedney and Novikov had their civilian driver's licenses."

"We think," Grigorenko offered hopefully.

Borushko leapt off the cot like he was shot out of a cannon. "What!? What the fuck was that *zhopa* doing?" he used the Russian word for asshole.

Only silence and blank stares answered his question.

"We have to go and find the buyer and get the money back. Feliks, can you set up another appointment with our double-crossing friend?"

"I can try."

"Good."

Things just went from bad to worse for the soldier and full time criminal.

CHAPTER FOUR

Friday, October 10, Paktika Province, Afghanistan

Once Len Puckett was removed from the cave, he was immediately flown to the huge American base at Kandahar to be stabilized and flown on to Germany. From there he would get more intricate surgeries to repair his broken body and finally to Walter Reed Medical Center back in the states.

Puckett's send off wasn't the end for Lt. Jack Dover. It had taken longer than he had thought, but his Rangers finally scoured every nook and cranny of the cave complex and removed the wealth of intelligence found there. There were more tunnels and chambers than what the floor plan had indicated. A smaller passageway was found at the end of the tunnel that Knapp was clearing and it had led to three more storage chambers. One held small arms ammunition, another was used for dry goods and food stuffs and the last was a general storage area that had a little of everything, ranging from toilet paper to AK-47s and mortars. A back door, so to speak, was also discovered.

Boxes of video tape and documents and computers all had to be removed, but unfortunately, not all of it had escaped unscathed. Some of the personal computers had battle damage. A few bullets had passed through bodies and smashed into the computer towers, damaging the internal workings. Those went right to the technicians who immediately went to work on them to extract as much information off the damaged hard drives as possible.

Dover, tired and emitting a ripe odor from not bathing in a couple of days, sat on a large boulder outside the cave's main entrance watching the last of the material being loaded onto the back ramp of the CH-47. He was writing notes on a clipboard for the after action report when Master Sergeant Chris Knapp emerged from the darkness of the cave opening.

"Cave's clean, sir." Knapp tiredly sat down next to Dover and took a long pull on the straw of his hydration pack. It was the third time Knapp swept the area.

"Good." There was something to say about being thorough and Dover made a mental note of the Master Sergeants work habits and the attention to detail he applied to his job.

"You have the final tally, Lieutenant?"

"Yeah," Dover let out a sigh and consulted his notes. He went through the list and when he was finished clapped Knapp on the back. "Well done Master Sergeant, mission accomplished."

"Yeah," Knapp said not too happily. "Lost some good people. Shouldn't have happened but thanks. It was a pleasure working with you. You led your men well, Lieutenant. Good job. If you need any help in the future, give my team a call. I'll put in a good word with the team commander, Captain MacDonald."

Dover swelled with pride from the praise the veteran soldier complimented him with. He sat up a little straighter. "Thanks, Master Sergeant." The two warriors then shook hands, knowing they would meet up again.

Saturday, October 11, Kiri, Chechnya

Major Mikhail Borushko stood next to the bank of radios in the tent and flipped through a new set of messages. He scanned through them, reading each one with a practice eye for which ones needed his immediate attention and which ones could be pushed aside. One message informed him the latest supply convoy was going to be late by six hours and another message was asking for a status report on two of the BMP's that were supposed to be heading out for repairs. All of the others were similar in nature, except for one and that caused him to smile.

The death of Colonel Anatoly Yezhov caused two sets of problems for Borushko. The first problem dealt with the battalion. In order to keep the unit working, he, in the capacity of the executive officer, had to report Yezhov, missing and assume command.

Of course, with Yezhov's disappearance, Borushko would be in command until Yezhov returned or they sent a replacement. That would prevent him from making the secret trip into Turkmenistan to find the arms buyer and straighten out what had happened during the sale and collect the money owed.

The second problem related to the Solntsevskaya. They were the distributor in the transaction between the buyer and seller, who Borushko believed to be a Saudi. As far as the supplier and distributor were concerned, the weapons were delivered and they were expecting payment. The Solntsevskaya's and Borushko's reputation, and possibly his life, were on the line if the money didn't change hands. A quick translation meant Borushko needed to get the money from the buyer and deposited.

He knew first hand the gruesome methods the disciplinarians in the Solntsevskaya used on people who stole money. They were on par with the Muslim extremists he was fighting. Though he believed he didn't have to worry about his health because he wasn't on the deal with Yezhov, he would be damned if he was going to take responsibility for the disaster and be subjected to the punishment. To be safe, he would try to recover the money before he reported the disaster.

Borushko liked to think in his armored vehicle. It gave him comfort and allowed him to collect and line up his thoughts. While in the BMP, he had decided on a bold approach to solve his problems. Since the battalion had momentarily pacified their sector of Chechnya and no operations were scheduled, the battalion was slated with just routine patrolling. He reported Yezhov missing and sought permission from Brigade to mount a limited search and rescue operation for him. Maybe, he suggested, he was in an accident or broke down on his way to or from Kiri. While he was conducting his search, he suggested the army could make contact with his family back in Russia and try to locate him there. He did, after all, have a fondness for vodka and it was quite possible that fondness got him into trouble.

The last message he held in his hand gave him permission to use two days to search for Colonel Anatoly Yezhov.

Borushko addressed the staff of the problem and quickly grabbed Captain Pyotr Agranov and Lieutenants Martov and Grigorenko and put a plan together.

Saturday, October 11, Loudonville, New York

Sara Kaderri's parents had called Friday afternoon and volunteered their services to take the kids for the weekend to spoil the heck out of them the way grandparents are entitled to. Sara jumped at the offer and immediately made reservations for dinner at a fancy restaurant. She selected a sexy black dress to wear and called her husband to let him in on the turn of events. Over the phone they discussed and planned on doing adult things all weekend, salivating at the opportunity to reacquaint themselves to the physical pleasures they enjoyed doing to and with each other on a more frequent basis BC, Before Children.

Dinner was in one of Albany's finer restaurants and since Kaderri was already downtown, Sara took a taxi and was waiting at the table when he arrived from his office. From the moment he laid eyes on the stunning brunette, the flirting began and progressed to the next level once they arrived home.

The master bedroom was one of four bedrooms in the three story contemporary house. Off to the side of the bedroom was a full bath, a two person Jacuzzi next to a stone fireplace and a pair of walk-in cedar closets large enough to be sitting rooms. Sara's closet was stuffed with so many clothes that she began moving into her husband's.

The center piece of the master bedroom was a king sized four poster ornately carved cherry bed with a step stool and matching night tables. Tucked off to one corner were a pair of upholstered wing chairs and a small rectangular cherry table between them. A shaded lamp perched upon it provided enough light to read by and not disturb whoever was sleeping. A deep luxurious rose colored carpet covered the floor.

The usual tidy room was strewn with clothes from two lovers who were in a rush to get them off and partake in carnal delights. Kaderri's tan cashmere sport coat lay draped over the back of one wing chair and dark trousers were crumpled in a ball on the floor. Socks and shoes were scattered about and a pair of boxer shorts was halfway across the room.

Sara's simple black spaghetti strap dress lay on the floor. Her tiny decorative lace thong and matching bra were scattered along with black thigh high stockings and three inch leather pumps.

The morning sunlight from behind the dark shades illuminated the heavy cotton rose colored drapes framing the windows, giving them a glowing aura.

Kaderri lay on his side with his eyes closed, drifting in and out sleep, the down comforter pulled up over his waist. He was in one of those stages of sleep where it was hard to tell if events were a dream or not. He thought he felt Sara's soft hand on his muscular chest, circle the hairs and slide down his washboard stomach till her long fingernails teased him.

"Ugh!" Sara cried in mock disappointment. "What's going on down here with this?"

It wasn't a dream.

"What do you mean?" Kaderri asked sleepily and opened a tired eye to see Sara lying on her side. Her head was propped up by her hand and the diamond and sapphire earrings glinted in the light. The twinkle in her eye matched the jewelry.

The Kaderri's physical pleasure was extremely important to them and they took great pride in fulfilling each other's desires. Ever since Sara's rape, Kaderri became extremely sensitive to her emotions and never pushed her to start or continue if she showed any signs of distress. The morning's dalliance didn't appear to be one of those times.

"There used to be a time when I played with this," she jiggled him then snorted, "you got right up! You must be getting old."

Disrespecting his manhood completely woke him up.

"Old, huh? The two long sessions last night didn't count for my virility?"

"That was then, this is now," Sara teased, stroking his now semi-hard cock. "Come on," she encouraged and stroked him a little harder. "Stand up!"

"Maybe," he rolled onto his back, put his finger to her red sensual lips and stated, "if you used these, it might get up a little faster." By now his erection was almost at full mast.

"Well," she sat up and threw the comforter completely off. Her large firm breasts swayed with her movements and pink nipples were erect with excitement. "I guess it's worth a shot, especially if you give me those awesome feelings again and put another big smile on my face." She moved between his legs.

With two hands she grabbed him, curling her fingers around his long, thick shaft. Teasingly, her warm tongue darted out like a snake's, striking the swollen head and quickly withdrawing. Then she put her mouth on the head, enveloping him with soft lips and began sucking gently.

"Hmmm," he moaned at her familiar touch.

Up and down she moved, blissfully working on him, varying the pace and pressure. The sensation sent shivers throughout his body.

"You like this?" she asked after disengaging her mouth, but her hands kept on stroking.

"Uh-huh," he breathed heavily as her tongue hovered above him. He eagerly awaited for what she was going to do next.

She smiled devilishly. "I like this too." Without another word, she opened her mouth and easily slid his entire length into her wanting mouth until her nose hit his pubic hair.

"Ohhh!" he cried and grasped the bed sheets as he watched her slowly repeat the maneuver. He felt himself grow even more at the excitement and the warmth of her mouth on his entire member felt as if he was wrapped in a hot towel.

A few delicious minutes later, she sat upright between his legs. Hooking a few strands of dark hair behind her ears, she pointed at his large throbbing member and exclaimed, "Now, that's what I call a hard on!" she giggled with a smile that spread from ear to ear. "It rivals the Washington Monument!"

Kaderri burst out laughing at her comparison. "I told you that would work!"

Firm believers in physical fitness, they both had sculpted hard bodies that they were proud of. Kaderri was obviously more bulked up with a broad, square chest and shoulders and thin wasp-like waist with a washboard stomach. He had the strength and appearance of being cut from stone, not in the way of a body builder, but sleek like a thoroughbred. Kaderri also earned the rank of black belt in the Korean martial art Tae Kwon Do.

Sara had an envious hourglass figure on a five foot seven inch frame. She did some weight training, but concentrated on aerobics, which she was also an instructor of. Her breasts were large, firm, and all natural. Even after childbirth, her hips and abdomen regained their form and her buttocks and legs were firm and elegantly shaped.

Using her strong leg muscles, Sara easily straddled him. No matter how many times he has seen her, Kaderri was still in awe of her goddess-like beauty. Her hair fell behind her shoulders and her breasts were calling for him to touch. Grabbing her hard nipples between his thumb and forefinger, he massaged them simultaneously, eliciting a soft moan from Sara's pursed lips.

Sara grasped the human version of the Washington Monument at its base and held it under her nearly bald baby smooth lips. A single strip of hair pointed to her erect clit like an arrow. She raised an eyebrow in a knowing tease, then slowly lowered herself on to him, his throbbing head piercing and stretching her moist warm folds of flesh.

"Ooh, yeah!" Kaderri moaned as her inner muscles gripped and then released his manhood. He kneaded her breasts in return.

"Mmmm," She cooed softly with his entire length in.

He let out a low satisfying moan as he relished in her warm tight grip.

Without warning, she pulled his hands off her breasts and held them tightly to the bed so he couldn't move. To his surprise and delight, she moved quickly up his shaft and slowly sank back down, repeating the muscle squeezing technique. Sara was committing torture on him and he loved every minute of it.

"Oh, wow!" he cried out as she continued. Each time she reached the top, she increased the speed on the next go around.

Using long fluid motions, Sara steadily rode him at a comfortable pace. Kaderri's hands, now free, glided over her soft skin and sought out her hot spots. One hand went back to her sensitive nipples and while the other moved down and stroked her erect clit.

"Hmmm, that's it!" she suddenly cried under his touch. Her breath came in short gasps and her body shuddered. "Keep doing it!"

Sara closed her eyes, her face a mask of ecstasy. Her movements became more deliberate and she bit her bottom lip as she rode him faster. Her hair tossed in every direction and her breasts bounced as the moans of their enjoyment echoed off the walls.

Kaderri grabbed her hips and held on as she bounced and met her downward thrusts, driving himself as deep as he could into her. Their hot sweaty bodies smacked together in a steady drumbeat. He saw her chest redden, indicating she was on the verge of an orgasm. He pulled her close so their chests met and quickly rolled her over and thrust his entire length into her.

"That's it, Marc! Oh, my God!"

Her fingernails dug into his back, but he ignored the quick stab of pain and focused on his movements. He found a steady pace and kept it going and watched the blissful mask on Sara's face as their bodies moved in a poetic dance. Minutes later, sweat formed on his brow and beaded on his face. He maintained the rhythm and soon felt the familiar tingling signs of his own approaching orgasm. His heart was racing and his breath came in short pants. He squeezed his own muscles to hold off a little longer.

Sara arched her back and met him thrust for thrust and yelled his name. "Yes! Yes! Marc! Oh my God!" she crooned over and over.

Kaderri loved it when she called out his name in the throes of passion. His own pleasurable release was imminent and he fought to hold off the inevitable.

Sara's chest turned to a crimson sunburn and her moans turned into delightful screams.

The tingling, burning sensation rushed from his loins. "Now!" he panted and pulled her closer.

"Ohhh!" she screamed and shuddered under him, her fingernails dug deeper into his flesh. She threw her had back and froze in a silent scream.

Sara's muscles went into spasm around his hard cock, gripping and releasing him countless times. The sensation sent him over the edge. All his energy and pleasure was focused on a single point and like a tidal wave crashing on shore, he let go inside of her with a satisfying yell and shudder of his own.

Exhausted, he collapsed on top of her and quickly rolled off as not to crush her. "So, Babe," he asked after catching his breath, "how was that? Get that feeling you wanted?"

"Oh, yeah, sure did!" she panted. "We are good together!" She wrapped her arms around his neck and gave him a long passionate kiss. "That was awesome!" She fell back into the down pillow and pushed the loose strands of hair from her face. She poked his shoulder. "It's your turn to get the coffee."

Kaderri let out a groan and put his head under the pillow. She poked him again. He playfully threw the pillow at her, wiped the sweat from his face, rolled off the bed and headed for the kitchen.

Kaderri brewed a pot of Kona, their favorite brand of coffee, and brought up some cheese and fruit danishes to replace their spent energy. When he returned to the bedroom, Sara was sitting in one of the wing chairs with a laptop on her naked thighs, stabbing away at the keys.

Surprised, he asked, "What are you doing?" He expected her to be back in bed, hugging a pillow and wrapped in the soft comforter. He put the tray down on the table and handed her a steaming mug.

"Thank you. I'm going over some numbers for the club."

"What for?" His curiosity now piqued, he sat down in the other chair and took a long pull of the flavorful Hawaiian brew. He held it in his mouth for a moment to savor the smooth, intense flavor before swallowing. Since he was a financial planner, he knew everything, money wise, that was going on at Sara's club, A Better Body.

She took a sip before answering. "I'm toying with the idea of selling the place."

"Huh?" he blurted and his eyes went wide in surprise. "Why?" Sara built that club from the ground up. Everything from securing the loans to supervising the first piece of exercise equipment was done by her. Kaderri gave her his full attention.

She looked up from the laptops' screen. "Being a mom, I want to spend more time with the kids."

From the moment Sara became pregnant, she stated she would be a stay at home mom, and Kaderri agreed with that. When he looked back at his childhood, his mom was home with him, and so was Sara's mother. Both of them believed in a traditional nuclear family and did not accept the intruding societal norms of anything goes for a family.

"May I point out that you spend most of your time with the kids now?" The thirty minute romp with Sara used up his energy and he hungrily sank his teeth into one of the cheese danishes.

"Sort of," she countered. "I take them to the club with me for a few hours a day, but it's not the same as raising the kids at home. I can't be at the club and run it the way it's supposed to be and raise them the way we want, especially now at the terrible twos." She slid her finger over the touch pad and cast her eyes to the screen.

Kaderri knew how much the club meant to her and it would be a shame for her to get rid of it. An idea popped into his head. "Is selling the club the only avenue you approached?

Ever consider bringing in a managing partner who can slowly buy into it?"

Sara looked up and swallowed another mouthful of coffee before she answered. "Not really. I don't know if I'd be willing to give up some control of the place. I put too much time and effort into it to have someone fight about changes."

"Have you set up a time frame for when you may want all this to happen?"

Sara shrugged and placed the computer on the table. She took a sip from her mug and grabbed a raspberry danish. "Six months, maybe," she shrugged again and softened her voice. "Hey, did you hear from Paul on your friend?" Her question about McKnight and Puckett had genuine concern in her voice.

Kaderri shook his head ruefully. "No, and I don't expect any good news. People in that country are barbaric." He saw the uncertain look on Sara's face. "No, babe, I mean real barbaric. Remember all those beheadings that were on the news? Well that's commonplace with extremist Islamic nuts." His mind drifted back to his time in Afghanistan and his mind's eye had laser vision on some of the horrific images he witnessed first hand. "Butchering people is an acceptable practice over there. If the bad guys caught Lenny, there's very little chance he'll be found alive and in one piece."

Sara covered her mouth and spoke through her hands. "How awful." Then she dropped her hands and asked quietly, "You saw some of that, didn't you?"

Kaderri wasn't one to talk about his war stories, especially since most of them were classified. He would talk about the relationships his Special Forces teams made with the armies and personnel he was training and the cultures and customs he learned and what he had to endure to be accepted by those people.

Once in a while, though, he would tell her about certain firefights he was involved in, but of course, they would be the sanitized version and the location was usually omitted. Sara didn't need to know in intimate detail what kind of destruction he encountered or caused.

"Yeah," he admitted. "It's not pretty and it's a lot worse than what you see in pictures or on TV." He drained his Kona and rose from the chair. In a few hours, they would have to pick up the kids. "Time for change of subject."

"Ok," Sara agreed and took another sip. "To what?"

Kaderri turned and stood in front of her. His eyes devoured her naked body, tracing his gaze up from her painted toenails, over the muscled calves to the firm thighs that were crossed right over left and concealed her womanhood. He gave a sly smile as his eyes worked farther up her body, past her breasts, up her long neck and slightly parted lips. He stopped roaming once his eyes met hers, twinkling from the light of the lamp.

She gave a inquiring look back.

Kaderri felt himself begin to stir, his erection growing as he dropped to his knees in front of her. Without resistance, he took the coffee mug and danish from her hands. He slid his hands down her smooth thighs to her knees, spread her legs and placed them over the arms of the chair. He moved his head between her legs, felt her hotness on his face and consumed her aroma. His tongue darted out and licked her tender folds of flesh.

"Hmmm," Sara moaned and gripped the back of his head, "I like this subject!"

Sunday, October 12, Chakmaklychanga, Turkmenistan

The situation had gone from bad to worse. Feliks Grigorenko had made contact with the weapons buyer, Nawaf Al Suqami and he had agreed to meet. Borushko had already devised a plan to meet near the original site in Turkmenistan that would allow him and his comrades to disappear from the false search and rescue for half a day without raising suspicions. The problem arose when Al Suqami said he could only meet at his compound near the border with Pakistan. That was on the other side of Afghanistan! To come up with a solution to travel across two countries and return in a day while pretending to be on a search and rescue mission for Yezhov was near impossible! NATO air forces controlled the sky over Afghanistan, preventing them from flying anywhere near Al Sugami's location. Driving wouldn't work either; the six hundred kilometers was too great a distance and he was sure American or NATO patrols would stop them.

Borushko then spent hours devising a new, ambitious plan to get to the far side of Afghanistan. Through his connections in the Solntsevskaya, old friends and a lot of money, he was able to get transportation to and from where he was to meet Al Suqami.

The first part of the plan was for a trusted NCO to take a unit into the field to conduct a pretend search mission for

Yezhov while Borushko began his journey. The men in that were to be paid off to keep their mouths shut and if they erred, Borushko made sure they knew they wouldn't live very long.

For the first leg of the trek, Borushko contracted with a privately owned helicopter company to carry himself, Captain Agranov and Lieutenants Martov and Grigorenko out of Chechnya before sunrise. They crossed the Caspian Sea in a former Soviet Army surplus Mi-8 Hip helicopter and reached the coastal town of Cheleken in Turkmenistan. There they switched rides in order to be less conspicuous and boarded another Mi-8 helicopter owned by one of the oil and gas companies drilling in the country. Emblazoned on the fuselage was the company logo of an oil well and flamed tipped smoke stack on a white circle. Natural gas and oil were Turkmenistan's main resources, so spotting one of the company helicopters darting across the sky or radar screens wouldn't raise any suspicions.

The Russians were then flown across the vast Garagum Desert, which comprised most of Turkmenistan, over the blue ribbon of the Amu Darya River and landed next to a collection of temporary work trailers for an oil drilling site ten kilometers from the western outskirts of Chakmaklychanga. The town was a few short kilometers from Afghanistan's western border and Iran's eastern border. They dared not getting any closer for fear of being shot down by either NATO or Iranian aircraft.

The next segment wasn't to be as fast.

The chopper settled down in a hurricane of dust and debris in the desolate landscape, blotting out the mid morning sun. Once the skids were firmly on the ground, Martov slid the door open and the four passengers jumped out and walked in a crouch over to the dust and mud covered Toyota Land Cruiser emblazoned with the same logo as the chopper. Shielding their heads from the wind storm created by the rotating blades, the men walked the thirty meters to the vehicle where the driver, a tall man with a dark complexion, black hair and sunglasses, exited as they approached.

Borushko felt the security of the Makarov pistol tucked in the small of his back, just in case events warranted its use. The other three men in his party were armed as well and discretely separated themselves in defensive posture.

No verbal exchanges were spoken as the men closed the distance.

"Nice day for a helicopter ride," the tall man greeted without a smile.

Borushko relaxed at the correct code words the man used. "Splendid, indeed," he answered back.

"Everything you asked for, it's all in here," the tall man stated and tapped the door.

"Good," Borushko nodded with a sigh of relief. Everything was working according to plan.

"Here," the tall man reached into the Land Cruiser and grabbed what looked like a pile of rags.

Martov and Grigorenko began to strip.

Borushko and Agranov both raised and eyebrow.

"We don't want to draw attention to ourselves," Grigorenko stated as he removed his shirt. "You should put on the clothes, it'll be much safer. And wear the kaffiyea," he added with a grin. "You have blond hair. It'll stand out."

Borushko realized that Grigorenko was right. The military uniforms had to go and begrudgingly he put the head scarf on his head.

Once everyone had changed, they handed their uniforms to the tall man, who put them in a bag. Then without a word, he walked towards the waiting helicopter and left. Borushko felt out of place wearing the loose fitting garments, but knew it was necessary, especially since he was sure there were still ill feelings among the populace towards Russians in the former Soviet Republic.

Stowed inside the Land Cruiser was indeed everything they had asked for. There were four AKM assault rifles and two hundred rounds of 7.62mm ammunition loaded in magazines for each. A bag of hand grenades, topographical and street maps, and most importantly, a satellite telephone to call the helicopter to pick them up. In addition, there was the equivalent of one thousand dollars each in manat and rials, Turkmenistan's and Iranian currency. The money was for the odd chance that they had to bribe their way out of or into one of the countries.

"Let's go. Feliks," Borushko nodded to Grigorenko, "you drive." They were heading west for approximately eighty kilometers. Their destination: Jannatabad, Iran.

"You better guide me," Grigorenko said and slid behind the wheel.

"Everything looks good," Agranov stated from the back seat, handing out the currency. "Here."

Borushko sat in the passenger seat and compared the topographical map to the lay of the land. Formidable mountains lay further to the south and east, the dangerous lands of the warlords in the border area of Turkmenistan, Afghanistan and Iran. He suddenly looked up in disgust and cursed at himself for not bringing a GPS. How stupid!

The dusty, uneven hard packed roads that crossed the countryside made for a slower than anticipated trip. Many times they had to brake suddenly because they came upon a slow moving horse or donkey drawn cart or the road disappeared and they had to reacquire it. All the while, Borushko concentrated on figuring out what went wrong in Yezhov's arm sale. Was he set up? Borushko kept asking himself. All signs pointed that way. He also thought about how he was going to deal with Al Suqami. Would it be easier to come right out and accuse him of setting them up and stealing the weapons and money? Or should a more tactful track be used? Either way, he had to play it carefully if wanted any chance to get the money back.

Yezhov's disaster wasn't the only thing running through Borushko's mind. The contents of the text message and e-mail he received from Eduard Tomsky and Aleksander Karsavin regarding the men who participated in his father's assassination was never far from thought. Excitement coursed through him, knowing he was at the beginning of fulfilling his promise.

Grigorenko broke his thoughts. "We're coming in to town."

Borushko read the map to orient himself and peered through the dirty windshield, spying the town of Jannatabad to his front. It wasn't a modern town with skyscrapers and office buildings, but it wasn't a collection of mud huts either. The buildings, homes, and stores were made from either wood, concrete or stone and dotted throughout was crude new construction. There were paved roads, telephone poles and electric lines, giving the town a sense that it was attempting to modernize.

Carefully they drove through the streets, following a mix of older, battered cars as well as mule drawn carts. Shops had neon lights glowing in the windows and café's had tables set up on sidewalks where customers were enjoying their meals. For every practical purpose, the town resembled any other third world town.

Some of the pedestrians stopped and stared as they drove past and some of those stares unnerved Borushko just a little, though he had no reason to believe he was being singled out. He had assurances from his contacts that they would be allowed to proceed unmolested to the far side of town to the small, one strip airfield. Assurances, he knew, didn't count on the solitary criminal not playing by the rules. He became acutely aware that his palms were damp and his heart rate increased. He tightened his hold on the weapon's pistol grip, chambered a round and kept his thumb hovering on the safety.

The sound of bolts slamming rounds into chambers from the back seat told him Agranov and Martov were spooked as well.

Grigorenko kept driving, his eyes constantly moving, searching for danger, but he seemed more relaxed than any of the others.

They were just reaching the western outskirts of the town when Borushko consulted the map again. "How much further do we have to go?" When he didn't get an immediate answer, he turned to look at Grigorenko and found him staring into the rearview mirror.

"Company," Grigorenko announced. "Red pickup a hundred meters behind."

The men were professional enough not turn around and look, but Borushko used his side view mirror to spot the tail.

"How long have they been there?" Agranov clicked the safety off.

"Long enough," Grigorenko answered flatly.

Borushko frowned. "Criminals or Iranian security forces in disguise?"

"Good question. And one I don't have an answer to."

The outer limits of town was just ahead and the buildings became more dilapidated. Garbage littered the streets and the pedestrians had downbeat gazes or hard stares at the vehicles that drove past, like a carnivore stalking its prey. Clearly this wasn't the safest part of town.

"He's still there," Borushko informed the pair in back. He turned to Grigorenko and asked, pushing the kaffiyea out of the way, "Can you lose them without getting us lost?"

Just before Grigorenko could answer, there was a sudden green flash from a side street off to the right. Another pickup truck darted out across their path and came to a skidding halt, filling the windshield.

"Shit!" Grigorenko slammed on the brakes and came to his own skidding halt, just inches from the pick-up.

Borushko dropped the weapon and got his hands up just to time to brace himself from smashing into the windshield.

The screeching of tires from behind indicated they were boxed in. One word raced through Borushko's mind–ambush! He reached for the AKM and shouted commands. "Pyotr, Osip cover the back!" He was going to fight his way out of this. "Feliks, smash through!"

But that wasn't going to happen. Sitting in the bed of the pickup in front of them were three masked men wearing flowing robes and kaffiyeas. Two were aiming AKs at them, and the third was standing behind a pintle mounted .50 cal. machine gun.

"I don't think we're going anywhere, Mikhail," Grigorenko said, staring at the receiving end of the large bored barrel. One burst from the machine gun would blow the vehicle, and them, to pieces.

Just as Borushko thought this was the end, the passenger in the cab of the pickup got out, slung an automatic weapon over his shoulder and walked towards the passenger side of Borushko's vehicle. Right towards *him*. The man put his hand up, signaling Borushko to stay put. The man had a kaffiyea covering his face so all Borushko could make out were hard, dark hard eyes staring at him. The man halted outside the window, pointed the muzzle at Borushko's head and twirled his finger, indicating he wanted the window down.

Borushko's heart raced. Tighter he gripped the weapon across his lap, calculating what chance they would have of surviving a firefight. One look at the .50 caliber machine gun didn't give them good odds. He spoke aloud to his crew. "If I shoot or get shot, take out the machine gun first then we'll get the hell out of here. Got it?"

"Right," they answered in unison.

Borushko lowered the window. "Yes?" he coolly asked the masked man.

"We are friends," the masked man stated in Russian. It was a greeting the Solntsevskaya used to identify themselves to one another.

Relief swelled within Borushko and he let out a loud exhale. "Yes! We are friends!" Borushko tried to suppress his grin and offered his hand through the window.

The masked man revealed his face and shook Borushko's hand. "Follow us to the airplane and the pilot will take you on your journey." Without waiting for a response he then turned and walked away.

Smiling at their good fortune, Borushko slapped Grigorenko on the shoulder. "You heard him, follow that truck!"

CHAPTER FIVE

Sunday, October 12, Kelif, Turkmenistan

"Pack your stuff, Weston," Russ Hannigan ordered walking through the storefront doorway to Hal Weston's closet-sized office.

The walls of the first floor office were bare and yellowed with age. Cracks in the plaster looked more like spider webs and the small window that allowed in some light was so drafty that if a candle flame was put anywhere near it, it would blow out. Outdated was one word that came to mind to describe the office, but, Harold Weston wasn't interested in the aesthetics.

Bewildered, Weston looked up from the papers scattered on his desk. He raised an eyebrow. "Why? Where am I going?"

"Forward Operating Base Warrior."

Weston thought for a moment then dropped his jaw. "FATA?" He used the acronym for the Federally Administered Tribal Area. "On the other side of Afghanistan?"

"Yep." Hannigan took three steps on the hard wood floor and sat on the edge of the old battered desk. "The Ranger unit that rescued Len Puckett found a tremendous amount of intel that I think you might be interested in."

Weston didn't like the change and was going to protest the move. He was still on the hunt for Saudi arms dealer, Ahmed Rashid Halabi, and didn't want to be pulled off his trail. He set his jaw before he spoke. "What about Halabi? I can't give up on him now." He defiantly folded his arms across his chest.

Hannigan was unimpressed. "Two reasons." He ticked off his fingers. "One, I'm sending you to replace Puckett."

Weston threw his arms over his head in an act of incredulity. "Come on, Russ! You've got to be kidding me!?"

Hannigan stared hard at his field officer. "Be quiet, Hal. This is not open to debate."

Weston was going to have none of this. Not that Puckett's work was any less important, in fact, he was doing the exact same thing that Weston was, finding weapons caches and the men trafficking them. But Weston was getting so close to Halabi he could smell his body odor. He was not about to give that up. He protested further. "All the work-"

Hannigan held up his hand, cutting him off. "Enough!" After a moment of silence to make sure Weston kept quiet, he continued. "The second reason is there is a belief that the two sites, the one you took out that bagged the Russian, Yezhov, and the one where the Rangers found Puckett are connected."

"What's the connection?" Weston asked sharply. "They both contained Russian designed weapons?" The AK-47 was the most widely reproduced weapon in the world.

Hannigan slowly gave a Cheshire cat's grin and held up two fingers. "The Rangers killed two Caucasians. Russians."

Weston's face immediately softened and he raised an eyebrow. "Yeah?" Suddenly the prospect of going to Afghanistan sounded much better.

"Yeah." Hannigan rose off the desk.

"What kind of intel?"

"All kinds of material. Videos, documents, computers. You'll have a field day with the information. The SF guys and the army's 10th Mountain Division are already planning operations from what was found. Langley and the Homeland Security people are getting revved up too."

"That good?" Weston began to get excited.

Hannigan nodded. "Do what you have to do with your contacts here. Your ride leaves tomorrow at 0800." He rose off the desk and paused before exiting and smiled once more, revealing a rare trait of a personality. "Don't forget about your nurse."

Sunday, October 12, Federally Administered Tribal Area, FATA, Pakistan

The twin engine Reims F406 turboprop plane had to fly in under the Pakistani radar net making for a roller coaster ride as it flew nap-of-the-earth. To Major Mikhail Borushko, the ride mimicked the movements of his BMP armored vehicle as it drove through the land with sudden rises and falls and bone jarring landings as it crested a hill and flew off the top. Because he was used to that type of ride, he was able to keep his mind focused on the fiasco Yezhov had gotten himself into and the list of men his comrades found in connection with his father's death. Looking over at his friends, the pale look on their faces indicated they didn't enjoy the ride.

Upon landing on a remote dirt valley floor, there was no runway, the group of Russians deplaned with their weapons at the ready and were met by armed men in a red dented, rust pocked Range Rover and a black Toyota pick-up truck. There was no mounted machine gun this time but the four kaffiyea covered men in the bed were armed to the teeth and two of them carried RPG's. Borushko knew these men weren't friends of the Solntsevskaya. They were either al-Qaeda, Taliban or some warlord's soldiers. One cloaked man approached Borushko, handed him the keys to the Range Rover and in harsh Russian, were told to follow. Borushko quickly handed the keys to Grigorenko and under the watchful eyes of their new escorts, climbed in.

Except for the general location of being in the Baluchistan territory of the Tribal Lands, Borushko had absolutely no clue where he was and that made him nervous. He also had no idea where he was heading or how he was getting back. He cursed himself again for not remembering the GPS. Somewhat comforting was the pilot's assurance that the airplane would be waiting for them when they returned. So far, everything was going according to plan but trusting people he did not personally know or take an oath with was something he did not like to do.

A half hour of rough driving had passed since the Russians were ordered to follow the truck full of armed masked men. Borushko had a map, but it didn't do him much good without a reference point. He rightly determined they were now in the rugged Toba Kakar Range and heading north on animal paths, dirt roads and just plain old cross country driving. How far they were going or how far they went was impossible to tell. He still wasn't sure if they were in Pakistan or Afghanistan? He grew concerned that the dust trails left by the vehicles may draw unwanted attention by American Predator drones.

They rounded a sharp corner on the donkey path and followed the lead vehicle into a deep ditch before coming to a halt. Borushko's first thought was this was the place they were going to be executed and expressed those sentiments to his fellow comrades. "I believe they are going to kill us here."

"I don't think so," Feliks Grigorenko countered. "They left us with our weapons, Mikhail. Not the thing one would do if they were going to carry out an execution."

"I'll have to agree," added Pyotr Agranov from the back. "Company from behind," he quickly warned.

Appearing out of nowhere, another pickup truck filled with armed men skidded to a halt ten meters behind them.

Borushko wasn't so sure about not being executed. He was under the impression that they were supposed to meet with the weapons buyer, not be taken prisoner by his men. At the moment, that appeared to be the case. It was a set up, like they did to Colonel Yezhov.

In front, one of bandits, as Borushko thought of them, stood in the bed and shouldered an RPG and trained the deadly weapon on their windshield. Others quickly got out of the vehicles and surrounded Borushko's.

One of them spoke harshly in a language Borushko didn't understand. He was gesturing with his thumb at the same time and Borushko took that for them to get out of the vehicle. The bandit waved the pistol and shouted something else, this time pointing to the hood and making a slashing motion across his throat.

"I think he wants us to get out and shut off the engine," Grigorenko suggested then looked at Borushko for instructions.

Borushko nodded in agreement and blew out a long breath. "Ok, let's do it slowly, and keep your weapons close."

Grigorenko killed the engine and they opened the doors. Showing they were not intimidated, the four Russians' confidently exited the Range Rover but remained behind the opened doors. Their weapons within easy reach on the seats.

To the Russians surprise, the thin man spoke in broken Russian and twirled his hand for added measure. "Turn around!" The men in the trail vehicle approached from behind, carrying what appeared to be rags.

The Russians traded concerned looks with each other and back at their weapons.

"Hands up!" the man ordered and the others closed in.

Seeing they had no choice, Borushko and his men did as they were told. Quickly their hands were tied behind their backs and tight fitting blindfolds placed over their eyes. This time, the weapons were taken away.

Borushko's heart raced as the blindfold was tightened, his mind believing this was the end, a bullet to the back of his head was forthcoming.

"In!" the captor shouted as one of Borushko's colleagues was pushed into the Range Rover.

Borushko stood in his spot and braced for his turn to be searched and shoved in. He was at the mercy of his captors and admitted to himself that he was scared. Scared of what type of hell these people were going to put him through. Sweat began dripping down his forehead and he clasped his hands to keep them from trembling. Without his sight, his hearing became amplified. When he heard the unmistakable sounds of AKs being handled, a moment of panic gripped him. Was the next sound he heard going to be the safety flicking off? The fear became so great that his legs became jelly and he fought hard to keep from urinating on himself.

Suddenly the fear vanished and he became angry with himself for acting like a scared little boy. He was a major in the Russian army! A combat officer who has killed other men and seen them die in front of his eyes. He should not be acting this way!

Death was something he had to come accept as a strong possibility, especially being a soldier. But he expected his demise to come, if the events warranted, in a firefight, either with Chechens or from a rival crime organization in Moscow, not this way, tied up like a bound pig and left in a shallow grave where nobody would ever find him.

"Where are we going?" he demanded in a commanding voice.

"Be quiet!" came the immediate response. Just then he was grabbed by the shoulders and pushed into the back seat, squished between two of his comrades.

"Mikhail?" Martov's quiet voice searched him out from his left.

"Yes?" Borushko answered quietly, hoping not to draw any attention to their conversation.

One of the bandits climbed behind the steering wheel and started the engine. The tires spun, kicking up dirt and rock that bounced on the underside of the wheel well. Then the big tires caught and the Range Rover leapt forward.

"What's going on?"

"I don't know, Osip. I don't think they want us to see where we are going to meet the weapons dealer. Hey," his voice went lower, "I can grab my pistol." His fingers wrapped around the metal handle of the Makarov still tucked in the small of his back, but he couldn't swing it around to the front so he could use it accurately. Why, he thought, didn't they search him for weapons?

Where they were headed to, Borushko had no idea, but he was starting to believe there was a God because he thanked Him for being alive.

After twenty minutes of riding over rough terrain, they finally stopped. The doors were pulled open and the men were given harsh commands in accented Russian and yanked out by their shirt collars into the crisp air. Once they regained their balance, their restraints and tightly wrapped blindfolds were removed. The sudden exposure to the bright sunlight acted like a flash bulb and caused them to shut their eyes tight and bow their heads.

Borushko blinked a few times as his eyes had adjusted to the light and took the opportunity to study the surrounding terrain. They were in a small valley, in which country he did not know, but it was colder here, indicating they were at a higher elevation. Stunted trees, scrub brush and some brown patches of grass dotted the rocky terrain out past the hills that bracketed the roughly fifteen acre compound. In the near distance, snow capped mountains surrounded the site, as did at least twenty mean looking sons-of-bitches armed to the teeth with assault rifles and machine guns. Off to his left in a shallow defilade covered with camouflaged netting were two worn and battered Soviet T-55 tanks streaked with rust. The tool compartment was open on one of them, indicating they may still be in working order.

Spread out across the compound were a half dozen buildings and sheds of various dimensions, made from plywood and corrugated tin and one or two from dried mud bricks.

Two of the one-story buildings on the far left appeared to be barracks and were approximately twenty meters apart from each other. There was one door in the center with two small windows on either side and men entering and exiting at irregular intervals. In the space between them, there was a small shed with electrical cables that extended out to them. Just behind them were two other windowless sheds.

To the right of the barracks was another windowless shed and a hundred meters further of open space was what appeared to be the main building. It was one story, twenty by forty in dimensions, made mostly of concrete block and flat roofed. Windows were evenly spaced with a solid wood door. White smoke curled from the top of the chimney, the burning wood permeated the air.

A muffled hum came from one of the smaller buildings and a faint whiff of diesel fuel was detected as well.

"Move," one of the masked bandits ordered, ending his surveillance. He thought he saw a firing range and obstacle course that was in use.

"Move to where?" Borushko asked snidely. He stared hard at the two men who blindfolded him and fought the urge to throttle them both.

The bandit pointed to the one story, concrete, building. "That way."

Holding his stare a moment longer, Borushko followed the armed escort and walked towards the door. His eyes wandered, trying to pick out any landmarks he memorized. His breath formed a cloud in front of his face as he took determined strides to the building where he believed the weapons buyer, Nawaf Al Suqami to be.

He paused at the door and waited. Wordlessly, Agranov, Grigorenko and Martov fell in line behind him. He knew their eyes were searching just like his and their muscles were coiled tight, ready to spring into action.

The bandit who escorted them pounded on the door in rapid succession, paused and banged on it again. After a moment, the door was pulled open and immediately filling the space was a giant of a man dressed in an old Soviet Red Army green colored uniform. He had a large sheathed knife secured through a thick leather belt hanging on one hip and an AKS-74U assault rifle hanging off his shoulder.

The big man moved aside as two men squeezed past from behind him to search Borushko and the others. These men were not amateurs like the ones who stopped them in town. They methodically patted the Russians down from head to toe, not missing any area and immediately found the hidden weapons. As if they were expecting to find them, the men tossed the weapons aside and continued the search without uttering a word. Once finished, the two men moved away to collect the weapons and the big man stepped aside and allowed the Russians to enter.

Just as the door was about to close, the big man said something harsh, followed by the unmistakable *crack!* of a jaw being broken.

Borushko surmised the bandit who escorted them to this place was in charge and failed to do a proper and thorough job. He was now paying the price for his shortcomings.

The interior of the building was dark and musty and it took a moment for Borushko's eyes to adjust to the change in light. The floor was constructed of plywood and there were no decorations on the concrete walls to speak of. The only light came from the windows and red glowing embers in the fireplace.

"So, these are the scum who stole my weapons!?" A deep gravelly voice growled in Russian from a dark corner. A battery operated table lamp was then turned on, revealing the face of the speaker.

Sitting at a large, crudely constructed table next to the fireplace was a stocky, rat faced man in his late forties with short cropped salt and pepper hair. He was wearing a dark sport coat under a white robe and his thick fingers were adorned with gold and jeweled rings. A bulge under his left armpit revealed he was carrying a concealed weapon and a satellite phone was on the table in front of him. Borushko instantly knew he was looking at Nawaf Al Suqami.

"I beg your pardon?" Borushko responded sharply. The hairs on the back of his neck stood up. He wasn't about to let a rat-faced man steer this conversation. He glanced around, counting seven armed men in the building, all with their eyes trained on him. He better play this one carefully or he wouldn't be around much longer.

Al Suqami rose from his seat and pointed at Borushko's chest. "You stole my weapons!"

"Hold it right there," Borushko ordered, feeling his face turn hot. "What do you mean we stole your weapons? I believe you set us up!"

"Nonsense!" There was fire in Al Suqami's dark eyes. "I would do no such thing!"

This was getting nowhere fast and a change in attitude had to happen now. Borushko calmly walked over to the table and stood, spreading his hands. The eyes of Al Suqami bore into him, and his jaw was clenched tight. Borushko attempted to ease the tension by starting over. "I am Mikhail Borushko, to my right is Pyotr Agranov, Osip Martov and Feliks Grigorenko."

The three men nodded their heads.

Al Suqami stared at each man, but did not speak. Borushko continued. "Feliks is the one who called to arrange this meeting to find out what happened during the last transaction." Al Suqami's nostrils flared and he opened his mouth to say something, but Borushko wouldn't let him. "By your reaction a moment ago, you believe we stole your money and the weapons we were supposed to sell you, correct?" It was a rhetorical question and once again he wouldn't let Al Suqami respond. "I came in here ready to accuse you of setting us up and ripping us off. We never saw any of the money and the weapons are gone. As you can see, my friend," Borushko spread his hands even wider, "we are both mistaken."

Al Suqami's features softened a bit, but he was still angry. Clearly he was mulling over in his mind what Borushko had just told him. Finally, he spoke in a cautious tone. "Sit down," he offered his hand, "please." He then called out to the guards for more fire wood and tea.

"Thank you," Borushko nodded. A warm drink would be nice, but some food would be better, he thought. They hadn't eaten since breakfast.

Three guards appeared with chairs and a fourth placed an armful of logs on the fire and coaxed it to a roaring flame.

"So," Al Suqami began in a business like tone "what can you tell me?" A guard appeared with the tea and some flat bread.

"I wasn't there," Borushko answered. Al Suqami's nostrils flared again and the embers in his eyes suddenly flashed but Borushko ignored the newly displayed anger. He pointed to Grigorenko and Martov. "But Feliks and Osip were and they will tell you what happened."

"Out with it," Al Suqami demanded.

Five minutes later, Grigorenko and Martov had completed the recount.

Al Suqami sat there in silence, staring hard at the Russians. He had listened intently, not saying a word, but absorbing the information like a sponge. His face had remained passive, the corners of his mouth turned down and his hands balled into fists.

Then he spoke, throwing the Russian delegation a curve ball. "What you say may be true."

"*May?*" The powerfully built Martov fired back, spittle flying from his mouth as he leaned forward. "We witnessed the destruction of our friends and your men, the weapons being carried away, the money never arriving and you say it 'may' have happened? You're an asshole!"

"Take a breath, Osip," Borushko cautioned. Diplomacy was needed here. He still believed that Al Suqami or one of his friendly tribes set them up.

Grigorenko angrily added his own thought. "I should slit your throat right here."

Before Al Suqami had a chance to respond to his death threat, Borushko asked in an even tone, "Tell me, Nawaf Al Suqami, since you don't seem convinced that we are telling the truth, what would I do with the weapons? We have no need for them. It is you who needs them to continue your fight with other tribes and kill whoever else."

Al Suqami bristled and didn't back down. "You could use them again to set someone else up! To make more money!"

"Don't be stupid!" Borushko snapped, showing his temper as he leaned across the table. "What would we have to gain by double crossing on a deal? That may be your method," he stabbed a accusatory finger at Al Suqami, "but not ours. We are conducting business. This loss cost us a lot of money and lives that will take time to replace. Now I ask you, where is my money? If you don't come up with a satisfactory answer, I will get word back to the supplier and tell him you are unreliable and stole everything." If Borushko knew where he was, he could threaten to come back here with armed men and handle the situation in one swift violent action. He only hoped that his threat would be enough to get to the truth.

"That will not be necessary," Al Suqami said confidently. "I believe your men's story. I know what happened to the money. There was a survivor."

"Where is the money? A survivor of what?" Agranov asked first, cutting the pompous idiot off. "And how are you going to get it back from the other side of the country?"

Al Suqami leaned back, a satisfied look on his face. "American aircraft attacked and destroyed the trucks with the money about five kilometers from the meeting site. One of our allies found the wreckage."

To a man the Russians sat there in stunned silence. Borushko clenched his jaw in anger that was ready to spill out like a pot of boiling water and stared hard at the man sitting across from him, his eyes boring a hole like an auger. Why would the son-of-a- bitch waste their time playing head games?

Borushko suddenly hit his boiling point and all the rage was focused on Al Suqami sitting across from him with a smug smile on his face. He shot straight out of his chair and pointed his finger at the man's nose. His outburst startled the guards. "Why the fuck didn't you tell us this when we arrived here? You motherfucker!" Borushko decided that Al Suqami wasn't playing with a full deck and didn't want to deal with this idiot anymore. The Solntsevskaya and supplier would just have to eat the money and they would understand once he relayed the events. "You may like playing stupid games, but I don't." He angrily turned to his men and stood. "We're finished here."

A dumbfounded look washed over Al Suqami's face. He quickly came out from behind the table. "What do you mean we are finished here? Please understand, I had to see if you were trustworthy! We have to set up another weapons sale! Where are you going? We have to negotiate!"

Borushko gave a hard stare, not trusting himself to say or do anything.

Agranov, who was silent for most of the conversation hit Al Suqami with a one two punch. "No, we don't have to negotiate anything, you dog's ass! You accuse us of stealing the money and weapons while the whole time you knew it was not true and still want us to do business with you? Why should we believe you that the money was really destroyed? I don't know what type of society you live in and what kind of negotiating tactics you think you possess, but dealing with you is out of the question! You cannot be trusted!"

The dumbfounded look on Al Suqami's face suggested that he completely miscalculated the reaction of the Russians. He pled, almost to the point of begging. "Wait! What am I supposed to do about my weapons? I, we, need those!" His face turned red in anger, "I paid for them!"

"As you said, everything was destroyed. We are out our money too. Deal with someone else," Martov answered flatly. "Not us."

"Tell your men to take us back," Borushko ordered, disgusted by the whole situation and knowing nothing was going to come of any more talk. "We're done."

Monday, October 13, Albany, New York

Slowly recovering from the lustful weekend with Sara, Marcus Kaderri was back at work, setting up and protecting the future wealth and financial security for hundreds of individual clients and businesses. Early in the morning he was to meet with a client to finalize a 401(k) program that would put no less than eight hundred dollars a month in commission in his pocket. This, he laughed to himself, was almost as exciting as exploring carnal delights with Sara. Then he thought about that and shook his head. No, it was nowhere near the excitement he explored with her.

The bump and grind weekend was over and it was time to focus on the matters that made the world go 'round. Sitting behind his desk as the morning sun illuminated and warmed his office, the sounds of business echoed from outside his door: Fingers stabbing on keyboards, copy machines humming their rhythmic drumbeat and the ringing of telephones.

Spread on his desk were copies of The Wall Street Journal and the New York Post. Adding to the noise from outside his office door, the television set was tuned to the Fox News Channel and the commentators were bringing the viewers up to date on current events.

A soft rap on the open door drew his attention. He looked up just as Louise entered with an armful of manila folders. "Good morning, Louise," he greeted with a smile.

"How was your weekend?" He reached for the television remote and pressed the mute button.

"Hi, Marc. It was wonderful!" Louise beamed. She had always been a bubbly, upbeat lady, but Kaderri couldn't help but notice how much happier she had gotten since her engagement.

Kaderri raised an eyebrow and smiled crookedly. "Should I ask?"

"Sure." The smile spread to her eyes. "We learned about the different things that can be done on furniture!"

He laughed, confirming his thoughts. "What have you got there?" he pointed to the stack in her arms. "It's not anything that needs attention right away, is it? I have–"

She dropped the stack on the corner of his desk. "No," she cut him off and rolled her eyes in exasperation. "Did you think I forgot about your meeting with Blanchett and Taylor this morning to finalize the 401(k) deal? Remember, I'm sitting in on the meeting with you?"

"I didn't forget," he admitted. "I thought maybe you did, especially since your engagement and being consumed with lustful bliss and all that."

She growled.

"Ok," he shrugged with a smile. "What's in these?"

"Resumes, basic New York State forms to fill out, client folders for you to follow up on this week."

He raised an eyebrow. "Resumes for what? I'm not hiring anyone. Someone leaving I should know about?"

Louise shook her head. "Future reference? You don't want to keep them on file?"

Without hesitation he answered, "No. I don't believe anybody is going to be leaving anytime soon." Kaderri was proud to make that statement and he knew it to be true. He treated his employees well and only once did he have to fire an employee, and that was for falsifying information on an insurance application. Because of the effort he put forth to see them succeed, they, in return, were loyal to him.

Louise looked at her watch and opened her mouth to speak when Kaderri's intercom buzzed.

"Marc?" The receptionist's soft voice came clearly over the speaker.

He pushed the button to respond. "Yes, Diane?"

"If Louise is in there, tell her the donuts and stuff have arrived."

"Will do, thank you." He pushed the button again and watched the frown grow on Louise's face. He knew what she was thinking and immediately tried to put her at ease. "She still needs a little work, but she's doing fine."

Louise threw her hands in the air. "Ugh! She could have brought them over to the conference room herself! Jesus, it's only a dozen steps away!" She shook her head and continued, the frown growing deeper. "And 'Tell her the donuts and stuff have arrived.' When does she tell the boss what to do? Whatever happened to asking and saying please?"

Kaderri nodded in agreement. "I'm sure you'll take that up with her." He knew Diane was about to get her ass chewed off. "You didn't order anything with powder, I hope?"

Louise placed her hands defiantly on her shapely hips and leaned forward. "You are such a smart ass. No. I ordered muffins and danishes." She glanced at her watch again. "Blanchett and Taylor should be here in a half hour. I'll have everything set up." She turned on her heels and added, "As usual."

Fifteen minutes later, Kaderri was double checking the figures for the plan when the secure line on his telephone rang. Without hesitation he picked it up.

"Yeah?" he asked cautiously.

"It's Paul. We found Len Puckett." There was relief in McKnight's voice.

Kaderri almost cheered aloud. "That's great news! Is he alive?"

"Yes. He's in Walter Reed now."

"Thanks for keeping me posted, Paul." Kaderri figured this was the end of the conversation and prepared to hang up.

"Marc," McKnight's voice sounded cautious, "when the Rangers raided the cave complex where Len was held, they found some interesting material."

Kaderri picked up on McKnight's tone of voice. Idle chit-chat from this man was very rare. "Like what?"

"First of all, Mike Karmal. He was with Len and was executed."

"Damn," he said sadly and recalled when he said good-bye to Karmal after they escaped from the operation where he killed General Borushko. "There's something else, right? What is it?"

"It's about your team in Afghanistan. Karmal gave them up under torture."

An unexpected chill ran down Kaderri's spine. "Whoa," he blew through pursed lips.

"That's an understatement."

"Shit, Paul, if it ever got out that we were there–"

"I know, believe me, I know," McKnight agreed to the seriousness of the information.

"Thanks for the info on Len," Kaderri said quietly, almost absentmindedly to the point where he didn't hear McKnight say good-bye and hang up.

Suddenly his mind wandered off, drifting back to his tour in Afghanistan with Karmal. All the missions came rushing back like a flash flood. He remembered Karmal's big lively eyes and toothy grin among a brown weathered face and how excited he was to be killing Russians and their puppet Afghan Government lap dogs. Freedom for his country was the only goal he strove for.

Kaderri could only imagine what internal turmoil Karmal was going through with the takeover of the country by the Taliban and their thugs, Osama bin Laden's al-Qaeda terrorist network. The transition from Russian rule to Islamic fundamentalism must have been eating him alive. First to kick out a world superpower only to have the victors turn more vicious and bring their society back to the Stone Age. One thing he knew for sure about Karmal, he would have been eagerly helping Len Puckett execute Operation Enduring Freedom.

Another chill ran down Kaderri's spine, this time causing his body to shiver. An ominous sense of foreboding descended upon him like an inescapable cage.

"Marc? Marc!?"

Louise's raised voice plucked him out of the past and an uncertain future. She was standing in the doorway. "What is it, Louise?"

"Blanchett and Taylor are waiting."

He read the hands on his Rolex. It was a quarter past nine, meaning he was fifteen minutes late. "I'll be there in a minute."

"But Marc, they–"

"I'll be there in a minute!" he uncommonly snapped and fixed a hard gaze.

He walked from behind his desk and closed the door on her stunned expression. Without saying another word, he strode over to his desk, picked up the phone and called his friend, teammate and CIA partner, Bob Wolff.

CHAPTER SIX

Tuesday, October 14, Riyadh, Saudi Arabia

The sprawling, thriving capital city in the Kingdom of Saudi Arabia was full of energy and life, as was typical of any modern city in the world. The inhabitants, tourists, shopkeepers and businessmen went about their daily lives, earning a living or taking in the city's grandeur and history.

The top floor, all twelve suites, of the ten story office building on Al Mather Street near the city center was occupied by Arabian Peninsula Transportation. Sixty full time employees in the office building were kept busy tracking and arranging shipments of goods and merchandise in, out and around Saudi Arabia to anywhere in the world using the company's fleet of long and short haul trucks, and two ocean going freighters.

It was midday, the temperature outside was already at one hundred fifteen degrees Fahrenheit and the employees took time out for their prayers, all except the owner of the company, Ahmed Rashid Halabi. He abandoned practicing the faith of Islam years ago when he realized that working made for a better life than praying to Allah for success. Of course, when he was in public, he followed the faith as prescribed in the Koran.

One wall of the office was a glass and teak display case filled with vases, urns and other museum pieces dating back to the Persian Empire. Some of the vases were crafted in solid gold while others were adorned with jewels of precious stone, some as large as quarters. Other pieces were crafted from ivory, onyx and jade. Framed oil paintings of Arabian horses and intricate Persian rugs hung on the other walls. Hanging on the center of one wall across from his desk was his favorite piece, a five foot by seven heavy teak framed painting of Salah al-Din's army recapturing Jerusalem from the Crusaders in the late twelfth century.

Someday, he always thought, the Muslims alone will be there again.

Back and well rested from his trip to Turkmenistan, he was behind the closed double doors in his richly decorated, seventy-two degree climate controlled suite staring angrily at the computer screen perched upon the corner of his desk. "Where is the rest of the money?" he said aloud, ignoring the history surrounding him in which he usually took comfort from and used the past glory of the empire for guidance. "Why hasn't it been deposited in my account?"

"Do you think he was delayed?" Marwan Al Dossadi, his personal aide asked from the other side of the desk sitting in one of the gold embossed ornate chairs.

"What?" Halabi looked up from his screen lined with column's full of numbers and letters, forgetting Al Dossadi was in here with him. He readjusted the kaffiyea. "My apologies, Marwan. I don't know what could have happened. Sergi Mirovich is a competent man. He has always paid the remainder of the sale on time. I do not know why he hasn't on this one."

"Ahmed, he is a Russian after all and the leader of their organized crime syndication." Al Dossadi spread his hands and they became lost in the sleeves of his robe. "He cannot be trusted."

Halabi tilted back in his own leather chair. "That is true to an extent, my friend, but even criminals do have some sense of honor, especially in a business transaction where repeat business is guaranteed."

"What are you going to do?"

Halabi spun in his chair and gazed out the window over looking the city, contemplating his answer. "I'll give him another day, then I will call."

Tuesday, October 14, Kiri, Chechnya

The past two days were full of internal turmoil for Major Mikhail Borushko. It cost him five thousand euros to keep the men quiet who were supposed to be on the patrol with him looking for Yezhov. He assured them that if any word ever leaked out of what really happened, they and their families would be dead. He was also upset the Solntsevskaya was out millions of rubles and he had the unpleasant task of reporting Colonel Yezhov missing.

The more difficult deed was the phone call he had to place to Sergi Mirovich. Reporting deals gone bad was not welcomed by Mirovich and on many occasions bodily harm was inflicted on the deal maker as a punishment for failing.

He sat behind the desk of his newly constructed office on a folding metal chair. The smell of fresh sawdust filled his nostrils every time he breathed. He pulled the cell phone from the cargo pocket in his field jacket and dialed Mirovich's number from memory. He rose from the chair and closed the door to shut out the sounds of the work detail hammering in the last of the nails in this portion of the building.

On the second ring it was answered. "Da?" It was Sergi Mirovich's deep voice.

"Sergi? It's Borushko."

"Misha, what's going on?" Mirovich asked skeptically.

Borushko felt no need to beat around the bush. "Bad news. Yezhov's deal went sour."

"How bad?" Mirovich asked sharply.

"He's dead," Borushko said flatly and immediately. "The weapons and bodies were taken and the money destroyed."

Borushko pulled the phone away from his ear, knowing that a thunderous blast was sure to come. Mirovich yelled so loud Borushko could swear the phone vibrated in his hand. *"What!?"*

Borushko took a deep breath before he informed Mirovich of the events and the recent meeting with the buyer, Nawaf Al Suqami.

There was a long moment of silence before Mirovich spoke again. "That's not the only problem in that part of the world, Misha."

Borushko suddenly became alarmed. He was directly under Yezhov, which could mean he was in hot water. He braced himself for being partially blamed.

"We've lost contact with Tomsky and Karsavin."

Borushko let out a sigh of relief. He wasn't in trouble! Losing contact with Eduard Tomsky and Aleksander Karsavin in Afghanistan was the last thing he would imagine. They were both experienced KGB/FSB field officers. "The money too?" Borushko asked, suddenly becoming concerned with the amount of people in the organization and money being lost.

Then another, more dangerous thought crept into his mind. The two operations Yezhov was in charge of had failed, and he, Borushko, was second in command. It just occurred to him that it may appear to Mirovich that he is trying to overtake Yezhov in the pecking order of the organization. It wouldn't be the first time that killing the guy ahead of you to take his place had occurred. Borushko had to quickly dispel any notion of that. "When did all this happen? They sent me an e-mail just a short time ago. I don't think I can get away from my unit here to go and find out what happened."

Mirovich answered immediately. "No. I don't need to lose anymore people, Misha." His next comment caught Borushko unawares. "I need you to take over for Yezhov and keep the business going. There are still plenty of people in this world willing to buy weapons. I'll get others to find out what happened to Tomsky and Karsavin."

Borushko remained speechless for a moment, letting the unexpected promotion sink in. Finally, he acknowledged his elevation in stature. "Right."

"What did Tomsky and Karsavin send you, Misha?" Mirovich asked guardedly.

Might as well tell him, Borushko thought, especially now that he just got promoted. He would need the resources of the Solntsevskaya's long reaching tentacles to help track down the men on the list he obtained from his missing colleagues. Telling Mirovich the truth was an absolute. Sometimes he played dumb, setting a trap to catch one in a lie. This could be one of those traps. "Eduard sent me a list with names of the men involved in the assassination of my father."

"How'd they get that?"

Borushko took a breath then continued. "Apparently they captured an American Green Beret and an Afghan–"

Once again, Mirovich's voice exploded through the phone. "What the hell did they do that for? They are playing with fire! *Zhopa's!*" He used the Russian word for assholes. There was a pause as Mirovich calmed himself down. When he spoke again, his voice was tight, but calm. "They better hope the Americans don't find them, for their good, and ours as well. Tell me Misha, did they say why they were interrogating the American?"

"No," Borushko shook his head as he answered. "I can only speculate."

"Then speculate," Mirovich ordered fiercely.

"I believe they were somewhere in the vast Tribal Area, I'm not sure, and my guess is they got stuck there because of American or Afghan patrols. I think that some of the Taliban, who Tomsky and Karsavin were selling the weapons to this time around, captured the American and Afghan and brought them to Tomsky and Karsavin to help in the interrogation."

There was a long pause. "You may be right, Misha. They weren't soldiers, as you well know. They were FSB."

"If they could get information out of the captured pair, then they would sell it to the highest bidder, the Taliban, al-Qaeda or some warlord. Who's really to say what?"

Mirovich let out a growl. "If that is the case, I admire their aggressiveness in business, but," he exploded again, "what were they thinking!? They should have remained out of sight!"

Borushko completely agreed and there was nothing they could do about it. He moved the conversation forward. "Two questions, Sergi." Because of the recent losses, he became concerned with the Solntsevskaya's reputation in their ability to deliver the goods and how it would affect future sales. "What are we supposed to do about paying the weapons supplier? It could look bad for us if we don't pay." Borushko was curious about who supplied the weapons but was always informed he didn't need to know. Now that he was taking over for Yezhov, he hoped that information would be forthcoming.

Mirovich dashed those hopes. "That is not your concern, Misha, but Tomsky and Karsavin's deal went through. You said two questions."

He didn't have luck with the first question and suddenly became hesitant with the second. This one was personal. Never had he asked the head of the Solntsevskaya for anything personal. He calmed the butterflies that took flight in his stomach. "I want to hunt the killers of my father and am going to need our resources."

"You mean the men on the list that was sent to you?"

"Yes."

"Call me later and we'll discuss it. I don't see a problem."

The line suddenly went dead as Mirovich clicked off.

Borushko stared at the phone for a minute and blinked, letting the good news sink in. A smile spread across his face, believing the revenge he had been waiting for his entire adult life was about to come to fruition.

Tuesday, October 14, FOB Warrior, Kashah, Afghanistan

The moment he touched down in the helicopter, Harold Weston went to work in the small prefabricated building used to house all the intelligence. Dubbed 'Research and Development', the building was located in the center of the base, adjacent to the headquarters building and heavily guarded. Any snippet of information that was gathered in the AO, area of operations, was stored there.

The bland interior was brilliantly lit with overhead fluorescent lights. Half of the building was open space with a few six foot tables set up so soldiers could sit and spread out their information. A few cubicles along one wall were occupied by the staff. Computers, telephones and desks made the cubicles appear like it was a sales office in a stateside city instead of a military base in a war. Along the opposite wall were a half dozen computer cubicles and towards the rear of the building, the files were housed behind closed doors and protected by armed military policemen.

Once he showed his credentials to the military police guard outside the door, Weston felt like a kid in a candy shop with all the intelligence information that was available to him.

Immediately upon entering, he was greeted by Captain Charles Adams, who was alerted to his arrival by Russ Hannigan. "Mr. Weston?" The tall thin man held out his hand. "Charlie Adams."

"Nice to meet you, Captain. You're here to help me, correct?"

"Yes, sir. I'm at your disposal."

"Great, lets get started."

For the past two hours, Weston had been sitting alone sifting through piles of paper hoping to learn something that would lead him to finding Ahmed Rashid Halabi. So far he hadn't had much luck. Part of the problem was having to translate the information on the documents. All of it was written in Pashto, Dari, and Arabic and needed to be translated.

"Mr. Weston?" Captain Adams called from a swivel chair looking at a computer monitor. Splayed around him were scattered files and Flash drives.

"What have you got, Captain?" With a huff, Weston dropped the map he was studying. He was getting frustrated trying to figure out what the red dots on the sides of some of the mountains represented. "Anything I can read without a translator?"

Adams shrugged and rolled out of the way. "If you can read and speak Russian, I think. You did say to call you if anything out of the ordinary showed up, right?"

Weston's heart skipped a beat. He rose from the chair and leaned over Adams' shoulder. "What do you mean, Russian?"

"Look," Adams pointed a bony finger to the screen and adjusted his wire rimmed glasses. The computer he was working on had been removed from the cave where Puckett was rescued. "These two names here," he pointed to specific items on the screen. "I believe they are Russian, correct? Or least some part of the former Soviet Union."

Weston leaned closer to the screen. The text on the screen was in Pashto, but where Adams was pointing, the names were definitely Russian. "Eduard Tomsky and Aleksander Karsavin," he said aloud.

Bingo! The mystery Caucasians shot by the Rangers appeared to have just been identified. Weston learned there was no identification on the bodies when they were searched.

"You do speak Russian," Adams said more as a statement than a question.

"Da," Weston smiled. Then his smile faded and his professional curiosity took over. "I can read it as well. What else do you have?"

"Nothing, sir. Sorry. I get to this point and the damn thing freezes. I'm also trying to convert the text to English. The language program has been corrupted so it's going to take me some time to get this corrected."

"Don't be sorry, Captain." Weston clapped him on the back. "Those names are very helpful. Holler if you find anything else like this."

"Yes, sir." Adams went back to the computer, his fingers flying over the keyboard.

Weston turned back. "Captain, could you get me a hard copy once you get the program to work?"

"No problem."

"Thank you." Weston jotted the names down on a note pad and turned his attention back to the map with the red dots.

"Mister Weston?" Adams called again.

Weston turned before he took his seat. "Yeah?"

Adams leaned back in the chair and folded his arms across his chest.. "This may be none of my business, but that videotape the Rangers found in the camera on the rescue operation of your buddy, what was that all about?"

Weston knew Adams saw it, hell everyone in the room saw it, and then some. Right now, half a dozen other men were watching, cataloging and disseminating all the other video tapes that were recovered. "I haven't figured it out," he answered truthfully. "Then again, I didn't find it that informative to what we are looking for so I didn't pay much attention to it."

"Oh," Adams answered somewhat surprised. "Our guys forwarded the info up the chain. That guy, Karmal, really spilled the beans on an A-Team he said he was with fighting the Russians back in the 80's. He named the entire unit."

One of the lessons Weston learned early in life was that he, nor anyone else, knew all the answers to anything and asking questions and bouncing ideas off of others could result in the answers you were seeking. "What do you think the interrogators were after?" he asked Adams, his curiosity suddenly piqued. Shit! What did he miss on the video? "What did they ask?"

"They kept asking who pulled the trigger."

"On who?"

Adams thought for a moment. He snapped his fingers in remembrance. "Borushko, General Vasily Borushko of the Soviet 65th Motorized Infantry Division."

An ice cold wind suddenly swooped in and hit Weston over the head like a two by four. He remembered the name of that general back in 1985 when he was new to Special Forces and heard whispers about a secret mission. A general being killed wasn't an everyday occurrence and it made international news. But the actual facts of the story were never revealed.

The rumored story was an American Special Forces trooper pulled off the hit. Allegedly it was one hell of a shot if he remembered the story correctly, something like a thousand meter shot on a moving target.

Weston decided he better go over the tape again, and try to discover why the two Russians were so interested in the past. "Did Karmal answer the questions?"

"He kept saying it was 'boss'."

Weston automatically assumed he knew what Karmal was referring to–the commander of the unit. It wouldn't be hard to research the personnel on that team and determine who the sniper was, but that wasn't necessary.

A picture in the puzzle was beginning to form in Weston's head. "I need that tape."

The dining facility, or DFAC, provided a tasteful carbohydrate laden dinner of fried chicken, mashed potatoes, corn and fresh dinner rolls smeared with butter that filled Hal Weston's stomach and recharged his batteries. He downed a few cups of coffee and went back to work in 'Research and Development'.

With the remote in hand, Weston stared at the flat screen TV and watched for the third time the video tape of Mike Karmal's interrogation. One of the tech guys had been able to 'wash' out the other sounds on the tape and isolate a conversation taking place off camera. Weston was now able to confirm that the two men off camera were speaking in Russian. Because the acoustics in the stone chamber caused distortions, he was only able to piece together enough of the conversation to determine that they were asking for information from a long time ago. The most exciting snippet he acquired from the tape was when they called each other by their names, Eduard and Aleksander.

Nothing else on the tape jumped out at him in relevancy for his hunt for Ahmed Rashid Halabi, but he did jot down the names Karmal had given up under duress. The names of an American Special Forces A-Team commanded by Marcus Kaderri.

"Mr. Weston?"

"Yeah?" Weston turned to find a sergeant holding a shoebox and a clipboard.

"Here are the personal contents of the two men that you asked for." The sergeant placed the box on the table next to Weston and then gave him the clipboard to sign for the contents. "On line three, please."

He scribbled his name and thanked the sergeant, handed the pen and clipboard back and opened the top of the box. The contents were kept in two clear plastic zip lock bags and the first one he grabbed and emptied was tagged, Aleksander Karsavin.

The usual contents that would be found on a person spilled out. A wallet, some euro's, keys, but the item that caught Weston's attention was the cell phones.

Like a little kid on Christmas morning, Hal Weston got very excited and turned the phone on.

Wednesday, October 15, Riyadh, Saudi Arabia

"Praise Allah," Ahmed Rashid Halabi parroted and hung up the phone, ending the conversation. Flipping through the rolodex, he quickly rotated the files to the unnamed phone number and dialed it. His patience was wearing thin and having to make this call was making him angry.

It was answered on the third ring. "Da?"

"Sergi," Halabi spoke in English. "I'm waiting for my money. I thought we had an agreement"

"Ahmed," Sergi Mirovich's voice was flat and emotionless, as usual when they spoke. "We ran into a problem."

"I don't like problems," he said curtly.

"I don't like problems either. Your money, like mine, and the weapons, are gone. Unfortunately, things like this happen in war."

Halabi could feel his blood pressure rise and he gripped the phone tighter. "Explain," he hissed.

Halabi listened as Mirovich went through the details of what happened. His suspicion about the Russian ebbed and flowed during the conversation but finally, he accepted the story from the leader of the Solntsevskaya as the truth. In the back of his mind he knew something like this was bound to happen at some point in time.

"It was the Americans you say?" He didn't like Americans.

"Yes, Ahmed, Americans along with the Turkmen army. That's what my people say and they were present when it happened."

"Very well," was all Halabi could say, though not at all pleased.

"Ahmed, despite the loss, I would like to believe our business relationship is still intact." There was a tinge of hope in his voice.

Halabi thought about that. He had plenty of weapons to sell and knew that the arms market, both legitimate and black market, were extremely competitive. By Mirovch asking if they still had a business relationship, that confirmed he still had a willing middleman and was telling the truth about the disaster in Turkmenistan. With the worldwide connections at his disposal, Mirovich could have easily found another supplier but decided he still wanted to do business. "Yes, Sergi," he finally answered. "Yes. We still enjoy our business relationship."

"Good! Good! Until next time."

Halabi hung up the phone gently and leaned back in the chair, his mind deep in thought. According to Mirovich, the operation in Turkmenistan was a precision operation, not a chance encounter. To Halabi, it was obvious there was a spy somewhere in Mirovich's organization that gave the information about the sale. No Muslims in the circles he worked with would ever betray him.

Though he had a vast network of his own, and welcomed the repeat business of the Solntsevskaya, Halabi was going to have to limit his exposure with them and deal primarily with Arabs, he corrected himself, Muslims, Sunni or Shia didn't matter, or Taliban, al-Qaeda and Chechens.

Thursday, October 16, Albany, New York

Detective Gary Trainor, dressed comfortably in a pair of cotton navy blue Dockers, a smartly pressed white and gray striped button down collared shirt and no tie, slowly raised his interlocked hands over his head and stretched. The muscles in the small of his back creaked and popped in protest after being tied to the swivel chair at his desk for most of the day. It was the end of another work day at the Albany Police Department, and a slow one at that. A low satisfying groan ended the stretch. "Ahhh." He ran his hands through the short black hair on the top of his head.

For the past six months his desk was clean. He smiled that he could actually see the dull wood finished top. It used to be such a mess with papers, folders, Styrofoam cups half filled with coffee and used napkins and sandwich wrappers. At one time it got to the point where the cleaning crew sent him notice that they refused to clean his desk. When he needed to find a scrap of paper with an important phone number or address on it, a search party was called in to locate it. But now, his pens and pencils were poking out of a mug he used as a holder, a pad of paper was on the corner and a framed picture of his fiancée stared back at him. It was because of her neatness at home and refusal to clean up after him that he finally changed his bachelor ways. His boss and partner were thankful that the foul odor was gone.

He rolled his wrist to read the hands on his watch, three-thirty, and announced the time of day. "Quitting time!" His hazel eyes looked across his desk at his partner, Joanne Bauer, for her immediate response. Instead, her head was bowed on a scattered pile of paper, her face partially hidden from her dark hair that gave the impression of hiding behind a dark screen. He crumpled a piece of paper and bounced it off her head.

That caused her to look up, confusion shone in her brown eyes. "What did you do that for?" She rubbed her head where the ball of paper hit and moved the strands of hair behind her ears.

"Time to go," he repeated and pointed to his watch. "What are you so engrossed in?"

She shuffled the papers into a neat stack, tapped them on the desk and closed the folder. "Ah, the fucking parole board is letting Deshayne Gilbert out after two fucking years! On goddamn good behavior! That puke should be tortured and strung up by his balls!"

Trainor stared at her. "I gather you don't like him or agree with the decision?"

"Hell no!" she exploded and slammed her fist on the desk. "That shit pled to a lesser charge for the killing of an eighty year old woman in a home invasion. She was pistol whipped, had her legs broken and shot in the head. He turned on his accomplice, blamed him for everything."

Trainor knew how she felt. Just about every detective had the same scenario happen to them, and there was nothing they could do about it. It was just the way the system worked. Sometimes it sucked. "Take a breath, Jo."

"Yeah, you're right. It's just that it was my first case as a lead detective–"

He could see she was getting hot under the collar again, her nostrils flared and the skin on her neck turned a dark shade of pink. "Jo."

"Sorry." She visibly relaxed and took a breath. "We're next on the rotation?"

"Yep." The next case that involved the need for a detective would be theirs. "Hopefully it will be something easy, like recovering a stolen bicycle. Anyway, quitting time!"

This time she smiled and responded, "We're outta here!" and she jerked her thumb over her shoulder. "Doing anything with Amanda tonight? More wedding plans?" She grabbed her purse from the bottom desk drawer and jacket off the back of her chair.

"Nothing set in stone," he said, pulling on his windbreaker. "But I think this weekend all we're doing is wedding stuff."

"You ok with that?"

He shrugged. "No," he finally admitted. "The football games are on, but I promised her I'd be a good participant. Saturday, December fourteenth is coming quick."

"Good for you, Gary, sticking to your promise of staying involved."

It was Trainor's turn to smile and he dramatically placed his hand over his heart then put the back of his hand on his forehead. "The things guys sacrifice for love and to keep their woman happy." He chuckled. "I'll see you tomorrow."

Joanne rolled her eyes and let out a laugh. "Now I've heard it all! Have a good one, Gary."

From the station at Police Plaza, Trainor headed off to A Better Body, where the Albany Police Department had a membership plan, to put in an hour's worth of sweat lifting weights and running on a treadmill. Besides the obvious necessity of staying in shape for the job, Trainor also wanted to look good for his wedding. His frame, just under six feet, looked much more masculine since he lost fifteen pounds that put him at one eighty.

The fifteen minute drive through the streets of Albany from A Better Body in downtown to his home in the adjacent town of Colonie was non-eventful. He didn't have to yell at any idiotic drivers weaving in and out of the rush hour traffic or stupid pedestrians crossing against the traffic flow. He just happened to get stuck at every red traffic light.

Finally, he turned into his development where there were no traffic lights. The neighborhood was succinctly middle class with older ranch and Cape Cod style houses that had been built forty years prior. Mature elm and dogwood trees were dominant in the well manicured yards as were young children playing.

Slowing down as he approached his driveway, Trainor waved to Elise, the elderly neighbor across the street who was plucking her marigolds that lined the walkway from her driveway to the front door. He pressed the button on the garage door opener clipped to the visor in his Jeep Grand Cherokee as he pulled into the driveway of his Cape Cod style house on the end of the cul-de-sac on Bonnie Ct. As he waited patiently for the door to rise, he glanced at the dashboard clock, noted the time was 5:45pm and wondered if his beautiful fiancée was home yet. She had been trying to recruit a manager for a prominent position in a major corporation and said she might have to work late to land her. If the deal was successful, she was looking at a five figure bonus.

As the door rose, he saw Amanda's Chrysler Concord parked in the other stall. His heart skipped a beat in excitement, as it always did when he laid his eyes on her.

After pulling the Jeep in, he walked up the three stairs, pressed the button to close the garage door and strode into the kitchen. Wonderful, swirling aromas buffeted his nose, curling from two plates of food on the counter. He could hear Amanda's voice, but couldn't see she where she was or who she was talking to.

Amanda Matthews, soon to be Amanda Trainor, suddenly appeared in the archway from the dining room holding a cell phone to her ear. She was wearing a short tan skirt that hugged her slender hips and ended at mid thigh, showing off her toned silky pantyhose covered legs. A cream colored mock turtleneck clung to her curves, accentuating her trim waist and breasts. She spotted Trainor and gave him a thumb's up.

"Thank you again," she spoke into the phone, her green eyes gleaming with delight, "but you didn't have to call. I'm just doing my job." She paused as the person on the other spoke. "Thank you for contacting me," she answered. "Let me know if I can help you again. Bye, bye."

She folded the phone and sprinted to Gary's outstretched arms. He effortlessly held her off the ground and wrapped his strong arms around her small waist. Her soft, thin pink painted lips zeroed in on his and gave him a long hearty kiss. He patted her tight buns and eased her down, but kept his arms around her waist and interlocked his fingers at the small of her back.

"Good day, huh?" he asked with a raised eyebrow.

"You betcha, baby!" she answered gleefully, bouncing in his arms as she wrapped her hands around his neck. She gave him another kiss.

"I take it you landed the big one?"

The smile on her oval face spread to her eyes. "Yes, I did!" she said proudly and pushed her long light brown hair behind her shoulders. "That was the CEO of the company who hired her."

"Congratulations honey," he gave her a huge bear hug and another kiss. "Good job!"

"Thank you, thank you!" she shook in excitement and bounced on her feet. "Our honeymoon is paid for… in cash!"

He turned his attention to the two plates on the counter. "Why don't we put the food away and go out to eat and celebrate? Let's go to The Steer House."

She looked up into his eyes and smiled but declined the offer. "How about tomorrow? It's going to be late by the time we get there and eat, besides, I just cooked."

"Ok," he shrugged. He gave her another kiss then turned towards the counter to study the colorful display of food. "What did you make?"

Amanda slid from his arms and held up one of the plates. "Chicken with a white wine garlic cream sauce, farfalle and a combination of green and yellow beans with baby carrots and sliced almonds."

He took the plate from her hand and inhaled the flavors. They immediately awakened his taste buds. There was no doubt that Amanda was an excellent cook, and could compete with many of the chefs in town. "Smells delicious."

After their first break-up, Trainor moved from Rochester to Albany and transferred to the APD to help get over the deep void left by her departure. Amanda, equally hollow, took up cooking classes and excelled in the culinary arts. She was talented enough to where some of the restaurants in the greater Rochester area began offering her jobs. Extremely flattered, she thanked them all, but turned them down, stating cooking was just an escape.

"What kind of wine are we having?" he asked, not knowing much about the pairing of food and wine. Wine was her territory as well. He was mainly a beer drinker, with Michelob being his favorite.

"A Washington State Chardonnay," she said.

"Ooh," he said, remembering he liked those. He removed his shoes, put them in the tray next to the door that opened to the garage and hung his windbreaker on the peg. "Need me to do anything, hon?"

"Pour the wine, please."

While he went to the drawer to find the opener and pull the wine from the refrigerator, Amanda set the table in the dining room.

"How was work today?" she called from the other room.

He pushed the corkscrew into the bottle before he answered. "Paperwork. There's nothing more that I hate than paperwork." *Pop!* the cork slid out.

"More than getting shot at?"

Getting shot at, he laughed to himself. Now there's a comparison. Most of the police officers he knows, and he knows many due to being the son of a Rochester, NY police officer and being on the Rochester force himself before he joined the Albany force, were never shot at or had to draw their weapon. He, on the other hand, was the unlucky one who was involved in multiple firefights. The first time was when he was chasing Moshe Koretsky, the Israeli Mossad officer who went by the alias Ariel Steiner. He and his partner at the time, Keith Bernard, were chasing Koretsky down a street in Albany when suddenly Koretsky spun around and fired, putting two rounds through his shoulder.

He was shot again while battling an Israeli commando team on Marcus Kaderri's property in the Adirondack Mountains where he administered the coup de grace to the mortally wounded Koretsky. It wasn't a shot done in the name of mercy.

Then there was the fateful day in Irondequoit where he and Amanda were the targets of the Black Warriors gang's initiation ritual. They were sitting on a bench in Eastman Park on the shores of Lake Ontario having breakfast discussing their relationship when a group of what turned out to be soon-to-be initiated gang members attempted to murder them. Amanda was grazed in the arm by a bullet, but Trainor killed two on the spot and later found a third member dead from one of his bullets. That incident led to more shooting and bloodshed in downtown Albany and again into the Adirondacks where an assault, with the help of Marcus Kaderri and the state police tactical unit, was carried out on the Black Warrior compound.

He rubbed the scars on his shoulder where the bullets entered. "I guess paperwork isn't that bad." He brought the wine to the table and paused before he poured it. "Are you ok with this? Still want to marry a cop?"

Amanda was standing behind the chair at the four seat cherry table. She gripped the back of the chair and rolled her eyes. "Yes." She fixed her gaze squarely on him. "We aren't going over this again are we?" There was a slight tremor in her voice, belying the attempted look of anger in her eyes.

Long ago she left him because of her inability to deal with the possibility that he may not come home from work one day. But after their life altering moment along the lake shore and the tragic events of September 11, she freely admitted that what he did for a living didn't matter. But the thought of her leaving again was always in the back of his mind, no matter how many times she said it would never happen again and that he was the love of her life and wanted to spend the rest of her days with him.

"No, just checking," he gave an disarming smile. He poured the wine and sat down across from her. He held up his glass in a toast. "To you, babe. Congratulations on landing your big fish!"

She held up her glass. "Thank you." Just as they were about to touch, she pulled her glass back. "Wait."

He raised an eyebrow. "What?"

She held up her glass for her own toast. "To you, Gary. May you stay safe and come home to me every night."

This time they touched glasses, took a sip of the white wine and enjoyed Amanda's exceptionally prepared culinary work of art.

The master bedroom was one of three on the second floor of the spacious house. It was period decorated in a nautical theme with the bottom half of the walls paneled in wainscoting and the upper half painted in a hue of sea blue. Heavy framed paintings of tall ships and photographs of Lake Ontario taken from the shores near their childhood homes in and around Rochester hung throughout the room. The furniture consisted of an ash armoire and dresser along with a leather wing chair tucked in a corner near the walk-in closet.

For the past half hour the four poster bed was pitching and rolling as if it was a ship on the stormy lake waters. Except the pitch and roll had nothing to do with weather.

Trainor knew he did everything right by the satisfied look on Amanda's face and the sounds of her moans of pleasure that still echoed in his ears. He was lying on his side next to her with his left arm cocked and hand holding up his head. With his finger, he lightly traced imaginary lines up and down her hip, over her flat, tight belly and down her smooth thighs.

Her smile seemed frozen in place and her eyes were closed.

His short pants of breath and rapid heart beat finally returned to normal after the vigorous and gratifying bout of lovemaking. He leaned forward and kissed her forehead, not wanting to disturb the last remaining moments of her pleasure.

"Oh my god, I love the way you fill me up and make me feel this way," she whispered and cracked open an eye. "That was amazing!" Her toned body shuddered one last time.

"Uh-huh," he wholeheartedly admitted, still reveling in the moment himself. He wiped the sweat from his brow. "It sure was, babe. Congrats again on your hire."

Amanda rolled onto her side and wrapped her arms around his neck, pulling him close. "I love you, Gary," she whispered as a tear formed in her eye.

He cradled her face with strong calloused hands. "I love you too, babe." He wiped the tear that clung to her eyelash with his thumb. "No need to cry, though. You told me I was good, but tears? I guess I should be impressed by my performance!"

Her eyes welled up even more.

"Sorry, babe, I was only trying to make a joke. What's going on?"

She wiped her wet cheeks. "I'm just happy I get to say those three words to you, and to hear you say them back to me."

"Me too."

"Sorry, Gary, for getting emotional. Sometimes I think about our past and realize what I fool I had been and how lucky I am I got you back."

"Hey," he said softly. "What's done is done. Don't dwell on it. We're here, together, now. Maybe it was fate or something that brought us back together."

"I am so happy, Gary, that we're getting married. like we planned years ago."

He stared into her warm eyes and saw genuine happiness. He knew that Amanda was the lady for him and there was nothing he wouldn't do to make sure he would always be by her side. His mouth zeroed in on hers and his tongue parted her lips, softly colliding into hers. She pushed back, then retreated as their tongues passionately fought and explored each other's mouth.

He pulled her closer as his hand slid down her shoulders to the small of her back. Their warm bodies touched from lips to toes, heating up as their embrace continued. His hand slid lower, over her tight buttock and into the folds of her moist flesh where his fingers stroked her. She moaned into his mouth at his touch.

"Nope," she whispered, but didn't pull away.

Startled, he opened his eyes and looked into hers. Repeat performances were fairly routine. "Why? No-way. We agreed we would cut off all nookie one month before the wedding and that month isn't here yet."

Amanda sat up as a mischievous smile spread on her face. Her nipples were erect in excitement and her breasts swayed with her movements. Grasping her hair, she pushed it behind her ears and positioned herself between his legs.

His erection was growing again.

"I know exactly when the cutoff date is," she said. "It's my turn to return the pleasure."

With her soft hands and long manicured fingers, Trainor watched as she took his large shaft at the base and took him into her mouth. "Hmm," he moaned.

Many pleasing minutes passed before she disengaged her mouth and straddled his erection. Holding it just under her tight opening, she smiled wickedly and lowered herself onto him.

CHAPTER SEVEN

Tuesday, October 21, Walter Reed Army Medical Center, Washington, DC

The massive medical center, which opened its doors in 1909, still had its original brick exterior on the main building. Inside, it was a state-of-the-art medical facility with a world renowned reputation for treatment, advances and research in all aspects of medicine. During peace time, it was a very busy hospital, but with the nation at war, it was a nonstop beehive of activity. Wounded soldiers fresh from the battlefields in Iraq, Afghanistan and other places the news media didn't know about, filled the hallways, recovery rooms, day rooms and every place imaginable. Many wounded warriors had the ability to walk on their own feet, while others used crutches and/or prosthetics. Sadly, others wheeled themselves around in their new mode of transportation. America's latest heroes were recovering from a job well done.

Leonard Puckett was one of those heroes. He lay on the bed in his private room, a luxury necessary because of his involvement with the Central Intelligence Agency. His were eyes closed and the covers pulled up to his waist as the morning sunlight poured through the open window, basking the room in a warm glow. A gentle autumn breeze ruffled the curtains. The television suspended from the wall at the end of the bed was on, but he wasn't paying much attention to the morning news programs.

His leg itched, just above the knee and he cursed. There was nothing he could do to scratch it and make it go away except using sheer will power. The larger lump under the blanket was his left leg wrapped in a cast that went from his ankle all the way to his hip. The femur was shattered by the 7.62mm bullet in the ambush and the latest surgery took six hours to put it back together. He was lucky with his right leg. The bullet missed the bone as it bored through the muscle and exited out the hamstring. It did, however, take dozens of stitches to repair the damage. A pair of IV lines snaked their way from the bags hanging on the silver tree and disappeared into his forearm.

There was a slight knock on the door, but he chose to ignore it, concentrating on attempting to will the damn itch away. He figured whoever knocked was going to enter anyway, so why bother inviting them in? Sure enough, a moment later the door creaked. He popped an eye open to see who entered.

Walking towards him was Paul McKnight.

It wasn't an everyday occurrence that someone of McKnight's statue would pay a visit to a field officer. "What brings you here, sir?" Puckett worked himself into a sitting position, trying to show the respect deserved of McKnight. He tried to smooth his short salt and pepper hair.

McKnight was wearing a brown pinstripe suit, white shirt and rust colored tie. An American flag was pinned to his lapel just above the heart. He stepped into the room and ignored the question for the moment, asking one of his own. "How are you feeling, Len?"

"No complaints, especially since I'm still on this planet." Puckett cracked a smile.

"You're looking better. Last time I saw you, you looked like shit."

Wasn't that the truth, Puckett said to himself. He felt like shit, too. He vaguely remembered McKnight, two or three other CIA officers and medical personnel meeting him at the end of the ramp of the C-17 cargo jet on the runway at Pope Air Force base when they brought him in from Germany. He had stitches in his swollen lips, bruises and cuts covered his body and his legs were splinted and wrapped in gauze and bandages. His body hurt like hell and all of this was *after* he was stabilized in Germany.

"Thank you, sir." He laughed and immediately held his broken ribs to ease the pain.

"Hopefully we can get you back in the field." McKnight pulled one of the chairs from the table near the window and sat next to the bed. He crossed his legs and held a note pad in his lap.

"I hope so too," Puckett agreed, "but it's going to take some time. My legs are going to need some serious rehab."

McKnight nodded. "Len, we need to go over a few things again. Specifically what you saw and heard in the cave."

"Again?" The prospect of retelling his tale of woe was not welcomed. "I was already debriefed. Twice, I remember.

Once in Germany and again here. I assume you read the reports."

"I did." McKnight ignored the subtle protest and retrieved a Cross pen from his suit jacket's inner pocket.

"Is there a problem with the debrief?"

"No. Did Marcus Kaderri's name ever come up?"

Puckett looked puzzled at first and then his eyes looked towards the ceiling as if the white sheet rock would give him an answer. "Captain Marcus Kaderri? My former commanding officer?"

"Same one."

Puckett shook his head. "No. Nobody asked me about him. Why do you ask?"

McKnight let out a sigh and dropped the pen on the pad. "There was a video tape found in the camera of Mike Karmal's interrogation with the two Russians. He let it slip that you were there, in Afghanistan, a long time ago with him and he gave up the names on Kaderri's team."

Puckett let out a long whistle. "Why would they want to know that?" he asked aloud, not expecting McKnight to answer. "They did start to question me about being in Afghanistan before, and I assumed they got that info from Mike. But they never asked me about Captain Kaderri. It's possible they were going to start, but the Rangers crashing their party may have prevented that from happening."

McKnight remained silent, his eyes suddenly distant as if he were staring into a void. This left Puckett wondering if he should have said more...or less. He needed to know, and as a good spook would, he ventured further into the real world of need to know, especially since the commander he respected most was thrown into the equation. "What does the Captain have to do with all of this?"

McKnight retreated out of his void and looked squarely at Puckett's face. "I don't know, Len. Tell me what you can about your mission in Afghanistan with Marc. One question the interrogators kept asking was 'Who pulled the trigger?"

Puckett hesitated to answer. He wasn't sure about this topic of conversation, even with the man in charge. His tour in Afghanistan was still classified a minimum of Top Secret. Most likely it was classified higher. As far as the world knew, there were no Americans in Afghanistan during the 1980s Afghan War. "Sir?" he answered with a straight face.

McKnight smiled gently, clearly understanding the man's conflict. "Len, I know about many of the missions in Afghanistan. I coordinated many of the ODAs."

Puckett stared back at McKnight, not sure what to make of the startling revelation that McKnight coordinated the A-Teams. When Puckett shipped out with Kaderri's team, he was new to Special Forces and wasn't familiar with all the personnel in the higher commands running the operations. He only knew their call signs. Just to make sure, he asked McKnight what his was. "Call sign?"

"Sly Fox," he responded immediately. Then before Puckett could ask the next obvious question, McKnight told him what Kaderri's call sign was. "Marc's ODA was 524 and he was 'Bear.'

Both were correct. Only the team and a few people involved in command and control would know the call signs.

Captain Kaderri had picked 'Bear' because he was hunting Soviets. Puckett asked, "What specifically do you want to know?"

McKnight leaned closer, resting his elbows on his knees. "What kind of contact did the Team have with the Soviets that would give rise to them suspecting we were there?"

"Well, sir, they weren't stupid. I suppose they had a strong inkling we were there, observing at the very least and engaging them or the Afghan government forces at the most." He chuckled proudly at a recollection. "Taking out an entire Spetsnaz unit doesn't go unnoticed. They lost too many troops in firefights not to believe they were fighting a trained force. Hell, the world knew we were supplying the rebels with weapons."

"The mission Marc got wounded on, what happened?" McKnight pressed.

The missions in Afghanistan flashed by in his minds eye, ending on the day his CO got wounded and almost killed. "Bingo!" he clapped his hands together. "He took out the Russian general riding in the armored vehicle with one squeeze on the trigger. It was at least a seven hundred yard shot. Brilliant."

McKnight nodded in agreement. "General Vasily Borushko."

"That's him!" A flood of memories came flying back of the day the team pulled off the hit. He quickly put two and two together from the line of questioning. "You think there's something going on *now* that involves Marc because of that mission?"

"I can't say for sure, but it's strange that the Russians would be asking about it."

Wednesday, October 22, Rangers, Paktika Province, Afghanistan.

Much of the newly discovered information from the cave from where Leonard Puckett was rescued pertained to the FATA region, which was legally off limits to American forces. With the Pakistani forces getting more involved in blocking some of the Taliban and al Qaeda forces from crossing the border, the American military now had greater opportunities to find, fix and destroy the remnants of the former rogue nation and the terrorists they harbored.

With the vast amount of rugged terrain covering thousands of square miles, blocking escape routes and finding the enemy to destroy him was easier said than done. To help locate enemy forces, every surveillance platform was brought in to sniff out the bad guys. Advanced KH-11 satellites, low flying Predator surveillance drones, high flying Global Hawk recon drones, piloted reconnaissance aircraft and eyes on the ground were all put to use.

The Rangers and light infantry from the 10th Mountain Division stationed at FOB Warrior were on the prowl as a result of one of the passes of the Global Hawk flying at thirty thousand feet. The four UH-60 Blackhawks and a pair of menacing AH-64 Apache helicopters heading east away from the setting sun towards Pakistan carrying the men of 1st Platoon, reinforced with two machine gun teams, skimmed along the valleys of the snow capped mountains and rocky landscape. The pilots were flying nap-of-the-earth, sometimes as low as thirty feet off the ground, twisting and turning around mountains and rising and falling with the elevations of the earth. Needless to say, the motions made for a bumpy ride for the Rangers strapped into the seats.

Lieutenant Jack Dover, in the lead helo of the four ship formation, was being dropped in a remote valley to conduct reconnaissance and ambush missions near the sites marked on the map that Harold Weston had found. Corroborating intel also suggested these sites linked infiltration routes from the FATA. Combined with real time images from Predator surveillance drones and satellite imagery, it was determined that the locations on the map were hotbeds of activity and needed to be explored. Dover's five day mission was simple. Gather intelligence and destroy the enemy if he encountered them. If enemy forces were larger than his platoon could handle, which was unlikely considering the training and firepower the Rangers possessed, air assets, mainly Apache helicopter gunships, Air Force F-16 Falcons loaded with precision guided munitions and A-10 Warthogs were just a phone call away.

As the helo pitched and bucked, Dover glanced over to Pfc. Josh Calpers, his RTO, radio telephone operator. The sunlight coming through the open doors highlighted the drawing of the Twin Towers on the side of Calpers' K-pot and his uncle's name, Kevin, written under it with the date of his death–9/11.

The horrific scene of the planes crashing into the buildings and the absolute destruction after they collapsed filled Dover's memory. A young teenager at the time, he fully understood that war was declared on his country and payback was warranted.

The pilot's voice crackled in his headset. "LZ ahead, Lieutenant. One minute." The co-pilot held up one gloved finger.

Looking between the pilots and through the windscreen, Dover spotted the flat plain where the helos were going to drop them off. A surge of adrenaline pumped its way through his veins. "Right. Lock and load!" he shouted to the nine men of First Squad over the engines whine and slapping rotor blades. They were crammed into the troop compartment dressed in full battle gear commonly called 'battle rattle' and their faces were smeared with green camouflage paint. Only the flashing whites of their hard eyes were visible as the young men readied for combat.

Dover traded the headset for his K-pot and stared at the picture of Renee taped to the inside before he buckled up. After hanging the headset on the hook above his head, he pulled the charging handle on his M-4, seating a 5.56mm round in the chamber.

"Get ready!" Sgt. Tomas Odessa, the First Squad leader, prepped his men.

The increase in power applied to the engines roared through the cargo hold as the helo slowed, flared out and dropped to the ground, their wheels striking the hard surface with a thud.

The four helos landed simultaneously. As their wheels rolled, the troops leapt out from both sides of the troop compartment, fanning away from the birds and swirling debris kicked up by the rotating blades.

Just as fast as the helos touched the ground, they increased their power and took off, leaving the deadly Rangers in hostile country.

Dover's heart pounded and the adrenaline coursed through his veins as his lean body hit the ground. He spat out a mouthful of dirt and grass and scanned the sector to his front. From the moment his feet hit the ground, he went into combat mode. His eyesight became sharper, his hearing intensified and every muscle in his body coiled, ready to react to any incident thrown at him.

The platoon remained motionless. The sounds of the helicopters faded in the distance, leaving an eerie silence. Dover felt Calpers at his side and half expected to come under fire. The Rangers were the most vulnerable when they disgorged from the helicopters.

Silence. Only the steady mountain breeze moved in the air.

Out of the corner of his eye, he saw Calpers peering through a thermal imager. Warm bodies would be hard to hide in the cold air. "See anything?" he asked.

"No, sir. All's clear."

Confident that they were safe, Dover's heart rate decreased and said to Calpers, "Send 'Drill Press'." That was the code phrase that indicated the Rangers were on the ground and encountered no resistance.

"Yes, sir, 'Drill Press,'" Calpers repeated back then clicked the handset. "Grim Reaper, this is Bravo One, over."

There was a pause as Calpers listened to the reply. "Grim Reaper, Drill Press. I say again, Drill Press. Copy?" A moment later he turned to Dover. "They got it. sir. Charlie Mike."

With the instruction to continue the mission, Dover rose to his feet and spoke quietly and succinctly into the boom arm microphone at his lips. "Orders group, on me," he said, circling his arm above his head.

Within thirty seconds, SFC Isles and the three squad leaders formed a small cluster around Dover. He was on a knee and already had a map spread on the ground.

"Gentlemen, we're here," Dover pointed to the spot on the map with his pen. "Over here is the Objective Rally Point, and here," he indicated the two other locations in the valley on the opposite slope of a mountain three peaks away, "is the first objective." The distance from their current location to the ORP was just over four and a half klicks away, with the objective, an ambush site, an additional three hundred meters. Not a far distance to travel for men of this caliber. "Second Squad's on point. First and Third follow. We'll be in Traveling formation except for Second Squad, you'll be moving in Traveling Overwatch. I'll be behind Second Squad. One machine gun team will follow me and the other will be between First and Third. Designate a compass man and a pace man. Everyone should know their compass headings." Despite the introduction of the GPS the platoon was carrying, Dover, as well as many of the commanders he knew, still made sure the Rangers under his command knew how to navigate over terrain using a compass and a map. Batteries did die and the

GPS could get lost or damaged. "Questions?" he asked the assembled leaders.

The squad leaders looked Dover in the eye and shook their head.

"Listen," he switched out of his command voice. "You guys saw the map. The border for Pakistan is a klick away from our first objective. We're deep in enemy territory and we're gonna run into some shit out here. I think it's going to be pretty fucking nasty. Keep your eyes and ears open and be smart about everything that you do. I want to make sure all the men in this platoon come back."

"Will do, sir," Isles spoke for the group.

"Let's go. We move out in five." Dover put the map away and withdrew the GPS from its case and checked the coordinates.

The leaders group broke the circle and Dover watched patiently as the Rangers moved into formation under Isles watchful eyes.

Once they were ready, Dover, with Calpers at his side, took his position behind the wedge created by half of Second Squad's nine man contingent known as Fire Team B. Sergeant Parks, Second Squad's leader, placed himself fifteen meters up front with Fire Team A, the other half of the squad. Dover made eye contact with Parks and gave him the signal while speaking into the microphone at his lips. "Move out."

Quickly squatting down, Dover picked up five pebbles. Four went in his right pocket and one in his left. That was his way of keeping track of the distance the platoon traveled, just in case something happened to the GPS. For every thousand meters they traveled, he would remove one pebble from of his pocket. The pebble in his left pocket was for the remaining half klick. When they reached the ORP, he would drop his last pebble.

Second Squad was just about far enough away for their spacing interval for Dover to take his first step. He pulled the compass from its pouch attached to his vest and checked the heading with the GPS. They were going the right way–east towards Pakistan and into the unknown.

Thirty minutes of steady progress over the bumpy, rocky terrain came to a abrupt halt. From the front of the formation, the distinct *pop, pop, pop* of a three round burst being fired from an M-4 split the air. A heartbeat later, it was followed by the heavier report of an AK-47. Suddenly, all of Second Squad's M-4's opened up. Hurried incomprehensible speaking came across the MIR.

Shit! The platoon immediately went to ground. Dover dropped to one knee and brought his weapon up, searching his front to see what was going on. "Set up a perimeter!" he yelled out automatically. "Two, what's going on?" he called Parks by his designation and spoke rapidly into the microphone.

"Contact!"

Dover and Calpers rushed forward to where Parks' excited voice was directing his squad in the firefight. By the time Dover had closed the fifty meters between him and Parks, the shooting had stopped. "What have you got?" Dover was breathing heavy from the short sprint. Second Squad was facing forward, four dead bodies were sprawled in grotesque positions behind large, man sized rocks and scrub brush.

"Well, sir, this guy here was sleeping when my guy spotted him." Parks used the muzzle of his weapon to point at the body partially wrapped in a thick dirty blanket. Brains and blood were still oozed from a gaping hole where the top of his head had blown away. "He was told not to move but brought his weapon up instead. My guy fired first."

"Good shooting," Dover acknowledged the quickness of the response.

"Then these three," Parks pointed to the other sprawled bodies and his eyes narrowed into slits, "thought they were good enough to tangle with us."

Dover nodded and quickly scanned the countryside for more fighters. "Anything else?"

"No, sir, we're clear." Then he added, "I think."

Dover took that for what it was. One could never be sure out here. He spoke into the mic at his lips. "Sergeant Isles, bring the platoon up and set up security."

"Hooah, sir," Sgt Isles responded in his ear.

While waiting for his platoon, Dover studied the broken body at his feet. The left hand was hanging by some flesh, the throat was shot away and the stock on the AK had a chunk taken out of it. He forced down a surge of bile and wondered what made these enemy soldiers believe that they could win a fight? Hatred, he told himself. Pure hatred.

He shook his head. Contact was expected on this mission, but if they got into a firefight this soon, what lie ahead?

Wednesday, October 22, Kiri, Chechnya

The reasons for the disappearance of Colonel Yezhov was no longer a top priority for the Russian Army, nor was finding him. That decision sat well with Major Mikhail Borushko and he was thankful for it. Though he and Captain Pyotr Agranov knew what had happened to Yezhov, they weren't about to let the Russian military know. As far as they were concerned, he was missing in action and that's what would be told to the family.

To continue the fight against the rebel Chechens, the brass brought in Yezhov's replacement. He was a hard ass colonel who, during the end of the Afghan War was a newly commissioned junior officer who competently led troops in combat. Colonel Leonid Travkin let it be known to every officer that he felt a personal embarrassment by the pull out and loss from that war. Because of that, he was going to save his and Russia's honor by fighting and defeating the Chechens and Muslim terrorists!

To back up his talk, Travkin immediately increased patrols and made them more aggressive. Borushko worried that in his vigor, Travkin would delay his release from the unit. But rumors through the grapevine went to the contrary. Borushko had a reliable source that stated his discharge papers had arrived early and were in Travkin's possession. Why they came in early Borushko did not know or care. Just as long as they were here. He was hoping, as he donned his field jacket, Travkin would be signing them at their meeting in just a few moments. Placing the helmet on his head and slinging the AK over his shoulder, Borushko opened the door from his barracks room and walked out into the cold night air. Snow began to fall, small flakes that flickered in the temporary lighting reminded him of a more peaceful time in his youth as he crossed the quiet compound to Travkin's office.

Once inside, he stepped past the empty desk of Travkin's aide and knocked twice on the closed door.

"Come," Travkin's deep voice called from behind the door.

As ordered, Borushko entered the twelve by twelve sparse, unfinished office, still bearing its newly nailed plywood walls. An electric heater plugged into the corner provided the warmth. He marched smartly into the office and came to attention at the two folding chairs placed in front of the metal desk. Taking a quick peek at the colonel's desk before he focused his eyes on a spot above the colonel's head, he noticed some discharge papers. He suppressed a smile. "Comrade Colonel, you wanted to see me?"

"Take a seat, Major." Travkin gestured to one of the chairs.

"Yes, sir," Borushko unslung his rifle and sat as ordered.

Travkin picked up the papers on his desk and tapped them into a neat pile. "Major," he began, "I want to thank you for all of your help since my arrival. You are a true soldier."

"Thank you, sir," Borushko tried not to sound too cautious. He was waiting for the 'but.'

"I'm sure you have heard that your discharge papers have arrived early and I have them in front of me," he gave a disarming smile. "I have signed them."

A wave a relief swept over Borushko. "Thank you, Comrade Colonel," he said with tempered enthusiasm. He didn't want to look too eager in front of the commander.

"I would have liked for you to work for me, but your decision is final, correct?"

Borushko nodded and felt a sense of pride from serving and knew the colonel was feeding him a line of bullshit. "The army has taught me many things, Comrade, including what my limitations are. I am at the point where I have reached those limitations and it is time for others to rise to the occasion." He lied through his teeth. Borushko knew if the lucrative dealings in the Solntsevskaya weren't at his disposal, he would be moving up the ranks and his success in the Russian Army would continue, especially after seeing combat and being the son of a general killed in the line of duty.

"Well said." Travkin swung the papers around and held out a pen. "Sign at the bottom. There will be a helicopter here tomorrow around noon to take you home and bring your replacement in."

Ah, there lies the answer to why the papers had arrived early. Travkin wanted his own man in the XO slot. Borushko shrugged inwardly. He would have done the same thing if he took command of another unit. Without any further thought, he took the pen from Travkin's hand and quickly signed the papers.

Travkin scooped the papers up and placed them in a folder. He rose from his seat and moved out from behind the desk and offered his hand. "Congratulations on a distinguished career, Major. In no time, you'll be back home. Good luck."

"Thank you, Comrade. I'm looking forward to it."

Wasn't that the truth, he laughed to himself. Money, power, women and the hunt for the man who was responsible for killing his father–Marcus Kaderri.

Just as Borushko closed the door to the Headquarters building, he stood bathed in the glow of the overhead light, footsteps on the frozen ground startled him.

"Is it official?" Pyotr Agranov asked as he emerged from a shadow and stopped at his side. Chilled breath formed a cloud in front of his face.

Borushko gave a wide smile. "Yes, Pyotr!" he said gladly. "I fly out tomorrow and my replacement will be flying in!"

Agranov excitedly grasped both of Borushko's shoulders. "You now move on to bigger and better things!"

Borushko adjusted the AK and pulled Agranov away from the door. Glancing over his shoulder, he lowered his voice and issued a warning. "Pyotr, I don't know who my replacement is, but I'm assuming he's like Travkin. It's his man that's coming in. My friend, you are going to have to watch yourself."

"Mikhail," Agranov eased Borushko by the arm towards the dining hall, "I have my ass covered so don't worry about me. Come on, let's go."

"To where?" he followed his friend.

"You'll see."

The snow began falling heavier as the two men made their way to the one story modular structure painted in drab green. Single bulb lights were atop the four corners and over the door, being threatened by the driving snow to have their glow blotted out.

Agranov grabbed the door handle and paused. He looked up into the night sky, appearing to stare at the falling snow then stamped his feet, causing small puffs to rise up. "There should be enough snow on the ground when we are done so that you can fall down drunk and not get hurt!" A big toothy smile spread across his happy face.

Confused, Borushko asked, "What are you talking about?"

Agranov opened the door, a wave of heated air spilled out along with a cheer from the gathered men inside.

"For you, Misha!" Agranov said with a sweeping wave of his arm and then pushed Borushko inside.

Borushko was greeted by most of his staff and close friends gathered around the mess tables. Bottles of vodka were on each table and the officers and certain senior NCO's each held a filled glass raised for a toast.

One of the company commanders approached with vodka filled glasses in each hand and passed one each to Borushko and Agranov. "Comrade Major! Welcome to your going away party!"

CHAPTER EIGHT

Friday, October 24, Rangers, Paktika Province, Afghanistan

The Rangers set up their second ambush site in as many days. The area of operations was crawling with enemy forces and since their insertion, they had engaged in four firefights, leaving eighteen enemy fighters dead and thankfully no Rangers killed or injured. The helicopter that brought in resupplies, especially ammunition and hand grenades, took out three wounded PW's who more than happy to talk. Lt. Jack Dover knew his luck wouldn't hold out. At some point, he was going to take casualties. As his deadly force lay in wait, that thought weighed heavily on his mind.

The platoon had set up thirty meters on the southern side of a well worn east-west footpath. At first, the path was thought to be an animal track, but further inspection revealed signs of human activity. Sets of sandaled footprints and a partially buried candy wrapper convinced Dover this was a prime target area.

Sections of grass, rock and frozen earth untouched from the rising sun were still coated with the light snow that had fallen over night. The mottled terrain allowed the Rangers to easily blend in. Dover set the platoon up in an L-shaped ambush with First and Third Squads used as the assault elements and Second Squad tasked with security. A fire team from Second Squad was positioned one hundred meters away at the ORP to guard the rear and if necessary, be used a reserve. The other fire team was tasked with establishing two listening posts, call signs X-ray and Zulu, located east of the ambush. The machine gun teams were anchored at the far ends of the L to create a murderous crossfire, and a half dozen Claymore anti-personnel mines were evenly spaced along the fifty meter kill zone. When the mines were detonated, hundreds of steel balls flew out in an arc, obliterating anyone unfortunate enough to be in their path.

Waiting. It was the worst thing for many of the men. Inactivity while waiting for the enemy to arrive allowed the Rangers to think, sometimes casting doubt on the plan or mission. It also allowed the mind to wander and when that happened it caused a drop in alertness and a rise in carelessness.

Many perceived problems crept into Dover's mind as he shifted his weight to a not so comfortable position to keep himself alert. Positioning himself in the center of the assault force, he looked both ways down the line of men, searching for any telltale signs of their presence. He spotted one Ranger right away, causing his heart to race. An exposed man would surely blow the ambush. He was about to tell the Ranger to reposition himself, but realized that he knew where every man was located, and it was going to be easy for him to spot them.

Calm down! He told himself. Everything they could possibly think of had been checked and rechecked by himself and SFC Isles. The ambush was laid out to the best of his ability and only when contact was made would he be able to tell if his planning worked. He shook his head and tried to clear out the anxiety and cursed for doing this to himself.

After four hours of lying in wait, Dover's stomach growled. Quietly he rolled his wrist to see the time, 0906 hours. Some crackers from the opened MRE he had in his pack would taste pretty good, but his gear, along with the rest of the platoon's, was back at the ORP under guard by one of the security teams. The Rangers only had their weapons, ammunition, hand grenades and mines. All the necessary tools to kill the enemy with maximum force.

"One Six!" came a whispered call in Dover's earpiece. "This is X-ray. Movement. Tangos," he used the label for terrorists, "heading your way."

Dover snapped his head to the right and looked east, in the direction that X-ray called from. X-ray, the two man team consisting of PFCs Dan Maxwell and Chris Conte, was approximately two hundred meters out on the far side of a ten meter tall hill. "This is One Six, X-ray, roger." Dover acknowledged Maxwell's call and brought the binoculars to his eyes. Holding his breath, he studied the terrain. Methodically he panned back and forth, slowly moving further out. Adjusting the focus he spotted movement. There! A brief glimpse of a pakol-covered head flashed between rocks and bare trees a hundred and fifty meters away. His palms began to sweat.

The MIR hissed in his ear. "This is X-ray, eighteen Tangos and counting."

"Roger, X-ray. Squads, get ready," Dover whispered into the mic trying to keep the nervous excitement from his voice. Rangers up and down the line did their final preparations for the fight. Dover reached for the Claymore mine's hand detonator laid out on the hard ground in front of him. When he felt there were enough enemy in the kill zone, he would spring the ambush by detonating the mine. If everything went as planned, there wouldn't be anyone standing in the kill zone when they were finished.

But he knew all military plans were subject to change, especially with an uncooperative enemy who tried to execute their own plan.

"Twenty-nine." X-ray called out the new tally. This time Maxwell's voice was lower. "I also count six pack donkeys, and they're loaded."

"Roger, X-ray," Dover whispered back in acknowledgment.

The kill zone of the ambush was fifty meters long and if X-ray already counted that many men, Dover suddenly became concerned that the kill zone wouldn't be big enough. Two minutes passed from X-ray's first report to the time that the lead elements of the enemy forces came into view. Dover held his breath, hoping his men wouldn't be spotted.

"One Six. Forty-seven, I say again forty-seven. Main force is bunched together."

Damn! He thought. There was a lot of enemy heading this way! Just as X-ray was finishing their report, the beginning of the enemy column stepped into the kill zone, moving from his right to left. The first six men wore long robes and blankets slung over one shoulder while their weapons were slung over the other. They were talking among themselves not paying attention to what, if anything, was going on around them. It was clear they were content in their surroundings and had no expectations of meeting an enemy force.

"One Six, this is X-ray, four more for a total of fifty-one." Maxwell's voice was stronger now, indicating that there were no more enemy fighters close by. "That's the total count. Over."

It was Dover's turn to whisper back, a simple, "Roger, X-ray. Stay put." His voice almost cracked. This was by far the largest enemy force they had faced and it was going to be one hell of a fight if they didn't kill the enemy quickly.

The front of the enemy column had walked past, with every Ranger weapon trained on them. The air was ripe with tension but the disciplined Rangers waited for Dover to spring the ambush.

Seconds that seemed like hours ticked by as Dover waited for the larger group of fighters to enter the kill zone.

"One Six, this is Mike One," came the barely audible call from a machine gun team. "Lead elements out of the kill zone."

"Roger," Dover acknowledged and he could feel Calper's eyes on him waiting for him to react. Keeping his focus, he watched the bulk of the enemy force enter the zone.

As was with the first group, this assembly had the same nonchalant demeanor. Some walked in clusters, and others alone. They were in no type of military formation, just a mass of people that resembled a herd of cattle. The small column of pack mules were clustered together as well, laden with boxes and gear that appeared to outweigh the small four legged creatures. Dover let out a grim smile and his fingers itched as they wrapped around the detonator. The enemy was cooperating. Perfect.

BOOM!

The thunderous explosion of the detonating anti-personnel mine split the air and rocked the ground. Hundreds of steel balls flew out in a wide arc, cutting down everything in its path. The dozen enemy fighters closest to the blast bore the brunt of the destruction. Flesh was ripped off bone and limbs torn from bodies. Some fighters were literally blown to pieces and others had their heads blasted off and torsos smashed into pulp.

The earth shook and teeth rattled as the horrific process was repeated an instant later when the platoon detonated the other five mines along the kill zone.

The wall of steel balls smashed into the unsuspecting enemy like a gigantic wave. Confusion reigned among the enemy. As they tried to figure what had happened, some stood there frozen in terror while others dropped to the ground in search of protection.

"Fire!" Dover yelled unnecessarily above the deafening roar of the mines. A lead rain poured out from the Ranger's M-4's.

The two machine gun teams had opened up at each end of the kill zone, drumming out steady controlled bursts of interlocking .30 caliber fire.

Blood curdling screams cried out in strange tongues as the Rangers kept pouring on the fire into the decimated enemy column. Smoke and dust had settled over the ambush site, partially obscuring the Rangers vision and blotting out the rising sun.

"Frag out!" A Ranger shouted. Seconds later the grenade exploded.

Unexpectedly, one of the pack donkeys disappeared in a huge explosion. A large orange and black fireball engulfed the animal and rose high into the sky. The ground shook under the explosion and chunks of the animal and men who were next to it flew skyward and outward.

"Barbecue!" a Ranger quipped as the rumble faded.

Suddenly stabs of light poked through the drifting smoke. Enemy survivors were beginning to fight back.

"Whoa!" someone yelled as bullets whip cracked nearby.

"Shift left! Shift left!" one of the squad leaders ordered, directing the fire to where surviving enemy fighters were shooting from.

"Die Motherfucker! Fucking raghead is dead!" a Ranger announced after firing a burst.

"Reloading!"

"Frag out! Frag out!"

A mountain breeze had carried most of the smoke away, revealing the carnage and enemy positions. Like metal drawn to a magnet, the Rangers shifted their fire, focusing on the newly revealed targets.

More shouting and yelling came from the Rangers as targets became identified, and a running commentary of the battle continued.

"I got 'em!"

"There's another moving up!"

"Get the fucker!"

A stab of flame then a *whoosh* as an RPG was launched from the far side of the trail in the center of the melee.

"RPG! Keep your fucking heads down!" Someone screamed as the RPG flew harmlessly overhead and exploded into the mountainside well behind the Rangers.

From behind a fallen mule, the smoke trail of the RPG ignition lingered around the enemy soldier who launched the deadly projectile and brought unwanted attention his way.

He was reloading the launcher when both machine guns and other small arms fire quickly concentrated on his location. Bullets slammed into the donkey, slowly chewing away its hide and meat. Two grenades thundered their explosions, adding more noise to the mix. The fighter stood, the launcher resting on his shoulder, providing an easy target. A barrage of bullets disintegrated his upper torso and head before he could fire again.

Further up the line, Dover spotted a bloodied enemy soldier crawling slowly towards a weapon. His left leg was mangled and useless, trailing a line of dark blood that pooled whenever he stopped. Dover brought his weapon up, sighted in on the man's head and let loose a three round burst. The weapon kicked against his shoulder. All three rounds slammed into the target and tore away the man's head. He immediately searched for another target.

"Frag out!" Another grenade exploded among the carnage.

Several Rangers tossed more hand grenades to finish off the ambush. The dark deadly objects bounced on the dirt or a body and exploded. Like the grand finale in a fireworks display, the exploding grenades ended the ambush.

Then without an order or shout, all firing ceased.

"I need another target!" A Ranger stated seriously.

Nothing moved as an eerie silence and a cloud of acrid smoke settled over the battlefield.

Cordite and the sickly smell of death filled the air. Bodies, whisping smoke and small fires from burning flesh, clothing and material dotted the kill zone. Like a far away echo, the moans of the wounded and dying floated on the air.

"Check 'em out," Dover ordered to everyone and made his way to the kill zone. He swallowed hard, trying to get rid of the lump in his throat that had suddenly formed. "Stay alert!"

He halted when he came to the edge of the destruction. Pieces of what were once human beings were scattered everywhere. Heads, headless torsos, legs, arms, every body part imaginable littered the ground that now ran red with blood. The devastation was so complete that it appeared that not one intact body was visible. That applied to the pack animals as well.

Transfixed at the scene spread before him, Dover slowly, almost hesitantly, stepped forward into the carnage. He wasn't paying attention to his footing when he felt his ankle give way. He caught himself before he rolled his ankle and when he looked down to see what caused him to misstep.

"Holy shit," Dover whispered and stepped aside from an arm blown off at the bicep. He tilted the K-pot on his head and fought down a sudden wave of nausea. In his worst nightmare, he never envisioned anything like this. The apocalypse had arrived. He hadn't noticed Calpers was at his side.

"Oh, sick!" the radioman spat.

"Clear on the left!" The Ranger at the far end of the ambush shouted.

"Right's clear!" the report from the other side came in.

"That'll teach these fuckers not to mess with the Rangers! Hooah!"

A wide eyed SFC Isles walked up to Dover and Calpers. He stood next to the men for a moment without saying anything. "Jesus, Lieutenant, there's not a thing out here… intact."

Dover forced himself to be the commander again and refocused his attention on running his platoon. "Any wounded enemy?"

Isles shook his head. "Doc's assessing some now, but it doesn't look like any are gonna to make it."

That sat well with Dover. "Casualties on our side?" his mouth went dry in fear. He scanned the battlefield for any Rangers tending to each other and braced himself for the bad news.

"None."

Dover shot a look of disbelief. "Really?"

"Really."

"Thank God!" He let out a huge sigh of relief and took a sip from the Camelbak hydration pack secured to his back.

"Amen to that!"

Dover held his hand out for the radio hand set to call in the situation report. "Calpers," was all he had to say.

As soon as he had the hand set in his gloved hand, an urgent call from X-ray came over the MIR that caused him to nearly jump out of skin. "One Six! One Six! This is X-ray. Tangos sighted! A shit load!"

Immediately Dover gave the handset back and instructed, "You call it in."

Dover's mind raced as he sprang into action. Another ambush at the same spot was out of the question so he decided a hasty defense was needed until he knew what was happening. He had to assume the new threat was a reaction force to the ambush and the enemy came to fight. There would be no surprises placed upon the enemy this time. He scanned the terrain to set up a suitable defensive position. Fifty five meters to the east he found the spot. The ground had a slight rise with scattered rocks and trees along the crest and then dipped slightly to where it leveled out for another one hundred fifty meters. Then it began to rise again to where X-ray was hiding on the hill. The location was high enough to give the Ranges the advantage of shooting down on the advancing enemy. "Platoon, set up a line on Archer extending right and facing X-ray. First Squad on the left and Mike One and Two anchor each end! Second Squad, haul ass up here!"

"Roger!" Came the response from Sgt. Bill Parks, the Second Squad leader.

PFC Archer had taken a position behind a rock and small leafless tree and immediately waved his hand above his head so the platoon could orient themselves.

Dover scrambled up the slope and took a knee behind a rock. He disengaged his safety, brought his rifle up and peered around the rock. Looking over the telescopic sight he called into the mic, "X-ray, this is One Six. Report." He needed to know what was coming. 'Shit load' as X-ray previously reported, could mean anything.

"One Six-"

Suddenly gunfire erupted from the vicinity of X-ray. The report of M-4s were quickly answered by AK-47's.

Dover's heart went into his throat when he didn't hear anymore outgoing fire. Did he just lose X-ray?

Anxious seconds ticked by.

"X-ray! X-ray! Come in!" Dover yelled into his mic.

There was a crackle in his ear and he held his breath. "One Six, X-ray. We're out of here!" The voice was harried. "We're coming back!"

Suddenly more gunfire filled the air near X-ray's position.

"X-ray, what's going on?" Dover pressed.

Maxwell answered in bated breath. "Large enemy force in pursuit…..shit!" The report of an exploding grenade echoed over the hill. He cut off his report to announce the dreaded words a comrade never wants to hear. "Man down!"

"First Squad!" Dover looked over in their direction as his heart raced. "Get up there and get X-ray out! Everyone else, give 'em cover!" He almost forgot about his other LP, Zulu! "Zulu! Zulu! This is One Six! Get back here!"

"Hooah One Six! Moving!"

"Let's go!" Sgt. Odessa, the First Squad leader rallied his men. In unison, the nine man squad rose from the ground and advanced from the rock and tree cover.

From around the left side of the hill just as First Squad moved forward, the two man team of X-ray appeared. Maxwell with Conte over his left shoulder, was running as fast as he could in an erratic fashion as to make himself a harder target. Bullets were kicking up dirt around his feet and Conte was firing back from the awkward position of being slung over Maxwell's shoulder. Suddenly Maxwell stopped, turned around and holding his weapon in one hand fired a burst, dropping an enemy fighter. More puffs of dirt blossomed near his feet, inching ever closer to his legs. He emptied his magazine at the increasing number of enemy infantry, then sprinted as fast as he could towards the Rangers with Conte screaming in pain.

Suddenly, a half dozen enemy fighters came over the hill, firing wildly from the hip.

"New contact!" came the warning.

"Fire!" In unison the Rangers opened up in protection of their own. Lead by the steady chatter of M-249 Squad Automatic Weapons, a hailstorm of bullets erupted, smashing into the enemy soldiers. Two fell immediately. Grenadiers joined the fray and lobbed 40mm projectiles towards the enemy, killing two more and causing the rest to dive for cover. The momentary lull gave Maxwell extra precious seconds to reach cover.

"Come on!" men in the platoon encouraged and waved them on.

Suddenly, more enemy troops appeared over and around the hill. Like ants at a picnic, they steadily advanced. Three Rangers sprinted from cover to set up a screen and let loose with their M-4s. The rest of the platoon provided covering fire.

"Move, Danny! Run!" A Ranger urged them on and fired off a burst.

The two Rangers of Zulu came sprinting in from the left as bullets licked at their heels.

"Medic! Medic!" Maxwell screamed as he neared the Ranger line. Once in the protection of his comrades, he fell to the ground as other Rangers eased Conte off his back and dragged him behind a large rock.

"Doc, up!" a deeper voice relayed the call. "Doc, up!"

Dover sprinted over just as Doc Reynolds tore at the bloodied clothing on the wounded leg. Bright red blood spilled out as part of his thigh was blown away from the grenade blast. Where the camouflage paint wasn't applied or wore away, Conte's face was ashen from shock and loss of blood and he began to shake.

"Stay with me!" Doc Reynolds yelled into Conte's face.

The young kid of nineteen years fought bravely to put on a good face, but the pain was too much and he grimaced and cried out when Reynolds moved him. "Ahhh, fuck!"

Getting out of Reynolds' way, Dover turned to Maxwell who was still trying to catch his breath and holding his side. Dover noticed a grimace and then saw blood trickling between his gloved fingers. Alarmed, he asked, "How bad are you hit?"

Maxwell shook his head. "Just a nick, sir. I'm good. A band aid will fix it."

Right. "Let's take a look at that wound and what did you see?" he knelt down and addressed the wound. The gouge under his right rib and the blood seeping out of it indicated it needed more than a band aid.

"Dozens more, sir," Maxwell began as Dover cleansed the wounded and taped sterile gauze over it. "They were pretty much taking the same route as the first group but they were spread out more and more alert. They must have heard the ambush. We had to open up. They were right on top of us!"

"Ok. Good job." Dover unfolded the map and asked, "Show me where you saw them and how many!"

"This way, sir," Maxwell winced in pain before he traced the route with his bloodied finger. "From the northeast. There was a long line of them. Twice as many as before."

Twice as many as before? Dover repeated to himself. That put the enemy at close to a hundred and meant that he was outnumbered more than two to one.

"Fuck! That hurts!" Conte suddenly screamed, catching everyone off guard. He threw his head back into the ground and scratched at the dirt with his fingers as Doc Reynolds worked.

Dover turned to see Reynolds with his fingers inside the open wound and then shoved a gauze pad inside to stop the flow of blood. "How is he, Doc?"

Reynolds gave a report without looking at his lieutenant. "He'll live, but we got to get him out of here. I'm not sure about his leg. He's losing blood."

With the wounded man under Doc's care, Dover turned his attention to where it was supposed to be, fighting the enemy.

"Lieutenant," came the call from Sgt. Parker. "We're right behind you. Where do we go?"

Dover turned to see Parks and his squad advancing at a fast jog. He pointed to the right side of the hill. "Take the right side and tie in."

"Contact!" The cry went out.

Incoming gunfire erupted again as more enemy fighters appeared over and around the hill. The cacophony grew as the Rangers returned fire. The heavier .30 caliber M-240B machine guns joined the fight, the gunners letting out short, controlled bursts now that the battlefield was ripe with targets.

From measured intervals across the Rangers front, a half dozen RPGs were launched. The tell-tale smoke of the ignition hung in the air.

"Incoming RPGs!" came the deadly warning just before the RPGs slammed into their positions. One missile detonated on a tree with an ear-splitting explosion, blowing it to pieces. The others slammed into rocks or the ground, sending rock, earth and dust clouds into the air.

The increasing staccato was punctuated by grenades exploding and Rangers calling out warnings and targets.

"Put some fucking lead out Rangers!" SFC Isles screamed.

Accurate shooting dropped a dozen fighters, but the enemy was still moving closer, spreading out on a wider front attempting to envelope the Rangers. Incoming fire was increasing and Rangers began to get hit.

Another RPG streaked in, its white trail billowing behind the warhead that exploded at the feet of a group of Rangers diving out of it's way.

"Doc!" A deep, harried voice called. One Ranger was writhing on the ground in pain, his left arm dangling and the side of his body had turned red.

Dover needed to make a decision. He was engaged with a superior force was and his options were limited. It was either retreat and run like hell or stay and fight. The problem with retreating was there was no defensive positions to fall back upon. They would have to fight it out.

"Calpers!" Dover scurried to cover behind a boulder Resting on one knee, he looked to his left and called for his radio operator, not realizing he was lying on his right. "Calpers!"

"Right here, sir," he said quietly and squeezed off a burst from his rifle.

"Give me the radio." Dover never believed in fighting fair and reached for the radio handset with one hand. "Bravo Six, this is Bravo One, Over." He called the company commander who was off to the north by ten miles with Second and Third Platoons of the Ranger company.

The answer from the commander was immediate. "Bravo One, this is Bravo Six, go."

"Bravo Six, be advised, we are engaged with a large enemy force and I am requesting a Flash Flood, I say again, I am requesting a Flash Flood, copy?"

"Roger Bravo One. You are requesting a Flash Flood. Do you need further assistance? Over."

"Negative at this time, Bravo Six. We'll keep you posted, out." Dover then pulled a small spiral notebook from his breast pocket. Flipping to the page with the call signs and code words, he depressed the transmit button on the handset. "Warrior, this is Bravo One, over." He had to shout over the sounds of battle.

The radio operator at FOB Warrior came on line. "Bravo One, this is Warrior, go."

"Flash Flood, I say again, Flash Flood, copy?" Dover used the code word to request an air strike. He was too far out for artillery support. To punctuate the request, bullets whip cracked past his head and slammed into the earth next him. *Shit!* He hunched his shoulders then dropped to the ground.

Normally the platoon would have an air force combat controller attached to them to handle any and all air strikes, but Captain Aaron Harris came down with an intestinal ailment and was scratched from the mission. There wasn't enough time to send in a replacement so the duties fell upon Dover.

Another cry went up. "RPG!" A half second later, the boulder Dover was hiding behind exploded with a thunderous, ear ringing crash that knocked Calpers to the ground. Rock fragments sliced through the air and pelted his helmet and body armor.

"Holy shit!" Dover screamed and curled himself into a ball, covering his head with his arms. When the ringing subsided enough, he put the handset back to his ear and toggled the push to talk button. "Warrior, did you get my last, over?"

Calpers opened fire, making hearing even more difficult. Dover pressed the handset to his ear and stuck his finger in the other. "Roger, Bravo One, acknowledge you are requesting a Flash Flood. What's the target description and location? Over."

"Infantry..." Dover gave the rest of the pertinent information, such as the Platoon's location, distance to the enemy and the direction the enemy is attacking from in a hurried voice. A moment later he learned the call sign of the air support that was already en route and ended the conversation. "Roger, Warrior. Tangos are close. Out." Dover gave the handset back to Calpers. "Call sign of the flight is Upper Cut." Rising to his knees, he looked down the line at the platoon still heavily engaged and put the mic to his lip. "Heads up. Air strike coming in." He traded the handset for a rifle and began picking targets.

The enemy had maneuvered closer, trying to envelope the line. All of a sudden from behind a boulder off to Dover's left, three enemy fighters sprang forward between him and the machine gunners, their bayonet tipped AKs held at the hip.

"*Tango left!*" Calpers screamed in a panic.

"Whoa, Shit!" Archer yelled, swung his weapon around and fired point blank.

The fighter thrust forward.

Without having the time to think, Dover reacted and dodged to the right, just as a frenzied fighter thrust the bayonet at his throat. Dover swept his rifle across and down as if he were using his lacrosse stick for a check, knocking the bayonet tip further away. Seeing the man's weight on his front foot, Dover immediately smashed the rifle butt down on the knee cap, hyper-extending it. The attacker dropped the AK, howled in pain and grasped the crushed knee with both hands and fell sideways in a heap. Dover immediately fired a three shot burst into his chest. The rifle jumped in his hand as he fired off another three round burst for insurance.

Calpers and Archer shot and killed the other two enemy fighters.

"Jesus Christ! That was too fucking close!" Calpers said what Dover was thinking. "Where did they come from?"

Dover's heart thumped in his chest at the realization of what just happened. The maniacal snarl on the attacker's face as he thrust the bayonet would be burned into his memory forever and it caused his hands to shake and sweat pour out of him.

He was still breathing hard when the radio crackled. Calpers kept the handset attached to the PALS webbing on his vest so everyone in earshot could hear incoming radio calls. "Bravo One, this is Upper Cut Lead, over." Dover breathed a sigh of relief that help had arrived.

"Sir," Calpers called and handed the headset to Dover. "Upper Cut is on the line."

Dover quickly took the handset without comment. Depressing the transmit button he automatically gazed in the clear blue sky, searching for the aircraft. "Upper Cut, this is Bravo One. Go ahead, over."

"Bravo One," said the pilot, "I have four sorties with CBUs. Verify target and location, copy."

Dover suddenly got nervous. He was never this close to an actual bombing run. Up to this point, every live bombing run had been under controlled conditions and he was far enough away from the actual strike he could have sat back and watched it like a Fourth of July celebration. Not wanting the fighters to drop the cluster bombs on his position, he pulled out his map to double check he had the correct grid coordinates. He hid his nervousness from the men and talked as professional as a Ranger officer should. "Upper Cut, we have infantry in the open. Location is Echo Hotel...." he gave the eight digit map coordinates along with the GPS position then the warning, "Danger close." That meant his Rangers were close to the enemy. "We'll throw out smoke. Bad guys to the east of the smoke, copy?"

He looked away from the map towards his engaged Rangers to make sure he made the right call.

"Roger Bravo One. Danger close. Keep your heads down."

Dover gave his next set of orders. "Pull back to the ambush site! Withdraw in squad order Three, One, Two!" He pulled a soup-sized canister off his PALS and waited to pull the pin. "Sergeant Isles!" Dover yelled over the battle din. He spotted Isles rising to his feet, bullets kicking at his heels.

"Sir?" Isles hunched over and sprinted to Dover's side.

"I'll hold here. You direct the squads from back there." He pointed to the ambush site.

"Right." Isled slid back twenty meters, clearly visible to direct the platoon's movements. "Third Squad! Let's go!"

Immediately, Third Squad pulled out of line to redeploy. The remaining squads increased their fire to buy some time for the move. As soon as the last squad withdrew, Dover pulled the pin on the smoke grenade and tossed it ten meters to the front to mark the Rangers location. As he waited in a crouch for the yellow smoke to blossom, bullets whip cracked past his head, some so close he could feel them whiz past. It took all his courage to stand there and wait for the smoke to billow out of the can before he sprinted away.

The withdraw went flawlessly and the Rangers reoccupied their previous holes and hide sites along the kill zone.

One long arduous minute later and over the constant rattle of gunfire, the roar of jet engines came thundering in from the west. Two pairs of speeding darts were seen on the horizon.

The radio crackled. Calpers handed the handset over. "Bravo One, we have you in sight west of the smoke. You're too close for a safe drop with CBUs."

"Negative, Upper Cup! We have wounded and they will overtake us if we try to run. Drop your ordnance."

There was a long deafening silence before Upper Cut came back on line. "Bravo One, this is Upper Cut. We're coming in. Is everyone clear?"

"Roger, Upper Cut. Take 'em out."

"Make like a gopher," the pilot warned.

"Cover!" Dover yelled to the platoon and dove to the bottom of he hole that he was in. The pucker factor increased tenfold. If the pilot miscalculated, the entire platoon could be wiped out.

The four F-16s split, one pair turned and leveled off coming in from the Rangers left. Bright white lights formed a hot trail behind the nimble fighters as they discharged flares to confuse any shoulder fired heat seeking missiles.

The pair then split again. One fighter turned up and away and the other dropped low, to low for a bomb run. His wings leveled off two hundred meters above the ground, a sudden ripping sound reverberated across the sky and a puff of smoke spewed from the side of the aircraft. The pilot fired hundreds of 20mm rounds from the M-61 Vulcan cannon.

The rounds chewed up the ground and cut down the leading elements of the assault. The strafing run had its desired effect. The enemy halted, leaving more space between them and the Ranger line and just long enough for the second F-16 to make its run. From a higher altitude, the fighter swung in. Dark canisters hanging underneath their wings fell away, hurtling towards the exposed enemy below.

"Down!"

Dover and his platoon simultaneously curled into balls, making themselves as small as possible and plugged their ears. Two hundred meters above the round the cluster bombs opened up. The small bomblets, fused for airburst, fanned out and exploded in an ear splitting rippling effect resembling a string of firecrackers. Black and gray clouds of smoke from the detonations hung in the air but beneath the hundreds of explosions, steel rain showered the exposed infantry. Screams from dying men could be heard once the roar of the explosion diminished. Anything that had been exposed in the blast cone was obliterated.

Ten seconds later, the second pair of fighters came in from the opposite direction. The nimble fighters engines let out a throaty growl as they began their bombing run.

"Cover!" Cries went up. Dover again curled into ball getting low to the ground and becoming one with the soil. He stuck his fingers into his ears to block the thunderous sound of the detonating bombs, squeezed his muscles to keep from urinating on himself, took a deep breath and braced for the second strike.

The roar of the fighters engines pressed him to the ground as they passed by exiting the area and instantly followed by the thunderous firecracker rippling of the exploding cluster bombs. The shock wave bounced his body in the hole and he suddenly wondered if the pilots dropped their ordnance to close to his men. A sense of urgency almost overcame him with the thought of friendly fire wiping out his platoon and he fought to keep from putting his head up before the last cluster bomb exploded.

And then it was over. All incoming fire had ceased.

He took the time to pat himself down and check for any holes. The ringing in his ears slowly dissipated and he spat out the dust that clogged his mouth.

The ringing in his ears subsided and he lifted his head off the ground. His first thought was for his men. "Squad leaders, check in," he called into his microphone. Before they began answering, he picked his body off the ground and rushed out to survey the battlefield. Smoke and dust suspended above the ground like a stagnant fog bank. Slowly it began to dissipate and as it did, the sunlight shone on the destruction. Bodies lay everywhere, scattered like rock salt on a winter road. The few dazed survivors turned tail, fleeing back over the hill where they came.

Calpers came jogging up. Dover held his hand out for the radio. "Upper Cut, this Bravo One, over," he spoke into the handset.

"Bravo One, what's the BDA? How'd we do?" asked the flight leader.

Dover knew that pilots, just like everyone else, wanted to know how well they performed. He gave them the battle damage assessment, or BDA. "Dead on, Upper Cut. Good shooting, you saved our asses. Thanks."

"Anytime, Bravo and thank you very much. Do you need further assistance? I have Scorpion ready to sting if you need him."

Dover shook his head at the terrible joke but was thankful that additional support was available. "Negative, Upper Cut. We'll call if we need him, over."

"Roger, Bravo One, Good luck. Out."

Dover didn't want to call in air strikes on the fleeing enemy that he knew nothing about in terms of numbers or where they were heading. It would be a waste of time and ordnance. He handed the handset back to Calpers and looked upon the grisly scene displayed in front of him. He thought the previous carnage his men inflicted during the ambush was horrible until he saw the landscape in front of him. The ground was pockmarked with holes and chunks of freshly churned dirt. Around them were remnants of the enemy soldiers. Bodies and pieces of bodies were strewn across the ground sown like seeds on lowed field.

Holding the binoculars to his eyes, Dover spied a few retreating enemy forces.

Isles saw them too and called out as he jogged to Dover's position, "Who's tracking them?"

"I'm on it, Sarge," Corporal Ross answered as he held a pair of binoculars to his eyes. "Counted about twenty haulin' ass heading east at about three hundred meters."

"Squad leaders, this is One-Six. Report in, any injuries?" Dover called a second time after no one answered his request. He feared the numbers were bad after the fierce firefight.

Isles delivered the news. "Six wounded, sir. Three seriously. Pedro," the nickname for a medevac helicopter, "is on its way."

A shiver shook Dover's spine. Almost twenty percent of his platoon was hit. "Are they gonna make it?"

Isles shook his head. "Doc says it's iffy. They lost some limbs."

"Fuck!" Dover kicked the dirt and swung a closed fist across his chest. He suddenly felt as if he was going to throw up.

Isles then pointed to Dover's microphone dangling by his chin. "Your mic is busted, sir."

Dover grabbed the dangling wire by his cheek. He didn't remembering smashing his head or the gear, so a bullet must have nicked it. Then he fingered a small tear on the collar of his jacket where the bullet grazed it. He felt the blood swiftly drain from his face and his knees grew weak as he grasped the notion *he* was millimeters away from meeting the Creator. He balled his fist to steady his nerves. That was the second time during the firefight that he almost lost his life. He wondered if the next time he wouldn't be so lucky.

Grabbing hold of his emotions, Dover mustered the energy, shook the feeling off and wiped a dirty hand over his sweaty face. No sense on dwelling what might have been, he reasoned. There was still more work to do.

Assessing his platoon, the men were taking care of each other and their gear. They seemed to be holding up ok. He spied where Reynolds was wrapping gauze around the upper arm of PFC Valens and jogged over. Calpers, in tow, was already on the radio checking on the status of 'Pedro' and other helos for resupply. Bloody bandages and wrappers were strewn about and three bayonet tipped M-4s stuck in the ground were being used to hold IV bags for the unconscious, seriously wounded soldiers.

Dover walked over to Valens. "Are you ok?"

"Yes, sir," Valens answered. "Just a scratch. I'm good to go."

"Good." He patted Valens on the shoulder and turned his attention to Reynolds. "Doc, how are we?" he asked referring to the other wounded.

"Breaux, Conte and Johnson," he pointed to the three men on the ground, "need to get out of here now. Breaux lost an arm and probably will lose his leg. They need surgery now. Everyone else can Charlie Mike."

Dover took one more look at the seriously wounded and said a prayer. The inevitable of taking casualties had happened There was nothing more he could do for them except wait for the evac. "All right, then, let's get it on."

Ten minutes after 'Pedro' and the resupply chopper lifted off, Dover issued new orders. "Let's go," he shouted. "Saddle up, lock and load. We're going after 'em!"

"Sir," Calpers called to Dover as he put the radio handset back on his PALS webbing. "Warrior says Minuteman will be the blocking force and is moving into place."

"Minuteman?"

Calpers shrugged. "Yes, sir, Minuteman."

Dover smiled, remembering who Minuteman was. "Minuteman are the SF guys we worked with on the search and rescue op."

"Hooah!" Calpers grinned. "Those guys can dish out a beating."

The horse grunts were something Captain Ian MacDonald, commander of SFOD A-301, became used to. He did learn, however, that when his mount, Horace, was nervous, the length of his grunt was extended. This particular grunt was not worth noting. Regardless, he turned and patted Horace acknowledging his grunt.

MacDonald had no idea what kind of horse it was, but Horace the Horse, as he named it, was big, muscular and all black. Horace had become MacDonald's primary mode of transportation in the mountains and despite a sore backside, he enjoyed riding him. The narrow mountain passes and trails were just not conductive to Humvees and while the powerful, agile ATV's were perfectly suitable for the terrain, they just drew to much attention for a group of soldiers trying to be invisible. Using motorized platforms when all other modes of transportation were of the two- and four-legged variety was not a way to blend in. Winning the hearts and minds and earning and maintaining the trust of the tribal leaders was MacDonald's primary mission with this tribe.

So far he had been successful.

One indicator MacDonald had known that his trust was earned and had been accepted by the tribe was Horace. The horse was the second favorite of Hazrat Fahim, the Pashtun tribal leader. On this mission, MacDonald led a composite unit of American Special Forces, tribal forces and a platoon of soldiers from the Afghan National Army. The aim, besides a successful military campaign to kill the enemy, was to foster trust between the different factions scattered throughout Afghanistan and the freely elected government.

"How are we looking, Mr. Couch?" MacDonald asked his second in command, Warrant Officer III Rodney Couch. Since a Warrant Officer did not hold a commission, he was called "Mister" instead of "Sir."

"Not bad, Boss," Couch replied enthusiastically, standing on the crudely made ladder leading out of the underground weapons cache. When he stepped off the rung and back onto the soil he adjusted his pakol and commented further. "Quite the weapons find here. A whole bunch of bad guys are going to be pissed we found their stash!"

MacDonald chuckled in agreement and stood on the rim of the hole, holding onto the reins. The cache was in a square pit that was twenty by twenty and went ten feet deep. It was filled with crates of newly manufactured AK-47s, RPK machine guns, rocket propelled grenades and thousands of rounds of ammunition. "These fucking people live like rats," he spat and shook his head. "They have more shit underground than above."

"Yeah," Couch agreed. "A nice nine point zero earthquake in the area would do nice. It'll bury everything forever."

"And the Taliban too," Ismatullah, one of the tribal soldiers who could speak English fairly well, said disgustingly as he stepped off the ladder.

"Mansour Sayyaf," MacDonald turned to the tribal leader standing beside him. He was a small, fragile, old looking man with a long white beard and mustache and leathery skin, but his eyes were projecting a different persona. They were brilliantly dark that had an eerie luminescence to them. The kind that said 'don't fuck with me'. "Do you want to take the weapons for your men and Hazrat?"

"I would like to do both, Captain. My men could always use more weapons and I would like to give some to Hazrat Fahim. It would be a gesture on our part, especially since he gave you one of his beloved horses."

"Very well," MacDonald answered, knowing Sayyaf was also going to sell some of the weapons and pocket the cash himself. Such was the way in this part of the world. What Sayaff didn't takeout on horseback, the rest would be flown out by helicopter.

MacDonald glanced around the surrounding hills and mountains, checking the perimeter to make sure his men were weaved in with the Afghans providing security. Though he didn't suspect it, Sayyaf was anal about the absolute loyalty of the people who he let around him, there was always the possibility that Taliban or al-Qaeda forces had infiltrated this group and were calling on friends to attack and seize the weapons. His experience taught him he was being watched. If they weren't being watched by enemy forces, some other tribe was.

The men started to haul the weapons out of the hole when SFC Michealson called over to MacDonald. "Boss?"

MacDonald turned to find Michealson kneeling on the ground a few yards away with the satellite radio to his ear and the umbrella like antenna pointing to the sky. "What is it?"

"Orders, sir. Request from Warrior to Valley Forge. They want us to move into position about five klicks south east of here." He waved the pad where he had jotted down the GPS and map coordinates.

"Are you sure?" MacDonald asked as he turned and closed the distance. "What do they want us to do?"

Michealson took the headset away from his ear. "They say there's the remnants of a large formation of Taliban and al-Qaeda forces are on the move towards us. A Ranger platoon, Bravo One, just beat the shit out of them and has them on the run. They're in pursuit and we're closest to interdict. Valley Forge wants us as a blocking force to keep them from running into Pakistan."

MacDonald let out a slow breath. "Right. How much time do we have?"

"They want us there ASAP." Michaelson stated.

MacDonald gave a quick nod and wiped his hands on the chakman coat. "Tell them we're on it." He then called into the hole. "Master Sergeant Knapp, get out of the hole, we're going hunting. Gather the troops. Sergeant Dorsey," the engineering NCO was in the hole as well. "Blow the weapons in place!"

Friday, October 24, Phoenix, Arizona

The two well-dressed men in taupe colored linen suits sat quietly and comfortably in the air conditioned rented Lincoln Town Car waited for the victim to exit the two story brick office building on the corner of W. Pima and South 7th Ave. They were parked under the hot, late afternoon sun two blocks away on W. Pima Street in front of the closed concession stand and empty ball fields of Harmon Park. They planned on this operation being quick and easy. In fact, there was no reason why it shouldn't be.

The man they hired to carjack Patrick Randall's car and take his life was supposed to be there any minute and take his position to follow Randall to the black Nissan Maxima parked on the curb twenty yards away.

"There!" said Lev Kalanin. "There's Juju." Kalanin, a short man with mid-ear length brown hair, blue eyes and keen eyesight, pointed to the skinny black man wearing tan cargo pants and a red tank top walking down 5th Ave. Gold chains and medallions adorned Juju's neck and a black skull cap sat low on his forehead.

"Good, he's on time," said Dmitri Rykov from behind the wheel. Rykov stood at just under six feet, three inches taller than Kalanin, and had light brown hair, cold brown eyes and a once athletic physique that had fallen into disrepair. "Do you think he can see the mark?"

"He should, unless he's a blind idiot." Kalanin left an 'X' marked in chalk on the sidewalk as a signal that he an Rykov were watching and the mission was still a go.

"I guess a thousand dollar advance was worth it, along with a promise of another four when the job is complete."

Kalanin shrugged indifferently. "My only concern, Dmitri, is the hospital right there." He scratched his ear and pointed to the massive structure of Phoenix Memorial Hospital on the corner. "There are usually police in hospitals and they may respond quickly, before we can finish the job. Plus, we're in front of a public park."

"We should be ok," was all Rykov said.

Lev Kalanin and Dmitri Rykov had received a list of American names by Mikhail Borushko, with the blessing of Sergi Mirovich, and ordered to find them. If they were still alive, Kalanin and Rykov were to eliminate them. They didn't know why and they didn't ask their leader of the crime organization for an explanation. It wasn't healthy.

Being former KGB/FSB officers with extensive experience in the United States before the fall of the Soviet Union, they took their assignments with very few questions. Old habits of not asking questions died hard. The difference this time compared to their work with the FSB was they were getting paid extremely well and didn't mind being kept in the dark. Since the target, Randall, was in his fifties and perceived as less of a threat, Rykov and Kalanin decided to pay a local criminal to do the job instead of carrying it out themselves.

The fact that Randall was a combat veteran and former member of the American Special Forces was figured as a non-issue.

Ten minutes after Juju arrived, the target, a tall, fit man with graying hair and wearing blue slacks and a white polo shirt walked confidently out of the buildings rotating doors and straight towards the Maxima.

Juju peeled himself away from the wall and casually fell in step behind Randall, quickly closing the gap.

"Here we go," Rykov put the car in gear.

Juju, a self proclaimed bad ass and tough guy on the streets of Phoenix since dropping out of high school in ninth grade a few years ago, didn't mind killing for money. As far as he was concerned, it was a way to make a living. He'd done it before and held no regrets or guilt. All he concerned himself with was lining his pockets with cash and filling his nose with cocaine and his veins with heroine. Five G's for this job, as he was promised, was going to get him a lot of both.

And the money was all he could think about. That amount would hold him over for some time, but not long enough where he wouldn't have to steal, mug, rob or murder again to feed his habit. Maybe, he thought, as he walked behind the victim, the two men who hired him to do this job would keep him gainfully employed.

As he closed the distance, he reached into his pocket and pulled out a snub nosed .38 revolver and kept it pressed to his body and out of sight.

From experience, Juju could predict the reaction of the victim from the second he would poke the gun into the man's body. Fear would instantly grip the man, his eyes would burst wide open and his jaw would drop. The paralyzing fear would render the man useless, allowing him to take the keys and drive the car away as easy as stealing a candy bar.

Juju closed on the man's left. Two more steps to go. Now!

Gripping the revolver tight, Juju jabbed the man in his left kidney. "Give me the keys motherfucker!" he ordered harshly. His heart pounded in his chest as he held out his other hand for the keys.

To his surprise, the man remained calm and turned to face him. Cold, determined brown eyes stared back at him. "I don't think that's going to happen." The man's voice was as hard as his stare.

The refusal and determined look from the gray haired man startled him. Panic, on his end, not the victims, was on the verge of breaking out. This was a scenario he hadn't thought of. Nobody had refused their keys before! "Give me the keys, motherfucker cracker, and get in!"

The man kept his hard stare. "You're kidnapping me?" You want me give you my keys and get in the car? Doesn't make sense, does it?"

Juju hesitated, not understanding what the man said. He only knew he had to get going before he was noticed. "Give me the keys, man!" He jabbed the gun harder into the mans kidney, causing the gray haired man to flinch.

He didn't give up the keys.

Juju's mind raced. What should have taken twenty seconds was going on a full minute. Pedestrians had taken notice. Panic was taking hold and his pounding heart echoed in his ears. Nervous sweat formed on his brow as a scream rang out. Time to make a decision. He was getting paid to kill the man standing defiantly in front of him. The carjacking was only a cover. If the man didn't want to give up his car, so be it.

The man's eyes turned into slits, almost daring him to shoot. With unexpected quickness, the old man threw a punch.

Being many years younger and an experienced street fighter, Juju was just a bit faster. He moved his head as the punch came, glancing off his cheek. With no other option, Juju pulled the trigger once.

The victim clutched his stomach where the bullet exited and blood oozed between his interlocked fingers. He stumbled backwards until he hit the car and collapsed to the ground, his hard eyes still fixed on Juju's.

Ignoring the pedestrians screams and believing his job done, Juju stuffed the gun back in his pocket and took off like a rabbit, sprinting down the sidewalk towards the rendezvous point in the abandoned warehouse blocks away on S. Watkins Rd.

"Shit!" Rykov hissed and slammed his closed fist on the door as he watched Juju shoot Randall. "What did that idiot do? He was supposed to kill him in a secluded spot!"

"There he goes! He must be headed for the warehouse," Kalanin pointed at Juju sprinting away, weaving through the pedestrians on the sidewalk. "I hope he's fast. It's going to be hard to outrun the police on foot."

"He better not screw this up by getting caught," said Rykov matter-of-factly. There was a tinge of disgust in his voice. "Fucking amateur!"

Kalanin nodded in agreement. "Right, Dmitiri. Go to the warehouse." He pulled a Makarov pistol from the shoulder holster and chambered a round.

Rykov eased the big car into traffic.

Juju's lungs burned. For the past ten minutes he sprinted down sidewalks, turned down alley's, zigzagged, and crossed streets in a haphazard manner in an attempt to lose the police that he knew were looking for him. When the sirens began to fade in the distance and he spotted no police cars, it was then he believed he would elude capture. If he made it to the warehouse and got his payment, he would go into hiding. He had enough friends in the city that would help him out, especially if he started waving cash.

He slowed to a walk and casually strode into an alley where he quickly switched the black skull cap for a royal blue one and donned an extra long baggy yellow t-shirt that he pulled from his back pocket. To catch his breath and let the adrenaline rush subside, Juju leaned against the brick wall of an apartment building, wiped the sweat from his face and lit a cigarette. He lit the tip and drew the smoke into his lungs, savoring the taste. Satisfied that he was in the clear, he walked nonchalantly back onto the sidewalk, bouncing with his bad ass gait and blended in with the crowd.

Twenty minutes had passed since he shot the man and the abandoned warehouse was around the next corner.

Maneuvering around dented aluminum garbage cans, empty crates and other scattered rubbish, he walked casually beneath the underpass of the busy Arizona Veterans Memorial Highway and into the industrial park. He spotted the warehouse where he was to meet the men who hired him and triumphantly stepped through the darkened doorway. It took a few moments for his eyes to adjust to the change in light.

"Juju," called Rykov when their hired gun walked through the door. He took one more step and stopped. His dark body silhouetted against the outside light.

"Yo, man, you got my money? I did what you want. I can't see you 'cause of the light." He nonchalantly folded his arms across his chest.

Rykov answered. "Yes, you did what we paid you for."

Kalanin, hiding in a shadow against the concrete wall used Rykov's echoing voice to silently slide up to Juju's side. He took advantage of Juju's admitted temporary vision loss and pointed the silenced Makarov a foot away from the back of his right ear.

"You've been a big help, Juju, thank you." Rykov said appreciatively, making sure his voice didn't betray his cold feelings. This was easier than he thought. Besides being an amateur, Juju was a complete moron. He came to the warehouse alone which made tying up the only loose end a breeze.

"Cool, man. I can just start to see you," Juju spoke to Rykov, unaware of Kalanin's presence. "Let's do this again, man, of course if the pay is right. Know what I'm sayin'?" His voice was upbeat and unconcerned.

"Hey, Juju, we know what you're saying," Rykov agreed in an easy going manner.

"Now, my money, man. This is a business deal."

"Absolutely. My partner is getting it as we speak. We had had to make sure you weren't followed."

"Right, right. No problem, man. That cool. Hey, man, what you real name? I know it ain't Mr. R."

Time to end the conversation. "Thank you for your services," Rykov said coldly.

"Huh?"

Kalanin pulled the trigger once, the round smashed through Juju's head and blew out his eye. He was dead before he hit the floor.

Rykov gave a passing glance to the crumpled man at his feet. "Let's go," he said to Kalanin and stepped over Juju's body. "On to the next one." He donned a pair of sunglasses when he stepped into the sunlight.

"Where are we going again?" Kalanin asked, pulling the cell phone from his suit pocket.

Rykov pulled the folded paper out of the inside jacket pocket and spotted the next name on the list. "California. San Diego."

Friday, October 24, Moscow, Russia

The dilapidated six-story office building adjacent to the massive sports complex of Luzhniki Park and overlooking the Moskva River in the heart of Moscow had been recently converted to luxury apartments. The dirty brown brick exterior had decades of grime washed away to reveal that the bricks were actually red in color. New thermal windows replaced the old drafty single pane ones and a brass and glass rotating door was installed in the entranceway. The hundred million ruble renovation caused some of the city's most influential and wealthiest movers and shakers to line up as the first tenants.

On the fourth floor, Mikhail Borushko rented a fifteen hundred square foot, three bedroom, two and one half bath apartment. He was sound asleep in the master bedroom when a strange chirping noise woke him.

Being a creature of habit, he reached out for his AK-47 rifle. It took a moment before he realized he wasn't in his armored vehicle or in the field and his rifle wasn't anywhere near him. There were no Chechens here that he had to defend against. He rolled over on the soft feather top bed and answered the cell phone on his night stand. "Yes?"

"Mikhail," Lev Kalanin spoke easily, "we got the first one on your list and are on the way to get another."

Borushko's mind was slow to comprehend, trying to figure out what Kalanin was talking about. He was still partially asleep and it took a few moments to get up to speed. Then he remembered! Lev Kalanin and Dimitri Rykov were given the assignment to hunt down his father's killers! He sat straight up in bed fully awake. "Excellent!"

Elation swelled in him as the promise he made to himself and his deceased father was beginning to come to fruition. The first one of the team of twelve that killed his father had met the same fate.

Without needing anymore information, he closed the phone, placed it back on the night stand and turned on the bedside lamp. Throwing the down comforter off, he swung his feet around and stood on the deep, soft beige carpet. Exiting the bedroom, with a cheerful gait, he walked the short distance to the den and went straight to the sideboard. Two crystal decanters and highball glasses sat centered on a marble tray. One decanter was filled with American bourbon and the other with Russian vodka. Off to the left was an eight by ten inch framed picture of his father posing proudly in his Red Army uniform after his promotion to general.

Despite being just past four in the morning, Borushko reached for the vodka, poured two fingers worth and raised his glass. Staring at the picture he spoke. "To you, father. The retribution has begun and I will not stop until all your murderers have met the same fate." In one gulp, he downed the vodka, slammed the glass on the sideboard and overjoyed, walked back to bed.

CHAPTER NINE

Saturday, October 25, Loudonville, New York

Marcus Kaderri strode through the door from the garage into the spacious kitchen wearing a dirty pair of jeans, old scuffed and worn Timberland work boots that he would not throw out, and a sweat shirt that was covered in dirt, sweat and wood splinters. "Did I hear someone say lunch?" he called aloud. For the past four hours, he had been splitting and stacking additional firewood for the upcoming winter.

Sara had set the kitchen table with glass plates for herself and her husband, while Sam and Sean were holding their spoons in a death grip, eagerly digging into the half filled, non-breakable plastic bowls of macaroni and cheese.

"What good timing you have," Sara teased and placed a ham and cheese sandwich on the plate. Then she poured a pint glass of his favorite beer, Samuel Adams Boston Lager.

"I'm good, aren't I," he stated with a smile and removed his boots, leaving them on the shoe tray next to the door. After he washed his hands, he made his way to the kids, who both smiled at seeing daddy and automatically puckered their gooey cheese covered lips. After a kiss and a nose to nose rub for Samantha and a kiss and rub on the head for Sean, he moved onto Sara who had already sat down. He bent over to give her a kiss.

She wrinkled her nose. "You smell awful."

"Thank you." He cocked his head, wrapped his arms around her shoulders and proceeded to give her a bigger kiss, locking his lips onto hers, and forcing her to breathe through her nose.

She pulled away and smacked him on the shoulder. "Gross!" she held her nose. "You…ugh!" She playfully pushed him away. "Go eat outside."

Kaderri raised his arm and inhaled deeply as he took his seat. "I don't smell that bad."

"You do," Sara countered immediately.

He slid under the table and bit hungrily into the sandwich, savoring the flavors as globs of mayonnaise squirted out the sides. Then a large mouthful of Sam Adams washed it all down.

"How much wood did you get cut?" Sara asked, keeping a cautious eye on the twins as she ate her own sandwich.

Kaderri paused before taking another bite to answer. "Two cords cut and stacked. There's probably another two more to go. I'll go back out and finish up after lunch."

Every fall Kaderri had huge logs, that looked more like shortened telephone poles, delivered so he could cut them up for firewood. It would have been easier to have the wood delivered already cut and stacked but he simply enjoyed the work.

"Will that be enough to keep me warm through the winter?" Sara arched an eyebrow and curled the corners of her mouth into a sly grin.

There wasn't a day in the winter where there wasn't one of the three fireplaces in the house burning, especially the one in the master bedroom which was used nightly.

"Yeah, Babe, there will be enough. If not, there's always me to fall back on."

Her shiny eyes twinkled. "True."

"Hey," he asked before taking another bite, "decided on if you're going to sell the club?"

"Not yet." She shook her head and bit into her own sandwich.

Kaderri grasped the pint glass and raised it to his lips. He looked over the rim with his eyes focused on Sean just as the beer touched his lips. Kaderri suddenly burst out laughing just as the beer entered his mouth and he sprayed it across the table.

Sean, apparently not happy with the spoon's small capacity to hold the macaroni, dropped it on the table and drove both hands into the bowl of macaroni and cheese. His tiny hands grabbed as much as they could and he moved to put them in his mouth. Concentrating to keep the macaroni from squirting out between his fingers, he squeezed them tighter as he attempted to simultaneously shove both hands into his mouth. Macaroni flew out the back end of his fists as he fought the losing battle to contain his lunch. Cheese sauce quickly turned his cheeks and chin yellowish orange as he shoved a handful into his mouth. Deciding this method was more useful than using a spoon, Sean went back to the bowl for another handful.

"What's so funny?" Sara asked.

Laughing out loud, Kaderri could only point to Sean as he put another fistful of squirting macaroni into his mouth.

"Oh my God!" Sara burst out laughing.

Samantha had been watching her father when he sprayed his beer across the table. Believing what daddy did was funny, she took a sip of her juice and sprayed it across the table and then began laughing herself.

"No, no, honey!" Sara reached for a napkin to wipe Sean's yellow cheese caked face. "Don't do that. Use your spoon!" She held it out for him to take.

"Sam, no!" Kaderri began wiping the sprayed juice from the table.

Sam gave a puzzled look and asked, "Why?" She smiled devilishly and brought the cup back up to her mouth.

"No more of that," Kaderri said snatching the cup just as it hit her lips. "Daddy didn't do that on purpose."

Meanwhile, Sean dropped the spoon and went back shoving the macaroni and cheese into his mouth, oblivious to what his sister was doing.

When the spectacle called lunch was finally over and the kids were cleaned up, Sara put them down for their nap and Kaderri cleaned up the kitchen. He was on all fours under the table picking the pieces of macaroni off the tiled floor when the phone rang.

"I'll get it honey," Sara said just as he was about to get out from under the table. "Hello?" she waited for the caller to speak. "It's for you, Marc." Then she added with a skeptical voice, "He's looking for Captain Kaderri?"

Kaderri paused before he eased himself from under the table. He put the pieces of macaroni in the garbage and wiped his hands on the front of his sweatshirt. "Thank you," he said with a raised eyebrow and took the phone from Sara's outstretched hand. A puzzled look was on her face as well.

"Hello?" he asked cautiously.

"Boss?"

Kaderri's mind raced. 'Boss' was what the men under his command in his Special Forces units called him. "Yes?" He tried to place the voice but before he could, the man on the other end quickly identified himself.

"It's Master Sergeant Ireland."

A mental picture of the short, battle-hardened man with black hair and a four week old beard dressed in BDUs with an AK-47 slung over his shoulder standing on a rock in the mountains of Afghanistan suddenly filled his vision. "Sam, how are you?" he asked cheerily but somewhat reserved. He hadn't spoken to Ireland in years. In fact, the last time was at another team member's, Steven Caron, funeral. The hairs on the back of his neck stood up.

"I'm doing well, Boss, but I'm calling with bad news. Patrick Randall was murdered."

A chill ran down Kaderri's spine as the smiling face of Sergeant First Class Randall immediately replaced the image of Ireland. "What?" The word shot out of his mouth. "When did this happen?"

"Yesterday, Boss, as he was coming out of his office in downtown Phoenix. Apparently it was an attempted carjacking. It's my understanding Pat didn't comply with the bastard's demands."

"That sounds like him," Kaderri admitted knowingly. Randall, like the rest of the men on the team, took a proactive approach when being threatened.

"Boss, the funeral is Wednesday at Arlington. I sure hope you can make it, along with the rest of the team."

There was nothing Kaderri wouldn't do or go to for his men. "I'll be there Master Sergeant." He motioned for Sara to get him a pad of paper and a pencil. "What are the details?"

Ireland spoke clearly and slowly, allowing time for Kaderri to write everything down. "Need me to do anything? Phone calls? I have Bob Wolff's number."

"That'd be great, sir."

"Anything else you need?"

"That's it, Boss. I wish is weren't so."

"Me too, Sam. Thanks. I'll see you Wednesday."

Kaderri's mind flashed hundred of pictures of his time in Afghanistan with the team as he solemnly put the receiver back in its cradle.

"What is it honey?" Sara asked, nervously putting her hand on his shoulder.

"One of my men was murdered in a carjacking yesterday."

She quickly covered her mouth with both hands. "Oh, no! Who?"

When Kaderri got married, he invited everyone who served on his A-Teams but for obvious reasons, not all could make it. Randall was one of the men on assignment. "Patrick Randall. I don't think you met him."

"I'm sorry, honey." She moved closer to her husband, wrapped her arms around his broad chest and shoulders and gave him a tight hug.

Kaderri hugged her back. "He was a good guy."

Sara knew of the bond her husband had with his men and it was a given that he was going to the funeral. "When are you leaving?"

"The funeral is Wednesday, so I'll get flight for sometime Tuesday." He let go of her and held her shoulders with his arms outstretched. He looked into her eyes before he gave her a kiss. "Let me call Bob Wolff," his voice trailed off as more memories of his teammate came rushing back.

"Do you want me to come along?" Sara offered. "I'm sure my parents would take the kids."

"Kaderri shook his head. "It's not necessary."

Sunday, October 26, Masozai Kili, Paktika Province, Afghanistan

Nawaf Al Suqami knew he was in a relatively safe area, especially with friends in the Federally Administered Tribal Area to the east, an area the Pakistani military shied away from and NATO forces hadn't yet entered into with any substantial strength. His compound was hidden in a small valley surrounded by steep hills and snow capped mountains. The collection of buildings spent a majority of the day swallowed in shadow and were difficult to spot unless whoever was looking for them was directly overhead or knew where they were to look.

"Bad news," Al Suqami's aide stated immediately upon walking into the main room of the building. A roaring fire blazed in the fireplace.

"What now?" Al Suqami asked curtly, chewing around a mouthful of goat stew. He was sitting at the table with maps and log books spread out in front of him. Bad news seemed to be the only news he received lately, so he took it in stride and kept on eating but kept his eyes on the short bearded Ustad.

The deep etched lines on Ustad's young weather beaten face looked like canyons and he had aged ten years past his current twenty-four. He actually appeared afraid to deliver the news. "We lost another cache," he stuttered and flinched as if he expected to get struck.

Al Suqami dropped his utensils and shot out of his chair, letting fly a litany of obscenities. Sentries from within rushed over to protect their boss. When Al Suqami finally took a breath, he sneered through tight lips drawn against crooked teeth. "Which one?" he demanded and waved the guards off.

"Emerald," Ustad answered quickly and took a step away from the table. It was not out of the realm of possibility that Al Suqami would jump across the table and inflict bodily harm.

Al Suqami felt his blood begin to boil and his face turn hot. He balled his fists in anger at the thought of losing his biggest weapons cache. Each cache, six in all, were named after jewels. Only a handful of people knew all of their names, emerald, ruby, diamond, onyx, jade and sapphire and their locations. "Who found it? The Americans?" he demanded. It very well could have been a rival warlord.

"I don't know," Ustad shrugged. "When we got there to pick them up, they were dug up and destroyed."

"Destroyed?" Al Suqami had a difficult time comprehending what he heard.

"Yes, destroyed. All that remains are burnt crates and pieces and broken guns. They were blown up."

Al Suqami let a long breath out of his nostrils and clenched his jaw. It had to be the Americans. Only the Americans could afford to blow up all those weapons. Al Suqami's stomach churned. How could he hold his grip on power in this territory if all of his weapons kept disappearing? His money was running low also, which would prevent him from replacing all that were lost. Credit didn't exist in the arms trade and a majority of his money was made from harvesting poppy seeds and selling opium. Unfortunately, opium harvesting happened only once a year.

Life under Taliban rule was good for Al Suqami. He thrived in his fief and was unmolested by the radical Islamist rulers, as long as he followed their vision of how life was supposed to be. Besides, he agreed with most of what they preached. The only adversaries he encountered were other warlords who attempted to move in on his opium business or settle decades or centuries old scores.

Then al-Qaeda became bold and believed they could hurt the U.S by carrying out attacks on American soil.

When the American president warned of the doom that would befall the Taliban if they did not give up those responsible for the attacks, Al Suqami believed the bluster spewing from Mullah Omar and his partner Osama bin Laden that it would cost tens of thousands of American lives to remove the Taliban. They were wrong! A world of hurt rained down upon them to the likes they had never imagined. As a result of their shortcomings, he was now making pacts with the surviving friendly warlords to merge their tribes in the hopes to kick the Americans out of the country and destabilize the current Afghan government.

But to accomplish that feat and keep his tribal enemies at bay, it required force protection and weapons. Lots of weapons.

In two weeks time, he was meeting with more sympathetic tribal leaders and representatives from both the Taliban and al-Qaeda to finalize a strategy to take Afghanistan back from the infidels. Besides strategy and tactics, weapons procurement would now have to be a top priority in their discussions.

Al Suqami turned his attention back to Ustad. "How are the other jewels? Are they safe?" He knew of one of the warlords losing a weapons site and the nearby cave complex was compromised with all the men killed. He didn't want that to happen to his cache's and secluded compound.

Ustad rapidly nodded. "Yes."

"Send men to protect all of them."

Ustad opened his mouth to say something but changed his mind. "Yes, yes."

Al Suqami caught the hesitation. "What is it, Ustad? Out with it."

The young bearded man shifted his weight from foot to foot. "What about the Americans?" he asked nervously. "They just butchered over one hundred men! If they spot us moving, won't we be giving away the weapons locations?"

Al Suqami heard about a recent massacre but didn't know whose men were killed. Ustad seemed to know. "Whose men were butchered? And what were they doing?" This could be a blessing or a curse. If it was a rival warlord who lost so many men, he would benefit from the fortuitous event. If it was an ally, the loss of men would most definitely hurt their cause. He drummed his fingers waiting for the answer.

Averting his eyes, Ustad answered. "That I do not know for sure. I haven't heard."

Al Suqami narrowed his eyes into slits. Ustad always knew what was going on, that's why he was kept around as an aide. He rose out of his seat, pointed a finger at Ustad's chest and hissed "Whose men and what were they doing?"

Ustad again shifted on his feet and tried to avoid his bosses stare. Hurriedly, he divulged the answer. "They were going to attack a UN food column and their Afghan escort."

At least twice a month, the UN sent in convoys of food and supplies into the villages that were located in this rugged, hard to reach terrain. It was part of the plan to win the people over from their former lifestyles and embrace the new Afghanistan. "What was the purpose of that?" Al Suqami instinctively knew there was more to the attack than the obvious.

"They wanted the food and to send a message to the Afghan Army that the Taliban was not done yet. They didn't plan on taking any prisoners."

"Ustad, *you* tell me whose men," he pointed directly at Ustad's face and threatened with a menacing growl.

Ustad visibly shook. "Zalmay Khan" he blurted.

Al Suqami clenched his jaw. Khan was usually one of the allies that could be relied upon to tow the party line. He must have been desperate for the food, because there was an agreement among the tribal leaders not to bring attention to themselves and attacking a UN food convoy was not the way to go about being anonymous.

"We're going to have to take that chance on being spotted," he referred back to his original statement of sending men to protect his weapons. "We need those weapons safe. Now go!" He pointed a chubby finger and with his stare bore a hole into Ustad. "You lead them."

"Yes." Ustad turned on his heel and nearly sprinted out the door.

Al Suqami stared at Ustad's back and thought hard on how he could get more weapons to achieve their goal. He was left with one option.

"Nobody comes in," he ordered the body guards standing dutifully in the corners of the room. Al Suqami came out from behind the table, turned past the fireplace to a concealed door in the hallway. He slid open the hidden door, walked down the concrete stairs and with two hands pushed opened a half inch thick steel door. Inside the ten by ten steel reinforced room was a prefabricated computer desk with a Sony

Vaio laptop plugged into the wall. A small generator outside provided the electricity. Overhead was a dual bulb fluorescent light fixture that flickered on. Bypassing the computer, he picked up the satellite phone and placed a call to the most reliable weapons dealer he knew.

"Yes?" Ahmed Rashid Halabi answered on the second ring.

"Praise Allah, my friend," Al Suqami opened the conversation.

Bagram Airbase, Bagram, Afghanistan

The Global Hawk unmanned aerial reconnaissance vehicle flew over the six locations Harold Weston found marked on the map that was discovered in the cave where Len Puckett was rescued. The Global Hawk was one of the various intelligence gathering platforms utilized by the American forces to look down on the rugged terrain. Satellites, other unmanned vehicles like the Predator and manned reconnaissance aircraft were used to keep a constant eye on those specific locations.

The amount of time and money spent on those six locations were beginning to payoff. One site under surveillance was found to hold a sizeable weapons cache buried underground in which Special Forces team A-301 blew up. With that discovery, hopes in the intelligence community, not to mention with the boots on the ground, the other locations would yield the same treasure.

On its second pass in as many days flying at twenty four thousand feet, the Global Hawk's powerful sensors and cameras captured movement on the ground approximately three miles east of Shinkay Kur which, in turn, caught the attention of the air force NCO controlling the vehicle. Sergeant Fisher sat upright in his comfortable swivel chair and peered closer at the screen in the center of the console. He manipulated the controls on the synthetic aperture radar and the ground moving target indicator to zoom in and get a closer look. There! Men with weapons. Keeping his emotions under control, he called over to the captain. "Ma'am, I got something."

"What is it, Sergeant?" Captain Ward walked over the side of the command trailer and leaned over Fisher's shoulder.

"Armed men on the ground at marker…Delta." Fisher punched a button to engage the infrared sensors for a different look.

"No shit? Let's take a look see." The captain leaned a little closer over the sergeants shoulder and stared at the picture. "What do we have, at least a dozen, eighteen?"

"Yes, ma'am, that's about right."

The captain studied the screen before she commented. "Looks like they're settling in."

"Digging hide sites," the sergeant clarified.

Ward ignored the remark and reached for a clipboard to note what was happening. "Download the images, Fisher, the higher ups are going to want to know about this. Well done." She reached for a phone.

Somebody was going to be busy in the next few days.

Monday, October 27, Albany, New York

With his feet up on his desk with his morning coffee in one hand and leaning back in his chair, Detective Gary Trainor finished reading the sports section of the newspaper. He tossed the NFL summary page on the cluttered desk and decided to attempt the crossword puzzle. He quickly became frustrated by crosswords. They never made any sense to him. He would get one answer correct, discovering the answer was a synonym for the given clue, but as he tackled the next string of boxes, the answer would be something the puzzle maker pulled out of thin air. Usually about half-way through the puzzle, he gave up on them.

"Trainor, Bauer," Lieutenant Robert Chiles called from his office doorway that was located in the detectives' section. Chiles had been the detective supervisor since Trainor had joined the force and was the only boss he had in the APD. He was in his early fifties and well into male pattern baldness. For a time, his build resembled more of a pear or Humpty Dumpty and his trademark red and blue suspenders were needed to hold up his pants instead of being worn for fashion. But over the past year, he dropped forty pounds by utilizing the police discount at A Better Body and now resembled a police officer instead of a politician.

"Yeah?" Joanne Bauer answered first.

"Got a case."

"'Bout time." Trainor dropped the paper and rose from his chair. Being the gentleman, he let his partner walk past then fell in behind as they walked to Chiles' office.

"What have you got?" she asked, stopping in front of Chiles.

"Surveillance." He motioned them inside his glass enclosed office and sat on the corner of his pine desk. He gestured for the two detectives to take a seat on the pair of cushioned chairs in front of the desk.

They both declined and stood in the doorway.

Trainor grunted at the thought of sitting in a car watching the same spot for hours on end. "Ugh. Who are we spying on?"

"Crack house on Hall Place." Chiles said it as if it were routine.

"That figures," Joanne stated the obvious. The Arbor Hill section of the city was full of criminal activity.

"What information do you have for us, Lieutenant?" Trainor asked. "How dangerous is the situation?"

Chiles picked up three photographs from his desk. "So far we know these three subjects are permanent residents of the house. Renters actually."

Trainor took the photographs from Chiles outstretched hand. The photos were of a black female, a Hispanic male and a black male. All were in their early twenties.

"What we need from you two are photographs of the other buyers and users frequenting the house. In particular, this man." Chiles handed over a set of photos. One was a mug shot from the NYPD and the other was of a close up of the man in an shadowed filled alley. "If he shows up, call it in immediately."

"What's so special about him?" Trainor asked guardedly then studied the photos of the meanest looking man he ever laid eyes on.

"Emergency Services will come in and take him down."

The Emergency Services Unit was the departments tactical team. "Bad dude, huh?" Joanne said and took the photo from Trainor. "What's his name?"

"Fletcher Jackson. A native Jamaican who's running narcotics out of Brooklyn and we believe he's supplying most of the heroine in the Capital District. We're working with the NYPD and FBI on this one."

Trainor realized this was a more important and serious operation than he first thought. He took one of the seats in front of Chiles' desk and grabbed the photo back from Joanne's hand.

"Hey," she protested weakly. "I wasn't done with that."

Trainor ignored her and studied the photo. Jackson had a bull neck, corn rows and a half dozen earrings in each ear. His nose was flat and came to a point just above his thick lips. He had high pronounced cheekbones and wide set eyes that were capped by thin brows. But the black, blank pupils that resembled coal floated in a sea of yellow streaked by thin red veins caught Trainor's attention. Even from the photograph, Fletcher Jackson seemed to be looking into your soul.

"Joint operation? Do they have officers up here or we just swapping intelligence?" Joanne inquired as she took the other seat.

Chiles answered right away. "As of now, it's just info sharing, but NYPD will send up detectives if we ask. The FBI, as you know, is just around the corner." The FBI had an office in the Federal Building in downtown Albany, making certain aspects of law enforcement much easier. "There are two surveillance cars," Chiles moved forward with the briefing, "on or near the corners of Second Street to the south and Tenbroeck to the north. When you get to the house, find a spot that's inconspicuous."

Trainor couldn't help but interrupt with a jab. "Gee Lieutenant, I didn't know we weren't supposed to be seen by the bad guys."

"Be quiet, Gary," Chiles ordered without a smile.

"Sorry," he said quickly. Chiles was more serious about this assignment than usual. Trainor's antenna went up. This guy Jackson must be a real bad ass.

Chiles acknowledged the apology with a nod, then continued. "There are two cars keeping watch now. Ralston and Adamson are on Second and Weiss and Griegs are on Tenbroeck. I also believe Karl and Dumptruck are nearby on the chance you need them."

Dumptruck was a German shepherd and Karl the handler. Trainor had worked with them before and enjoyed playing with the canine, especially roughly rubbing his ears and face. Dumptruck seemed to like it as well. Every time they met, the dog would run up to Trainor and rub his head against his knee to begin playtime.

"Get there now and we'll send your relief at the next shift. Make sure your radios are on and the batteries are charged." Chiles rose off his desk, ending the meeting.

The detectives stood. "Can we keep the pictures?" Joanne asked, holding them up.

"They're yours. Get going. Call when your in position. Here," Chiles handed over a few sheets of paper.

"What's this?" Trainor asked, taking them.

"For your reading enjoyment. Be careful."

The papers turned out to be the rap sheets and the one on top happened to be Jackson's. "Shiiit," Trainor whistled softly as they walked back to their desks. "This guy is nasty. He's wanted for six known murders, suspected in eight others and has...twenty- something assault charges."

Joanne snorted. "And we wanted a case."

Trainor slowed the Grand Marquis when he spotted an opening on the curb just short of the target house on the opposite side of the street. Looking over his shoulder, he maneuvered the car in a perfect parallel park then killed the engine.

"Nice park job. I'm impressed," Joanne complimented.

"You're just jealous." He shifted his weight on the seat and settled in for a long, boring shift. "Ready for this?"

"Yep. Hey, how are the wedding plans going?" Joanne asked while she put the 55x200mm zoom lens on the Nikon D200 10.2 mega pixel digital camera and opened the slot to make sure the memory card was in there. She then turned on the power and the camera came to life.

"Great, as far as I know. Amanda handles most of everything, I just say yes or no to colors, food items, times, that sort of stuff."

"What color is your tuxedo?"

"Charcoal gray, with...." he paused, searching for the word, "I forget what color cummerbund." He turned his attention outside. "Do you have the card in there?"

Joanne gave him a dumbfounded look. "Yeah, duh."

"Good," he said and pointed out the window at the two men walking up the sidewalk. "Start taking pictures."

She brought the camera up to eye and adjusted the lens. "This didn't take long. Maybe it's not going to be so boring after all." The camera clicked as she began taking pictures.

Marcus Kaderri had been sitting at his desk since seven in the morning preparing files for Louise to follow up on while he was in Virginia for Patrick Randall's funeral. An unusual third mug of coffee was on the corner of his desk, the steam that once curled into the air had long since dissipated and gone cold. He was compiling a punch list for her in the case his absence was longer than anticipated.

As he went about his task, he couldn't help feel that something was amiss but he couldn't put his finger on it. Was it the simple fact that he was going to the funeral of friend whom he formed a solid bond with in combat and felt a deeper loss?

The unmistakable sound of a purse being dropped on a desk outside the open door caught his attention. His eyes were immediately drawn to the clock on the wall. Louise was right on time.

"Louise," he called from his desk.

A red mane of hair leaned into the doorway. "What are you doing here so early?" She walked into his office.

It actually wasn't that unusual for him to get in before her. He held up a small stack of files. "I need you to follow up on these."

"Ok," she narrowed her eyes and then locked eyes with him. "Why? Where are you going?"

"I'm leaving tomorrow morning for Virginia. A friend of mine was killed and I'm going to his funeral."

She took the files from his hand. "Oh, I'm sorry, Marc," she strode over and gave him a strong, heartfelt hug. "Is there anything I can do? Do you want me to watch the kids or something?"

"Thanks, but no. It's just me that's going."

"How long are you going to be away?"

"I'm not sure. The funeral is Wednesday and I should be back here Thursday. In the event that I'm not, I'll have another list for you to follow up on. As usual, you'll run the office. Got any questions?"

Louise shook her head. "No. I think I can handle it."

He produced a broad grin. "That's what I thought." Without question, he could rely on Louise to handle just about anything.

Louise turned to walk away and suddenly stopped, concern covering her pretty face. "Marc, are you alright?"

He looked at her suspiciously. "Yeah, why?"

Louise shrugged but didn't back away from her question. "I don't know. You just seem…different. Not 'here' is a better way to say it."

He suddenly became aware of that sixth sense again. It always appeared when danger was around the corner. He forced the feeling aside. "I'm ok, Louise. I've got a lot to take care of, that's all, but thanks for asking."

"Ok," she smiled weakly and took the files, twirled on her heel and left.

She was right. Kaderri leaned back into the leather chair and interlocked his fingers across his abdomen. The conversation with McKnight and the bombshell revelation of his team's presence in Afghanistan, he realized, was gnawing at him. Was he subconsciously linking Randall's death with the timing of his team's discovery? If so, why? What was the connection? Was there a connection or was he being overly suspicious?

Kaderri left work early to pick up his Green US Army Class A uniform from the dry cleaners. Because he was such a good patron–having all of his and Sara's clothes cleaned and pressed with the same establishment for the past five years–when he called in the morning and said he needed a favor, the owner didn't hesitate to comply with his request.

Once he arrived home, Kaderri laid the uniform on the bed and spent twenty minutes meticulously reattaching the ribbons and badges he had earned. The black name tag with white lettering was secured just above the button on the right breast pocket flap and above the pocket were two rows of colored ribbons.

Above the left breast pocket was the 'salad', a dazzling display of multi-colored ribbons arranged in rows that climbed to the top of his shoulder. Each 'salad' gave a brief history of the campaigns he participated in and the medals and decorations that he had earned. There was no doubt that Marcus Kaderri had a lot of history. The highest award he had received was the Distinguished Service Cross, the country's second highest award for valor, for actions taken during Operation Urgent Fury, the invasion of Grenada. Other ribbons were for the Silver and Bronze Stars, both for valor. Atop the salad was the blue and white musket surrounded by a wreath denoting the Combat Infantryman's Badge.

Below the ribbons on the pocket flap were two badges, one denoting his Master Jump Wings and the other the Air Assault qualifying badge. Both shoulders bore the Special Forces shoulder patch. The insignia was teal in color shaped in an upright arrowhead. Centered in the patch was a gold sword standing on its handle with three lightning bolts across the blade. The patch on the right sleeve signified he served in combat with that unit. On the left sleeve, it signified the unit he was assigned to.

Above the patch were three tabs, Airborne, Ranger and Special Forces. Each tab had been earned by passing each grueling course.

The epaulets were adorned with two accessories. One was the highly polished silver 'railroad tracks' of his rank, captain. In the middle of the epaulet, was a green felt tab with the Special Forces crest, an erect knife covering the junction of two crossed arrows and at the base of the knife, the motto *De Oppresso Libre*, To Liberate From Oppression, pinned through it.

Almost satisfied that everything was up to snuff, he rechecked the distance between the ribbons and badges with reference points on the uniform with a ruler. Finally, from a black vinyl bag, he removed his green beret and checked its shape. When worn, the unit's flash sat directly above the left eye and the 'railroad track' pinned to the center of the flash still had its high gleam.

Standing back from the bed, he gazed upon the uniform, reflected on what it meant to him and what it still stood for. 'Proud' and 'honored' were the two words that described his emotion for that uniform and what it represented.

Carefully picking the tunic up, he placed it back in the garment bag as a sudden rush of memories came flooding back to him. The next day he would be among his former colleagues and the memories as they reminisce after they bury one of their own.

Monday, October 27, San Diego, California

John Evers, retired Master Sergeant, U.S. Army Special Forces, sat behind the wheel of the red Dodge Viper with the powerful engine idling listening to a soft rock station. He waited patiently for his wife, as he always did when they were going on a trip, to check and recheck everything in the house to make sure it was off or closed.

He glanced at his watch, noticing five more minutes had passed since the last time he looked. He and his second wife of six years, Trish, had a plane to catch to Reagan International Airport because they were saying goodbye to his dear friend and brother-in-arms, Patrick Randall.

Trish finally exited the garage and hustled to the car, her long locks of auburn hair flowing behind like a trailing flame. "Sorry, honey, I had to make sure everything was off and all that stuff."

He looked into her green eyes and smiled. It was hard to get annoyed with her. "I know, I know." He backed out of the driveway, drove through the neighborhood and finally onto the main roads.

It didn't take long to get on the San Diego Freeway, and head south on Rt. 5 towards San Diego International Airport's Lindbergh Field.

Ten minutes of driving on the highway, traffic began to congest and slowed, but nothing that Evers had to be concerned about with not making the flight. He had allowed extra time for such circumstances.

Trailing behind their target in a massive, dark tinted Yukon was Dimitri Rykov and Lev Kalanin. This time Kalanin was behind the wheel, his sunglass covered eyes never being off their target for more than two seconds and that was only to check the mirrors. He kept the Yukon equidistant behind and to the left of the flashy red sports car as best he could and when the time was right, Rykov would fire the shot that would end the life of their target, John Evers.

"Things aren't looking promising, Dimitri," Kalanin said as he watched the volume of traffic build and the speed slow down.

"No?" Rykov was slouched on the rear bench seat, a sleek black scoped Dragunov SVD sniper rifle held in his strong, calloused hands. Even with the windows tinted, he was lying below the window, remaining out of sight from passing motorists.

When the time was right, he'd lower the window, aim at Evers' head and fire the shot. The SVD was equipped with a silencer and flash suppressor which would limit the muzzle signature to any witnesses and save their ears from the report. Firing a weapon in an enclosed space was a surefire way to lose one's hearing. Once the shot was taken, they would put their escape and evasion plan into effect and vanish, immediately moving on to their next target.

"No," Kalanin parroted. "The traffic is getting too crowded. We might not be able to evade once you take the shot."

Rykov sat up in the seat and studied the congestion. Kalanin was right, the traffic was getting thin. "Humph!" he snorted. "We may have to wait. Anyway, keep following," he instructed, "if I can get a shot I'll take it."

Spacing between the cars became erratic as drivers jockeyed for position to pass or change lanes. Two cars ahead, the driver quickly changed lanes, leaving a long stretch of open road in the left lane. Rykov saw an opportunity. "There!" He pointed out the windshield past Kalanin's ear. "A long space. Can you find a way out if I shoot?" He brought the weapon up and sighted the cross hairs behind the target's left ear.

Kalanin saw what Rykov did. "I think so."

Rykov lowered the automatic window and fit the rifle butt to his shoulder. The target's car was much lower to the ground so Rykov had to sit up in the seat to get a clean shot. He inched towards the center of the cabin to keep the barrel from protruding out the window. Steadying his aim, he placed the crosshairs just above the left ear.

"Ok, I'm taking the shot. Keep this speed." He applied pressure on the trigger.

"Not going to happen! Hang on!" Kalanin stomped on the brakes to avoid a collision as traffic suddenly slowed.

Too late.

Rykov squeezed the trigger but was unprepared for the sudden stop. The rifle jumped in his hands and he flew forward into the back of the front passenger seat. Because his hands were on the weapon, he was unable to brace himself and his face smashed into the seat and the rifle flew from his hands.

He didn't see if his shot was true but what followed did the job.

"Honey?" Trish called from the passenger seat. She gave a broad, beaming smile that immediately sent Evers' heart fluttering. "Do you think it's possible we could stay an extra couple of days? I've never been to Washington. It's something I'd like to see."

Evers quickly brought his eyes forward and focused on the sea of brake lights that glowed in front of him. "We might!" he answered and then stepped hard on the brake pedal as the car in front of him swerved to avoid colliding with another vehicle. "Shit!"

Tires screeched and smoked across the highway, resulting in a manmade fog. Evers' hands and feet worked in unison on the clutch, break and gear shift as he downshifted quickly to keep the powerful engine from stalling. The growling engine and transmission protested the sudden decrease in power and the brake pedal pumped under his foot as the anti-lock brakes engaged. The nose of the Viper came to a halt inches from the rear bumper of the car in front of him. He was just about to breath a sigh of relief when he instinctively checked the mirrors for an impending collision from behind. In the rearview mirror, a Mack semi-trailer rapidly filled his view. The truck's tires were engulfed in white smoke and screeching on the blacktop as the driver applied the brakes and attempted to keep the trailer from jackknifing.

The blaring air horn emitted a foreboding mournful wail.

Evers didn't have time to think anything past 'We're dead.' He turned quickly to Trish and blurted, "I love you!"

Trish turned her head to see what he was talking about but what she saw out his window made her scream.

Evers began to turn to look out his window to see what caused her panic. A searing pain suddenly exploded on his cheek as the bullet passed through his mouth and blew up the dashboard on its downward descent.

Before he had time to register what had happened, there was a horrendous roar as the truck he had been watching smashed into the rear and then up and over the Viper. Glass exploded with a thunderous roar and metal and fiberglass twisted and became entwined as the force of the truck crushed the Viper like a tin can under a steamroller. The momentum shoved Evers, Trish and the Viper into the car ahead, crushing that one as well. Hot engine parts sliced through and into both vehicles gas tanks. With a *whoosh,* the gasoline ignited and the cars burst into flames.

John and Trish Evers died instantly and would later be identified by dental records.

Tuesday, October 28, FOB Warrior, Kashah, Afghanistan

There was a wealth of information extracted from the computers discovered in the cave where Len Puckett was rescued. Infiltration routes, faction leaders, tribal alliances, weapons cache's and sales and a host of actionable intelligence. Harold Weston even found a link to the Saudi arms dealer, Ahmed Rashid Halabi, selling arms stolen from a Saudi Arabian military base. He firmly believed he now could take the evidence through the proper diplomatic channels to get the guy arrested in his home country. Of course he was assuming the Saudis were willing to cooperate. Since reviewing again the video tape of the interrogation of Mike Karmal and accessing the information found on the two Russians, Karsavin's and Tomsky's, cell phones, a clear picture of the gun running operation came into focus.

Weston sipped at a cup of hot chocolate sitting on his cot in the small, two-man CHU and thanked the advances in modern technology and the people that invented microchips and SIM cards.

He turned his attention to the note filled yellow legal pad and the documents Captain Adams printed, among other files and the SIM card, that were spread across his cot. After spending hours sifting, arranging and piecing through the intelligence, Weston believed he knew why the Russians were in Afghanistan – black market weapons sales. And to top it off, he had names of both buyers and sellers to go along with them. Halabi was one of them.

Satisfied with the progress on the Halabi aspect of his mission, Weston detoured for a moment and followed his curiosity to see why the Cave Russians, as he referred to

Karsavin and Tomsky, were so determined in finding out who shot General Borushko. After sifting through the text messages and e-mails, Weston simply believed the Russians were just curious to know who carried out the mission in killing the general. That appeared to be the only plausible explanation.

After getting a refill of hot chocolate at the dining facility, DFAC, he dug deeper and began connecting bits of information, coupled with the videotape of Puckett's interrogation, Weston's trained mind knew there was more to this than just curiosity. It was obvious the two men were more than hired thugs. These guys knew how to interrogate, leading him to believe they were trained intelligence officers. They had the trademarks of KGB/FSB or GRU officers.

Then he read the most telling piece of information that solidified his thoughts. In his hand was a message printed from Tomsky's cell phone. It was a message sent to Mikhail Borushko and the contents of the message were the names of Marcus Kaderri and his A-Team that served in Afghanistan in nineteen eighty five.

"Damn," he said aloud. "This could be a national security issue if it ever got out."

He needed to get this information to Hannigan ASAP. He looked at his watch, decided not to call and instead rushed over to flight ops and get a ride to Kabul.

Wednesday, October 29, Arlington National Cemetery, Arlington, Virginia

The bright sunshine in the cloudless bright blue sky warmed the skin, but it could not alter the somber mood. The final note of Taps carried on the cool autumn breeze drifted from the bugler standing perfectly erect among the gray headstones of the fallen heroes. The honor guard finished folding the American flag that draped the coffin into a tight triangle of stars and handed it to Randall's oldest child, Mike, seated on a cold metal folding chair. Seated next to him was, Karen, Randall's daughter, his ex-wife, Barbara and his only sibling, Mary.

"Order arms!" the command came quietly yet sharply from the immaculately dressed honor guard commander who performed this impressive ritual a few times a day.

White gloved hands from the honor guard slowly returned to the gold vertical stripe on the blue uniformed trousers and their fingers curled into palms as straight faced soldiers returned to attention. Military personnel, both active and retired, attending the service followed the orders as well.

"That concludes the service," the chaplain stated quietly as he clutched the Holy Bible to his chest. In a louder voice, he proceeded, "Mrs. Randall would like all of you to gather at the hotel Marriott Crystal City to celebrate Patrick's life."

Marcus Kaderri fought to kept his emotions inside as he stared at the gleaming mahogany casket adorned with beautiful sprays of flowers and ribbons that contained his friend for eternal rest. Tearful mourners, many in uniform, placed roses on the casket and then walked away in sorrow, quietly stating how tragic it was for a good man's life to be cut short. A tear formed in the corner of his eye and slid down his cheek as he remembered his friend.

Just as they did at Steven Caron's funeral many years back, the remaining survivors of Kaderri's team in Afghanistan, wearing either their dress blue or green class A uniforms festooned with medals and decorations and their green berets, stood shoulder to shoulder at the side of the casket. Leonard Puckett sat in a wheelchair at the end of the line. In silence they waited by themselves as the last of the mourners melted away and with members of Randall's family, they watched as the casket was lowered.

"Sergeant First Class Patrick Randall," Retired Master Sergeant Sam Ireland began. He pulled a flask from his jacket pocket and waited until everyone else retrieved theirs before he continued. "Though you are no longer here on Earth walking among us, you, an honored Green Beret and man that we all are honored and privileged to call our friend, our brother, will always be part of the team and never forgotten. May you rest in peace."

Then, with tears in their eyes, they all took a long pull.

Kaderri's team knew the internment site was not the proper place to reminisce and catch up on each others lives. They were there to say good-bye to a beloved comrade, commit his body to the good Earth and ensure his soul was sent to God in heaven.

The gathering at the Crystal City Marriott hotel afterwards was the location for the reminiscing and catch up to occur. Men who shared a unique common bond were genuinely happy to see each other, evidenced by the warm embraces but, of course, not because of the sorrowful circumstances.

Marcus Kaderri, like many of the out of town guests, checked into the hotel before heading downstairs into the richly decorated conference room where the reception was taking place. He was one among hundreds swimming in a sea of uniforms of both active and retired military personnel. Despite the large crowd and the years that passed, Kaderri was able to spot old acquaintances and the members of every Special Forces team he commanded, especially the ones he took into combat in Lebanon, Afghanistan and Grenada. As he figured, it was turning into an informal reunion.

Traditionally in the Special Forces community, a slice of one's estate was left to purchase drinks after the funeral, and Patrick Randall's estate was no exception. The bartenders poured drinks until the limit was reached and then a cash bar would ensue. Only the bartenders and the Randall family knew what the limit was. But that didn't matter to these men. If the Randall family needed money, transportation or just about anything, it was going to be provided by this special group of men.

Finding a spot at the bar, Kaderri maneuvered himself in and flashed a five dollar bill. Immediately the tuxedo clad bartender came over. "What can I get you?" He placed a paper cocktail napkin on the bar.

"Do you have Sam Adams?" Kaderri asked hopefully, eyeing the beer taps.

"We have that in a bottle."

"I'll take one, with a room temperature glass." Kaderri never drank a beer from the bottle, of course, unless circumstances dictated otherwise. Pouring the beer into a chilled glass caused small ice crystals to form and water down the beer, altering the flavor.

The bartended poured the beer perfectly, putting an inch and half thick, foamy head on top. "Here you go," he said and put the glass on the bar.

Kaderri held up the glass for inspection. "Well done." He read the gold plated name tag on the bartender's lapel. "Jack, I'll be back soon," he warned and tossed the tip on the bar.

"Thank you," Jack smiled. "I'll keep an eye out for you."

Taking a sip, Kaderri turned away from the bar and spotted a large, uniformed, bald black man engaged in a conversation at a nearby table. On his thick biceps were chevrons with three rockers and a star in the middle indicating the rank of a Sergeant Major. He was so big and muscular that he nearly occupied two place settings at the table set for eight. "Sergeant Major James Andrews," Kaderri announced as he came upon the two men.

The large man looked up and immediately recognized his accuser. He stood to his full six foot four inch height. "I'll be damned!" he said with a booming voice and a genuine smile. "Captain Kaderri!" He offered a hand that was as big as a bear paw. "It's nice to see you, sir."

Kaderri shook the massive outstretched hand, giving it a firm shake despite the fact that Andrew's hand enveloped his. James Andrews was one of Kaderri's instructors at the Q Course, or qualifying course, that was one of the stages needed to pass to become a member of Special Forces. Andrews was one of the meanest and toughest son-of-a-bitches that he ever met, but he was also the fairest. Kaderri finished top of his class and was one of Andrew's proudest students. "It's nice to see you too, Sergeant Major. I heard you made your rank a couple of years ago, congratulations."

"Thank you, sir. How'd you hear? Through the grapevine?"

"No," Kaderri shook his head. "I met a Major Matthew Bennington in Albany a while back and we struck up a conversation. I mentioned your name and that's when he told me you made Sergeant Major."

Andrews bowed his head slightly. "He was a good man."

Kaderri cocked his head at the use of the term 'was.'

Andrews caught the questioning look and offered, "Lost him on assignment right after he must have talked to you."

Kaderri nodded his head in understanding. Bennington must have truly been a good man for Andrews to say so because praise from the old soldier was hard to come by.

The soldier Andrews was sitting next to, a fit young looking first sergeant, stood up. "Pardon me, sir, it's an honor to meet a legend like yourself. I've heard many great things about you. I'm First Sergeant Adam Housley."

Kaderri tried to ignore the remark, but his reputation was always brought up whenever he met someone new and his 'salad' was always a magnet for praise and admiration. He offered his hand. "Thank you, Top," he used the accepted nickname for first sergeants. "It's nice to meet you as well."

"Boss!" a voice Kaderri recognized called from behind. He turned to see David Tillman, his executive officer of Team 524, bobbing and weaving through the crowd heading towards him.

Kaderri gave a wave in acknowledgment and turned back to Andrews and offered his hand. "It was a pleasure seeing you again, Sergeant Major."

"It was my pleasure, sir. I wish you were still in. We could always use leaders like you."

Kaderri nodded, touched by compliment. "Thank you, Sergeant Major." He then turned to Housley and shook his hand. His eyes gravitated to the first sergeant's salad and spotted the newly authorized ribbons for the Global War on Terrorism (GWOT) and the Afghanistan Campaign Medal. A combat veteran, Kaderri noted. "Glad to have met you, Top. Best of luck in your career."

"Likewise, sir, and thank you."

Kaderri turned and took a few steps towards Tillman and noticed the silver eagles of a full colonel on his epaulets and the size of his salad extended all the way to his shoulder. They included the campaign ribbon for the GWOT, the Afghanistan Campaign Medal and the Iraq Campaign Medal. "Jesus, David," Kaderri smiled and shook his hand warmly, once again genuinely happy to see his fellow teammates. A warm heartfelt hug immediately followed. "When does a full colonel call a lowly former captain, Boss? I think you jumped too many times without your 'chute."

"I've been told that before," Tillman commented.

David Tillman, in Kaderri's opinion, was an outstanding officer and knew he would be going places. It just seems strange that he was only a colonel instead of wearing the stars of a general officer. So he asked, half jokingly. "I figured you would have at least a star by now."

"I'm in the reserves, now. Actually been there for the past half dozen years."

That explained why he had eagles instead of stars. Going into the reserves slows down promotions. Kaderri clapped him on the shoulder and steered him towards the bar. "Reserves, huh?" He pointed to Tillman's salad, specifically the new campaign medals and the second silver star. "I see you've been busy. Let me get you a beer."

"Sounds good to me. Hey, Boss," Tillman said as they approached the bar, "this sucks you know, burying one our own for something stupid."

"Yep," he agreed. As they waited for a spot at the bar, Kaderri felt a pang of loss for not being involved in the current military operations. Since the attacks on September 11, on more than one occasion, he seriously thought about trying to get back into the Forces. He pointed to Tillman's salad. "How many tours for OEF?"

Without hesitation, he held up three fingers. "Two in Afghanistan and one in the Sandbox." He used the slang term for Iraq. He then cracked a crooked a smile. "I can't tell you the other places."

Kaderri chuckled. "Successful?"

"Very! Did a lot of good work and took out shit loads of ragheads."

Kaderri patted him on the shoulder. "Well done, I knew I taught you well!"

"You did, Boss, you did."

"What'll you have, gentlemen?" Jack, the bartender threw napkins on the bar.

"Hey, Jack," Kaderri greeted then deferred to Tillman. "David?"

Tillman smiled and shook his head. "Give the man next to me another Sam Adams and," he paused for a moment then added, "I'll take one of those too."

The bartender placed the beers on the napkins and offered Tillman a glass, which he declined. "No charge yet."

"Thank you," Kaderri said and grasped the beer bottle and carefully refilled his glass, putting a one inch head on it. He placed the empty bottle back on the bar, he held up the pint. "To the Team."

"To the Team," Tillman echoed and touched his glass.

After taking a healthy swallow, Kaderri pointed to the bottle in Tillman's hand. "That's sacrilegious, you know. Drinking a quality beer from a bottle."

"Uh-huh," he smiled and took another swallow.

"Boss!" a still handsome, though older Mike Wagner called, holding out his hand. He stood as tall as Kaderri, but put on about ten pounds since the last time they met and his dark, short cropped hair was going gray around the edges. There was an attractive, curvy blonde in her mid thirties standing at his side, about twenty years younger than he.

Kaderri took the outstretched hand. "Hey, Mike!" This greeting was followed by an embrace and firm pats on the back.

When they let go, Wagner introduced the woman next to him. "Boss, I'd like you to meet my wife, Liz."

Kaderri offered his hand and smiled. "Nice to meet you, Liz." He wondered what happened to Wagner's first wife, Abbey. Failed marriages were more common than not in Special Forces. It was just the nature of the business.

"Nice to meet you, too," she cocked her head, looking for a name.

"Marcus Kaderri," he introduced himself.

"Jesus!" Mike slapped himself on the forehead. "I'm sorry, Liz. I'm so used to calling him Boss, as is everyone else is in the unit. I just assume everyone knows who he is."

"I'll bite," the smile spread to her eyes. Kaderri had that effect on women. "Why Boss?"

Kaderri shrugged and playfully answered. "They didn't want to call me 'sir'.

Wagner snorted and proudly proclaimed, "There's more to it than that."

"Boss! David! Mike!" The arrival of the rest of Team 524 saved Kaderri from further embarrassment about his exploits and the adoration from his team. Some of the men arrived alone, others had a female companion hanging on their arm.

The first to arrive were the team sergeant Master Sergeant Sam Ireland and Sergeant First Class Tom Gallagher. Both men had retired. Behind them was Bob Wolff and Jesse Hughes, one of the team medics and who was involved in the firefight with the Israeli's at Kaderri's house in the Adirondacks. Hughes' medical skills had saved both Kaderri's and Wolff's lives on the mountainside after they took multiple gunshot wounds. Interlocked with his arm was a pretty brunette that stood a few inches smaller than him. Finally arriving was Zack Newcomb and his wife.

Sadly, though a third of the team was missing. Steven Caron was killed years ago in a drive-by shooting while sitting with Kaderri and Wolff on the steps that led into Caron's apartment in downtown Albany. He was simply in the wrong place at the wrong time. Leonard Puckett was back in Walter Reed, the doctors only allowed him out for the funeral, and now Patrick Randall had passed.

The only member not accounted for was John Evers.

"Jack," Kaderri called over the growing crowd at the bar. When the bartender arrived, Kaderri continued, "these people need drinks," he pointed to his teammates and spouses standing behind him and this time threw down a twenty dollar bill.

Jack grinned and began tossing napkins on the bar. "You got it."

With drinks in hands, the mourners began to grab tables to eat. The noise level stabilized at a low hum and the attentive servers hovered nearby, waiting for everyone to sit so they could begin to bring out the food. It wasn't difficult for Team-524 to get tables next to each other. While dinner was being consumed, the conversation steered to their missing comrade.

"Anybody see or hear from Evers?" Tom Gallagher asked aloud.

There was a collective shaking of the heads.

"I know he was coming," Sam Ireland stated. "I talked him the same day I called the rest of you. He told me he was bringing his wife, too."

A sense of foreboding hit Kaderri and he did his best to hide the look on his face. Bob Wolff, the only person who was able to pick up on the brief reaction, did. Kaderri gave a barely perceptible shake of his head to not mention anything.

"Anyone try calling?" Zack Newcomb asked. He pulled a cell phone from the inner pocket of his uniform and flipped it open. "Who knows his number?"

"I already left a few messages on his answering machine and his voice mail." Ireland answered. He was still acting as the team sergeant, taking care of his men. He then pulled out his own cell phone and checked for messages. "No messages," he said and put the phone back in his pocket.

"That's not like him," said Gallagher.

Concerned glances were exchanged between the men.

"I'm going for more drinks," Wolff said trying to lighten the mood. "Who's ready?"

CHAPTER TEN

Thursday, October 30, Kabul, Afghanistan

In general, the once dangerous cities in Afghanistan were stabilized and the fully armed multinational force patrolling the streets had been a major factor in restoring order, despite threats of mass violence from Taliban members and terrorists. Free elections have taken place and the nation was taking baby steps on it's way to becoming a self sustaining democracy.

In the countryside, things were different. Warlords, drug dealers and terrorists were still on the loose and controlled large swaths of territory with a heavy hand and a sharp blade. These were the places where the Taliban and their skewed beliefs were still percolating and in some locales, growing stronger.

Since Hal Weston was sent to work in the eastern reaches of the country, he no longer had the luxury of being able to report to Russ Hannigan back in Turkmenistan on a moment's notice, which he was grateful for. He always believed scheduled meetings were a waste of time and meetings were only needed when important information had to be disseminated. To attend meetings now would mean a long, expensive and non productive helicopter ride. Besides, long helicopter rides were something he never liked. Hannigan would now make the trips for the meetings, allowing Weston to remain in the field and draw less attention to his comings and goings.

Weston sat behind his desk in a non-descript, oft-used ground floor office on a relatively quiet Kabul street. The sounds of impatient drivers honking their horns could be heard through the small, dirty single pane window, as well as the normal hustle and bustle of the growing city. A fluorescent light suspended from the ceiling provided the only light. The floor was constructed of wood planks and the concrete walls were bare. Electric heat was provided, but the system was temperamental at best. For warmth, Weston used a portable kerosene heater. A bottle of water and an unopened laptop computer were on the desk. He was loaded with a wealth of information on what he discovered in the cave and was eager to offer an analysis and conclusions.

"You sounded too excited on the phone, Hal," Hannigan stated as he leaned back in the chair across the desk. "I figured a trip out here was worth it."

Weston correctly took it as the cue to begin. "Remember the conversation we had with Colonel Cavallo after my last mission?"

Hannigan frowned and then nodded. "Yeah," he snorted.

Apparently he was still perturbed by the way the Green Beret took him to task. When Hannigan didn't say anything else, Weston continued. "I found a definitive link with Ahmed Rashid Halabi and another with the Russians."

Hannigan leaned forward, his eyes narrowing. "Like what?"

"Ok," Weston began ticking off fingers. "Russians first. The two guys killed by the Rangers in the cave were Eduard Tomsky and Aleksander Karsavin. I had one of the guys in Intelligence back at Langley run their names, and sure enough they came back as former KGB/FSB. As for the others, Bedny and Novikov, the Russians killed in Turkmenistan, they have come up blank, but we're still working on it."

"So," Hannigan said skeptically. "There are thousands of former KGB and GRU officers running around the world offering their services, just like our spec ops guys in our country. All those PMC's working here and in Iraq." PMC's were private military corporations, or a more looser term that could be applied would be modern day mercenaries. "Could they be similar?"

It was a fair question and something Weston considered. "Possible, but I doubt it. It's pretty clear these guys are running weapons on the black market. No, these guys are criminals at the very least. This guy, Tomsky, was the one who texted the names of Kaderri's team to someone."

"Did you get that name?"

Weston nodded. "Mikhail Borushko." He didn't go any further than that. The compromised A-Team wasn't his concern to pursue. That would be Hannigan's call.

"Now, what about the link to Halabi?"

Weston gave a Cheshire cat's grin. "These Russians were buying the weapons from him and reselling them to the Taliban and al-Qaeda, and get this, Chechen rebels."

Hannigan let out a whistle. "Holy shit! These guys are supplying weapons to their country's enemies?"

Weston nodded and shrugged. "It appears that way."

"Who are the Russians working for? Is their operation financed by the government?"

Weston shook his head. "I don't believe so. My bet is the Russian Mafia. Those guys got their hands into everything and it's a perfect career move for former FSB officers to continue the game. Where else can they employ their skills and use their contacts and make a hell of a lot of money? I'd say they're players in the arms trade with a vast and better equipped distribution network. "

"Well done, Hal." Hannigan stood, signaling the end of the conversation. "Send me copies of your intel and I'll send it up the line."

"Here it is." Weston flipped Hannigan a flash drive. "What about sending the evidence the Russian cops? Think they would want to catch the bad guys?"

"I'll pass that along, too."

"To quote Colonel Cavallo, 'it's time to call the fucking Russians on it?"

"That's right, and the Saudis too." Hannigan agreed. "What's on the agenda?"

Weston understood this to mean what his next step was going to be. "Back in the field. I've found the locations of a bunch of weapons caches that our troops are now raiding. Those weapons are going to have to be replaced and I'm going to find out where and when."

Hannigan offered his hand and stood. "Great work. Keep me updated. Good luck."

Thursday, October 30, Walter Reed Army Medical Center, Washington, DC

"Hey, Len!" Marcus Kaderri smiled the minute he walked through the door into the hospital room.

Leonard Puckett, still wrapped in bandages and casts, turned away from the television set with a surprised look on his face. "Boss?" he recognized Kaderri after a short pause and then sat up right in the bed. "What are you doing here?" He asked with a wide smile that displayed missing teeth.

"I decided to take a morning stroll. How are you, Len?" Kaderri offered his hand and Puckett shook it immediately and enthusiastically.

"Recovering, Boss. Slowly, but recovering. How'd you get past the guards?"

There were uniformed guards posted outside Puckett's room with orders not to let anyone see the man recovering in the room. The guards didn't know Puckett worked for the CIA and they weren't going to. They only had their orders. Kaderri flashed a disarming smile. "Glad to hear you're feeling better." He tapped Puckett on the shoulder. You can call me Marc, Len. We're not in uniform anymore. And me getting in? I have my ways." An identification card that says he works for the CIA goes far.

Puckett nodded, conceding he wasn't going to learn the secret. "Ok, Boss."

Kaderri's smile widened and he chuckled. Old habits die hard. The smile quickly faded as he got down to business. "I'm here for a couple of reasons, Len," he answered Puckett's question. "First, to see a former teammate and brother."

"I appreciate you coming down."

"Well, since you couldn't stay last night for the get together," he pulled a bottle of Jack Daniels out of the paper bag he was carrying, "I figured we'd bring a drink to you!" The doctors had told Puckett he had to get back to the hospital immediately after the funeral. When the services were over, the team had said good-bye to him as the orderlies loaded him back in the ambulance. "I know you like this."

"Sounds like a plan!"

He untwisted the cap, found a water glass and poured the dark liquid in. He handed the glass to Puckett and held up the bottle. "To Patrick."

"To Patrick."

A saddened look crept into his eyes. "Did they get the son-of-a-bitch who killed him?"

Kaderri shook his head. "Can't answer that, Len." He put the bottle down and moved onto the other reason for his visit. He sat on one of the cushioned seats nestled between the round table top and open window. He crossed his leg and began with the questions he needed answers to. "Len, I know you were wounded in Afghanistan. I need to know what you found pertaining to our team."

"Boss," Puckett hesitated, clearly taken aback by Kaderri's statement. He shouldn't have though, one needed not to be a rocket scientist to figure out why he was in Walter Reed.

"Paul McKnight kept me and Bob Wolff in the loop right after you went missing," he stated to alleviate Puckett's apprehension. "But I need to know from you what you found. I don't need to hear your mission or operational details, just what you discovered on us."

Puckett briefly mulled it over. Finally he nodded and said, "Ok, Boss. What do you want to know?"

Good. "The list of our names. Where was it found and who had it?"

"I was captured by the Tangos after an ambush and brought to a cave complex for interrogation. I only heard about the list from McKnight. Actually, Boss, there's not a lot I can tell you. The curious thing that perked up my ears was the two interrogators who were speaking Russian."

Kaderri uncrossed his legs, leaned forward and rested his elbows on his knees. His eyes narrowed. "What did they want?"

"They were very curious about our team. Who we were, what was our mission, those sorts of things."

"What did you tell them?"

"Nothing. They never suspected I worked for..." he trailed off then realized Kaderri knew and gave a smile. "But Mile Karmal broke under the interrogation and told them a lot. Probably everything you just asked me. I got to tell you, Boss," Puckett held his thumb and index finger a millimeter apart. "I was this close from lights out."

Kaderri raised an eyebrow. "Meaning?"

"I believe they already had the information they wanted from Mike and were just trying to verify it from me. They weren't interested in anything current. They killed Mike in front of me and made it clear I was next."

Kaderri leaned back into the chair but continued his questioning. "Why were the Russians there?"

Puckett shook his head. "Don't know, Boss. I'd have to speculate it was in an unofficial capacity. But they were trained interrogators."

"How do you know?"

"Their methods. Deliberate, methodical. They mixed in psychological with physical. They would take a pistol, place it at the back of your head and pull the trigger. You would hear the *click*, but of course, the chamber was empty. Then they would smack you up side your head, curse and state the weapon misfired and go through the whole process again. They talked about family and getting home, really played on the heart strings. They mimicked the methods that were used on us when we went through the POW course. The ragheads on the other hand were just plain physical. No rhyme or reason. They would ask a question, of course about current ops, and then *pow!* They'd lay one into your gut or on the side of your head." He pointed to a spot in his mouth where there was a missing tooth. "And they sliced off half my ear!" He turned his head to show the bandaged wound.

"It hurt, huh?"

Puckett laughed. "Hell yeah!"

The door opened after a quick knock and in walked a middle aged nurse pushing a cart full of needles, vials and an assortment of other medical material. "Hi, Len," she greeted with an indifferent smile. "Time for the morning blood letting."

"I guess time's up," Kaderri noted and stood, discreetly placing the bottle of Jack Daniels back in its bag. He offered his hand to his former RTO and received a firm grip. "Speedy recovery, my friend."

Kaderri put the bag on the table and held up a business card.

Puckett shook his hand firmly. "Thanks, Boss, and thanks for coming by."

Kaderri tapped Puckett on the shoulder. "You're welcome. The rest of the team will be filtering in throughout the day. You have my number. Call me if you need anything."

"I will."

Kaderri let the door close behind him and turned for the direction of the elevator knowing he was going to have to talk to Paul McKnight about his team's presence in Afghanistan being discovered and how it pertained to him. An uneasy feeling began to grow in the pit of his stomach.

After suffering through two morning rush hour tie ups on his way back to the hotel that added forty minutes, Marcus Kaderri walked into the hotel lobby and spotted Master Sergeant Sam Ireland leaning against the restaurants door jam with a Bloody Mary in one hand and a perplexed, saddened look on his weathered face. Kaderri assumed he was still mourning the loss of Patrick Randall.

He veered in the direction of Ireland to see how he was doing. Behind Ireland, movement at the bar caught his eye and found it filled with Green Berets downing drinks. It appeared as if they were warming up for another infamous party. And at half past ten, it was perfect time to continue the drinking.

"Bad news, Boss," Ireland announced. "I didn't want to call your cell phone."

Kaderri took a quick intake of breath and his heart skipped a beat as his first thoughts were something happened to Sara or the kids. Alarmed, he asked quickly, "What news?"

"We just found out that John Evers was killed in a car accident on his way to the airport."

Goose bumps rippled across Kaderri's skin. He breathed a sigh of relief the news wasn't about his family but shook his head in disbelief that another team member was killed. "Jesus," he said aloud. "Everyone else knows?" He pointed past Ireland towards the bar.

Ireland nodded. "Yes, sir. I had the men gather at the bar and got the manager to open up for us."

"I see." Kaderri put his hand on Ireland's back and gently guided him into the bar. That uneasy feeling began to grow. "C'mon Master Sergeant, you need another drink."

It was a good thing Kaderri's flight was at two in the afternoon.

Friday, October 31, Loudonville, New York

From the moment he received the news that John Evers was killed, Kaderri couldn't help but believe that something sinister was afoot and it had to do with his mission in Afghanistan.

That thought had never left his mind and caused a restless sleep. Maybe, he thought, as he rose from the bed and moved to the shower, the business day would occupy all his time and push his dark thoughts aside.

It didn't work. From the moment he informed his staff he was leaving for another funeral, the feeling grew stronger and he found it hard to concentrate on the business. So at four in the afternoon, he called it a day to spend extra time with the kids on Halloween.

As he drove through the streets of the upper scale suburb of Albany, he paid extra attention to not squish any of the little ghosts and goblins darting from house to house with bagfuls of candy in search of more.

Pulling into the driveway of his three story contemporary house, he guided the powerful Porsche into the left stall of the three car garage. He grabbed his bag from the passenger seat and depressed the button to close the garage door. He entered the kitchen, excited about seeing how Sara and the kids looked in their costumes. Just as soon as he closed the door, the pitter-patter of small feet preceded a half pint sized knight in shining armor and his fair maiden as they sprang their ambush and charged at him from around a corner.

"Daddy!" Sean exclaimed and charged, trying to hold the plastic helmet on his head.

Sam wasn't far behind with her flowing pink satin gown and white lace overlay and silk streamer flying from the top of her conical hat.

Kaderri dropped his bag, bent down and held out his arms, thankful Sean wasn't armed with a broadsword. Like a one-two punch, the twins slammed into his chest.

"Hi guys!" Kaderri scooped them up and gave them each a kiss as they nuzzled into the side of his neck. "Are you slaying dragons to protect your sister?" he asked Sean, who had to straighten his crooked helmet.

The tiny knight gave his father a quizzical look. "Dragons? Where?"

The doorbell rang just as Sara, dressed in a sexy witches outfit, complete with a wide brimmed, pointed hat and a solid black cloak that draped her torso and down to her ankles, emerged from the same corner where the ambush was sprung. The kids began squirming in his arms and pointed in the direction of the front door. "Candy!" they cried and wiggled to get free.

Kaderri let them loose and they took off at a full sprint towards the door. Sara walked up to him with puckered lips, but he surprised her by wrapping his arms around her waist and gave a long soft sensual kiss. "Mmm, nice," she cooed. Staying in his arms, she described what was supposed to happen. "Their ambush didn't go as planned. Sean was supposed to hold you at sword point while Sam zapped you into a frog with her magic wand."

"What went wrong?" He interlocked his fingers at the small of her back.

"They decided hugs were better."

"Wait," Kaderri furrowed his brow. "When does a princess carry a magic wand?"

Sara patted him on his chest. "When she's two." Then the doorbell rang again.

"Mommy!" Sam's voice screeched through the house. "Candy!"

"Duty calls," the beautiful witch smiled and chased after the twins.

Regrettably, he had to let go of the witch for the important function of handing out candy.

Kaderri changed out of his suit, donned a pair of jeans, sweatshirt and sneakers and made a few stops throughout the house for certain items before going trick-or-treating with Sara and the kids.

He caught up with them in the foyer. "Here you go," he handed Sara a travel coffee mug.

"What's this?" She took the mug with a quizzical look.

He held up one of his own. "Wine for you, beer for me and this," he produced a Hoyo De Monterrey double corona cigar.

Sara sipped her wine. "Ever so thoughtful, hon."

"I agree!" he gave a crooked smile. He turned to the kids who had opened the front door and were getting anxious. He grabbed Sam's hand. "Ready to go?"

Sam nodded cautiously, taking care not to knock her hat off. Sean, on the other hand, with his sword drawn in one hand and an empty plastic pumpkin to fill up in the other, immediately bolted out the door before Sara could catch him.

After an hour of scouring the land for sweets and chocolate, the half-pint sized knight and princess had their fill and protested any further walking on their quest. Sean ran out of energy first. At the end of the last driveway, which happened to be their next door neighbor, he halted, dropped his helmet, sword and candy filled pumpkin and raised his arms. "Up," he said to Sara with heavy eye lids.

"I guess we're done." She grabbed his belongings and lifted him up where he immediately put his head on her shoulder.

As soon as Sam saw her brother call it a day, she immediately followed suit. "Daddy, up." Effortlessly, Kaderri hoisted her up and held her in one arm. Tilting his head to avoid the pointed top of her hat when she put her head on his shoulder, he offered a suggestion for dinner. "Pizza and chicken wings?" He already had the cell phone out and pushed a speed dial number before Sara could answer.

The pizza and buffalo chicken wings were delivered from their favorite pizza restaurant within the half hour and it took another half hour to eat because they were constantly interrupted by the trick-or-treaters ringing the door bell.

Another hour later, the Kaderris sat on the floor in the warm, inviting, spacious living room. A deep, soft maroon carpet covered every square inch of the floor except for the stone slab in front of the burning fireplace. Low watt recessed lights dotted the off white ceiling, washing the room in a soft, warm glow.

Flanking the cut blue stone fireplace on the back wall were floor to ceiling plate glass windows, heavy decorative drapes were tied back, displaying the illuminated landscaped grounds outside. Off to the left were glass paned French doors that swung open to the patio and a path that snaked its way to the in ground pool and natural pond beyond.

Pictures of land- and seascapes hung on the remaining walls above the cherry wainscoting and chair rail. The furniture consisted of a leather couch pushed up against the wall with the matching love seat forming an L. Two leather recliners, each with their own table, bracketed the fireplace.

The busy night was just about over. Sean and Sam had changed into their pajamas and ate enough candy to keep a dentist busy for a month. Their full bellies combined with the excitement of the evening caused them to crash on the living room floor among their hard earned candy.

"Which one do you want?" Sara rose from the couch. She was still wearing her costume, minus the pointed brimmed hat and cape.

"I'll take 'em both," Kaderri answered and scooped them both off the floor. After Sara gave them a kiss, Kaderri bounded upstairs to put them to bed.

When he returned downstairs, Sara had the candy picked up, a glass of wine for her and a snifter of twelve year old Macallan single malt whisky for him.

He fell into the couch next to her. "Thanks, babe." He sipped the nectar, savoring the complex flavors that was the benchmark brand for all single malt whiskys.

"You're welcome. You've been quiet more than usual," she took his hand into her hers. "Thinking about your guys?"

He nodded as memories flashed in his mind. "Yeah, it's hard not to," he admitted.

"I know those guys mean a lot to you. How come you never stayed in touch with them like you did with Bob and Steven?"

He took a sip before answering. "That's a good question, Babe. I don't know." His answer was solemn and he regretted not maintaining contact. Meeting over funerals was not the preferred way to keep in touch with people that he loved. "I wish I had."

"What time is your flight again?" asked Sara.

"Seven thirty." He met her caring eyes. "That's ok with you?"

Sara gave him a perplexed look. "Of course. Why do you ask?"

"I didn't know if you had anything planned with the kids or if I needed to do something."

"Marc," Sara reached out with her soft, delicate hand and cradled his cheek. "You go to the funeral of your friend. Don't worry about what's going on here."

He wished she was going along with him, but as chance would have it, none of the baby sitters they had were available, nor their parents, and it would be more work to bring the twins across the country.

"There's something not right," he offered. His ominous feeling was getting the better of him and he needed to discuss it.

"What's not right? About what?"

"I have a strange feeling that Patrick's and John's deaths are connected and it has something to do with my tenure in the army."

Sara's face suddenly turned pale. "What do you mean?"

Kaderri really didn't want to get into detail, mainly because he didn't have any facts to back up his suspicion. Everything that he was about to say was pure speculation and the few facts that he did have he couldn't say because it was classified material. He took a sip of the whisky while he contemplated his thoughts. "I have a suspicion that someone is trying to eliminate my team, and the guys that are doing this are very clever."

"How do you know all of this?" Sara asked with a slight tremor in her voice.

Kaderri understood her fear. Her life was put in jeopardy many years ago because of his past and it looked as though they may be going through that again. The difference this time is he doesn't know the *who* and the *why.* After the last episode, he vowed that if anything like that ever happened again, he would keep her apprised of the situation.

He chose his words carefully. He didn't want to unnecessarily alarm her and because of the classified nature of the topic. "Something happened recently in a far away place that brought the past up to the present."

"We're talking in riddles?" Sara asked, annoyance shone on her face. Then she caught on. "This has something to do when you were on assignment overseas, right after Beirut?"

His silence was deafening. She immediately knew it was Afghanistan.

When she spoke the tremor was back in her voice. "Marcus, I need to know if the kids and me are in danger. What has happened?"

"You know I'll protect you and the kids. If you are in danger now, I can't honestly say." He took a breath, shuddering at the thought. "God, I hope not." He decided she needed to hear more. "Apparently, the identities of one of my teams was revealed on a current operation. Since that information was discovered, both Patrick Randall and John Evers have been killed."

Sara sat straight up and moved to the edge of the couch. "And you think that's not a coincidence?"

Kaderri shrugged and shook his head. "I'm only going on a gut feeling."

"How long ago was the information revealed" Sara quizzed.

"A few weeks ago when Len Puckett was rescued."

Sara leaned forward. "Marc, let's think about this. In three weeks' time, your guys identities were discovered, presumably in Afghanistan, it got out of that country, into the hands of some bad people, they came over to America, tracked down and killed two of them?"

Kaderri paused and took a sip of his drink, contemplating her logic. Since she put it that context, it did seem improbable. "Maybe you're right," he agreed with her. But there were some lingering doubts and he didn't want to try to sway her since she seemed at ease with her conclusion.

Sara leaned back into the couch, visibly relieved. "See."

"Yeah." He turned his wrist to read the hands on his Rolex. "I'd better get upstairs. I have to repack for tomorrow's flight." He inched forward on the couch to get up.

"Hold on," she gently pushed him back. She stood in front of him and quickly removed her costume, revealing her voluptuous body. Her breasts were cradled in a black sheer and lace bra and erect nipples poking through the fabric. A matching micro g-string barely covered the thin strip of dark pubic hair and baby smooth lips. The strings of the garment snaked over her hips and when she made a pirouette, the string disappeared between the firm cheeks of her delectable derriere. Black thigh high stockings wrapped her toned shapely legs. She pushed her long hair behind her ear. "This witch needs to cast a naughty spell!"

Kaderri's heart skipped a beat and he drew in a breath. "Time for trick or treat?" He smiled and stirred at the sight of the goddess in front of him. For the entire time in their relationship, they always made it a practice to make love before and after one of them left for and returned from a trip. Tonight was going to be no different.

Sara moved in, her nimble fingers unbuttoned his shirt, long fingernails lightly teasing his chest hairs as she worked her way to his belt buckle.

"Where's your broom?" he asked curiously.

Hot breath flowed into his ear as she freed his erection and began stroking it with her soft fingers. "A treat for both of us. I'm riding this tonight!"

Saturday, November 1, Masozai Kili, Afghanistan

The previous conversation with Ustad about moving the weapons ate at his intestines and it caused him to change his mind. The twenty-odd men he sent with Ustad to the 'Ruby' weapons cache were still there guarding them. They were exposed to overhead surveillance and that meant the weapons caches were vulnerable. It didn't take anyone with a little bit of brains to figure out that a group of men remaining in a remote area were up to something and were worth checking out. 'Ruby' was the largest of the four remaining caches, therefore, the most important.

"We have to get these weapons moved out of there!" Nawaf Al-Suqami banged the table with a closed fist. He was tired and his patience had worn thin. He had been awake for the past twenty hours dealing with the mounting problems caused by the United States Army. It was two in the morning and sleep wasn't on the horizon any time soon.

Mohammed, one of the aides Al Suqami summoned, appeared to shake with every spoken syllable. "Yes, we will," was all he could stammer out in response to Al Suqami's outburst.

"How many men do we have to spare?" Al-Suqami barked.

"We can get one hundred," Mohammed answered after a moments thought. "No more without getting attention." The Taliban, warlords and al-Qaeda sympathizers had slowly been gathering in scattered locations for the massive assault to push the infidels out of FOB Warrior and were trying to keep their movements a secret. Low profile was the phrase often used in close circles.

"Then do it! Without those weapons, there will be no chance to achieve victory!" Al Suqami could feel his face redden and his heart pound in his chest. He visualized the map burned into his brain where all the weapons cache's were. He put X's on 'Emerald' and 'Diamond,' the sites that were lost and silently prayed he wouldn't be crossing off any more.

Mohammed raised an eyebrow. "Isn't Ahmed Rashid Halabi going to provide us with weapons?"

"Only some, unless we have cash. He is, after all, a businessman." Al Suqami pointed to the door. "Now go! Go to Ruby and bring the weapons and Ustad back here!"

With Mohammed mentioning Ahmed Rashid Halabi, Al Suqami wondered why he hadn't received an answer yet from the arms dealer about providing weapons. A phone call would potentially get him an answer but cell phones weren't available in that part of the country and the satellite phone, which the Americans track very well, would sooner or later invite the Americans in. He mulled over his options. Risk exposing his well hidden camp and growing number of fighters to get an answer on the weapons or do nothing and wait for an answer that may never come?

Time was of the essence and he needed to take action.

Finally, Al Suqami decided the risk was worth it, but he would have to keep the conversation short on the very real chance the Americans had their tracking equipment in use. He dashed down to his basement bunker to get the SAT PHONE and dialed Halabi's phone number.

"Yes?" came the curt salutation.

"My friend," Al Suqami began, keeping his voice friendly. "Have you had time to think about my request?"

"Which request is that?" Halabi asked coldly.

The tone in Halabi's voice caused Al-Suqami to hesitate. He knew the arms dealer didn't like to be pestered. "The weapons," he answered quickly. "Will you help supply us so we can continue our jihad? We have run into some difficulty lately."

"I will be at your meeting." Without further comment, Halabi hung up.

Al-Suqami looked at the phone as if something was going to jump out at him. A slow smile spread across his face. There was no way Halabi was going to go through all the trouble and waste his time to travel from Riyadh without the intention of selling or, as Al Suqami prayed, donate the weapons. He could begin to taste the early fruits of victory!

CHAPTER ELEVEN

Saturday, November 1, FOB Warrior, Kashah, Afghanistan

The sand and dust blew with the cold wind, the small particles stung any and all exposed skin. Harold Weston pulled the collar up on his field coat and tried to bury his head like a turtle as he walked over to the Operations building.

Off in the distance, more than a dozen Blackhawk helicopters of Charlie Company, 1st Battalion 32nd Infantry of the 10th Mountain Division sat on the tarmac with their rotors spinning and engines idling, ready to take flight. Standing by each helicopter were nine fully armed soldiers, waiting for the order to board. The company had to set down a few hours earlier because of a delay in their mission. Instead of wasting time and gas heading back to their base, command decided to land at FOB Warrior. Besides, when the base was completed, elements of the 1/32 would be moving in so why not get a preview of their new home?

Further on down the flight line were two deadly Apache gunships. The pilots were rechecking the missiles and rocket pods slung to the stubby wings. They were going to escort and cover the Blackhawk's on their insertion.

Weston reached for the door but it opened just as he was about to turn the doorknob. A combat ready soldier with an etched face and hard eyes peered out from under the K-pot, stood in the way. "You're late, Mr. Weston," said the expressionless major with an M-4 carbine strung across his chest and another in one hand. He also carried an extra K-pot and Interceptor body armor vest. "I was just coming to get you." He dumped the helmet on Weston's head.

"Uh,-" Weston was about to say something but the major sped past him towards the flight line and waiting helicopters.

"Move it," the no-nonsense major ordered over his shoulder.

Without any choice, if he wanted to know what was going on, Weston jogged to catch up to the major. "What's the rush?' he asked as he pulled aside, reading the name tab above the breast pocket– Hutchinson.

"Word has it that you wanted to get in the field to find the arms supplier, right?" Hutchinson said it more as a statement.

"Correct." Weston felt a sudden surge of adrenaline.

"We have intel that there's a shipment of weapons and a bunch of bad guys are headed for one of the locations on the map. Reference point Delta." Hutchinson handed a folded map to Weston. He instantly recognized the location. "We're going to head them off at the pass, so to speak. Maybe you'll get a chance to get some field interrogations in. I understand you got history."

Weston knew Hutchinson was referring to his past military experience. "That's right. A dozen years with Special Forces." He studied the location on the map and then gave it back.

As they stood next to a fully loaded Blackhawk, Hutchinson handed Weston the M-4, a bandolier of magazines and body armor. Hutchinson had to shout over the noise of the rotating blades and engine. "Good. You'll be needing those and are riding in the chopper with me." Once Weston had the gear on, Hutchinson held out his strong hand and gave a cheery smile. "Pete Hutchinson, XO of the one thirty-two. Nice to meet you and welcome aboard!"

Weston clasped the hand and shouted, "Thanks."

A few moments later, Weston, armed and ready for combat, sat in the seat next to Hutchinson with a full combat ready infantry squad, waiting to lift off.

While Weston was boarding the choppers with the 1/32, Lt. Jack Dover was on his way over to Operations for a routine briefing. Checking his watch, he figured he could spare a few minutes to take a detour to The Chat Room and check his e-mails. It had been awhile and he was sure there would be some messages from his fiancée, Renee. He quickly veered away from Operations for the adjacent prefabricated building.

The Chat Room was a large prefabricated sheet metal warehouse where a dozen telephones were set up on a long countertop and separated by small partitions and twice as many computer terminals were located for the soldiers to call home or check their e-mails. A cluster of vending machines offered soda or sports drinks and snacks.

He closed the door behind and immediately signed in on the clip board and waited for the duty NCO to assign him a terminal. He was in luck, there was an open terminal against the near wall.

The Chat Room was busy but not crowded. Rangers and soldiers were talking on the phones, stabbing away at keyboards or just carrying on general conversations. A staff sergeant came up to Dover. He had his helmet and body armor off but kept his M-4 slung across his back. "What's it gonna be, sir? Phones or computers?"

"Computer, Sarge." Dover pointed to the empty terminal, but the sergeant ignored his hint.

The NCO scanned the room and pointed to the same terminal Dover pointed to. "Take station six." He picked up the clipboard and waved it while reading Dover's name. "Did you sign in, sir?" He scanned the sheet.

"I did, Sarge."

"Got it. You're all set."

"Thanks." Dover raced over to Station Six and plopped himself down in the hard metal chair and moved the mouse on the pad with the image of a waving American flag. A couple of clicks and his fingers flying over the keyboard, he logged on to his account and waited eagerly for it to come up.

When it did, there were thirty-three messages in his inbox and twenty-seven were from Renee. The most recent one, sent that morning, had fear in the subject line, "I'm worried."

"Whoa," he said aloud at the number of messages. He didn't have time to read them all. He selected a few and smiled. They were gushy and telling him how much she missed him and what was going on back at home.

Five minutes had gone by since he sat down. With only a few minutes left before the briefing, he composed a letter informing her he was ok and would call later when he got off duty. In the subject line, he typed a simple 'Hello'. His calloused fingers breezed over the keyboard and in under a minute he finished. He hit the 'send' button, immediately logged off and arrived at Operations just in time for the briefing.

Saturday, November 1, Paktika Province, Afghanistan

The powerful Blackhawk helicopter flew nap of the earth, twisting, turning climbing and diving with the rocky terrain. Through the windshield between the pilots, Weston could see the other Blackhawks land under fire. Mortar rounds blew holes in the ground yards away from the helos as they disgorged their troops and lifted off. Streaks of smoke from rocket propelled grenades nearly found their mark on one helo but the pilot deftly maneuvered the bird that caused the RPGs to sail past.

With awed fascination, Weston watched as an Apache gunship circled its prey, lined up a shot and fired off a salvo of the 2.75 inch Hydra 70 rockets slung under the stubby wings. In a blinding flash of explosions and earth that looked like a volcano erupting, an enemy mortar team was obliterated.

Seemingly out of nowhere, the second Apache slid into firing position and let loose a burst of the nose-mounted M230 30mm chain gun at the dug in enemy below. The massive shells ripped the ground open and tore the defenders in the foxhole to shreds.

Satisfied for the moment with the destruction they caused, the Apache pilots put their birds into a tight turn and pulled away, making room for the rest of the Blackhawks to land.

Without warning, Weston's pilot turned to port and put the helo in a steep bank and raced to the ground. It had a been a long time since he felt the rush of excitement of a heliborne assault and his training immediately took over. The helo slowed a dozen feet above the ground and he inched closer to the open door as a hurricane of debris from the rotor wash engulfed the helo. The instant the wheels skimmed the ground, Hutchinson ordered with a pumping fist, "Out! Out! Out!"

Gunfire could be heard above the noise of the turning rotors and engines as it increased power to take flight. Bullets pinged off the green metal skin and plastic windows. Weston dropped to a knee and brought his weapon up, searching for targets.

"Contact Right!" a soldier called out the direction he saw the enemy. Incoming small arm fire suddenly increased.

"Contact fucking everywhere!" another soldier warned. They were under heavy fire.

More helos touched down. Each pilot making sure they were clear of each other as they unloaded their men. Dirt and debris from the rotor wash and exploding ordnance flew everywhere as did incoming and outgoing lead. Door gunners on the helo's let loose with their M-240B's and rockets screamed out of their pods. The cacophony of men and machine in battle increased with every deadly second.

The Apache's once again dove on strafing runs, attempting to keep the head down of the entrenched enemy while the assault forces began their advance.

The assault teams were moving up a slight rise, taking heavy fire from a dug in enemy. Grenades and mortars started raining down on the assault force, causing the men of the 10th Mountain Division to seek cover. Some never got the chance.

Hutchinson turned to Weston. "Keep your head down and eyes open. The bastards are going to fight for this one."

Saturday, November 1, Moscow, Russia

Mikhail Vasilyevich Borushko sat comfortably in a brand new soft Italian leather recliner sipping at a Stolichnaya vodka on the rocks in his new apartment over looking the Moskva River. The money he always had access to but had to conceal from the military was no longer the case. And he loved spending it on himself. Surrounded in comfort and luxury, Borushko had no regrets of leaving his former profession.

Life for him was improving exponentially and there was no slowdown on the horizon. He immediately began setting up a pair of hardware stores that he was going to use as a front for his Solntsevskaya business and by all accounts the first one should be opened by the end of the month. Borushko smiled as he sipped his vodka and marveled at how fast paperwork and bureaucratic bullshit can move when you flash a wad of euros or American dollars. Rubles didn't have the same affect.

To make life even better was the wonderful news that Rykov and Kalanin had eliminated two men from Marcus Kaderri's Special Forces team. But he wasn't satisfied. His thirst for revenge was not to be quenched until he knew all the surviving men that were responsible for his fathers death met the same fate. Borushko's aim was to torment the commander of the American unit and make him sweat. Make him constantly look over his shoulder and wonder if he was going to get it next. Borushko put word out that Kaderri was to be the last man eliminated and that he personally was the one that was going to pull the trigger and end Kaderri's life.

To make this issue move faster so he could concentrate on business, Sergi Mirovich gave him a free hand in this 'side' operation and allowed Borushko to send another team to America to help Rykov and Kalanin.

Saturday, November 1st, Albany, New York

Amanda Matthews and Gary Trainor had just finished dining on and cleaning up another one of Amanda's delicious meals. With a full belly, Trainor would have liked nothing more than going out to a bar or a movie. Instead, with little enthusiasm, he looked forward to spending the remainder of the night finalizing the plans for their fast approaching wedding.

After changing into sweats and lighting a warm crackling fire, the soon to be newlyweds retired to the spacious living room and sat next to each other on the brown leather couch. Trainor had his arms folded across his chest with his legs crossed, left over right and constantly wiggled his foot.

Spread on the table were the catalogues and menus that they would be perusing and two glasses of Pinot Grigio. The chilled bottle was in a marble cooler.

Amanda had her slippered feet resting on the oak coffee table and excitedly opened the festivities. "Ok, Gary, what do you want to do first?"

"Whatever you want to do is ok with me."

She shot him a look of displeasure. "No way, baby. You are going to participate in the final details of *our* wedding." She snatched up the pile of menus and dropped them on his lap. "Pick a restaurant for the rehearsal dinner," she ordered. A jab with a long fingernail into his chest accentuated her point.

"Ugh," he sighed, read the name of the restaurant on the first one then stared at the appetizer section of the menu. "How many restaurants have you narrowed it down to?"

"Six."

There had to be a way out of this, he thought. Wouldn't it be easier to just pick a good restaurant that they liked and make a reservation? How hard could that be? "How many people are going to the dinner?"

"The wedding party," she answered with a raised eyebrow. Amanda began ticking off her fingers. "Your parents, your brother and his girlfriend, your sister, my parents, my sister and her husband, all the ushers," she took off a slipper and began counting toes as she continued. "Bridesmaids, best man, maid of honor…"

Gary held up his hands in surrender. "That's a lot. Do my parents know it's that many?" Both parents insisted on paying for the traditional items, meaning his parents would pay for the rehearsal dinner and her parents for the wedding and so on.

Amanda rolled her eyes. "Yes, Gary, they know."

He gave a sheepish grin. "Oh." He realized there was much more to planning this than he imagined but still didn't like it. Under his beautiful fiancée's glowering gaze, he picked up the menus and gave the task his full attention.

An hour later and well into their second bottle of wine, they had accomplished what they wanted. The ushers and bridesmaids gifts were selected as well as which limousine company they would use and of course, the restaurant for the rehearsal dinner.

"Done!" Amanda said with an air of satisfaction and clasped her hands.

"Thank God!" Trainor couldn't agree with her more and let it show by being overly dramatic and falling back into the couch. Of course her statement was for a sense of accomplishment and his was for that it was finally over.

"Stop it," Amanda cautioned and took a sip of her wine. "That wasn't so bad."

"I guess not," he admitted not too convincingly. He still preferred watching a college football game. He rose from the couch to put another log on the fire and stretch his legs. He discovered he had a slight buzz going.

Amanda collected and straightened out the papers, put them into a neat pile and leaned back into the couch. "What's new on the surveillance?" she asked and plopped her feet back on the table.

"Nothing. It's very boring actually." He fell onto the couch with a grunt. "Joanne and I just sit in the car and take pictures of all the drug dealers and junkies."

"Have they spotted you?"

Trainor thought about that and took a sip from his glass. "I don't think so. The criminals still come and go as they please."

"If they did spot you," she pointed a wavy finger, "what would happen?"

He shrugged. "That I don't know." He wondered about that a few times himself. "I don't think it'll be violent if they do. The bad guys would probably turn and walk away and tell everyone they know that the cops are on the corner. I can say that I'd rather be doing something else instead of sitting on my ass in a car all day."

She drained her glass and placed it on the table with a thud. She showed signs of inebriation. "It's better than sitting at your desk? You hate sitting there doing nothing."

He couldn't argue that point. Besides, on the street, it was always interesting to see the various aspects of the public. "Yeah, I guess not." He pointed to her empty glass and emptied the bottle.

"Thank you," she feigned exasperation. "It's about time you fill me up."

Trainor thought he caught a double entendre. When he looked over at her, she gave a thin smile with the tip of her tongue sticking out and a sparkle her eyes. His mind dashed to racy thoughts.

She rested her head on his shoulder and playfully nibbled on his neck. "I'm getting tipsy," she giggled.

Chills shot down his arm with each nip and a shudder came when her warm tongue tickled the outline of his ear. Her hand slowly slid down his chest and across his stomach. Little by little her fingers snaked their way under the elastic waistband of his sweats. "Hmm," he cooed.

Amanda paused momentarily to compliment him on the evening's work. "You did well, tonight, Gary. We got everything done. I'm impressed." There was a slur in her voice as the effects of the wine took hold.

She went back to work on his neck and her hand inched further down into his pants, rubbing his semi-erect cock. "Am I getting my just desserts?" he asked hopefully.

She freed his manhood from the confines of the sweatpants and her fingers wrapped around his long, thick shaft and stroked him until he was fully erect. She teased him by scratching him lightly with her fingernails, causing another wave of shivers. Her glassy eyes looked into his, a hint of sexual wickedness shining in them. "I get it!" she exclaimed, "Dessert! Yep," she lowered her head and swirled her tongue around his swollen tip. "Isn't this a fun way to finish the night?"

Before he could answer, she hungrily put her mouth over his now throbbing head and took him in. "Ahh," Trainor moaned as her mouth worked on him. Expertly she moved, alternating between sucking gently and licking, to nipping with her teeth to give him multiple sensations.

After a few minutes of the wondrous delight, she looked up with a grin. "You like that?" she asked, still stroking him.

"Very nice," he admitted while taking deep breaths.

"Yeah, it is."

Amanda then stood in front of him, seductively lifting her sweatshirt, exposing her braless breasts and erect, rosy nipples. After dropping the sweatshirt, she fluffed her long brown hair, teasingly licked her lips and dragged her hands down the sides of her body. Swaying her hips, she slid her fingers into the waistband and seductively lowered her pants. Trainor's erection grew bigger still and began to throb as he enjoyed her show.

Finally, she ended the striptease and stepped out of her pants, displaying her trim, curvy figure in front of him. Amanda posed with her hands on her hips, legs slightly spread and her head tilted to one side with her chin resting on her shoulder and froze like a statue. A fiendish smile spread across her pretty face. "You like?"

"Oh, yeah," Trainor panted. His heart raced as he wondered what she was going to do next.

She reached for the glass of wine, took a healthy sip and momentarily held it in her mouth. Before swallowing, she sank to her knees and took him into her mouth.

"Holy shit!" he cried, grasped the edge of the couch and curled his toes as the sensation of her hot mouth and cold wine engulfed his member. Chills and goose bumps exploded instantly across his body.

When she pulled her mouth off, she happily exclaimed, "That's a cocktail!" She gave his shaft a shake before whisking his pants off. "What do you think?"

"Awesome!"

Amanda locked eyes with him then climbed on top, straddling his waist. He reached out for her, placing his strong hands on her slim hips as she simultaneously wrapped her hand around the base of his cock and guided him into her.

He pulled her close, inhaling her perfume and the wine on her breath. She lowered herself onto him, and he could feel her heat moments before her slick wetness easily allowed him in.

"Oh!" she moaned and sank all the way down. He cradled a delicate cheek with his left hand and slid his right down to her smooth, tight buttock. He wantonly pulled her face towards his, zeroing in on her alluring, parted, lips.

Their mouths met briefly, then a wrestling match of their tongues began in a heated passionate kiss. Amanda opened her mouth wide, allowing Trainor to explore. She pushed his tongue back with her own going on the offensive. Back and forth they went, attacking, retreating meeting in the middle. All the while Amanda moved her body in a practiced rhythm up and down Trainor's rock hard cock.

Breathing hard, she suddenly pulled away. She locked her fingers behind his sweaty neck and arched her back, thrusting an erect nipple into his face. Eagerly he took it into his mouth, alternating between flicking it with his tongue and sucking it between his lips.

"Ah!" she shrieked in passion.

Amanda's moans increased as she rocked on his lap. Trainor held on tight, making sure she didn't fall off. "You feel great, Amanda!" he managed to say between pants. Sweat beaded on his brow and a shiny sheen covered their heated bodies.

"So...do...you," she gasped between moans and maintained her rhythm.

He kissed the nape of her neck and noticed her breathing had changed to a pant. A sure sign she was heading towards an orgasm. Knowing what she liked, he slipped his hand between her legs and began rubbing the delicate, exposed organ. She shuddered in delight under his touch.

"Oh my god!" She pressed her pelvis harder into his hand. "Faster! Gary, faster!" Her fingernails sank into his neck. "Yes!"

Trainor was close to the point where he couldn't hold back anymore. Her movements and knowing he was doing everything right brought him right up to the edge. He began thrusting, finding a comfortable and compatible tempo while still using his finger on her.

Just as soon as he thought they were in sync, Amanda's movements increased. "Oh my god!" she shrieked and writhed in ecstasy.

Trainor tried to hold back. He pulled her close as she bounced harder and faster on him. His heart raced and his breath came in short pants. The sensations became too much. "Here it is!"

"Ahhh!" she howled louder than ever before.

He felt the sudden rush and the need to release all of his love. Fireworks danced before his eyes as he erupted in her.

Suddenly she went rigid in his arms. Her head flung back as she arched her back and her lips parted in a silent scream. She involuntarily pulled his head into her sweaty breasts, muffling the pleasure scream of his own.

"Whoa." He finally stammered.

"Not a bad way to spend a Saturday night, huh?" Amanda asked as she cuddled with him. "I love you, Gary."

"Not bad at all," Trainor agreed. "I love you too, honey." They kissed passionately for a few moments. "Next time can we skip the planning and just go to the dessert?"

She gave him a gentle smack. "You are terrible!"

"I know, but is was good!"

Amanda locked her hands behind his neck and pulled him onto her. "It sure was. I can't wait to do it again!"

Sunday, November 2, FOB Warrior, Kashah, Afghanistan

It was 2200 hours and Lt. Jack Dover was finally off duty. He stood in line behind four other soldiers, checked his watch and yawned. It was late and he knew he should be sleeping, but he was eager to call Renee.

In The Chat Room, rank didn't mean anything in regards to who accessed the communication devices and when. It was like being on a buffet line. Everyone waited their turn. Because of the time differential with the states, this time at night every cubicle was occupied, but the flow was steady, thanks to the pacing corporal keeping watch and time over everyone. Each soldier only had three minutes to take care of business and vacate for the next person or else a not too friendly tap on the shoulder was felt.

"You're next, sir," a sergeant acting as an usher said and pointed to the corporal standing behind an empty chair. He scratched his name off the sign-in clipboard. "Did you remember your calling card?" he asked as an afterthought. "Or need one?"

Dover pulled the plastic card from his jacket pocket and held it up. "I got it."

The corporal waived him over. "Hurry, sir."

He made a bee line for the empty chair, not wanting to lose his time. "Thanks."

"Three minutes, Lieutenant," the corporal said matter-of-factly.

"Right." Dover picked up the receiver and started punching buttons, listening to the instructions from the recording and punched more buttons. Finally he got a ring.

"Hello?" an upbeat voice answered. It was one in the afternoon back in the states.

"Hi, Renee," Dover's face lit up when heard her voice.

"Jack!" she screamed into his ear.

"How you doing?" He visualized her jumping up and down like she did when she became excited. "I miss you!"

"I miss you too, honey. How are you? Is everything ok?" The questions came out in rapid fire and in one breath.

Her sweet voice was music to his ears. "I was hoping you'd be home for lunch. This is the only chance I had to call. I've been busy, but everything is ok." Well, not really. The news on PFC Breaux was grave. Word filtered back to him that Breaux wasn't going to recover and he only had a couple of days left. The comforting thought was he was going to be stateside and his family would be with him when he goes.

"I noticed on the news things have really picked up over there. The news says the Taliban and al-Qaeda are growing again." Concern crept into her voice.

He couldn't lie about that. "Yeah, they're carrying out more attacks. It gets a little dicey around here. Anyway," he changed the subject. He was more interested in her life. "What's new with you?"

"I've been sending you e-mails telling you what's going on, haven't you read them?"

"Of course I have, but I want to hear it from you. I love you, Renee." He felt giddy telling her, acting like a young teenager caught between love and lust.

"I love you too. I can't wait till you come home. How are your men? Do they like you?"

Dover knew for a fact he was well-liked. There were many times his men had gone out of their way to say hello to him, ask if he needed anything and most telling of all was Sergeant First Class Isles informing him flat out that the men listened and respected him. With that confidence, Dover walked a fine line from becoming friends with his men and maintaining his position of commander. "They're great. I couldn't have better group of guys. How's work going?"

A tap on his shoulder caused him to look back. "Less than a minute, Lieutenant," the corporal informed him.

He held up his thumb in acknowledgment. "I'm running out of time, hon."

"What do you mean?" she asked a little confused. "Oh, right, sorry, the time limit. Do you know when you'll call next?"

"No, I don't but I'll call again. I promise."

"Keep an eye on the mail, I sent you a package and a bunch of guys from the office sent one to your platoon."

"Cool. When did they send it and--" He got another tap on the shoulder and turned to find the corporal tapping his watch and standing with another soldier. His time on the phone was up. Shit. "I gotta go, Babe, my time is up. I love you."

"I love you too, I'll dream about you all day and tonight. I miss you. I love you. Be safe."

He could hear she was trying to hold back the tears and a lump formed in his throat. "Me too. Bye."

Dover left The Chat Room in a light fog, his mind was clearly focused on his soon-to-be-wife. During the brief conversation his mind was transfixed on images of her–what she was wearing when they first met and the last night they were together before he shipped out. The sound of her voice and the last few phrases she spoke at the end of their conversation repeated over and over again in his head.

A tear suddenly formed in the corner of his eye, and that surprised him. There was no doubt that he missed her but he didn't think her voice would affect him that way. Maybe it was the way she said she loved him or since the imminent loss of a soldier reminded him that his life could end in a flash. A chill brought him to realize he didn't have his field coat zippered. He fumbled with the zipper, got it secured and slid it up to his chin.

Suddenly the silent cold night air rippled with a loud *whoosh* and a streak of light raced from the eastern side of the base, quickly followed by at least a half dozen more.

Rockets! The base was under attack!

Without bothering to see where the rockets would hit, Dover instinctively ducked, trying to make himself smaller. He unslung his rifle and sprinted for the slit trench carved out of the earth near his CHU. The first rocket impacted on the other side of the base, harmlessly blowing a hole in the open ground. The other rockets went wild in uncontrolled flights. One rocket screeched on its descent and burrowed into the ground but didn't explode. Two collided in mid-air and went tumbling and twisting off in different directions. One flew into a storage building and exploded with a dull pop, while the other veered off towards the tarmac. Two more flew straight and impacted with the ground, short of any structure and the last one soared into the air and exploded like a Fourth of July fireworks display.

A second salvo was launched a few seconds later, but this group was more accurate. Two rockets slammed into a nearby trailer, blowing it apart with a loud, ear shattering boom and immediately set it on fire.

Mixed in with the rockets, was the familiar and unnerving *bloop* of mortars being fired. Mortars didn't leave a blazing trail in the night sky to give away their position or give the defendants a few precious seconds to react and find cover. All along the eastern perimeter of the base, the mortar shells started to explode.

The guards on duty raced into action. A .50 caliber machine gun emplacement on the perimeter near the main gate opened up, quickly followed by another a hundred meters away. A half klick away, red angry tracer rounds converged on the spot where the rockets were fired from.

A line of armored Humvees mounted with the M-2 .50 caliber machine guns raced out of the gate towards the threat and soldiers sprinted to and fro, taking up their assigned positions to repel any attack against the base.

Not bothering to look, Dover blindly dove over the dirt filled three foot high wire mesh and canvas HESCO barrier and into the trench as another salvo of rockets flew in from the north. He crashed into someone, smashed his helmet down onto his nose and dropped his rifle.

"Oof!" the voice blurted in the darkness. "Who the hell hit me?"

"Sorry, Phil," Dover apologized, recognizing the voice of Lieutenant Phil Case, the Second Platoon leader and rolled off onto the hard dirt.

"What's going on?" The question came from his CHU mate and Third Platoon leader, Lieutenant Ramone Hernandez. All three platoon leaders were in the same trench.

"A rocket and mortar attack, you idiot." Dover then moved to a more comfortable position on his knees. He groped around for his rifle and when he found it, pulled the charging handle, seating a round in the chamber. He then poked his head above the HESCO barrier, a replacement for sandbags, to see what was going on. Steady chattering from the powerful M-2 machine guns echoed from afar. The troops in the Humvees found the enemy.

"Man," Hernandez offered, "how many bad guys are still in this fucking place? This shit is happening too much."

This was the twelfth time in the past two weeks that insurgents had attacked the base with crude home made or old Soviet rockets. The results were usually the same with the rockets missing anything important. But every once in awhile, a rocket would blow something apart or injure or kill a soldier.

Dover stood so his eyes were above the barriers and scanned the base, searching to see if the Ranger Company was taking up its assigned defensive positions in preparation to repel an attack. The incoming fire ceased, replaced by a cold ill wind that blew in from over the horizon. "All's quiet, I guess we should get to our platoon's."

"For now."

Monday, November 3, FOB Warrior, Kashah, Afghanistan

Hal Weston returned from the assault with the 1/32 and hadn't changed out of his dirty and blood-stained ACUs. The nasty fight had lasted more than a day and he came close to losing his life on more than one occasion. The determined enemy fought like a caged tiger and almost to the last man trying to safeguard what turned out to be a sizeable weapons cache. The last encounter he had with the enemy was one of surprise that nearly made him shit his pants. As he and Hutchinson were huddled together conversing over how they were going to secure the lone prisoner in the midst of the battle, an enemy fighter appeared from nowhere with a grenade in his hand and charged towards them. Instantaneously Hutchinson shot the Tango as Weston pulled the prisoner away and dove for cover. The enemy stumbled as the bullets tore into his chest, halting his momentum ten meters away but he fell forward. Just as he fell, the grenade exploded, blowing his upper torso apart and showering the two Americans with bloody pieces of flesh.

Now inside the cramped interrogation room, Weston sat on the metal folding chair with a legal pad and ball point pen placed in front of him on the table. The ten by ten concrete block room called "The Box" had no windows and a jail cell door welded from scrap iron found on the base and the nearby town. In the ceiling were recessed lights, protected by chicken wire, and a small camera and microphone tucked up in a corner.

The two empty, wooden arm chairs on the other side of the table made Weston grow a bit more fidgety. He glanced at his watch, wondering where his prisoner was. The man captured on the battlefield had been directing the defenses, which made him a prime target for capture. A marksman killed two men standing next to the target and then shot out his knee, disabling him and allowing for the capture to take place.

Footsteps and chains rattling signaled the arrival of his prisoner. He turned, looked over his shoulder to find an American MP enter the cell. He was followed by the bearded limping prisoner wearing a flight suit that someone had spray painted orange and in black paint stenciled 'Bad Guy' on the back. The orange jump suits for prisoners hadn't arrived yet so someone got creative. The prisoner was trailed by another MP and behind him was an aged Afghan National Army Intelligence officer, a small man with dark, piercing, cold eyes Weston knew as Mansoor. He was to act as the interpreter, if necessary, as well as an interrogator. In his hand was a large bucket of ice. The Soviets had left an impression in their interrogation techniques.

Weston shook his head at the sight of the ice and felt a shiver. He knew what that was to be used for and for a fleeting moment, he felt sorry for the prisoner. But that moment subsided quickly. He was a fucking terrorist.

The prisoners hands and bare feet were shackled and he walked with a considerable limp because of the shot to his knee. He was guided to the empty chairs where he was forcefully pushed to sit down. He fired off a hard look at the guards who were unmoved by his act of defiance as they secured his wrists to the arms of the chair and his ankles together with tie wraps. Mansoor sat on the prisoner's left, staring into his hardened, weathered face. He placed the bucket next to the prisoners feet and saw a brief flash of fear.

"Your prisoner, sir," one of the MP's said. "We'll be outside the door."

"Thank you, Sergeant," Weston said and picked up the pen. He kept his eye on the prisoner's face, watching him glance between Mansoor and the bucket of ice. "What's his name, Sergeant?"

The sergeant paused and gave a shrug. "Mohammed, what else?"

Every die hard fighter who was captured gave their name as Mohammed. Weston laughed. "Of course. We'll see soon enough what his real name is." He turned his attention to the prisoner and asked his first question. "Is your name Mohammed?" he asked once the MP's closed the door.

There was no response, only a hard stare.

A tough bastard, Weston thought. He'll break in time. "Do you speak English?"

The Afghan Intelligence officer looked over at the prisoner with contempt, let out a low growl and gave the prisoners pinky a quick jerk.

Snap!

"Ahhh!" Mohammed howled and tried to recoil against the pain of the dislocated finger. Sweat immediately came pouring out of his skin and his face twisted in pain. The one hand balled into a fist while his other grabbed the arm of the chair with only the four working fingers.

Weston winced the moment he heard the snap. Some back home in the States would strongly disapprove of the interrogation techniques, but those people weren't in this war. Besides, he shrugged inwardly, he was in a foreign country and the interrogation was being conducted by a native. More importantly, it was effective.

"Wrong answer," Weston informed Mohammed. Weston leaned forward on the chair, resting his elbows on his knees. "Lets try again." His voice was cold and unemotional and his eyes never blinked. "Do you speak English?"

Mansoor stood before Mohammed and clenched his fist. With lightning speed, he stepped forward and landed a solid punch to the solar plexus of the unsuspecting prisoner. Mohammed's eyes bulged outward and his mouth opened wide like a drowning fish gasping for air before he fell forward till his chest hit his knees. Mansoor yanked Mohammed's head by the hair, slammed him back into the chair and quickly slapped his injured knee.

Mohammed gave a piercing scream and white knuckled the arms of the chair. Taking deep breaths in an effort to breathe, he stammered. "Yes," he gasped. "I speak English."

Mansoor folded his arms. "That was a warning shot for the next incorrect answer." He locked eyes with the man tied to the chair.

Weston showed no emotion at Mohammed's pain. He didn't have time to play mind games and coax the information out of him. American lives were at stake and he was damned to play by some fucking politicians naive goody agenda. He turned to Mansoor. "Put his feet in the ice. Maybe it will keep him from sweating and smelling like a fucking goat."

Without hesitation, Mansoor slid the bucket over and grabbed the ankles.

"No! No!" Mohammed protested, wildly kicking his bound feet. "Please!" he cried as he tried to kick the ice away.

Mansoor, visibly pissed, stood and withdrew an American Army issue combat knife from its sheath. Mohammed's eyes went wide in fear and opened his mouth to scream. A sharp blow to his head with the steel butt end of the handle shut him up. His body sagged and chin rested on his chest.

On the dazed and confused side of the issue, Mohammed didn't put up any further resistance and his feet were put in the ice.

"What is your real name?" Weston pushed Mohammed's head back.

Mohammed's eyes rolled as his head lolled back and forth.

"Shit." Weston turned to Mansoor. "I think you hit him too hard." There wasn't anger in his voice, but disappointment that they would have to wait to continue.

The Afghan sneered and shrugged nonchalantly. "He'll come around."

They had to wait a half hour for the effects of the blow to the head to wear off before they were able to begin again. During that time, Mohammed was thoroughly checked out by a medic, given the ok to continue the interrogation and had his finger reset. Weston used the lull to grab a bite to eat, drink a cup of coffee and shower and change his ACU.

The minute the prisoner woke, the interrogation continued in earnest. Four hours of mental and physical interrogation, mostly having Mohammed's bare feet placed in and out of the ice, a technique the Soviets used on prisoners in the Gulags, was beginning to have is desired effect. The biggest telltale sign of the prisoner's impending breakage was the revelation on his real name. Ustad.

Ustad's feet were back in the bucket of ice. The skin halfway up his calves had turned pale and he couldn't control his rattling teeth. The early stages of frostbite had set in and the cold was affecting his brain.

"Ok, Ustad, where is the meeting supposed to take place?" Out of the corner of his eye he noticed Mansoor ball his hand into a fist. Ustad noticed it also. He cringed and braced himself for an imminent blow. Weston turned to Mansoor and held up his hand just as Mansoor raised his fist. "Easy."

Ustad didn't respond. He avoided Weston's eyes and stared at the floor, bracing for the strike.

Though he didn't get an answer to the question, he also didn't get a nasty response either, which had been the case in the past. This, Weston thought correctly, was making progress. He switched to a different tact.

Weston took the chair from behind the table and placed it directly in front of Ustad so they were just a few feet apart. "Ustad, listen," Weston spread his hands. "I'm going to ask you some questions, and think of them logically, ok?"

Ustad stared at Weston, trying to comprehend what was being asked. "I don't understand, 'logically,'" he admitted. His teeth chattered and body shook from the ice.

Mansoor rattled something off in Pashto that Ustad understood.

"Ok," Ustad nodded. Then to Weston he said, "I understand."

"Ustad, you believe in your cause, killing Americans, unbelievers, and anyone else that doesn't believe in the same thing as you. Killing yourself in the process and by carrying out your believed duty, do you really think you are going to paradise and have a whole bunch of virgins waiting for you to bed?"

Ustad stared hard at Weston, but in his eyes he was thinking about what Weston had asked.

"Allah doesn't look favorably upon you!" Mansoor sneered and slapped Ustad on the back of his head.

"If the virgin thing is true," Weston continued, "why are there many millions of old Islamic men still in the world? Why are the wise clerics old men? Don't you think they would want to bed all these virgins? Why are they still on this Earth instead of in paradise? What does that tell you? Shouldn't they have led the way and been an example to you?"

Ustad stared hard for just a second and then blinked. His mind was working, but his mouth was deafly silent. He couldn't come up with an answer. Finally, he said weakly, "Because Allah commands us to be martyrs."

"You have believed in lies! Lies!" Mansoor roared and delivered another blow behind Ustad's ear. "All those years you lived learning to hate. For what? Some dog to tell you what you should do that he won't do himself?"

Weston gave him a few moments to think it over before he asked his next question. "Ustad, where is the meeting supposed to take place?"

Ustad hung his head in shame or sorrow.

Weston knew Ustad was a broken man. What caused it he didn't care, just as long as the man talked. "Where, Ustad?"

"In Paktika," he answered weakly. His body was convulsing and his teeth were chattering nonstop.

"Near the border with the Tribal Area?"

"Yes," he whispered, looking down at his frozen feet.

A sense of victory was creeping up on Weston. Ustad was broken and the impending flood of information was about to spill over the dam. "Where exactly is the meeting? Paktika is a big area."

"In Masozai Kili." His body shuddered violently.

Weston was not going to take a chance on the recording devices missing anything Ustad was saying. He grabbed the pen and paper, ready to write down everything Ustad was about to say. "Who's going to the meeting, and why?"

His head lolled back and forth. "Tribal leaders and warlords."

"What about Taliban and al-Qaeda?"

"Yes, them too."

"Mansoor," Weston turned to his counterpart. "Take his feet out of the ice." He believed that Ustad was telling the truth and a reward was to be given.

"Ahhhh!" Ustad cried when his frozen feet were removed.

Weston then threw a towel on them as another gesture, but he wasn't going to let up. "Give me the names of these people, Ustad. Just saying 'tribal leaders and warlords' isn't going to cut it. I'll put your feet back in the ice if I have to." That was a promise he intended to keep.

Ustad shuffled his feet under the towel and winced in pain as they began to warm and the blood flowed. He let out a long breath then began talking. "Afzal Hafeez from Pakistan," was the first name he spilled through still chattering teeth. "Nawaf al-Suqami, someone from Chechnya, I do not know his name. A leader from Ansar-al Islam from Iran will be there. Hezeb Islami Al Gulbadin and some others that I do not know."

Weston let out a whistle. Holy shit! he said to himself. This was the mother load! What a blow they could deal to the terrorists if they could take them out in one swoop! "Who else? There has to be more leaders coming to the meeting."

Ustad closed his eyes and grunted in pain, shuffling his feet to warm them up. He did not answer the question.

"Ustad!" Weston shouted, causing Ustad to jerk his eyes open. "Who else?"

"No more warlords," he said through clenched teeth. The pain in his feet was getting worse as the once frozen blood began to flow freely through his veins. "Taliban. Mainly Taliban."

Weston stared at Ustad as he tried to cope with the pain. "Ok, Ustad, what about weapons and supplies? You have to know your fighters lost a lot of weapons recently. What are you doing about those?"

With a pained expression, Ustad looked at Weston and winced again. He was clearly struggling to keep from crying out. "Ahmed Rashid Halabi is supposed to be there to discuss weapons."

Weston's jaw dropped. Pay dirt! Excitedly he asked, "When is the meeting scheduled?"

"On Sunday. The sixteenth."

"What's the purpose of the meeting?"

"To form a battle plan to kick you, the Americans and the coalition forces out of your base Warrior and eventually Afghanistan."

Weston hesitated a moment, trying to let sink in what Ustad had just said. "Do they really think they are going to be able to achieve that?"

"Yes, they do." he hissed through clenched teeth. "They are going to attack your base. They believe that if they can take over that base and kill many Americans, the Americans will have to pull out. They believe your country, your politicians, will run away when there are many casualties. You have done so in the past, so why won't you do so again?" Ustad seemed exhausted after saying so much in one breath. He gritted his teeth and clutched the arms of the chairs until his knuckles were as white as his feet.

This was it! He had them! Weston was ecstatic and he did everything he could to keep his enthusiasm contained. He wanted to jump and down and run in circles like he scored the winning touchdown with no time remaining on the clock. He leaned back in the chair and shot a glance at Mansoor who had a sly, evil grin on his face.

"Hah! Many bad guys are going to die!" Mansoor clapped his hands.

Weston smiled back, agreeing with Mansoor's statement. They sure are. "What else are they planning, Ustad?"

Monday, November 3, Langley, Virginia

Paul McKnight let out a soft whistle and dropped the five page report submitted by Harold Weston on his paper strewn desk. Criminal elements being involved in espionage was nothing new, but what he just read about the Saudis and the Russian Mafia was incredible. There was no doubt that elected officials on the hill were going to have to be brought in on this.

First he was going to have to run the report past his boss and he glanced at his watch, noting the time and believing Thomas Lawrence, the DCI, Director of Central Intelligence, was already back from the President's Daily Brief. He tapped the papers together, placed them in the file with a red and white striped taped border and walked past his long time secretary, Julie Eastman. "I'm going down the hall." He knew she knew what that meant.

"Right, Paul." When they were alone, Julie had permission to call him by his first name.

It didn't take long to walk the short distance on the carpeted floor, nodding to a few people in the hallway with who he made eye contact with. "Good morning, Barbara," he said to Lawrence's secretary once he stepped into the DCI's outer office. "Is Tom in?"

"Good morning, Director," the attractive older lady countered as she met his smile. "You may go right in."

Getting in to see the DCI was never a problem for McKnight, but usually he had to wait a moment or two to get buzzed past the secretary's desk. Not this time. "Thank you."

He politely knocked on the heavy oak double doors and waited for a reply. He assumed correctly that Barbara was on the phone alerting the DCI he was the one knocking on the door.

"Come in," came the command voice from the other side of the door.

Stepping into the ornate office, he found Lawrence, a graying, slightly overweight man, sitting in the leather wing seat behind the massive mahogany desk that was piled with papers and files. Lawrence looked up from the computer screen with half glasses perched on the end of his nose. "What brings you in, Paul?"

"I have a report from Hannigan, one of my officers in Afghanistan. I believe you'll find it interesting."

Lawrence turned his wrist to glance at his watch. "Give it to me in a nutshell."

"Right." McKnight noticed the DCI was pressed for time. "One of the field officers in Afghanistan discovered the

Russians, probably their Mafia, are running weapons to the highest bidder."

"You've already informed me of that," he answered flatly.

"Yes, sir, I did. Now we have a link that Ahmed Rashid Halabi is the supplier."

Lawrence looked at him with dead pan eyes. "You sure?"

"Yes."

Lawrence thought for a moment and gestured to one of the chairs across from him. "Any relation with that dead Russian, Yezhov?"

McKnight felt confident in his answer as he took a seat. "It's promising. There's another twist."

"What's that?" Lawrence asked with a raised eyebrow.

"When the Rangers rescued my field officer-"

"Puckett, I recall?" The DCI showed he had a good memory.

"That's him. They discovered the identities of a Special Forces A-Team that was assisting the Mujahadeen in the mid-eighties." McKnight paused to let that sink in.

Lawrence folded his hands on the desk. With trepidation he said, "Go on."

"For some reason, this is of interest to the Russians."

"The Kremlin?" His eyes went wide. "Jesus Christ, I hope not."

McKnight quickly shook his head, dispelling that thought. "It doesn't appear that's the case, but all indications point to the Russian Mafia."

"Why would they have an interest in an A-Team?" Lawrence asked the obvious question.

McKnight didn't like not knowing particulars when he spoke about such things and what he was about to declare was tough on him. "That I can't answer."

"Then that tells me the Russian Government needs to get involved. Do they know we have their dead Colonel?"

"No. But we can't acknowledge that we had our people in Afghanistan back then. To this day we are denying it."

Without hesitation, Lawrence issued instructions. "Get the State Department involved on this. I'm sure the Russians want to know who's selling weapons to the Chechens and probably from their military stocks. Also, I'm going to guess that crime organization doesn't share intel with the government so we may avoid and international incident." Lawrence began to push away from the desk, signaling the meeting was over. He amended his statement by saying, "Bring it to the attention of the National Security Advisor as well."

McKnight didn't move. He wasn't finished.

Lawrence paused and eyed his deputy. "What else, Paul?"

This aspect of the conversation was just as important to him as the national security part. He held up two fingers and spoke. "Two men on that A-Team were recently killed."

"Which A-Team? From long ago in Afghanistan?"

"Yes, sir."

Lawrence coolly eyed McKnight. "And you believe there's a connections?"

"Yes. One man was murdered in a car jacking and the other supposedly in a traffic accident."

"What is it that you want?"

"I'm not sure what's going on, but I would like to send some people to keep an eye the rest of the team, very subtly of course." For emphasis he added, "Some of those men have worked for us."

Lawrence leaned back into the chair, steepling his fingers under his chin. Not much time passed before he answered. "I don't believe we have the manpower to offer protection. Besides, men of their caliber and experience, do you believe they need protection? Especially since there is no evidence of what you are suggesting?"

McKnight took Lawrence's final question as his answer. No. "I guess you're right."

This time Lawrence pushed away from his desk and rose to his feet. "If something changes, let me know and we'll take it from there."

"Will do. Thanks for seeing me."

Back in his own office, McKnight stood next to his gleaming desk and picked up the phone, intending to place the call to Ridley Donovan, the National Security Advisor.

But he hesitated for a moment before pushing the speed dial button on the direct line. This situation with the Russians was no doubt a powder keg and the lid was about to be blown into the stratosphere. What kind of ramifications would come about once this information was released and more importantly, would it be believed? He shrugged his shoulders, that was a political decision, all he was doing was putting forth information. Besides, if it got the Russians in hot water with the administration, so be it. He hated the fucking Russians with a passion. He spent most of his life learning to fight against and to destroy them.

He put the phone back in its cradle, sat down in the leather chair and withdrew an Arturo Fuente cigar from the humidor he kept on his desk. He clipped the end off with a razor sharp stainless steel cutter and placed it in his mouth. Being a purist, he withdrew wooden matches from his desk drawer and struck one. In a brilliant blue and orange flame, he touched the lit match to the end of the flavorful, medium bodied cigar. A few puffs to make sure it was lit, he shook the match out and turned on the smoke eater.

Ready now to place the first phone call, he pushed the speed dial button.

The phone was picked up on the second ring. "Donovan."

"Ridley, It's Paul." The two men, like many tasked with national security, worked on a first name basis.

"What can I do for you, Paul?"

McKnight took a breath and gave him the condensed version, knowing Donovan was intelligent enough to piece together the rest.

"Are you sure you have the proof?" Donovan asked with bewilderment in regard to the weapons.

"Yeah," McKnight answered and wondered how the NSA was going to handle what he was going to say next. "And we still have the bodies."

"What?" Donovan's voice roared through the phone. "Are you shitting me? What the hell do you mean you still have the bodies? Why wasn't I told about this earlier, Paul?"

McKnight anticipated this outburst, and it didn't faze him in the least. "We waited until we knew why the Russians were in Turkmenistan and Afghanistan. We weren't just going to call the Kremlin and say 'hey, we just blew away a bunch of your people, where do you want us to deliver the bodies? And by-the-way, one of them is wearing the uniform of a colonel from a mechanized unit.'" Diplomacy wasn't one of McKnight's strong suits.

"Ok, Paul," Donovan said with a slight edge to his voice. He then chuckled. "I get the point. I'll take both issues up with the President. Most likely State will handle the most of it."

"I kind of figured. I'll give them a buzz when I hang up with you and let them know the ball is in their court."

"Right. Paul, no more surprises like that, ok?"

"I'll see what I can do, but no promises." He hung up the phone without hearing Donovan's reply.

McKnight inhaled on the cigar again, savoring the taste in his mouth before he exhaled a white cloud. He then pushed the speed dial button for the Ruler of Foggy Bottom, the Secretary of State.

"Secretary's office," the friendly southern-twanged male voice greeted.

McKnight tried to think of the secretary's name, but it escaped him. "This is Paul McKnight. I need to speak to the Secretary."

"One minute please."

A moment later, the raspy voice of Karen Schmidt came on the line. "Mr. McKnight, why am I blessed to receive a call at this early in the morning from one of our top spies?"

"Ma'am, there's this little thing that happened with a few Russians," McKnight began.

"Oh, shit. I believe I better sit down for this one."

Tuesday, November 4, Albany, New York

As Marcus Kaderri sat at his desk, he realized his mind was getting overworked like a plow horse during planting season. He knew it wasn't just the emotion of losing friends and comprehending the uncertain immortality of one's life, it was the fact that he couldn't shake the feeling that Randall's and Evers' deaths were intertwined and somehow connected to him. He needed to find out if it was true or put it to rest. It was beginning to consume him. That, he knew, was not good. When situations like that happened, he fell into a protective shell and shut out everything around him until he remedied the situation. He didn't withdraw from society, but concentrated so much on the problem, he lost his personality.

To put his mind at ease, to either confirm or deny his suspicions, he needed to bounce his thoughts off someone. Someone he could discuss classified material with. He plucked the phone out of its and cradle and pushed one of the speed dial buttons.

"Director's office," the pleasant female voice answered.

"Bob, please."

After a moment's hesitation, she asked, "Is this Mr. Marc-us?" Clearly she remembered their first conversation.

Kaderri chuckled. "One and the same."

"I'll put you right through."

A moment later Bob Wolff was on the line.

"Marc, you're not calling with another death, are you?"

"No, lunch at the Steer House. It's important." Kaderri was never an alarmist, but his teammates and friends knew that when he said 'It's important,' it really was.

Without hesitation, Wolff answered. "See you in a half hour."

He hung up the phone and donned his suit jacket. It was a beautiful, crisp, sunny day with the temperature hovering in the mid-fifties and Kaderri decided to walk to the restaurant. It afforded him the chance to gather his thoughts without having to worry about wayward pedestrians and automobile traffic if he drove.

"I'm going to lunch," he said aloud as he walked past the receptionist counter. He assumed it was Louise, but didn't bother to look or register her response. He rode the elevator down and put all thoughts of his business aside and concentrated on what he was going to say to Bob without sounding like a paranoid idiot who's ready to get committed.

The doors 'dinged' and he strode across the lobby's marble floor and through the revolving glass doors into the cool air. As he bounded down the stairs to the sidewalk, he paused at the curb and waited for the traffic signal to turn.

It took him fifteen minutes to get to the restaurant and he waited outside for Bob Wolff to arrive.

Dimitri Rykov and Lev Kalanin sat in the warm midnight blue Chevy Impala forty yards away from The Steer House and waited for their target to leave. Not having to use any tricks of their tradecraft, the two former KGB/FSB officers were able to follow their target, Robert Wolff, from his office a dozen blocks north of where they parked to the restaurant on Broadway.

"Are we going to take him out here?" Kalanin asked unemotionally from the passenger side seat.

"I'm not sure it's him," Rykov admitted with a slight shrug.

"How can you not be sure?" Kalanin challenged. "We tracked him from the office where he works and it looks like him!" He shook the photo in his hand. "What more do you want?"

Rykov felt the blood rush to his face. "Because I'm not sure! The photograph of Robert Wolff that we have is not that clear. I don't want to shoot the wrong man!" He slammed an open hand on the steering wheel. "C'mon!" he snapped. "We need to discover if he's got a pattern and exploit it. You know better!"

Kalanin snorted. "Dimitri, I say it's him and we shoot him and get out of here."

Partly, Rykov agreed. It would be good to get out of America and back home to Moscow for a few weeks. He was getting tired. Over the past few weeks they flew halfway around the world and then headed back in the opposite direction. Departing from Moscow to San Diego, California then east to Albany, New York to carry out their assignments was wearing on him, and he knew it was wearing on Kalanin as well. He also knew that when you got tired, you make mistakes. In his business, you couldn't afford to make mistakes. The mistakes could either put your future employment in jeopardy because you screwed up, or it could end your life.

Because he didn't want any of those unfortunate events to occur, he was going to err on the side of caution and track his targets movements to find a pattern and then use it to his advantage.

They were lucky in Phoenix and even luckier in San Diego. Luck was something he couldn't rely on because sooner or later it ran out.

The Steer House lunch crowd, as usual, was bustling. Men and women in business suits out for lunch break or sales reps schmoozing potential clients to land the big deal waited in line to be seated at one of Albany's better restaurants.

Marcus Kaderri and Bob Wolff were two people that did not have to wait in line. Kaderri opened the heavy oak door, walked in and leaned around the corner past the line and spotted the dark haired, middle aged woman wearing an impeccably tailored brown suit. "Hi, Leslie," Kaderri said quietly and waved to the owner as she stood behind the podium.

"Hi, gentlemen," she smiled and discreetly held up two fingers.

Kaderri nodded, indicating there were just the two of them. Being a very frequent guest for both business and pleasure always guaranteed him a table.

Leslie grabbed two leather bound menus and a wine list. "Follow me, please. Your table is waiting."

Smiling, they moved to the front of the line.

The restaurant was divided into two sections. Upon walking in, the main dining room was off to the right and the bar to the left. The dining room had a capacity for ninety patrons and the tables were draped with white lined tablecloths. The walls were paneled with planks of barn wood and were decorated with materials one would see in a blacksmith's shop and a hunters cabin. The bar section had a half dozen wooden high back booths and four bar tables. The bar itself had a dozen leather seated barstools.

Just as soon as Leslie sat them in the dining room, Kaderri's regular dinner server, Jennifer, a cute red head college coed wearing black slacks and a tuxedo shirt, appeared at their table with a pitcher of water.

"Good afternoon, gentlemen," she said with a warm smile and filled the stemware. She turned to Kaderri after she filled his glass, "Where is your beautiful wife?"

Kaderri held his finger up to his lips. "Shhhh. Don't let it get out that I'm married. You're going to ruin my image."

Jennifer smacked him on the shoulder with the note pad. "That's terrible!"

Kaderri laughed. Every opportunity he had he made it known that he was happily married, especially when other women began flirting. "She's probably at home with the kids or at the gym with the kids."

"Oh," Jennifer feigned surprise, "you mean she's working."

"You are correct, smart ass," he always enjoyed joking with her. "Why are you here? Shouldn't you be in class?"

"Tim couldn't make it and I was able to cover. I have class at four. What may I get you to drink?"

Bob answered first. "I'll take a Ketel One martini on the rocks."

"And for you, Mr. Kaderri? The usual?"

"Yes, please."

"I'll be back in a moment." Jennifer turned on her heel and left.

"So what's on your mind, Marc?" Wolff immediately asked and opened the menu.

No sense on dragging this out, Kaderri thought. This was the reason why he asked his friend to come down. "I didn't want to bring this up at either of the funerals, partly because I'm going on gut instinct and because I didn't want you guys to think I was going nuts. I believe Randall's and Evers' deaths are related."

Wolff looked him straight in the eye. "Boss, every guy on your team trusts your gut feelings. Why do you think they're related?"

Kaderri relayed what Puckett had told him and what little information McKnight had provided.

Jennifer arrived with their drinks and placed them on the cocktail napkins. "Are you ready to order?"

"No, Jen, give us a few moments, please."

"No problem." She turned and headed for another table.

"You really believe there's a connection?" Wolff asked after taking a sip of his martini.

"I do," Kaderri admitted and finally opened the menu. "You know as well as I that there are very few coincidences when it comes to events that deal with people in our profession, especially deaths."

Wolff cracked a smile. "Don't you mean former profession?"

Kaderri nodded, sipped his whisky then cautioned. "I have learned, and so have you, that we are never out of this profession, we just slip into the 'inactive' file."

Wolff lifted his head out of his menu. "I'll buy into that. Now, Marc, is there anything you plan on doing? Call the team and give them your theory?"

"I'm not sure. That's why we're here." He took a sip of his whisky before continuing. "I want your thoughts on that." It was a rare showing of a lack of confidence for Kaderri.

Wolff took a sip of his own drink and gathered his thoughts. "I think you should let everyone know. A few guys may actually have the same thoughts as you and if it is true, you may save someone's life. Marc, if nothing else comes of it, so what? No harm will be done."

Kaderri placed the menu down and contemplated what Wolff had said. He was right. What would be the big deal? "That's not a bad idea."

"You may even get some feedback, especially if we start looking over our shoulders." Wolff pressed further. "What about McKnight? You going to let him in on your theory?"

"I haven't decided."

Jennifer reappeared at the table with the pad out and pen poised to write. "Ready yet?"

"I am, Jen." Kaderri nodded and deferred to his trusted friend.

Wolff rechecked the menu before he ordered. "I'll start off with the French onion soup then the buffalo sausage."

"Good choice," Jennifer offered then asked Kaderri. "For you?"

"It's a chilly day so I'll have the New England clam chowder then the flank steak, medium."

"No wine today?" she asked surprised.

"No, have to get back to the office," Kaderri said with a hint of disappointment. He always enjoyed a bottle at dinner and a nice Bordeaux would have gone great with the steak.

In stark contrast to the food being consumed inside The Steer House, Kalanin and Rykov filled their bellies with dirty water hot dogs and cans of soda from the street vendor on the corner. In silence, they ate them in the car.

An hour had passed since they watched Wolff walk into the restaurant. Many times the door opened and patrons entered or left, but none resembled the man they followed or fit the description of Robert Wolff, PhD.

"Do you think he left?" Kalanin read his watch.

"No, I don't think so." Rykov shifted in his seat to work out a kink in his back.

They exchanged concerned glances. "It's been a long time–".

One more time the door opened, and out walked a man with short wavy salt and pepper hair wearing a black overcoat that strongly resembled their target.

"That's him, I'm sure of it," Kalanin sounded cool and confident and withdrew the Makarov pistol from it's shoulder holster under his left arm. "Are we going to take a shot?" He removed the silencer from his coat pocket and screwed it into the barrel.

"No, you fool! Put that away!" Rykov hissed and pushed the gun into Kalanin's lap. "We have nothing in place. We have no escape route, a safe house, and we don't know where the police or security officials are located. Where's your head, man? We went over this an hour ago!" He angrily tapped the notepad on the seat between them. "Take notes!"

Kalanin grunted and holstered the pistol. He let out a big sigh before he spoke. In a conciliatory voice he disclosed, "I'm tired, my friend. You are right. Maybe I need a break from this spy and assassin game."

"I'll keep you straight," Rykov comforted his friend and patted him on the knee. Sometimes he felt the same way.

Their target paused a few steps away from the door and waited for another man to come out and join up with him. Pedestrians walked passed the two men, but they paid no attention to them. They appeared to be engaged in a conversation.

"Who's the target talking to?" Kalanin asked. "Is that someone we should know?"

The two men focused their attention on the man wearing a dark suit and no overcoat. He sported short brown hair and had an aura of confident authority about him.

"I don't know," Rykov answered hesitantly and leaned closer to the window. His breath caused a faint cloud when it hit the cold glass.

From the back seat, Kalanin grabbed the stack of photographs that Mikhail Borushko gave them and shuffled through them. He stopped on the fourth one and held it up. Excitedly, he said, "Ooh, I think he's the big prize, the guy who Wolff is talking to."

Rykov snapped his head around. "The one Borushko wants? Kaderri?"

"Yeah, I think so." He handed Rykov the photographs and picked up the binoculars stowed on the armrest between them to get a close up view.

"Well?" he asked impatiently.

"It's hard to make out. Wolff is standing in the way."

The two men under surveillance began walking down Broadway towards State Street, the opposite way the car was facing.

"Damn!" Rykov punched the steering wheel again and looked out into traffic.

Kalanin wondered what his friend cursed about then realized they were facing the wrong way! How could they forget to realize the two men were going to head back the same way they entered?

"They're moving," Kalanin stated the obvious and brought the binoculars up again and adjusted the focus. Wolff stepped aside and Kalanin, with a clear, unobstructed view, looked directly into the face of the other man. "That's him!" he declared before Kaderri turned away.

Rykov started the car. "No shit. Keep an eye on them while I turn around." Impatiently he waited for a break in the traffic, tapping his palms on the steering wheel. "Shit!" There was little chance of making a u-turn across four lanes without drawing attention. A half dozen cars drove past before an opening appeared. With no other choice he pulled out and drove in the opposite direction.

"Come on!" Kalanin urged. "We're going to lose them! Turn around!" He twisted his head, searching out the back window to find the two men. "I'm losing them in the crowd!"

"I know!" Rykov shot back. He had to drive down a few blocks before he was able to turn around and get going in the right direction on Broadway. He carefully weaved in and out of traffic, being careful not cut off anyone that would cause them to blow their horn and draw attention to themselves. "Do you see them?"

Kalanin searched frantically, scanning the sidewalk. They couldn't have gotten far in the short time it took them to turn around. "There! I think." He pointed to spot on the sidewalk in front of an electronics store front. "Hurry up!"

They drove a few more yards when he came to a red traffic signal that had halted the line of traffic. "Shit!" Rykov hit the breaks hard, causing Kalanin to thrust his hands out to prevent him from slamming into the dashboard. "We're going to lose them! Can you still see them?"

"No!" Kalanin spat disgustedly and slammed his fist on the dash. "You keep going down the road. I'm going on foot." He opened the door and jumped onto the sidewalk, his fast gait propelled him through the throng of pedestrians.

Rykov impatiently tapped the steering wheel, waiting for the light to turn green and the traffic to move.

Wednesday, November 5, Masozai Kili, Afghanistan

It had been four days since Mohammed had been sent out to Ruby to bring the weapons and Ustad back. The lack of contact with them over the past few days wasn't that much of a concern, telecommunications was almost non-existent. Nawaf Al Suqami wanted limited contact for fear the Americans would be able to zero in on their signal and locate both the weapons cache and his hidden camp. But some sort of communication, like using a runner, would have been nice to keep him updated on the progress.

Finally, as he contemplated sending another fighter out, news reached his ears and it was not what he wanted to hear.

Standing hunched over across the table in his building was Mohammed. He was covered in dirt and grime from head to toe and his tan payraan tumbaan tunic had turned to the color of mud. Dried blood, apparently from someone else, was splattered across his chest and neck and his eyes were hollow and bloodshot. An AK-47 was slung over his shoulder along with an empty bandolier that had once held a dozen fully loaded magazines.

Al Suqami was so angry that his balled fists were shaking, but he couldn't direct his anger at Mohammed. He did his job to the best of his ability and was ready to pass out from exhaustion.

"Gone? All gone you say?" Al Suqami hissed in disbelief and gestured to him to take a seat.

"All of it," Mohammed whispered and pulled a chair over to sit before he fell. "Most of the men, too." Seventeen had returned and some of them would not live much longer.

Al Suqami blew a gasket. He rocketed out of his seat which crashed to the floor behind him. "How is this happening?" Before he let Mohammed answer, he strode around the table and motioned for his bodyguards to follow. "Get up, Mohammed, we're going to Ruby!" He needed to see what happened with his own eyes.

Mohammed turned in the chair and stared in disbelief. "What? Why? There is nothing there!"

Al Suqami stopped in his tracks, turned and gave Mohammed an icy stare. "Are you afraid to go back there? Why?" He put his hands on his hips and leaned forward so his nose was in Mohammed's face. "Is there something you are not telling me?" His tone was sarcastic and accusatory.

An expression of fear exploded across Mohammed's face and balled his fists. He rose defiantly from the chair. "Afraid? Yes, I am afraid," he nodded emphatically. "Afraid we will meet the same fate for no reason! All that's at Ruby are pieces of our brave fighters or bodies that the Americans have not buried."

"Let's go," Al Suqami demanded. "You will show me."

Just over an hour later as the rounded a tall, rock hill, Al Suqami ordered Mohammed, "Stop here." They had driven the battered Isuzu Trooper over the rough terrain to a location two hundred meters above and five hundred meters away from the small plain where the Ruby weapons cache was located. In the event that American forces were still in the area, Al Suqami played it safe and remained far enough way as not to get spotted. He stepped out of the vehicle and moved to stand in front of it. He brought a pair of binoculars to his eyes and surveyed the scene below.

The ground looked as if it was plowed and tilled and ready for planting. Everywhere he looked were scars of a battle. Scorched rock and earth where grenades and RPG's detonated and bigger, deeper holes from helicopter fired rockets. Spent shell casings littered the ground, the brass glittered in the sun like thousands of fireflies floating in the night. A few bloated bodies were there as well. Most disturbing was the freshly turned dirt where the weapons were hidden. A sense of fear shook him.

"Like I said, there is nothing here," Mohammed offered quietly, leaning against the hood.

"I see," Al Suqami mumbled crossly. He set the binoculars on the hood and rubbed his chin. "All the bodies. I only see a few. Where are they? And the pits with the weapons?" Seeing the evidence, Al Suqami erased all doubts he had of Mohammed not telling the truth. "Tell me what you can. What happened here?""

Mohammed let out a long breath and moved next to Al Suqami. He stared out over the battlefield and gathered his thoughts before he described the fight. "After I gathered the men like you asked-I was able to get almost one hundred-we came up this way," he pointed to the direction they traveled. "I sent fifty out right away before I gathered everyone else-"

Al Suqami cut him off. "How much time passed before you were able to catch up with the rest of the men?"

Without hesitation, Mohammad answered. "About and hour."

"Go on."

"I was able to get six horse carts to bring the weapons back. When we got to this point," he pointed to the ground at his feet, "we saw the battle. American helicopters were circling and firing and their soldiers were attacking. Most of us rushed down to help but others decided that the battle was already lost and left. We tried to defeat the Americans but…they killed many of us. Few were able to get away. After the Americans killed us and removed the weapons, they buried most of the bodies in the weapons pits."

Al Suqami remained silent, his emotions simmered. He then turned to Mohammed and pointed to the dried bloodstains on his clothing. "That is not your blood?"

Mohammed shook his head. His hollow eyes focused on the distance. "It's Yousefs. He was next to me when he was shot in the head. His blood and brains splattered all over me." His voice trailed off. "I tried to wipe it off."

Suddenly a frightening thought came to Al Suqami. Alarmed, he asked, "Where is Ustad?"

Mohammed shook his head and scratched his beard. "I don't know. Dead probably." He pointed to scorched section near the turned dirt of the pits. "He was leading the defense from that location the last time I saw him."

Al Suqami's body shuddered like he was shot with electricity.

Thursday, November 6, Albany, New York

Surveillance was boring. Period. Especially if there was no activity to watch on the target. But there were many forms of entertainment taking place outside the car to distract Gary Trainor and Joanne Bauer from their assignment. Of particular enjoyment for the pair was an elderly drunk man leaning against a lamp post who tried to serenade every woman who walked passed. A few slaps to his face was the only reward he had for his efforts. Finally, he stumbled away to another location.

"This sucks," Trainor confessed as he unwrapped his roast beef and Swiss cheese sandwich.

"What does?" Joanne Bauer asked, still watching the house through the passenger side window. "This case or your sandwich?"

"The case. I know we wanted to take one, but shit, this is worse than sitting in the office listening to Weymer bitch and moan." He took a healthy bite and wiped the excess Russian dressing from the corners of his mouth with a paper napkin.

"You're right. He does complain about everything. What's the tally so far for today?" she asked, meaning the number of people who entered the house.

Trainor glanced at the tick marks on the clipboard wedged in between the two front seats. "Six," he answered around a mouthful of food. He swallowed before continuing. "Same as yesterday. I even think it's the same people."

"Think they figured out they are under surveillance and moved to another location?"

That was a possibility. They took precautions to prevent being spotted, such as changing cars, altering their appearance, and wearing clothes that was indigenous to the neighborhood. At the moment, Trainor wore baggy pants, a worn leather jacket and baseball hat with its bill canted sideways. Joanne slipped on tight jeans with an oversized sweatshirt under a down vest and a purple knit cap. Despite their safety measures, being exposed was a real possibility, primarily because they were two white people in a predominately black neighborhood.

"Could be," he accepted. Trainor adjusted his sunglasses and focused his attention on a tall black man headed their way on the sidewalk. He wore a black, unbuttoned trench coat and a red knit cap over long dread locks that swayed with every step. Trainor could see and *feel* the man staring at them as he walked past. This was a man to watch out for, Trainor told himself.

"Great," Joanne spoke without noticing Trainor's concentration was focused elsewhere. "I haven't seen any inclination that this guy, Jackson, is near this house."

"Humph," Trainor grunted and put his attention in the rearview mirror. The man who walked past a moment ago turned around and was on his way back. This time a shorter man joined him on the sidewalk. They were staring icily at the car. Calmly, Trainor alerted Joanne. "Company, Jo. Use your mirror and put the camera away."

"Right," Joanne said, pointed the camera at the mirror and snapped a few frames before she put the camera on the floor. "I see 'em. Mean looking sons-of-bitches."

"Looks like Dreadlocks is coming to my side and you got Shorty." He came up with the two names to differentiate between the two. "Let's keep our identities quiet unless it's necessary, ok?" Trainor reached for the door handle while his other hand lowered the jacket zipper for easy access to the pistol. "Maybe they're just pissed we're in their parking spot or something."

"Yeah, that's it," she snorted. Her hand felt for her sidearm on her hip.

Trainor's heart jumped as Dreadlocks pulled open his coat and withdrew a baseball bat, wound up and slammed it into the side of the car. *Whump!* The car rocked on its tires. "Get out motherfucker!" he slammed the car again, the quarter panel crushing under the heavy blow.

The two detectives immediately exited the car. Trainor stood in the street in front of the opened door and fought the instinct to pull the gun from the shoulder holster and level it at Dreadlocks forehead. "What the fuck you doin' man?" Trainor yelled in a street voice. He spread his arms in bewilderment and to show he wasn't armed. Dreadlocks readied the bat for another swing. "Stop! What the fuck is wrong with you?"

"Why the fuck you here, cracker?" Dreadlocks challenged. "I been watching you, man! You tryin' to move in on my territory? I gonna split you fuckin' head!"

Trainor eyed the few people who looked in their direction, but most minded their own business and kept going. He was more concerned with the other thug, Shorty, who was on the passenger side facing Bauer with his hand hovering near the opening in his black overcoat. Trainor was sure he was hiding something more dangerous than a baseball bat.

"Easy man," Trainor tried to calm the excited drug dealer. "Hey man, who are you? What's your name?" He attempted to build a rapport, calm the guy down and get some information out of him before this erupted into a firefight.

"None of you fuckin' business man!" Spittle flew from his lips and he raised the bat higher, ready to deliver another blow. "Just get the fuck outta here before I fuck you up good, man!"

"Yo, easy man!" Trainor shot back. The urge to pull his weapon was becoming stronger. There were times when Trainor's patience was paper thin and he sprang into action, usually resulting in bodily harm for a suspect.

"We meant no disrespect," Joanne quickly threw out the popular phrase, attempting to ease the tensions and calm the excited nut. The pissed off sneer on Dreadlocks seemed to soften a bit and he lowered the bat to his waist. "Know what I mean? No disrespect," she repeated.

Out of the corner of his eye, Trainor saw two other detectives who were on the surveillance get out of their car and start walking towards them. With Joanne garnishing the attention, he deftly waved the help off. Trainor immediately decided against trying to establish anything with Dreadlocks and his goal now was to get out of there alive and without their identity being discovered. He threw up his hands and eased back towards the open car door. "Hey, no prob, man. We'll get out of here." He slowly backed into the car, keeping a watchful eye on the two thugs.

"Uh-huh, that's right, cracker!" Dreadlocks chanted, tapping the bat into his hand. "Yous get your fuckin' white asses out of here."

Without another word, the detectives closed the doors, their hands still hovering around their pistols. Trainor started the engine and pulled into traffic.

"Now what?" Joanne asked, fear and anger in her voice.

Trainor kept one eye on the two men and one on the road until they were out of danger. "We go back to the station and see what Chiles wants us to do next."

CHAPTER TWELVE

Thursday, November 6, Albany, New York

"What are you two doing here?" Lieutenant Chiles stopped in his tracks and asked not to pleasantly when he walked into his office and found Gary Trainor and Joanne Bauer sitting in front of his desk.

"We have a problem," Joanne answered, playing with the pull strings on her sweatshirt.

Chiles closed the door and sat behind his desk. "What problem?"

Trainor scratched the back of his neck. "We were chased out of the area."

"By who?" Concern crept into Chiles' voice.

"A couple of local drug dealers."

"Were you made?" Chiles winced in anticipation.

Trainor shook his head. "I don't think so. This druggie was under the impression we were trying to move into his territory and he decided to rearrange the appearance of the car to make us leave."

"Do you know who these guys are?"

"Nope," said Trainor, then added, "when I asked him his name, he threatened me with bodily harm and I thought it best not to press the issue."

"We left him with the idea that he was right," Joanne interjected, "about moving in on his territory. We obliged with his demands and got out of his territory. It was the only plausible story to come up with without revealing our identity or bringing other officers to our plight. But I think he had a suspicion. You don't see too many white chicks in the area."

"Ok," Chiles nodded, clearly seeing their point. He looked at Trainor and gave a sly smile. "Glad to see you made it out of the situation without shooting or roughing up anyone. A damaged car is easy to take care of."

Trainor knew Chiles made light of the prior shootouts he was involved in, specifically the case where he wanted to arrest Marcus Kaderri for the murders of a handful of drug dealers but an intercession from the federal government on Kaderri's behalf stating he was on assignment with their authority prevented that from happening. The public result was the bad guy got away and it was a ribbing among the force that Trainor had to put up with. Only a few on the force knew the truth and it was difficult for them to not come to Trainor's defense. "Gee, thanks Lieutenant. I figured you didn't want to go in front of the civilian review board again on my behalf," Trainor retorted with a jab at another incident he was involved in where he happened upon a bank robber and beat him up. It didn't matter he recovered the money. The public activists cried foul about police brutality and Chiles stood behind his detective.

Chiles chuckled. "Good thinking. I do truly appreciate your concern."

Joanne was keen to pick up on the private joke and she heard rumors what had really happened and smartly shied away from the topic. "What do you want us to do now?" she asked.

Chiles rubbed his chin and put his feet on the desk. "You said the other surveillance units are still on scene, correct?"

"Yeah. I think we were an isolated incident. Oh," Joanne held up the camera. "I snapped a few frames of the subjects in the mirror as they approached the car. I didn't check to see how they came out." She moved to turn the camera on to view the pictures in the view screen.

Chiles waved her off. "Get them printed out and distributed. In the mean time, sit tight. Word on the street may have spread about you two."

Thursday, November 6, Loudonville, New York

Three out of the four members of the Kaderri family were sound asleep. The bulky down comforters and soft flannel sheets were pulled up tight to protect them from November's cold wind and in the master bedroom, a soft fire crackled.

Marcus Kaderri sat at the polished desk in the first floor den. A once roaring fire that spewed warmth and light had died to bright red embers and ashes. Only a few pops were heard instead of the continuous crackle of the burning wood. But he ignored all that as his fingers flew over the keyboard, entering the last of his team's e-mail addresses.

Before he sent the letter regarding his theory about the deaths of Patrick Randall and John Evers, he reread the letter one more time. Satisfied with the content, he moved the cursor to the 'send message' box and clicked the mouse.

A long deep sigh escaped his nostrils as he leaned back into the soft leather chair and stretched, interlocking his fingers behind his head. He looked at the screen and wondered what kind of replies was he going to receive? His first thought was that his team was going to think he was nuts.

Slowly his thoughts changed regarding the letter. What's done is done. If they thought he was nuts, so be it. He sincerely believed the deaths of Evers and Puckett were assassinations. His CIA training and military experience taught him to think in other ways, to look at what was *not* there and what in the past could be relevant for the present. The more he thought about it, the more he began to think in terms of personal security. Beginning tomorrow, he would alter his daily routine, begin looking over his shoulder, and keep an extra eye on Sara and the kids.

He let out another concerned sigh. Once again, his past was catching up to his present and this time he didn't know why. A long, jaw locking yawn snuck up on him, signaling it was time to turn in for the night. The clock on the computer indicated it was almost midnight. He shut the computer down and pushed out of the chair. He made sure the mesh screen was secure so no embers could pop out of the fireplace, and checked the doors and windows one more time.

Friday, November 7, Albany, New York

Dimitri Rykov and Lev Kalanin shared the two bedroom suite on the tenth floor of the Crowne Plaza Hotel on the corner of State Street and Pine Street. They had booked the room for ten days, though they believed they wouldn't need it for more than a week. Their next target, Robert Wolff, should be dead within the week.

What had started out as a promising day two days ago, had turned into something of a problem. They found and tracked their intended target, Robert Wolff and accidentally stumbled upon the jackpot, Marcus Kaderri. Then just more than an hour after that discovery, the two men were lost after they exited the restaurant. Through prior surveillance, Rykov and Kalanin could easily pick up the trail of Wolff, it was Kaderri who they had very little information on and gathering it caused a dilemma.

Mikhail Borushko kept Kaderri's information all to himself and he gave specific orders not to do anything regarding Kaderri until or if he gave the go-ahead. The problem they faced was what to do if Kaderri was around Wolff when they were ready to kill him? By appearances, Kaderri worked in the city as well, evidenced that Wolff walked to the restaurant alone and Kaderri and he walked out of the restaurant together.

Because of those strict rules laid down by Borushko, the two assassins waited until now to call Borushko and inform him they spotted Kaderri. Until they received new orders, they were going to concentrate on their primary task of tracking and killing Robert Wolff and hope that Kaderri didn't make his appearance at the time of the hit.

Kalanin stuck his head out of the bathroom. "Are you ordering breakfast?"

Rykov was on the love seat sipping coffee and reading the hotel provided local newspaper. Without looking up, he pointed to the coffee pot on the counter. "I made a pot of coffee. Help yourself."

"That's not enough." Kalanin dabbed his face with a towel and wiped away the excess shaving cream. Wrapped in a towel he made for the desk telephone. "I need something more substantial."

"You're right," Rykov agreed. "I'll take two eggs over easy with a side of sausage. And get a large pot of coffee with cream and sugar."

Kalanin grumbled under his breath then dialed room service. When he hung up, Rykov put out the agenda for the day. "I think it's a good idea to track Wolff a little more. I'm also going to call Borushko and tell him a few things."

"Like what?" Kalanin frowned upon contacting the boss.

Rykov folded the newspaper and dropped it on the table. "I've been thinking about our assignment. It is too much for us to handle alone. To be hopping around this country and pulling off all these assassinations is crazy. Most of our contacts over here have dried up since the Wall came down, leaving us short of help. We don't have access to the intelligence databases like we used to to get detailed information on these men. We don't know what kind of history they have or what they are capable of." The Internet could provide many of the details they needed but the true information obtained from secure networks and classified information was what they needed to make a sound plan. Rykov was going to be adamant about slowing down their task.

"What do you think Borushko's going to say, Dimitri?" Kalanin asked, easing himself down on one of the chairs.

Rykov gave a shrug. "I don't know and I don't care. If we keep this up we are going to get sloppy. If we get sloppy, we get hurt." He shook his head and gritted his teeth. "I'm not going to get hurt. If I have to, I will call Mirovich."

"That's playing with fire my friend," Kalanin warned.

Rykov nodded in agreement. "I don't care. We were foolish in not planning this better and I'm done being foolish for a man who wants to rush things and does not know what he is doing."

Friday, November 7, Moscow, Russia

Dinner time had come and gone without him eating a thing. Unlike in the army where all meal times were regulated, Mikhail Borushko enjoyed the simple luxury of choosing when and where he wanted to eat. The transition from military life and the old regimented communist system went a lot smoother than he anticipated. Once he was finished with his task for the evening in Borushko Hardware, he was looking forward to a delicious venison dinner and a few glasses of vodka.

Laboring inside the store with him were mostly legitimate employees. They were busy stocking shelves with various tools and other hardware, placing fixtures, washing windows and doing everything else necessary to get the store open. Sprinkled in were a few low ranking members of the Solntsevskaya.

As the work continued, Borushko stood in the middle of the receiving dock scattered with loaded pallets of merchandise. He scanned the list of invoices of delivered hammers, saws, toggle bolts, cabinet handles and just about anything else that could be found in a hardware store. "There you are," he said aloud and pulled the one invoice that meant the most. He dropped the rest of the papers on a pallet of boxed light fixtures and strode over to another shrink wrapped pallet. "Hey, you two," he called over to the two men unpacking boxes of electrical wire.

They looked over at the sound of the owner calling to them. "Yes, Mr. Borushko?" They weren't more than twenty years old and working on their first job.

"Go take a twenty minute break, you've been working hard." They weren't members of the Solntsevskaya and Borushko didn't want them around when he dismantled the pallet.

The two young men smiled at their boss' praise. "Right! Thank you!" they beamed and headed for the swinging door that led into the store.

Satisfied the two men were out of sight and ear shot, Borushko motioned to one of the Solntsevskaya men to close and lock the door. "Open that one," Borushko ordered and pointed to the pallet he wanted. The men went to work on the six-foot high stack of ninety kilo bags of sand held together with clear plastic shrink wrap.

One man produced a box cutter from his trouser pocket and began cutting the wrap with quick deliberate slices. Another man arrived with a flatbed cart to restack the sand. After all, it was merchandise that would be on the sales floor.

"Take it apart," Borushko said a little impatiently. He needed to know if his special, untraceable merchandise was in there.

Immediately the men began dismantling the stack, heaving the bags onto the cart. Borushko tapped his foot, biting his tongue to encourage the men to move faster.

Five minutes and half the stack later, one of the men wiped his sweaty brow, stood and pointed to the two wooden crates amid the bags of sand. "There they are, Misha."

Borushko's eyes fell on the rectangular gray-green boxes. The top one had white stenciling, identifying the contents as property of the Russian Army. "Open them."

Simultaneously they wiped the sweat from their brow and retrieved crow bars from a collection of tools on the dock floor. Squeaks resounded off the walls as the wood top was pried open. A final pop signaled the last nail gave way and the top was off. Borushko reached in and pulled out one of twenty brand new Makarov PM pistols and a dozen silencers. "Good," he said and placed the pistol back in the crate. He pointed to the other crate. "Now open the other."

The same squeaks and pops were repeated as the top was opened on the second box. In this box his eyes fell upon fist sized bags of white powder. "Excellent." He clapped his hands together as a smile spread upon his face. His contact came through! A half million dollars in heroin and weapons. His new business venture was off to a smooth start. "Test it," he directed, "make sure it's real."

"Right."

The cell phone on his belt chirped. He removed it from its cradle and stared at the numbers on the display screen. "Rykov, do you have good news for me?"

Rykov's voice was upbeat. "It's possible, depending on how you look at it."

"What do you have for me?" He asked guardedly.

"We are making progress and need more men to handle this assignment. If we keep going the way we are, we are going to get sloppy and something bad will happen."

"What do you mean? You successfully took out the first two, so why can't you continue?"

"We were lucky, that's all. You should know, Misha," Rykov said in a reasoning and firm voice. "When you had troops in the field, you knew their limitations. Well, Lev and I have reached ours."

Borushko remained silent, letting what the former KGB officer said sink in. Rykov must have taken the silence for him to continue.

"Anyway, we also believe we found your man, Kaderri."

Borushko's heart skipped a beat and he felt a tingling sensation in his fingers. He swallowed the lump that suddenly formed in his throat. "Are you sure?"

"We're confident," came the answer in a self-assured voice.

"What do you mean?" he growled. Borushko liked solid information, especially when it pertained to this.

"We were tracking Robert Wolff and the two men met. Since we weren't looking for Kaderri, as per your request, we didn't study up on him. But we believe he met with Wolff for lunch."

"Find out if that was Kaderri you spotted," he said immediately and forcefully.

"Fine," Rykov said without urgency. "What about sending other men to help out?"

Borushko's excitement was about to bubble over like a covered pot of boiling water. He had his prized possession within his grasp and wanted to leap across the Atlantic Ocean to make the kill. If he acted upon this information, he knew the original plan to demoralize Kaderri and make him paranoid would fall apart. But so what? Why prolong what he wanted when it was there for the taking? As commander of the unit that killed his father, Kaderri would know who actually killed the general. He would get the information out of him one way or another. He issued new instructions. "Back off of Wolff. Don't take him out yet. I don't want you two to alert Kaderri to your presence. Keep both of them under surveillance and I will see you soon. There is another team already in America."

There was a long pause. "So you are coming here?"

"Yes," Borushko confirmed. "I'll be there in a few days. Send me the data on where you are."

"Right."

Borushko disconnected the phone call and absentmindedly placed the phone back on his hip. His mind raced on how to accelerate to the final phase of his plan that no one but he knew about. He wanted Rykov and Kalanin taking no part in that phase but the three men he counted on to go along with him in killing Kaderri were still in Chechnya.

Saturday, November 8, Albany, New York

The smell of his favorite breakfast, sizzling bacon, sautéed home fries and scrambled eggs woke Gary Trainor. The mouthwatering flavors curled into his nose, and stimulated his taste buds. He raised his groggy head from the pillow and inhaled once again.

He threw the covers off and swung his feet over the bed and put on his shorts. Sleeping naked was something he ordinarily didn't do, but he and Amanda had less than a week before all carnal delights were voluntarily suspended until their wedding night and they were pleasuring each other as much as they could.

The weekend was planned for sex. All kinds of sex. They were going to make tender love in the bedroom to no holds barred fucking around the house and only their imaginations were going to hinder their efforts.

Like a bloodhound led by his nose, Trainor tracked the smell of freshly brewed coffee. The closer he got to the kitchen, the stronger the aroma, and the more his mouth watered. His stomach suddenly growled in hunger. He followed the scent and when he entered the kitchen he stopped dead in his tracks. Amanda was at the stove, stirring the home fries wearing only an apron which was secured at her waist. The ties were dangling over her naked backside looking like a Christmas present ready to be unwrapped. Leather moccasins were on her feet.

"Whoa!" he gasped, taking in her hourglass shape. Her attire caught him completely off guard. His manhood began to stir.

"Good morning, honey." She spun around with the spatula in her hand and her breasts jiggled under the bib of the apron. "Do you like my apron?" She gave him a kiss.

Trainor felt his erection grow. "If the food is comparable to the way the chef dresses, I'm going to like the way the food tastes!"

She wiggled her bottom and went back to the sizzling home fries. "Take a seat."

After he poured himself a mug of coffee, he did as instructed by the goddess queen of the kitchen and sat sideways on wooden spindled chair at the table.

"Today we are having brunch."

"Brunch?" He looked at the wall clock and the hands read eight in the morning. Then he turned to the counter for any sandwiches or something else that would resemble a traditional brunch but didn't spot anything. "Um, are you sure we're having brunch? Aren't we missing a few items. Like the lunch part?"

"This is my version of brunch," she turned with a smile and lifted her apron. "This is the lunch part for you and" she pointed to his growing erection, "I see you have your lunch entree ready for me!"

She dropped the apron and turned back to the stove where she plated the food.

Trainor's erection grew to full mast at her stunt. He was going to like this kind of brunch! "Nice!"

Amanda puts the plates on the table and stared at Trainor's erection. A devious smile spread across her face and she hooked her long hair behind her ears. All of a sudden, she bent down, freed his cock from his shorts and swirled her tongue across the tip. A few delicious moments later, she ended the tease and sat down. "It's time to eat your breakfast."

"This isn't fair!" he stammered. "First you flash me and then give a few teasing licks!"

"I'm sorry, honey, here, maybe this will refocus your mind." She pulled the apron string over her head, dropping it into her lap and exposing her breasts.

"Yeah, sure!" He groaned. "Sitting there like that is only going to help drive me crazy!" He swung the chair and his legs around so they were under the table.

"Don't forget, dear, you're sitting there with a hard-on. What do you think that's doing to me?"

He asked with a smile of his own, "I don't know. Why don't you tell me?"

Amanda bit her bottom lip. "It's getting me all excited." She pointed a finger at him and changed her facial expression. "Eat your breakfast. You're going to need your energy."

Their desire for each other caused the almost newlyweds to rush through the meal. In record time, Trainor finished the last of his eggs and with a clang, dropped the fork on the plate as if he'd just won a race. "I'm done," he stated, eager to begin the brunch part.

"I'm not," Amanda pointed to the small pile of perfectly seasoned home fries. She placed her toes on his erection under the table and wiggled them.

The teasing was too much for him.

"You're done now!" He shot from the table, grabbed the plates and put them on the counter. When he turned around, he found Amanda sitting on the table, leaning back with her heels on the edge and legs spread wide. A beckoning grin and gleaming smile in her eyes caused his pounding heart to miss a beat and his manhood to throb.

She flicked her long chestnut hair behind her shoulders and signaled a 'come hither' motion with her index finger. "Lunch is served"

Excitedly, he moved between her legs. But instead of diving right in like she wanted and expected, he began kissing inside her raised knee, soft, light kisses that gave her goose bumps.

"Oh, you tease!" she sighed.

He left a trail of kisses down her inner thigh, getting closer and closer to her womanhood. "You think you call all the shots?" he challenged between kisses. Slowly he moved closer, giving tiny nips to her toned muscle. His fingers tickled her moist lips, circling them, tracing the outlines of her folded flesh. She moaned again, enjoying his touch.

By now her clit was swollen, protruding from under its protective hood, and he gave it a slight lick as he continued the kisses up the other leg.

"Oh, God, Gary! You're driving me nuts!" Amanda gasped and gripped the edge of the table.

A grin formed on his lips. "I know."

The exhaustive first round of their morning romp came to an end just under a half hour later. Not once did they leave the kitchen, and utilized the counter, table and chairs. They sat at the table and replaced their spent energy by drinking a large glass of fruit juice. Orange for him, and cranberry for her.

"You know," Trainor said while still breathing deeply, "I'm never going to look at the kitchen the same way again."

Amanda giggled. "Me either, especially the next time I'm chopping something on the counter."

Trainor leaned forward and pursed his lips. "I love, you babe."

She met his lips. "I love you too. What's new at work?" She dabbed at the beads of sweat that still clung to her forehead from the vigorous escapade.

"Joanne and I got pulled off our last assignment."

"Why?"

Trainor shrugged and sipped his juice before answering. "We were made."

She furrowed her brow. "What do you mean, 'made'? You mean compromised?"

"Yeah, sort of," he disclosed. "A couple of drug dealers thought we were dealers moving in on their turf and persuaded us to move our business."

"What do you mean 'persuaded'?" Apprehension sounded in her voice and her eyes grew a little bigger. "Do I really want to know?" She waved her hand and shook her head. "Never mind, forget I asked."

He didn't want to keep her completely in the dark, she had a right to know. "It was a little tense for a moment or two. One of them had a baseball bat and beat up the car to scare us away." Mentioning the other dealer with his hand near the opening of his coat apparently ready to use a gun wasn't necessary.

"I guess it worked?"

"Uh-huh." He jerked his thumb over his shoulder. "We high tailed it out of there and let him keep his territory."

"When did this happen?"

"Thursday."

"Humph," Amanda grunted. "What's your next assignment? Did you get one yet?"

He shook his head. "No, but I'm sure something will come up. It always does."

CHAPTER THIRTEEN

Monday, November 10, Albany, New York

Since the duo got pulled off the crack house surveillance assignment, Gary Trainor and Joanne Bauer were back at their desks and on the rotation. Trainor had his feet up and was reading the sports pages while Bauer leafed through old files. Styrofoam cups filled with lukewarm, bitter coffee were on the desks. It was another day on the job.

"How was your weekend?" Joanne asked from across the desk.

"The answer is still the same as the last time you asked." It was the second time in twenty minutes. She was fishing for details and he wasn't about to take the bait. He was never one to kiss and tell.

"Oh, I already asked?" she furrowed her brow.

"Uh-huh. Are you lost in space or something? What did you do this weekend that's made you forgetful?" Her behavior was unusual so he studied her for a moment. Maybe she wasn't fishing for lurid details, she wanted to say something but didn't know how to go about it. "You drunk or something?"

"No!" she shook her head quickly. "Well," she blushed. "I met a guy-"

Trainor cut her off. "You're love struck!" He was instantly happy for her. She wasn't the most attractive lady and sometimes had difficulty getting dates. She had low cheek bones, a non-descript chin and pair of brown oval shaped eyes that were just a little too close to the bridge of a somewhat long pointy nose.

"Sort of," she blushed a little more like a teenager instead of a thirty-something mature adult.

He could tell she wanted to talk about her encounter and was ready to listen. He dropped the paper. "Ok, Jo, tell me about–,"

She gladly launched right into it. "I went out with my lady friends on Friday-"

"Hey, Gary, Joanne," Chiles interrupted from his office doorway, ending her tale. "Come in here."

Trainor swung his feet off the desk and pushed himself away from the desk. He picked up his coffee cup and looked over to his partner. "Tell me about him later."

"I will," she beamed. The redness in her cheeks faded as they got closer to Chiles' office.

"What is it, Lieutenant?" Trainor asked, pausing in the doorway, blocking access to Joanne. A push from behind caused him to move. "Sorry, Jo."

"Close the door," Chiles instructed with a concerned look.

Trainor grabbed a seat, knowing they were going on another case. Joanne closed the door then sat in the chair next to him. They exchanged cautious glances.

Chiles sat behind his desk. "I have an assignment for you two."

"Ok."

Chiles looked directly at Trainor. "I got a phone call a little while ago from Paul McKnight."

Trainor felt as if he were hit with a hammer to his chest. "Oh, shit." He shook his head and rubbed his temples with his thumb and middle finger and sank further into the chair. Memories came rushing back from last time he worked on a case or better coined, a mission, that involved this man.

"Who's Paul McKnight?" Joanne asked.

"Tell me," Trainor directed his question to Chiles. "Does this next assignment involve Kaderri and Wolff?"

"Who's this guy McKnight?" Joanne repeated the question.

Chiles and Trainor carried on their conversation. "That's a given, Gary. I don't believe this is anything like the last couple of dealings you had."

"What's going on?" Joanne insisted, putting an edge to her voice. "Who are McKnight, Kaderri and Wolff?"

The two men continued their conversation, oblivious to Joanne. "Should I hold you to that, Lieutenant?" Trainor didn't believe him. Experience tells a different story.

Joanne exploded out of her chair and shouted. "What the hell are you two talking about? Is it ok if I get in on the details since I'm supposed to be in on this?"

Dumbfounded, Trainor looked up at her. "Huh?"

"Sorry, Joanne," Chiles stammered and scratched the bald spot on the top of his head. "You had a question?"

She visibly relaxed with a long exhale through her flared nostrils then sat back down. "Who's McKnight?"

"A man who won't allow us to be bored anymore." Trainor answered smartly.

Joanne held her hands out, palms up. "Why?"

"He's CIA."

Joanne's eyes nearly popped out of her head in both confusion and astonishment. "What? We're going to be working for the CIA now?"

"In a matter of speaking," Chiles informed them. "He's in charge of all the spy operations for the country."

"What does that mean?" she inquired cautiously.

Trainor spoke from experience. "That means we're going into harm's way."

Chiles held up his hand to alleviate Trainor's concern. "Not this time, Gary. McKnight called to see if I could spare you and another detective to watch Kaderri's and Wolff's back...discreetly, while they are at work in Albany, if you weren't working on anything else."

"More surveillance?" Joanne asked. She pointed out their last surveillance assignment didn't go well. "Lieutenant, do you remember the last time we pulled a surveillance job? Just what are we supposed to be looking for this time?"

Chiles held up his hand again and nodded. "I remember. This is different. Just look for anything suspicious, like someone following them."

Trainor leaned forward, resting his elbows on his knees. He didn't like the sound of this. He wasn't particularly fond of being put on an assignment and not knowing exactly what he was supposed to do or be looking for. It didn't appear to be a sound plan. He'd worked with Kaderri and Wolff before and found them to be the most capable and thorough individuals to work with. There was no one else he would want on his side in a fight or to face if they were his foe. The shit really hits the fan with those two. That was the drawback. "You're kidding right? Keep an eye on Kaderri and Wolff? Lieutenant," he sat up straight and spread his hands. He let out a sigh before he continued, "If Kaderri and Wolff need their backs watched, what kind of trouble could they be in?" Trainor answered his own questions. "Deadly trouble. If there are two people in this city who can take care of themselves, it would be those two." Trainor was talking from first hand experience. "Christ, Lieutenant, those two could take on our entire tactical team and win."

Chiles leaned back in his own chair, picked up a pencil and began tapping it on the desk. "I agree with you, Gary, but from what McKnight told me, there really is no danger. Granted he didn't go into much detail." He dropped the pencil and gave a shrug. "It was more of a favor that he was asking."

Trainor shook his head. "I don't like it," he said flatly. "There *is* something more with those two. There always is"

"You're probably right, but that's all McKnight told me."

"Uh-huh," Trainor grunted, still not liking the situation. "Who's following them? Can you tell us that?"

Chiles drummed his fingers on his desk. "It may be the Russian Mafia."

Trainor blinked, letting the information sink in. He leaned forward again. "What? Did you say the Russian Mafia?"

After he repeated it, he became angry. "Are you shittin' me? The fucking Russian Mafia?"

"Yeah–"

"Just great!" Trainor snorted and threw his hands up. "Just great."

"Think you can handle it?" Chiles asked honestly and leveled a steady gaze. "You don't have to do this. You can turn it down."

Trainor met his gaze. Confidently, he stated, "Lieutenant, if I can track a Mossad officer and his commando team and win a fight against them," he thumped his chest, "and take down a racist thug and his minions, I can handle the Russian Mafia."

Chiles gave a sly smile. He expected Trainor to respond that way. "Good." Then he reminded his detective of an important fact, "But don't forget," he waggled a finger, "those times you had the help of Kaderri, Wolff and their other friend."

Trainor shrugged nonchalantly. "A small detail."

"Anything on those pictures, Lieutenant?" Joanne asked regarding the photos she took in the mirror of the two drug dealers that smashed the car on their last assignment.

"Matter of fact, yes. Those two are wanted by the State Police."

"Good. So something good came out of our short stay," she said proudly.

Chiles moved the conversation back to the new task and handed over a piece of paper to each of the detectives. "Here are the business addresses of Robert Wolff and Marcus Kaderri. You two decide who will watch whom."

"We're not going together?" Joanne asked surprised.

"No, it doesn't seem necessary," Chiles said. "Like I said, it's just surveillance."

Trainor quickly determined that Kaderri would the be the one that would most likely have the dangerous turn of events and didn't want his partner to be involved. "I'll take Marc."

"I guess that leaves me with the other guy, what's his name-Robert Wolff? What does he look like?"

Trainor recalled the picture form his mind. "About six feet, one hundred eighty. Short light brown hair with a touch of gray and a beard. He also has intense eyes. Well, he looked like that the last time I saw him." He vividly remembered the intense firefight at the Black Warrior compound, referred to as Coates' Kingdom, named after the leader of the racial group The Black Warriors. The bad guys were just about wiped out, and Wolff stood triumphantly in full combat gear above the mortally wounded chapter leader, Rashan Mobutu.

"When was that?"

"A few years ago."

"Jerk," she gave a playful punch. "I'll pull up his picture from Motor Vehicles to see if there is a more recent photo."

"Be safe," Chiles offered, indicating the meeting was over.

"Thanks," they said in unison and rose from their chairs and headed towards the door.

"One more thing," Chiles said, stopping them in their tracks. "Wolff and Kaderri don't and must not know you are following them."

Trainor rolled his eyes as he left the office thinking, yeah, right, follow a CIA officer and former Green Beret without being spotted! He didn't like this at all, not one bit. He was going to be playing a dangerous game of spying on Kaderri who doesn't know he is being watched and may be in danger. Great, just fucking great. He paused before he sat down at his desk. "Joanne?"

"Yeah?"

"How's your marksmanship?" There wasn't any hint of a smile on his face or sarcasm in is voice.

"I'm current on my training. Why?" she asked.

"I'll schedule us some time at the range. I think we're going to need it." As an afterthought, he added, "And get some heavier body armor too."

Monday, November 10, Durham, North Carolina

Jesse Hughes, a slender built man of average height with brown hair that was graying at the temples, sat at the kitchen table in his upscale center hall colonial sipping a mug of lukewarm coffee. He stared out the window into the spacious back yard but his brown eyes saw nothing in front of him.

His mind was hard at work, relieving his tour in Afghanistan with Marcus Kaderri and trying to determine what happened during his tour that would prompt his former commander and friend to issue that cautionary e-mail.

"Jesse?" His wife, Jill, called for the second time.

He turned around to find her standing next to the dishwasher dressed in a emerald green business suit that flattered her attractive figure and displayed her shapely legs.

"What?" he answered, automatically looking down at his white shirt and green and gold striped tie. He thought he spilled something down the front, which was usually the case.

"You're going to be late if you don't move it." She spoke matter-of-factly as if she were addressing the court defending the corporation she worked for.

He glanced at his watch. She was right. "Ugh," he grunted and pushed away from the table.

"What were you staring at outside?" she asked as he put the mug in the dishwasher. Her long, light brown hair shimmered in the sunlight pouring through the window.

"Just thinking about my meeting," he answered in a half-truth. Hughes was a medic in Special Forces and he made the easy jump to being a physician's assistant in the civilian world. Besides being a physician's assistant, he was also in charge of the Duke University Medical Center flight nurses. He was also a helicopter pilot and managed to get himself on the pilot rotation for a few days every month.

The first thing on tap for the day was a meeting with the hospital administration to discuss the possibility of adding two more flight nurses, and it was going to be a battle because money was tight.

"Good luck, honey. I'm sure you'll get what you need. You have a way of getting what you want." She gave him a kiss. "I'll see you later."

"Have a good day," he patted her firm behind. "Love you."

"Love you, too."

Hughes quickly coursed his way from the kitchen through the hall and bounded up the stairs to the master bathroom where he brushed his teeth and rinsed with some mouthwash. Once he finished his routine, he walked through the house, checked and double checked all the doors and windows and verified the security system was armed.

Satisfied that all was well, he threw on the tan LL Bean jacket, walked back through the kitchen and into the two car garage. He depressed the button and the garage door clanged and slowly slid open on its rails. Normally he would have jumped into the Chevy Blazer, backed out and gone straight to work without so much as a care except for passing traffic or pedestrians.

Not this time.

Hughes walked to the edge of the garage and peered out onto the quiet neighborhood street. His hawk-like eyes searched for anything out of the ordinary. Was there a strange vehicle parked on the corner? Did someone have a guest where there was a different car parked in the driveway? Was a vehicle backed into a driveway instead of facing forward? Everything seemed to be as normal as everyday. Neighbors were heading out to work, some even waved when they drove by.

Satisfied he wasn't being watched, Hughes climbed into the Blazer and proceeded to work, wondering if the surviving teammates of SFOD-A 524 had just done what he had.

Monday, November 10, Albany, New York

With a squeal of the rubber tires hitting the concrete and a puff of smoke that signaled the Boeing 737 made contact with the tarmac, the pilot reversed thrusters on the powerful engines and the aircraft shuddered against the sudden deceleration. The crew and passengers had arrived safely at Albany International Airport.

The passenger in seat 1A was tired and knew jet lag was going to set in, especially since he was unable to sleep on the flight from Moscow into New York and then on the connecting flight to Albany. Mikhail Vasilyevich Borushko let out a yawn that was so long that he thought his jaw would lock. He stretched out in the first class seat once the yawn subsided and smiled embarrassingly at the flight attendant.

"I feel the same way," the pretty black woman said from her folding seat directly across from him. She then unbuckled the strap and stood, grabbing the microphone.

The aircraft approached the jet way and the same flight attendant made the customary announcements welcoming the passengers and thanking them for flying with their airline.

Borushko rose and grabbed the worn leather carry-on bag from the overhead compartment and made his way toward the door where the captain and flight attendant were stationed.

"Thank you for flying with us," the attendant said with a practiced smile.

"Have a nice day," said the young blonde haired pilot.

"Thank you," Borushko nodded at the crew and slowly walked up the ramp, ignoring the throng of people speeding past him. He emerged from the group and immediately spotted the blank faces of Lev Kalanin and Dimitri Rykov, right where they said they would be, standing at the end of the jet way. Rykov offered his hand first.

"Good morning, Dimitri," Borushko spoke in Russian then grasped the outstretched hand.

"I assume you are tired?"

Borushko grunted, shook Kalanin's strong hand then handed him the small suitcase. A man of Borushko's statute in the Solntsevskaya was not going to carry his own luggage. Though he was tired, he was eager to get started on finding Kaderri. He searched for the signs to direct him to the luggage claim and began walking. "Is there any additional intel since we last spoke?"

"Not much," Rykov answered with a shrug. "We confirmed where Kaderri works and just obtained the address of his residence. We haven't verified that yet."

"Excellent." Good news on the hunt for his father's murderers was just the thing he needed to put his restless mind at ease, at least for the moment.

In silence the group took the escalator to the ground floor and retrieved Borushko's suitcase from the luggage claim. From there they exited through the automatic sliding doors with Kalanin leading them to the multi tiered parking garage where the car was parked on the ground level.

"The car's right here," Kalanin pointed and pressed the remote. The headlights flashed, the doors unlocked and the trunk popped open. He heaved the heavy suitcase into the trunk and his eyes gave a quick scan for any signs of danger. By the time he closed the trunk, Borushko was seated in the rear.

Rykov stood near the passenger side door. "We're clear."

"Right." By the time they drove down the ramp and halted at the gate to pay the parking fee, Borushko was fast asleep.

Kalanin looked in the rear view mirror at his motionless boss and then turned to Rykov. "I guess we won't stop to get something for lunch."

Monday, November 10, Durham, North Carolina

Jesse Hughes sat comfortably in the den in front of the desktop computer and checked his e-mail one more time before he turned in for the night. He was curious to see if there were any updates or correspondence from other team members regarding Kaderri's concern. There weren't.

Hughes had been looking over his shoulder ever since and so far hadn't found anyone or any signs that he was being followed. But to play it safe, he began carrying a Glock 9mm pistol.

Believing that all was well, Hughes shut down the computer, checked the doors and windows in the house and turned off the interior lights. A comforting glow from the exterior lights caused enough illumination for Hughes to see the stairs on his ascent to the bedroom and fitful nights rest.

Two men in shirtsleeves sat in the forest green Ford Explorer fifty yards down the road facing the house that had just shut off the interior lights. They were in no rush to do anything as their task for the moment was to observe and take notes.

"You're sure that's his house?" The driver asked.

The passenger checked his paperwork for the fifth time. "That's it. That belongs to Jesse Hughes."

"How long until we take him out?"

The passenger thought about that before he answered. "No more than four days. Five at the most. It mostly depends on what habits he shows us."

"This should not be difficult," the driver said confidently. "He has no reason to be concerned for his life."

Monday, November 10, Albany, New York

Gary Trainor laid under the covers wearing only his maroon colored shorts. The television was on and the remote lightly gripped in his hand but his eyes and ears weren't focused on the program. His mind was preoccupied with the new assignment he was going to undertake. Over and over in his mind he repeated what Lt. Chiles had told him and Joanne, 'There really is no danger.' Bullshit, he thought. Marcus Kaderri and Robert Wolff may not go out and seek any danger, but sure as hell it follows them whether they want it or not.

His assignment was simple enough. Follow Kaderri and report any suspicious activity, as in someone following him. Two options came to mind as Trainor tried to figure out how to go about his job. Option A was to stay in the shadows, acting like a spy and trail Kaderri whenever he was in the city. Option B was to go right up to Kaderri and tell him he was watching his back on the request of Paul McKnight.

Of course, problems presented themselves with both options. First and foremost, Kaderri was most likely trained in counter surveillance and it wouldn't take long for him to spot Trainor, quickly ending the assignment. The lack of evidence that suggested Kaderri was in danger made Option B pointless. It might also put Kaderri on the offensive and when that happened, people got hurt and that was what he wanted to avoid.

As he mulled over what he was going to do, a poke to his chest got his attention.

"Hello? Are you home?" Amanda asked, lying next to him wearing one of his navy colored t-shirts with the Albany Police Department coat of arms on the left breast and *police* stenciled on the back.

"What?"

"You. What are you thinking? You're staring off into space."

"Oh, sorry." He blinked his eyes a few times then focused on her. "I was thinking about my new assignment and how I was going to go about doing it, that's all."

"What is it, may I ask?"

If he mentioned Kaderri's name to her, she would get all worried and rightly so. She had visited Trainor in the hospital after the first time he dealt with Kaderri at his Adirondack cabin against the Israeli's and then again with the Black Warriors. A lot of people ended up dead in those two incidents, and he received a few extra holes in his body that weren't there when he was born. Vagueness was the preferred way to go this time. "It's more surveillance work, that's all."

"Oh, sounds like fun," Amanda joked.

"Yeah," he said and pushed a button on the remote. The deadly kind of fun, he thought. The Russian Mafia had a reputation for being extremely violent and ruthless.

"Oh, forgot to tell you!" In her excitement, she slapped his bare, bullet scarred shoulder. "I have to go to Rochester on Saturday. The company is having issues with a long time client so I have to go out and settle things."

"The office or the client's work site?"

She folder her legs and sat Indian style. "Neither. We're going to one of the country clubs. Neutral ground."

Trainor had known about Amanda's trip for the past week but he kept that information to himself and his face impassive. Amanda's best friend, Cassie, called him to see if she was free for a surprise bridal shower that the crew at the Rochester office of Amanda's company wanted to throw. He was all for it and made sure that nothing was planned for the weekend to interfere. Since Amanda was one of the executives of the headhunter company, she wouldn't question why they needed her out there to handle a problem and allowing the surprise to work. "Which club's it at?" he asked.

"I have it written down at the office," she waved him off and placed her hair behind her shoulders. "We don't have anything going on, right?"

"No, unless we have more wedding stuff to go over?"

"That's all done. Hey!" she poked him in the chest again and dove her face into his neck. "Drop the remote" she directed after a few licks on his ear.

Shivers shot down his arms, causing him to drop the remote. "Whoa! Chills!"

She unexpectedly yanked the sheets away from his body and quickly straddled his thighs. "Four days to the cut off. Let's get busy!"

CHAPTER FOURTEEN

Tuesday, November 11, Albany, New York

Mikhail Borushko woke with a start. He sat bolt upright in bed, breathing heavy and his heart thumped in his chest. Rivers of sweat flowed from his brow and his hands were shaking.

Like a horror movie, Borushko's mind replayed the memory of the day when in the seventeenth year of his life, two grim faced men, who identified themselves as friends of their father, knocked on the door just before he and his mother were to sit down for dinner. One man wore a military uniform with the rank of general and the other wore a dark wool suit who identified himself as a member of the communist party. They came to report the dreadful news that Major General Vasily Borushko had been killed in action in Afghanistan.

When the general informed them of his father's death, Borushko was standing behind his mother and caught her as she fainted.

It was always at that point in the nightmare he woke. Most nights had been like this ever since Pyotr Agranov informed him that Tomsky and Karsavin discovered the men responsible for the death of his father.

Borushko wiped the sweat from his face and took deep breaths to slow his breathing. For a moment, confusion swirled around him as he gathered his wits and took in his surroundings. Slowly, it came back him. He was in the Crowne Plaza Hotel in downtown Albany. The jet lag hit him harder than he thought. He found the clock on the nightstand and the green digital numbers glowed seven twelve in the morning.

Borushko threw off the covers and walked to the desk phone. He called the front desk and asked the attendant to connect him to his underlings. On the fourth ring the phone was answered.

"Yes?"

"Who is this? Borushko asked in English, not recognizing the voice.

"Beg your pardon?" The accented voice on the other end snapped.

Borushko let out an audible sigh. He knew Rykov or Kalanin wouldn't involuntarily give out their name. He was still a little fuzzy from the long sleep. "Is this Dimitri or Lev?"

"It's Dmitri. Mikhail, a suggestion." There was no delight in his voice in speaking to his boss. "Next time speak in Russian."

That was something he should have thought of, his English was barely passable and would be unable to carry on a conversation in English. "Next time I will. What room are you in? I'll be over by eight and make sure you order a pot of coffee. Also, what's your room number?"

Tuesday, November 11, Albany, New York

"Are you ready for this?" Gary Trainor asked his partner over the cell phone. He was en route in an unmarked police cruiser to the Times Union Center's multi-tiered parking garage on South Pearl Street, just around the corner from Kaderri's office. Joanne was further north in the city, up on Elk Street, near the Cathedral of All Saints.

"Doesn't sound to difficult. Unless there's something I don't know about?"

"Nothing more than what I already told you. Keep alert."

"I'll do my best." She disconnected the call.

At this time in the morning, the city was just coming alive and Trainor found plenty of parking spots available before the commuters rushed in and fought for the limited spots. He turned onto South Pearl Street, angled the Grand Marquis into a metered spot along the curb and killed the engine.

He got out of the car a little slower than usual. He was tired from all frivolity he and Amanda partook in that lasted into the wee hours of the morning. He pressed the remote to lock the car, stepped on the curb and headed towards the parking garage. He was dressed warmly in a dark gray micro fleece lined nylon jacket, navy blue Dockers and insulated hiking boots. In his jacket pockets were a pair of ski gloves and a wool hat. He didn't know what to expect in his dealings with Kaderri and he was prepared to stay outdoors if necessary.

Trainor rounded the corner and went straight to the parking attendant in the glass enclosed booth. He flashed his badge. "Good morning."

"What's up?" the young black male asked. He had a look of concern in his dark eyes that stared out under a worn and stained orange knit cap.

"Do you know if Marcus Kaderri pulled in yet?"

"Who's that?" he answered defensively.

"He usually drives a Porsche or a Corvette." Trainor pulled a piece of paper from his back pocket and read off the license plate numbers.

"Kaderri? Is that with a 'C' or 'K'?" the attendant asked.

"It's a 'K'"

The attendant punched the keys into the computer and waited a few seconds. The numbers for his parking permit appeared on screen. "Oh, the Porsche guy! I didn't know that's how you spelled his name. He's cool, man. Nice guy. Good tipper, especially at Christmas. No man," he turned his attention back to Trainor, "he ain't here yet. He's been driving a Jeep Grand Cherokee lately. I give him a spot right here when I'm working." He pointed to the location four spots up from the exit.

That figures, Trainor sighed. Kaderri decided to take one of the vehicles that he didn't write the license plate down for. "What time does he usually get in?"

"Around eight."

"Ok."

"Hey, dude, is the man in trouble or something?"

"Nope." Trainor pulled a small roll of cash from his pocket and gave the attendant a ten dollar bill. The short conversation and exchange of information didn't warrant a bigger denomination of currency. "We go back a ways, but he doesn't need to know I was here. Understand?"

The attendant cast a weary eye then shrugged and took the cash. "Sure, you got it."

"Thanks." Trainor turned and walked across the street, found an inconspicuous spot on a sidewalk bench, donned his hat and gloves and watched for Kaderri to arrive.

Mikhail Borushko's suite was conveniently located across the hall from Kalanin's and Rykov's. Dressed in a pair of gray slacks and a white button down collared shirt made in England, he grabbed his files, pulled open the door and took the three steps to reach the door. He gave it two quick knocks.

Before he could bring his hand down, Rykov pulled the door open. "Good morning," Rykov greeted. He wore tan slacks and a maroon crew neck sweater and stepped out of the way.

"Good morning," Borushko parroted as he was walked past and sat down in the middle of the couch next to Kalanin. A pot of coffee and a tray of pastries and other treats were on the table. He set his files on the vacant spot on the couch to his right.

"Morning," Kalanin said gruffly and took a sip from the mug.

Borushko nodded and pointed to the small circular bread with the hole in the middle. "What is that?"

Kalanin raised a questioning eyebrow. "It's a bagel."

"I know it's a bagel," Borushko snapped, "What kind?"

"Onion. There's more over there with cream cheese." Kalanin pointed to another silver tray on the larger dining table piled with the bagels and danishes.

He followed Kalanin's direction and selected a sesame seed bagel.

"Mikhail," Rykov spoke as he poured a mug of coffee for Borushko and refilled his own. He sat on a chair next to the window. "Is this your first time to America?"

"Da," he answered and bit into his breakfast. It was ironic, Borushko thought. Growing up, he spent his entire life being taught America and capitalism were the enemy and he trained to fight and destroy its army and way of life. The Soviet Union and its socialist ways fell into ruin and embraced capitalism so it could reemerge as Russia and a world leader. Now he sat comfortably in America, eating breakfast and plotting to kill one of its former military officers.

"Ok, Mikhail," Rykov spoke with a no nonsense tone and a stone face. "What's the situation we're involved in?" He made it perfectly clear he was not to be bullshitted.

An air of tension suddenly filled the room. Borushko's familiarity with Rykov and Kalanin was established only through the crime organization and they weren't men he considered friends. He wasn't sure how they would react to the disclosure that the assignment they were tasked with was solely a personal one, even with Sergi Mirovich's backing. Borushko knew they would carry out their task because of whom the direction came from and the oath they took upon entering the Solntsevskaya. He also wasn't naive to the possibility that they would refuse, kill him and return to Moscow stating the assignment was a failure and Borushko was killed. Nobody would be the wiser.

Borushko knew both Kalanin and Rykov were former KGB/FSB officers and could spot a set up and detect a lie the second something was out of the ordinary. Giving them the truthful explanation would be best, he thought, and in the process earn their trust for who he is and the position he holds. Borushko realized he wasn't smart or crafty enough to come up with such an elaborate plan that would escape the experience of the two intelligence officers.

Borushko took a breath. "The men you are eliminating were involved in the assassination of the commanding general of the Sixty-Fifth Motorized Infantry Division while he was serving in Afghanistan in nineteen eighty-five."

"What?" Rykov blurted and leaned forward in his chair, the coffee sloshed out the mug. The look of disbelief on his hard face quickly turned serious.

"Who's the general?" Kalanin asked calmly.

"Major General Vasily Ivanovich Borushko."

Looking into Borushko's eyes, Kalanin asked without missing a beat. "Your father, I presume?"

"Yes," Borushko answered, holding Kalanin's stare. "That's why I want the American bastards dead!" He pounded a fist into his palm.

Kalanin leaned back on the sofa and asked, "Is this man, Kaderri, the one who pulled the trigger? Is that why you want to take him out by yourself?"

Borushko shrugged indifferently. "I don't know who pulled the trigger but Kaderri was the commander of the special forces unit and that makes him responsible."

Rykov stood and walked around the suite. "So this assignment is personal?" He came to a stop behind the sofa and stared down at Borushko.

Borushko had to turn around to face him. He didn't know if Rykov's position was supposed to be an intimidation tactic or not. If it was, it didn't work. "Yes, it is. Do you have any issues with that?" Borushko challenged.

"No, none at all," Rykov shrugged and sat back down in his chair. "I just like to know why I'm doing something, that's all. Being the good little sheep who gets fucked in the ass without ever knowing why gets old real fast. That is one thing I do not miss from the Soviet Union!" He leaned over and rubbed his buttocks for emphasis.

"That explains why Mirovich wouldn't tell us why we were coming here," Kalanin put in coldly. "This is a personal job."

"Do you have a problem with this?" Borushko challenged Kalanin.

"No. Actually, I welcome it." He bit into his bagel.

These were comments Borushko didn't expect. "Why is that?"

Kalanin swallowed the mouthful of food before answering. "It gets us," he pointed at Rykov and then himself, "at least me, back in a version of the game we were trained to participate in. Another reason is," his tone suddenly deepened, "growing up I shared a room with my cousin who was maimed in Afghanistan. Unconfirmed reports stated it was an American Special Forces unit that carried out the ambush. There were only three survivors from the thirty-man unit."

"I agree with Lev," Rykov offered. "I want to do what we were trained to do."

He didn't outwardly show his emotion, but Borushko was ecstatic that he had these two men on board. "Good." He grabbed the files and strode over to the dining table. "Let's talk," he said and spread out the papers.

"Ok," Rykov said in agreement and turned away, heading into one of the bedrooms. He returned a few seconds later with a note pad. "Here's what we have collected on Wolff and Kaderri."

Borushko nodded and began once they sat down at the table. "You have reached your limit, correct?" Borushko asked as a reminder of their prior conversation.

"That is correct. We don't think we can keep up the pace and sooner or later we are going to screw up."

"I can understand that," Borushko sympathized. He knew where these men were coming from and appreciated their candor. "Here's what's going to happen. From this point on, you two will be concentrating on Wolff. I sent another team here to help out."

Rykov cocked his head and took a sip. "Who is the other team?"

"Nikolai Chernov and Pavel Filonenko. Do you know them?" Borushko asked.

Both men shook their heads.

"Who are they going after?" Kalanin found the target list and prepared to cross another name off.

Borushko consulted his own list and gave the name. "Their first target is Jesse Hughes. His last known address was in North Carolina. Anyway, that is not your concern right now. Tell me," Borushko pointed to the stack of papers Kalanin brought out, "what do you have?"

Borushko listened intently as Kalanin and Rykov alternated divulging the limited information they found. It was early in their surveillance so the information mainly consisted of where both Kaderri and Wolff lived and worked and what times they began and ended their days. They produced a map to show Borushko where their residences and places of employment were located.

Borushko remained silent as he processed the information. By all appearances, both Kaderri and Wolff should be easy targets to take out. Borushko could feel his excitement rise. "Great job!" he clapped both men on the back. "Ok. Here's what I have on Kaderri and Wolff."

Kalanin and Rykov prepared to write down everything Borushko said.

"Here's some additional information you will find useful. Kaderri and his company were highly skilled soldiers. They are all special forces trained and combat veterans. But they are also older now, so their skills have probably diminished. The information about these men came to me from two of our people in Afghanistan who happened to be interrogating a captured Afghan and an American named Leonard Puckett.

Both men were on Kaderri's team." Borushko glanced at his notes for confirmation. "The Afghan confirmed he was with Kaderri's team in Afghanistan in nineteen eighty five *and* was involved in my father's assassination. He just didn't say who it was that pulled the trigger."

Rykov and Kalanin shot glances at each other but remained silent.

Borushko noticed their action and assumed it was for the information he just provided. "That's all that I have. Do you have any questions?"

Rykov took a sip and held the mug in both hands. He leveled a gaze at Borushko. "Who were the men in Afghanistan that got the information on this American military unit? Is it credible?"

"It is." That's all Borushko was going say on the matter. Tomsky and Karsavin's business in Afghanistan was none of their business and he wasn't going to get into it with them. Rykov and Kalanin had their information and orders and it was time to get on with it. "Anything else?"

Neither Kalanin or Rykov answered.

"Ok, then," Borushko looked at his watch and ended the conversation. "I have Solntsevskaya business to care of that will take me about an hour. When I am done, I will return and begin our plan to kill Kaderri and Wolff." Borushko then rose from the chair and walked out of the suite. Before he opened the door, he halted, turned back and stated with a grin, "when we are done here, there are fifty thousand Euros for each of you."

****

Rykov stared at the closed door with his arms folded across his chest. "I don't like this," he declared to his partner.

Kalanin faced his friend. "I agree with you. These men we are hunting are far more dangerous than we were led to believe. Combat veterans in guerrilla warfare! It also makes us that much, much more luckier in eliminating the first two men."

"It does. That also leaves many more questions," Rykov pointed out and circled the suite and thought out loud. "Like how many of these men are still involved in the military or other professions with weapons? Active military, police? There is at least one that we know of. The guy they captured in Afghanistan," he held out his hands, "where is he now? Dead? Borushko didn't tell us."

"I can't answer that, but the only two men that I am worried about now are Kaderri and Wolff. What special talents do they have that we need to be aware of?"

Rykov halted his lap near the window. "There has to be some way to get more detailed information on these men. The information that Borushko got us is not good enough. How can we get access to their military records?"

"The first thing we can do is search the Net and see what that turns up. Hey!" Kalanin snapped his fingers as if a light bulb went off. "I got it! Yuri, do you remember him? He was always finding out ways to hack into computers and getting into other classified materials that we never could. I wonder if he can still help us out?"

"Good idea! Find out!"

CHAPTER FIFTEEN

Tuesday, November 11, FOB Warrior, Kashah, Afghanistan

Lt. Jack Dover, bootless in the warm sixty-six degree CHU, sat on his cot and finished cleaning his M-4 rifle. He loaded a magazine, chambered a round and put it on safe before he leaned it against the wall within easy reach. He then swung his feet up and laid back in the opened sleeping bag, grabbed the latest copy of *Inside Lacrosse* magazine and settled in for what he hoped would be an uneventful night.

"Got any Gatorade over there?" Lt. Phil Case called from the folding camp chair. Case, who bunked on the other side of the wall in the CHU with the XO, First Lieutenant Brett Lyde, was visiting.

Dover wasn't sure who Case was asking. Lt. Ramone Hernandez was supine on his cot near the door with one ear phone from his Ipod plugged into his right ear. For obvious reasons, the left ear remained unobstructed to hear the outside world. "Who me?" Dover asked.

"Yeah," Case pointed to cooler at the foot of the cot. "You have the cooler at the end of your cot."

Dover shrugged. "I don't know what's in there. Move your ass the three feet and go look yourself," he turned a page in the magazine. "Vodka's up there if you want to mix." He pointed to the bottle on the shelf between the two cots.

"You're the friendly type," Case jabbed and leaned out of the chair to the cooler. "Is there any beer in there? Vodka doesn't like me."

"I *am* the friendly type," Dover corrected without taking his attention away from the magazine. "Beer would be just fine about now. If you find one, I'll take one."

"What are your reading?" Case then read the cover of the magazine. "Is that the game where you can beat the crap out of someone with a stick?"

"Yeah, dude. I need to keep updated on what's going on in the game. You should try it. It's a lot of fun."

Case shook his head. "I'll pass. I've seen a few games. I think it's safer in a firefight!" He held up an extra blue colored Gatorade. "Want a drink?"

"No, thanks."

Just as Case unscrewed the cap, there was a knock on the door.

"Sirs?" First Sergeant Wright called from outside.

"Come in, First Sergeant," Case called, recognizing the deeper voice of the company sergeant.

Wright walked through the door. "All three of you are here? Perfect. Briefing with the captain in ten minutes." He reached down and slapped Hernandez's foot. "Wake up, Lieutenant."

"For what?" Case asked, holding the Gatorade to his lips.

Hernandez stirred and propped himself up on his elbows, the white earphones dangled. "What gives?" he asked groggily.

"Something to do with new intel about the bad guys attacking us, sir," Wright answered Case's question. "The captain will let you know. We meet in Operations."

"Hmmm. Want a drink, First Sergeant? They're over there in the cooler. Help yourself."

"No thanks, sir." He then turned and left the CHU, but not before slapping Hernandez's foot one more time. "Shake your ass, Lieutenant."

Dover swung his feet off the cot, stepped into his boots and laced them up. "You guys ready?" he asked standing and stretching his cramped, tired muscles. He donned his dirty field jacket, dropped the K-pot on his head and slung his rifle.

"Hooah!" Case answered in the affirmative. He looked over at Hernandez who managed to get into a sitting position. "C'mon Ramone, you heard the first sergeant, give it a shake and let's go."

"Screw you. I'm ready," the droopy eyed lieutenant shot back.

The trio made it over to Operations without having to duck for cover from incoming fire. They engaged in small, personal chit-chat along the way, until Hernandez reached for the door to enter the Operations building.

"Hey, what do you think First Sergeant Wright meant by bad guys attacking us? Do you think he meant here, at the base?"

"I guess we'll find out when the Captain gives his briefing," Case huffed and then blew into his cupped hands. "Now open the fucking door, it's cold out here."

The three lieutenants were the last to arrive and immediately upon entering, the briefing began.

"Take seats, gentlemen," Captain Jonas Hanks, a five foot eight inch black man and the commander of Bravo Company, 1st Battalion 75th Ranger Regiment said from the front of the small conference room. He had at least six more years of service than his newly commissioned second lieutenants and four more years than his XO. Only the company first sergeant and two of the platoon sergeants had more years of service.

Hanks was standing next to the wall with Lyde and Wright seated next to him on folding chairs. A solitary black telephone was attached to the wall behind Hanks. There were no additional maps, aerial photographs, computers, flat panel television screens or anything else that what would normally be present in an operations briefing. That equipment, along with a staff, was set up in the main conference room where it was maintained around the clock.

The three lieutenants found their respective platoon sergeants and sat down at the six foot long tables.

"Ok, everyone's here," Hanks began. "This isn't going to be a long briefing. I'm going to bring you up to date on a few things. First, as you well know, enemy activity has picked up significantly in our area. The reason, according to intelligence that was extracted from a PW, is that enemy forces are planning to attack Warrior in an effort to drive us out of Afghanistan." He clasped his hands and waited for the information to sink in.

Dover, with Isles seated at his side and shaking his head in amazement, asked what everyone else was thinking. "Sir, bad guys are going to attack us? At the base?"

"That's what was discovered during the interrogation. It doesn't seem like a bright idea, but then again, who knows what their tactics are going to be and what type of weapons are going to be used."

The last comment about what type of weapons sent a chill through the room.

"Are you implying NBC, sir?" Dover asked somewhat alarmed.

Banks responded with a shake of his head. "There is no indication that a nuclear, biological or chemical weapon will be used. More likely suicide bombers, more sophisticated and coordinated attacks and I'm assuming better rockets." That drew a laugh.

"What's the bad guys' point? They want to meet Allah real soon?" Hernandez' statement was met with chuckles.

"Apparently they are under the belief that if we suffer many casualties, we will turn tail and run away."

"That's bullshit, sir. That won't happen." SFC Johnson, 2nd Platoon's sergeant stated defiantly.

A quick agreement was murmured by everyone in the room.

"I, for one," First Sergeant Wright started, "will hope and welcome the sons-of- bitches if they want to attack us here. It'll be a hell of a lot easier to kill the fuckers."

"We may not be inside the wire when the attack occurs." Hanks began to sow the seed of an upcoming operation. "Since we don't know when the attack is coming, or what direction or the number of forces involved, there's good possibility we are going out to look for them. Our mission then, gentlemen, will be a combination of long range patrolling and/or being the quick reaction force depending on when the attack will occur. UAVs and Special Forces teams are currently scouring the countryside looking for the enemy, hoping to pinpoint their location so we can assault them. Jack," Hanks nodded in Dover's direction. "The intel that your unit discovered in the cave complex has proved priceless. Lots of weapons caches have been located and the 10th Mountain has been having a field day taking them out, along with the enemy forces trying to protect and defend them."

"Hooah!" Dover pumped a fist in jubilation.

"Cap'n?" Isles called after Hanks took a breath.

"Sergeant Isles," Hanks acknowledged.

"You mentioned assaulting the enemy. Has the S-3 said how we are going to do that?"

Banks shook his head. "Specifically, no. We're either going in on an airborne or heliborne assault."

A combat jump? Dover remained quiet but inside him his emotions ran wild. The prospect of a combat jump excited him and scared the shit out of him at the same time. It was the ultimate experience for a Ranger and he would love nothing more than leading his platoon out of the aircraft. There were murmurs from the other men, but he ignored what they were saying. He assumed they were going through the same emotions as he was.

Banks cleared his throat that brought the room back to silence. "I don't have anymore specific information to pass along. If you don't have any questions, we're done here." He waited for questions and when there weren't any, he dismissed them. "When things get going, I'll let you know. Start preparing your men."

Dover walked back to the CHU with the other platoon leaders in silence, contemplating what Hanks had said. He made a mental checklist of what he was going to need because this upcoming operation was going to be a major fight and it would test his abilities.

Tuesday, November 11, Albany, New York

It was after dinner and the kids were dressed in their footed pajamas, pink for Sam and blue for Sean, and had a half hour to go before their eight o'clock bed time. Marc and Sara Kaderri sat on the leather couch in the family room as the crackling fire spilled its warmth and the twins' mischievousness and laughter filled the room.

Samantha sat on the floor contently beating on the portable xylophone, playing music that only she could admire.

Sean completed the last floor of a two foot tall skyscraper built out of multi colored wooden blocks. When the last block was set in its place, he would yell *"crash,"* and push the tower over. Immediately he would jump up and down in excitement and then begin the rebuilding process all over again.

Kaderri laughed at the enjoyment Sean had every time the blocks fell and decided he wanted to get in on the fun. He put the whisky filled crystal snifter on the end table and crawled to his son. "Hey, bud," he said and scooped up Sean with one hand and kissed him on the cheek. "May I play too?" he asked the demolition master.

Sean smiled and handed his dad a block. "Build a tower, Daddy!"

Kaderri took the yellow block from his son's outstretched hand and proceeded to build a tower. "Ok, let's build a big one!"

"Yeah, a big one!" Sean clapped his hands in excitement then raised them above his arms as if signaling a touchdown.

Samantha, seeing that her dad was playing with her brother, stood, grabbed the pull string on the xylophone and walked over to her mom who sat on the couch and scrambled up on her lap.

"I guess you're in music class," Kaderri said to Sara.

"This should be fun. The music over here and the crashing blocks over there." She pressed her hand to her forehead and announced, "Pain relievers in twenty minutes!"

When Kaderri was settled comfortably on the floor, one by one Sean handed over a block and like a foreman, instructed his father where to put it. Dutifully, Kaderri did as he was instructed.

After at least a dozen towers were built and then razed, Kaderri had decided that this was going to be the last one. Partly because his legs were cramping up from sitting Indian style for so long.

The last tower was shaped like a pyramid with a rectangular spire and stood over three feet tall, above Sean's head. Just like all the previous towers, Sean handed each block and finally came to the last one. It was a blue one. "Blue,"

Sean said triumphantly at identifying the correct color. Then with his tiny finger, he then directed were it was supposed to go. "On the yellow."

Kaderri surveyed the design and knew instantly the big blue block wasn't going to remain on top of the building. The thin yellow block spire simply wasn't going to hold the big blue block. "If we put the blue one on the yellow, it's going to fall over. It's too big."

Sean looked at the tower, processed what he had just been told and looked at his dad. A smile spread on his face. "Crash!"

Kaderri laughed out loud. "Yep, it will crash."

"Me do it!" Sean squealed excitedly and grabbed the blue block back from Kaderri's hand. Carefully he placed it on top of the yellow block and the second he let it go, the building toppled.

"Crash!" Kaderri yelled and raised his arms above his head.

"Crash!" Sean mimicked and began jumping among the scattered ruins.

"Sam," Kaderri called over to his daughter who still banging on the xylophone. "Do you want to help crash the buildings?"

"No," she answered without looking up and tapped the colored metal strips. "I'm playing with Mommy."

"I say we switch," Sara suggested and massaged her temples. "I'll help Sean build a real cool tower and Dad can play musician."

"Ok," Sam nodded and moved away as her parents traded places.

"Hey pumpkin," Kaderri called as he placed Sam on his lap after he sat down. His legs were grateful for the renewed blood flow. Just as he did with Sean, he gave Sam a big kiss. "What are we going to play?" he asked.

"Listen, Daddy!" Sam ordered as she began to bang on the colored metal. "This is 'Mary had a little Lamb'"

Three minutes later, Sam had finished her version of the classic song, which sounded nothing close to it. "Well done, honey!" Kaderri clapped his hands in applause. "Do you have another song you like to play?"

"Yeah! Listen!" she happily screeched and energetically played the song. She banged haphazardly on the instrument and looked like a drummer in a punk rock band. Her head bounced in sync with every strike on the metal plates and Kaderri cringed with every hit.

When she finished, Kaderri took the opportunity to prolong the silence and asked, "What's the name of that song?"

"Sam's song," she said proudly. "I made it up."

Kaderri gently clapped his hands on her back. "It was great, honey! That was the best song I've ever heard." He wrapped his arms around her and kissed her head.

As if on cue, Sean exclaimed the impending doom of another building. *"Crash!"* The latest tower of blocks scattered across the floor.

"Well guys," Sara called as she got up off the floor. "It's time for bed. Clean up first."

"Did you guys brush your teeth yet?" Kaderri asked as Sam climbed off his lap.

"I did!" Sean called as he dragged the plastic container over to put the blocks in.

Sam smiled and pointed to her teeth, indicating that she had, to which Kaderri gave a quick inspection. "Well done. Let's go." He rose off the couch, squatted down with his arms spread wide and caught each kid as they jumped into an arm for the trip upstairs into bed. Sara followed, tickling each kid in their ribs and eliciting a giggle and a twitch.

Once Sean and Sam were tucked in, and hugs and kisses were delivered, Kaderri and Sara changed into their bed clothes, dark shorts and t-shirt for Kaderri and a teal silk pajama set for Sara and went back to the family room where they regained their spots on the love seat. Kaderri sat in the corner next to the armrest and Sara leaned back into him, swung her legs up and stretched herself out. In his right hand he held the whisky glass and his left draped around her shoulders.

"Comfy?" He slid his hand along the silk material.

She wriggled further into him. "Uh-huh."

"So," he opened their nightly conversation. It was usually difficult to carry on serious or important conversations during dinner. The twins just took up to much concentration. "How'd your day go?"

"I think I decided on what I'm going to do with the club."

"Yeah? What's that?" He stared at the top of her head and took a sip of his drink.

Sara turned her face up. "I think I'll bring on a managing partner."

"Who or how are you going to do that?"

"Put an ad in the paper," she said jokingly. "I'm kidding. I want to try to keep everything in house and I put a feeler out to Bill MacIntyre. He seemed pretty interested."

"Bill, huh?" Kaderri visualized the thirty-five year old former competitive swimmer and the longest tenured of the four managers. "How are you going to split?"

"We've had some preliminary conversations and offered to split the club sixty-five thirty-five. He didn't balk."

"You sure this is the way you want to go?" He wasn't questioning her business sense, she held an MBA and knew more about business than he did. It was the emotional aspect he was concerned about. She put most of her life into building the business.

"Yeah. It keeps me involved in the club and Billy knows how everything is run. This way there will be little changes and very little fighting."

"Are you sure about that?" Kaderri asked guardedly. "People change when they get into power and the decision making positions."

"I'm sure. Bill was my first manager and I know how he is. We both think alike, that's why he's still with me. Besides," she snuggled back into his chest, "I will still own a large majority of the company."

Kaderri laughed and knew Sara was smirking. She was a smart business woman and wasn't going to do anything dumb to jeopardize everything she had done to build the most successful health club in the capital district.

"What about you?" It was Sara's turn to ask about his day. "How was your day? Anything new on the...your team?"

"No, actually, there hasn't been." He didn't know if that was a blessing or not. No funerals announced was certainly a blessing and he hadn't received anything that suggested any members of his team were in jeopardy. The absence of information and further incidents made him think that maybe he had overreacted and the deaths of his friends were, in fact, purely coincidental.

Tuesday, November 11, Durham, North Carolina

A fierce autumn storm had struck earlier in the evening that so far had dumped three inches of rain and assaulted North Carolina with forty mile per hour winds. Slick road conditions, flash floods, down trees and limited visibility made driving treacherous. Warnings were given to stay off the roads until the storm subsided. Unfortunately, not everyone heeded the warnings or because of the nature of their work, they couldn't.

All of that made Jesse Hughes' job very busy.

There had been motor vehicle accidents scattered across the area, putting Hughes in the air as the pilot of the hospital's second Bell Jet Ranger helicopter. His third call of the night was for a serious car wreck on a flooded creek side road outside of Durham. The car hydroplaned and flipped into the creek, trapping the passengers inside. The driver was a thirty-one-year-old male and his passenger was a twenty-nine-year-old female. When he arrived on scene, he learned the victims were pulled free by other motorists after being underwater for at least five minutes. Paramedics had restarted the male's heart twice and the female was barely breathing on her own.

The victim's plight didn't end there. The harrowing conditions made the landing on the hospital's roof extremely difficult. Maintaining the helicopter's flight stability as he descended and hovered to land on the roof took all of Hughes' skills and cost him at least three pounds in sweat. He landed hard but managed to set the chopper down while the passengers were still breathing. When the staff wheeled the gurneys away, the victims were alive, but he didn't know what their chances were. The 'Golden Hour' in medical speak was just about up and so was his time on duty.

He let a monstrous yawn run its course as he sat behind the steering wheel of his Chevy Blazer. Once it subsided, Hughes started the engine and slowly drove out of the 'staff only' parking lot at the Duke University Medical Center. The deluge had let up, extending visibility on the black night out to one hundred yards and he could use his wipers on the low setting. After he drove his way through the nearly deserted campus, he prepared to turn south onto the two lane Anderson Street and head home.

He came upon the stop sign and checked for oncoming traffic and glanced in his rearview mirror. Headlights in the near distance caught his attention.

The fact that there was another car behind him, especially around the University, was nothing out of the ordinary, after all, Duke was a busy place, but instinct sent him an urgent message that told him to keep his guard up.

Hughes took his time driving through the predominately residential areas. Traffic was light and only twice did he stop for cross traffic. All the while, one eye was kept on the trail vehicle. If the vehicle was a tail, he didn't want to alert the bad guys that he was onto them.

Not yet alarmed but wary, Hughes continued to drive towards his home. At the end of Anderson, he turned right onto Chapel Hill Road where a strong gust of wind blew the SUV towards the edge of the slick road. A speedy reaction, helped by his pilot's training, and a tight two handed grip on the wheel kept him from losing control. He brought the car back into the lane and once he was sure of his control, his eyes darted to the rear view mirror to see the same headlights still following. A short distance later he approached Vineyard Street, the entrance to his neighborhood. Just as he was about to tap the brake to make the turn, he decided against it. A check in the mirror showed the same headlights were still behind him.

"All right," Hughes spoke to the headlights in his mirror. "Let's see who you are." It was time to confirm or deny his suspicions. He accelerated slightly and continued for a few more miles to a Kangaroo Convenience store that was perfectly suited to perform counter surveillance. That is, of course, if they had any electrical power. The storm had knocked out the power in other parts of area, but by the house lights that were on, this area seemed to be ok.

He was in luck. The red and orange Kangaroo sign was lit as was the interior of the building. Hughes tapped the brakes, slowing down to keep from hydroplaning and coasted into the empty lot. He slid the SUV into a spot near the door and shut the engine off. He removed the Glock pistol from the glove compartment and tucked it in the small of his back. He flipped the hood up on his rain coat before he jumped out and sprinted through the driving rain into the store.

"Hey, man. How's it going?" asked the acne covered teenager behind the counter asked after he turned the blaring music down. "Pretty crappy out there ain't it?"

Hughes pushed the hood off his head and wiped a few drops of water from his face. "You can say that." He peered outside to see if the vehicle followed in. Keeping his focus outside, he walked over to the cooler and took a Coke off the shelf.

The reflection of headlights off the wet ground caught his attention as he moved to the counter. A green Ford Explorer slowly pulled into the lot and stopped next to the gas pumps. A chill shot through him and he caught himself going for the pistol.

"Will that be all?" the teenager asked after Hughes put the soda down. "Man, you're the first customer I had in an hour."

"That's it," Hughes answered with a forced smile. Nobody had exited the vehicle to begin pumping gas. "I don't think you're going to get many more for a while."

The clerk tapped the keys on the register. "Kinda figured. Sucks out there. A dollar twenty five, please."

Hughes withdrew the exact amount from his pocket and handed the money over. To confirm his suspicion, he asked the clerk, "Hey, can you tell if that guy out there started pumping gas?"

"Sure," the clerk looked at the terminal next to the register, happy to be talking to someone. "No, man, not yet. I wonder if he knows how to work it? If not, sucks for him 'cause I ain't going out there in that shit to help him. "

Hughes laughed. "I don't blame you. Thanks. Have a good one." Hughes flipped his hood up and started towards the door.

"Stay dry, man," the clerk said to his back as he stepped out.

Using the hood to shield his eyes, Hughes focused his vision to determine how many people were in the SUV. The glare from the overhead lights and the rain splattered on the windows made it difficult. All of a sudden there was movement in the passenger seat. Then a blurry face looked in his direction but still, no one had gotten out to pump gas. Hughes's heart skipped a beat. He was being tailed.

The moment he climbed into the Blazer, he opened the bottle and took a long pull. He withdrew the Glock from his waistband and instead of putting it back in the glove box, he placed it on the passenger seat, within easy reach on the chance he had to use it. The waterlogged engine coughed to life and he began to formulate his next move.

"This is bullshit," Nikolai Chernov exclaimed. He was having ever increasing difficulties following Jesse Hughes in the storm. They were on unfamiliar roads from the moment they pulled out of the Kangaroo and the windshield wipers were on the highest setting, struggling to keep the water off the glass. Compounded with the rain and the glare from the few streetlights, the road striping was almost impossible to see.

"Don't get to close," Pavel Filonenko suggested. "Ease off."

"I'll try, but we are going to lose him if I don't get closer. Where's he's going? His house is back that away about three kilometers."

"I don't know. Maybe he's got a mistress."

Chernov snorted. He kept two hands on the wheel and leaned closer to the windshield to see out. "Do you think he's spotted us? He's never gone this way before."

"No. Don't get paranoid," Filonenko cautioned, then added, "how can he know?"

The rain came down in driving sheets, making a car wash machine look like a spring shower. A heavy burst of rain caused the windshield wipers to disappear. "I'm going to break this off," Chernov said angrily as the rain pounded loudly on the roof. "We can catch up with him later." He pulled over and pointed to the map "Find out where the hell we are and get us back to the hotel before we get washed away."

Wednesday, November 12, Albany, New York

Marcus Kaderri spent most of the night with his eyes open, staring at the ceiling and listening to Sara's soft breathing as she slept. Over and over, images of his past kept flashing by, and they all had to do with his combat operations in Afghanistan. He saw combat in Beirut and the invasion of Grenada but none of those experiences presented themselves.

It was only his time in Afghanistan that reared its head. He would doze off for a few moments and then wake up after another image appeared. It was as if someone was trying to tell him something or point to clue. But what?

On his way to the office to counter the lack of sleep, Kaderri stopped at Dunkin Donuts and picked up his third cup of coffee for the morning. Once in the office, he turned on the TV to the Fox News Channel and fired up the computer. He drained the last of the coffee, sat down at the keyboard, logged in on his account and went straight to his e-mail. Twenty-seven new messages were indicated and he scanned through them, looking for anything in the subject line that would catch his attention.

One did and it gave him goose bumps. It was time stamped at one minute past eleven last night and it came from Jesse Hughes. The subject line stated one threatening word 'followed.'

Kaderri opened the message and saw that the message went to every member of the team. The message itself was short and to the point. 'Guys, I was followed last night by two men in a green Ford Explorer. Evaded them on my way home. Boss, I believe you were right about the team being in danger. Use extreme caution, guys. Anybody have anything to share? I'm taking appropriate measures.'

Kaderri exhaled and sat back in his chair, a sense of foreboding shook him. He instinctively glanced over his shoulder and gazed upon the city below him to see if he was being watched.

Wednesday, November 12, Albany, New York

"Are you sure he said that?" Rykov became alarmed. He fell into the sofa at the hotel suite and shook his head.

"Yes, I am sure," Kalanin answered solemnly. "Look, it's right there." He leaned against the table and put the lap top computer on it for Rykov to see. Their friend, Yuri, the computer whiz who had also been employed by the FSB as well as the GRU–the intelligence arm of the Russian military– had dug up some military service information on Marcus Kaderri and Robert Wolff. Most of the information Yuri passed on to Kalanin was awe-inspiring and unsettling. Especially Kaderri's record.

They had learned that both men had indeed served in the US Army's Special Forces, the Green Berets, and were veterans of combat operations. Those two facts alone presented a serious challenge. But what they trained for was alarming. For Kaderri, he was the top in his class in three of the training schools he attended, which included Airborne, Ranger, Special Forces, Air Assault and the US Marine Corps Scout/Sniper Course, arguably the best sniper training in the world. He was also selected to try out for the US Army's elite counterterrorism unit, Special Forces Operational Detachment-Delta, commonly know as Delta Force. For that class he was medically discharged before he could complete the course but once again, he was near the top of his class. If his knee hadn't been shot out, there was a very good chance he would have made it through the extremely difficult selection process and once again, towards the top of his class. There was also speculation, Yuri concluded, that Kaderri and Wolff were employees with the Central Intelligence Agency.

Those two men were a force to be reckoned with and not surprisingly Kalanin and Rykov were having doubts about carrying out their mission. By all intents and purposes, Kaderri and Wolff were the cream of the crop in their former profession.

"So what are we going to do?" Rykov asked his partner. Before Kalanin could respond, he posed another question. "Do we tell Borushko and let him make the decision? I for one don't know him well enough to believe he is going to make the right call regarding *our* best interest and safety." He swung his finger back and forth between each other for emphasis.

Kalanin processed the proposal, looking past the wagging finger and Rykov's intense eyes before answering. His partner was right and he agreed with him. Borushko was probably not going to make the correct call on this one. "I think," he finally answered, "that we keep this information from Borushko and we'll do this the way we were taught. The FSB way. I don't know if an old Russian infantryman will understand patience and stealth. He sure as hell knows how to charge straight ahead with guns blazing, that I know. No, my friend," his voice rose in confidence, "we'll apply our tradecraft on this."

Marcus Kaderri had skipped lunch to finish a financial proposal for a potential client. He completed it at three-thirty in the afternoon and called the prospect to let her know it was done, as promised, and to set up a meeting time to discuss the particulars.

As luck would have it, the prospect was not in the building and he was to call back tomorrow.

He tossed the proposal on his desk, pushed himself away in the leather chair and put his feet up. With the financial business out of the way, he immediately moved onto a more serious issue. Pulling out his cell phone, he found Jesse Hughes' number and pressed the keys.

"Jesse Hughes," he answered after the third ring.

"Jesse, it's Marc, I read your e-mail. How are things?" Kaderri got straight to the point.

"Hey, Boss," said Hughes. "Things are good so far."

"Anything else pop up?"

"I spotted them again this morning. Same vehicle with two guys in it. This time they were a little more discrete. Probably because it was daylight. Anything on your end?"

"Nothing that I'm aware of. Listen," when Kaderri spoke, he always commanded attention. "I'm thinking about coming down and lending a hand in eradicating the situation. You good with that?"

"I'm on board with that," Hughes agreed. "When?"

"Friday morning," Kaderri said. "I'll call you with more info later."

"Right. Bob coming with you?"

"I'll ask him, but I doubt it. He's extremely busy at work." Kaderri knew if Wolff was still under contract with the CIA, a simple phone call would get him out of work. Besides, Hughes and he could handle the situation. "Keep your eyes open and head down."

Hughes chuckled. "Will do."

Kaderri closed the phone and turned towards the window overlooking the city. Hughes' message solidified his belief about his team being targeted and he was going to do something about the danger before any more of his men were killed. There was very little he wouldn't do to aide his fellow brothers. Like flipping a light switch, Kaderri switched into soldier mode.

Hughes was in danger and Kaderri was going on the offensive. But before he could leave on the trip, his only concern was how to get his custom fit M-40A3 sniper rifle to North Carolina without having to drive.

The sun had set, passing the job of illumination to the street lights which cast an orange-white glow across the city. Detective Gary Trainor, who had been sitting for the past two hours on one of the green benches bolted to the concrete sidewalk, noticed the steady uptick in pedestrian traffic and figured it was close to the end of the business day. He pulled the jacket sleeve away from his wrist to read his watch. He was right. It was five minutes after five.

Trainor rose off the bench and rubbed the soreness out of his backside. What a boneheaded move he made by not placing his police cruiser on State Street outside Kaderri's office. He could have been sitting in it where it was comfortable and warm. Idiot, he called himself. The only consolation was he made a couple of hours of overtime.

The cell phone on his belt rang and it took him a few moments to remove his gloves and lift up the parka to remove it from its holder. It rang three more times before he was finally able to answer it. He cursed himself for another boneheaded move. Next time he would put the phone in his parka pocket. "Trainor," he greeted the caller.

"'Bout time you answered it," Joanne greeted.

"Hey, Joanne, how's it going?" He wondered if she had as much fun as he had. "I was just going to call you."

"Boring is how it went. I almost fell asleep. I need some excitement."

"Maybe tomorrow you'll get something." It was time for their closing routine. "Hey!" He had to yell into the phone because a delivery tuck rumbled past. "Quittin' time!"

"We're outta here!" she fired back.

"See you at the station."

CHAPTER SIXTEEN

Thursday, November 13, Albany, New York

Mikhail Borushko rode the hotel elevator down to the lobby, holding onto the piece of paper on which he had scribbled the address of Kaderri Financial Services. Although he had limited understanding of English, he understood and didn't mind listening to the excited family of four talking about how long the flight was going to be to reach Orlando, Florida and which ride they were going to hop on first when they entered MGM Studios theme park. He could understand their excitement. He liked going to amusement parks when he was a kid as well.

The two businessmen in the elevator, on the other hand, were obnoxious and annoying. They were getting animated in their conversation about the presentations they were going to give and the brown haired man couldn't keep his hands still, constantly, though inadvertently, slapping Borushko's shoulder. The first time Borushko understood the contact to be an accident, but the subsequent tapings and lack of an apology began to piss him off.

The elevator slowed and came to a halt just as Borushko was about to turn around and demand an apology. The door chime dinged then the doors slid open. The two businessmen tried to rush past Borushko to get out, but he blocked their path, causing them to knock into each other and with a smile, he let the excited family go first. He then timed it so he would exit the elevator simultaneously with the brown haired man and bumped shoulders with him, nudging him into the door. "Pardon," the business man said sarcastically.

"Zhopa," Borushko smiled sardonically and strode purposefully through the lobby. He exited the main doors and into a chilly wind. Turning the collar up on his black wool overcoat, he recalled from memory the route to Kaderri's two blocks down State Street on the opposite side of the hotel. Out the doors, he turned left and walked to the corner of State. Heavy traffic was flowing in both directions on the four lane State so he turned left again and proceeded down the hill to the point across from Kaderri's towering office building.

He stopped on the curb, away from any crosswalk or traffic light and watched the traffic moving from his left to right. He paused for a break to cross the two west bound lanes, aiming for the painted divider until traffic would allow him to cross the east bound lanes.

Spotting a break in the traffic, he stepped between two cars parked in the diagonal metered spaces. He thought it strange that the car on his right was pulled in backwards. He momentarily locked eyes with the man sitting in the drivers seat.

The window was halfway down. "Good morning," the younger man said, taking a sip from his paper cup.

"Good morning," Borushko mimicked. He stepped past the car, waited for the traffic then crossed the entire four lanes without stopping.

"Moron," Gary Trainor said aloud as he watched the blond haired man he just said good morning to cross the busy street. "Use a crosswalk, that's what they're there for."

Trainor took another sip from the hot coffee and let out a yawn. A gust of wind blew through the half opened window and he smiled. He was happy at his decision to sit in the cruiser instead of on the hard sidewalk bench like he did yesterday. The car's heater was running on low so he wouldn't overheat and he placed the phone on the dash. If the phone rang, he would be able to answer it on the first ring, unlike yesterday when he had to search for it under the layers of clothing. Suddenly… it rang.

"Ha!" He answered the phone on the first ring. The numbers on the phone indicated the incoming call was from Joanne Bauer. "Trainor," he greeted anyway.

"How's it going so far? Nice and warm?" she asked mockingly. He bitched to her yesterday about how cold he was and how sore his feet and ass were.

"Yep. Toasty and comfortable. What's up?"

"Wolff hasn't arrived yet. What about your guy?"

"Not yet," he answered and scanned the sidewalk again. It was getting crowded.

"What do we do if they don't show up?"

It was a question he thought of himself but never asked Chiles for an answer. "Foot patrol? Lunch? Beers?" He attempted to stifle another yawn.

Joanne heard the involuntary action. "Am I boring you that much?"

"No, of course not." He and Amanda were once again engaged in decadent behavior all night and he was worn out. Cut off time was closing fast but he wasn't going to tell Joanne that. There was only so much he was going to tell his partner, especially when she was of the opposite sex. "I just didn't get much sleep, that's all."

"Wedding stuff keeping you awake?" she probed.

Trainor laughed. "Yeah, you can say that." The vision of Amanda sitting in the middle of the bed, naked motioning with her index finger to 'come here' popped into his mind. It was how they started the night off when he walked into the bedroom after shutting off the house lights.

Joanne's voice in his ear interrupted the memory. "Wolff is here, I gotta go."

She hung up before he could respond, but his eyes darted to the spot on the sidewalk where he knew Kaderri would come from.

Mikhail Borushko bounded up the short flight of concrete stairs and through the revolving brass and glass door of the office building. The glass enclosed lobby floor was black tile speckled with white and finished with a high gleam. The first thing he noticed besides his shadowy reflection on the floor was the security officer stationed behind a tall horseshoe shaped desk. To the right of the officer's desk on the marble wall between two elevators was a directory. At the bottom of the directory he spied Kaderri's name and waited patiently with the dozen or so employees for the cars to arrive.

Like a lightning bolt out of the blue, it dawned on him that maybe his target, Marcus Kaderri, might be in the lobby waiting like everyone else for the elevator. His eyes scanned the small group of business people, searching for the face of the man that murdered his father.

Nothing. Kaderri wasn't among this group of eight men and five women.

The elevator dinged and the doors glided open. Everyone but he rushed to get in. Being the last one in, he pressed the button for the seventeenth floor and stood staring straight ahead as the doors closed.

After eight stops on the ascent, he was the last passenger when the car reached the seventeenth floor. He stepped out of the car and paused, thinking he would be in a hallway. Instead he found himself stepping into the warm, welcoming lobby of Kaderri Financial Services.

A four foot wide marble floor led from the elevator and turned left to the cherry veneer receptionist desk that looked more like a bar. Sunlight streamed through the plate glass windows that overlooked the city.

Taupe colored Berber carpeting flanked both sides of the marble path and a love seat and two armless chairs were placed around a coffee table. Large green leafy plants were placed in the corners and financial magazines and pamphlets were neatly piled and stacked.

Behind the desk was an office with the door open. A brass name plate next to the door jam read Louise Faith. To the left of the desk was a conference room and a hallway that led to the bathrooms and offices for the other agents on staff. Next to the hallway was another door that was closed and no name plate was posted.

"Hi," greeted the short blonde haired attractive young lady behind the desk. "Can I help you with something?"

Borushko stood their for a moment, stunned like a deer in the headlights. He saw the lady's lips move and heard the words she asked but he had difficulty understanding them. He instantly realized that coming here was very, very stupid. He had no reason to be here. Why did he come? He asked himself. What would the point be? To see what Marcus Kaderri looks like up close and personal? He didn't even bring a gun to shoot the son-of-a-bitch who killed his father. This was wrong coming here! He had to think fast. He stepped toward the desk and spoke in heavily accented English. "I am in need some money planning." He stumbled for words and was thankful the lady cut him off.

"Sure, we can help. I can ask one of our representatives to sit down and talk with you if you'd like?" Smiling, she reached for the phone.

Borushko rapidly shook his head and held up his hand to stop her. He didn't completely understand what she said, but he knew meeting someone was out of the question. "No, no," he frantically waved his hands. "I don't have time for Mr. Kaderri. Just some," he hesitated a moment. He couldn't pronounce brochures or pamphlets so he simply said, "Papers, a business card, please."

"I'd be happy to get those for you," she said and emerged from behind the desk. She made her way around the lobby picking up booklets and brochures. When she was done, she placed them in a blue folder with the company name embossed in gold. "Here you go." She offered the folder to Borushko.

"Thank you," he said with a nod and promptly turned towards the elevator.

Kaderri stepped out of his office into the reception lobby and froze when he spied the short cropped blond haired man dressed in slacks and black overcoat anxiously waiting for the elevator. Kaderri gauged he stood about five ten but his head was turned just enough to prevent him from seeing the man's face. But as the man stepped onto the elevator, he turned slightly to give a profile. The hairs on the back of Kaderri's neck stood up.

He was about to ask Diane who that man was, when he heard Louise's ask the same question.

"Was that someone looking for Marc?" Louise asked as she popped her head out of the office from behind the receptionists desk.

"Um, I'm not sure."

"What do you mean you're not sure?" Louise snapped. It was a simple question to answer. Louise clearly wasn't that thrilled with Diane's job performance up to this point. Diane retook her seat on the bar chair behind the counter and began to answer.

"Good morning, ladies," Kaderri greeted with a deadpan face. "Anybody know who that guy was?"

Louise folded her arms and leaned against the door frame. "Diane was just going to explain that."

"Oh. Was there a problem?" Kaderri raised an eyebrow.

Diane faced Kaderri to answer. "That guy came in and said he wanted information on investments. So I gave him a packet like Louise has told me to do."

Louise jumped into the conversation. "He mentioned your name, Marc. I would like to know if he was here to see you. That's what I was asking Diane and she told me she wasn't sure." A personality conflict was beginning to show between the women.

Diane let out a sigh and went on to explain. "This guy comes in looking lost. I asked him if he needed help. His English was bad but I understood he wanted investment info. I–"

"Did you get his name?" Louise cut her off.

"No," Diane rolled her eyes in frustration. "I didn't get a chance to. He walked away."

Kaderri needed to end this now, Diane did what she was supposed to and Louise was looking for a fight. "Ok, no harm done. Keep up the good work, Diane." He turned back towards his office and whispered to Louise. "You need to lighten up on her." He then directed a question to Diane. "What kind of investments was he looking for?"

She shrugged with a smile, glad that the big boss backed her up. "He didn't say. I asked him if he wanted to talk to one of the reps and he quickly said no and that he didn't have time to talk to *you*," she pointed to Kaderri. "That was the first time your name was mentioned. He asked for materials and a business card and high tailed it out of here. But," she added as an afterthought, "he definitely didn't look like someone who was really interested in finances. He was sort of hard to understand because he had an accent that sounded Russian."

Kaderri's cheek began to twitch.

Lev Kalanin and Dimitri Rykov spent six hours casing the large concrete Crawford Enterprise building that spanned most of the block on Elk Street where Robert Wolff worked. Through their professional opinion, they determined that the only real way for Wolff to enter and exit the building was through the front door. Because of the sensitive nature of the business that was conducted in the building, along with the effects of September 11, security measures prevented employees and visitors alike from using any other door. There were no windows anywhere below the top floor, which in comparison to other buildings was at least the equivalent of the fourth story, and the emergency doors were made of steel with no access from the outside. Only the receiving dock allowed both ingress and egress but that was tightly controlled with surveillance equipment and armed security guards. With access being tightly controlled, that made the assassination plan easy.

For twelve solid hours driving the streets over the past couple of days, the two members of the Solntsevskaya had planned their escape route and had determined that they had a ninety percent chance of success.

Presently, they sat in the hotel suite to celebrate their upcoming success. "We are set, yes?" Kalanin stated surely, feeling a whole lot better now that things were being done their way. He poured vodka into two glasses and handed one to his partner.

"Da." Rykov nodded and took the glass. "Thank you."

"Tomorrow." Kalanin pumped his fist in anticipation. He moved to the dining table and brought the half filled vodka bottle with him.

"Correct, my friend. The morning gives us a better opportunity." There was no emotion in Rykov's voice. It was flat and deadpan like he was discussing how to brush his teeth, not assassinate another human being.

Kalanin leaned forward and held up his glass in a toast. "To luck."

Rykov touched his glass. "To luck," he parroted and they swallowed the drink in one gulp.

"Another?" Kalanin poured with out waiting for an answer.

"What time was Borushko supposed to get here? It was about now, wasn't it?" Rykov snorted contemptuously and looked at his watch. "He is supposed to bring lunch."

"Dimitri," Kalanin said seriously, almost conspiratorial as if Borushko was in the same room. "I don't like Borushko very much. He's too much of an amateur. Very impatient and changes plans all the time. That's dangerous."

"I agree, Dimitri. That's why we decided to this our way."

A quick rap on the door ended their short conversation. "That must be Borushko." Kalanin pulled the door open. "Ah, Mikhail, what did you bring for lunch?" he stepped aside to let Borushko pass, holding a pair of brown paper bags.

Borushko placed the bags on the table and withdrew the contents. "I brought Gyros and these," In addition to the roasted lamb meat and cucumber sauce pita sandwiches, he held up a bag of Fritos corn chips and sour cream and onion potato chips.

"Vodka?" Kalanin poured a glass for Borushko before he answered.

Borushko took the glass and held it up in a silent toast before downing it in one gulp. "Thank you. Let's eat."

They waited until lunch was finished before they moved to the living room section of the suite and got down to business.

"Where do you stand with Wolff?" Borushko sat by himself on the couch and threw the question out to both men sitting on the chairs across from him. The vodka bottle was on the table between them.

Rykov leaned against the chair and answered in a nonchalant manner. "We we have enough information on Wolff's movements that we can take him out tomorrow."

Borushko's eyes went wide in anticipation. "What time?"

"We are planning for the morning. His arrival time is the most consistent. But," Rykov cautioned, "if the opportunity is not perfect we will wait for another time."

Borushko nodded and remained silent for a long moment. "This should be a productive next few days."

Kalanin offered details of the plan and made it perfectly clear that Borushko was not joining them in its execution. "We will call you with the results of the operation. If it is successful, we will use the word, 'sputnik.' If there is a problem, we will say 'hang up.' In that case, we will meet you back here. 'Race' will indicate that we are in trouble and on the run and will contact you at a later date."

Borushko committed the words to memory. "Understood."

"Good," a satisfied Kalanin nodded once.

Borushko drew his lips tight. "While you are carrying out your plan, I am going to recon Kaderri's house."

Rykov raised an eyebrow. "Are you changing plans?"

"Meaning?" Borushko answered the question with one of his own.

Rykov put an edge to his voice. "It sounds as if you are going to take Kaderri out now. I thought the plan was going to eliminate his team first and he was going to be the last one. Has something changed?"

"That was the original plan," Borushko agreed. "But since we are here and so is Kaderri, it would make sense to take him out next. Wouldn't you agree?" Before the two former FSB officers could respond, Borushko continued. "Things may be wrapping up sooner than anticipated. Chernov and Filonenko will be removing Jesse Hughes this weekend. That, I believe, will leave six members of the team that killed my father. Now that we have found Kaderri, we may not have to eliminate the rest. If the quarry is in the trap, why give him a chance to escape?"

Rykov and Kalanin stared open mouthed at Borushko.

"Something wrong with that?" Borushko sneered.

"No," Kalanin slowly shook his head, holding his contempt. "Nothing at all."

Rykov folded his arms and crossed his legs. "How are you going to do it and what is our role going to be?"

Borushko set his jaw and thrust a finger out. A wild look flashed in his eyes "You will kidnap and hand him over to me."

"Time frame?" Rykov asked while Kalanin stewed at the operations change.

Borushko picked up his glass of vodka and drained it in one gulp. "Soon."

Thursday, November 13, Riyadh, Saudi Arabia

In his prestigious, tenth floor air conditioned office, Ahmed Rashid Halabi took care of the final details to make sure his company, Arabian Peninsula Transportation, was able to run without him while he made the all-important trip to Afghanistan. The large framed painting of Salah al-Din's army retaking Jerusalem from the non-believers gave him strength in the belief that the planned assault by the Muslim groups on the American base Warrior in Afghanistan would be a success. His strong belief in the goal moved him enough to donate four hundred AK-47s with three hundred rounds of ammunition for each and one hundred RPG launchers and three hundred warheads.

At the meeting in Masozai Kili, he was going to make it perfectly clear that his donation was a one time deal. He didn't want the fighters in Afghanistan to look to him for a free bail out every time they lost a weapons cache. He was a business man and needed to make money.

"Marwan," Halabi called to his ever present bodyguard seated quietly in one of the ornate chairs reading a magazine.

"Yes, Ahmed?" The large man closed the magazine and placed it on the end table, giving his boss his full attention.

Halabi tapped a few more keys on the keyboard, finishing the sentence before he looked up. "Are we set with the travel arrangements?"

Marwan answered without having to consult the itinerary he carried in his blazer pocket. "We leave tomorrow by air and land in Quetta, Pakistan. From there we meet up with Saleh, who should have the weapons, and travel overland by horse cart to Masozai Kili. We will have a low profile which also means we will have minimal protection."

Halabi gave a curt nod. "I don't believe that will be much of a concern. When will we arrive at Al Suqami's?"

"Without any delays, Saturday morning."

Halabi smiled. "Excellent. Well done, Marwan. We will be partly responsible for the deaths of many Americans."

Marwan smiled in return. "I like that."

Thursday, November 13, Loudonville, New York

Kaderri put a few more birch logs on the fire in the master bedroom and adjusted them so the flames would spread evenly. The dry wood caught and the flames grew instantly, throwing out a wave of heat. Satisfied the fire wouldn't need his attention for the remainder of the night, he placed one of the store bought, chemically treated, slow burning logs on top of the stack so it would burn through most of the night. He secured the mesh screen and turned away.

Sara was changing in the cedar lined walk-in closet on the other side of the room. "Honey, you really think someone connected with your time in Afghanistan is after your team?" She called through the open door.

Kaderri could hear the clothes hangars clanking on the bar but was caught off guard by the calmness in her voice. In the past, when confronted with potentially dangerous situations, there was always a quiver when she spoke. There was no use in going into his closet to undress so he began, like usual, removing his clothes next to the fireplace. "Yeah, I do," he said and unbuttoned his shirt and tossed it on the nearest wing chair. "Jesse said he was being followed and spotted the tail a couple of times." He didn't believe it would serve any purpose to tell her about the Russian speaking man asking about him in the office, at least not yet.

"I don't know which is scarier," she said and stepped out of the closet, "you intentionally going into harm's way or me getting used to it."

Kaderri had his back turned to her and was draping his tailored slacks over the back of the chair. He half snorted and chuckled and removed his socks and underwear. "I sure don't like having a target on my back."

When he finally turned around, Sara was standing next to the bed. Her right arm was coiled around the bedpost at the foot of the bed. Like him, she was stark naked. His heart jumped and fluttered upon seeing her breathless beauty and his eyes devoured her.

"Come, take me," she smiled and spread her arms wide like a child wanting to be picked up by a parent.

He quickly strode over and scooped her up, one hand around her waist and the under her knees. Right away her fingers interlocked behind his neck and their lips zeroed in on each others as he placed her on the bed.

The night before one of them, usually him, was going away, they took the time to make love to each other. Despite a fire roaring in the bedroom, the loving couple had the ability to create more heat than any fire could produce. What had started out as tender lovemaking with soft, teasing foreplay, more akin to poetry in motion, had turned into pure unbridled lust. For the past ten minutes, they were going at it hot and heavy with the lust of newlyweds combined with years of experience.

When they finished, they collapsed on the bed wrapped in each other's arms. Sara's head was on Kaderri's sweaty chest, her hair tickled his nose. He stroked her hair and inhaled deeply, her scent filled his nostrils and he savored it as it may be the last time he would be able to do so.

"Wow, hon, you were pretty wild. That was a lot of fun!" Kaderri breathed heavily and his heart thumped loudly in his chest. "I thought you would wake the kids."

"Yeah, that was a lot of fun," she agreed and ran her finger along the outline of his square chest. "I haven't had an Earth shattering orgasm like that in a long time! At least a week!" she kidded. "You wore me out." She turned her head and gave him a light kiss on the tip of his nose.

He pushed a few strands of hair away from her face and stared into her eyes. "Love you," he stated quietly.

Sara put her head back down. “Marc?” Her fingers moved to the bullet scars on his shoulder. She traced the outline of them.

“Yeah?”

“What are you and Jesse going to do?” This time her voice wasn’t as controlled as it was earlier. Fear was evident.

Kaderri reassuringly patted her bare shoulder and then traced a finger along her sweaty collar bone. He spoke quietly, almost in a whisper so not to alarm her. “Find out who’s doing this and why.”

CHAPTER SEVENTEEN

Friday, November 14, Scotia, New York

The dark sky hid the fact that dawn broke a half hour ago. A solid sheet of ominous gray clouds spread over the horizon, but the forecast did not call for any storms or precipitation. Marcus Kaderri guided the Porsche through the main entrance of the quiet Schenectady County Airport and steered towards the two small silver hangars off to the left. The airport's operation was split between the private section and the Stratton Air National Guard Base that housed the 109th Airlift Wing of the New York Air National Guard. There were no commercial flights that used the airport.

Once he put a little mind power to the issue, the solution was simple to get himself, his weaponry and gear down to North Carolina without having to drive or use his CIA credentials. The latter option was the last resort since this exploit had nothing to do with his contract work for the Agency.

Kaderri had picked up the phone and called his client who owned a small aviation and pilot training company at the airport that specialized in executive charters and asked if he could charter a plane down to Raleigh, North Carolina for an urgent matter.

Without hesitation, his client agreed to take him.

Following the instructions his client had given him, Kaderri turned left through the gate and followed the service road to the hangars. On the tarmac, dozens of small private aircraft, a mixture of jet and prop, were tied down in neat rows waiting to be woken from their slumber.

As he approached the hangars, three aircraft painted sky blue with the stars and bars logo of a five star general on the fuselage were chocked in front. Not knowing much about aircraft and aviation, Kaderri didn't know what types of aircraft they were, but one was a small jet, the other a twin engine prop and the third was what he thought of as a Cessna, just because it looked like one. He turned in front of the first hangar and pulled into an empty slot next to the glass door. The overhead sign read Five Star Air. The company logo matched the same ones on the aircraft. A man in a pair of slacks and a sweatshirt with short cropped auburn hair pushed through the door and waived.

"Good morning, John," Kaderri greeted when he exited the car. "Hey, thanks again for taking me." They shook hands in a firm grip.

"Anytime, Marc," answered John 'Rusty' Doyle with a smile. Doyle had spent twenty years as a pilot in the U.S. Air Force, the last twelve flying F-15 Eagles and Strike Eagles. Four of those years were over Iraq and Afghanistan.

"I really appreciate this-"

Doyle held up his hand and cut him off. "Stop. We've gone over this. I need to log some hours and flying alone in anything but a fighter is pretty damn boring. Do you need help with your gear?"

Kaderri shook his head. "No, thanks, I got it." He moved to the trunk, which was in the front of the car, and pulled out the long flat black case that held the latest version of the US Marine Corps sniper rifle, the M-40A3, and two black duffle bags. One bag contained his change of clothes and toiletries and the other, larger one contained his gear for the mission. Inside that bag was a Beretta 9mm pistol, ammunition for both weapons, combat boots, a set of ACU's and a snipers Ghillie Suit. Kaderri closed the trunk and stared at the airplanes. He waved his finger at them. "You have three airplanes out here, which one are we taking?"

Doyle smiled and pointed to the twin prop plane. "We're taking the Beechcraft King Air. It's the plane I use the most."

"It's yours?" Kaderri surmised he was going to get a quick description of the aircraft that Doyle had at his disposal.

Doyle leaned against the car and gave the expected summary. "Not personally. Everything here is company owned," he shrugged, "well along with the bank or the aircraft company holding the paper. Which reminds me we need to talk business later."

"Ok," Kaderri acknowledged and knew now was not the time to talk financial business.

Doyle continued talking about his airplanes. "One of my partners, Steve, primarily flies the Hawker 800," he pointed to the sleek jet that could carry eight to ten passengers, "on the longer charters with Dan as the co-pilot. It's a sweet airplane, but when I fly it, I tend to forget I'm flying passengers instead of my Eagle." He chuckled and began doing dances with his hands to mimic combat flight maneuvers. "High G turns don't mix well with stuffed shirts in the cabin conducting a meeting or whatever they are doing."

Kaderri laughed and could easily picture the scenario his client was painting. "I guess not."

Doyle then pointed to the last plane, the single engine Cessna Station Air. "This little one is for short hops, sight seeing and training pilots. And that's the quick low down on our airplanes." He pushed away from the Porsche. "Let me get a few things and I'll meet you inside the cabin."

"Right." Kaderri slung the bags and ambled to the airplane. The cabin door was open and the retractable stairs were locked down. With one foot on the lowest rung, he turned and called over his shoulder and pointed to the bags. "Hey, John," Kaderri shouted before Doyle reached the door. "Should I bring these inside or do they go somewhere out here in a cargo hold?"

"There are storage bins inside. You can't miss them." Doyle then disappeared into the office.

The cell phone on Kaderri's belt chirped. Still standing on the stair, he removed it from the holder. The screen indicated the call was from Bob Wolff. "Hi, Bob."

"Hey, Marc, I just wanted to wish you and Jesse luck. Are you airborne yet?"

"Thanks. Not yet. I'm just getting on board. We should be leaving in few minutes."

There was a trace of disappointment in Wolff's voice. "Sorry I'm not joining you two." The project he was working on was at a critical stage and he couldn't take the time away from it. Millions of dollars were at stake.

Wolff was just as protective of his friends as anyone. "Listen, Bob," Kaderri consoled. "I hear you. Jesse and I should be able to handle this without much of a problem." If Kaderri thought it was necessary, Wolff would be there at the drop of a hat, regardless of the consequences.

"Keep me updated, will you?"

"Roger that." Kaderri heard approaching footsteps and turned to see Doyle twenty feet away. "Gotta go."

"Right. Good luck."

"Thanks." He put the phone back on the belt just a Doyle arrived with a folder in his grasp.

"Ready? Let's go." He motioned with the folder to board.

Kaderri nodded. "All set." He ascended the stairs into the cabin and found four wide leather chairs, two on each side with a center aisle and a blue carpet. Each side of the fuselage was lined with wood cabinets and three round windows. A bathroom was in the rear and a black curtain separated the cabin from the cockpit.

"It's only you and me," Doyle said from the cockpit. "If you want, you can take the controls once we get aloft."

Kaderri smiled excitedly and dropped his bag onto one of the leather seats. "Yeah?" He never flew an airplane before.

His experience with aircraft was either riding or jumping out of them. This, he thought, could be a lot of fun. "That'll be great!"

"Sure. I'll give you a lesson."

"Can I do a barrel roll?" he asked eagerly.

Doyle laughed. "I should of expected that from a snake eater!" He used one of the unofficial terms for a Green Beret. "We'll see."

"Stow your gear then come up front." He pointed to a coffee maker and a package of bagels. "There's breakfast if you want. Help yourself."

Friday, November 14, Albany, New York

Gary Trainor had been sitting in the car for over an hour waiting for Marcus Kaderri to arrive at work. To pass the time, his weighed options for his weekend while Amanda was out in Rochester at her bridal shower. Would a night out with his buddies be in the works or would he spend the time checking off the honey do list that Amanda was sure to leave? A big yawn snuck up on him and he was too lazy to cover his mouth. When the yawn subsided, he realized he had to find something to keep him focused or else he would fall asleep.

He shook his head to clear his mind and focus hit attention to the job at hand. The clock on the dashboard read eight forty-two and he frowned. Another ten minutes had gone past and no sign of Marcus Kaderri. There was one way to find out where he was. He pulled out his cell phone and Kaderri's business card and called.

"Kaderri Financial Services. How may I help you?" The female voice was young and pleasant.

"Marc, please."

"Mr. Kaderri is out of the office until Monday. May I take a message?"

Shit. That explains why he hadn't seen him. "No thanks. I'll call him Monday." Now what? he asked himself and looked out the windshield at nothing in particular. This would be the time to move on to plan B, if he had a plan B. He let out a sigh and came to a decision. Elk Street and Joanne were only a few blocks away.

Friday, November 14, Albany, New York.

Once all the notes were compiled and studied, Dimitri Rykov and Lev Kalanin confirmed that the best time to eliminate Robert Wolff was in the morning after he parked his car and walked to his place of employment. His time of arrival varied by ten minutes in comparison to the times he left for lunch, if he did at all, or when he exited the concrete building at the end of the business day.

The two men had spent hours pouring over maps of the city to plan their escape route and committed them to memory. The plans were so ingrained the assassins could recite in their sleep which streets went one way, the names of cross streets and intersections and which ones had construction or were detoured. They made one last final run through just after dinner last night to make sure they had missed nothing.

They were set, the assassination was a go. Each man had a duffel bag packed with two sets of clothes, an extra pair of shoes and a thousand dollars in twenty dollar bills for any contingency. The last thing they did was alter their appearance, Rykov had applied a mustache while Kalanin went a step further and added a beard.

They sat in the warm car on Elk Street and waited for their prey. They hadn't said a word since they parked an hour ago. Their vigilant eyes constantly scanned the growing number of pedestrians on their way to work to spot Robert Wolff as quickly as possible.

Elk ran east-west and the two men parked on the eastbound side between South Swan and Dove. A couple of large parking lots on the north side of Elk were quickly filling and the commuters flooded the crosswalks to get to the opposite side where a host of business and buildings were located that housed New York State agencies.

Rykov sat behind the wheel of the Impala and cast his eyes down to the dashboard clock and then back to the sidewalk in the direction Wolff usually traveled. He brought the small binoculars up to his eyes.

"Any moment now," Kalanin said after he noticed Rykov's actions.

"Uh-huh," grunted Rykov. "I think I see him. Half way down the next block. Tan overcoat, briefcase in left hand. He's late today and coming from farther down than where he usually turns the corner." He handed the glasses over to Kalanin. Wolff had shown a pattern of appearing on the corner of South Swan and Elk.

"That's him," Kalanin confirmed after staring for a moment. "Let's go."

Calmly and simultaneously the men exited the car. Rykov kept the engine running to make their escape much easier. They didn't believe they had to worry about anyone stealing the car. The hit was only going to take a couple of minutes.

Kalanin was the one tasked with pulling the trigger and Rykov was the lookout and backup. Kalanin was to approach Wolff from behind and to the right. Being a right handed shooter, Kalanin would bring the silenced pistol up to his chest and without using the gun sights, shoot across his body into Wolff's head, placing the bullet just under his ear in an upward angle. It was a shot he had practiced until he could do it in his sleep. It was also a shot he used successfully in the past in carrying out his KGB/FSB duties.

Once the shot was taken, he would move onto the nearest cross walk, circle back to the car and drive away.

Meanwhile, Rykov would hang back about twenty meters, look for anything out of the ordinary and be in position to cover Kalanin's back in the rare case something went wrong. Once the shot was taken, Rykov would get back behind the wheel and wait for Kalanin.

As the men stood by the car, Robert Wolff approached their location, minding his own business and keeping his line of sight straight ahead, plotting his path to the office as he stepped around slower moving people.

Suddenly Wolff was adjacent to them.

Rykov and Kalanin both avoided eye contact and the moment Wolff was three steps past, they put their plan in motion.

Friday, November 14, Loudonville, New York

Mikhail Borushko drove through the quiet streets of the upscale development of Loudonville and was instantly impressed. With the wealth he could now openly display from his dealings in the Solntsevskaya, he could relate to the affluence he was looking upon. Large stately homes of various design and construction were well maintained and professionally landscaped. Only his imagination could picture what the grounds looked like with the foliage in full bloom.

The closer he drove to Kaderri's house, the more the distance increased between the houses and they sat further back from the road. Some houses were obscured by natural fences, trees or thick green arborvitaes, while others had brick walls and wrought iron fences to keep unwelcome eyes out. The neighborhood's design was not what he expected. He went on the assumption that Kaderri lived in neighborhood where the houses were built on preplanned lots and were similar in design. This posed a challenge for him as he slowed the rental car just past a neighbor's driveway and stopped a hundred feet from Kaderri's driveway. There wasn't enough traffic on the quiet street for him to park and hide in plain sight and became concerned that one of the neighbors may take notice.

Not left with any options, Borushko, decided to park the car along the side of the road and walk through the wide copse of woods that separated the houses to learn what he could about the man that murdered his father.

Friday, November 14, Albany, New York

Joanne Bauer had the police cruiser parked on the westward lane of Elk and from the driver's seat, watched Robert Wolff walk past heading east on the opposite side of the road. She had never bothered to locate the spot where he parked, but assumed it was around the corner on Washington Ave. It was a main road lined with busy office buildings, shops and restaurants that cut through the city and ran parallel to Elk. If Chiles had stated the assignment was more serious, Joanne would have had Wolff's parking information and would be trailing him from the time he left his car up to the point where he entered the safety of his work place. By not taking the case as serious, Joanne had spent more than one night feeling guilty in not giving her assignment her best.

That changed. She decided to do what she knew was the right thing to do and what she was paid to do-to protect and serve the public. Without hesitation, she exited the unmarked police car, felt for the gun on her hip and the walkie talkie in her left jacket pocket. Lastly, under her leather jacket, she repositioned the new body armor that Trainor had insisted she wear. Watching for traffic, Joanne crossed the road and slowly followed Wolff down the sidewalk. Matching his pace, she kept twenty steps behind, her eyes scanning for anything out of the ordinary. When she came upon the bright red fire hydrant poking out of the sidewalk, she knew it was approximately a two minute walk until Wolff reached his destination.

After ten steps, all seemed normal. The sounds and flow of traffic and pedestrians on their way to work had picked up as expected, but didn't impede her surveillance.

Ten more steps and she would be adjacent to the lamp post that was her next marker at a minute at a half from Wolff's destination. Joanne continued to follow at the same distance and passed a midnight blue Chevrolet Impala parked at the curb that was running. I hope the idiot who just left the car knows it's running, she thought, as she continued past it without another thought.

A feeling she couldn't explain suddenly gripped her. Like low hung rain soaked clouds threatening to open up any moment, foreboding loomed overhead. All her senses went on high alert. Her eyes were instantly drawn to Wolff and the immediate area. She noticed that Wolff's over coat was unbuttoned, the waist belt hung from the back belt loops and swayed with his gait. That was odd, she though, it was cold outside and every one else had their coats or jackets closed.

Movement off to Wolff's right suddenly caught her attention. It was a man who didn't seem to quite fit in. Not a pedestrian, or sightseer or someone going to work. He was wearing a gray wool over coat and had dark hair. He walked with a purpose but not the kind to get to one's destination on time.

He was focused. He was on a quest. He was the man who got out of the blue Impala!

Joanne's heartbeat quickened and the hairs stood on the back of her neck. Something was wrong! The man in the gray coat moved closer to Wolff and slightly picked up his pace.

Joanne's heartbeat raced and her eyes open wide.

The man in the gray coat pulled his hand out of his pocket and she caught a glimpse of a silenced pistol.

Oh my god! she thought, as she watched the man in the gray coat move closer still. Her mind raced through many thoughts all at once. The one that was the most pronounced was Trainor's chilly warning that now roared like a gale that they were going into harm's way.

Joanne's training instantly took over. For the first time in her police career, she had to draw her weapon with the intent on firing it. She swiftly pulled the pistol out of it's holster and started running forward, rapidly closing the gap and screaming, "Wolff! Move left! Get down! Down! Gun!"

Then events moved at breakneck speed but to Joanne, they moved in slow motion and were extremely vivid.

Pedestrians froze in place. Without hesitation, Wolff immediately spun and ducked to the left and the man in the gray coat raised his pistol.

She heard the distinctive metallic click of a pistol's working slide and the dull, muffled pop from the bullet being fired. Wolff had spun to the ground, his hand hidden inside his open coat.

Joanne skidded to a halt, grasped the pistol in a two handed grip and lined the sights up on the man's back. Sure her aim was true, she pulled the trigger. The 9mm pistol jerked in her hand. Strong wrists absorbed the recoil and she pulled the trigger again and again. Puffs of smoke exploded across the upper back and shoulders on the man with gray coat. His legs buckled and he slowly fell to the ground.

As the gray coat man's knees hit the ground, his pained face turned towards Wolff's direction, but suddenly his head was jerked rearward, a hole exploded from the back of his head and a red mist hung in the air. The echo of a single gunshot slowly faded.

The scene in front of her still played in slow motion. Wolff was on his back, his arm outstretched with a gun of his own pointed at the man with the gray coat. Smoke enshrouded his hand.

From behind, she unexpectedly heard Trainor's voice scream a warning. "Joanne, get down!"

Startled by his shout, all she could mutter was, "Huh?"

But it was too late.

Two hard blows slammed into her back and propelled her forward before she crashed to the ground, gasping for air. The pistol fell from her grasp and rattled on the sidewalk as the world began to spin before her face hit the cold concrete sidewalk.

Gary Trainor felt rejuvenated in the cool air as he walked up Washington Ave. towards the intersection of South Swan. Lafayette Park was on his right, a one block quiet expanse of trees and grass that ended at North Hawk. The massive multi story marble structure of the New York Sate Education building loomed a few hundred feet ahead. Dozens of workers were entering and exiting the building, resembling ants attacking a unattended picnic basket.

He turned right on South Swan and the stone walls of the Cathedral of All Saints rose above the other modern concrete and steel buildings. On the far side of the cathedral was Elk Street and the solid concrete building with the one row of glass on the top floor that housed Crawford Enterprises, the building where Robert Wolff was employed.

With Kaderri out of town, Trainor had planned to join up with Joanne and keep her company during the surveillance of Wolff. Two sets of eyes were always better than one and they would be able to keep each other focused on their task. When his feet carried him onto Elk, the scene unfolding before him caught him totally by surprise. Joanne had sprung into action of some kind, and she was pointing her gun at someone. His heart rate went into overdrive and his fingers tingled with the surge of adrenaline.

Suddenly there was a loud string of gunfire and his mind processed what his eyes were seeing. Joanne had shot at a man in a gray coat, Wolff was falling to the ground and shooting at the same man while pedestrians were running and screaming in every direction.

Instantly, Trainor sprang into action. He withdrew his pistol and raced towards his partner searching for any signs of danger. It was then he spotted a second man, this one wearing a tan over coat standing a half dozen steps behind Joanne and take aim at her.

His heartbeat accelerated even faster, threatening to beat out of his chest. "Joanne, get down!" he screamed in warning. He stopped running, brought the pistol up, took aim on the center of the man's back and pulled the trigger a half dozen times. From thirty feet away he couldn't miss. All six bullets peppered the man's back, dropping him into a immobile heap.

It was then that he saw that Joanne was lying on the ground. He had shot too late.

"Fuck! No! No!" he roared. "Officer down!" he frantically called into his walkie talkie as the adrenaline surged through him. "Officer down! On Elk Street near the Cathedral of All Saints." He fought the immediate urge to rush to his partners side to see if she was alright. He gave a quick scan to make sure there were no more shooters. When he didn't see any, he stepped over the man he just shot, secured the pistol and felt his jugular vein for a pulse. There was none.

When he looked up Wolff was checking over Joanne who still lying on the concrete. He had her jacket off and his hand under her body armor. He also had taken the shooter's pistol away from his lifeless body.

"No bleeding, Gary. I think she's ok." Wolff offered in his characteristically calm voice as Trainor approached.

"I sure as fucking hell hope so." He stepped past the body of the first shooter and knelt next to Joanne who was attempting to sit up. He already lost one partner to gunfire and he wasn't going to lose another. "Easy, Joanne, stay put."

A crowd had begun to gather around the trio and offers of help were forthcoming. 911 calls were being made by just about everyone present.

Joanne grimaced and winced and forced herself to a seated position. Small cuts on her left cheek and chin from hitting the concrete were seeping blood. "I'll be ok, Gary. Damn, that hurts." She fell over to one side and both Wolff and Trainor caught her before she hit the pavement again.

"No blood. You may have some damage to your ribs," Wolff suggested as he helped her to a more comfortable position. "Hey, thanks for the warning."

Joanne cracked a weak smile. "Sure. What happened?" Her hands began to shake as her body reacted to the realization that she was shot.

Trainor had been in the most advantageous spot to see what unfolded so he was the one to answer. "There was another shooter. You and Bob took out the first guy. I got the one who shot you." His voice dropped to a whisper, a bit ashamed that he couldn't prevent his partner from getting hurt. He put a consoling hand on her shoulder. "Sorry, Jo, I didn't get him quick enough."

Trainor turned to Wolff and snipped. "Do you know who these guys are?"

Wolff rose to one knee and shook his head. "I–"

Curtly, Trainor cut him off and felt the anger of his partner being shot flowing out of him. "Bullshit, Bob! You probably know damn well who they are and you just won't open your fucking mouth about it or spew some sort of bullshit that you can't tell me or something like plausible deniability–"

It was Wolff's turn to get angry. He reached out, grabbed a fistful of jacket by Trainor's neck and pulled him close. Joanne was still on the ground with them coming nose to nose above her. "Hey!" Wolff barked loud enough to shut Trainor up.

Trainor took a breath and looked into Wolff's menacing eyes. He forgot what kind of people Wolff and Kaderri were. They were two men that had total control over their emotions at all times and had the rare ability to go from passive to deadly in the blink of an eye.

"Take it easy, Gary," Wolff snarled. "I was going to answer your question." He dropped his hold of Trainor's jacket and his eyes softened a bit. In a quieter voice he said, "Take a breath, Gary. Your partner is going to be fine. It's over."

Trainor alternated his focus between Wolff and Joanne and began to calm down. He got caught up in the emotional aspect of the firefight and let his emotions get the better of him. He brought his boiling anger down to a simmer. "Are you sure? Is it really over?" He challenged. "Nothing with you or Kaderri is over until bodies litter the ground."

"Easy, Gary," a flash of fire returned to Wolff's eyes. "Gary, to answer your question, no, I don't know who they are or why they are here, but had a suspicion they would show up."

"That's why you were armed?"

"Yeah." He then jabbed a finger at Trainor's chest. "By your presence here, I am to assume you know more than I do. *You* tell me who these guys are! Who put you up to this?"

Trainor huffed. "Guess."

Wailing sirens were heard and suddenly the area was filled with police cruisers and ambulances. Shouts and running footsteps echoed from all points of the compass.

"Help is here, Jo." Trainor said encouragingly, never answering Wolff's question.

Friday, November 14, Raleigh-Durham Airport, Raleigh North Carolina

The ride was uneventful as far a weather and turbulence were concerned and the sun was shining bright in the eastern sky as the Beechcraft descended on final approach into

Raleigh-Durham. With a gentle touch, Doyle brought the plane down and steered it to a hangar away from the main terminal. Dozens of aircraft, ranging from large commercial jet liners to small two seat private planes, taxied about, smoothly working their choreographed dance as they moved on the tarmac to and from the runways and terminals. Kaderri listened intently on the snug headphones as the tower communicated with the pilots and marveled at how all of this was carried out without planes crashing into each other.

Doyle brought the plane to a halt and Kaderri felt a tinge of sadness as the engines were shut down. Part of him wanted to ask Doyle if he could turn the plane around and take it back up in the air for another half hour.

That was the first time that Kaderri had ever ridden in the cockpit of an airplane and he instantly fell in love with flying. From the moment they taxied to the runway back in Scotia, through the takeoff sequence, the actual flying and finally the landing, Kaderri was giddy with excitement. Twenty minutes into the flight, Kaderri had his first flying lesson. It was a five minute show and tell from Doyle on what instruments he needed to pay attention to and how to steer the aircraft.

Once he understood what Doyle had instructed, Kaderri was left to fly the plane for forty-five minutes. He performed steep dives, climbs, loops and sharp turns, putting the plane through his limited acrobatic skill. The one stunt he wanted to perform, a barrel roll, was beyond his limited skill and he didn't even ask for an attempt. To his delight, Doyle surprised him and performed at least a half dozen for him. Because Kaderri was having such a grand time, Doyle extended the flight an extra forty-five minutes so Kaderri could enjoy his moment.

As Doyle began the sequence for shutting down the engines, Kaderri turned to look out the window and saw Jesse Hughes standing at a safe distance with his arms folded across his chest. Kaderri gave a short wave and turned back to Doyle. "Thanks, John, that was fun." Kaderri smiled broadly and hung up the ear phones.

Doyle's smile matched his passengers. "You did well for a rookie. You didn't puke as I thought you may when I did the rolls."

Kaderri laughed heartily. "That's what you were trying to do? I've been every which way you can think of from jumping out of these things. From thirty five thousand foot HALO jumps to eighteen hundred foot LALO jumps, my stomach is used to that sort of stuff." HALO was the acronym for High Altitude Low Opening parachute jump while LALO stood for Low Altitude Low Opening.

Still smiling, Doyle shrugged. "Shit, that's right! I forgot you were a special operator! You guys are nuts."

Kaderri maneuvered his way out of the cockpit and patted Doyle on the shoulder. "Whenever you're ready to try again, just call."

The pair left the cockpit and Kaderri went to retrieve his gear while Doyle opened the cabin door. Bright sunshine and warm air flowed in through the oval doorway. When Kaderri stepped in the doorway and prepared to descend, Hughes was already waiting at the bottom.

"Hey, Marc," he waived and took the duffle bag from Kaderri's hand.

The fun of flying was over and Kaderri immediately refocused his attention on the task of why he was there. "Hey, Jesse," he greeted and turned back to Doyle and offered his hand. "Thanks again, John."

Doyle firmly gripped the hand and barked, "Stop. We've gone over this before," he said a bit annoyed. The smile reappeared. "But you're welcome. Fly back at noon on Sunday?"

"I'll be here."

Friday, November 14, Loudonville, New York

Borushko studied the woods from the warmth of his car and picked his spot to begin. He grasped the binoculars off the passenger seat and checked that the safety on the pistol was engaged. An accidental discharge would ruin everything, including his life if he wasn't careful. His original plan was to first completely circle the residence and locate the most advantageous spot to conduct the surveillance. From what he could see from the road, thick woods framed the land between the houses and because Kaderri's land sloped away from the rear of the house, it was impossible to determine the distance to the far tree line. A well manicured lawn sprinkled with plants and bushes stretched like a sea from the tree line to the house. Figuring he'd move in a counter clockwise direction, he would use the binoculars to peer in every window that afforded him a view to the interior and attempt to spot something that would give him some insight into the man he wanted to kill.

Not knowing what, if any, alarms or cameras were used for security, he dared not venture any closer than the tree line.

With his plan set, he exited the car and stepped into the woods on the right side of the house, taking care that every step he took was carefully placed so he wouldn't make any noise by breaking a fallen tree branch or twig or rustle the fallen leaves.

After five minutes of walking through the leafless tress, he was almost a hundred yards into the woods and adjacent to the three stall garage and realized he was wholly unprepared for his surveillance mission. That was the second time he headed off on a fool's errand in regards to Kaderri and cursed himself for not thinking things through. First, he didn't have proper warm clothing. Instead of wearing a warm field coat and insulated boots, he was dressed in a suit with an overcoat and wingtip shoes. He wiggled his cold toes to generate some heat. Secondly, he didn't have a defined plan or was prepared if contingencies arose. He was flying by the seat of his pants.

For a fleeting moment, he seriously thought about walking out the way he came in, get in his car and drive back to the hotel and wait for word from Rykov and Kalanin. It was only the decades-old loss and anger at who killed his father that prevented him from leaving.

He found a spot that he believed would be advantageous and leaned against a sizeable white birch tree. He brought the binoculars to his eyes and peered into a pair of first floor windows on the side of the house. He had a difficult time discerning what he was looking at inside the unlit room and it didn't help when he rolled the focus. With a grunt and a shiver, he moved past some saplings and found a spot where the next set of windows were. Once again, he brought the binoculars up and was rewarded with the same result.

Slowly he moved towards the back of the property and became a bit excited when he saw all the windows and glass doors. The back of the house was just as impressive as the front. From what he could see, the large windows, sliding glass and French doors overlooked a spacious patio and in-ground swimming pool. But there was an open grassy lawn that sloped down to a pond that would prevent him from getting any closer than a few hundred feet without the very real possibility of being spotted.

The more he studied the landscaping around the patio and swimming pool, the more his expectations of discovering anything useful faded. A wrought iron fence and shrubs created a wall that made the house very private. The Kaderris didn't want prying eyes in their backyard and his weren't going to see anything either.

Defeated in his surveillance effort, Borushko retraced his steps all the way back to the car. Angrily, he tossed the binoculars in the back seat. He started the car and smacked the steering wheel a thud. While he waited for the heater to crank out some warmth, Borushko admitted he had accomplished very little and what an amateurish stunt it was. He wondered if Rykov and Kalanin had better luck than he did.

Friday, November 14, Masozai Kili, Afghanistan

Immediately after Ustad gave the vague description of the territory where Nawaf Al Suqami had his hidden base, satellite, UAV and other fixed wing aircraft flew photo reconnaissance missions over the suspect area to locate it. Added to the intelligence was a signals intercept from a satellite telephone that was not in the allied inventory.

Hundreds of photos and videos were downloaded and studied, the intelligence people looked for of any signs of human activity that may give them a clue to where the bad guys were hiding. Once locations were identified, Special Forces teams were sent out to verify or rule out the suspect locations.

Special Forces Operational Detachment A-301 was assigned four locations to investigate. After two days of searching the hidden valleys looking for the elusive base, the team had cleared three sites. The first one was an abandoned terrorist training site that was destroyed by a cruise missile strike some years ago and never reopened. The second and third sites were a collection of small stone and mud huts that showed signs of human activity and were most likely used for storage in the opium trade.

"I think this one's it," Sergeant First Class Dorsey said with a hint of excitement. He had a pair of binoculars to his eyes.

"Why would you say that?" asked Staff Sergeant Wicker, shoveling the contents of an MRE, Meal Ready to Eat, into his mouth.

"Because, numbnuts," Dorsey lowered the binoculars and turned to Wicker, "there are two, I repeat, two," he held up two fingers, "mother fuckin' tanks down there."

"Two? Like this many?" Wicker held up both middle fingers in return.

Captain Ian MacDonald listened from the rock he sat on and laughed as the two sergeants traded barbs. The team was two hundred meters above and five hundred meters west of the enemy camp. The twelve Americans and two Afghans were well hidden in crevices and under camouflage netting on the military crest of the ridge to observe the activity below.

MacDonald brought his own binoculars to his eyes to study the movement below and confirmed what Dorsey had reported. The compound was full of motion, armed men were scurrying about and one glaring, missing item that helped confirm his belief that this was the camp they were looking for–there were no women or children. He also noted that closer to them was a firing range with ten shooting lanes and an obstacle course carved out the ground with a set of monkey bars.

"Boss?" SFC Michaelson called from MacDonald's right.

"Yeah?" MacDonald acknowledged but kept looking through the binoculars.

"I don't see any fixed weapons. They must think they are pretty secure in here."

Before MacDonald could respond, Master Sergeant Chris Knapp spoke his exact thoughts. "There's going to be a fucking world of hurt descending on this place."

"Listen up," MacDonald ordered. "This looks like the place. Get settled in and watch below. The sun will be setting soon so make sure you stay warm. Mr. Couch?"

"Sir?" The XO called from somewhere hidden in the rocks.

"Check the perimeter. You guys know the routine."

"Right, Boss."

"Gimme the radio," MacDonald called to the RTO crouching nearby. "Time to notify Valley Forge and let 'em know what we found."

CHAPTER EIGHTEEN

Friday, November 14, Raleigh, North Carolina

Marcus Kaderri and Jesse Hughes exchanged handshakes and a heartfelt hug at the bottom of the stairs from the aircraft before they loaded Kaderri's gear in the Blazer.

"Nice airplane," Hughes cracked smile and started the engine.

Kaderri closed the door and put on the seat belt. "It is. It's comfortable and flies real well. Too bad it cost me an arm and a leg to get down here," he stated with mock indignation. "You see, I had a friend who used to be able to get his hands on a helicopter who I thought would fly up to get me."

Hughes feigned shock. "A friend who wouldn't do that for you must be an asshole."

"He is, sometimes." Kaderri agreed and slapped his friend on the knee and let out a laugh.

Years ago Kaderri called upon Hughes to help him out by keeping an eye on Sara while he and Bob Wolff hunted the rogue Mossad officer, Moshe Koretsky in the Adirondacks. Without a second thought, Hughes grabbed a bird and flew himself up to the Adirondack Airport near Lake Placid, NY to help out.

Kaderri remembered he had to call Sara to give her an update on his status. He pulled the cell phone out and speed dialed his home phone number. On the second ring it was answered.

"Hi, honey, you made it ok?" Sara said before Kaderri could speak.

"Yeah, I'm with Jesse now."

There was a moment's hesitation before she continued. "Be careful, Marc." There was fear in her voice. "I love you."

Kaderri had no intention of getting hurt, maimed or killed but he understood her fear. "I will," he answered assuredly. "I love you, too."

After their lust session last night, Kaderri and Sara had talked a bit more about what he and Hughes were going to do. Being secretive had always been in his nature and combined with the classified missions he operated on and his involvement with the CIA, he still hadn't been able to completely open up to Sara. He did his best to limit the amount of information but gave her enough to satisfy her curiosity and ease her anxiety. He informed her he was going to do everything he could to remove the threat that descended upon his friends, which to him were family and possibly to himself.

Without having to tell her, Sara had understood that it was more likely than not that he was going to be eradicating a bad person or people and that was a fact of their lives that she accepted. It wasn't that Kaderri liked killing, but at times it was a necessary tool for survival and justice and he had no qualms about using it.

"Everything good?" Hughes asked.

"Yep."

Hughes drove through the gate, exited the airport and weaved his way through traffic to get on the highway. Kaderri noticed Hughes' head and eyes were in constant motion, checking the mirrors or lingering a little longer on an individual car. His guard was up.

Hughes got right down to business. "You want to go to my place now, or check out the site I picked out for the ambush?"

Before Kaderri could answer the question, his cell phone rang again. The phone he carried with him was for family and friends only. The other phone he carried was for business only and he left that one at home. Only Louise had his private number and she would only call in cases of emergency. Bob Wolff's name and number were displayed on the screen. "Hey, Bob."

"Listen up, Marc," Wolff's words were spoken calmly but clipped. "The motherfuckers just tried a hit on me near my office. We took them out. Gary Trainor and his partner were mixed up in it as well. Took out the two bastards. Trainor's partner was also shot."

Kaderri's blood ran cold. "Is Trainor's partner dead?" His eyes immediately scanned the area around them, searching for signs of an ambush.

Hughes's head snapped in Kaderri's direction after he asked the question.

"No, she isn't," Wolff answered. "Vest saved her but she's sore."

Kaderri faced Hughes and pulled the phone away from his mouth. "Bad guys tried to hit Bob. He's good." He spoke into the phone again and asked Wolff, "Any idea who tried to pull this off?"

"Don't know," he answered curtly. Without a doubt he was pissed at the situation. "But Trainor and his partner, Joanne something, were following me to make sure that I was protected. Actually, he had been following you and she had my back for some time. Because you were out of town he was up this way. It was a good thing he was there. That's all I got out of him so far."

Kaderri creased his forehead at the news. "They say why we needed protection?"

"No, but it was McKnight who asked them to keep an eye on us. I tried calling him but didn't get an answer."

Kaderri's heart raced as a terrifying thought engulfed him. "Bob, when you're done, could you swing by my house and look after Sara and the kids?" Moshe Koretsky and the Israeli commando team had no problem going after him and Sara while they were in his cabin and there was no reason to think these people would be any different.

"I know what you're thinking. No problem. I'll keep you updated with everything."

"What's there to add?" Hughes asked once Kaderri hung up.

"It appears a couple of detectives from the Albany PD were assigned to watch us. Gary Trainor, remember him?" Kaderri asked.

Hughes nodded. "I remember. Took a bullet or two in his shoulder and administered the coup de grace to Koretsky. I dressed his wounds."

"Same guy. Anyway, Trainor was assigned to watch my ass while his partner was assigned to watch Bob's."

"Sounded like a good thing," Hughes stated then asked with a cocked eyebrow, "How would the Albany police know to watch out for a hit on you and Bob?"

Kaderri unhooked his seatbelt and crawled in the back of the vehicle to retrieve the 9mm pistol from his duffel bag. "Paul McKnight is behind that." He held the gun below the windows so no passing motorist could see and chambered a round.

"Well, Boss, your instincts have always been right on. I can't see why they would be wrong now."

Friday, November 14, FATA, Afghanistan-Pakistan Border

Ahmed Rashid Halabi sat in the cramped, covered wagon with an extra blanket over his shoulders to keep warm and swore under his breath. Traveling on a horse drawn cart was not his preferred method of travel. Private jets and limousines were more to his liking but he knew local transportation was the only way to go. At least the cart was made up as comfortable as possible with a small mattress.

The party of eight horse drawn carts resembled a wagon train from the American west. Except the party weren't homesteaders with all their belongings seeking a better life, only hard men transporting weapons and ammunition for use in the destruction of others.

Darkness, along with the cold, had come quickly to the mountains. The darkness wasn't much of a concern, it was the cold that bothered Halabi the most. Though he didn't know the actual temperature, to him anything below ninety degrees Fahrenheit was cold. His thin Saudi blood had a difficult time coursing through his veins.

He tucked the wool lap blanket under his thighs and readjusted the seat cushion. "Saleh," he called out to the man tasked with bringing them to Masozai Kili.

"Yes?" Saleh answered and poked his head inside the rear of the cart.

It was too dark to make out his features and it wasn't necessary to turn on the flashlight. "How many men do we have for security?"

Saleh answered immediately, as if he was expecting the question. "Six."

Halabi understood any more security would draw attention, especially with this convoy. "And how much longer until we get to Nawaf Al-Suqami's?"

Again, Saleh answered immediately, "Eight hours at best. I made a spot in the back for you lay down if you would like. You may want to get some sleep. We should be safe."

Halabi let out a big sigh. Eight hours over rough terrain causing the cart to bobble and sway would make sleep difficult to come by.

Friday, November 14, Albany, New York

When Mikhail Borushko got back to the hotel from his folly, the first thing he did was pour himself a large glass of vodka to warm his insides before he soaked under a hot shower. After the shower, he checked his phone anticipating a message from Rykov or Kalanin but none was there. His anxiety increased as the minutes turned into hours with no word from the duo. Like an expectant father, he paced the hotel room and alternated sitting on the couch and the chair, never being able to remain still in the same location for more than a few minutes.

For the fifth time in the past hour, he checked his cell phone for any messages or missed calls. Like the previous four times, there were no messages or missed calls.

Maybe, he thought as he stared at the phone, Rykov and Kalanin weren't able to pull off the hit and circumstances may have prevented or delayed the mission. But why not let him know? Impatiently, he began dialing Rykov's number then stopped. Once again he fought the urge to call, fearing that he may jeopardize or compromise the mission. With nothing else to do but wait, Borushko poured himself another vodka, fell into the couch and turned the television on to one of the local stations just a few minutes into their noon newscast.

He brought the glass to his lips and paused when he saw the screen. Scrolling on the bottom of the screen was 'Breaking news coverage.' The pretty face of the short haired blonde news reporter filled the screen. In the background was a sea of police cruisers and ambulances with flashing red and blue lights.

"For a recap of this incredible, still unfolding story," the reporter said with a shake of her head and an incredulous look on her face, "a shoot out on Elk Street just a few hours ago between Albany Police and two gunmen has left a female plain clothes officer shot and wounded and the two alleged perpetrators dead. Sources tell me that the wounded officer, whose name has not yet been released, will be ok and has been taken to Albany Med to be evaluated. No identification on the alleged perpetrators as been released, nor has a motive for the this incident."

"Brenda?" the view switched to the black male anchor. In a deep concerned voice, he asked, "Did the police mention how they happened to be there when the shooting began? Were they tipped off as to something that may happen?"

The television screen went to a split picture of the anchor and reporter. Brenda, on the right, shook her head. "No, Alec. It appears that the officer just happened to be in the right place at the right time."

"This is a developing story, so stay tuned…"

Borushko froze and stared. He didn't fully comprehend what the reporter was saying but he did get the gist of it, especially the part about Elk Street. He knew that was where the hit was supposed to take place. "Oh, shit!" he said aloud and leaped out of his seat. Instantly he knew the two dead perpetrators were Rykov and Kalanin and their intended target, Bob Wolff, was still alive.

His mind, along with his heart, raced in an attempt to assess the danger that threatened him. Was there a link that the police could find on Rykov and Kalanin that could lead them to him? He doubted there was an immediate risk to himself, Rykov and Kalanin were trained KBG officers and seasoned Solntsevskaya members so he was sure they covered their bases.

No matter, though, he knew it was time to leave. He flipped open his laptop and looked for flights to Moscow. Getting out of the country was the safest thing for him to do. Though one part of his quest to get retribution on his father's killers had suffered a serious setback, the operation was far from over. His other team was still on track. Pavel Filonenko and Nikolai Chernov were set to assassinate Jesse Hughes.

Like a shark smelling blood in the water, Borushko knew where his prey was and wasn't about to give up.

Friday, November 14, Durham, North Carolina

Immediately after the phone call from Bob Wolff about the attempted assassination, Marcus Kaderri and Jesse Hughes had kept a constant scan of the highway for any signs of an ambush or tail. So far the ride had been clear.

"How much longer to your house?" Kaderri asked as Hughes turned off the main road and into a residential development.

"Couple of minutes."

"Still clear?" Kaderri asked. Hughes would know better than he what would be out of the ordinary in the neighborhood.

"Yeah. I'm going to assume the bad guys know where I live." Hughes paused and amended the comment. "I've seen their vehicle around here so I wouldn't be surprised if I see them now."

"What precautions have you taken?"

"I'm always armed and slightly change my route and time to and from work. Other than that, not much. I didn't want to alert them that I was on to them."

Kaderri eyed his friend. "What about Jill? Have you told her anything?"

Hughes shook his head. "No, not yet. I can't answer the *why* we're being targeted which I know she will ask, and I'm also not sure how she will react. For her, this kind of stuff only happens on television and in books."

Kaderri knowingly shook his head in agreement. He went through it with Sara. When he told her he was a contract employee with the CIA and sometimes dispatched bad guys, she had a hard time digesting it. Her first thought was that her husband was a cold blooded murderer and it took her some time to understand his part time job. "How much does she know about your military career?"

For the second time, Hughes shook his head. "Not much. She knows I was a Special Forces medic but most of the missions we were on are still classified so I've kept mum." He thought a moment and looked reflectively out the window. "That may have to change, I know." He slowed the SUV and turned into his driveway. "Lunch and a beer and then I'll take you out to the ambush site?"

"Sounds good to me."

Hughes beat Kaderri to the rear of the SUV and opened the door. "Let me help," he said and grabbed the larger of the two duffle bags.

Kaderri carried the rifle and slung the small duffel bag over his shoulder and followed Hughes into the garage. "Jess," Kaderri stated in his commander's voice.

Hughes halted and turned around. "Yeah, Boss?"

Kaderri's face was etched with serious but caring lines and looked his friend in the eye before he spoke. "It may be a good time to tell Jill before we go out and execute the mission. You know as well as I there is a chance that one or both of us may not be coming back in one piece or not at all." He tapped his friends shoulder. "Don't leave her wondering."

Hughes drew his lips tight, contemplating what Kaderri said. He nodded. "Yeah, Boss, you're right. I'll just have to find the right time tonight."

Hughes led him through the empty stall where Jill parked her silver Cadillac STS and through a door into a small mud room. The floor was laid with a patterned white and Terra Cotta tiled floor that extended into the kitchen.

Off the kitchen, Hughes gestured with his hand as he stood outside a door.

"This is where you'll be staying." He stepped in and dropped the bag on the bed.

"Thanks." Kaderri nodded.

The room was well kept and nicely decorated with teal wallpaper dotted with ruby red roses and a soft tan carpet. There was a queen sized bed and a lone night stand with a table lamp. A pair of double hung windows washed the room in plenty of light. A dark stained pine desk with a small flat panel TV and a bureau rounded out the furniture.

Kaderri tossed the bag on the bed and then carefully laid the rifle case that contained his M-40A3 sniper rifle next to it. Though he knew it would be difficult to bump the scope in the hardened, cushioned case, he didn't want to take the chance. The slightest misalignment of the scope could result in a missed shot.

After stowing their gear, Hughes gave Kaderri a quick tour of the two story house. The upstairs den was the last room on the tour. Two opposite walls were designated the 'I Love Me' walls. Hughes' was decorated with his many military awards, including citations for bronze and silver stars, his flight and medical certifications and pictures of him with his military buddies. Jill's wall was adorned with academic and law credentials.

"That's the whole place," Hughes said proudly and stepped on the stairs.

"Very nice, Jesse," Kaderri complimented. "Jill does a nice job."

Hughes laughed. "Yeah, she does. She keeps after me and I have to admit, I am improving. How 'bought those beers?" he asked halfway down the stairs. Mockingly, he stated, "I only have Sam Adams. I hope that's ok?"

"Lead the way!" Kaderri pointed happily, already tasting the beer.

They walked into the open, spacious kitchen where Hughes went directly to the refrigerator and extracted the beers. "Glasses are in that cupboard," He pointed to the third one on the left above the counter.

"Got 'em." Kaderri placed the glasses on the counter just as Hughes popped the tops and jump shot them into the garbage can.

Hughes handed on bottle over. "Here you go."

"Thank you." Kaderri took the bottle and slowly poured it into the tilted glass. He held up the glass for Hughes to touch. "To us."

"Right. And making sure this works."

Kaderri leveled a steady gaze. His normally shiny steel gray eyes turned flat and his voice went stone cold. "It will."

"Right."

Lunch consisted of turkey sandwiches and potato chips on paper plates. The conversation was light and focused on current events and what parts of the world they would be fighting in if they were still in Special Forces. They decided to keep the more heavy conversation for the ride to the ambush site. After downing one more beer each, they prepared for the recon mission.

Kaderri changed into navy blue rip-stop cargo pants, a brown long sleeve Under Armor shirt and waterproof hiking boots. To ward off any chill, he had a green windbreaker. When he was done, he grabbed his weapons and met Hughes in the garage. Though they were only supposed to go out to reconnoitering the ambush site, Kaderri wanted to make sure he was prepared for any situation.

When he stepped into the garage, Hughes was fiddling at the back of the Blazer. His wore black cargo pants and wore a fishing vest over a tan sweatshirt. To an outside observer, it would appear that the two men were going fishing or a hike in the woods, which was their ploy. "Ready?" Hughes asked after Kaderri put his weapons in the back. "I already loaded the tackle box and fishing poles."

Kaderri nodded then asked, "Do you have another weapon besides your sidearm?"

"Yeah, I have an -A2 inside." He referred to the standard issue M-16A2 rifle used by the U.S. military. Hughes cocked an eyebrow. "You want me to go get it?"

"It might not be a bad idea. We don't know if our friends are going to follow and an opportunity may arise for us to take them out or defend ourselves."

Hughes let out a long slow breath. "I didn't think of that. That's why you're the commander. I'll be right back." He spun on his toes and jogged back into the house. A couple of minutes later he appeared holding the sleek black rifle with a pack filled with extra magazines and extra boxes of 5.56mm ammunition. He held up the ammo and said, "You'll have to load the mags while I drive. I only keep one mag loaded."

"Got it. Are we ready?"

"Yep. It'll take us about an hour to get there. Hop in."

"An hour?" Kaderri blurted as he climbed into the Blazer. "Jesse, you've got a helicopter and know the vehicle the bad guys use. Why not just mount some weaponry on it and we'll take the fuckers out from the air?"

Hughes started the engine and answered with a straight face. "I thought about it but figured it would be a bit oxymoronic to use a Med-Flight bird for death and destruction."

Kaderri couldn't help but laugh. "Drive."

Friday, November 14, Albany, New York

Gary Trainor had just left Joanne's bedside at Albany Medical Center and walked into the waiting area where Lt.

Chiles entered from the opposite side. "Is she ok?" Chiles shouted across the room. Between them was a sea of officers in blue and a few civilians waiting for their turn to see a physician or get some news about a loved one Both men ignored their fellow officers' frantic questions and closed the distance.

Trainor halted to answer. "The doctor says she'll be fine," he said and jerked his thumb over his shoulder to the swinging double doors, indicating where Joanne was.

Chiles came to a stop and had a concerned look on his face. He put a caring hand on Trainor's shoulder. "You ok?"

Trainor nodded and was about to bring up a sore point with his boss.

Chiles didn't give him the chance. "I'll catch up with you later, Gary, I'm going to see Joanne," he stated and then was gone.

Trainor stood, his blood simmering as he watched Chiles vanish behind the swinging doors. "Damn right there will be time later!" he mumbled.

An hour later at One Police Plaza, that time had arrived.

Two floors above the detectives level, Trainor sat across the white veneer table from Chiles in one of the interview rooms at the station. They attempted to have a conversation in Chiles' office but that turned out to be impossible. Despite the door being closed and blinds drawn tight, there were too many people that knocked on the door and window to ask Trainor how he and his partner were doing. After the fourth interruption in as many minutes, they left for the interview room.

"Ok, Gary, tell me what happened." There was less than a professional tone to his question and more of a personal concern.

Trainor had been waiting for this moment from the time Joanne had been loaded into the ambulance. He exploded out of the comfortable chair and banged his fist on the table. "The same fucking shit that happens every time I deal with Kaderri and his friends! Gunfights and death! All the fucking time! Bullets are flying and bodies litter the ground." He pointed a shaky finger at Chiles and continued. "I told you this was going to happen. It always fucking does!"

Chiles didn't flinch at the outburst. "You're right." He leaned back in the chair and folded his hands. "Feel better for getting that off your chest?"

Trainor leaned forward, gripped the edge of the table and stared hard into Chiles eyes. He was breathing heavily out of his nose and could slowly feel the blood drain from his face. He knew Chiles wasn't the one to blame for what happened on the street. "Yeah," he admitted in a calmer voice and sat back down. "Sorry, Lieutenant."

"No problem, Gary. Do you need to see the department shrink?"

Trainor shook his head and waved his hand. "No, I'm good. I'll get through this like I have all the other shootings."

Chiles tried to lighten the mood. "Look at it this way, at least you aren't Wolff or Kaderri. Those two are being targeted once again. Imagine how they feel?"

"That's one of the things I like about you, Lieutenant. I just killed a man, saw my partner blow away a guy, watch her get shot and you find the positive outlook on things. Goddamn!" He leaned back in the chair, interlocked his fingers behind his head and let out a loud breath. "That's why you're the lieutenant!"

Chiles smiled. "I do my best. Anyway," he turned serious, "tell me what happened." He placed a micro recorder on the table along with a yellow legal pad and pen. He turned the recorder on.

Trainor recounted every step he took from the moment he arrived at the sidewalk on State Street outside Kaderri's office. Chiles let him tell the story without interruption.

When Trainor was finished, Chiles shut the recorder off. "You did everything right, Gary. I'm glad you and Joanne are ok. I'm putting you two in for citations."

"Uh, I don't think that's necessary, Lieutenant," Trainor stammered, a bit embarrassed. "I was backing up my partner, that's all. Nothing different then what anyone else would have done."

"Uh-huh," Chiles rolled his eyes. He quickly changed the subject. "Do you know where Kaderri went?"

Trainor shook his head. "His office said he would be back in to work on Monday." Then a thought occurred to him, "Shit! I wonder if he's still alive?"

"If anyone would know, it would be Bob Wolff. Do you have his number?"

Trainor jerked his thumb over his shoulder. "I have his cell phone number at my desk. I made sure he gave it to me before I rode with Joanne in the ambulance. I'll go call him now." He pushed the chair away from the table and stood.

"Gary," Chiles said informatively and glanced at his watch, "Internal Affairs will be over in about fifteen minutes to talk to you. You know, all that routine bullshit that happens after a shooting."

"Gotcha," he acknowledged and reached for the door handle.

"Gary," Chiles called again. "One more thing,"

Not again, Trainor thought and dropped his head to his chin. He still held onto the door handle when he turned around. "What?"

"You have quite the resume, you know that?" Chiles rose from behind the table, came around to the front and sat on the corner.

Trainor cocked an eyebrow. Puzzled he said, "I don't get it?"

Chiles began ticking off fingers. "All the organizations you tangled with. First it was an Israeli Mossad officer and commandos. The Black Warriors gang and now, the Russian Mafia. Better be careful, ours or the state police tactical unit or even the CIA will be calling to recruit you. How would Amanda like that?"

Trainor said nothing in return. Suddenly pain surrounded his racing heart and his breathing became shallow. It was beating so loudly he could hear it in his ears. Sweat began to bead on his forehead and upper lip and his vision began to blur. He had to leave, now! All he did in response to Chiles was shake his head and open the door. He darted out quickly before Chiles could see what was happening. Ignoring the fellow officers in the hallway, he made straight for the emergency stair case. He yanked hard on the steel door and once inside the stairwell, he stopped and leaned his back against the door's cold metal. His vision began to fade to gray, closing in from the corners of his eyes. Deep breaths, he told himself, take slow deep breaths to calm his nerves and shaking hands. "Easy, Gary," he said aloud, hoping his own voice would help. He closed his eyes and concentrated on his breathing.

He fought the urge to curl up on the floor and pass out. The long deep breaths seemed to help and he kept telling himself to keep doing them. Slowly, his breathing and vision had returned to normal. The pain around his heart faded and the shakes had stopped. Sweat soaked his collar and under his arms. The anxiety or panic attack-at least that's what he assumed had happened to him-had passed. It wasn't the first time he had been in a firefight and it baffled him why his body had reacted that way. He wasn't shot or even shot at. Dead bodies were nothing new either. So why did that happen?

Alone in the silent staircase, he searched his inner feelings to try to come up with the answer. Lost in his confusion, he forgot about calling Marcus Kaderri.

CHAPTER NINETEEN

Friday, November 14, Chatham County, North Carolina

South of Durham, the population and signs of civilization thinned, replaced by the thickening pine forests and rolling hills of sand. The site that Hughes had picked for the ambush was on the eastern shore of the Shearon Harris Reservoir in the southwest corner of Wake county and northeastern corner of Chatham county. The large reservoir, southwest of Raleigh and approximately twenty miles long, looked like a spiny fingered left hand. On each finger, there were countless inlets that resembled piers and docks at a marina.

The nook between the thumb and forefinger was the spot Hughes had selected and the only road that had access to that location was the Bartley Holleman Rd. that ended a few yards from the shore.

"Where the hell is this place?" Kaderri asked looking at the monotonous scene running past the window. It took him ten minutes to load all six of the thirty round magazines and that was the only time he hadn't looked out the window. Since then, all he saw was scrub brush, patches of sand, dense pine forests and not another human being around. "And how did you find it?"

"It is out of the way to say the least." Hughes checked the rearview mirror again. The section of the concrete road was straight with a slight decline as they got closer to the water. "I was on a Med-Flight the other day and spotted it. It's in the middle of nowhere. Pretty good, huh?"

Kaderri had to admit it, it was the perfect spot for what they planned. "So far you've done well. The area will suit us perfectly. I am going to assume that the actual site is just as apt? Now," Kaderri turned to face Hughes, "how much longer till we get to our spot?"

"Not much longer. Fifteen minutes then a ten minute walk."

"How are we going to lure them here?"

"The bad guys have been somewhere in the vicinity of my house every morning and I am going to assume that tomorrow will be no different. If I make it conspicuous that I am going fishing, I'm sure they'll be chomping at the bit to take me out. It'll be a perfect set up. By the way, you'll get in the Blazer while it's still in the garage, that way they won't see you."

Kaderri thought about the plan for a moment and decided it was as good as any but some doubt knocked at his conscience. Something seemed amiss. "Jess, were the bad guys outside your house this morning or when we left to come here?"

Hughes pursed his lips, recalling his memory. "No," he answered shaking his head. "I didn't see them. Shit. This may not work then." Just then he glanced in the mirror and spotted two dark sedans closing in fast. "Marc," he said cautiously. "Coming up quick."

The fact that there were two more cars on the road was nothing to be concerned about. Speeding or drag racing on the desolate road seemed like the thing to do since it was relatively straight and level and no or other civilization was to be seen. In all probability, the two cars were being driven by stupid teenagers racing each other.

Kaderri turned around and watched as the distance from the lead car rapidly closed. He instinctively reached for Hughes' M-16A2, pulled the charging handle and let it go, loading a round in the chamber. Mechanically he tapped the forward assist to assure the round was seated. Instinctively, he thumbed the weapon's selector lever out of the 'safe' position into 'burst.' If he squeezed the trigger a three round burst would be fired.

The first car approached, a burgundy Chevy Malibu with one male driver. The second car, a gold Malibu, remained close behind. Kaderri's heart had a slight increase in beat while adrenaline began to push through his veins. "Easy does it," he unnecessarily instructed Hughes.

Suddenly the burgundy car pulled into the opposite lane and accelerated, rocketing past the Blazer. The gold Malibu fell in behind. Hughes slowed, not trusting the capabilities of the drivers.

When the burgundy car was a hundred yards ahead and the gold only twenty, Hughes and Kaderri gave a collective sigh of relief as they assumed the two cars were drag racing.

All of a sudden the burgundy Malibu decelerated, the anti-lock brakes preventing it from skidding, but the driver turned the wheel and blocked the lane. Before Hughes could react, the gold Malibu hit its brakes and fell in behind Hughes.

They were boxed in.

"Ambush!" Kaderri shouted as he watched the driver of the burgundy Malibu point a pistol at them through the passenger side window. A flash indicated the man fired.

Kaderri stuck the barrel out the window and began to lean out for a shot, but Hughes' strong grip pulled him back.

"Hang on!" Hughes yelled in disgust and jerked the wheel hard to the right. The Blazer careened off the road and Hughes stood on the brakes. Sand and brush erupted in their wake and swirled around them as they came to a stop thirty feet from the road and ten away from the tree line.

"Get out this side!" Kaderri ordered. They were still facing the same direction in which they were traveling and Kaderri had the tree line on his side. Wanting to take advantage of the dust that engulfed them, Kaderri pushed the door open, grabbed the bag of magazines, jumped out and dropped to one knee behind the door. He immediately brought the rifle up to his shoulder and pointed it in the direction of the burgundy Malibu. "Hurry up, Jesse!" He was taking to long to get out! A pang of fear stabbed him. "Jesse?" concern crept into his voice.

The dust began to settle and he could hear voices yelling from one car to the other, but he couldn't make out what they were saying.

A moment later, just as Kaderri leaned back to look inside, Hughes dove out and landed on his face. Gripped in his hands was Kaderri's sniper rifle. "Ready!"

The dust that helped them was also a hindrance. The bad guys couldn't see them and at the same time, they couldn't see the bad guys approach. They had to get away. "Tree line, on me!" Kaderri stood, looked over his shoulder and sprinted for the trees with Hughes was on his tail.

Three powerful strides brought him just inside the tree line, but he continued another twenty yards deeper into it. He spotted a thick gnarled pine tree a few yards off to his left that would provide good cover and he made a dash for it. With a thump, he dove to the ground and brought the weapon up. He trained it on the Blazer, anticipating the enemy would check it out.

"Jesse?" he whispered, not knowing where Hughes had dropped. Kaderri knew he was close because he heard the rifle case being opened.

Immediately Hughes called back. "Ten yards on your left. Two back."

Kaderri risked a glance and spotted Hughes in a prone position behind another pine tree. He was loading the sleek, powerful rifle all the while keeping his focus on the two men that approached the Blazer. He and Hughes were in a good position, each one covering the front and back of the Blazer.

In the woods, with a weapon in his hand, Kaderri was in his element. That was his home. He was a warrior at heart and he knew it and there were few better than he. Kaderri had the -A2 set in his shoulder and peered through the scope onto the torso of the man that approached the Blazer from the front.

Then the other man appeared at the rear of the Blazer. Both had pistols in their hands and walked with a confidence that only men who were accustomed to violence do.

Kaderri's mind raced. It would be easy to shoot and kill both men right now, but he decided against it. He wanted information from one or both of them. An idea formed and he turned to get a quick survey of the land. His experienced eyes scanned the terrain, looking for a spot to set up an ambush. Panning right there was nothing. Turning to the left, he thought he spotted a place that would suit his need, a dip in the terrain that created a small depression and it rose to a higher point, about eight feet, on the far side. It'll have to do. He checked back on the two assailants, they were at the Blazer now and quickly discovered that nobody was inside. They turned their attention to the woods and after a few words, began walking cautiously towards them.

"Jesse," Kaderri hissed. "Let's go, on me."

Nikolai Chernov, the driver of the gold Malibu, stared dumbfounded at the opened door and empty interior. Nobody was inside. The plan that he and Pavel Filonenko, the driver of the other Malibu, devised should have worked. It was simple and the location was perfect! They couldn't have planned it better. Box in the target, shoot the driver and drive away. They couldn't have asked for a better opportunity!

Except that didn't happen. Filonenko's shot missed just as the driver turned away. And in the ensuing sand storm from the skidding vehicle, the driver and his passenger escaped undetected into the pine forest.

"Do you know who that other man was?" Filonenko asked, waving his Makarov pistol in anger.

"Fishing buddy?" Chernov suggested with a shrug. "There's fishing gear in here. Do we go after them?" Chernov asked, already knowing the answer. He offered another option anyway. "Or do *we* get out of here, now and wait for another opportunity?"

"We have no choice now," Filonenko stated the obvious. "We must. We must get them both. We can't let them go to the authorities."

Chernov grunted in agreement. Untold consequences would be meted out if they were caught. "Do you think they are armed?"

Filonenko thought about that for a moment. "Good question. But it doesn't matter, we still have to go get them."

With that said, they turned, pistols in hand and headed towards the woods.

The ambush site Kaderri selected should work well. He and Hughes were twenty yards apart, hidden in the shadows on the tree dotted rise, overlooking the route that the two pursuers should take. Kaderri made sure he left a trail that anyone could follow. The accumulated pine needles were a soft cushion that could hide footfalls, but they also left rich dark soil underneath when pushed aside. So every third step Kaderri took, he shuffled his foot, exposing the dirt underneath. He used that method to lure them where he wanted then he expertly hid his tracks and moved to his current hiding spot. Having the advantage in higher elevation and surprise, Kaderri already knew the outcome of the meeting.

During their short trek, Kaderri and Hughes had switched to their own weapons. Kaderri had his M-40A3 sniper rifle and Hughes had the M-16A2. A quick plan was discussed. Hughes would shoot to kill and Kaderri would shoot to wound and disable. They needed one of the men alive for interrogation.

Five minutes after they left their initial position, Hughes indicated with hand signals he spotted their prey. Two fingers were held up, identifying that both men were spotted. He then moved his hand from left to right, indicating which direction they were traveling. Next, he inverted the fingers and motioned they were walking and then flashed five fingers twice, signaling they were ten feet apart.

They were following the path just as Kaderri planned.

Kaderri nodded in acknowledgment. His heart had a slight uptick in speed and he snugly fit the fiberglass rifle butt to his shoulder. His right eye peered through the Unertl 10X scope and he regulated his breathing.

Partially hidden by the pine trees, the first man came into sight. Kaderri scanned him through the scope. He was wearing blue jeans, a red long sleeved buttoned shirt and black sneakers. The pistol, Kaderri pegged it as a Makarov, was being carried in the right hand, the shooters arm out at a forty-five degree angle from the ground and the trigger finger resting on the trigger guard. Ok, Kaderri thought, the guy was trained in firearms. He was ready to use the pistol but not careless enough to have an accidental discharge. Kaderri, typical with snipers, then noticed the targets' eyes. They were shiny and alive and then he quickly dismissed the idea of him as a human being.

He was a target. A threat to his life and his friends.

Kaderri loosened the safety with his thumb and rested his finger on the trigger. He slowed his breathing and felt the rhythm of his heart beat. Timing was everything for an accurate shot. The shot would come when he was at the end of an exhale and when his heart was between beats.

He trained the crosshairs on the gun hand. The shot would blow off most of the hand and if things worked out correctly, the powerful one hundred seventy three grain bullet would continue on and penetrate one of the legs and disable the shooter. Once Kaderri shot, Hughes would immediately follow by taking out the other man.

Closer they came. The trees were no longer an obstruction as the two men followed the path Kaderri set up. Kaderri trained the crosshairs on the hand, which was gripped tight around the pistol handle and held motionless down by his knee, ready in an instant to be brought to use. He let his breath half way out and felt his heart at rest. One more beat.

Now! Kaderri exhaled and squeezed the trigger. The weapons report resounded in his ears and echoed through the woods.

Kaderri watched the 7.62mm bullet hit the center of the hand, blowing off the three interior fingers and thumb, causing the pistol to fall. Instantly the man screamed louder than the shot and fell to the ground and writhed in pain, clutching the shattered, blood spurting remnants of his hand to his chest.

A three shot burst from Hughes' weapon immediately followed.

Knowing his target was down, Kaderri swung his rifle onto the second target in the event Hughes missed. Through the scope, he could see the body of the second man lay crumpled on the pine floor, blood oozed from the three shot burst to his chest and neck. Kaderri sprung to his feet, slung his rifle and quickly walked to the screaming man. He withdrew the 9mm pistol from the shoulder holster and kept it pointed at a non-vital part of the man's writhing body in the event he tried to flee or use another weapon.

A check on Hughes found him standing over his kill and he put one more burst into the man that had tried to kill him. With a grim, satisfactory look, he strode over to Kaderri.

Kaderri looked down upon the man at his feet with pitiless eyes and a cold heart. The bullet must have missed the man's legs on the descent because he was moving them as if he were walking. The man held his bloody stump of a hand close to his chest, blood covered the front of his shirt and trousers and fresh blood continued to seep out from the wound. The pistol was lying a couple of feet away and in no danger of being used. Kaderri brought his foot back and with considerable force, landed the kick in the man's ribs with a thud. "Shut the fuck up and look at me."

The man turned and focused his eyes on Kaderri and grimaced with every breath he took. There was a look of defiance in the man's dark eyes.

To make sure the man didn't have any tricks up his sleeve or have a chance to escape, Kaderri pointed the pistol at the right knee and pulled the trigger.

An animalistic scream erupted from deep within his belly and he tried to clutch his shattered knee. Instantly fresh flowing blood darkened his pants.

"Sit up," Hughes ordered. He roughly grabbed the man by a fistful of hair and jerked him up. "And shut up!"

"Ahh!" the man screamed in protest.

"I am going to assume you know what's coming so let's do this the easy way." Kaderri then pointed to the dead man. "He isn't going to help so don't try to show any bravado." The man looked over at his comrade and then back at Kaderri but remained silent. "Who are you?" Kaderri barked.

"I don't speak English," the man spat in Russian absorbing the pain in his hand and knee. He then held up his bloody stump in a way of asking for help. The pinky pointed skyward.

Kaderri set his jaw and offered in flawless Russian. "Then we can speak in Russian if it suits you better." Every member in Special Forces was required to speak two languages. Russian was one of the languages that both Kaderri and Hughes had mastered. Kaderri shook his head and pointed to the bloody stump. "You're not getting any help," he said without any emotion.

The man's eyes went wide in a flash of fear before Hughes kicked him to the ground. With the sole of his foot pressing the man's head into the dirt, Hughes retrieved a wallet from a back pocket. He tossed it over to Kaderri and patted the man down. "He's clean."

With his pistol pointed at the man's head, Kaderri opened the tri folded wallet and discovered a driver's license.

Holding it up, he read the name out loud. "Dennis Avery." He cast a hard stare at the man. "Dennis my ass." He lowered his voice and hissed, "Who the fuck are you?"

The man flinched but said nothing. Sweat beaded on his face and trickled into his eye but he did not blink.

Kaderri cut to the chase. In Russian, he offered in no uncertain terms, "Listen, you're not going to live much longer. Don't you at least want your family to know what happened to you? Get a proper burial? I promise you that your body won't be left out here," he gave a sweeping motion with his arm and paused to let that sink in. "If you tell us what's going on. If you don't, you will experience pain that is unimaginable." Kaderri pick up some nasty techniques over the course of his military career and on a few occasions, he put them to use.

The man on the ground gritted his teeth in pain and turned away.

Kaderri didn't use any theatrics or intimidating gestures. He simply pointed the pistol at the man's foot and pulled the trigger. "See."

The man howled in agony and tears streamed down his dirty face. He switched his glance between Kaderri and Wolff standing over him and made his decision. "Da," he then switched to accented English. "My name is Pavel Filonenko."

Now we're getting somewhere, Kaderri thought, at least he gave a Russian name this time. "Well Pavel, why are you trying to kill us?" Kaderri asked.

Filonenko shook his head. "I was not trying to kill you," he pointed to Kaderri. He then pointed a shaky finger at Hughes. "I was hired to kill him."

Hughes' nostrils flared and he visibly became angry. He clenched his jaw and gripped the rifle tighter. He took a deep breath, and then another to calm himself down. "Why?" he asked through clenched teeth. "I don't know you."

"Who hired you?" asked Kaderri.

"Mikhail Borushko hired us. For what reason, I do not know."

Hughes exploded and stepped forward, bringing his face inches away from Filonenko's and thrust the barrel of the rifle into his sore ribs. "You're a fuckin' hired assassin?"

Filonenko grunted in pain and cowered at the rage directed at him. Clearly he expected to be clobbered again.

Kaderri stood frozen at the mention of Mikhail Borushko's name and could feel his muscles tighten throughout his body. Borushko. He and Hughes traded knowing glances. The image of the commanding general of the Soviet 65th Motorized Infantry Division standing high in the hatch of the APC on that dusty, windy road in Afghanistan flashed in front of his eyes. Kaderri shook his head to clear the vision. When he regained his wits, he asked, "Why did Borushko hire you?"

"I do not know the reason."

Hughes exploded again. "Bullshit!" This time he kicked Filonenko in the ribs that ended in a sickening crunch.

"Ahh!" Filonenko shrieked in agony that filtered through the pine trees. He immediately fell to the opposite side and curled into a ball, trying to cradle his right hand and right rib cage with his good hand. His knee was immobile and still oozed blood.

Kaderri didn't give him a reprieve. "Get back up." He waited for Filonenko to work his way back into a sitting position before he spoke again. "I suggest you be more forthcoming with information or my friend here, the one you failed to kill, will make your last moments on earth extremely painful."

Filonenko twisted his face in pain and tried to hold his ribs and bloody stump with the same hand. It wasn't working too well. His face, streaked and matted with dirt and pine needles, was becoming pale and the amount of sweat pouring out of his face looked as if he was caught in a rain storm. Finally, he nodded and around a thick tongue spoke. "We were given a list of men that Borushko wanted dead. He didn't give us the reason why and we, in the Solntsevskaya, don't ask questions when given a directive by someone superior than us. We just do as we are told and get paid for our services. You," he pointed to Hughes, "were the first one we were told to kill."

"Do you have the list?" Kaderri asked. He wanted to ask questions about Borushko. His lineage in particular, but now wasn't the time. "I'd like to see it."

Filonenko shook his head and answered in a weakened voice. "No. Nikolai has it." He tilted his head in the direction of his dead comrade. The blood loss and shock were beginning to have its affect.

Hughes instantly darted over and began searching the body.

Friday, November 14, FOB Warrior, Kashah, Afghanistan

Another sixteen hour exhaustive day ended for Lt. Jack Dover and his Rangers. He fell into his cot after a three minute hot shower and a dash across the camp from the shower trailer to his tent in the thirty five degree night air. Lt. Ramone Hernandez, Third Platoon's leader, had the heaters going and was snoring loudly on his own cot, taking advantage of the time to get as much rest as he could before he left on a three-day patrol.

Dover kicked off his boots and placed the M-4 behind his head against the wall and eagerly climbed into his sleeping bag. Sleep he knew, would be almost instant. Except sleep in a war zone was anything but restful. One ear was always listening for the screams of incoming fire or a guard shouting that insurgents were attacking the base.

He pulled the zipper up to his chin and hunched down into the warmth. He folded his arms across his chest and rolled onto his side.

"Lieutenants!" a voice preceded right before a rapid pounding on the door.

Both Chase and Hernandez reached for their weapons then sat bolt up right.

"Easy, no need to shoot, sirs," a dark figure cautioned, stood in the door and turned on the overhead lamp.

"What the fuck?" Hernandez said first.

"I'm Master Sergeant Tegan. Briefing ASAP with your captain in Ops. Copy that, sirs?"

"Hooah, Master Sergeant." Dover said tiredly and wiped a hand over his stubbled face and watched the senior NCO leave. "Guess I'm not getting any sleep tonight."

Hernandez faced Dover and spoke. "Who was that guy?"

"Duty NCO, I guess."

Five minutes later in the briefing room, the entire cadre of Bravo Company sat in rapt attention as a hard faced Captain Banks began the briefing. "Gentlemen," Banks spoke authoritatively. "I'll be brief. This is an alert order. More details will follow, but I want to inform you that a Special Forces team believes they have found the hidden camp where the meeting of the warlords and terrorists will be taking place. It's a given we will be attacking them in a day or two. All scheduled patrols from here on out are cancelled. The operation will comprise most of the combat force stationed here at Warrior. All the tactical details are being worked on as I speak to you and I can say with certainty we will use a heliborne assault while the 10th Mountain will seal off all escape routes. We have UAV's and satellites providing imagery as well as the boots on the ground. Gentlemen," Banks' eyes turned into slits and he set his jaw. "This isn't going to be easy. Be ready for a fight. Start preparing your men. That is all I have for now. We'll get together for a final briefing with the base commander, Colonel Stouffer." Banks held up his hand to halt any questions. "Dismissed."

This was it, Dover thought. A straight-out-of-the-book Ranger mission and casualties could be significant.

Friday, November 14, Shearon Harris Reservoir, North Carolina

Kaderri hadn't moved from his overwatch position on Pavel Filonenko. His ire was growing inside him and he flexed his grip on the pistol's handle. He kept repeating to himself the name that Filonenko gave up. Borushko, Mikhail

Borushko. Again a name from the past has resurfaced. His mind flashed back to Afghanistan and the mission where he terminated the commanding general of the Soviet 65th Motorized Infantry Division, a man named Vasily Ivanovich Borushko. Coincidence? Kaderri thought not. It was becoming more of a reality that his past had once again come into the present.

A whimper of pain from Filonenko drew his attention. When he looked down, Filonenko was gritting his teeth and holding his forearm as another wave of pain hit. He coughed and spat out blood. Hughes must have punctured a lung when he kicked Filonenko in the ribs. "Just an FYI," Kaderri said scornfully. "the men that attempted to take out Robert Wolff in Albany, New York," he looked for signs of recognition at that statement. When he thought he saw an eyebrow go up, he continued. "They failed, just like you did. I got the call from Wolff earlier this morning saying he and the Albany Police Department killed the two men who were attempting to shoot him. Looks to me your Solntsevskaya need better training."

Filonenko attempted to shoot a dirty look at Kaderri, but the fire in his eyes had faded. The blood continued to flow out of his mangled hand and knee and soaked the dried pine needles under his legs.

Hughes came to Kaderri's side and held out a bloodied sheet of white paper. Ever the medical professional, Hughes wore surgical gloves to protect himself from blood borne pathogens. "Here's the list."

Wordlessly, Kaderri held a corner of the paper and scanned the names. The entire list comprised the twelve men of Kaderri's Special Forces team in Afghanistan. Just as Paul

McKnight had told him. There were check marks next to Hughes', Gallagher's and Newcomb's names. Kaderri shook the paper at Filonenko. "Are the marked names the ones you are supposed to eliminate?"

Filonenko nodded. "Da." In the darkened woods his ghostly pale face was getting whiter, looking like a dim spotlight.

"How many teams are in America assigned to carry out this mission?" Kaderri wanted to know.

Filonenko groaned and closed his eyes to another wave of pain. When he opened them, he answered. "Two, that I know of. I am not sure."

"What are their names and who else did they try to kill?" The harsh toned question came from Hughes.

Filonenko blinked a few times and took a shallow breath. In a weakened voice, he revealed the names. "Rykov and Kalanin. I know they killed one man."

Kaderri felt the blood rush to his face and fought the urge to shoot the bastard at his feet. His instincts on this whole affair were confirmed. "If there were only two teams, they have both been rendered ineffective. What is Borushko's plan?" He exchanged concerned glances with Hughes.

Filonenko drunkenly shook his head. "Borushko didn't tell us the big plan. I only know he wants to kill the top man, Kaderri, all for himself. We are not to go after him."

If there was another level above boiling, Kaderri's blood was there. He gritted his teeth. "Why?" he barked. The urge to beat the man to a pulp threatened to erupt but he was only the messenger.

"I don't know. Like I said before, he didn't tell us everything. We were to kill everyone else." Filonenko's voice grew weaker and the grip he had to stem the flow of blood out of his wounded hand had slackened.

Hughes asked the next question. "What were your instructions if you spotted Kaderri."

"Call Borushko…tell him" Filonenko spoke softly between shallow breaths "…where Kaderri was." His head lolled around before his chin fell to his chest. A vicious cough rattled his body and blood ran down his chin.

Kaderri gave Filonenko a nudge with his booted foot. "Hey." When Filonenko looked up, Kaderri kneeled down and looked into the sunken dying eyes. Proudly, Kaderri declared, "I am Marcus Kaderri."

Filonenko's eyes momentarily shot open at the revelation.

"I wonder what he's thinking now?" Hughes didn't expect an answer.

"Hey!" Kaderri wasn't finished with the interrogation and slapped Filonenko on the shoulder. "Where is Borushko, now?"

Filonenko tried to focus his stare on Kaderri. "Um," his eyes rolled and he teetered on consciousness. "New York."

"City or State?"

"Not city," he whispered.

A shock blast smashed into Kaderri like a crashing wave. In an instant, the image of the man walking into the elevator at his office came into view. That was him! That was Mikhail Borushko! He had the same eyes as the general!

Kaderri took one last look at Filonenko and abruptly stood, knowing that any further conversation would be fruitless. He turned to Hughes. "Do you want him? He was, after all, here to kill you."

"He's mine," Hughes answered curtly.

Kaderri leaned next to Filonenko's ear. "Pavel," he called quietly. "What is your father's name?"

Filonenko tilted his head in curiosity and answered in a whisper. "Ivan."

"Pavel Ivanovich Filonenko," Kaderri addressed him in the traditional Russian manner, "if you believe in God, say your prayers." He then stood and moved back a half dozen paces.

Hughes pointed the rifle above Filonenko's ear and squeezed the trigger. The three shot burst took less than half a second to blow off three quarters of Filonenko's head. Soundlessly, the body simply slumped over on its side.

Hughes looked at the lifeless bodies and slung the rifle. "Marc? How are you going to get the bodies back to Russia?"

Kaderri pulled out his cell phone and dialed. Waiting for the call to go through, he answered. "The CIA is going to handle this."

"McKnight," said the voice on the other end.

"It's Kaderri. We need to talk ASAP, at Jesse Hughes' house tonight if possible. The shit you must have been concerned about has hit the fan. Hughes and I are standing next to two bodies that you need to send back to Russia. There're also two in Albany. "

There was a deep sigh on the other end. "Where are they?"

Kaderri quickly relayed the pertinent information because he wasn't talking on a secure phone. Once McKnight said he understood and confirmed he would get to Hughes' house, Kaderri ended the conversation. The last thing Hughes and Kaderri did was pull the two would be assassins' cars off the road and placed them to be used as a reference point. The CIA would be taking them as well.

"You good?" Kaderri asked once they got back to the Blazer. He had his hands on top of the roof while he stood in the open door. It was a question he always asked his men after a firefight or traumatic experience. Each incident was never a duplicate and neither was the reaction. Hughes deliberately blowing off Filonenko's head was much different than killing him in a firefight.

Hughes turned and faced Kaderri before he got behind the wheel. "Yeah, Boss, I'm good."

Kaderri studied his friend, searching for the slightest crack in his demeanor. Satisfied Hughes was telling the truth, he nodded. "Ok. Let's get out of here."

An hour later, Hughes pulled the Blazer into the driveway, pressed the garage door opener and paused while the door opened. "I could use a few more beers," Kaderri hinted.

"They're inside," Hughes said in agreement and pulled into the bay. "I have a refrigerator full." Jill's Cadillac STS was parked in the other bay. Wordlessly, they unloaded their gear. Hughes stowed the fishing gear and then ran his rifle upstairs while Kaderri walked into the guest room and stowed his.

"Beers," Hughes said when they met outside Kaderri's room and proceeded to lead him into the spacious kitchen.

Kaderri grabbed Hughes by the shoulder and stopped him. "Jesse?"

"Yeah?" Hughes cautiously eyed his friend.

"Listen," Kaderri spoke as a concerned friend, not as a combat commander. "I don't want to overstep, but now may be a good time to tell Jill what's going on. Prep her for when McKnight gets here." Kaderri nodded towards Jill, a pretty brunette with shiny straight hair that fell past her shoulders. She was at the kitchen's island, chopping at a small pile of green onions wearing snug faded blue jeans and a black zippered sweatshirt that was opened halfway down her chest.

The wheels were spinning in Hughes' mind, weighing his options. He traded glances between Kaderri and his wife. "You're probably right, Marc, I just don't know."

Kaderri double tapped Hughes' shoulder. "Let's get those beers."

"Hi, honey," Hughes greeted Jill. "We're back." He strode over to her and gave her a small kiss before she could look up.

She turned her head up to meet him. "What kind of kiss was that?" she asked a bit perturbed.

"I guess it wasn't a good one." He grabbed Jill around the waist and shoulder and dipped her, giving her a long passionate kiss. When he brought her back up he asked, "Is that better?"

Jill giggled and pushed her long flailed hair away from her face. "It'll do." Her tone suggested she knew something was amiss.

Hughes turned to Kaderri who was in the doorway. "Marc's here, remember him?"

Kaderri stepped forward and extended his hand. "Nice to see you again, Jill." He and Sara attended the Hughes' wedding and was sure she didn't remember him. Jill's soft manicured hands held a firm grip.

Jill gave a warm, welcoming smile. "Likewise, Marc. Jesse said you may be staying the weekend and looking for some property."

Her comment caught him unawares. He never established a cover story and apparently Hughes forgot to inform him of what he told Jill. He ran with it. "Yeah, Sara and I aren't sure if we want to move out of New York or just buy another home."

"Right," Hughes said steering the conversation away. "How 'bout those beers?" He moved towards the refrigerator. "Jill, what would you like?"

"I'm set, thanks." She resumed her chopping.

"What can I help with?" Kaderri asked, not wanting to be left out.

Jill shook her head. "Nothing, thanks. I've got ribs ready to go on the grill," she pointed to the platter piled with boiled half racks of baby back ribs on the counter, "cole slaw in the fridge and am finishing up on the barbeque sauce." She tossed the chopped onions into a bowl of thick brown liquid and stirred.

Hughes interjected himself into the conversation. "Barbeque sauce! Grilling? That's my job!" He closed the refrigerator door and cracked open the beer tops, handing the first one to Kaderri, along with a pint glass. "I do the barbequing!" he exclaimed and then snatched the mixing bowl from Jill's grip, whisked the ribs from the counter and marched out onto the patio where the grill was already heated.

When Hughes was done on the grill, he placed the ribs in the center of the patio table with the cole slaw. Kaderri sat with Hughes to his left and Jill across from him. The seat to his right remained vacant. The patio lights were turned on to impede the growing darkness.

"So, Marc," Jill began just as they sat down to eat, "are you just looking at land down here or a house? By the looks of you two," she pointed to the dirt and grass stains on their clothes, "it appears you were really checking out the land."

Kaderri took a long pull from his glass, using the time to create a solid cover story. The dirt stains were something he couldn't hide and he would have to think of some explanation. He also waited a moment to see if Hughes was going to use this opportunity to inform Jill of the situation they were in. He glanced sideways and caught a very imperceptible shake from Hughes-not yet. Kaderri nodded towards Jill and put the glass back down. "Land, most likely. I'm not sure what I want to do yet."

"We get a lot of that down here," Jill acknowledged. "Any place in particular?"

Kaderri didn't know the names of many locales in North Carolina, outside of Ft. Bragg where he did extensive training, and was at a loss with an answer. Hughes stepped in with a laugh. "Marc doesn't play well with others so I'm taking him where there is less population!"

Kaderri laughed along and added, "I live on a sparsely populated street and also have a cabin in the Adirondack Mountains. So I guess what Jesse says is true."

Jill took the answers for what they were worth and conversations moved to small chit-chat and Kaderri proudly told the Hughes' about the addition to his family, Sean and Sam. They reminisced a bit about their military service and comrades and of course the fallen ones whose funerals they attended.

All the while, Jill had been taking it all in, learning a little bit more about her husband and a past life.

Kaderri finished off the last rib on his plate, sat back in the cushioned chair and wiped his sticky fingers and mouth with the cloth napkin. "My god, guys, those ribs were great! Jill, that sauce was to die for! You should sell it."

"Thank you," Jill smiled. "I can give you the recipe if you'd like."

"I'd love it. Thank you."

Hughes pushed his empty plate to the center of the table and stared at his hands for a moment. Kaderri knew what he was about to say. Jill looked upon him with a furrowed brow.

"Jill," Hughes said quietly and then paused.

The nuances of married couples are learned over the course of time and Jill immediately picked up on the slight change in the way her husband called her name. "Yeah?" she said cautiously.

Kaderri leaned back in the chair and sipped at his beer, eyeing his friend.

"You learned a bit more about me tonight sitting here with Marc."

"I did," she admitted a bit guardedly.

"There's quite a bit more..." Hughes mumbled, which caused Jill to become alarmed.

"And?" She leaned forward in the chair, her eyes becoming wide with concern.

Hughes rubbed his chin, pursed his lips and blew out, causing a soft whistle. "Ok, there's a lot more but I'll hit the highlights. As you know I was a Special Forces medic and Marc was the commander of one of the Teams I was on."

Jill cut him off. "That part I know."

Nuances worked both ways. Hughes leveled a steady gaze at his wife and stated in no uncertain terms, "Hon, I don't need you to play lawyer with me on this."

Kaderri watched for Jill's reaction and saw her a bit taken aback by her husband's demeanor. He presumed she never saw him like this before. This was the 'no bullshit' side Kaderri saw in the field all the time, the professional soldier. "I'll leave you two for this." Kaderri rose from the chair, stacked the dinner plates and carried them and his empty beer glass into the kitchen.

Friday, November 14, New York City, New York

For three hours, Mikhail Borushko wandered the international terminal at New York's JFK International Airport. His mind was a quagmire of what he was doing and how he should finish the job of killing Marcus Kaderri. He even admitted to himself that it was one big conflict of actions and wondered if he bit off more than he could chew. He simply had difficulty in making decisions. At first he informed the assassination teams that he was the one who was going to kill Kaderri because he was the commander of the unit that killed his father. Then in Albany, he changed plans and vacillated between using Rykov and Kalanin to help him kill Kaderri. In fact, he told them he wanted them to kidnap him. He also planned on using his friends, Pyotr Agranov, Osip Martov, and Feliks Grigorenko, if they could get out of Chechnya. Approaching Sergi Mirovich for more men to help was out of the question. If he informed Mirovich of Rykov and Kalanin's death, he knew for certain that Mirovich would deny his request and in all likelihood, would put an end to his pursuit to get his father's killer.

No, Borushko decided. Getting back to Russia was what he needed to formulate a sound plan. He would have the time to do it correctly and think things through. He also decided that he was going to get his three friends, the ones that he trusted with his life, to finish the job and keep it from the head of the Solntsevskaya until it was over. To get those people required a trip to the headquarters of the 15th Motorized Rifle Division, parent unit of the 70th Motorized Rifle Regiment or to the Ministry of Defense in Moscow.

"May I have your attention," the female voice came over the speakers in the waiting area. An immediate hush overtook the crowd. The attendant was at the podium by the jetway and the door leading to the aircraft was open. "We will be boarding in just a few short minutes for Aeroflot flight SU zero three one five to Sheremetyevo, Moscow, Russia. First Class passengers will be boarded first. Please…"

Borushko rose to feet, ignoring the rest of the instructions that were being delivered. If someone from Albany connected him to the deaths of Rykov and Kalanin, they were going to detain him before he got on the plane. He gave a quick scan of the waiting area for law enforcement approaching or at least fixing their sights on him. Completing a full rotation, he was relieved that nobody had paid any attention to him. Like the other travelers, he held out his boarding pass as he paused next to the podium.

"Thank you," the woman attendant said robotically, taking the slip of paper and putting it under the scanner. "Have a nice flight."

"Thank you," he parroted and walked confidently down the jet way.

CHAPTER TWENTY

Friday, November 14, Albany, New York

What a fucking day, Trainor thought, as he sat behind his desk toying with a pencil. The furthest thing from his mind was the shooting and he was most concerned with what caused his anxiety or panic attack in the stairwell. He started from the beginning of the ordeal to try to pinpoint its cause. After the shooting, he rode with Joanne in the ambulance to Albany Medical Center. A thorough examination revealed deep bruises where the bullets hit and thankfully nothing broken.

Following his chat with Chiles came the interview with Internal Affairs which was nothing spectacular. It took a total of twenty minutes and most of the concerns addressed was the welfare of himself and Joanne. There was absolutely no chance that Trainor was going to be charged with any wrongdoing and the IA inspectors passed along the message from Chiles that he could go home for the rest of the day.

He stood, pushed his chair under the desk and took a long look at Joanne's empty seat before he walked away. He turned and bumped into Chiles. "Hey Lieutenant."

"Got a call from McKnight when you were with IA expressing his thanks."

Trainor shrugged it off. "Ah."

Chiles eyed the detective. "Think what you want, Gary," he lowered his voice so no one can hear. "But I think it's a big deal when someone of McKnight's rank and position calls to thank you. He said he'd try to call you later."

Trainor didn't know how to respond. "Ok."

Chiles clasped Trainor's shoulders. "Take off, Gary. Go home."

He left, but didn't go directly home. A few pints of beer at The Steer House and a Reuben sandwich for lunch was more to his liking. During the course of consuming the pints, meal and the drive home, his mind remained occupied with questions about why he had the anxiety attack and how would Amanda react when he told her he was one of the officers involved in the day's shooting. He cursed himself for not talking to her and letting her know that he was ok. A simple message left on her voicemail stating he was going to be late was all he left. Then again, if she wasn't aware of what had happened, telling her would be pointless and in fact it would probably do more harm by making her worry.

This shit is getting complicated, he thought, as he turned into the driveway. Lights were ablaze inside the house and white smoke curled out of the chimney. Snow flurries began falling and were illuminated in the beam of the headlights, lifting his spirits. The change of seasons, especially snow, had that effect on him.

He pulled in the garage and killed the engine. He stared at the interior door and could picture the scene inside the house. Amanda would have quite the romantic setting in place. The dinner table would be set with long tapered candles burning and wine in an ice bucket. A roaring fire would be crackling in the fireplace and Amanda, making herself look exquisite, would be ready to serve one of her culinary masterpieces and set the mood for the night.

He just hoped he wouldn't disappoint her.

It was just as he expected. The moment he walked in the house from the cold garage into the kitchen, he was blasted with the sounds and smell of a crackling fire and mouth watering flavors. He kicked off his shoes and hung his coat on the peg rack and stepped into the kitchen.

"Hi, Amanda," he said as normal as he could. The setting was just as he imagined. Amanda was at the stove, wearing black tailored slacks and a pink cashmere turtleneck sweater that accentuated her curves, doting over the pots and pans. Off to his left, candlelight from the candles on the table flickered on the walls of the dining room.

Amanda turned, her sparkling eyes lit up when she saw him. She dropped the wooden spoon and in her fuzzy pink slippers shuffled over to him. "Hi, baby!" She leapt into his arms and wrapped herself around him and gave him a deep passionate kiss.

Suddenly his apprehensions began to melt away. Her tongue filled his mouth and her perfumed skin infiltrated his nostrils. Perfectly, her body fit into his and he squeezed her tighter. There's no way he could disappoint her, he told himself.

"Mmmm," she cooed and pulled her mouth away but remained wrapped around him. "I am so excited about tonight!"

Trainor gave a quizzical look and challenged, "It's the cut off. What is there to be excited about?" She finally uncoiled her arms and legs and stood.

She turned to give attention to the sauce on the stove. "You, me and sex! Lots of it!" She shut the burners off and prepared the dinner plates.

Normally Trainor would have gotten excited but his mood was tempered. "Since you put it that way, I guess that's a reason to be excited. Do you want me to do anything? Besides pour the wine?" He learned long ago that pouring the wine she had on the table or in the refrigerator was his job when it came to preparing dinner.

"It's on the table," she thumbed over her shoulder.

Trainor removed the foil cutter and corkscrew from the utensil drawer and grabbed the wine. It was red. A zinfandel. He associated red wine with beef and assumed that's what they were having. But past experience had told him not to make those assumptions so quickly and the aromas that were swirling in the room told him otherwise as well. "What are we having?"

As soon as the cork popped she turned holding two plates. "Duck with a blackberry sauce."

Trainor's mouth instantly began to water and he happily poured the wine.

"Did you get the message I left on your phone?" She flirtatiously rubbed up against him, gave a devilish smile and set the plates down.

He shook his head and moved to the other side of the table and sat down. "No, I shut my cell phone off earlier." In the ambulance with Joanne, the calls were constantly coming in asking how they were doing. Not interested in talking to anyone other than Joanne, he shut the damned thing off and never turned it back on. "What did it say?"

"You would like it." She winked and raised her eyebrows a few times. "It was very dirty and I gave a hint of what we might be able to do tonight!"

"Sorry I missed it," he said with little conviction.

Amanda dropped the utensils on the table and gave him her full attention. "What's the matter, Gary?"

"Tough day on the job" he admitted. He hoped she could handle what he was about to say. Suddenly his hand began to shake and his heart beat faster. Not again! He tried to hide the attack from Amanda and began taking long deep breaths. Then it hit him like a two by four on the side of his head. That was it! That had to be it! That was the reason why he had the anxiety attack back at the station. His subconscious feared that Amanda would leave again because of the danger of the job. Please, God, don't let it happen! He closed his eyes and prayed silently and fought to control the growing symptoms.

"What happened?" she pressed.

He took some deep breaths which seemed to help. "I guess you haven't been watching television, huh?"

"No." Now alarmed, she wrapped her hands in the apron. "Gary what happened? Is everything ok?" Her voice trembled.

The moment he feared had arrived. He hid his trembling hands on his lap and could feel his forehead breakout in a sweat. He closed his eyes and said another prayer that when he was done telling her, Amanda would still want to marry him, not run away like the last time. When he opened his eyes, he stared across the table into her fearful eyes, swallowed and told her the story. "Where to begin," he paused, collecting his thoughts. "Shitty day, actually. Kaderri, the guy I was supposed to keep an eye on, wasn't around so I went to help out Joanne on her surveillance and wound up getting into a shootout."

Stunned, all Amanda could blurt out was, "*What?*"

"Yeah. There was an ambush." Trainor recited the whole incident, holding out the gory details. "Joanne is home, resting and I stopped by The Steer House for a few beers." He felt a tear form in his eye. He was afraid she would call off their relationship and that would be too much to handle.

Amanda sat in open mouthed silence, unable to speak. Finally, the whole incident registered. She shot out the chair and bolted over to him. Sobbing, she squatted next to him and pulled his head to her chest. "Oh, my God, honey! Are you ok? You sure you didn't get hurt, did you?"

"No, I'm fine." He spoke into her breast.

"Really?"

He pulled his head out of her chest and held her shaking hands. He couldn't tell who's hands were trembling more. "Yes, really. My concern, Amanda," he took a deep breath, "is how are you and what your reaction to this is going to be." He stared at her face, trying to gauge her reaction. She just stared back, not saying a word. "I actually had a panic attack over this."

Amanda gently sat on his lap and clasped her hands. "I'm ok." Then she understood what he was saying. "Ah, I get it, that whole me running away thing."

Trainor fidgeted nervously under her. His eyes welled up. "Yeah."

She held his cheeks and put her nose up to his. "I'm here for you, forever," she whispered with assurance. "After the Black Warrior thing, I accepted the fact, as you pointed out numerous times, that danger can be anywhere. I'm staying put." She gave a lingering kiss on the forehead. "Is that what you wanted to hear?"

"Yes." He had been holding his breath and let out a heavy sigh of relief. "That's what I wanted to hear," he confirmed and the tears flowed freely down his cheeks.

Amanda's face grew serious. Concern dominated her features. "Do you want to talk about it?"

The thought crossed his mind. It did feel better when he shared the story with her. "There's nothing else to tell. Can we eat?"

"Ok, hon." Amanda kissed him again and slid off his lap to retake her seat.

All through dinner he talked and she listened intently, only asking him to repeat a name or clarify a point. When he was done, dinner and the bottle of wine were finished as well. "That's what happened." He admitted to himself he felt much better.

"Scary shit," she acknowledged.

Trainor laughed. "Scary shit is right. It's worse when its over. During the incident itself, you don't have time to think. You only react. Hey," he turned the focus off himself and put it on to her. "What time are you leaving tomorrow for Rochester?"

"I'm not sure, now."

"Why? What do you mean?" She had to go. It was the surprise wedding shower her friends were throwing for her!

With a straight face, she answered immediately, "I might be too tired."

Trainor became totally lost. "Huh? Tired from what?"

"Honey," Amanda gleamed proudly, "tonight I get to sleep with a hero!"

Friday, November 14, Durham, North Carolina

Two beers later, Marcus Kaderri had the kitchen and dinnerware cleaned and put away in the proper locations. Not once had he ventured out onto the patio to check on how things were going between Jesse and Jill, though he did manage to steal a few glances through the glass doors and was happy to see that they were holding hands. He took that as a good sign.

The door bell chimed and Kaderri instinctively knew who it was. Being cautious for there may be a chance that Filonenko wasn't being entirely truthful about the number of assassination teams in America, Kaderri quietly moved to the front door. He located the light switch and flipped it on, hoping to catch the caller off guard. He didn't have his weapon handy so he balled a fist and partially hid behind the door when he pulled it open. With his training in martial arts, he was prepared to strike, hard and fast, if necessary.

"Hi, Marc," Paul McKnight greeted as if it were a routine meeting. He wore a navy pinstripe suit and holding a manila folder with red and white stripped tape across it and no smile on his face. Kaderri relaxed his fist and shook hands with his former boss. "Come on in, Paul." He stepped aside and closed the door after McKnight passed. "Jesse is on the patio explaining things to his wife. This way." He turned to lead McKnight to the patio, not giving him a chance to protest or question why Hughes was spilling the beans.

As they passed through the kitchen, Kaderri retrieved two more beers and the bottle of chardonnay. Experience told him McKnight wasn't staying long but offered a drink anyway. McKnight declined with a wave.

"Paul's here," Kaderri announced after sliding the doors open and stepping onto the patio.

Hughes stood and offered his hand. "Thanks for coming." He turned to Jill and introduced her. "Paul, this is my wife, Jill. Jill, Paul McKnight."

They shook hands. "Hi, Jill."

Jill remained seated. Her once smiling upbeat look had been replaced by confusion and worry and dried tears streaked her face. "Hello," she said quietly.

McKnight cast his glance back to Hughes and discretely pointed his finger in Jill's direction, indicating if he wanted to hold this conversation in front of her.

Hughes nodded.

With the introductions out of the way, they all sat down and as usual, Kaderri got right to the point. "Needless to say, I'm..." he held his tongue against the litany of curses that were about to roll off because of Jill's presence. "Pissed off. Paul, what's going on?"

"You have every right to be," McKnight agreed. "This is something that nobody could have predicted. Here's what it looks like." He stopped and directed his statement to Jill. "Jill, could you excuse us for a few minutes, please?"

With a hard stare, Jill shot back as if she was cross examining a witness. "Why? I have a right to know what's going on with my husband. If people are dying and it involves him, I'm staying."

McKnight donned his professional demeanor. In a flat, serious tone he responded, "It doesn't work like that all the time, Jill. There are things going on here that are bigger than us and you are not privy to the information."

Her eyes narrowed and her lips drew tight. "Are you going to tell me that this has something to do with national security?"

McKnight pulled no punches. "The beginning does and it's CIA business. So please, Jill, when we are done with that part, I'll send your husband in to get you." He steepled his fingers under his chin and waited for her to leave.

The three men at the table all held the same serious look and Jill understood there was to be no compromise. Quietly she rose from the table and gave her husband a confused and troubled look when she walked past.

Hughes reached out and grabbed her hand. "I'll get you in a couple of minutes, honey."

Just as soon as the doors were closed, Kaderri launched right into the questioning. "Paul, did your people remove the bodies?"

McKnight nodded. "They did, along with the rental cars. They sanitized the place as well. Good directions. Have no fear, you guys are in the clear."

Kaderri had no fear about legal ramifications but it was reassuring to hear. The second question he asked went to Hughes. "Jesse, how did things go with Jill? Did you tell her what happened by the water?"

Hughes nodded and breathed a sigh of relief. "It went well. I gave her a quick rundown of what I did in the teams and my limited participation in the CIA." He shrugged before he answered the second part. "I think the jury is still out, especially on the CIA bit, but when I told her we were being targeted by bad guys and we acted in self defense, she kinda understood. I think she's scared I'll go to jail or something."

"She has nothing to worry about," McKnight assured him. "I'll tell her that."

"You guys gonna be okay?" Kaderri was genuinely concerned about their relationship. He went through the same scenario with Sara years before when he and Wolff were working on a mission. With him becoming open about his involvement with the CIA, it actually strengthened their relationship because he didn't have to hide it from her anymore. That was why he was insistent on Jesse talking to Jill.

"We'll be ok," he said guardedly.

"Ok," McKnight began, steering the conversation to the issue at hand. "From all the intel we have gathered, this thing began from the day you assassinated General Vasily Borushko in Afghanistan."

Kaderri nodded knowingly. "I'm getting that sense." He wasn't ready to let on that Filonenko revealed in his dying moments that Mikhail Borushko wanted him and Team A-524 dead. At least until he heard all of what McKnight had.

"Marc, from what we could figure, the Russians, particularly the Russian Mafia, are after yours and A-524's asses. Remember I told you about your team being discovered to be in Afghanistan? Mike Karmal gave it up under interrogation by the Russians. We have it on video tape."

"Yeah, I remember." He thumbed in Hughes' direction. "He found a printed list of our names on one of the dead bodies." He then recalled the conversation he had with Len Puckett in his hospital bed. "I also spoke to Len after you were there and he confirmed it."

McKnight frowned on that news. Even though Puckett was talking to Kaderri, it wasn't good that an intelligence officer was giving out information without permission. "What did he tell you?"

"Very little. I'm hoping you could clear this up so *I* can take care of matters."

It wasn't lost on McKnight that Kaderri emphasized *I*. "Ok. Here's what we got. It appears the Russians, I should clarify that, the Russian Mafia, is in business with a Saudi arms dealer named Ahmed Rashid Halabi. Halabi is the Agency's primary target and it looks as if the Russians are middlemen.

They will sell weapons to anyone. Anyway, we figured that's how the Russians came to be in the cave in Afghanistan. They were on a business trip and got caught up in one of our ops."

Kaderri rubbed his chin and took a mouthful of beer. Still puzzled, he asked, "What does that have to do with A-524 and me?"

"These guys were interrogating Len Puckett and Mike Karmal and Karmal broke. During the interrogation he let it out that Puckett was in Afghanistan before killing Soviets and was on the team that assassinated General Borushko. After that, he gave up your team. The reason why? That we still don't know."

Hughes leaned forward. "How do you know all of this? Is it credible?"

McKnight nodded. "It's credible, Jesse. I watched the videotape of the interrogation. There was more to it than the Russians asking about your team. The Taliban were asking about current operations and somehow, we're not sure, Karmal let it out that Puckett was fighting the Russians in eight-five. From that point on, all the Russians' focus was on that. The only thing that Karmal didn't give up was who the shooter was that killed Borushko. The Russians were intent on knowing that. Give the little guy credit, he didn't give that up."

Kaderri followed up with, "Do you know if our presence in Afghanistan made it to the Russian government? That could cause one hell of a headache."

McKnight shook his head. "We don't believe so. First, we don't believe the Solntsevskaya would give that information to the government. It wouldn't serve any purpose. Second, our tech guys have been able to penetrate the computer systems and cell phones of the men who sent the information electronically and it seems to have limited dissemination."

"That's encouraging," Kaderri declared.

"Anything else?" When the two shook their heads, McKnight turned to Hughes. "Jesse, you can get Jill now."

"Right." Hughes rose from the table. "Beers on the way," he called over his shoulder and disappeared inside.

Kaderri was getting annoyed. McKnight still hadn't answered his question about how all this pertained to him. "Paul-."

McKnight held up his hand, anticipating the question. "The two Russians, um," he opened the folder that he carried in and scanned one of the sheets. "Their names were Eduard Tomsky and Aleksander Karsavin. One of them sent the names via e-mail from a cell phone while they were still in or near the cave. Was this a specific operation with the aim of interrogating Americans? It doesn't appear to be. My guess it was an 'Oh, shit! look what we found' moment."

Hughes and Jill came back and retook their former seats. Jill's forlorn look had softened considerably. Hughes handed out the Sam Adams and this time McKnight took one. Out of his jacket's breast pocket he removed three Arturo Fuente cigars, cutter and matches and passed them out. "I know these guys like cigars. Jill, I have another if you'd like?" he asked and removed a fourth and held it out for her to grab.

She waved it off, "No thanks. Are we going to get into what is going on? I'm a bit confused right now. All that Jesse had explained to me earlier was that his military career was a lot more, uh, complex than I thought and has had some involvement with the CIA since he got out. "

McKnight and Kaderri both alternated their gazes between Jill and Hughes. "Sure," said McKnight. "First, Jill," he reached out and patted her hand, "let me assure you that your husband is in no legal danger from the incident earlier today. Period." Jill's face visibly relaxed upon the news. "Ok, taking things to current time," McKnight addressed the group, "after A-524 personnel fell into the wrong hands and the deaths of the two men on your team, Randall and Evers, I got suspicious that you guys were being targeted for elimination. It was pure speculation on my part and I took it to the DCI and asked if we, the Agency, could put a few pair of eyes on you guys. Unfortunately, the answer came back no, especially without any hard evidence to release the manpower from their duties. So I made some phone calls to local police precincts and asked a few favors."

Kaderri toyed with the cigar. "So you were able to get Gary Trainor and his partner to watch mine and Bob's back." It was more a statement than a question.

"I called Lieutenant Chiles and asked for help. I didn't know who he would assign, if anybody. I'm glad he did send Trainor. He's a smart kid."

"Who else is being kept an eye on?" asked Hughes.

McKnight flipped a few sheets of paper in the folder. "Zack Newcomb and Tom Gallagher. After today though, I think we'll be covering everyone's back."

Kaderri was digesting the information McKnight had just given him and poured the beer. It all began to make sense!

He pieced all the Intel and came up with one conclusion. It was hard to believe but not out of the realm of possibility. One more piece of information would solidify his conclusion. McKnight left out that important piece during his short summation. "Paul, the Russian who sent the text or e-mail, who did it go to?"

McKnight gave a deadpan look and rubbed his chin before answering. Long, drawn out seconds ticked away before he answered. Finally, he spoke. "Mikhail Borushko."

"That's who sent the hit squads to kill us," Hughes confessed.

McKnight eyed Hughes guardedly. "Where'd you get that from?"

"Filonenko gave it up on his death bed." Kaderri had previously given McKnight the names of the two men who tried to kill them.

Hughes leaned forward. "Do you know if there is a relationship between him and the general?" He was on the same page as Kaderri.

McKnight gave a tepid shrug. "Possibly, but we haven't confirmed it yet."

Kaderri clamped his jaw and huffed. Calmly, he simply stated, "Yes, Mikhail Borushko is the son of Major General Vasily Ivanovich Borushko."

McKnight held the glowing match to the tip of the cigar clenched between his teeth. "Could be."

"Holy shit," Hughes said softly.

McKnight lit the cigar and white aromatic smoke swirled around his head. He eyed Kaderri knowingly. "You have a theory. Let's hear it." McKnight tossed the box of matches to Kaderri.

Kaderri explained. It all seemed so simple. He had to watch what he said because of Jill's presence. "It adds up. Put everything together from what you told us you saw on that tape and combine it with the information we extracted from the guys…by the water. Mikhail Borushko is the son of the general and he wants his revenge for what happened. He was in my office the other day." He struck the match and in a dramatic effect, the flame flared and highlighted and cast shadows on his rugged, angry face.

"Revenge?" McKnight suggested easily. "You think that's what this about? The kid wants revenge?"

"Yeah, I do."

McKnight rubbed his chin in thought. "I have to agree with your assessment that Borushko junior is coming after the team." McKnight cleared his throat indicating there was more to come. "It looks as if they have succeeded in two hits."

Kaderri and Hughes reacted immediately and sat straight up. "Whoa. Two?" Kaderri hadn't received any phone calls stating that another member of his team had been killed. "Who else besides Patrick Randall? Did those bastards get John Evers as well?"

"It appears they tried to kill Evers. McKnight said. "I asked for a review of the autopsy and eyewitness accounts of the accident. There had been one report that a man in the back of a darkened SUV had a rifle pointing towards Evers' Viper. The autopsy noted that there was a hole in Evers left cheek. Because of tissue damage from the intense fire, the medical examiner couldn't determine what had caused it but believed that the entrance wound came from an object outside the car and it strongly resembled a bullet hole. A forensic team is going over the car to find a bullet."

"Oh, my God!" Jill uttered. Up to this point she hadn't said a word.

The anger in Kaderri was beginning to turn into rage. "He wants me and my men." He balled his hand into a fist and gnashed on the cigar. In no uncertain terms, he let it be known in a steely voice, "And *I* am not going to let that happen again."

CHAPTER TWENTY-ONE

Saturday, November 15, Masozai Kili, Afghanistan

Nawaf Al Suqami had been awake since the sun's first rays cracked the dark sky. Though tomorrow was the big meeting, some tribal and jihad leaders had already arrived and most were due in later that day. Nobody had given him a time in which they would arrive, men living that life simply didn't publish their ETAs for the simple fear of being killed or captured.

He stepped outside his quarters, wrapped in a warm woolen blanket and holding onto a steaming mug of green tea. The cold air smacked his face, which caused him to take a quick inhale of breath and wrap the blanket tighter. He stood just outside the doorway as the bright morning sun peeked over the mountains and illuminated his compound in a golden hue. He scanned the compound and noticed more tents had been erected overnight. More leaders and soldiers had arrived for the meeting.

This is it, he thought. The leaders were gathering here, at his place, to form an alliance once and for all to kick the

Americans out of his country, just as they did to the Soviets more than two decades earlier. With the gathering, decisions on leadership and tactics were going to be made. He knew for certain that he wasn't going to be the man to emerge as the military leader for such a great undertaking. He didn't have the military experience of the Chechens or the leaders of Ansar Al Salam. Sure, he fought his battles against other tribes and small units of the Afghan Army, but attacking a fortified American military base was way out of his league. That was better left for someone else to handle.

The best way to handle this, he decided, was to play his part as the host and manager. Listen to what everyone had to say and see how he could turn the situation to his advantage in receiving more weapons, a larger distribution area for his opium and maybe find a way to settle an old score or two.

Out of blue a loud *pop!* caused him to jump and reach for his sidearm. A puff of smoke rose above one of the tanks and then another *pop!* quickly followed. A cheer from the unseen men working on the tank was heard as the engine roared to life.

Movement across the compound caught his attention. A few fighters on foot entered, quickly followed by a horse-drawn wagon. Trailing was a small caravan of horse and donkey drawn carts. The first wagon in the train broke off and headed straight for him. It stopped five meters from him and out from the back jumped a man. A scarf and knit cap covered his face but when he approached Al Suqami, he removed the warm protection from his face and offered his hand.

Al Suqami couldn't help not smiling. Ahmed Rashid Halabi had arrived!

Above the compound hidden in the rocks and out of view from below, eight of the twelve men of SFOD-A 301 were asleep, or in some level of sleep. They were nestled in their sleeping bags, staying warm for as long as they could. The four men assigned the last watch rotation remained on the military crest of the hill. Through night vision equipment, they kept a watchful eye on the compound below and the surrounding ridge, notating every movement. SFC Peter Mohr, the spotter for the sniper team, was one of the men on watch. He had a powerful set of binoculars glued to his eyes and the sight of the horse drawn wagon caravan and armed men on foot advancing into the quiet compound drew his attention. "Check this out," he said softly and chuckled, "we're back in the old west." He traded the binoculars for the more powerful spotting scope for a better look. The first wagon halted in front of the main building and a passenger hopped out of the rear, only to be greeted by another man standing in the doorway.

"Captain," Mohr called.

"What have you got?" Captain MacDonald rolled out of his sleeping bag and sat next to Mohr on a flat rock.

"Pioneers heading into the homestead, Boss." He pointed to the wagon. "More bad guys arrived last night, too. I'd say another thirty men. Tents are springing up all over."

The sudden double *pop!* of the tank engine coming to life got everyone's attention.

"What the fuck was that?" Dorsey asked, shaking the sleeping bag off.

"Tanks starting their engines," Mohr answered. He swung the binoculars from the wagon to the tanks and put them under observation.

"Hey Captain, take a look," SFC Ryan Hill, the team sniper, called from MacDonald's left. He was peering through the powerful 30X Swarovski scope mounted on the Barrett M-107 .50 cal sniper rifle. Lying between him and Mohr was a laptop with images of the men who were supposed to be at the meeting.

"What do you have?"

With a gloved finger, Hill pointed to one of the images on the screen. "I think this guy just got out of the lead wagon." He then pointed down into the compound.

"Oh, yeah?" MacDonald got down on the ground and peered through the scope of the sniper rifle. "I'll be damned. That's him." He let Hill retake his position behind the rifle. "Let's get on the horn and call in the tally with who and what we have so far. That OGA Weston is going to be happy his prized possession is in town."

"Sure this guy is supposed to be captured, Boss?" Hill asked with his eye glued to the sight and finger hovering near the trigger. "I can blow him in half right now."

MacDonald tapped Hill's boot. "I'm sure you'll get a few shots in once the Rangers assault this place."

Saturday, November 15, Moscow, Russia

Mikhail Borushko was surprised he had such a sound sleep on the transatlantic flight to Moscow. In fact, he put the roomy seat back and fell asleep once the plane reached its cruising altitude of thirty five thousand feet and missed the delightful roast beef dinner served in first class. He awoke moments before the stewardess announced that they were on final approach into Moscow's Sheremetyevo 2 airport.

Immediately upon landing, the first thing Borushko did was check his cell phone for messages. Eagerly he scrolled through the fourteen messages, his fingers itching to open the messages from the teams of Nikolai Chernov and Pavel Filonenko and Lev Kalanin and Dimitri Rykov. His heart sank when he reached the bottom of the list. There were none from either team.

Borushko went through the motions of deplaning, grabbed his luggage and hailed a taxi for a ride to his apartment in the city. He could have had a member of the Solntsevskaya pick him up, but that would have alerted others he was back in country and raised questions. During the taxi ride he kept thinking what might have gone wrong with the two hits. In his heart he knew Kalanin and Rykov were dead, but the fate of Chernov and Filonenko had yet to be determined. He took comfort in the old saying that no news was good news and believed that Chernov and Filonenko were still carrying out their mission.

But he was growing weary and impatient. Damnit! He whipped out the cell phone and dialed Chernov's number. One ring, two... On the fourth ring, Chernov's voicemail picked up. "Shit!" he cursed aloud, angrily closed the phone and tossed it aside. Then it dawned on him that it was the middle of the night back in the States and Chernov was probably sleeping and didn't hear the phone.

Borushko stared out the window as the taxi made its way through the lighter than normal traffic and drummed his fingers on his thigh, contemplating his next move.

Saturday, November 15, Raleigh, North Carolina

The conversation the prior night at Jesse Hughes' house ended with McKnight offering to fly Marcus Kaderri back to the Stratton Air National Guard Base in the morning instead of waiting for Doyle on Sunday. Since he accomplished his mission earlier than expected, Kaderri took him up on the offer. He called Doyle to let him know he was off the hook and in no uncertain terms he would still pay him for the lost revenue.

Kaderri thought it would be easier to take a cab to the airport and let Hughes and his wife carry on any further discussions they may have with the recent revelations, but Hughes insisted on driving his friend and former commander to the airport.

A restful sleep for Kaderri never came during the night. He lay awake, staring at the ceiling working through scenarios of how he was going to get Mikhail Borushko before he killed any more of his men. With all the evidence, McKnight promised he would get the CIA more involved in protecting Kaderri's team and gather information on Borushko's whereabouts so Kaderri could take care of business. By offering assistance, that made whatever Kaderri decided to do pseudo-sanctioned by the CIA.

The hardened combat warrior in him had been awakened and he would not stop until the threat was eliminated. That threat now had a face, a name and a reason and Kaderri would see it through to the end.

Kaderri and Hughes got an early start and the first priority was to stop at a Dunkin' Donuts for coffee and bacon egg and cheese breakfast sandwiches to go.

"Hey, Jess?"

"What's up?" He turned his sunglass covered eyes from the road.

"I can't see the Solntsevskaya sending more and more teams to America to continue their folly, especially with two teams being eliminated. Indications are Borushko is still in my home area and he hasn't completed his mission."

Hughes put forward the question. "You're going after Borushko, aren't you?"

Kaderri stared at his friend behind his own sunglass covered eyes and without delay, answered, "I am."

"Thought so," Hughes knew how his commander worked.

With a hard voice, Kaderri offered, "Do you want in on this?" It was a tough question for Hughes to answer, Kaderri knew. Hughes had the same deep loyalty to the team just like he did and knew Hughes would normally drop whatever he was doing to help out. But the situation with Jill was still not resolved and he didn't know if Hughes wanted to take the risk that his marriage may end if he went along.

Without hesitation, Hughes turned and met Kaderri's gaze. "Name the time and place, Boss. I'm there."

Kaderri offered his hand in which Hughes grasped tightly. As he expected, their bond, which was forged from spilled blood, was still unbroken.

The next time they spoke was when they pulled alongside the sleek, white Gulfstream IV aircraft that Kaderri was to take back home. They shook hands as Kaderri stepped onto the ladder. "Thanks for the ride, Jess. I'll be in touch."

"You know where to find me."

Saturday, November 15, FOB Warrior, Kashah, Afghanistan

"Gentlemen, the HVTs have arrived." The platoon leaders and sergeants of Bravo Company, 1st Battalion, 75th Ranger Regiment sat in silence and listened to their CO, Captain Jonas Banks, give the warning order. "At 0400 tomorrow, we will be carrying out a heliborne assault on an previously unknown terrorist compound in Masozai Kili," Banks said from the front of the briefing room. Two large flat panel screens mounted on the wall flickered on, showing an aerial view of he compound. "There will be no preparatory bombardment. We're going for surprise. Nevertheless, there are approximately one hundred to one hundred fifty enemy forces in the compound, including armor. Expect a hot landing."

Banks paused while one of the staff members began passing out stapled packs of paper. Lt. Jack Dover took two packs from the sergeant to his front and handed one to SFC Isles, seated on his left. The quarter inch thick packet contained photographs of the compound, both aerial and almost ground level, and photos of the HVTs along with a brief biography.

"Shit," someone muttered under their breath.

"What was that?" Banks asked sharply.

Lt. Phil Case spoke up. "Sir, doesn't doctrine call for at least a three to one advantage to the assaulting force on a dug-in enemy? From what you have told us, we're a bit shy of that ratio."

Banks nodded in agreement. "It does, but from the intel reports we have been given, the enemy doesn't have prepared defenses and doesn't seem to be an organized and trained force." Banks could see the concern on his men's faces and addressed the issue. "I understand your concern and brought it up at the meeting with the mission planners. Recon photos." Banks nodded to a specialist working with a laptop. Two close-up images of the compound appeared on the flat screens. Banks pointed to the one over his left shoulder and continued the briefing. "The compound is designed more like an outdoor festival than a military facility. We should be ok, but be prepared for anything.

"Now, these photos were taken over the past few hours by Predators and a special forces team on site. The high value targets are what we are after." Banks got into the meat of the mission and directed the staff to follow along with the photos in their packets. "Intel has placed most of the HVTs in these buildings. On the left is the barracks," he pointed to the screen, "and the building on the right is the HQ where Nawaf Al Suqami lives. The rest of them are scattered among the tents. Those men in your packets are the prize. If at all possible, don't kill the fuckers." Banks shrugged, knowing the difficulty his company faced. "Jack."

"Yes, sir," Dover gave his full attention.

"Your platoon's assignment is to take down the HQ."

"Hooah, sir." Dover momentarily felt a surge of pride that he was singled out for one of the jobs, but that quickly faded when he realized Banks was handing out assignments to all the platoons. He just happened to be first.

"We have to bring our 'A' game on this one," Isles whispered in Dover's ear.

Dover nodded in agreement.

Banks continued with the briefing for another fifteen minutes. Call signs were reinforced, order of movement and everything else that was needed for a heliborne assault. Finally, he closed the briefing with a question and answer period. After the last question he made his final address. "Listen, men, this isn't going to be easy. Go now and get prepared. Check your gear, get your ammo and…you know what has to be done. Be ready to go at a moment's notice. May God be with you."

The staff was dismissed and Dover immediately turned his attention to his ever trusted platoon sergeant SFC Isles. "Ok, Sarge," Dover walked stride for stride with him until they got caught up in the bottle neck near the door, "what insight do you have for me? You've been doing this longer and have done it before. This I know is going to be a lot different than a training mission." Dover was smart not to assume he had all the answers and leaned on the more experienced soldier.

"Lieutenant," Isles began with a smile, "so far you've done well for a butter bar." He used one of the slang terms for a second lieutenant. "You know what has to be done. The only thing that I can add is bring extra water and ammo and make sure everyone has their body armor."

Dover swelled with pride at Isles' compliment and he knew it shown on his face. He tried hard to conceal it by turning away. "Thanks, Sarge."

Isles clapped him on the back. "C'mon Lieutenant, let's get the platoon ready."

"Jack," Hanks called over the din of the speaking voices. "Come here, please."

Dover and Isles stopped on a dime at the sound of Banks' voice, pivoted on their toe and fought against the exiting crowd to get to the commander. "Yes, sir?" Dover asked once he reached Banks.

"You two did a great job in the cave complex and I though it would be rewarding for you to take down this group of terrorists." The smile faded and was quickly replaced with a hard stare. "You up for it?" Banks challenged.

This was the second time in two minutes that Dover received accolades. Without hesitation Dover accepted the challenge. "Hooah, sir! Rangers lead the way!"

"Atta boy! That's what I was hoping for." Banks slapped him on his shoulder. "One more thing. The OGA guy," Hanks used the military slang for the CIA, Other Government Agency, "Weston, he'll be attaching himself to your unit. His main mission is capturing the gunrunner Halabi."

"Shit," Isles blurted. "Just what we need. A tag along to baby sit."

"Don't worry, Sergeant," Banks alleviated his concern. "Weston is the real deal. He was a Green Beanie for quite a few years before he jumped ship into spookville. He won't be a hindrance to you."

"That's good to know, sir."

Banks gave a curt nod. "Get your men ready, Jack," he said by way of dismissal.

"Yes, sir!"

The duo turned away and Isles informed Dover that new material was going to be needed. "Sir, we now have to add flex cuffs, flash bang grenades, blindfolds, and few more items for a snatch job."

Dover smiled crookedly. "Good thing I have you to keep me in line."

"If you say so," Isles smiled in return.

Saturday, November 15, Loudonville, New York

Marcus Kaderri was the only passenger on the plane and he liked it that way. The solitude allowed him to put his mind frame in complete mission mode. There was so much that needed to be done and the most important item was to locate the whereabouts of Mikhail Borushko. Kaderri savored the thought of how the hunter had turned into the hunted and was completely unaware the tables had turned. He could feel the blood pressure rise as he thought about the friends he lost and the ones slated for death at the hands of Mikhail Borushko.

When Kaderri shot General Borushko, there was nothing personal about it. It took place on the battlefield where people die very frequently. It was a risk that all combatants knew and accepted when they served. But when it came to the general's son, Mikhail, it was personal. The murderer was going to *know* who killed him and why.

About a half hour before landing, the frame work of a plan took shape. Kaderri called Bob Wolff for a meeting later in the day to discuss what he wanted to do and go about getting it done. Without hesitation, Wolff agreed.

The minute he left the aircraft, Kaderri phoned Sara to let her know he was back on the ground and heading home. When he pulled into the garage, she was standing there poised, like a sprinter in the starting blocks waiting for the gun to go off. As soon as he exited the car, Sara leapt in his arms and held on for dear life.

"I'm so glad you're home safe!" She fought to choke back the tears that welled up in her eyes.

Kaderri held her tight, keeping her feet off the ground. With a deep inhale, he breathed her in, the fragrance of her shampoo and natural scent filling his nostrils. "Me too, Babe." Their lips locked, giving each other a long, loving kiss.

"How did it go?" Sara asked with trepidation after he put her down.

"Quite a few surprises," he admitted and moved to get his bags and gear. He guided her out of the chilly garage and into the house. "Where are the kids?"

Sara grabbed a bag from him and led him into the kitchen. "They're inside." Suddenly she announced, "Daddy's home!"

There was a pair of shrieks, a crash of toys and the fast pitter patter of little feet running. From the living room Sam and Sean jockeyed for position to get to daddy first. "Daddy!" Sam screamed and took the lead.

"Daddy!" Sean wasn't far behind and pulled along side her.

Kaderri squatted down and opened his arms. Simultaneously they slammed into him and like a gate, his arms closed around them and he effortlessly lifted them off the ground. "Hey, guys!" He puckered his lips to kiss them both at the same time. Like a magnet, both kids zoeroed in and gave him a big, loud kiss. "What are you two doing?"

"Playing with blocks!" Sean answered first and wriggled to get down and continue his playing. "Big towers!"

"Yeah, wanna play, Daddy?" Sam asked. She was more content remaining in his arms.

Kaderri put her down and patted her behind. "I'll be there in a minute. Let me put my things away."

"Ok!" The kids zoomed off to continue their construction project. Kaderri picked up his bags and turned to Sara. He knew she wouldn't be pleased with what he was going to say but he knew she would not protest. "I'm going to meet with Bob later."

Sara's face became a worrisome mask and her eyes showed fear. "This thing isn't over yet, is it?" She push a strand of dark hair away from her face.

Kaderri shook his head and took the bag from her hands. In a voice that betrayed no emotion, he simply said, "It's not. I'll fill you in after I put these away."

Saturday, November 15, Albany, New York

Sleep for Gary Trainor was as elusive as a fox. Considering the tiring bouts of lovemaking he and Amanda engaged in and combined with the horrendous day he had, he figured he'd fall asleep in a heartbeat. It didn't happen. Every time he closed his eyes, he had a vision of Amanda leaving him once again, this time for good. Also in vivid clarity he could see Joanne getting shot and falling to the ground just before he pumped rounds into her shooter. No matter how hard he tried to think of something else to get his mind off of the both visions, it failed.

At seven in the morning, he had made the second pot of coffee while Amanda finished getting ready for her trip to Rochester for what she thought was an important business engagement. Barely capable of keeping his eyes open, he walked Amanda to the garage door, gave her a warm hug, a long passionate kiss and a tap on her behind before she got in the car and drove away.

When Amanda turned out of the driveway, he gave a limp, final wave and she beeped the horn in return. He closed the door and turned to go right back to bed. Maybe a long uninterrupted rest was waiting for him. As he trudged up the stairs, his legs were so heavy they felt as if he was walking through quicksand. He fell into the messed bed and within two minutes of crawling under the covers, he was snoring.

Four hours later, Trainor woke to the ringing phone. Amanda had called to let him know that she had made it to Rochester and excitedly told him that she didn't have a meeting but her friends had given her a bridal shower. They had a whole day and night of fun planned for her and she wouldn't be coming home until tomorrow. That was, of course, if he was alright from yesterday's shoot out. If he wasn't, she would leave to come home and take care of him.

Trainor let it be known in no uncertain terms that he was fine and she was to enjoy herself and not to worry about him. When he hung up with her, he realized sleep was not going to come, he decided to take a shower and grab something to eat.

Marcus Kaderri and Robert Wolff exited the car and strode purposefully up the walkway and rang the doorbell on the well-maintained Cape Cod house.

A few silent moments ticked by and there was no response from inside the house. Wolff then asked, "You think he's here?" He switched the six pack of beer to the other hand.

"I peeked in the garage when we walked up and saw one car in the garage. I don't know if he has two cars and he's driving the other."

Wolff pushed the doorbell again. "You think he'll go for it?"

Kaderri heard footsteps approaching the door from inside the house. He turned to Wolff and shrugged. "I guess we'll find out."

Tired, alone and nothing to do, Gary Trainor grabbed a beer and plopped himself in front of the television to watch some college football games. The first beer went down easy halfway through the first quarter and a call for chips and dip was heard when he went for another cold Michelob.

On his was way back from the kitchen, the doorbell rang. With beer and food in hand, he strode to the door, yanked it open and was stunned to see who was standing there. He took a inhale of breath and held it a moment.

"Hey, Gary," Marcus Kaderri said with a slight smile. His piercing steel gray eyes betrayed that smile. Trainor immediately knew he was here for strictly business. Standing right behind Kaderri was Robert Wolff holding a six pack of beer.

"Uh, hi," he managed to respond after a moment's hesitation. "Come on in." He moved out of the way and let them pass. "What brings you guys over?" Once inside the warm house, Trainor closed the door and offered his hand.

A strong shake was given and Kaderri was the first to speak. "Gary, we need to talk."

"Right," Trainor acknowledged and led them into the kitchen.

Both Kaderri and Wolff removed their jackets and placed them on the arm of the couch in the living room and followed Trainor into the kitchen. They grabbed a seat in no particular order but ended up sitting next to each other and across from Trainor.

Trainor opened the beers that Wolff brought in and passed them around. First, he had to get Kaderri a glass.

"Gary, how are you doing?" Wolff asked, shaking his hand. "Good?" Wolff referred to Trainor's mental state regarding the shooting.

"I'm fine. You making out ok?" Because of their dealings in the past Trainor knew there wouldn't be any personal issues with Wolff.

"Ah," he shrugged it off. It was just another day to him. "Listen," Wolff began, "I want to thank you again for saving my life."

"Hey, I was just doing my job. No hard feelings for me yelling at you?" Trainor referred to the incident on the sidewalk while they were attending to Trainor's partner.

Wolff shook his head. "No hard feelings. I completely understand your emotions but if you continued I would have had to shut you up."

Trainor laughed heartily. "I'm sure you would have."

"How's your partner?" Wolff inquired and folded his hands together.

"She's ok. Bruised ribs and still has the small cuts on her face. Thanks for asking."

"First," Kaderri held up the beer glass. "Here's to you doing a commendable job saving your partner," he gave a sideways glance to Wolff, "and Bob's ass too!"

"Amen!" Wolff shouted and then all three touched glasses and bottles.

"Thanks, guys. Now, what brings you over?" Trainor wanted to know.

"An offer," Kaderri simply stated.

Trainor's antenna went up. The dealings he had with Kaderri and his friends were always violent and deadly. But the oath he swore to uphold the law weighed heavily on his mind. An uneasy feeling appeared in the pit of his stomach. The whole situation he was in, he corrected himself, allowed himself to become involved in, could end here and now. But knowing the men seated around the table *are the good guys,* he would at least hear them out. He felt their stares on him and he met their eyes. What he saw in them was fierce loyalty to their friends and a reminder not to cross them unless you were prepared to pay the consequences. They were men to be honored for their beliefs in right and wrong. "Ok, I'm listening."

"Gary," Kaderri then leveled a gaze that could freeze ice. "You have never backed down from a situation that involved us and have called on us for our assistance. I believe you like working with us, no matter how much you want us to believe the contrary. You get the adrenaline rush, just like we do."

Trainor was speechless. He tried to counter what Kaderri had told him but he knew deep inside that Kaderri was right. Kaderri and Wolff were always on the right side of things and he liked being a part of righting wrongs and doing good. That was the main reason why he became a police officer.

He listened in fascination as Kaderri and Wolff tag teamed in delivering the information on what led up to his and Joanne's assignment of watching Kaderri's and Wolff's back and the subsequent shooting of Joanne. That was then followed up with the information that was extracted from the would-be assassin in North Carolina. Obviously there was more to the story than they told him. He understood things were classified or top secret or whatever levels the military had for secrets and they couldn't tell him. If Kaderri's and Wolff's objective was to get him angry about Joanne getting shot, it worked. "What is it you want from me?" he asked once they were finished.

"McKnight called me on the way over," Kaderri said. "They traced Borushko to Moscow from Albany to JFK. Oddly enough, he used his own passport. He's there now. He placed a call that went unanswered to one of the men Hughes and I confronted."

You mean, the boor bastard you interrogated, Trainor thought. "So you guys are going into Russia to kill Borushko, is that it?" He got up for another round of beers.

Without a blink or a sense of hesitation, Kaderri and Wolff both answered. "Yes." Kaderri expanded. "He's not going to stop until he gets to me and I assume my team. We want to know if you want to come along. We have everything you need to get in and out of the country."

Trainor, not completely stunned by their actions, shook his head. "I'm a detective in Albany. I can't do what you're asking– murder. That goes against the oath I took as a police officer!"

"Murder? It depends on how you look at it," Wolff contested. He took a large sip and eyed Trainor. "To us, it's prevention because Borushko plans on killing us. At the same time, justice will be served for the crimes that he committed."

Trainor admitted to himself that is was a sound argument. It did make sense, but didn't that go against his oath? He leaned back in the chair and understood Kaderri was going for the preemptive strike. More blood was going to be shed but Kaderri and Wolff were going to do it on their terms. In actuality, there was no difference between what they were planning and how the military went after terrorists. Part of him believed in the whole notion, especially since he did some background checking on the Solntsevskaya. He believed they needed to be dealt with by using an eye for an eye response.

Trainor had a few questions that needed to be addressed. "Question. If I tag along, what kind of protection will I have?" He spread his hands. "I mean, you guys, and I'm sure your buddy, Hughes, have CIA or diplomatic, protection. What about me?"

"Fair question," Kaderri admitted. In his confident and knowing demeanor, he stated, "We'll take care of that."

Trainor suspected Kaderri would say that, but if that fell through, he had an ace up his sleeve that he was unwilling to play at the moment. "Ok. How are you getting into Russia?"

"I'm working on it. I have a few options."

Trainor chuckled. "You have thought of everything, hadn't you?"

"Definitely not." Kaderri's blank face cracked into a smile. "But I'm working on it." With the beers gone and the purpose of the meeting coming to an end Kaderri wrapped it up. "Thoughts?" he asked Trainor.

"I don't know guys, there's a lot to digest," Trainor shifted in his seat. "I have to think about this. When do you need an answer and when do you plan on heading out?"

"An answer by Monday and we'll be leaving later in the week."

"Is there anything else I can do to help? Detective work, not tactical stuff? Do you know what this guy Borushko looks like?" Trainor asked, truly wanting to help.

Kaderri nodded. "I have an idea of what he looks like. He was in my office the other day and I'm going down to my building as soon as I leave here to look at the security tapes."

Trainor whistled softly. "You guys have your shit together."

Kaderri and Wolff rose from the table. "We do," Wolff answered.

Kaderri offered his hand. "Let me know by Monday." All three shook hands and made their way to the door.

"Thanks for the beers and the invite," Trainor said with a crooked smile. "I'll be in touch."

"You think he'll tag along?" Wolff asked reaching for the car door.

Kaderri slid behind the wheel and closed the door before answering. "I think he will." He started the Porsche and backed out of the driveway. "Trainor, I believe, knows he thrives on the excitement of the danger but won't freely admit it. I don't know why he won't just come out and say it and I don't care, but he is very capable and would be an asset to us." He looked over at Wolff. "I'm going to my building to study the security tapes of when Borushko was in the building. Want to join me"

"Yeah," Wolff nodded. "I want to see how much junior looks like his old man."

Joanne Bauer lived in the same town as Trainor and the moment Kaderri and Wolff left, Trainor drove to the grocery store, picked up a six pack of beer and a bag of chips and went to his partner's house to see how she was doing. There weren't any signs of life in the house when he pulled into the driveway but he decided to ring the doorbell anyway. A person who was just shot, he reasoned, wouldn't venture far from home.

He rang the doorbell on the ranch style house and listened for any movement from within. He waited thirty seconds before pressing the button again.

"Hold on!" Joanne shouted from the other side of the wood door. She pulled the door open and revealed a welcoming yet tired smile. Her dark circled eyes seemed to brighten when she saw him. "Gary! Come in!"

"How are you doing?" he asked and stepped on the hard wood floor, immediately concerned for her. She led him to the living room where he took a seat on the three cushioned couch.

He placed the bag on the coffee table and dropped his coat on the love seat. Flower bouquets of every size, color and scent covered all the flat surfaces in the room. The only open space was in front of the flat panel television. Curious, he went over to the largest display and found it was from Bob Wolff.

"What brings you over?" She winced in pain when she sat in the straight back chair across from him.

"Still hurts a lot?" he regained his seat

"Yeah. Deep bruised ribs. Hurts like hell sometimes. Just hurts all the time."

"I'm sorry, Jo. I came over to see how you were doing and if you needed anything. You good?"

Joanne nodded. "I'm good."

"Here," Trainor reached into the bag and pulled out the beer and chips. "You can use one of these and I want to have one with you." He twisted the tops off and handed one to her.

"Thanks."

"Speedy recovery, partner," he toasted and they touched bottles.

She took a small sip and put the bottle down. "That's all I dare to have. I'm on pain killers and I took one ten minutes ago."

"Oh, I get it, bad mix." He made a falling motion with his hand. "Ok," Trainor acknowledged then smiled, "I'll drink them both." He put the mouth of the bottle to his lips looked over the butt at Joanne as he took a sip. She grimaced and flinched in pain again when she placed the bottle on the table. He quickly stood. "You have to drink something with me. What can get you? You have soda?"

Joanne smiled. "I really wish I could have that beer, but yeah, soda will work." She nodded with her head instead of pointing with her hand, "It's in the fridge. Thanks."

"How are you doing?" Joanne asked after he handed her the can of Coke. There was concern in her voice about how he was handling the fact that he killed a person.

"I'm good," he admitted more nonchalantly than he expected. The comment Kaderri made to him about getting the adrenaline rush sank in. It was true. He was also aware of the fact that he had become indifferent to killing. In the forefront of his mind he reasoned it was a bad man who he had killed and it was completely justifiable.

"Sure?"

He brought the bottle up to his lips again and nodded while mumbling, "Uh-huh."

"Ok."

They made some small talk and only briefly did they touch on the subject of the Russian mafia and her being shot. It was just too close to the incident to bring it up in conversation. She was still pretty shook up about it. Trainor also made it a point not to bring up the possibility of him tagging along with Kaderri and his buddies to go to Russia to catch the bastard who ordered the hit in which she was shot. He knew she would protest loudly and besides, he didn't want her to get in trouble in the event things went wrong. The less she knew, the better off she was.

As their conversation moved along, Trainor kept a watchful eye on her movements. If she moved a certain way or reached to far, she would grimace in pain. At first, Trainor felt a pang of sorrow for her and the pain and discomfort she was in. But as their conversation progressed, she went on to tell him her tightly wrapped ribs hurt when she took a deep breath, laughed or coughed or moved the wrong way. It didn't take long for the sorrow he felt to turn to anger. Steadily, he was working towards his decision.

Trainor drained the second beer and decided he had stayed long enough. Joanne's eyes were getting heavy, one of the side effects of the pain killer. "I'm going to take off," he said and collected the empty bottles. "I'll put these in the fridge," he held up the remaining beers. "They're ready when you are."

"Can't wait," Joanne smiled weakly.

Trainor put the beers away and found a box next to the garbage can for empties. He returned to the living room and donned his coat. "You need me to do anything for you?"

"Nope, I'm good, thanks. I'll be ready to go in a couple of days." She gingerly rose to get out of the seat.

"Sit," he said harshly and placed his hand on her shoulder. "I can find my way out."

Joanne gave a tired smile. "I'm going to the couch to lay down. Don't let the door hit you on the way out."

CHAPTER TWENTY-TWO

Sunday, November 16, FOB Warrior, Kashah, Afghanistan

The order to go came at 0153 hours for a 0400 launch. In a flurry of activity, the Rangers masked their faces in camouflage paint and checked and rechecked their gear one more time before moving out to the tarmac to the board the big CH-47 Chinook helicopters. Forming up in platoons, the units marched out to their assigned helos and waited for orders to board the birds. Each man handled the passing time differently. Some grabbed more sleep while others sat quietly and reflected on their lives. Others boasted about what they were going to do when they met the enemy while others carried on conversations as if it were another ordinary day.

For Lt. Jack Dover, this could be a defining moment. This was the first combat air assault he was involved in. Prior to this, all of his assignments were patrolling and ambushes. This time they were going to conduct a mission in which the Rangers were specifically designed and trained for and were going into the teeth of the tiger. Thoughts about his confidence ran the gambit. Why was he tasked with assaulting the main building and capturing or killing the men in charge? Could he lead these young men, many only teenagers, on the assault and be successful and bring them all back? Would he survive and be able to go home to his beautiful fiancée?

In his gloved hands he held an eight by ten aerial photograph of the compound and under a flashlight, committed every detail to memory. Clearly he could see the two tanks and the growing number of tents that housed the enemy his company would be engaging.

Using a finger, he traced the route to the objective, knowing that once the shooting began, he would have to adjust on the fly. No plan ever survived contact with the enemy. He thanked God in Heaven the report from the special forces unit on site had stated that there were no crew served weapons or heavy machine guns spotted besides the ones mounted on the tanks. The assault should only be met with small arms fire and the special forces team had a sniper unit in overwatch with a .50cal rifle to handle any problems that may arise.

"Sarge," Dover called to Isles sitting next to him on the tarmac.

"Yes, sir?" Isles was leaning against his equipment and had a knit cap pulled over his eyes. The veteran soldier slept whenever he could.

"Squads good to go?"

"Lieutenant, they were good to go ten minutes ago. And ten minutes before that and a half hour before that. The squad leaders have their shit squared away. Every man has their body armor, night vision goggles, rifle, ammunition, flex cuffs, water, food, compass, GPS, maps and condoms for the ragheads their going to fuck. Relax, sir. We just need the word from Captain Banks to board."

"Radio works, sir," Calpers said, seating on Dover's other side, heading off the next question.

Suddenly the helo's engines spooled up and the big rotors began to turn, quickly spinning the calm air into a tornado. The radio crackled and Banks' deep voice came through the speaker loud and clear. "All Romeo Bravo elements, this is Bravo Six. Load 'em up! I say again, load 'em up! Rangers lead the way!"

"Hooah!" Dover leapt to his feet and shouted to his men who were already forming up. "First Platoon! On your feet!"

Sunday, November 16, Masozai Kili, Afghanistan

Nawaf Al Suqami awoke after a peaceful sleep, knowing that everything was in place. He sat in his favorite spot at the table next to the roaring fire and wondered excitedly how things were going to unfold in his compound over the course of the day. All the important people had arrived in the camp and when he greeted each man, they were eager to work together and kill the Americans at their new base named Warrior. Though he personally greeted each leader when they arrived, he had paid special attention to the weapons supplier Ahmed Rashid Halabi. He was one of the two most important men at the meeting. The other was the one who would emerge as the commander of the force that was going to lead the attack.

Since Halabi's arrival early yesterday morning, Al Suqami remained in the arms dealer's shadow, praying to Allah that he would remain in his favor and be rewarded with extra weapons for his men. Al Suqami set up a lunch for just the two of them to discuss those extra weapons. At the conclusion, Halabi gave overtones that he may be able to help out with an extra shipment, of course, depending on how the assault on the American camp went.

As the fire roared, Al Suqami drained his Turkish coffee and summoned an aide for a refill. Yes, he thought, today was going to be a glorious day!

Ten minutes into the flight, Captain Banks worked his way down the helo's cramped center aisle filled with battle ready Rangers in search for Dover. Despite the red lit interior, Banks didn't have any problem finding the First Platoon leader. Following him was Harold Weston. "Jack," Banks shouted over the noise of the engines, spinning rotors and Toby Keith's patriotic song 'Courtesy of the Red White and Blue' playing over the speakers, "this is Harold Weston, OGA. He will be joining your platoon on the assault."

Dover, sitting on the seat along the airframe, looked up in surprise to see his commanding officer standing above him. He didn't remember seeing Banks board the helo.

Weston was outfitted like every other Ranger with the new Army Combat Uniform and MOLLE system. He had the M-4 slung over his shoulder and extended his hand. He leaned forward, his facial features were hidden behind the green camouflage paint, and shouted, "Nice to meet you Lieutenant!" The other hand was placed on the airframe to steady himself from the pitch and yaw of the helo's flight.

Dover firmly shook the offered hand and started to get up. "You can take my seat but it's a little cramped."

Weston declined with a wave. "No, thanks. When we get on the ground, I'll follow you. And don't worry, Lieutenant, I won't get in the way."

"From my understanding, Mr. Weston, I may learn a few things from you!"

Weston let out a hearty laugh. "I'm not sure about that!"

Off the starboard side an Apache gunship took up station and fired a pair of Hellfire antitank missiles. The bright flash of the missiles ignition lit up the interior of the cabin as the white hot fingers of fire streaked towards their targets.

"Showtime," Banks said. "Good luck, Jack. I'll be in touch." With that said, he turned and led Weston back to their seats as the crew chief started issuing instructions.

The strange slapping sound outside in the predawn darkness was foreign and unfamiliar and grew louder with each passing second. With his coffee in hand, Nawaf Al Suqami rose from his warm seat next to the fire and walked towards the door to investigate the ominous noise. In the back of his mind he knew what it was and he couldn't believe it. It just wasn't possible! Just as he reached for the door, Mohammad, his trusted aide, smashed through it, almost knocking him off his feet. There was panic in his eyes.

"Helicopters!" he screamed and pointed to the sky. Many tiny red pulsating lights could be seen flickering against the dark sky.

Just then, a pair of comets hurtled from the sky and slammed into the parked tanks. Thunderous explosions shook the ground and brilliant flashes of sparks and a bright orange and black fireball turned the predawn darkness into daylight. The tanks were instantly turned into hulking masses of flame and twisted metal.

Before the echo of the initial explosion subsided, secondary explosions on the tanks erupted as on board ammo began cooking off. Then there was a ripping sound never heard before by Al Suqami's ears and the concrete walls of his building began to disintegrate around him. Fist-sized holes were punched through and in some spots entire sections of cinder blocks and sheetrock were destroyed. Chunks of block and dust flew about the room as if a furious wind storm suddenly hit.

Al Suqami and Mohammad dove for the floor and covered their heads as bullets peppered the structure and tore out chunks out of the wood floor. Mohammad screamed in fear.

When the hail of lead subsided, Al Suqami yelled to Mohammad, "Go get the leaders and bring them back here!" He pushed and shoved his petrified aide into action. "Now! Hurry!"

The CH-47 Chinook, which had been flying nap-of-the-earth, banked hard to port and made a rapid descent. Bright, hot white flares were discharged to confuse any surface to air missiles that the enemy may have. The rear ramp opened as the helo descended and ushered in a blast of cold air that quickly filled the cabin.

Dover blocked the sudden chill with a rush of adrenaline speeding through his veins. Through the ramp opening and the fuselage windows, the men of First Platoon watched the battle joined below as the other helicopters disgorged their brothers and engaged the enemy.

Second and Third Platoons were assaulting the area dubbed the 'campground.' Dover was thankful he didn't get that job. The labyrinth of tents would be a nightmare to navigate through and death would be lurking behind every flap. Dover's First Platoon anchored the right flank of the assault and his task was to clear his front and take down the main building and capture the HVTs that were present. His hopes for an uneventful landing was quickly dispelled. Incoming rounds began clinking off the helos fuselage while some bored holes through it. The sudden chatter of the door gunner's M-240B on the starboard side of the helo returning fire made the assault real. He flexed his hands in nervous anticipation and asked God for the strength and guidance to succeed.

Captain Banks made his way to the ramp and called attention to himself. "We're going in hot! Get ready!" All eyes were on him, waiting for the signal to race out the helicopter and join the fight.

Dover felt the presence of Hal Weston and stole a glance over his shoulder and found him waiting as if he were at a bus stop. Instantly he knew that he would not have to worry about the CIA officer getting in the way. "Hey, guys," Dover yelled over the sounds of the engines. "Put the Noggs on and lock and load!"

The slamming of bolts seating rounds in the rifles was the immediate response. The Rangers were ready for battle.

In the ghostly green light of the night vision goggles, Dover eyed Banks and waited for the 'go' signal.

The helo's rear wheels bumped the ground and Banks waved his arm forward and shouted, "Go!"

Without hesitation, Dover and his platoon raced down the ramp and jumped to the ground. The Rangers immediately oriented themselves to the sporadic and inaccurate incoming small arms fire and waited for Dover to issues orders. The insertion was successful in maintaining surprise and command and control was to be established.

Like a trusted and loyal dog constantly at its masters side, Calpers knelt next to Dover. He held the radio handset out for Dover to take. "Bravo Six wants a check, sir."

Dover knew Banks was making sure all his platoons had inserted and were ready to attack. With Banks riding the same helo as Dover, he found it pointless to answer. He waved Calpers off to let him answer.

The helo increased power for takeoff, forcing Dover to lower his head and shield his face from the swirling debris caused by the rotor wash.

While Calpers had the radio to maintain contact with the other platoons and Banks, each platoon had their MIRs for intraplatoon communications. "Squad leaders check in," Dover called over the MIR. Each squad was assigned a sector of ground to cover after they exited the helo.

"Delta's good," First Squad's Sgt. Odessa said calmly. To avoid any confusion, all the units used their identification signs for communications.

"Echo is set," Sgt. Parks, of Second Squad, spoke as if he was answering the offer for another beer at a bar.

"Foxtrot is in position." Sgt. Jervis, of Third, sounded bored.

Dover scanned the deployment of his squads as they called in. Second Squad was on his left, First Squad on the right and in the middle just behind from where he would lead, was Third Squad. They were where they were supposed to be. The platoon's order of movement into the battle was wedge-shaped with Third Squad in the lead. Trailing on the flanks would be Second Squad on the left and First Squad on the right, just as they had exited the helo and set up a defensive perimeter. Off to the platoons' left, the volume of fire suddenly increased as Second and Third platoons became fully engaged in the 'campground.'

Dover ignored the other platoon's fight and focused on his job. The burning tanks acted like a beacon and he decided to use them as a waypoint to his objective. A constant light breezed blew the smoke away from the building so it didn't obstruct the target. Dover stood and ordered his men forward. With the rifle held high above his head, he waved the men into action citing a Ranger motto, "Rangers! Follow me!"

Nawaf Al Suqami nearly crapped in his pants when he witnessed his precious tanks being blown apart and barely survived the strafing of his building. In stunned fascination he watched the hulking American helicopters land in his compound and assumed correctly they were offloading infantry. Never had he thought that his secluded compound would be assaulted. Now that it was, he became almost too paralyzed with fear to react. His life as a warlord had been leading ambushes and small raids and defending against the same. He was not equipped to withstand or repel an attack by such a force of overwhelming firepower.

How did the Americans find him, he wondered and more importantly, what should he do now?

Running away was never something he had done before, at least not without putting up a fight first. He couldn't just turn tail and hide. But fight to do what? And with how many men? There were never more than seventy-five of his men in the compound at one time, and they were usually training raw fighters. Take away the numbers killed in guarding the weapons caches and those who went back to their homes to lick their wounds and he was left with much less. There wouldn't be enough time to get the other men from the outlying villages under his reign to help in the defense of the compound. It was already too late for that. Taking up positions within the building were only his bodyguards and a handful of fighters.

The other tribal leaders and commanders in the compound traveled light so as not to attract suspicion to their movements and only brought personal bodyguards. That at best numbered another fifty men.

Al Suqami's primary defensive weapons in the compound had been the main guns and machine guns on the tanks. They were the extra firepower he had to make up for the low numbers in manpower. But as he cast his gaze to the bright burning hulks of steel, the prospect of repelling the American assault looked dim. He could pray to Allah for intervention or hope that supporters in the town of Masozai Kili heard the assault and raised the alarm.

As he watched through the doorway, there was movement all over the compound. Small arms fire had increased in its intensity around the barracks and store rooms. Fierce fighting erupted where the tribal leaders and their men had set up their tents. At least they were fighting back. A sense of hope and a slight window of opportunity presented itself. He checked his watch and silently urged the other leaders to get to his place so they could discuss their course of action–escape!

There wasn't much time.

The distance from where Dover and his platoon were inserted to the target building was just over five hundred meters. They traveled the first two hundred without getting shot at or anyone in the platoon firing a shot. All the action had been to his left where Second and Third Platoons were assaulting the 'campground' and barracks.

At two hundred meters, the thick smoke from the tanks was still blowing away from the building but the fires lit the battlefield in an orange glow. It also highlighted the advancing Rangers. AKs from in and around the building suddenly opened up on his platoon. The first rounds whizzed past, causing the Rangers to go to ground. Dover belly flopped on the frozen ground and brought his rifle up, searching for targets. Immediately other Rangers returned fire and began maneuvering to eliminate the force that was arraigned against them. Like flashbulbs in a darkened arena at a rock concert, muzzle flashes betrayed the positions of the enemy defenders. A sustained flash from a hole in the wall caught Dover's attention. He placed the red dot from the PAQ4 infrared sight on the muzzle flash and for the first time that night, he squeezed the trigger. Firing from that position ceased.

The incoming fire was inaccurate with bullets whip cracking overhead or thudding into the ground. The sky also wasn't light enough for the naked eye to identify individual Rangers in the camouflaged uniforms. As far as the Rangers knew, the bad guys weren't equipped with night vision goggles to put out effective and deadly fire.

Sometimes indiscriminate firing finds a target.

"Man down!" The terrifying phrase echoed across the battlefield.

Then a scream for, "Doc!" was heard above the fire and through the earphone on the MIR. "Doc! Get your ass over here! Davies is down!"

Dover's heart nearly stopped. Davies was a nineteen-year-old kid in First Squad. Dover began the mission three men down and now he was down one more. Keep control! He told himself. Casualties were going to happen. He wanted to race to Davies' aid but he had to press the attack. Davies was in Doc's good hands. "Rangers, keep going!" he ordered into the mic. Mad that another man was hit, he bellowed, "Press Forward!"

His head was on a swivel, searching for another target as he moved closer to the objective. Any target would do to unleash his fury on. Like an emanation, a ghostly green figure rose from the uneven ground seventy meters to his front.

Except this was no ghost. It was an enemy fighter armed with an AK and it was pointing at him. Dover snapped the rifle to his shoulder, placed the targeting red dot on center mass and squeezed off a burst. The rifle kicked against his shoulder and the bullets hit square in the chest. The green figure crumpled to the ground. Dover stepped forward, one sure footed step after another and sought another target.

Two quick kills later, he needed to know about his wounded Ranger. "Doc, this is One Six," he called over the IR.

"Little busy right now, sir, what do you need?" His voice was calm but hurried.

"Status on Davies."

"Uh," there was a pause. "Alive. Assessing now, let me work." Then he added "Sir."

"Keep me updated." Through the night vision goggles, Dover took notice of an additional half dozen men moving to his target building from the barracks and campground areas. "Sergeant Parks! Tangos moving from your left!"

Chatter over the MIR became confused as conversations, enemy sightings and warnings meshed. Dover didn't know if Parks heard his warning.

Either the Rangers in Second Squad saw the same movement that Dover pointed out or they heard the warning. The immediate increase in fire sounded as if the whole squad opened up. In a hail of bullets and exploding grenades, three enemy fighters immediately fell. The survivors turned to face the Rangers and fought back.

Isles tapped Dover on the shoulder. "I'm going over to Second squad and make sure the tie in with Third is good so they don't separate. I'll direct the fight over there."

"Right." Dover agreed and thanked God that he had a very capable platoon sergeant. A short staccato of shouting was immediately followed by a string of bullets that kicked up dirt between Dover and Calpers.

"Fuck!" Calpers shouted. He jumped away and sighted his rifle.

Dover snapped his head and spotted the terrorist who shot at him. A small green outline of a man's head was poking up from a clump of scrub brush. Dover leveled the M-4, put the aiming dot on the terrorists head and watched him fall before he could fire.

Like an exploding watermelon, the target's head disintegrated. "Dick head," Calpers spat.

In the midst of the firefight, Dover completely forgot that the OGA spook was with his platoon. He urgently spun on his heel in search for Harold Weston. The green images of his men appeared in his sight but he couldn't make out who was who with their night vision goggles over their eyes. His heart raced and he called out over the MIR. "Weston, where are you?"

"To your left, Lieutenant," Weston answered calmly. "Ten meters."

Dover focused on two men, one kneeling and the other prone. The prone soldier was changing magazines and other paused in his firing, turned to Dover and gave a quick wave. "Got ya."

Up to this point, Dover was satisfied with the results of his sector in the attack. The insertion went smoothly, his platoon advanced on their target without losing momentum and Dover hadn't lost Weston. Casualties were a given on this type of mission and he only knew of one, Davies. No other calls for Doc Reynolds had been heard. In actuality, they met little resistance.

An eerie lull settled on Dover's sector of the battlefield. Targets suddenly dried up. Only over the MIR did the activity continue as Rangers called out looking for something to shoot at or asking what was going on.

Then a single shot rang out, breaking the silence.

"Sniper!" came the call over the MIR.

The chatter among the platoon picked up. "Anyone see him?"

"Where did that come from?"

Then another shot rang out.

"Motherfucker! That was close! I'm moving!"

"Everyone get down!" Dover ordered as he scanned the terrain and the buildings for the shooter. Nothing appeared in the Noggs.

Cradling the rifle in the crook on his elbows, Dover propped himself on his elbows and searched for the sniper through his night vision goggles. The scope would be beneficial if he knew approximately where the sniper was located but for spotting him the field of vision was too narrow.

A third shot rang out, followed by sickening thud as the bullet penetrated a Kevlar helmet.

"Doc!" another Ranger screamed. "It's Geerling!"

"Someone see the son-of-a-bitch yet?"

A few Rangers let loose, hoping their shots may get that lucky hit or cause the sniper to expose himself by moving and drawing attention.

This was bullshit, Dover said to himself, as he frantically searched for the gunman. He didn't come this far to get stopped by a fucking sniper! He had to do something and it had to be fast before this guy picked off more of his platoon. Then he remembered the briefing and the information that a special forces team was up in the hills overlooking the compound. Because of their vantage point, maybe they could see the sniper. He rolled to his side on the hard dirt and removed the spiral notebook from his pocket that contained the code words, call signs and radio frequencies for all the units involved in this operation. He flipped on the red filtered flashlight to read the pages. He ran his gloved finger down the list and stopped at the call sign the special forces team was using. He smiled when he read the name. "Calpers," he reached out and tapped his trusty RTO. "Radio."

A moment later he had the handset pressed against his ear and the push to talk button depressed. "Minuteman, this is Bravo One Six, come in, over?"

As soon as he released the button, Minuteman came on line. "This is Minuteman, Bravo One Six. Go."

Dover recognized the voice of SFC Michaelson. "Minuteman, I'm on the southern edge of the battle area and am taking sniper fire from my front. Can you spot from your location, copy?"

"Roger, One Six. Give us a moment, over."

Tense moments ticked by for Dover. The battle next to him was increasing and he felt like a sitting duck waiting for Minuteman to respond. His patience was wearing thin. He actually hoped that the enemy sniper would take another shot so Minuteman's spotter could spot the muzzle flash. He also prayed that the enemy sniper would miss.

A few Rangers took pot shots, trying to goad the sniper into firing.

The sniper responded.

"Ha, missed motherfucker!"

A deep southern drawl called out, "Anybody see it?"

The radio crackled. "Bravo One six, this is Minuteman, come in, over."

"This One Six. What have you got for me? Over."

"Hang tight One Six. We spotted him on the roof top next to the chimney."

Once again Dover waited out the tense moments. Unable to hear the actual shot from the .50cal sniper rifle, the sound the bullet made when it went through the tin chimney sounded like a large firecracker exploding in a metal can.

"Bravo One Six, this is Minuteman, over."

"Go ahead, Minuteman."

"Scratch one Tango. You're in the clear, Lieutenant."

Dover cracked a smile. Minuteman recognized who he was. "Thank you, Minuteman. We'll call if we need you again. Out. Rangers! Forward!"

When Al Suqami offered Ahmed Rashid Halabi the private room in the barracks, he graciously thanked his host and immediately accepted the offer. Any type of creature comfort was welcomed, even if it was small and Spartan. The room consisted of a cot, a small folding table with a battery operated light and a chair. An ammo box was used for storage. The room belonged to the leader of the training cadre who had no issues with moving out for a few days. Someone also found a portable kerosene heater for him to use and turned it on an hour before he retired for the night so when he got to his room, it was already warm.

The other warlords and tribal leaders, along with one bodyguard, were offered bunks in the barracks bays among Al Suqami's men but the remainder of their entourage had to remain outside in their tents. Few of them took up his offer, choosing to remain with their group. All that sat well with Halabi. Since he was the most important man at the meeting, he deserved special treatment. Without him, the offensive the warlords and Taliban planned would be short lived. It would be hard to fight a war without weapons.

After a long day of meeting and getting a feel for the leaders, Halabi sized up who he thought was the weakest and less influential to who was the strongest. Afzal Hafeez, representing the Tehrik Taliban-i Pakistan, was clearly the weakest while Alu Akhmadov from Chechnya was the strongest and would most likely emerge as the military commander of the assault on the American base. He was hardcore and a true believer.

When Halabi put his tired and achy body down to sleep on the rusting cot and flat mattress, with Marwan sleeping right outside the door, he felt as if the warlords were all on the same page. Only good things were to come out of the official meeting. There was a real possibility that the gathered men would be able to kick the Americans out of their base or at least hurt them real bad. Close to a thousand men would be used to assault the base.

The unexpected and sudden *whoosh* of missiles being fired and the immediate explosions that rocked the building launched him out of bed. He raced to the small window in the room to see what was happening outside. The compound was lit in an eerie orange glow as the fireballs over the tanks launched skyward. Just then the secondary explosions of the onboard ammunition of the burning tanks cooked off, adding brilliant streaks of white across the compound. His heart raced and his palms became sweaty as his tired mind began to sort out what was happening.

As the roar of the initial detonation subsided, it was replaced by the strange, haunting *whop whop whop* of helicopter blades slapping the air and the growing whine of powerful engines. The sounds struck fear into him as he realized what was going on. He had his introduction to combat.

"Ahmed get down!" Marwan burst through the door and dragged him to the floor just as volley of bullets from the Apache attack helicopter's nose-mounted 30mm chain gun tore through the walls.

Halabi hit the ground hard and Marwan fell on top of him, using his body as a shield. Stomach-turning thuds were followed by a piercing, inhuman scream. Halabi could feel warm sticky blood dripping down his neck and frantically tried to push Marwan off of him. Panic rose to a higher level in him, thinking he might have been hit.. "Get off! Marwan, get off!"

All he got in response was a weak, gurgling groan.

Using all his strength, Halabi pushed himself up, causing Marwan's body to partially roll to one side. By the light of the coils in the kerosene heater, he could see Marwan's right arm had been blown off at the shoulder. Feeling around on the ground for leverage to release himself from under the rest of Marwan's weight, his hand found a pool of blood. Bile raced up his throat and he realized he wet his pants. The chatter of weapons firing spurred him to move and he went for a final shove to push Marwan off his legs. It was then he noticed Marwan's shredded pants were soaked in blood, internal organs were hanging from a massive hole in his abdomen and his destroyed right leg was hanging by a thread. The chain gun had strafed his body. Nausea rocketed up his throat and this time he couldn't hold it back.

A flurry of activity was going on outside his room as the surviving fighters ran to repel the attack. Suddenly there was a voice calling his name. "Ahmed Halabi! Where are you? Ahmed Halabi, where are you?"

"In here!" Halabi screamed, finally getting out from under Marwan's dead body.

"Are you ok?" It was the voice of Mohammad, Al Suqami's aide. He stood in the damaged doorway to the main bay as armed fighters rushed by.

Halabi stood on shaky legs and swiped the blood and vomit from the front of his shirt. "I'm fine," he said, attempting to hide the fear in his voice.

"Come with me! Al Suqami's house is safer!" Mohammad said with urgency and ran out the door.

"Wait!" Halabi screamed over the increasing roar of battle. "How are going to get through?" Another volley of bullets tore through the walls. Chucks of wood, concrete and dried mud sent Halabi back to the floor.

Mohammad called back over his shoulder. "Back door!"

Not having to be told twice, Halabi slipped on his shoes, grabbed his coat and raced after the sprinting man. Fighters were still rushing to and fro to defend the compound and scattered across the ground were the bodies of the ones that had already become martyrs. Halabi stepped on or around these bodies and had no desire to pick up a rifle and shoot back. He caught up with Mohammad and together they ran behind the buildings, away from the firefight and what they expected was safety.

With the sniper out of the way, Dover using a maneuver called bounding overwatch, where one group of soldiers covers another as they move forward, to methodically moved his platoon forward, past the burning tanks and ever closer to the target. The tanks licking flames were slowly dying but thick greasy smoke continued to pour out of the open hatches and from the burning tires on the road wheels.

Dover attached himself to Third Squad to direct the advance. He was propped on one knee and peered through the rifle scope seeking targets as First Squad finished its twenty meter bound. "Third Squad, stand by," he readied the next bounding squad. Another eerie silence settled on First Platoon's section of the battlefield. They were thirty meters from the building and since the last volley of grenades was hurled at them, there hadn't been a single incoming round of fire. This is it, Dover thought excitedly, time to enter the building. Then he realized what the lack of fire could mean. Shit! What if they killed everyone inside? He was supposed to capture the HVTs inside, not kill them. A hand on his shoulder startled him.

"Lieutenant, are we going in?" The hand and question came from Hal Weston. By the tone in his voice, he didn't like the pause that was being taken.

"Yeah, we are." Dover pushed the microphone closer to his lips. "Squad leaders, this is Six. Come in, over,"

"Delta here," Sgt. Odessa replied, using First Squad's radio designation.

"Foxtrot here," Sgt. Jervis followed out of sequence, beating Sgt. Parks of Echo.

"Echo's on."

"We're going in," Dover stated. "Once we come abreast to First Squad's position, First and Second squad move to set up the perimeter around the building, copy?"

"Copy," they said in unison. Both their confident voices came clearly through the headset.

"Foxtrot, we'll form up on the left side of the front door, copy?"

"Roger. Ready on your call."

Satisfied all was in order, Dover gave the command to go. "Move out."

Even in the dark, it didn't take long for the other squads to reach First Squad's position and form a line abreast.

First squad was going to move to the right while Second squad was going to move to the left and encircle the building while Dover and Third Squad moved straight ahead.

Dover surveyed his deployed platoon through the Noggs. If there was any movement in or near the building, the entire platoon would open up. Satisfied all was set, he gave the order. "Rangers, Go!" A short burst of fire led off the sprint. Dover zigzagged his way to the building at a half sprint, his strong legs propelled him forward over the frozen and scarred terrain.

Off to the left, the cacophony of the battle increased as the Ranger company advanced. Second and Third platoons were facing stiffening resistance as the Tangos were desperately holding on. Red and green tracer rounds crisscrossed the dark sky, their colorful trails looked like a laser show.

Suddenly, disaster struck. One of the ammo sheds placed between the barracks and Al Suqami's headquarters detonated. An ear splitting explosion roared, drowning out the small arms fire over the battlefield. A huge churning fireball rocketed high into the air, turning the predawn sky into day. Those fortunate enough to be out of the immediate blast range survived the explosion but were knocked over the by the shock wave.

"Holy fuck!" a Ranger screamed and pressed his hands to his ears.

"What the hell was that?"

"Ammo dump! Get the fuck out of the way!" In the blink of an eye, the exterior wall of the barracks closest to the shed disintegrated along with scores of enemy fighters.

Frantic calls for help went out over the company radio net. Rangers were also caught in the explosion.

"Lieutenant!" Calpers called to Dover.

Dover, like all the Rangers, was flat on his belly, shielding himself from the blast and exploding ammo. The ringing in his ears prevented him from hearing Calpers.

"Lieutenant!" This time Calpers slapped his lieutenant on the shoulder.

"What?" Dover yelled louder than usual so he could hear himself.

Calpers held out the handset and spoke loudly. "It's Bravo Six."

"Oh." Dover took the call from Captain Banks. He pressed the handset hard to his ear and stuck his finger in the other one. "This is One Six, over."

"Dover, Third Platoon is in trouble. Can you get a squad over there to help out?"

Dover looked in the direction of where Third Platoon was supposed to be. Their right flank was where the shed detonated. Images of hell flashed before his eyes. He could only imagine pieces of destroyed bodies littering the ground and some of those were going to be Rangers. Lost in his thoughts, he didn't hear Banks repeat his order.

"One Six, do you copy? Dover! Do you hear me?"

Shaking himself out, he simply responded. "Roger, Bravo Six. I'll send a squad, over."

"One Six, continue your mission. Out."

A flash of fear hit Dover. Second Squad was on the platoon's left flank! He never checked to see if his men were ok!

He may not have a squad to send for help! Just shy of frantic with his heart now stuck in his throat, Dover called over the MIR, "Sergeant Parks, come in."

"Parks here," came the immediate reply.

"Your squad ok?" He held his breath.

"Yes, sir. A little hard of hearing but we're good."

The biggest sigh of relief washed across Dover's body. Exhaling to calm himself, he issued new orders. "Take your squad over to Third Platoon. They need help."

"Uh, could you be a little more specific, sir? Help in the fight or," there was a pause, "help with casualties?"

Dover wondered the same thing but didn't want to ask Captain Banks over the radio. He gave Sergeant Parks the only answer he knew. "I'm assuming both. Report to Lieutenant Hernandez or whoever is in charge. Keep me posted."

"Hooah."

Dover wasn't comfortable with sending one third of his unit away into the unknown, despite that they were only going a short distance. The size of the explosion could have taken out the leadership of Third Platoon and there was only one way to make sure someone was in command. "Sergeant Isles, come in."

"Right here, Lieutenant."

"Go over there with Second Squad and keep an eye on things. I don't know who survived the blast. Take command if necessary."

"Hooah, sir."

Dover ignored the chatter on the MIR as Parks relayed their new orders. He formulated a new plan and decided it was the time to take down the target while the enemy forces were still in a daze. "Delta and Echo, listen up. Were going in. Delta, you're now tasked with setting up the perimeter. Understood?"

"Roger," Sergeant Odessa complied.

"Echo, let's finish this."

There were five men sitting on the floor of Al Suqami's hidden basement. Al Suqami sat on the chair with his arm resting on the desk. Four of the men were the remaining tribal leaders and warlords who had gathered for the meeting. The last man was Al Suqami's bodyguard, Mohammad. Everyone else remained outside in an attempt to repel the American attack. From the sounds of the battle, Al Suqami didn't expect to see them alive. One who he knew that was already dead was Zalmay Khan, the local tribal leader who attempted to attack the UN food convoy and lost scores of men. He was shot and killed just as soon as he exited the barracks. He had paused in the doorway to yell for the others to run when a bullet smashed into the side of his head mid-sentence. Bahadur Marashi, the long bearded representative from Ansar Al Islam was slumped against the wall and bleeding heavily from a fist sized hole in his right shoulder. Scores of smaller holes from a grenade blast peppered his chest. His arm was immobile and his olive colored skin had gone pale. Loss of blood and shock would soon end his life if he didn't get medical attention quickly. The rags stuffed in the hole to slow the bleeding wasn't working and the blood was running down his arm and forming a puddle on the floor next to him.

The fluorescent lights that lit the room prevented the men from concealing the fear that shone on their faces. Only one of the group had participated in combat on the scale the Americans were inflicting on the compound and its defenders. Alu Akhmadov, the lone man dressed in a uniform, had fought the Russian military machine for years in Chechnya and knew the destruction that was being rained down upon the compound. His hard stare conveyed the message that the other men in the room had every reason to be afraid.

"What happened, Nawaf?" Halabi asked angrily. "Why are the Americans attacking here?"

Besides telling the Saudi arms dealer the obvious, Al Suqami was at a loss for an explanation of how the Americans found his compound. He sat staring from his chair, nervously rapping his knuckles on the desk.

"What do we do now?" Afzal Hafeez, the representative of Tehrik Taliban-i Pakistan, asked aloud, his eyes wide with concern. "Nawaf, is there another way out of here?"

Al Suqami felt dizzy and his stomach began to churn. He never imagined that his compound would be assaulted and that he would have to take his last refuge in the hidden basement. "No," he muttered and avoided the eyes staring at him.

Akhmadov shot to his feet and ripped the wool cap off his head. "You mean we are going to die in this box?" he hissed and wrung the hat.

Al Suqami, taken aback by the wild look in the Chechen's eyes, stammered a feeble answer. "My fighters and your bodyguards," he swung his hand over the collection of men, "will defend against the attack!" He hoped his delivery sounded more confident than he felt.

"Apparently your men have never faced an air assault." Disgust dripped from Akhmadov's voice.

"What are we going to do?" Halabi asked. The fear in his voice matched the wide eyed expression on his face.

The sounds of battle outside the door increased in its intensity. Suddenly there was a loud explosion that shook rock particles from the ceiling and the ground under them.

"What was that?" Halabi nearly screamed. Sweat beads dotted his forehead.

The men turned their attention to Halabi. For a man that was bold and ruthless in the arms trade and gave the appearance he was fearless and believed in the cause, his voice showed how meek he really was.

"That," Akhmadov pointed to the ceiling "is the sound of battle."

"You, Halabi, are weak," Marashi said softly and in a coughing fit expelled from his throat some of the dust that had fallen from the ceiling. The loss of blood and the body going into shock had rendered him nearly unconscious. He took a shallow breath before continuing his trashing of Halabi. "You have proved that you are the same as the Americans and Jews! You," he attempted to raise his pointed finger but it fell into his lap, "are motivated by money and greed." His voice was getting weaker and he paused once again to catch his breath. A violent cough shook him and bile spilled onto his beard. There was rage in his cold, unflinching eyes as he labored over his breathing.

Halabi took in a quick breath. The accusation of him being weak and a non-believer among these men scared him as much as the assault.

Afzal Hafeez glared at the arms dealer and gritted his teeth.

"Save the allegation for another time," Akhmadov interjected and took control of the situation. "What is important now is for us to get out of here." He turned his focus to Al Suqami. "Nawaf, how hidden and secure is this basement?" Without waiting for Al Suqami to answer, his next comment sent chills down every man's spine. In a hardened and sure voice, he stated, "I can tell you this, your men outside will not be able to defend against the attack. They will die."

To accent his point, a pair of muffled bangs could be heard upstairs.

"The door, it is hidden well, my friend," Al Suqami tried to assure everyone and head off the comment that Akhmadov was sure to state next. "They will not be able to find us down here."

Akhmadov sneered. "Listen to me. We are going to die in here if we do not try to escape. We cannot live down here for days. There is no food or water. Air is going to be a problem unless there is a ventilation system installed and I don't see one." He turned to Al Suqami for an answer.

Al Suqami shook his head and muttered, "No."

"The Americans out there," he pointed to the steel door. "They will find us and kill or capture us. I prefer to live and fight than become a martyr. You may be on jihad but I am not!"

"What are you proposing, Alu?" Hafeez asked. His voice was calm. He too had seen combat on a larger scale, not against the Americans, but the Pakistani Army. "I am in agreement with you. We cannot stay here."

Akhmadov gave a curt nod. "We leave now while the battle is still going on. With help from Allah, we can sneak away and head for the village."

"Yes! Yes!" Al Suqami stood and clasped his hands in agreement. He was thankful more that the Chechen took control and came up with a plan.

"What about Marashi?" Halabi asked, pointing to the dying representative of Ansar Al Islam. "What are we going to do with him?"

Mohammad, armed with an AK, broke his silence. "It is God's will that he dies."

Without further comment on the situation, Akhmadov stood, unholstered his pistol and pointed to the door. "Open it and let's get out of here."

Mohammed, the first one to the door, held the AK at the ready.

Without warning, the lights went out.

CHAPTER TWENTY-THREE

Sunday, November 16, Masozai Kili, Afghanistan

Third Squad was positioned against the damaged front wall of the building in a 'train' with Sergeant Jervis on point just outside the smashed door. Dover was in the fifth spot in line directing the insertion. Jervis had been peeking through the smashed doorway wearing the night vision goggles while other Rangers peeked into the interior from holes blown through the concrete blocks. Dover was waiting for Sergeant Odessa's First Squad to complete its task in securing the rear of the building before they entered. Intel indicated there may be a back door and he didn't want their prey to escape.

"One Six, this is Montana," came the call over the MIR.

"Go ahead," Dover responded.

"I don't see anyone alive inside, just bodies."

"That's not what we wanted," Weston said what Dover thought.

Dover cursed under his breath. If the HVTs were dead, his mission was a bust. "Where are you, Montana?" he asked, keeping his focus on the door.

"Three places behind you, sir. Just behind Mr. Weston."

Dover quickly turned around, looked past the ever present Calpers and Weston and saw Montana with his head stuffed through a hole in the wall. "Nothing moving?"

"Nothing sir, just bodies. But it's warm. There's a fireplace that's still burning."

"I don't see anything either, sir," Jarvis said from his position looking in the door. "I got a body here just inside the door. He's dead."

"Shit." Dover said to himself. The Tangos were either dead or playing opossum waiting for his men to enter so they could ambush them. Either way they had to go in and find out.

"One Six, this is Delta." The call came from Sergeant Odessa.

"Go, Delta."

"We're in position. There is a back door that's closed and a running generator but no signs of activity."

"Right," Dover acknowledged. "Everyone listen up. We're going in. If anyone inside is pretending to be dead, I want to rattle their brains. We toss flash-bangs then we go in, hooah?" After the acknowledged hooahs came back, Dover continued. "Sergeant Jarvis, toss one through the door and Montana, put one through the hole where your head is at. Everyone, check ammo. "

"Right, sir."

"Got it."

The clinking of half filled or almost empty magazines being extracted and the snap of full ones being inserted was followed by the slide and snap of charging handles seating rounds in well worn chambers.

"Delta, on my call, kill the generator," Dover ordered.

"Roger that."

Dover inserted a fresh magazine and gripped his rifle tighter. Readying himself, he fit the butt into his shoulder. He shuffled his feet and shifted his weight as he moved into a ready position. He checked the train. All were ready. Despite the cold temperature, his body was sweating from every pore in his body. He took a deep breath and counted. "Three, two, one, *now!*"

Simultaneously, Montana and Jarvis threw the grenades in and turned their heads and shielded their eyes from the blast. The grenades exploded, lighting up the interior of the building in a bright stunning flash and at the same time the debilitating bang echoed off the walls.

"GO! GO! GO!" Dover shouted.

In a flawless execution, the squad entered in one fluid motion. Each man had his weapon up and covered their assigned sectors. The search for the HVTs had begun. Dover shuffled inside, his rifle tucked snugly into his shoulder and finger on the trigger. He stepped over the debris and body strewn floor to a far wall where a table had been overturned. The Rangers fanned out inside the building, checking every room for enemy soldiers.

Dover stood by the overturned table and dying fire in the fireplace and waited. One by one, teams of Rangers called in. The thankful, yet disappointing phrase was spoken. "Clear!"

It didn't take more then two minutes to secure the three room, single story building. Not one live body had been discovered and the task of identifying them began.

Dover moved the MIR mic to his mouth. "Delta, this is One Six. Are you there?"

"This is Delta."

"Anybody come out the back door?" Dover wished that they did. It wasn't looking good for a successful conclusion to the mission.

"Negative. Nothing's going on out here."

Shit! Dover shook his head in resignation. "Roger, sit tight."

With the building secure, there was no need to sneak around. Dover flipped up the goggles and turned on the Maglite attached to the barrel of his weapon. "Search the bodies for identification," Dover ordered as his eyes drew him to four broken bodies. "Be careful," he reminded, "they could be booby trapped."

One by one bright rays of light crisscrossed the dirty, smoky interior of the debris filled building as the Rangers turned on their flashlights. Immediately Hal Weston went to the first dead fighter lying near the doorway. The body was on its back with his feet closest to the door and his left arm folded grotesquely under him. His face had been blown away, leaving a bloody pile of goo and making an identification impossible.

"I can't read this guy's name," a Ranger kneeling next to another body said holding out identification papers, "but I don't think he's anybody important.,"

"How do you know?" Weston asked after dropping the papers he found on the body he was searching.

"This guy is my age, no more than twenty."

Weston nodded in agreement. Halabi was in his late thirties or early forties.

Outside the battle continued but the ferocity seemed to quieting down, indicating the outcome was going to be in favor of the Rangers. Inside the building, though, Dover became concerned. A sinking feeling formed in the pit of his stomach as be began to figure that the mission was a bust.

"There are no HVTs here, sir," Sgt. Jervis said disappointedly.

"Damn!" Dover kicked a chunk of concrete block that was on the floor. He began to pace and look for something else to take his frustration out on. Then his mind clicked and a sense of excitement tingled through his body. Sgt. Odessa mentioned there was a running generator outside. Generators were used for producing electricity. He shined the light on the walls that were still standing, looking for any electrical outlet or light or heating unit. He began moving through the building, searching, shining the light everywhere he thought would be something that needed electricity.

"Sir, what are you looking for?" Jervis asked somewhat alarmed as he watched Dover dart about. All the Rangers went back on alert.

"There has to be more to this place than what we see. Odessa said there was a working generator outside."

Jervis picked up on what Dover was saying. "Rangers, tear this place apart! Look for hide sites and concealed rooms or a basement! Look for a light or heat source or anything that would use electricity."

Resembling a demolition crew, the Rangers began moving debris and destroyed furniture and tapping on walls or punching holes through them. Carefully, they peered through hollow spots or a loose board that might reveal a secret room or passage.

It didn't take long for the cry of discovery. It came from one of the fire team leaders, Corporal Dylan Gunderson. "I got something over here!" He was kneeling next to the fireplace, his fingers prying at a crack in the wall.

Weston was the first one at his side. "What have you got?" Right after him came Dover and Jervis. All three stood behind Gunderson, spotting the tiny crack that he had his fingers wedged into.

Gunderson was about to answer when he flung the door open and nearly lost his balance. Weston trained his flashlight in the opening and discovered a staircase.

Suddenly there was a loud shout in Pashto and a man holding an AK was climbing the stairs. He froze when the light focused on him.

"Shit!" Weston yelled.

"Don't shoot!" Dover ordered and moved just behind Weston, "he may be an HVT!" Dover already had his rifle up and sighted on the man frozen at the base of the stairs. "Stop!" he yelled in Pashto and put pressure on the trigger.

Frantic yelling from below spurred the man into action. He either caught his nerve or reacted to orders coming from behind and swung the AK in their direction.

A sustained, unaimed burst was fired up the stairs. A full thirty round magazine of bullets sprayed wildly off the walls as the shooter couldn't see in the darkness where his target was at the top of the stairs. Holding their ground as the bullets zinged past, Weston and Dover returned fire simultaneously, hitting the man in the chest. The body tumbled back down the stairs.

Dover thought he heard a grunt then pointed to the basement. "Flash-bang down there!"

"Fire in the hole!" Jervis announced and tossed a flash-bang grenade down the stairs. For an agonizing three seconds, the grenade clanked down the concrete stairs and off the walls and bounced over the dead fighter's body.

Multiple screams of terror echoed up the staircase milliseconds before the grenade detonated. The intense flash and bang effects in the small confine expanded exponentially. The light carried up the stairs and into the main floor and the bang rattled the walls.

Before the disorientating effects of the flash-bang grenade wore off, the Rangers moved quick to secure whoever was down there. "Two men go!" Dover ordered and kept his rifle and flash light trained on the doorway at the bottom of the stairs.

Hal Weston took the lead and nearly sprinted down the rickety stairs. Close on his heels were Jarvis and Gunderson.

"Hold here," Dover addressed the remainder of the squad then raced down the stairs himself.

From the sounds below, the Rangers had complete control. Commands in English and Pashto were ordered and the occasional thud of a body being smacked was heard. Protesting voices responded but they were quickly silenced.

"I said down you stupid ass motherfucking raghead!" Gunderson's voice rose above the rest. "Don't you understand fucking English?"

Carefully Dover stepped over the body of the fighter who shot up the stairs and entered the small room, the strong Maglites gave the room a surreal aura. His eyes quickly adjusted and he found the situation well in hand. Gunderson had his knee on the back of the neck of his prisoner and was securing a flex cuff around the prisoner's wrist. Weston and Jarvis had three prisoners under foot, lying prone.

Dover noticed the fighter slumped against the wall and reached for him. The skin was pale an waxy and the eyes were dull. Blood covered the entire side of the fighters body but no more was leaking from the covered wounds. Dover reached for the stash of flex cuffs on his PALS. Gunderson's statement halted him.

"He's dead, sir. No need to cuff him."

Dover turned towards Gunderson as he stood triumphantly over his subdued prisoner and shone the flashlight on the prisoners face. The fierce eyes of the man on the ground bore hatred towards Dover.

"That dude is pissed!" Dover snorted. "I wonder who his is? He's the only guy with a uniform." He turned to Weston. "Mr. Weston, do you have your guy?"

Weston let out a wet, gurgling cough and highlighted the back of a prisoners head and tapped his back with a heavy foot. "I do," he said quietly.

****

The last tap of the boot didn't come down as heavy as he would have liked. The enormous satisfaction Hal Weston felt at finally capturing Nawaf Rashid Halabi was tempered. One of the bullets fired from the Tango at the bottom of the stair found its way under his body armor and penetrated his lung. He tried to ignore the pain and the growing weakness as he attempted to focus on his prize and all that he went through to capture him. What started with a name given to him by an informant evolved into months and months of painstaking work, and along with a bit of luck, ended in a dark hole in the ground.

"Up!" Weston grunted and jerked his prisoner by the collar and repeated the command in Arabic. He let out another wet, gurgling cough and had difficulty hauling his prisoner up. Halabi, with his hands secured behind his back, struggled to his knees and then got to his feet. Weston held on to Halabi's collar not just to keep him under control but to keep himself from collapsing. "Lieutenant," Weston grinned proudly and put the light on Halabi's face, "meet Ahmed Rashid Halabi."

"No shit?" Dover clapped Weston on the back. "Awesome! Good job!"

Weston waited for the rest of the prisoners to be put in single file before he took up the rear. His legs became heavy and weak and he fought to catch his breath. Slowly his vision blurred and went black. He knew he wasn't going to make it.

Dover eyed the wanted gun runner and was not impressed. He was wimpy looking and didn't have the fire in his eyes that he expected. "Who else do we have here? Anybody know?"

"No clue, sir," Gunderson answered and hauled his prisoner up with effort. The man was not being helpful. "But this guy has hatred in his eyes. Look." Gunderson grabbed a fistful of hair and turned the dark, hate filled eyes towards Dover. The prisoner sneered. "He's one pissed off raghead."

"Take them out of here." He stepped away from the stairs for his Rangers to move the prisoners out. Dover moving the microphone to his lips he called, "I need two men down here to help with the prisoners."

In a few seconds, two Rangers bounded down the stairs and Dover directed one each to help out himself and Jarvis. "Take this guy out," he said to the Rangers.

Dover breathed a sigh of relief. They did it! They got the HVTs! The mission was a success! He watched as the prisoners were pushed up the stairs and then felt a hand on his shoulder.

"Your prisoner, Lieutenant," Weston said weakly then collapsed.

"Doc!" Dover screamed and he immediately searched for a pulse. He didn't find one. "Doc! Get here now!"

Both Dover and Doc Reynolds carried Weston's listless body up the stairs and out into the field where Reynolds immediately began performing CPR. Frantically they worked on him but to no avail. The stripped off his body armor and found where the bullet entered at his waist, just under the edge of the body armor and in its upward path, exited out his back under the shoulder blade. There was nothing they could have done for him.

The entire compound had fallen silent with only sporadic shooting. With anger and sadness in his heart, Dover stood over Weston's body and held out his hand. "Calpers."

"Sir." Calpers put the handset in Dover's outstretched hand.

Dover nodded in thanks and depressed the talk button. "Bravo Six, this is One Six, come in."

"Go ahead One Six," answered Captain Banks' RTO.

"Four Touchdowns. I say again, Four Touchdowns, copy?" Touchdown was the code word for an HVT.

"Roger One Six. Four Touchdowns. Wait one."

A moment later, Banks came on line. "Well done, One Six! Secure the prisoners and call in the birds to take 'em out. When finished, head over to the campground, copy?"

"Roger that. TD extraction then head over to the campground. Out." Dover gave the handset back to Calpers without saying a word.

"Hooah, sir! Got the fuckers," Calpers said with little conviction.

"We did." Dover gave a tired smile. "Call the helos in to take out the PWs. Gentlemen, let's get out of here." When he looked up, the sky had brightened. The first rays of the new dawn broke above the horizon. He took a deep breath and rubbed his dirty face. Part of him was elated that the mission was a success but he knew his platoon and company had taken casualties. He steeled himself for the carnage he was about to face in the Campground and get a tally on his losses. The realities of war hit home.

Sunday, November 16, Albany, New York

Gary Trainor didn't think it was possible to have two sleepless nights in a row, but once again, a good night's sleep was as elusive as ever. It was a strange and lonely night in bed without Amanda by his side. His mind was also occupied with the offer made by Marcus Kaderri to bring the men to justice who were responsible for shooting his partner.

It seemed every half hour he would check the digital clock on the nightstand and the glowing red numbers increased at a snail's pace. Finally at three in the morning, he fell asleep.

Five hours later he awoke. Disappointed that his rest was so short, he lay in bed and tried to fall back to sleep for another few hours but had no success. Giving up, he threw the covers aside and got on with the day and waited eagerly for Amanda to come home. He laughed at himself a few times over the course of the morning when he found himself staring out the window, waiting to catch her car heading towards the house…towards him. He couldn't deny the excitement in his core for her return and he realized how much he didn't like her not being around.

It was after lunch and on the third time he looked out the window, Amanda's car pulled into the driveway. He tried to hide his giddiness by making himself appear busy in the kitchen when she walked in from the garage.

"I'm home!" Amanda called then closed the door.

Trainor's heart raced and he fought the urge to rush to her. "In here, babe!" he called with his head in the refrigerator. He closed the door and met her eyes with a smile. Her hair was in a ponytail and she was wearing a blue warm up suit with white piping. "You made great time." He reached out for her and took her in his arms. He breathed her in and kissed her soft puckered lips.

"I wanted to get home to you!" She kissed him again and bounced on her toes.

He thought she would tease him about being a not so tough cop and all that if she knew how much he missed her so in response he cracked a smile and said, "Good answer." Amanda was holding paper shopping bags in addition to her luggage. "Here, let me take those. What did you get?"

"You're not looking in there!" she warned and handed him the suitcase. "You have to wait for our honeymoon for that stuff!"

Trainor arched an eyebrow in excitement and attempted a peek. "Oh?"

Amanda pulled the bags out of reach. "Uh-huh." She kicked off her shoes and headed towards the stairs. "I'll put my stuff away and then I'll tell you all about the party! Will you get the rest of the gifts out of the car?"

"Sure."

"Thanks." She turned and darted up the stairs.

Trainor took an armful of bags and boxes from the car and brought them into the living room. He was happy Amanda had a good time but he envisioned what was coming next. He placed the gifts in an out of the way corner then went back to the refrigerator and pulled out a beer for himself and a poured a glass of white wine for her. He went back to the living room and waited for Amanda. He already had the fire roaring.

After a few moments, Amanda joined him on the couch. "Wine for me, awesome. Thanks." She leaned her shoulder into his and gave him a kiss on cheek and then asked, "So, what did you do when I was gone? Did you miss me?"

"I went out with the guys last night and didn't get back to about three this morning." He faked a deep yawn before he continued with his story. "Actually, we were at The Steer House for lunch, had a few beers at the bar and then went to a couple of other places before turning in. Guy's night out, you know?"

Amanda gave a sideways glance. "Guy's night out always means trouble. What strip clubs did you go to?"

Trainor silently counted and ticked off his fingers. One by one he extended them from a balled fist. He stopped at three. "Three. Those places are expensive!"

"Gary!"

"What? We have our cut off in place. I needed a reminder of what a naked, sexy woman's body looks like! Guy's night out, am I not allowed to do that kind of stuff anymore?"

Amanda let out a sorrowful sigh. Her body sagged like a deflating balloon "I can't tell you not to go out with your friends. I know how important bonding is with your police friends. Who drove?" she quickly got off the subject.

Trainor waived his hand in dismissal. "We called a couple of cars that were on patrol to take us home. We asked if we could arrive home in style with the sirens and lights going but were shot down. I hit the pillow and was out."

"So you didn't miss me?" the dejected way she asked the question matched the saddened look on her face. "At least a little?" She spread her thumb and index finger a quarter inch apart.

Trainor never had the ability to carry on with a fib with Amanda. His face cracked and he caved in from his macho persona. "Yeah, I missed you. A lot. I didn't sleep too well either."

"Aw, honey, I missed you too." She leaned over and gave him a big wet kiss on the cheek.

"I have to confess, I didn't go out last night. I spent the night here watching television."

"You jerk!" she slapped him teasingly on the shoulder and fell back into the couch. "Strip clubs! Ugh!"

"Tell me, how'd the shower go?" He took a long pull on the cold beer and waited for the stories of male bashing. He assumed that's what went on at an all female party. The moment he dreaded was upon them. She was now going to show him all the gifts she received and the story behind it and the reaction of all the women.

"Great! It was such a total surprise!" Amanda then went into a lengthy discourse on what guests where there, the décor of the room, what food was served and how much alcohol was available. She then gave a brief account of the gifts she received, except, of course, the ones she had in the bags that she raced upstairs with. Those were the ones he was most interested in.

"Did they make you wear a stupid hat made out of bows and ribbons?"

"Yes, and it's not stupid!" she countered playfully. "Many brides to be wear the ribbons and bows."

"That's because they are drunk. Speaking of," he poked her in the ribs, "how drunk did you get?"

Amanda pursed her lips and gave a grin. "I had a bit."

"Hmmm. And the bachelorette party?" He raised both eyebrows on that question. "Where did you go and what did you do?"

Amanda avoided his stare and shifted uncomfortably in her seat.

A lump immediately formed in Trainor's throat and his stomach began to churn. The beer bottle almost slipped out of his hand. He swallowed hard, forcing the lump a little farther down. Nervously he asked again, "Amanda? What did you do?"

Slowly Amanda turned to meet his worrisome stare. "Gary, I, um…I'm not supposed to tell because it was a bachelorette party. Like the same thing that goes on at bachelor's parties. "

Trainor leaned forward wanting to hear what she had to say and at the same time he wanted to cover his ears and run. Emotions swept through him like a tornado through a trailer park and her answer could be just as destructive. "Amanda?" His voice quivered.

"I…uh...did…well," she wouldn't look at him and fiddled with her fingers.

Fear, betrayal and a twinge of anger took root in Trainor's belly. He couldn't believe what he was going to hear. His hands trembled and his breathing was shallow. A scary vision of Amanda in bed with someone else formed in front of his eyes.

Suddenly Amanda blurted out, "Nothing! I only got a kiss on the cheek from the stripper." Her face broke into a huge smile and she pointed at his nose. "Gotcha!" She clapped her hands and giggled. "Two can play that game!" Seeing the stunned look on his face, she gave him another kiss on the cheek and cradled his face. "Oh, honey I could never do anything that resembles cheating on you for any reason!" A big smile preceded her recollection of the dancer. "But he was hot!"

Trainor stared open mouthed, filtering the joke that she played on him. The saying of turn about is fair play hit him hard dead center in his forehead. A sudden wave of warmth flowed over him at her admission and all his emotions subsided. "You had me worried for a moment," he acknowledged.

"I know, your face turned white!" She laughed.

Amanda then showed all the gifts to him and who they were from. Trainor had as much interest in kitchen appliances and sheets and towels as he did watching birds hunt for worms in the yard. But seeing how happy Amanda was, he put on a good face and sat through the show and tell. When the last of the gifts were shown, Trainor tried one more time to get her to reveal what the gifts were that she brought upstairs.

"So," he cast his eyes upwards, "can I see what was in the bags you brought upstairs?"

"Sure you can," Amanda said ruefully, "starting on our wedding night!"

Shot down again, Trainor drained his beer, pulled another one from the fridge and brought the bottle of wine out for Amanda. He refilled her glass and then sat. "Important stuff to talk about." He waited to make sure he had her full attention before continuing. "I was busy this weekend. Police work."

"A new case?" she asked quizzically.

"No, the same one that Joanne was shot on. I visited her yesterday."

Amanda quickly covered her mouth with both hands. "Oh my god, Gary, I'm so sorry!" Her eyes immediately welled up with tears and threatened to spill over like a dam. "How are you and Joanne doing? Please forgive me for not asking about you. I'm sorry! I'm such an ass for not remembering what happened Friday! I got so wrapped up in..." She buried her face in her hands and began to sob.

Trainor grabbed her shaking body in his arms. "It's ok, babe," he assured her and stroked her hair. "Everything is fine."

"Are you sure?" she turned and looked pleadingly in his eyes. "Gary–"

He put his finger to her lips, cutting her off. "Stop."

"Ok." she sniffed, wiped the tears off her cheeks and regained control of her emotions. She sat upright, clasped his hands between hers and asked, "What were you going to tell me?" She sniffed again and wiped her tear streaked cheeks with her shoulder.

He was still a bit unsure of how Amanda would react when he talked about dangerous police work and what he was going to do was near suicidal. He took a deep breath to steady his nerves. "I was offered the opportunity to go and get the group of people that shot Joanne."

"What does that mean?" Amanda nervously drummed her fingers together and pulled herself away from his warm embrace. "Offered the opportunity? To do what and go where?" Her puffy eyes looked fearfully into his.

"Simple. Bring the people to justice who are responsible for shooting my partner and carrying out at least two other murders. I will be going overseas."

"When is this going to happen? Gary, we are getting married in a month!" Tears cascaded down her cheeks. Her chest began to heave as she desperately fought to keep herself in control. Her lips quivered and fear shot from her eyes. "Aren't we?"

Trainor cradled her head in his hands and looked directly into her terror filled eyes. "Yes, Amanda," his smile immediately spread across his face, "we are still getting married. I wouldn't miss it for anything."

At that moment she lost control and fell sobbing, shaking into his chest. Her arms wrapped around his and squeezed him in a death grip.

"Hey," he whispered softly after a few minutes, "I'll let you know tomorrow when I'm going. It'll probably be later this week."

Amanda's red rimmed eyes stared into his. The fearful look hadn't subsided. "Gary, how dangerous is this?"

Trainor reached out and pulled her back to his chest, enveloping her in his arms. Stroking her hair he assured her, "Don't worry, you've met the guys before who I'll be going with. I'll be in good hands."

Monday, November 17, Moscow, Russia

Mikhail Borushko had spent Sunday at his dacha in Romanovo recouping from his stay in America and the setbacks that had befallen him. He still hadn't been able to contact Chernov and Filonenko in North Carolina and that increased his concern tenfold. Something had gone terribly wrong. He was going to have to go on the assumption that they too had failed. Just as well, he thought, all the more reason to bring in his own, trusted, people. The plan he came up with was sure to succeed.

Which led him to where he was, at the Ministry of Defense, dressed in his uniform as a major in the Red Army. He sat patiently in the outer office of Major Andrei Uritsky and watched the sergeant at the desk type away on the keyboard waiting for the call to speak with the officer who was in charge of personnel. If this part of his plan failed, everything else was useless and he would be back at square one.

He was banking on some things never changing.

The telephone on the sergeants desk rang only once before it was answered. "Yes, Comrade Major?" The sergeant listened for a moment, nodded his head as if the major could see him, and then hung up. Turning his attention to Borushko, he said, "You may go in, Major." The sergeant stood and opened the door that was three paces to the rear.

Borushko stood and automatically straightened his tunic. Clutching the thick envelope, he purposefully marched through the door, across the gray carpet and halted at the major's plain wooden desk. The door closed with a click. "Thank you for seeing me, comrade."

Major Uritsky stood and offered his hand. "Take a seat, Major." He gestured to the chair. "What can I do you for you?" The windowless office was small with white painted walls and had a few framed pictures of modern weapons systems hung on them.

Borushko wiped his sweaty palms together. If Uritsky wanted to run his name through the computer sitting on the desk, it would clearly point out that he was no longer in the army. Uritsky's most likely reaction would be to call security and that would be the end of him and his plan to get Marcus Kaderri.

Borushko eased himself down and grasped the envelope with both hands. "I need three men pulled from the field for an important assignment."

"Ok." Uritsky tapped the keys on the computer. "Who and where are they?"

"First Battalion, Seventieth Motorized Rifle Regiment."

Uritsky stopped tapping and stared at Borushko. "That unit is in–"

Borushko cut him off. "Chechnya."

Suspicion crept into Uritsky's eyes. He leaned forward on the desk and stated. "I need to know what the mission is, Major, and do you have orders to show me so I can cut new orders releasing them from their combat duties?"

Borushko felt the sweat drip down his back. He nervously licked his lips. "I cannot tell you what the purpose is nor do I have orders."

Uritsky glared. In a harsh tone, he began to lecture. "Major–"

Before Uritsky could carry on any further, Borushko held up the envelope. "I have this."

"And what is that?" Uritsky asked in the same harsh tone.

Borushko dropped the envelope on the desk. "A reason why I need those men."

Uritsky eyed the envelop for a moment before he picked it up. He then alternated his focus between the envelope and Borushko. "A reason, huh?" This time his voice was softer.

Borushko held out hope that Uritsky would not call security. If he was going to, he would have done so by now. Borushko nodded. "Yes."

The curiosity got the better of Uritsky and he opened the flap. What he saw inside caused him to whistle. He withdrew a stack of euros and fanned them. "Must be a good reason."

"Thirty thousand. Ten thousand for each."

Uritsky put the money back in the envelope and placed the envelope in the inner pocket of his tunic. "What are the names of those men and for how long do you need them?"

Borushko thought his smile was going to be permanently frozen to his face. Something's never change as bribery still worked well in the Red Army.

Monday, November 17, Albany, New York

Gary Trainor arrived at the station at his normal hour of seven, but didn't plan on being there for the whole day. The plan was to ask Chiles for an extended vacation with the reason to gather his wits as a result of the shooting. But until Chiles got in, Trainor sat at his desk, fingering the tickler file searching for a specific name. Occasionally he would glance up and stare at Joanne's empty seat across from him and feel the anger in him begin to rise. Going after Borushko was the right move.

The activity in the station began to pick up as the overnight shift filtered out and the day shift began their rotation. Every officer in the station had made it a point to seek Trainor out and ask about his well being and how Joanne was doing. He thanked them all and avoided any lengthy conversation about the shooting. Then he saw detectives Adam Dunne and Taylor McNeil. They were the detectives assigned to the case.

"Adam!" Trainor called across the room when he saw Dunne walk in.

Dunne turned and waved. "Hey, Gary."

Trainor slid out from behind his desk and met Dunne at his. "How's the case going?" He asked with a hopeful smile. He knew there wouldn't be anything to report but he had to pretend. The whole thing was going to be closed as a cold case because nobody in the department, except for Chiles, himself and Joanne knew why the shooters were in Albany. Lieutenant Chiles would be handling this one behind the scenes.

Dunne slammed a fist into his open palm and shook his head. "Like running into a concrete wall. That intended victim, Bob Wolff, hasn't the foggiest idea who these guys are. The driver's licenses the perps were carrying were fake and they were wearing a disguise. We haven't been able to come up with anything new, either. We released the photos on the licenses and have a request in to Homeland Security. Hopefully something will pop up. I'd like to know who these motherfuckers were that tried to shoot Joanne."

Trainor didn't want to get any deeper in conversation for fear of spilling any additional information. "Keep me posted?" he asked by way of ending the conversation.

"Absolutely," Dunne agreed enthusiastically.

"Thanks, I'd appreciate it." Trainor went back to his desk to find the name and number in his tickler file when Chiles walked in. "Lieutenant, I need to talk to you."

Chiles halted at his door, turned and faced Trainor with pursed lips. "Give me five minutes."

Monday, November 17, Albany, New York

Marcus Kaderri was in his office with all intention on taking on the business day with a full head of steam. There were clients to serve, accounts to attend and the never ending prospecting for new business. Money was to be made. Except his business intentions were distracted by the hungry desire to move forward with the payback to be exacted for his fallen teammates and put an end to the looming threat on his and the lives of the surviving members of SFOD-A 524.

In his hands he held a picture of Mikhail Borushko. Junior, Kaderri liked to call him. He had the same eyes as the man he shot decades ago who was riding in an armored vehicle in Afghanistan. The print out came from the digital surveillance tape he and Bob Wolff watched the day before from the camera positioned on the front entrance of Kaderri's building. The segment of the video where the photo came from had Junior practically looking straight into the camera as if he were posing. Kaderri simply froze the image and printed out hard copies. Déjà vu struck Kaderri as he studied the man but he dismissed the notion. This mission with Junior was personal, the mission with the father was in the line of duty. His hands tightened on the photo. "You will meet a more painful death than your father."

The day prior he had spent most of the time confined to the den in his house, planning out the operation. He had accomplished most of what he needed, but there were still details that needed to be finalized. Paul McKnight would provide him with those details and Kaderri had been promised that they would be delivered to him within the next two days.

Perfect.

Thursday was the day he selected for the day of departure.

Kaderri swiveled in the leather chair and stared out over the city. The gray November day matched his mood. He turned his wrist to read the hands on the gold and diamond Rolex and snorted. It was four thirty in the afternoon and he had expected Gary Trainor would have called by now with an answer. He counted on Trainor joining in and could have used his ability to get the job done. Now, it appeared, he would have to tweak his planning. The goal was still attainable, especially with the skills possessed by himself, Wolff and Hughes, it would just require a different approach.

The phone rang.

Absentmindedly Kaderri spun in his chair and lifted the receiver out of its cradle. "Marc Kaderri," he spoke in his business tone.

"Hey, Marc, it's Gary." There was no excitement in his voice either.

With no fluff, Kaderri simply asked, "Hey, Gary, you come to a decision?"

"Yeah, I'm coming along."

"Good," Kaderri said impassively. There was nothing to get energized about. They were in the serious business of doling out justice and there was the real chance of one or more of them not coming back whole or at all. "I did expect your call earlier."

"Oh, sorry," Trainor said a bit surprised, "I didn't know you wanted to know by a certain time. Anyway, a few questions."

Kaderri leaned back in the chair. "Fire away."

"Departure?"

"Thursday evening. I'll have a more updated schedule later in the week."

"I'm getting married in a month, we gonna be back in time? I'd sure as hell hate to be late to my wedding!"

Kaderri laughed. "Is it the same girl that was involved with the Black Warrior crap?" Kaderri pursed his lips and thought he remembered her name. "Amanda, right?"

"Same one!"

"Conrgatulations to you both!" Kaderri offered then reassured the police officer, "Yeah, we'll be back by then. I'm anticipating not more than three or four days. Got to find the fucker first. I have–"

Trainor cut him off. "I have intel that will help, that's why I'm calling you so late. I was waiting for it to come in."

Kaderri sat up straighter in his chair. "Go ahead," he said cautiously.

"I have connections with Interpol and was able to get two addresses of Mikhail Borushko. One is in Moscow and one is in Romanovo."

"No shit?" Kaderri blurted. He knew Trainor was the man for the job! A connection with Interpol, the International Police Organization! This was part of the information that McKnight was supposed to get. "Where's Romanovo?"

"About fifty miles north of Moscow. I'm getting a packet sent to me from my contact. I'll forward it on once it arrives."

"Well done, Gary! I knew you would be an asset! You are a man of many talents and surprises!"

"Thanks," Trainor chuckled. "Just get me back by my wedding and in one piece!"

CHAPTER TWENTY-FOUR

Tuesday, November 18, Romanovo, Russia

Mikhail Borushko had spent the work day in the hardware store ironing out wrinkles and unforeseen issues that were typical with the opening of a new business. As he tended to the business and prepped the managers for his departure for a week or two, his mind quickly focused on the arrival of his three friends from Chechnya. Keeping tabs with cell phone calls and text messaging, Pyotr Agranov, Osip Martov and Feliks Grigorenko were due into Moscow's Vnukovo International Airport just before sundown. To ensure the last leg of their travel went smoothly, Borushko would have a limousine provided by the Solntsevskaya waiting and then whisked to his home in Romanovo.

Of the three men, Agranov was the only one who knew what Borushko was planning, killing the man that led the unit that shot General Borushko. He had instructed Agranov to inform Grigorenko and Martov that they were needed on Solntsevskaya business and would get the details later. With electronic surveillance and hackers accessing cell phones and computers, Borushko didn't spill any pertinent information to his friends while they were in Chechnya. The risk was too high.

Almost alone in his spacious two story four bedroom rustic dacha in the quiet pine and fir woods, he sipped at his third glass of vodka, waiting for the call from Agranov. The cell phone lay quiet on the cedar end table next to the studded brown leather recliner. Borushko had his feet on the matching ottoman and stared into the flickering flames of the fire.

He turned his head and gazed out into the woods through the grid paned window. Heavy red drapes were tied back with a gold rope. Snow was falling which gave him a relaxed, comforting feeling and he felt protected as he watched one of the armed guards walk past on their foot patrol. There was a house keeper and five guards always at the dacha when he was on the premises. The number dropped to two when he was away. One of the guards was stationed inside the residence and he had a small bedroom off the kitchen–right across from the front door and at the foot of the stairway that led to Borushko's upstairs bedroom. The other four guards lived in a trailer fifty meters away from the house, partially hidden in the woods near the stream that marked the northeastern boundary of the ten acre property.

The cell phone emitted its chime.

Borushko scarped it off the table and studied the numbers of the incoming call. He expected it was from Agranov but desperately wanted it to be from either Chernov or Filonenko, the two men he hadn't heard from in North Carolina. It wasn't. "Yes, Pyotr, you are ten minutes out?" he said by way of answering the phone.

"We are," Agranov answered in a tired voice, "if the spot you told us to call from is ten minutes away. I hope you have food and drink for us."

"There is plenty of both." Borushko closed the flip phone and made preparations for their arrival.

He put more logs on the fire and then walked into the kitchen. "Galena," he called to the housekeeper stirring the contents in a pot on the stove. "My friends will be here in ten minutes."

The fairly attractive lady in her mid-forties turned to face Borushko. She brushed a strand of dark hair away from her face. "Da, everything is ready."

She pulled a beef roast out of the oven, the aroma causing Borushko's mouth to instantly water. "Hmm, that smells delicious!" he complimented then stole a slice of black bread from the fresh baked loaf on the cutting board.

"Thank you," she answered casually. Galena was newly assigned to Borushko's staff and kept her comments short and formal. She was aware of his involvement in the Solntsevskaya but not what he did in the organization. She would come in, clean his dacha, cook his meals and leave. No questions were asked and very little conversation took place. For a guaranteed fifteen thousand rubles a month, Galena knew how to keep quiet.

There was a knock on the door and as Borushko moved from the kitchen to answer it, Karl, the bodyguard stationed inside the house, was already at the door. One hand was grasping the door handle while the other hovered at the pistol in the worn shoulder holster. He made eye contact, waiting for Borushko to give him the ok to open the door.

"Mr. Borushko, Pavel called and confirmed these were your friends," he tapped the receiver in his ear. "Should I open the door?"

The security at the dacha was tight. The driver, Leonid, had confirmed the three men when he picked them up at the airport and, as Karl informed him, Pavel, stationed in the guard shack at the end of the driveway, confirmed the three passengers again. Borushko nodded, but stood away from the opening of the door just for good measure. "Yes, yes, let them in."

With a heave, Karl pulled the solid wood door open and blocked the opening with his body, giving the trio outside a once over with a sharp eye. The three men were dressed in their winter military clothing and each held a duffle bag. "Mr. Agranov, it is good to see you again."

"You too, Karl," Pyotr Agranov offered his hand which Karl immediately shook. "Please come in, gentlemen," Karl said with a practiced smile. He stepped out of the way to let them pass then closed out the cold autumn air.

Borushko stepped forward and clasped his hands together. "It is good to see you men!" He embraced each one in a bear hug. Upon seeing them, he confirmed his belief he had right men for the job in finding and killing Marcus Kaderri.

"Misha!" Osip Martov smiled. The short, powerfully built man grasped Borushko in his own bear hug and lifted him off his feet. The normally dark, dangerous eyes had a gleam to them. "Thank you for getting us out of Chechnya!" The gleam suddenly dulled and he posed the question, "Why did you get us out? The real reason? Not just what you have stated in messages and what Pyotr has said that it is Solntsevskaya business."

"I am glad I was able to get you out!" Borushko answered truthfully. Though his reasons were purely selfish he didn't want to let his comrades know that just yet. That would wait until they had rested heads and full stomachs. "Tomorrow," he spoke calmly and authoritatively, "tomorrow I will tell you everything."

The members of the Solntsevskaya knew when not to press an issue, even though Mikhail Borushko was their friend.

"Vodka?" Agranov asked with raised eyebrow. "I could use a drink."

Just then Galena arrived with four glasses on a tray filled to the rim with the clear liquid. Wordlessly she held the tray for each man to take a glass. "So, Pyotr, how do you know Karl?" Borushko asked as Karl gathered the luggage and took it upstairs to the bedrooms.

"We've known each other for years. Started just about the same time in the organization."

"Da," Karl grunted and went upstairs. Galena had disappeared as fast as she arrived.

Borushko left it at that. He could tell that neither man was going to give up any more details. "Well," he held up his glass, "to us. I'm glad you all made it!"

They toasted and in one gulp the men swallowed the glass.

"Where to now?" Grigorenko raised his empty glass. "I hope I can get a refill on this!"

Borushko laughed aloud and clapped Grigorenko on the back. "You can, my friend! There is food as well. A big roast beef that I'm sure will taste better than any food you had in the field! Come, let's eat!"

"Good, because after dinner I am going to bed." Agranov stated.

"Me too," chorused Grigorenko and Martov.

Tuesday, November 18, FOB Warrior, Kashah, Afghanistan

The assault on Al Suqami's compound in Masozai Kili was a success. All one hundred sixteen terrorists, fighters and warlords were either killed or captured and Hal Weston's grand prize, Ahmed Rashid Halabi, was sitting somewhere in a cold concrete cell. The surviving HVTs, who were just as big a prize, were in similar detention facilities being interrogated at least twenty hours a day.

Lieutenant Jack Dover sat on the edge of his cot with his head in his hands. A half empty bottle of Gatorade was at his feet. He was sore and tired beyond belief. After he completed the grueling Ranger training he believed he could never be as tired. He was wrong. That paled in comparison to the way he felt now. Part of the reason why he was so tired was the mental anguish he was experiencing with the loss of men the Rangers suffered in the attack, including two dead and seven wounded in his platoon, not including Weston. Two men had been evacuated to Germany with their lives hanging by a thread. Two more were in the hospital at the base in Kandahar and the other three were treated and returned to duty. When he added up the numbers, over one third of his platoon had been killed or wounded.

And the job wasn't close to being over. There was still more fighting ahead, hard fighting and the greater chance he was going to take more casualties. Dover knew this would happen, it came with the job he loved. He also accepted the fact that the men under his command, men he was responsible for, kids, some not even out of their teen years, would not come off the battlefield alive. He would have to suck it up and Charlie Mike, continue the mission.

Twisting his body to get the kinks out, he stared at the poster of the Twin Towers superimposed over an American flag tacked on the wall that Renee had sent him. That was the reason why he attended West Point. What he volunteered for. What he believed in. Put simply, the bad guys needed to be destroyed. Peace would only come at their destruction and he was going help it come about and a high price was being paid. The empty bunk of his CHU mate, Ramone Hernandez who was killed attacking the Campground, was also a stark reminder. Despite that, he took comfort in kicking the enemy's ass and putting a serious hole in their leadership.

There was a hard knock on the door. "Lieutenant!" SFC Isles called.

Dover shot off his bed and reached for the door. Isles stood in the door geared up in full battle rattle. "What's up, Sergeant?"

"Another strike mission, sir!"

Dover took a deep breath and blew the air out his nose. He dropped the K-pot on his head, donned his body armor and vest and slung the M-4 over his shoulder. "Ok, Sarge, let's go get 'em!"

Wednesday, November 19, Romanovo, Russia

The conversation during dinner the previous night was upbeat and limited to the goings on in the motorized rifle battalion. Not that is was by design, it was just the way the conversation progressed. Borushko had asked how life was under Colonel Travkin and he got an earful. Agranov took the lead in answering and stated the patrolling had gotten more frequent and aggressive which led to more violent confrontations with the Chechen rebels and of course, higher casualties.

Funny, Borushko thought, he hadn't heard much about that in the papers. There were some things that hadn't changed with the switch over from communism. The state still controlled the media and the truth still had difficulty finding its way in print.

After dinner and two bottles of vodka, the three guests slept soundly. They awoke to Galena cooking bacon, sausage and eggs which they energetically wolfed down. When breakfast was finished and cleaned up, Borushko dismissed Galena so they could openly discuss and plan the elimination of Marcus Kaderri.

With a fresh pot of coffee on the kitchen table around which the men were still seated, Pyotr Agranov wiped his mouth with the linen napkin and dropped it in a ball in front of him. He clasped his hands together in his lap and leaned back in the chair. "So what is the plan you have in mind?" he asked their leader.

Borushko first addressed Martov and Grigorenko. "The reason I got you out of Chechnya was to help me kill a man." After he received understanding, though tepid, nods from the men, he continued, "We are going after a man named Marcus Kaderri," he stared at each man for a moment and then added, "the four of us." Borushko then went on and explained the situation, how it evolved and where it currently stood. He kept the latter portion very vague.

Grigorenko raised an eyebrow. "Does Mirovich know about this?"

Borushko nodded. "He does." It wasn't technically a lie, Mirovich did approve of Borushko's quest and the use of Solntsevskaya men. But Borushko also hadn't informed Mirovich of the suspected loss of the original teams sent to America and taking Agranov, Grigorenko and Martov out of Chechnya. Besides, he reasoned, their current duties of fighting the Chechens precluded them from any Solntsevskaya business.

"Good!" Grigorenko smiled. "I didn't want to have to sneak around his back like the way we did in the army! It would be painful if we're caught!"

"Right!" Borushko was relieved that his friends wouldn't give him a hard time about his hunt. If they did, he didn't know how to proceed.

"Tell us Misha," Osip Martov, who hadn't said much since their arrival, spoke up. "How are we going to kill this man?"

Borushko had thought long and hard how to make this work. He used his knowledge of planning military operations and applied them to what he wanted done. In a determined and menacing growl he stared at each man as he spoke. "We are headed to America and I am going to kill Marcus Kaderri, with me looking him in the eye." Borushko could feel his blood pressure rise and his face tighten. "I want my face to be the last thing on earth that he sees!" He banged his fist on the table for emphasis.

Emotionless faces stared back at him.

"What are we to do?" Agranov questioned. "If you are doing all the work, why are we needed?"

"You will help me capture him. But," he cautioned with a wag of his finger, "it will not be easy."

"Misha?" the question came from Feliks Grigorenko. He leaned forward, resting his elbows on the table. A troubled look creased his face. "What happened to the other men that were sent to America? There were two teams, yes?"

Borushko slowly nodded. These were the details he omitted in his earlier explanation. "Yes, two teams. One was eliminated and the other is missing."

A collective gasp was heard around the table. "How? How did that happened?" Grigorenko inquired.

The explanation was uneasy for Borushko to offer, partly because he didn't know, especially Chernov and Filonenko's fate. They could be either dead or simply quit their assignment. Anything could have happened to them. "I don't know." He passed out the roster of Kaderri's team in Afghanistan and the men in the Solntsevskaya tasked with killing them. "Rykov and Kalanin had succeeded in eliminating the first two men on their list. The first man was in California and the second in Arizona. When they arrived in Albany, New York, to get the third man, Robert Wolff. they spotted Kaderri. I flew out to meet them with the aim to kill Kaderri while they killed Wolff."

Agranov, holding the paper, cut Borushko off. "What happened to them?"

Borushko readjusted himself in his seat before answering. "I do not know for sure. I was gathering intelligence at Kaderri's house when I believe they were killed." He relayed the breaking news story he watched on the television. "Rykov and Kalanin were not carrying their identifications with them so I am confident it will take the authorities a long time, if at all, to discover their real names. After the shooting, I immediately left the county. I believe they failed in killing Wolff."

Martov snatched the paper from Agranov and studied it. He rubbed his chin in thought and breathed loudly through his nose. "Humph, Rykov and Kalanin. I know their names." He looked up from the paper, narrowed his eyes and asked, "Weren't they KGB?"

"They were," Borushko said tight lipped.

"And what happened to..." Martov studied the paper again, "Nikolai Chernov and Pavel Filonenko? They went to North–," he paused and fumbled over the pronunciation of 'Carolina'?"

Borushko resigned himself to the probability that they were dead as well. "They were after Jesse Hughes. I don't know what happened to them and I have not been able to contact them either. They don't answer their phones and text messages and have not contacted me. I believe they are dead as well." Borushko shrugged. "Then again, they could call at any moment with an update."

Agranov let out a long whistle. "You don't think they'll call, do you?"

"No," Borushko shook his head. "Anyway," Borushko moved on and pointed to the list in Martov's hand, "as you know, those men were in a special forces unit and you know they are very, very good at their tradecraft. Once combat and survival techniques are learned and used, they are never forgotten. Those skills may diminish as we age, but never forgotten."

"Well, we'll keep that in mind," Martov assured Borushko.

"Mikhail," Agranov spoke, "when do we leave to kill the men that assassinated a great Soviet general, your father?"

A rush of pride and sorrow suddenly filled Borushko. "Monday." he balled his fist and slammed it on the table. "Monday!" he repeated forcefully. "Until then, we will plan and rehearse how we are going to kill them. I," he paused, then corrected, "We, will not fail!"

Wednesday, November 19, Albany, New York

Marcus Kaderri had spent the day tying up loose ends, gathering information, equipment and clothing for the trip overseas. Maps, including road and aerial, and finding the exact location of Borushko's addresses, all had to be secured. Road maps and aerial photos were readily available on the Internet so a simple click of the mouse provided all he needed. Thankfully, the man who took the lead on most other items was Detective Gary Trainor. His Interpol contacts have proved invaluable.

Somehow, and Kaderri didn't want to know, Trainor had gotten permission for them to stay at an Interpol safe house in Moscow. To keep the safe house location secret, they would only receive the address once they were on the ground. That made matters much easier because it saved Kaderri the trouble and risks of booking and staying in hotel rooms. Ground transportation was being arranged by Interpol as well and their rides would meet their private aircraft at a somewhat secluded section of the airport upon landing. That would allow Kaderri and his company to bring in their weapons without any scrutiny. Trainor also got them Interpol identification badges, which eliminated the use of a cover story, and diplomatic credentials.

When all the planning was finalized, a dinner out with the family was called.

The Kaderri's, each with a child in hand, briskly walked against the light wind that dropped the forty five degree temperature into the high thirties. "It's cold out here. C'mon, faster," Kaderri urged Sean to the door of The Steer House.

Sean pursed his lips and pretended he was a car and made a noise like a revved up engine. His little legs ran faster as he tried to keep up while his father pulled him along.

Kaderri opened the door and shooed Sean inside, who promptly stopped and caused a traffic jam when Sara and Sam attempted to enter. The door remained open, allowing the chilly air to follow them in.

"Move it, dude, keep going," Kaderri directed.

Sara, with a small bag of toys slung over her shoulder, nudged him forward with her knee. "Go, honey."

"Good evening, Kaderri family," Leslie greeted once the family was inside the door. "Got everyone tonight!"

"Hi, Leslie," Sara returned the greet. "Ready for us?"

Kaderri gathered the coats and hats and Leslie hung them on the rack. "For you guys, anytime."

Kaderri then moved to tuck in the tail of Sean's turtleneck that worked its way out of his corduroy pants then brushed a piece of lint from the front of his own brown wool commando sweater.

Sara, in the meantime, fluffed Sam's red dress and retied the ribbon in her ponytail. She then gave her pink cashmere turtleneck a once over and brushed at the knee length black leather skirt.

"All set?" Leslie grabbed the menu's and waved with her head, "Follow me." She led them through the dining room to the linen covered table where two high chairs had already been added.

Each adult placed a child in a chair and then automatically removed the knives from the place settings. Once the table was mischievous proof, they sat down across from each other and placed the linen napkins on their laps.

Leslie took the knives, handed out the menus and put the wine list in the center of the table. "Here you go," she said with a smile and rubbed Sean on his head. "Jennifer is on tonight so she will be your waitress. Enjoy."

"Thanks, Leslie," Kaderri said and opened the menu.

As soon as Leslie departed, Jennifer arrived at the tableside with a pitcher of water. "Hi, everybody," Jen said with her usually cheery smile. "Oh!" she screamed, "you brought the kids! Hi guys." She knelt next to each one and tickled their bellies, causing both of them to giggle and squirm.

"Hi, Jen," Kaderri chuckled as he watched the kids enjoy the tease.

"Hello," said Sara.

Jen filled the water glasses then flipped open the note pad to take their order. "What can I get you for drinks?" She turned to Sara first.

"I'll take a glass of pinot grigio, please."

"Ok, and for you," she directed her question to Kaderri. "The usual?"

Kaderri nodded, smiled and shrugged. "Of course."

Jen pointed to the kids. "For them?"

"Ginger ale, please," Sara said. "Could you bring them in small glasses?"

"Oh, absolutely. We have kiddie cups. I'll be right back." She paused after a step, turned and said to Sara, "It's nice to see you with him tonight."

Sara raised an eyebrow while she removed a toy car from the bag of goodies for Sean to play with and a doll for Sam. "Hmm, is there a story behind that that I should know?"

"Uh," Kaderri feigned innocence, remembering the comment he made to Jen about his reputation while at lunch with Wolff.

Sara immediately knew. "Oh, you had a date with Bob."

Kaderri just nodded and kept a watchful eye on the twins.

"Marc," Sara called quietly.

The tone of her voice signaled she wanted a serious conversation. He turned all of his focus on her. "Yeah, hon?"

"How long are you going to be gone?"

This was the never ending conversation and he could see the concern in her passionate eyes. Since he made the decision to go after Borushko on his home turf, he kept Sara appraised with most of the details. Tomorrow evening was the day of departure and she was looking for reassurance that he was going to be coming home to her and the kids. He had every intention of coming home, and in one piece. "I'll be home Monday or Tuesday at the latest. I don't foresee this as a long process."

Sara was about to say something but Jennifer arrived with the drinks, halting their conversation. "Here you go."

"Thank you," Sara said.

When she put the sodas down, she asked knowingly, "I assume you want more time to place your order?"

"Uh-huh," Kaderri nodded and helped Sam with a sip from the glass.

"I'll be back." Jennifer then spun on her toe and walked to another table.

"A toast to you, honey." Sara raised her glass and held it out for her husband. "May you return safely to me and the kids."

Before Kaderri touched her glass, he used a spoon to put few drops of water in the whisky to release its flavors. "I will." He then took a sip of his favorite whisky, feeling the warmth and complex flavors fill his throat.

"I'm scared," Sara suddenly said and pushed a strand of hair behind her ear.

Kaderri reached across the table and grasped her soft hand. Holding it tightly he spoke in an encouraging tone. Her eyes became glassy, their shine matching the sparkling diamond and sapphire earrings. "If I don't go over and put an end to this, he," meaning Borushko, "will not stop until he gets me and my team. I'm taking the fight to his own turf where the element of surprise will be in our favor. It's safer this way, babe. I don't know if he is going to target you and the kids as bait to get me." He set his jaw and in no uncertain terms he vowed, "I won't let that happen. Ok?"

Sara gave an easy smile. A single tear dropped from the corner of her eye. "I know you won't, honey. I just worry about you."

He squeezed her hand tighter. He became lost in her beauty and knew no matter what, he would return to her to be held in her warm embrace. "Let's enjoy the night."

Thursday, November 20, Scotia, New York

The sun had just set in the late afternoon and already a few stars began to twinkle in the darkening night sky. The Schenectady County Airport's perimeter and security lights winked on, giving off enough yellow-orange light to see without having to strain. The three men stood next to the sleek Hawker 800 jet with their luggage and equipment neatly piled in front of their feet.

The aircraft's cabin door was open and a soft white light emitted from the interior, a beacon for the hard men ready to begin their pursuit.

The *thump, thump, thump*, of running footsteps echoed from the parking lot soon materialized into a figure of a man.

"I was getting worried," Marcus Kaderri admitted to the new comer.

A little out of breath, Gary Trainor dropped his bags with a thud at his feet and held two pizza boxes in his hands. "Then your worries are over," Trainor said with a nervous laugh. After he caught his breath, he added, "Actually, I was worried too. There was an accident that had traffic tied up. I was hoping you wouldn't leave without me."

"Hey, Gary," Jesse Hughes called. "It's nice to see you again. You're looking much better than the last time I saw you." He shook Trainor's hand after he balanced the pizza boxes on the bags.

The first and last time they met it was at Kaderri's cabin in the Adirondacks battling the Israeli commando team. Trainor had taken two bullets in the fight and Hughes was the one who administered the medical care until the helicopters arrived to take him, Kaderri and Wolff to the hospital.

"Jesse," Trainor shook the offered hand. "I never did thank you for plugging the holes in me. Thank you."

"People saving your ass seems to happen a lot, doesn't it?" Bob Wolff joked.

"Yeah, sure. Look who's talking about getting his ass saved! Be nice or you don't get any dinner." Trainor warned.

Kaderri cleared his throat, getting their attention. "Is everyone all set? Have all their gear and most importantly, no reservations?"

"We're good, Boss," Hughes answered for them.

A pair of flashlight beams swayed on the ground and footsteps approached the group from the rear of the aircraft. "Good evening, gentlemen," said John 'Rusty' Doyle. "Ready for a long flight?"

Kaderri stepped forward and shook Doyle's hand. "Hi, John, let me introduce you."

"Ok, Marc," Doyle said but stole the lead. "First, this is the actual pilot, Steve Blackwell," Doyle introduced the man on his right.

"Hiya," Blackwell, a medium height man with close cropped jet black hair said in an easy going manner.

Kaderri began the introductions. "Starting on my right, is Bob Wolff, then Jesse Hughes and Gary Trainor." The men shook hands all around. "We good to go?" Kaderri asked Doyle. He was anxious to get off the ground. There weren't many people privy to what he and his friends were embarking on but Murphy's Law had a habit of making its presence known. The sooner they left, the better.

"Yep," Doyle confirmed, "the plane checks out. Climb aboard and get comfortable, it's going to be a long flight."

"John," Trainor posed, " How long is it? We going non-stop?" The second question was asked with a laugh.

"Please, call me Rusty. I'm glad you asked. Gary, right?" When Trainor nodded, Doyle continued. "It's just under four thousand nautical miles if that gives you any indication. If not, it's about ten hours, factoring in winds and all that aeronautical stuff."

"Long fucking flight," Trainor blurted. "When do we land?"

"We will be stopping in Iceland for refueling and maybe Norway or Sweden depending on our fuel status, etcetera. Touch down time is around ten am."

"Just an FYI," Kaderri interjected, "Jesse here is a helicopter pilot."

Hughes nodded in acknowledgment then added casually, "In case you need a spell or something in flight. You can give me a crash course and I would understand what's going on."

"Good to know," Doyle acknowledged. "Let's hit the sky."

They were committed.

The team picked up their bags and gear and filed into the aircraft. Blackwell started the engines and Doyle closed the cabin door. The team stored their equipment, picked a leather swivel chair to sit in and snapped the seat belts shut.

Doyle climbed into the cockpit and left the door open. There was no need for safety measures to keep those passengers out. After he strapped himself in, he turned and issued final instructions. "Buckle up, we're rolling."

The engines increased power and the plane began to roll. Being at a small airport, the Hawker didn't have to wait in line for take off. Blackwell taxied to the runway and without stopping pointed the nose down the center of the runway. The engines roared and the plane gave a slight shake as it hurtled down the strip. Seconds later, the nose lifted off the ground and the landing gear doors closed with a thud.

Minutes later, the plane leveled off at their cruising altitude of thirty three thousand feet. "Cold beer," Wolff announced and unbuckled the clasp. He ripped open the twelve pack of Samuel Adams and passed them out to all but the pilots.

Kaderri found a glass in one of the side stowage cabinets and poured the beer in. He pulled a laptop out of its case along with a small file of papers. "Ok, guys, let's get down to business. We need to plan for his apartment in Moscow and house in Romanovo. Let's plan this op to make it simple and deadly so we can all get home to our families. We are going to hit hard and hit fast."

"We going for a kill, here?" The question came from Hughes with a hard set face and determined voice. Wolff had the same steely look.

Kaderri knew where his friends were coming from. They were already targeted and wanted to make sure justice was meted out. "Yes, unless something prevents us from doing so."

Hughes turned to face Trainor. "You're a law enforcement officer, you going to have an issue when the moment arrives? This is a lot different than police work."

Trainor shook his head. "Nope."

CHAPTER TWENTY-FIVE

Friday, November 21, Moscow, Russia

By the way the men carried themselves and their fit physical appearance, Doyle pegged Kaderri's friends as former military. So for a wake up call, Doyle thought he would be clever and placed his IPod in the onboard sound system and played Reveille.

"Are you shittin' me?" Jesse Hughes groaned at the sound of the music that woke him. "This guy think he's fuckin' funny or something?"

One by one the men stood and stretched and worked the kinks out of their stiff muscles.

They lifted the window shades to let in the morning sun. Trainor found the coffee maker and brewed a pot.

Kaderri poked his head into the cockpit. "Good morning guys," he said to the pilots. He looked out the windscreen onto the patchwork quilt of browns below. The higher elevations had a blanket of snow.

"Have a good sleep?" Doyle asked from the right seat, taking the headset off his ears and wrapping it around his neck.

Blackwell, with the headset over his ears, was talking into the microphone and nodded to Kaderri.

"Not bad. We still on time?"

"Actually we're ahead. We touch down at Sheremetyevo Two in an hour."

"Great." Kaderri then added smugly, "Nice wake up call."

Doyle laughed. "I thought it might be appropriate."

The men had kept mostly quiet during that hour, eating packaged muffins and bagels Doyle had on board.

"Buckle up, gents," Doyle called from the cockpit. "We're on final approach. We'll be on the ground in ten minutes."

The Hawker glided gently, smoothly on its downward slope speeding towards the ground. The nose came up slightly and Blackwell eased onto the runway. Only a slight bump was heard and felt when the wheels made contact with the tarmac. The nose wheel followed and the engines reversed thrusters, slowing the plane with a shudder.

They were safely on Russian soil.

None of the team felt it was necessary to state they had arrived and there was no visible relief that they had made it. To a man, they unbuckled but remained seated and waited to get up once the plane came to rest after taxiing to a secluded spot at the far end of the airport. They halted near a pair of small hangars and the engines were shut down. Small piles of plowed snow were pushed against fences or snow covered grass.

Doyle popped his head into the cabin from the cockpit. "We're here, gents, and your ride is waiting outside. Local time nine thirty-two." He saw the puzzled look on some of the men's faces and explained their early arrival. "We had a good tail wind."

"Cool." Wolff said.

Kaderri shook his head at the irony of the situation. He turned to Wolff and Hughes who were still sitting in their seats. "Quite a different method of getting into Russia than what we expected, huh? The big bad Bear has allowed us in its den."

"You got that right," Agreed Wolff who then stood. "Didn't have to shoot anybody," then under his breath so Doyle couldn't hear, added dryly, "yet."

The men grabbed their winter coats and gathered their gear. Doyle opened the fuselage door and lowered the stairs. A rush of cold air flooded the cabin. "Impressive welcoming committee," Doyle nodded out the door with his head.

Kaderri was closest to the door and spied what Doyle referred to. He leaned out the door and found waiting at the foot of the stairs an attractive woman with shoulder length dirty blond hair. She was dressed in black slacks and flat soled shoes and a black leather jacket. A white scarf was coiled around her neck. She waved a leather gloved hand and smiled tentatively. "Detective Gary Trainor?" she called in accented English.

"No, but I'll get him." Kaderri turned to Doyle. "You're right, it is nice. Gary," he called to the detective, "there's a good looking woman asking for you."

"Yeah?" Trainor said and zipped his coat. "That should be the Interpol rep on the Moscow police force."

Trainor picked up his luggage and gear and descended the stairs.

"Don't forget anything," Kaderri reminded his team, unintentionally sounding like a parent.

"We won't, Boss," Hughes huffed and led Wolff out the door.

Kaderri leaned his head into the cockpit. "Great flight, thank you." He shook hands with Blackwell first, who was fondling some of the switches and buttons on the console.

"You're welcome."

"Good luck in whatever you are doing," Doyle said offering his hand. He had spent years in the military and knew on sight what the cases Kaderri and his team carried. "Thanks for the vacation!"

"Yes, thank you!" Blackwell mimicked.

In addition to paying the cost of the flight to Moscow, Kaderri also paid the way for the two pilots to remain in country until it was time for the team to depart. Kaderri was thankful Doyle didn't ask any questions and firmly shook the offered hand. "My pleasure. I'll be in touch." He turned and deplaned.

There was man to kill.

When Kaderri descended the stairs, the team had declined the help from the two drivers and loaded their own gear into the rear cargo hold of two running GAZ all wheel drive SUVs. He joined Trainor and the female Russian police officer standing next to the lead vehicle. She was prettier than he first thought. Her pale skin was blemish free and her deep blue eyes were captivating. "Hi," he offered his hand, beating

Trainor to the introduction. "Marcus Kaderri." He made it a point to speak in English. He didn't want to get into any unnecessary conversations and by speaking in the native tongue, curious questions were sure to arise.

"Inspector Kristina Peshkova. Nice to meet you." Her grip was firm.

"Likewise. Are we set?"

"Almost," she cast a disarming smile. "First, I will need to see your Interpol credentials before I take you to where you will be staying." Her English was good, but not as fluent as Kaderri's Russian.

Suddenly, a speeding GAZ skidded to a halt ten feet away, causing everyone to freeze in place. Curious glances spread among the Americans. Two armed, uniformed men quickly exited out of the rear doors of the GAZ. The third man, wearing a suit, stepped out of the passenger side and had his face twisted in anger. He had a fast gait, giving the uniformed men a tough time keeping up. The lead man halted and glared at Katrina with flared nostrils. "You were to wait for me before meeting the plane!" he snarled in Russian and pointed a finger at her.

Kaderri, Wolff and Hughes all understood Russian and exchanged glances among themselves and wondered what was going on. Trainor shot a nervous glance over to his teammates. Kaderri gave a slight shake of his head.

Katrina looked unfazed by the man's outburst. She folded her arms and answered confidently, almost as if she was annoyed. "I called you immediately after the control tower informed me their plane would be on the ground within ten minutes. You weren't at your desk. I am not going to keep fellow police officers from a foreign country who are working on a case waiting around because you had to take a crap."

It took every fiber in Kaderri's body not to laugh or even crack a smile. He stole a glance at Wolff and Hughes who both turned their heads away smiling. The man stared openmouthed while the two guards snickered. Katrina then turned to Kaderri and Trainor with a hint of a smile on her full lips. "My apologies, gentlemen," she switched to English. She pointed over her shoulder. "This is Andre Beria. He works in customs."

"So we show our IDs to him?" Trainor pointed to Beria and asked with a raised eyebrow.

Beria regained his composure. "You do," he spoke in harsh English. He stepped forward and withdrew a stamp pad from his jacket pocket.

"Andre," Katrina switched back to Russian, "they do not have passports that need to be stamped. They have ID cards with magnetic strips on the back to verify who they are. You cannot stamp a plastic ID card."

Once again the three Americans held their laughter in check. Kaderri liked what he saw in how Katrina operated.

Katrina pulled a small electronic device out of her pocket to swipe the cards. "I will handle this, Andre. Just look important." She turned back to the gathered men. "I'll take your cards now."

Beria's eyes flared in anger but he kept quiet. He put the stamp pad away and glared at the back of Katrina's head.

One by one the men approached and produced the Interpol ID cards Trainor acquired for Katrina to swipe. The screen displayed their brief bio and picture and she matched each one up with the picture on the card and the live man.

"Very good gentlemen, we are ready to go." Kristina clapped her gloved hands and excitedly exclaimed, "Welcome to Russia!"

"Thank you," they said collectively.

Katrina walked a few feet away to talk to Beria. Wolff, Kaderri and Hughes laughed quietly at the exchange the two Russians had.

Trainor knew the others spoke Russian so he asked, "What was that all about?"

Hughes laughed a little louder and relayed the conversation.

"What a shithead. She's good!"

The group laughed at Trainor's collective assessment.

The customs official and the guards got back into the GAZ and drove away. Katrina joined the men as if nothing had happened and swept her arm towards the two running vehicles. "Whenever you are ready."

Kaderri and Trainor paired off and rode with Katrina in the lead vehicle.

Ten minutes into the ride, Katrina, of course, tried to gather information on the case that Kaderri and his company were working on.

Katrina turned from the front seat and directed her question to Trainor. "So, can you tell me who in the Solntsevskaya you are looking for?"

The question put Trainor, Kaderri as well, in a tight spot. They had to give up some information to get the credentials and be allowed into Russia to continue their 'case,' but giving up a specific name made them both leery. Trainor looked to Kaderri for guidance.

Kaderri cleared his throat. He didn't completely trust Katrina, even though she was an Interpol affiliate. As far as he knew, she could be working with Mikhail Borushko and would either tip him off that there were Americans after him or she could make their trip to Russia short lived. Deciding it wasn't worth the risk, he shook his head and flat out told her, "Can't do that. Security reasons."

"I understand. I hope you catch him. That group grows more powerful everyday. If you need help in any way, please call me."

"Will do and thank you." Kaderri was even more impressed with her when she didn't press the issue.

Katrina changed the subject and asked some general questions about life in America and described the changes Russia went through from its emergence out of communism into a free society. Mixed in was a brief tour of the city as they passed certain points of interest and well known landmarks.

As Katrina conversed mostly with Trainor about police work, Kaderri studied the city as they drove. Moscow was old but modernizing at a fast rate. Capitalism had taken hold, evidenced by construction crews erecting new buildings or refurbishing old ones. Western food chains were noticeable, not as abundant as back home in the States, but they had a large presence there. Foreign car makers, GM, Ford and many European companies far outnumbered the Russian made ones.

Kaderri's stomach suddenly rumbled, his body called for breakfast. The bagel he had on the plane didn't last long. If his stomach was hungry, he was sure everyone else's was as well. "Hey, Katrina, think we could stop somewhere and get a bite to eat?"

"Sure," she said happily and relayed instructions to the driver.

Breakfast was at a diner where they had consumed eggs and sausage and lots of coffee. Heading off jet lag could be an issue for some so timing their bodies with the clock was desirable. Forty minutes later, Katrina picked up the bill as a treat for her fellow officers and then they were back in the SUV's.

Once they were off the main highway, the urban sprawl slowly thinned out to mostly residential structures and one and two story office buildings and store fronts. Few were in better condition than most and it was evident that capitalism hadn't had much of an impact in this part. "We're almost there," Katrina informed.

Kaderri stole a glance behind to make sure the other SUV was still there. The location of the safe house was a small residential development just inside the northern limits of the city. She pointed to the driveway covered with a light coating of snow, not for the driver's sake-he knew where he was going-but to give Kaderri and Trainor the heads up. The one story house was old and in need of repair. The brick and wood exterior was crumbling and the shingles on the roof were curling. It looked just like the rest of the homes in the neighborhood. Kaderri hoped that the interior was in better condition, especially since this was where the police were supposed to house and protect witnesses.

The two GAZ SUVs pulled into the driveway. "This is where you will be staying," Kristina looked over her shoulder from the front passenger seat.

Simultaneously the team exited the vehicles and removed their gear. Burdened like pack animals, they followed Kristina who held the front door open. She moved out of the way for the men to enter and they put their gear and luggage down in the middle of the wood plank floor living room. There was a worn brown couch and chair and a table with an old tube television set on top. On the left side of the room was a small fireplace. A doorway was in the corner between the couch and fireplace.

She closed the front door against the cold and gave a verbal tour. "What you see is what you get. There are two bedrooms with two beds each," she pointed in their direction. "I am sure you will find the accommodations lacking compared to what you are used to," she said with a disarming smile, "but we are getting there. The stove is gas and the refrigerator works." She handed Trainor the key to the front door. "Once again, if there is anything that you need in apprehending your wanted man, just call me."

"Will do, thanks."

"Oh, here is the key to the GAZ." She dangled it in front of Trainor.

"Thank you," Trainor said and took the second key.

Wolff stepped to the door, sensing correctly the meeting was over. He put his hand on the knob and waited for Kristina.

Katrina flashed a smile knowing she was being dismissed. "Good luck."

Once the door was closed, the men got right down to business. "Let's get going," Kaderri said and studied the house. It was as he thought it would be. The interior was in better condition than the outside, remodeled with drywall and a coat of white paint. The door jam was reinforced and the two windows in the living room were newly installed. He tapped one, assuming it was going to be much thicker than a standard pane window. "Bulletproof," he said aloud.

The eat-in kitchen was to the right of the living room. It was furnished with a square wood table and four wooden chairs. The stove and refrigerator were white and out dated. A single window on the side let in some light. The bathroom was also on the right and behind the kitchen. The bedrooms were next to each other, with the one door opening into the living room while the other opened across from the bathroom.

"Me and Jesse have this room," Wolff pointed to the one off the living room.

"I guess that means we have the other." Trainor grabbed his luggage and put it on the metal framed bed. When he came back out, he asked, "You guys think this place is bugged?"

Kaderri wondered that himself. He also wondered if they were going to be watched by the local police or the federal authorities or what ever the latest version of the former KGB was called.

"Most likely," Wolff snorted. "The minute they found out Americans were coming here, they probably loaded up on the listening devices. Old habits die hard."

"No matter," Kaderri said and read the hands on his Rolex. "Let's get a recon done." He pulled out his cell phone and called McKnight.

McKnight answered the phone. "You there, Marc?"

"On location." That was the way Kaderri acknowledged they were in the safe house. "You have the Bear's location?"

"We can confirm he is at Site Two. Cell phone call originated from there."

"Roger, thanks." He hung up and relayed the information. "We're going north," he indicated Romanovo. On the assumption the place was bugged, they would avoid using names and locations as much as possible.

"Right, Boss."

The team convened to the kitchen table. Hughes produced a map and Kaderri took out the highly detailed satellite photos he had received from the CIA. He leafed through the small stack until he found the one he wanted. He dropped it on the table and began the meeting. "These photos were taken a couple of days ago." The satellite images of locales that are readily available on the Internet were a good reference but they didn't compare to the capabilities of spy satellites. "Here's Bear's house," Kaderri pointed to the main structure in the center of the photograph. Sparse foliage was within twenty yards of the house but outside that radius, the woods became thicker and more dense. The house was a good two hundred yards north of the road. The only other feature near the property was a stream to the northeast approximately seventy yards from the house. "As you can see for yourself," Kaderri pointed out, "it's isolated, away from any roads and perfect for us to approach. Over here," he pointed to a trailer with a large patch of snow scraped away about twenty yards from the house, "piques my interest. We need to find out what this is." He paused and pulled out another photograph, this one was taken by an infrared camera. One part of the photograph glowed red, indicating a warm spot. Kaderri called that out. "Hot spot, here. I think it's a chimney. My guess it's inhabited by his thugs."

"Or just a workshop or garage," Wolff suggested.

"Could be," Kaderri acknowledged the point. One of the most important aspects he learned being a commander was to listen to his men. Many times they would see things in a completely different light and their suggestions, ideas or comments were dead on. "We need to find out. Here's how we'll handle the recon. Each one of us will take a compass point and observe. We'll watch for a couple of hours and then compare notes. Questions?"

Nobody had any.

Kaderri set his jaw. "Let's go hunt some bear! Jesse, you want to drive?"

"You got it, Boss."

Friday, November 21, Romanovo, Russia

Mikhail Borushko's friends were solidly on board with his plan to kill Marcus Kaderri. They too had a bond and friendship that went beyond loyalty to the criminal organization. Their first order of business was booking flights and hotel rooms in the United States. With no direct flights into Albany, NY, the route they had to take brought them first into Philadelphia with a connecting flight north to Albany International Airport. ETA for Albany was three fifteen in the afternoon. Borushko knew from the last trip he took to America that they would need rest immediately after they landed and before they hunted down Kaderri.

After the flights and hotel accommodations were confirmed, Grigorenko, Martov and Agranov went out shopping for supplies and clothing to take to America. Because they left directly from the battlefield in Chechnya, the three men only had spare uniforms and one change of civilian clothing. They would need more than that for their stay in America.

While his comrades were out, Borushko sat in the chair by the fireplace, remembering his childhood with his father when he wasn't away on military business. He recalled the times of he and his father kicked a ball in the park, traveled to Romania to visit the carnivals set up by the Gypsies or fished on many of the lakes that dotted the Russian countryside. The slow burning fire in the pit of his stomach grew stronger and stronger with each passing tick of the clock. He could now taste the revenge that was at hand.

The final planning phase of how they were going to kill Kaderri, plot the escape route and get out of the country before the authorities were alerted was planned when his comrades returned. When that phase was finished, they were going take a celebratory dinner at one of Borushko's favorite restaurants in Moscow.

"Mr. Borushko?" Galena interrupted his thoughts.

He cast his glance in her direction. She was standing near the stairs drying her hands on a towel. "Yes, Galena?"

"Lunch at the usual time?"

Borushko nodded once. "That would be fine." Galena, seeing there would be no further conversation, turned to leave. "Galena?"

"Yes, Mr. Borushko?"

"When we are done with the meal, you may leave. We are going out for dinner tonight." He didn't want any chance of her overhearing their planning.

Galena tried to hide a smile as she turned away. "Yes, thank you."

It took Kaderri and the team fifteen minutes to change into their winter camouflage and warm clothing, pass out and test the Cobra MIR RA3185 communications devices, the same model the American military used on the battlefield, and a set of binoculars for each man. Since they were only going on a recon, they left their major firepower in the safe house and opted to take their 9mm Glock G19 pistols instead. Each magazine carried fifteen rounds and they brought along two spares apiece for assurance. The sixty odd mile drive north to Romanovo took just over an hour. Once outside Moscow, the patchy snow covered country became low, snow covered rolling hills with leafless tress and thick pine trees dusted with clingy snow. Houses became sparse, often standing alone amid the trees or an open field. The men remained quiet as they prepared against potential threats and how to respond. Kaderri sat in the passenger seat and studied the map and aerial photographs planning the teams insertion points and where to park the SUV without being spotted. One thing became obvious. There was going to be a lot of walking.

The rural road they traveled on approached the property from the southwest and curved eastward about a mile west of Borushko's driveway and continued on. Kaderri checked the coordinates on the GPS and oriented himself with the map and began issuing instructions. "Jesse, continue past his driveway and we'll see what we have. You are also going to recon the eastern side of the house and keep the SUV."

"Right."

Kaderri traded looks between the aerial photograph, the terrain and GPS. "The driveway should be coming up on the left. It's the only driveway."

Hughes slowed on the slushy road so all four sets of eyes could spot any signs of the residence through the thick forest.

"There's the driveway on the left," Hughes called, pointing to a slight opening between the trees.

"Keep a sharp eye," Kaderri instructed.

"Guard shack!" Hughes called out. Being a pilot, he had the best eyesight among them. It was fitting that he spotted something first. "Twenty yards in."

"Someone's in there," Wolff added. A stream of smoke wafted out of the tin chimney.

Trainor immediately pulled out a pad and jotted down what the team had spotted.

"Keep going, Jesse, don't slow down," Kaderri urged. They couldn't risk the chance of being spotted.

Hughes drove another mile and a half and pulled off onto the shoulder. "What's next, Boss?"

Kaderri consulted the map to double check that what he wanted to do could be done. He traced a finger on the route and then tapped the map. It would work, he decided. "Surveillance assignments around the house are: East, Jesse. South goes to Gary. Bob, you have the west and I'll take the north." He showed the map and aerial photos first to Hughes and traced what he wanted done. "Turn here and follow this around. Once we get to this spot, Bob and I can get out." He gave the map to Hughes who used the steering wheel as a table.

"I got it," Hughes said after reading the map. " I can drop Gary off here, then I'll retrace back along this route." He used his finger to show where he'd pull over so Trainor could hop out and watch the southern end.

Kaderri turned in the seat and pointed to the location on both the map and photograph for Wolff and Trainor. "You guys see?"

Wolff studied the location. "Right. Just as we planned."

"Yep." Trainor said.

"Careful," Hughes warned, "that's where we saw the guard shack. You up to avoiding that or taking it out?"

The question wasn't meant as a dig on Trainor's capabilities. Policeman simply weren't trained in stealth or shoot first tactics.

"I can handle it," Trainor said assuredly. "Surveillance in a not-too-friendly spot and I are like peanut butter and jelly. We work well together."

Kaderri grinned at Trainor's comparison. "Good. Get the comm gear out and do another check. Last thing we need is for these to go in the shitter. Make sure you have your balaclavas on covering your face."

The men did so and the check went off without a hitch. Satisfied that all was in order, Hughes made the human deliveries.

Within a half hour of the first drop off, all four men were in position to carry out the surveillance on Borushko's residence. Kaderri had the longest trek on foot, taking a long sweeping arc northwest, working his way through the woods to the rear of the house. Along the stream bank, he spotted several fallen trees that would provide cover. Just behind one trunk, he discovered a rotting stump that he could use to sit on that would keep his torso hidden and just allow his head to poke above the tree. He brushed the snow off, sat down and got an unobstructed view of the two story house. He shifted the shoulder holster so it didn't dig into his armpit and adjusted the black balaclava over his mouth to hide his breath. Lastly he flipped open the small spiral notebook, clicked the ballpoint pen and began taking notes.

It was in the field that Kaderri was at home. The warrior in him rose to the top. It was where he transformed from the loving husband and father to a fearless experienced combat leader who would succeed in his mission, no matter what obstacles were thrown in his path.

"This is Kilo," Kaderri called into the microphone. "I'm in position. Check in." For practicality and ease, the team identified each other by using the military identifiers for the alphabet for their last name.

"Whisky," said Wolff.

"Hotel," Hughes said after Wolff.

"Tango is set." Trainor added.

"Roger. Call if you spot anything that causes concern. Don't fall asleep," Kaderri warned.

Twenty minutes after the initial check in, Gary Trainor saw nothing out of the ordinary. He shook his head and mumbled in a whisper so no one else on the MIR could hear him. "Surveillance sucks." Though he was dressed warmly in wool and thermal layers and had the wool hat pulled down over his ears and eyebrows, he wished for the warmth of his heated patrol car. Russia in November was cold! To keep the blood flowing and to prevent cramping, he had alternated between sitting and kneeling in the snow to standing behind a thick pine tree. The longer he remained out in the snow, the more appreciation he had for the men and women in the armed forces who did that kind of work on a daily basis.

From Trainor's location, the guard shack was behind him at least one hundred twenty yards. Borushko's house was sixty yards in front and was devoid of activity. Worthy of note was the small two door red vehicle that was the size of a Matchbox toy car and the big shiny, brand new black four door Mercedes S class sedan parked near the house. Trainor also noted the static security cameras on the corners of the house and one over the front door.

Getting comfortable, he knelt on his right knee and leaned his left shoulder against the pine tree. He brought the binoculars up to his eyes and peered into the window just to the left of the door. He manipulated the focus and spotted a flicker of flame in the fireplace. Then…movement. Suddenly a blond head appeared in the lower corner of the window and looked straight out in his direction! Trainor took in a bite of air and his heart raced in fear that he was spotted. He felt for the Glock.

He fought the urge to duck behind the tree. The human eye reacted quicker to sudden movement, increasing the possibility of being spotted. He froze but kept the binoculars to his eyes, studying the man and trying to determine if it was Borushko looking out the window. The reflection of the snow off the window made it hard to identify, but the man had his hand up to his ear as if he were talking on a phone. Vying for a better angle, Trainor shifted to his left. The glare melted away and materializing behind the pane was the face of Mikhail Borushko.

Then like a gopher ducking back into its hole, Borushko's face disappeared.

The sudden rumble of an engine and the crunch of snow under tires from his rear broke Trainor's concentration. Through the trees he spied a silver Mercedes as it slowly made its way down the driveway towards the house. "Shit," Trainor spoke softly, forgetting everyone could hear him over the MIR.

"Who said that? What's the matter?" Kaderri's concerned voice whispered in his ear.

"Trainor," he answered, forgetting to identify himself as 'Tango.' "Got a vehicle coming down the driveway." He shrank in his posture, hunched his shoulders and made himself small behind the tree he was leaning on. He was only fifteen feet away from where the car would pass him.

He reached for the pistol and held his breath as the car drove slowly past. There were two men inside, both in the front seats. Trainor gripped the pistol tighter, ready to use it if necessary. Fortunately, the driver kept his eyes forward and continued down the driveway to the house.

The car stopped next to the black Mercedes and to Trainor's surprise, three men got out: two from the front and one from the rear. Trainor noted the driver put a pistol in the waistband of his pants before he covered it with his jacket. All of them went to the trunk and removed shopping bags and boxes before they made their way to the front door. Just as soon as they reached the step, the wooden door opened from the inside. Trainor made a note of that as well. Someone was watching the outside.

"Tango, what's going on with the car?" Kaderri voice flowed in his ear.

"It's parked and three men went inside. Borushko met them. He was looking out the window when they arrived."

Silence greeted Trainor's remark.

A few moments later, Kaderri spoke. "Roger, keep watching."

Activity wasn't just taking place in the south or front part of the house.

The absence of a whistling wind rustling the branches and the frozen stream allowed for sound to carry. Marcus Kaderri hadn't moved from the stump since he took up residence. He didn't want to risk it. Cameras on the corners of the house kept him static and that was also the only useful information he had gathered, besides the design of the rear of the house.

Without warning that all changed.

The muffled crunch of snow carried through the air from his right. He turned his head, narrowed his eyes and scanned for the source of the noise. Not knowing what wild animals were indigenous to the area, he kept his mind open to the fact that a bear or other large animal may be near. The steady noise grew louder, sounding like the steady gait of a man. The footfalls became louder, but still Kaderri couldn't see.

Then came the voices in a conversation. They were muffled, difficult to understand but clear enough that there were at least two men. Quickly his eyes scanned the trees, darting back and forth, looking to spot anything out of the ordinary. Still, nothing. Slowly he pulled the Glock from the holster and became alarmed about his footprints. He rested his thumb on the safety.

A sudden prolonged coughing fit gave away the position of the men. Not more than forty feet away two men emerged between a copse of trees. They wore black knit caps and thick leather jackets with cigarettes dangling from their lips. One had a thick scarf wrapped around his neck. Slung over each of their shoulders was an automatic weapon.

Kaderri pegged them as a security patrol. He loosed the safety and froze, silently shooing the patrol away. "This is Kilo," he whispered into the microphone. "Contact."

One by one the team acknowledged.

The two man patrol slowly moved from Kaderri's right to left across what would be the back yard. He held his breath as they continued on, engaged in their conversation. Tighter he gripped his pistol calculating which man, if necessary, to shoot first. The man with the scarf coughed again and stumbled over a downed tree limb. His partner laughed and reached out to catch him and pulled him towards the house, away from Kaderri. Oblivious to the man in the woods, the two man patrol continued on. Not once did they look in Kaderri's direction.

Not until they turned the corner of the house did Kaderri breathe a sigh of relief. He holstered his pistol and called Hughes over the MIR. "Hotel, this is Kilo."

"Go."

"Two man patrol headed your way."

"Roger. Thanks for the heads up."

It was readily apparent that the two men on patrol weren't very good at their job, or the least bit interested in doing it correctly. Kaderri dismissed them as hired thugs who didn't pose a serious threat.

"Welcome back," Borushko closed the front door, curious to know the outcome of his friends shopping spree. "Did you get everything we needed? I see you found a nice car to drive."

Borushko could have let them use his car, but he wasn't going to be left without any means of transportation. He hadn't bought a vehicle yet to be left at the house for use by the guards or Galena. Granted he could have taken one of the guards' private vehicles if he needed to, but he preferred not to drive one of the lesser vehicles. Instead, he had one of the guards use their private automobile to take Agranov, Grigorenko and Martov to a car dealership that was on very friendly terms with the Solntsevskaya to lease them a car for the time they were in country.

Pyotr Agranov stood next to the fire, nodded and dropped the shopping bags. "Yeah, we got everything we needed."

Everything they needed included the clothes and toiletries and more importantly, false bottom luggage where they could hide their weapons and ammunition on the plane. Martov inhaled deeply and looked towards the kitchen. "Lunch?"

"Yes, it is ready. Galena will set it out for us. Grab a bottle of vodka from the closet will you? Then we will finish our planning for this."

The only excitement Marcus Kaderri encountered while sitting on the cold rotting stump was the security patrol. And that was ok with him. There wasn't much to observe on the surveillance of the house. The time of year caused very little reason for anyone to be outside, which eliminated most chances of discovering how many people were in the house.

After two hours, Kaderri figured they were going to get all that could and decided to get his team back indoors and compare notes. He wiggled his toes against the growing cold. "Hey, guys," he spoke softly into the microphone, "this is Kilo. Ready to call it a day?"

The men answered just as softly and in sequence.

"Whisky's ready."

"Hotel is done."

"Ditto for Tango." Trainor remembered this time not to use his name.

Kaderri closed the small spiral notebook and tucked it away in the pocket in his camouflaged field coat. It would take approximately twenty minutes for Hughes to get to the GAZ and another ten for him to pick up the men as they slowly exfiltrated from their observation sites. "Let's go."

Relieved that time was up, Trainor shivered and slowly moved away from the tree he had grown accustomed to leaning against. Satisfied with his notes, he put the spiral notebook in a pocket and readjusted the wool cap for the trek back to the road.

Carefully, he began retracing his footprints to minimize any chance of being discovered. He had made slow and steady progress when he heard the sounds of another car. This time the sound originated from the direction of the house, heading up the driveway towards the road. Curious, he decided to check it out. Maybe Borushko was on the move and he knew Kaderri would want to know. Trainor picked his way through the trees, straight to where he believed the driveway was.

He didn't know exactly where the edge of the driveway was at that point in the woods but thought he was in the clear. He was about to take another step then suddenly froze. Ten feet to the left was the guard shack. He could see through the small window the guard was smoking a cigarette.

Gingerly, Trainor stepped back, careful not to make any noise or sudden moves that would catch the eye of the guard. The little red car that was parked at the house slowed to a stop at the shack. The guard stepped out, an automatic weapon was slung over his shoulder and he held a radio in one hand. He put the other hand out to stop the car and raised the radio to his mouth.

The driver came to a stop, leaned across the passenger seat and rolled down the window. Trainor noted the driver was a woman but couldn't discern her approximate age. The guard leaned into the open window and they smiled to each other and carried on a conversation.

Because it wasn't Borushko, Trainor felt there was no need for any more observation. While the guard and driver were occupied with each other, he took the opportunity to sneak away. Instead of trying to navigate his way back on course, Trainor opted to parallel the driveway all the way to the street. There he would turn and walk along the road until he made it to the extraction point.

Up ahead, he could see the trees thin. The road was in sight. Another car engine was heard off to his left and he looked at his watch. That, he thought, should be Hughes coming down the road. Trainor had to pick up the pace to make it to the road before Hughes drove past him. Then he remembered he was wearing the MIR. "Hang on, Jesse," he forgot to use his call sign again, "I'll be exiting the woods at the side of the driveway in a second. Don't drive past."

"I'm not near there yet," Hughes said with a questionable tone.

Trainor stepped out of the woods and realized too late the mistake he just made. The driveway was a mere forty yards to his left and the red car turned onto the road, right at him. "Shit!"

The driver's and Trainor's met eyes.

A million thoughts on what to do raced through Trainor's mind. There was no doubt that something had to be done with the driver. He was sure that she would immediately turn around, go directly to the guard shack and report that she had just seen a man in camouflage clothing emerge from the woods. That would put the entire operation in jeopardy.

Trainor had to stop her. He ignored the calls from Kaderri and Hughes over the MIR, jumped directly in front of the car, withdrew his pistol and pointed it at her. His heart pounded in his ears and he yelled, "Please, you better stop!"

The woman's mouth opened in fear at seeing the camouflaged man pointing a gun at her. She swerved to avoid hitting him and skidded to a halt.

Before she could recover, Trainor leapt into action. He ran to the passenger side door and yanked it open. Immediately he leveled the pistol at the drivers head. She instantly threw her shaking hands up and yelled and screamed in wide eyed fear. He pressed the pistol to her temple, climbed in and put a finger to his lips to shush her. "Do you speak English?" he asked, hoping she would say yes. He quickly looked over his shoulder to see if the guard came out to investigate what the screeching tires was all about.

The woman stared at him. Her green eyes were wide in horror and her bottom lip was quivering. She kept her shaking hands up in the air. When she didn't answer, he took it that she didn't speak English. Not being able to communicate, Trainor pointed out the windshield hoping she would understand he wanted her to drive.

The lady put the car in gear and slowly depressed the accelerator.

"Tango! What's going on?" Kaderri urgently called over the headset.

This time Trainor answered. "Got a prisoner," was all he could come up with.

"What? Who is it?"

"Some lady. I don't speak Russian." He passed the location where he inserted into the woods and thought it best to meet Wolff and Kaderri at their location. "I'll meet you at your insertion point."

A sense of urgency took over. Instead of slowly making his way through the woods, Kaderri began a steady jog. Bobbing and weaving his way around the trees and under low branches, he followed his tracks that he produced on the way in. Quickly he came upon the location where Wolff had positioned his surveillance point and noticed from the stride of his tracks that he too had jogged out of the woods.

Abruptly he came to the edge of the woods and spotted the little red two door Russian built Lada pulled over to the side of the road. He ran up to it and found Wolff sitting behind the wheel and Trainor and the woman squished in the back seat. Kaderri climbed into the passenger side of the cramped car and nearly ate his knees.

He knew that Wolff would have already began questioning the lady. "What have you found out so far?"

"Her name is Galena Surikov, that's all I asked so far." Wolff answered. He had the MIR draped around his neck. "She's scared shitless."

Kaderri turned to face the trembling, terrified woman. The first thing he had to do was allay her fear that she was going to get hurt. "Galena," he spoke quietly in Russian and removed the MIR and balaclava from his head. By revealing his face, he hoped that she would understand that there was nothing to fear. Smiling, he tried to reassure her, "we are not going to hurt you, I promise that." The next thing to do was get out of there before someone spotted them. He put the MIR back on. "Hotel, where are you?"

Hughes immediately responded in a clear voice. "Half a mile from your pick up spot."

"We have a red Lada at that location. Drive past and we'll follow you back." He could have had Hughes stop so someone could ride with him so they would be more comfortable, but the less conspicuous they were, the better.

"Roger."

Kaderri turned to Wolff. "Can you drive this thing?"

Wolff twisted his face. "I hope it can carry all of our weight."

Trainor had been watching for Hughes out the back window. "Here he comes."

Hughes slowed down as he passed and smiled broadly. "You guys look like the clowns in a circus car!" He joked over the MIR.

"Real cozy." Wolff put the car in gear and followed.

Kaderri tossed his balaclava to Trainor. "Put this on her. I don't think your friend in the police department wants the whereabouts of the safe house known."

"Right." In one motion, Trainor covered Galena's terrified face. "Hey, Marc. That guy Borushko–"

Kaderri turned around in the cramped seat. "Yeah?"

"He walked past me in Albany when I was sitting the car watching your building. I actually said good morning to him!"

"Well, he doesn't have too many mornings left."

CHAPTER TWENTY-SIX

Friday, November 21, Moscow, Russia

The ride back to the safe house was uneventful and surprisingly Galena hadn't made a sound. She was too terrified to even ask what the men wanted or where they were taking her. She was a petite woman who didn't weigh more than a hundred and ten pounds and posed no physical threat to any of Kaderri's team.

Kaderri wanted to get the questioning of Galena going immediately because jet lag was beginning to set in and he wanted to get as much information out of her regarding Borushko before they got much needed rest.

Once the team was in the safe house, the balaclava was removed and he made her sit in the corner of the kitchen. The shades were drawn to prevent her from looking out or prying eyes looking in. Kaderri sat across from her and Trainor strategically placed himself between her and the front door to prevent any chance of escape. They saw no reason bind her hands.

While Kaderri and Trainor began the interrogation of Galena, Wolff and Hughes set out to find food for dinner and the next day's breakfast. Even though Trainor didn't speak or understand a word of Russian, Kaderri wanted the detective present for his experience and knowledge with those types of interviews. Kaderri used tactics that were designed for immediate results and wouldn't be the proper method for use on Galena. At least not yet.

To put Galena at ease, the first thing Trainor did was to give her a glass of water, which she immediately drank.

"No harm will come to you," Kaderri spoke in Russian and handed her a second glass of water.

"What do you want with me and who are you?" Galena asked nervously, interlocking her fingers around the half empty glass.

Kaderri relayed the question to Trainor. "She wants to know who we are. I'll show her the Interpol ID but I want you to show her your shield, ok?"

Trainor nodded.

They both showed her their respective ID's. "This is who we are." Kaderri was careful not to mention his or Trainor's name and knew Galena couldn't read the print on the cards. Her eyes went wide at seeing Trainor's badge. It was common knowledge across the world what a badge stood for.

She threw her hands up and sat straight up in the chair. "I've done nothing wrong!" she protested and moved her long dark hair behind her shoulders.

Kaderri waved his hand in dismissal. "We know," he spoke softly. Then his eyes narrowed into slits and with chilling clarity commanded, "We want to know about Mikhail Borushko."

The muscles in Galena's face relaxed upon learning she wasn't the target of an investigation. At the mention of Borushko's name, though, her eyes turned downward towards the table.

Kaderri and Trainor traded glances at her actions and came to the same conclusion. She was afraid.

"Ask her why she is afraid of him," Trainor instructed Kaderri. "Ask if it's because of the Solntsevskaya?"

The mention of the criminal organization caused Galena's head to snap up with fear in her green eyes.

Kaderri presented the question and Galena's head bounced like a bobblehead.

"Let's start with simple, friendly questions," Trainor suggested. "Make sure she knows that we are not interested in her activities outside of her relationship with Borushko."

Kaderri nodded his understanding. "Galena, what do you do for Borushko?"

"I'm a housekeeper and cook, that's all," she revealed.

Kaderri felt a surge of excitement. Galena would have the answers to all the information he needed! The layout of the interior of the house, how many people were inside, Borushko's schedule and the list could go on. He hit the jackpot! Kaderri relayed her position.

Trainor then asked, "For how long?"

Kaderri asked and was intrigued by her answer. "Just over a year, but he's been in the army so I haven't seen much of him until a couple of months ago."

Kaderri didn't translate but immediately followed with, "What did he do in the army?"

Galena shrugged. She seemed more at ease now and took another sip of water. "I don't know. I don't talk to him about such things, only my job. But I–" she hesitated and put the glass back down. She clasped it with two hands and looked Kaderri in the eye. "I don't think I should say anymore." She tried to mask her fear with a bit of defiance. "What is going to happen to me?" she asked in a stronger than expected voice.

Kaderri hadn't gotten that far in his planning so he turned to Trainor thinking he may have some insight. "Do the Russians or Interpol have a witness protection program or something along those lines?"

Trainor furrowed his brow and shrugged. "Beats me. I would think so since we are in a safe house."

"Good point," Kaderri acknowledged. "Galena, you'll be ok." To end any further discussion about her future and dissuade more attempts of defiance, Kaderri placed his pistol on the table.

Galena stared at the gun and got the message. "Ok, I hope you are right."

"What were you going to say about Borushko and the army?"

Galena eyed the gun and nervously tapped her fingers on the table. "I overheard him and his friends talk about their time in Chechnya."

"What were they doing there?"

"I don't know for sure, but I assume fighting rebels."

"How many friends are in the house with Borushko?"

Galena stared past Kaderri and moved her lips in a silent count. "Three and Karl."

"Who's Karl?"

"Karl is security that lives inside the house."

Trainor cleared his throat. "Uh, Marc, can you fill me in?"

Kaderri rubbed his tired face and scratched at his head. "Sorry, Gary. In a nutshell, there are five guys inside the house. Borushko and his three friends appear to have combat experience in Chechnya. The fifth guy, his name is Karl, is a bodyguard."

"Who is probably not afraid to shoot anybody," he added.

"Right." Kaderri looked questioningly at Trainor. "Is there anything up to this point that you want to ask?"

Trainor shook his head. "Nope, you're doing fine."

"Ok." Kaderri stifled a yawn then got back to the questioning. "Galena, where is Borushko going to be tomorrow?"

"I think he will be at the dacha. I know he was going out to dinner tonight with his friends. That is why I left early today."

Kaderri leaned back and this time the yawn came out. "Do you have to cook for him tomorrow?"

Galena shook her head. "No. They said they would be sleeping in because they would be late getting in and I wouldn't have to cook. I have to go back Sunday before they leave for their trip."

"Trip?" That swept away the creeping tiredness. "Where to and when?"

Galena gave one of her shrugs. "I don't know. All I know is they all leave on Monday."

Kaderri fished the small spiral notebook from his field jacket, tore out a page and handed that and a pen to Galena. "Draw me a map of the two floors, please. Oh," he almost forgot, "is there a basement?"

She took the paper and tapped the pen on the table. "Yes, there is."

Kaderri removed another piece of paper and handed it to her. "Draw that as well, and I need to know where the door is that leads from the basement to the outside, if there is one."

A knock at the door stole his attention. Kaderri and Trainor both reached for their pistols. Trainor moved to open the door while Kaderri stood behind him with the pistol ready. Kaderri put a finger to his lips as Galena froze in terror.

"Delivery for the Bear Hunter!" Hughes announced from the other side.

Trainor looked quizzically at Kaderri, who chuckled at Hughes term for Kaderri's call sign when he commanded the team in Afghanistan and hunted Soviets. "Let them in."

Hughes entered carrying two large paper bags. Wolff had one bag and a case of bottled water over his shoulder. They brushed past Trainor and dropped everything on the counter.

"What the hell did you guys buy?" Trainor asked, closing and locking the door behind them. A very familiar odor filled his nostrils. Fried hamburgers and French fries permeated the small house. "I come all the way to Russia for hamburgers?"

"Didn't want to risk getting the shits from the local fare. We also picked up a six pack of Czech beer," Wolff said to balance out the meal. "Good stuff."

Because of the mission, one six pack of beer was their self-imposed limit. There would be no chance for a hangover to impede their abilities to carry out their tasks.

They handed out an assortment of food and fries and offered Galena her pick. She declined a beer but drank a bottle of water with the thirst of someone who had spent the day in a desert.

Friday, November 21, Romanovo, Russia

Mikhail Borushko felt more at ease now that everything to avenge his father's death was on track. In a way, the dinner was going to be an early celebration of their success, his success, in holding to his promise he'd made many years before. Once they returned from America after killing Kaderri, they would celebrate again, only then time it would be a bash.

"Mikhail?" Agranov walked into the living room where Borushko sat in his familiar seat sipping a vodka.

"Yes, Pyotr?" He shook himself away from his thoughts. "Would you like a vodka before we go to dinner? Help yourself." He pointed to the decanter and the extra glasses on the sideboard in the corner.

"Thank you." Agranov helped himself and as he poured, Grigorenko and Martov walked in. He automatically filled two more glasses.

"Gentlemen," Borushko stood and smiled at the impromptu gathering. "This is such a wonderful night! Drink!" He lifted his outstretched arms, raising them high above his head.

"Mikhail," Agranov called for him. "I want to ask you before I forget. Are we taking automatic weapons to America?"

Borushko was delighted to see that his men were still focused on the job. He shook his head. "No. Pistols should be fine. Automatic weapons are harder to smuggle in using our luggage. We do, though, have AKSs here." Borushko referred to the compact automatic weapon.

"Extras? Not just for the guards?" Grigorenko asked surprised. "Why?"

Borushko shrugged dismissingly. "You never know when they may come in handy."

A muffled cough interrupted. "Sir?"

Borushko turned to see Boris standing next to the door. He was the driver and bodyguard for the night. "We are ready!" Borushko said enthusiastically. "Come, my friends, lets eat and celebrate!"

"Good!" Martov clapped his hands together. "I think I am going to get drunk tonight. It has been a long time since I had vast amounts of good vodka and I am due!"

"Yes, we all are!" Grigorenko agreed. "Especially after serving and surviving in Chechnya!"

"And don't forget visiting the warlord in Afghanistan! I thought for sure we were going to die there!"

"Yes, my friends," Borushko happily herded them towards the door, "We have much to celebrate tonight!"

Friday, November 21, Moscow, Russia

Hughes elected to lean against the Formica counter while everyone else sat around the table and consumed their fried gourmet feast. Kaderri used the opportunity to debrief the team on the recon. He wiped the ketchup from the corner of his mouth before he began. "Jesse, let's start with you. What did you see?"

Hughes, who observed the east side of the house, pulled out his notes and began reading them. One by one each man followed suit and described what they had seen regarding the house, its security system, where the electrical and telephone wires entered the house and the guards that patrolled the grounds. Most notable about the guards was the AKS-74U assault rifles they carried slung over their shoulders and lack of attentiveness on their patrols. It took twenty minutes for all four men to present their findings.

Kaderri jotted down all the pertinent information as his colleagues spoke, then compared the notes with the very detailed floor plan that Galena had drawn. The four bedrooms upstairs was where Borushko and his three friends were sleeping. Karl, the bodyguard, had his room downstairs strategically located next to the stairs with his door facing the front door. Once Kaderri had evaluated all the material, a clear picture came into focus.

While in the army, Kaderri had the reputation of being a gifted tactician with an eye for the unorthodox as well as simplicity. The key to making his plan work was speed and silence.

"Ready to rock, Boss?" Hughes said.

"Boss, what are you thinking?" Wolff asked after Kaderri didn't respond.

"Right. Here's what we're looking at if everything we discovered and what Galena," Kaderri nodded at her sitting in the corner picking at a pile of fries, "gave us is true. We have five armed men in the house, probably with combat experience, and five armed men around the grounds and in the trailer. Of those five, two or three should be inside the trailer." Kaderri made eye contact with them all. "Yes?"

They all nodded in agreement.

"Four against ten." Kaderri knew what protests were coming and saw the reaction on Wolff and Hughes' face. He held up his hand to silence them. Being outnumbered was nothing they haven't experienced before in firefights. Their skill, training and a sound plan always made sure they came out on the winning side. "Here's where I'm going. It's not the numbers per se, it's the dispersement of the bad guys that has me concerned." He drummed his fingers on the table and explained his plan. "We have to hit two targets. Ideally at the same time and splitting us up for an assault is risky."

"Main target is in the house," Wolff began his thought out loud. It was common for these men to work through ideas like that. "If we…no, then that'll leave….shit, Boss, I see it."

"Huh?" Trainor blurted.

Wolff smiled and gave brief chuckle and went to explain. "If we assault the house, ignoring the guards outside, especially the ones in the trailer, we risk having them ambush us on the way out or attacking us once we are inside."

Trainor completely understood. "Got it."

"If we attack the trailer and engage in a firefight there," Hughes chimed in, "it'll alert the target inside and make for a rougher go. We don't want to split up two by two to attack both targets simultaneously, either."

"We need more men," a worried Trainor said

Wolff immediately tried to alleviate Trainor's fears. "Don't worry, Gary, we'll get this figured out."

Good, Kaderri nodded. They all understood the situation. "Here's what we'll do," Kaderri announced. "We take down the trailer first, eliminating the guards inside. Two men, Gary and Bob, enter the trailer and take 'em out. Jesse and I will overwatch for the other guards on patrol." Kaderri had reservations about Trainor on this. He would have to eliminate the guards who weren't a direct threat. In the past he had no trouble shooting people who were shooting at him, but this time, it wouldn't be the case. He needed to know if Trainor could do this. "Gary?"

Trainor leaned his elbows on the table. "Yeah?"

"Obviously we're setting this up like a military op. You ok with killing the guards?" Kaderri leaned back in the chair and folded his arms, looking for any signs of hesitation in Trainor's reaction.

All eyes stared at Trainor.

"I am," Trainor confirmed straight-faced without hesitation. "Fuckers got it coming."

"Good," Kaderri thumped the table. "After the trailer is secured, we enter the house through the French doors in the rear of the house and take care of business."

"The guard in the shack?" Hughes inquired. "What do we do about him?"

That man was the one intangible that was left. "We leave him alone. I'm taking the risk that he won't know what's going on and we'll be gone before he does. If he decides to show up and get involved, we'll take care of him."

Trainor signaled towards Galena with his thumb. "And her?"

Silence settled over them. That was a big problem. "You have handcuffs?" Kaderri asked the detective more by way of a statement.

Trainor nodded and held up two fingers. "Two sets."

"We handcuff her until we return and then we'll let her go." He scanned the gathering. "Anybody have a better idea?"

Trainor shrugged while Hughes shook his head. Wolff was the only one who spoke. "Works for me."

Kaderri clapped his hands once and yawned. "Let's wrap this up. I'm beat. Morning, I'm sure, will come quick."

It took another half hour for the team to finalize their assault plan and every avenue of approach and counter was discussed. Borushko's trip on Monday forced the timetable. A decision to attack before sunrise was selected. Lastly, they set up a watch to keep an eye on Galena.

The men cleaned up dinner and moved Galena over to the couch where they put the television on for her. Hughes had her bring her knees to her chest where he cuffed her right wrist to her left ankle and left wrist to her right ankle. She began to protest but when Hughes gave her a stern warning that he would gag her and put her outside in the GAZ naked, she shut up.

Saturday, November 22, Romanovo, Russia

The team rose just before five o'clock in the morning. They had just over three hours before sunrise to pack their gear and drive the hour to Romanovo in order to catch the targets while they were still sleeping. Jesse Hughes made instant coffee and opened a box of pastries for anyone who wanted them while they went about their morning routines and packed for the assault. There was no joking or bantering, just complete concentration on their task. Wolff woke Galena and had her use the facilities and fed her breakfast and then handcuffed her again. This time, instead of leaving her on the couch, they tied her to a chair in the kitchen and then secured her and the chair to the pipes under the sink.

They did one final check before they packed their Heckler and Koch MP5SD submachine guns attached with sound suppressors and brought three extra thirty round clips of ammunition for each weapon. The MP5 used the same round as the Glock pistols which saved on packing and carrying two types of ammunition. Finally, they inserted batteries and tested the AN/PVS night vision goggles.

Thirty five minutes after waking, they donned the Interceptor body armor under the winter camouflaged field coats and climbed into the frozen GAZ.

Once again, Hughes jumped behind the wheel. The roads from Moscow had been deserted for most of the trip which made for an easy, uncomplicated ride. The only exception was for a car that appeared to be following them but turned off after a half hour. The plan was to park on the east side of the house in the previous spot where Hughes had parked they would progress to Borushko's house from there. The first objective they would tackle would be the guards trailer.

"Coming up," Hughes broke the silence.

As they approached Borushko's driveway, all eyes in the GAZ turned to get a glimpse of the guard shack. A dull glow emanated from the window. The light was on and someone was inside. "Light's on for business," Trainor noted from the back seat behind Hughes. "Hopefully he's asleep."

"It's right up here," Hughes referred to the parking spot.

The headlights illuminated the tire tracks from Hughes' previous visit and shone through the woods like a spotlight. Immediately Kaderri's senses became more focused. It was game time.

Hughes turned off the road and immediately shut off the headlights. He drove twenty yards into the tree line then killed the engine. "This is it."

Almost as if it was rehearsed, the four men donned their balaclavas, strapped the Cobra MIR's to their heads and chambered a round in their pistols. This time they strapped the holsters to their thighs for easier access. "Hey," Kaderri chuckled when they were done, "that was good, all done at the same time."

"All on the same page, Boss," Wolff commented. "That's a good sign."

"Ok, listen up." Kaderri immediately received everyone's attention. "Remember why we are here. The son-of-a-bitch in that house has caused the death of our family members and attempted to take the lives of others. He wants us dead. Let's stomp his fucking ass."

"Let's do it," Wolff said with an edge in his voice. It was easy to tell he wanted payback for the attack on him.

Hughes shut off the dome light so whey they exited, the GAZ would still be dark. Quietly they got out into the cold Russian air and dark, silent woods. Carefully they closed the doors so just a barely audible *click* could be heard when they shut. Wolff was the first one to make it to the back and opened the rear door, handing out the MP5s and night vision goggles. Lastly, despite their gloved hands, they easily chambered a round and engaged the safeties.

Hughes also slung the medical kit to his back in the event one of the team members needed his services. He wasn't concerned about Borushko and his men.

The team turned on their Noggs and formed up in single file behind Hughes. Kaderri was second in line and checked over his shoulder at Wolff and Trainor. "We set?" he asked.

A mixed response returned. "We're good."

"Roger."

"Yep."

Kaderri tapped Hughes on the shoulder. "Move out. Watch your spacing."

Hughes led the faceless, deadly group into the darkness and Kaderri waited until Hughes took ten paces before he took his first step. There was no rush to get through the woods so they took care to work their way around trees and under branches. As much as possible, they tried to step in each other footsteps to hide their tracks and make as little noise as possible.

With his senses on high alert, Kaderri swept the terrain looking for any movement. The ghostly green light through the night vision goggles displayed everything in clarity and he vigilantly stepped in Hughes' tracks. Off to the left, flood lights from the corners of the house and trailer winked through the thick foliage of the pines. They were close. The hold on his weapon tightened around the pistol grip and the closer he got to the house, the more he began to think of what he would do once he saw Borushko. Would he shoot him outright, or let him know that he failed in his plan? Hughes' hushed voice interrupted his thoughts.

"Hold up, we're here," Hughes' voice sounded in the earpiece.

The rally point was to the rear of the trailer and house. From there, the men would split into pairs and would use the same codenames for identification as they did on the earlier recon. Kaderri and Hughes would place themselves as a blocking force between the rear of the house and trailer, stopping any of Borushko's men who exited the house to assist, while Wolff and Trainor took down the trailer.

Wordlessly, the four men closed ranks. The trailer, as Hughes pointed out, was to their left approximately thirty yards away. The blazing white lights over the front door of the trailer and the corners of the house were the guiding lights to the target. Three parked cars were off to the side of the trailer.

Slowly, Hughes guided the team up to the tree line where they halted and crouched in the snow. Before them the ground opened up and they had an unobstructed view to the house. No lights were on inside, but the outside lights were bright enough that the team didn't need the night vision goggles to see.

Silently, they studied the two structures. Lights glowed from the small windows and over the door of the trailer. Thick wood burning smoke curled out of the chimney, the scent filling the forest. The trailer was alive and dangerous.

"Hold tight," Kaderri whispered and knelt in the snow. The only sound he heard was his own breathing.

"See or hear anything?" Hughes asked over the MIR.

"Negative," Wolff answered.

Kaderri waited another thirty seconds before he spoke. His nervous anticipation increased knowing the end of the calamity that had befallen his friends was at hand. "Move into position to take out the lights on the corners of the house. Then we move on the trailer."

"Roger," Hughes answered.

Hughes' job was to slink up to the far side of the trailer and shoot out the light on the front corner of the house. Kaderri would shoot out the rear light while Wolff and Trainor moved into position along side the trailer.

Kaderri surveyed the scene. All was set. He gave the order. "Go."

The teams split and moved into position. Wolff and Trainor moved towards the trailer in a crouch along the wood line and Kaderri and Hughes snuck towards the house.

After only two steps, there was loud noise that rattled the night. Like a car crashing through a storefront window, the door to the trailer slammed open. Out stepped a guard with his AKS slung over his shoulder. He wore a thick wool jacket, heavy boots and a ushanka, the traditional Russian fur hat, pushed low on his head.

The team froze in place and collectively held their breaths. All four brought their weapons up and trained them on the figure standing outside the open door. Index fingers immediately went on the triggers and thumbs flicked off the safeties.

"Hold!" Kaderri whispered harshly.

The guard, bathed in the light from the overhead lamp, descended the three step stairs and fished a cigarette out of his winter coat. He was just about to light it when a shout came from inside the trailer. The guard turned, mumbled something then stepped on the first stair and closed the door. He then walked a few steps away and lit the cigarette.

Kaderri pondered his next move. What to do with the smoking guard? He could wait for the guard to go back inside the trailer and then carry out their original plan or risk shooting him now and attempt to hide the body. Undoubtedly the guard's appearance was most unwelcome but the team could now account for three guards. There was the one in the shack at the end of the driveway, the one smoking and the one who yelled at him from inside the trailer.

"Kilo?" Hughes called. He was the closest to the trailer and had the best shot.

Kaderri made the decision. "Let him go back inside, then we'll move."

"Roger," Hughes answered without question.

Patiently they watched the guard enjoy his cigarette. Nobody had moved from the shadows so there was very little chance they would be spotted. After ten minutes, the guard stomped his feet to fend off the cold and took one last long drag on the cigarette. With great satisfaction, he inhaled it deeply and blew it out his nose. With a flick, the butt went flying.

Just as the guard reached for the door, another call caused the guard to turn towards the front of the house.

The team froze once again as one of the foot patrol guards appeared, this one sporting a heavy trench coat and a close cropped beard. A ushanka sat low on his forehead and he too carried an AKS. The newly arrived guard waved to the one by the trailer and joined up.

"Shit," someone whispered into their mic. "Don't these guys sleep?"

"Hold again," Kaderri said through clenched teeth. Things weren't going as planned. He could deal with one guard and wait out what was going to happen and adjust his plans but the arrival of another guard really limited his options. The team couldn't wait much longer without risking themselves or possibly losing the opportunity to get Borushko.

"Kilo, what are we doing?" Hughes asked urgently. He also knew the options were limited.

Without further thought, Kaderri gave the order. He put the red dot from the sight on the bearded guard "Hotel, you got the smoker."

"Roger that."

"On my call, take 'em out. Whisky, Tango, take down the trailer once the lights go dark, copy?"

"Roger," both Wolff and Trainor acknowledged.

"On your left," Wolff said tapping Kaderri on his shoulder and crouched next to him. Trainor took up his position directly behind Wolff.

"This is Tango," Trainor remembered to use his code name. "I have the door light."

"Roger," Wolff replied.

Everyone was set. Kaderri executed the order. "Now!"

From their crouched positions, Kaderri and Hughes fired their suppresed weapons at the unsuspecting guards. Not knowing if the guards wore body armor under the thick winter coats, Kaderri and Hughes aimed for the head. A short burst from each weapon blew the guards heads apart and dropped them without uttering a sound. The once pure white snow was suddenly stained red. Immediately, they turned and shot out the lights on the corners of the house, leaving only the one light above the trailer door.

But suppressed weapons aren't completely silent. Neither are bullets that shatter glass or pass through human skulls and bore through thinned-skinned metal trailer walls.

Trainor and Wolff sprinted towards the trailer while Hughes checked the bodies, giving them an extra dose of lead. Kaderri positioned himself between the house and trailer, covering Wolff and Trainor as they entered.

Wolff reached for the door. Without warning the door flew open, smashed into him and knocked him backwards in a summersault. Filling the doorway was another guard, the AKS held ready in both hands. His head moved on a swivel and came to rest on Wolff's sprawled body. He quickly brought his weapon up and took aim.

Trainor was quick on the trigger. He leveled his MP5 and fired. The burst slammed the guard in the chest and neck, knocking him backwards through the doorway with a loud crash. But his finger twitched and pulled on the trigger. The AKS discharge resounded like an alarm and the muzzle flash pulsed liked a strobe light.

Trainor reached down to help Wolff up when all of a sudden another guard appeared in the doorway. Without pausing, he bounded over the body of his comrade.

"Tango, get down!" Hughes shouted and fired.

The guard fell in hail of bullets and landed with a heavy thud.

Kaderri sped past Trainor and over the two bodies and raced into the trailer. A quick search revealed there was nobody else inside.

Lights came on inside the house. The element of surprise was lost.

"On me!" Kaderri ordered upon exiting, "Let's move!"

Unexpected automatic gunfire from outside immediately awoke Mikhail Borushko from his needed sleep. At first he thought he was back in Chechnya and nearly reacted as if he was. He caught himself just before he dove out of bed. Realizing he was home, he tossed the bed covers off and strode out of the room. Angry at being woken, Borushko stood at the top of the stairs in his pajamas and tried to focus his alcohol-affected vision. The lights downstairs were on and he saw Karl hurriedly walk past with a pistol in his extended arm. "What the hell was that?" Borushko shouted down the stairs. The idiot who discharged his weapon better have a damn good reason, he huffed. The guards were known to have hunted with their automatic weapons before. If that was the case, someone was in big trouble!

Karl appeared at the bottom of the stairs, looked up and said. "I'm checking on it now."

Borushko believed he had little to worry about in regards of a rival organization trying to kill him or the police arresting him, especially at his rustic dacha. He snorted, turned to get back into bed and sleep off the alcohol. He was sure that whatever was going on, Karl would be able to handle just about any contingency. Then he paused in the hallway. Something just didn't sit right with the situation. He decided to check out things on his own. He got down to the bottom of the stairs and looked out one of the front windows. Not all the lights on the corners of the house were on, illuminating the grounds in a forbidding harsh white light. The left side of the grounds outside the house was dark, threatening.

Karl had moved to the kitchen in the rear of the house and Borushko could make out his footsteps on the hard wood floor. Suddenly there was a loud shatter of glass and sharp thuds, the unmistakable sounds of bullets boring into a wall. Immediately the interior alarm screamed its warning.

Barefoot, Borushko raced to the kitchen to investigate, only to find Karl squirming on the ground among thousands of pieces of glass that were once beautiful French doors. Cold air rushed in and the sight before him sent a chill through his body. Bright red blood covered Karl's face and neck, flowing out of dozens of cuts. He gripped his chest with one hand, trying to stop the blood freely flowing over his spread fingers. With his other hand he was reaching for the pistol that fell out of his grip. A sucking, whistling sound escaped from the holes in his chest every time he breathed. Karl turned his head, his pleading eyes beckoning.

From combat experience, Borushko knew that Karl was not going to survive much longer with a sucking chest wound. He dropped to the floor and crawled towards him, grabbed a fistful of shirt and tried to pull him back from the smashed door. When he looked out where the glass once was, he saw two winter camouflaged figures move onto the patio heading towards the house. Heading towards him!

"Mikhail!" Agranov shouted from the doorway into the kitchen. "What is happening?"

Borushko let go of Karl's shirt, went prone and crawled away from the door. "Get out of here! Get the weapons, we are under attack!"

The lights turned on inside the kitchen was the perfect visual aid Kaderri needed. Resembling a TV screen that was on in a dark room, everything outside the light was cloaked in shadows. Kaderri stood on the patio and kept the stock of the weapon snugly into his shoulder with his finger lightly touching the trigger. The burst he just let loose was true to his aim. The armed man who was inside the kitchen and walking towards the French doors had no idea what hit him.

Immediately upon the glass breaking, the alarm sounded. Its shrill sound was capable of waking the dead. The code Galena gave him to disarm it before they breached was now useless. "Keep going!" Kaderri encouraged and the foursome hustled forward. Silently they moved into single file, the best way to move through a doorway, with Kaderri in the lead.

"I got left," Wolff stated, indicating the direction he was orienting his weapon.

"Right," said Hughes, the next in line.

"I've got the rear," Trainor said lastly.

They stepped onto the patio when another man appeared in the kitchen. The man dropped to his knees and prevented Kaderri from getting a shot off but he thought he recognized who he was. The twitch began in his cheek and his blood boiled. Time stood still for Kaderri. Mikhail Borushko was in sight. The moment was at hand where Kaderri could end it all right then. "There's the fucker!" Kaderri hissed as he prepared to sprint into the house when more movement in the kitchen caught his eye. Borushko, was on his knees with his head and chest close to the ground, suddenly turned away from the door. The movement gave Kaderri a flank shot. Jumping at the brief opportunity, he sighted the scope on Borushko's upper torso and squeezed the trigger. Just as he squeezed the trigger, Borushko dove to the floor and scampered away. The burst of bullets flew inches above him and bored through the far wall. "Damn!" Kaderri cursed his miss and moved into the house.

In half a dozen steps, Kaderri and the team were in the kitchen. Broken glass crunched under their boots and bright red blood smeared the floor and splattered on the bullet ridden wall. The team fanned out, covering the different corners of the room. Kaderri and Wolff took the right, where they saw Borushko disappear. Hughes and Trainor took the left, watching the dining room.

"Eyes open!" Hughes warned above the wailing alarm.

Burned into Kaderri's memory was the map Galena had drawn. The dining room was the only room on the left and that circled around to the front of the house where it opened into a formal living room, just on the other side of the kitchen wall. What Kaderri considered a family room with the fireplace was forward and to the right. He held up his hand and issued instructions. "Hotel, Tango, go left. We'll meet you by the front door."

"Roger," Hughes acknowledged. He signaled to Trainor who was behind him. "On me."

Without looking over his shoulder, Kaderri signaled Wolff to follow. Slowly, step by step they moved forward, eyes peered over their weapons sight and stepped over a dead body as they moved through the house. Kaderri's head was on swivel, his hawk-like eyes searched for movement. Kaderri tensed and silently cursed. The blaring security alarm drowned out any sound in the house.

He cautiously stepped into the small hallway, the front door was straight ahead. Light from the outside overhead bulb seeped through the vertical window that paralleled the door. From his left, Hughes and Trainor should be approaching any minute but a wall to his right that divided the stairway and the room with the fireplace blocked his sight. No lights were on in that part of the house and the heavy drawn drapes blocked the outside security lights. With his right shoulder against the wall, he slowly inched forward, careful not to have the rifle's muzzle protrude past the wall, giving away his position. A combination of adrenaline and heat from his winter clothing caused sweat to form on is forehead.

"Kilo," Hughes called over the MIR. "Room's clear."

"Roger," Kaderri acknowledged.

Out of the corner of his eye, Kaderri watched Hughes and Trainor turn past the wall of the dining room and walk in a crouch through the archway towards him. "Hold," he almost shouted. With the kitchen light to their back, it gave them the perfect silhouette as they moved forward and made for an easy target. "One of you guys kill that light! And put your goggles back on!" Operating in the dark with the Noggs was the preferred method.

Then like a blessing, the alarm went silent and the light in the dining room went off.

All of a sudden a burst from an automatic weapon was fired from the living room and footsteps stomped on the stairs that Kaderri was leaning against.

"Aw, fuck! Not again!" came a yell from the dining room and then return fire spewed back.

Kaderri whirled and fired multiple bursts through the wall where he heard the footsteps. Immediately he was rewarded with a grunt followed by a hard thud. Instantly, he changed magazines and called, "Who's hit?"

"Me, Tango." Trainor groaned then quickly added through clenched teeth, "I'm good. I think."

Concerned, Kaderri asked, "You sure?"

"Yeah," Trainor answered after taking a deep breath. "There's still someone in the living room. That's the bastard who shot me."

Kaderri had to think fast. He didn't know if the guy he shot on the stairs was the same shooter who hit Trainor or if there was someone else. He had no idea how many people were killed compared to the number that was supposed to be in the house. "Do you know where he is?"

"There's a couch in front of the fireplace. He's behind it."

Kaderri moved to peer around the corner. "How do–" a suppressed burst from either Hughes or Trainor cut him off.

Trainor answered the question Kaderri was going to ask. "I just saw him pop his head up like a gopher. I missed."

Kaderri wasn't about to doubt the man. "Listen up," Kaderri addressed the team and readjusted the Noggs. He gazed upon the surroundings in the familiar green ghostly light. He kept his focus on the edge of the wall while he spoke, vigilant against any of Borushko's men making a sudden appearance. "Here's what we'll do. Tango, Hotel, get up here on me. You two plus Whisky charge the couch and take him out. I'll fire up the stairs while you go."

Kaderri heard the muffled footsteps of Trainor and Hughes on the hardwood floor as they approached. Wolff inched past Kaderri and took a knee.

"Did you hear that?" Wolff whispered a warning. "Shh. Someone's talking."

Kaderri pulled the MIR off his ear and strained to listen. He inched closer to the end of the wall, straining to hear what Wolff was talking about. An unnerving quiet stillness filled the house. The darkness seemed to get deeper, threatening to swallow them. Then he heard it.

"Feliks? Feliks? Are you ok?" The voice spoke in Russian.

Kaderri immediately knew that there were two bad guys in the vicinity and one, Feliks, was hurt or dead. He decided to risk a look around the corner of the wall. He kept the MP5 low to the ground and slowly poked his head out. Keeping himself in the shadows as best he could, he tried to look up the stairs without exposing too much of himself. Two stairs up from the floor he could see a bare, bloody, foot. Blood ran over the ankle bone and dripped down the stairs. Moaning came from the body.

Mikhail Borushko and Pyotr Agranov readied themselves in Borushko's upstairs bedroom at the end of the hallway. They shut the lights off and waited for Feliks Grigorenko and Osip Martov to return from their dash downstairs to investigate what was happening and to get more ammunition for the assault rifles.

"Misha, what is going on?" Agranov asked. There was alarm in the way he asked. "Who is doing this? Is Mirovich out to punish you for something?"

Borushko swallowed his fear and tried to grasp the situation. He couldn't think of anyone or any reason who would be attacking his home. After nearly getting killed in the kitchen and abandoning the attempt to drag Karl to safety, Borushko ran to the weapons locker at the foot of the stairs, grabbed the AKS-74U's and then barricaded himself in his upstairs bedroom. At first he asked himself where the guards were to protect him and his friends but then realized that the noise that woke him was their deaths. The one thing he knew for sure, the men that were attacking him were professionals. They displayed discipline and used suppressed weapons. And that scared him.

Intelligence was one of the top items needed to succeed on the battlefield and at the moment, Borushko was completely in the dark. In order to hear what was going on outside his bedroom, the first thing he did was shut off the alarm. He punched the code in the keypad next to the bed and shut off the light. He crouched on the floor and answered Agranov's question. "I don't know, Pyotr. I don't know who is doing this and why."

A burst of automatic weapons fire, answered by the muffled shots of a surpressed weapon, caused him to jump. He heard a groan and a heavy thump on the stairs. Someone was hit. His hands began to shake and his heart pounded in his chest. His gut told him the thump he just heard was the death of one of his friends.

"We can't stay here, Misha, we're sitting ducks." Agranov stated the truth.

"I know, I know!" Borushko agreed angrily. "We have to find out what happened to Osip and Feliks. Let's go, Pyotr."

Borushko loosed the safety on his weapon and reached for the door.

Agranov stood next to him and put his hand on the door, preventing Borushko from opening it. In a reasoned tone, he suggested, "Why don't we try to find out who these men are, what they want? We can ask them from up here and we would have the tactical advantage if they try to come up."

Borushko thought hard about Agranov's suggestion. It couldn't hurt and he did want to know why he was being attacked. The delay would also would allow for any surviving guards to come to the rescue. Maybe he could negotiate with these people for whatever it was they were after. He nodded and opened the door. "Ok, let's try it." He clicked the safety off the AKS in case negotiations failed.

Crouched and ready to leap out from behind the wall as if he were on coiled springs, Kaderri prepared to go. "On three," he instructed. "Ready?"

"We're set."

Kaderri repositioned his weight and fit the MP5 into his shoulder. He took a breath to steady his nerves. "One, two, three!"

Kaderri stepped out past the wall while the other three got on line and advanced towards the couch. In a fluid motion, Kaderri sprayed the body on the stairs with another burst to make sure he wouldn't be a threat and in continuation, fired a few short bursts up the darkened stairs. He fired in short bursts from right to left and put rounds through the stairwell walls and into the hallway. He heard a scream after his last burst.

The other three fired simultaneously at and over the couch, flushing the target out of his hiding spot. Chunks of the foam cushions and wood frame flew in every direction as the bullets shredded the furniture. Suddenly from behind the right side, a man rolled out, rose to his knee and fired a long sustained burst. In the darkness, the man didn't know where the intruders were and fired high, missing his targets and spraying the ceiling.

With a clear target presenting itself through the Noggs, the former special forces troopers and the Albany detective didn't miss. No less than a dozen rounds smashed into the body, blowing away his head and shoulders.

"Bad guy down," Wolff stated, then issued instructions. "Tango, cover. Hotel, go right."

"Roger."

Wolff then swept the left side of the room. "We're clear," Wolff called unemotionally after he reached the other side.

"Find out if that body is Borushko," Kaderri ordered. "I'll check this one." Wolff came over to assist Kaderri and provide cover in the event someone on the top of the stairs tried to shoot down on them. Kaderri grasped the bloody ankle pulled the body down, the head thumped on each step until it came to rest on the floor. Kaderri had Borushko's image burned into his memory and it only took one sweep of the flashlight across his pale, waxy face to determine the guy wasn't him. He said the same. "Negative on Borushko." There was no need to whisper anymore.

"It's hard to tell on this guy," Hughes said after he checked on the body behind the couch. "Not much of his head is left but I don't think it's him. This guy's too short and stocky."

Galena affirmed Borushko had three friends with him and they were all staying upstairs. Counting the bodies littered inside the house, that left two men, including Borushko. With the elimination of the man behind the couch, the downstairs was cleared. The dangerous attempt of attacking upstairs was left.

Kaderri was ready to finish the fight. "Upstairs."

"Pyotr!" Borushko called after his friend fell back onto him and they crashed to the floor. Agranov was leading the way towards the stairs when the bullets began popping through the walls and into him. "Where are you hit?"

"It hurts," he said through clenched teeth. "My right side and leg."

Borushko had his arm draped over Agranov's chest and could feel warm sticky blood flowing freely. "Can you get up?" he asked. "We have to move!"

"I don't know." Agranov attempted to roll off but let out a painful, throaty groan.

The lack of gunfire downstairs bode ill for Borushko's friends. Fear's icy grip took hold of him. The voices he heard wafting up the stairs were alien to him, which compounded his dread. Borushko tossed his weapon aside and began extracting himself from under Agranov's almost dead weight. "C'mon

Pyotr, we don't have time!" Agranov would have to fend for himself.

Borushko and Agranov didn't hear or see the men ascending the stairs.

Kaderri, quiet as a mouse, ascended the stairs with steel nerves and an itchy trigger finger. He paused on the second to last step and peered left around the corner. Three feet away on the floor were two men sprawled and entangled with each other. Even through the Noggs, Kaderri could tell which man was Mikhail Borushko. "Don't move," Kaderri snarled in Russian.

The two men froze in shock at the command. Both stared open mouthed at the faceless, camouflaged clothed figure looming over them with a weapon pointed at their head. Borushko suddenly reached for the weapon he pushed aside.

Kaderri anticipated the move and fired a burst, a round shattering Borushko's hand. He recoiled in pain with a guttural howl, clutching his hand to his chest. "I told you not to move," Kaderri said coldly and loomed over them.

"Who are you?" Borushko demanded, trying to act as if he wasn't frightened.

Wolff and Hughes brushed past, Wolff stepped on one of the wounded men to search the bedrooms down the hall. Trainor turned right at the top of the stairs to search in that direction and watch over the stairs.

Kaderri ignored Borushko's question. "Find a light switch," he spoke in Russian to Wolff and Hughes. He didn't want to tip his hand to his identity just yet.

"Help me," came the hoarse, whispered plea from the wounded man. He was curled up in a fetal position, rocking in pain. The entire right side of his body was stained in blood and it was spreading on the floor.

His pleas were ignored as well.

"I ask again," Borushko said a little less defiantly, the pain from his hand was evident in his voice, "who are you and what do you want?"

"Found a switch," Hughes called out as warning. They didn't want to be looking through the Noggs when the lights came on. "On in three, two, one."

Kaderri flipped the goggles up but kept them on his head. The hallway lights suddenly came on and Kaderri looked upon the blond haired monster who set this whole operation in motion. "Mikhail Borushko," Kaderri said with contempt and kicked Borushko in the stomach, the toe sinking deep into his abdomen.

Borushko forcefully grunted and curled into a ball gasping for air.

Hughes and Wolff stood at the far end of the hallway while Trainor stood guard behind Kaderri at the top of the stairs. "So that's the bastard," Wolff spoke in Russian.

Each man with Kaderri had a reason to hate and take revenge out on the pitiful man lying on the floor in his pajamas but their discipline kept their physical reactions in check. It was their commander's show now.

The grimace on Borushko's face gave away that he was trying to absorb the pain in his hand and abdomen. He worked himself into a sitting position and looked nervously at the heavily armed, camouflaged men with state of the art weapons and gear who surrounded him. His shoulders slumped. "How do you know me?" His eyes narrowed in an attempted show of defiance. "What do you want? Thanks to your shooting, I am no longer a threat to you. Tell me, who are you and your men?"

Kaderri removed his balaclava, hoping Borushko would recognize his features. After a few moments, it was clear Borushko didn't know who he was. Kaderri continued to speak in Russian. "Special Forces Operational Detachment, Alpha Five Twenty Four." He waited to see if Borushko would understand.

Borushko shrugged and shook his head. "What does that mean? I don't know anything about Spetsnaz units. I was in a mechanized brigade."

Kaderri gave a sly smile. "Not Russian special forces." He then spoke in English. "United States Army, motherfucker." With lightning speed, Kaderri pivoted on his left toe, pointed his right knee at Borushko's midsection and whipped his foot in a powerful roundhouse kick. The boot contacted with the ribs that resulted in a loud *crunch*.

Borushko wailed in pain, his eyes bulged and his face went completely white as he doubled over and clutched his broken ribs. "Americans?" he blurted, gasping for breath.

Borushko's wounded friend stirred at the admission and picked his head up to see who it was and groaned again. His face was just as pale but it was hard to tell if it was because of the loss of blood or the revelation that Americans were at the house. One thing was for sure, the wounded man knew who was standing over him.

In Russian, Hughes asked out of curiosity, "Who's your friend?"

Borushko turned to Hughes and then back to his friend. "Pyotr Agranov."

Unexpectedly, Kaderri stepped forward and planted the sole of his boot dead center in Borushko's chest, knocking him backwards and away from Agranov. He was about to feel Kaderri's fury. Borushko was gasping for air when Kaderri leapt on him, grabbed him by the shoulders and effortlessly lifted him off the ground and slammed him into the wall. He held Borushko up by the throat so that he stood on his toes and put his nose inches away from Borushko's. For Trainor's sake, Kaderri kept the conversation in English. "That's right, Americans. Detachment Five Twenty Four, Afghanistan, nineteen eighty-five. That man to your left," Kaderri pointed, "is Jesse Hughes. Name ring a bell?" Spittle flew from Kaderri's mouth.

Borushko squirmed under Kaderri's iron grasp and his eyes grew even wider in recognition of the name. He shifted his eyes to see the man who Kaderri was pointing to. With his good hand, Borushko tried to loosen the grip but all Kaderri did was squeeze tighter, choking off his airway. "Please," he pleaded.

"I'm not done with the introductions." Kaderri gave him another shove into the wall and his voice grew into a deep growl. "The man next to him is Bob Wolff and the man over here," he indicated with is head, "is Gary Trainor." Kaderri bared his teeth and the adrenaline picked up momentum. "These men killed the amateur thugs you sent to America."

Suddenly the front door burst open with a loud crash. Trainor, positioned on top of the stairs, whirled, brought his weapon up and fired a sustained burst. Nonchalantly he ejected the magazine and replaced it with a fresh one. He shrugged. "I guess that was the guy from the guard shack."

"I was wondering when he would show up," Hughes said. "Good shooting."

Borushko was gasping for breath and his eyes were rolling into his head as Kaderri's tight grip closed his windpipe. Borushko tried to say something. "Who..."

Kaderri knew what Borushko was asking. He released his grip and Borushko immediately fell to the floor, gasping for air. With his good hand he rubbed his throat and worked himself into a sitting position against the wall. "Look at me!" Kaderri sneered. Borushko lifted his head and Kaderri thumped his chest. "Look closely!"

Recognition slowly dawned in Borushko's eyes. His face paled. "No...."

Kaderri cut him off. "Me, I'm the guy that you wanted to kill yourself. I," he spoke slowly and deliberately to make sure Borushko knew who he was, "am Marcus Aurelius Kaderri."

Borushko went white and his mouth dropped to his chest. In a raspy voice he stammered, "You! You killed my father! I promised him I would get his killer!"

Kaderri looked upon him with contempt. "Your hatred should be towards the Politburo. They ordered your father on the mission. They knew the risks. He knew the risks. He was doing his job in a war and I was doing mine."

Borushko slumped further down not knowing what to say or do.

"Going after my team was a mistake. It cost you and your friends their lives."

"Please, help," A delirious Agranov cried in Russian. He waved his hand in the air. He was still curled up in the fetal position and the pool of blood under him grew so it covered much of the hallway.

All of a sudden, Wolff stepped forward, pointed the MP5 at Agranov and fired a burst into his chest, killing him. "I helped. Feel better?"

Borushko jumped at Wolff's action and with terror filled eyes stared at Kaderri. He began shaking his head, slowly at first and then more rapidly knowing he was next. "No! Please, no!"

With pitiless eyes, Kaderri stared into Borushko's fear filled ones. These were not the same confident eyes he saw looking through a scope back in Afghanistan. "You murdered my men and tried to murder others and me! You will meet the same fate as your father. The difference is your father died as a soldier in the line of duty and was not a coward. You, you are just going to die as a fucking criminal."

"No!"

The smiling faces of John Evers and Patrick Randall flashed before Kaderri's eyes. Nothing they did in life justified their murder and they were killed because Mikhail Borushko lost his father in a war and wanted revenge. Kaderri felt at ease in his actions. He was returning the payment. Without any more thought, he swiftly put the barrel of the MP5 on

Borushko's heart. In Russian he said, "You lose, zhopa," then pulled the trigger.

Borushko's lifeless body fell to the side, a blood stain streaked down the wall. With his mission accomplished, Kaderri simply turned away and walked down the stairs. "Let's go home."

Saturday, November 22, Moscow, Russia

The sky was still dark when the foursome departed Borushko's dacha. Once they put the Noggs back on, not a single eye was turned to view the carnage that they left and not a single word was spoken as they trudged through the forest back to the GAZ.

On the ride back to Moscow, Wolff drove so Hughes could tend to Trainor's wound. He was hit twice in the left shoulder with one bullet taking a few layers off the top. Hughes cleansed it with some antiseptic and closed it with a butterfly bandage. The other bullet glanced off his vest, leaving a quarter sized bruise. Otherwise, the men remained silent, there was nothing to say. They accomplished what they set out to do and there was nothing more to it.

Sunrise wasn't for another half hour but the sky had lightened and a thin red line grew on the eastern horizon. In the driveway of the safe house next to Galena's car was another GAZ, the same SUV Katrina was in when she met them at the airport.

"Interesting twist," Wolff said upon seeing the vehicle.

"Yep," Kaderri agreed hoping he wouldn't have any issues in getting out of the country.

Wolff parked the GAZ behind the other and shut it down. The men grabbed their gear that had been stowed in the duffle bags and walked into the house. The door was unlocked which put them on edge.

"Good morning, gentlemen," Katrina greeted in English without a smile. She was sitting on the couch next to Galena who had a pissed off look on her tired face. Katrina was wearing a red fleece pullover and black pants. Her leather coat was draped over the arm of the couch.

"Good morning," they parroted. Hughes was the last one in and shut the door.

They all slung their bags and stood still as Trainor took the lead since he was the actual police officer. "What brings you here, Inspector?"

"Detective Trainor, where have you been this early in the morning? The sun hasn't risen yet."

Trainor cleared his throat and spread his hands. "We are working on a case," he reminded her.

She stood, folded her arms and began pacing the floor. The heels of her boots made a steady rhythm with every step. "I received a phone call from a comrade that said there was quite a mess in Romanovo." She made it to one end of the living room and turned, paced back to the group and stopped. Anger etched into her face. She pointed to Galena and drew her lips tight across her teeth. "I had a nice conversation with her, after I untied her from the chair and pipes!"

"Ok." Neither Trainor or anyone else was going to give up information.

Kaderri looked around and found something odd. Katrina was here by herself. He started to think that if they were in some sort of trouble or to be apprehended, the place would be crawling with officers. She wanted something. He kept his thoughts to himself and waited for the two cops to finish.

Katrina threw her hands up. "That is all you can say, 'ok?' I had you men under surveillance since you got here. There are ten bodies at a house in Romanovo and you had one civilian as a hostage! There has to be more than 'ok!'"

Hughes was the first to break the silence. "Yeah, figured that. Your first tail left us about forty kilometers outside of here this morning. Didn't see a second one. He must have been better."

"Some things get messy," Trainor admitted about the bodies. "Like I said, we are working on case."

Kaderri saw the anger flare in Katrina's eyes and was about to ask her what it was she was after when Trainor beat him to it.

"Katrina," he said with a calm voice, "what are you upset about? That Interpol didn't include you on our case? Apparently you believe you know where we were and what happened. In that house were some very bad people." He paused, tilted his head and looked directly at her. "You knew that, didn't you? Something else is pissing you off. What is it?"

Kaderri was about to slap Trainor on the back of his head for revealing where they were but Trainor appeared to know what he was doing.

Katrina crossed her arms then let them drop. "Ah!" She threw her arms back in the air and let out a sigh.

Trainior gave a knowing smile and reached out for her. He put his hands on her shoulders and said, "You were working on a case against them, weren't you?"

"Yes," she nodded dejectedly. Then the anger returned, though not as intense. "For two years I have been trying to bring down those members of the Solntsevskaya and you did it in less than a day! I am grateful that those men are off the streets but...."

Trainor finished her sentence. "I know, you wanted the satisfaction of doing it."

She clapped her hands in one loud smack. "Yes, exactly!"

"Well, it's a big organization and you have Galena here who is full of information. She worked for Borushko."

Katrina eyed the former prisoner and smiled. "That is true."

Relief flowed over Kaderri and seeing things were ok, Hughes and Wolff left to put their gear in the bedrooms.

Kaderri stepped forward. "What is going to happen to Galena?" He was concerned about her welfare. "She gave us a lot of information that was very helpful. Will you protect her?"

"Yes, she will be taken care of," Katrina admitted. "You will be leaving soon?" The question came out as a statement.

"Yes," Kaderri nodded. "We will be leaving tomorrow."

"Fine." Katrina donned up her jacket and turned to Galena, who hadn't moved from the couch. "Come Galena, we're leaving. Detective, gentlemen," she addressed Kaderri and company, "thank you for what you did. I mean that. You achieved what we may not have been able to." She walked towards the door which Wolff held open for her. Before she stepped out she said one last thing, "I will be back with a driver to take you to the airport. I'll be in touch."

Once the door was closed, Kaderri addressed his company. "Well guys, we did it. Everybody good?"

"Good, Boss. Nice to know justice was served." Wolff said.

"Got to agree with that," said Hughes.

Kaderri then turned to Trainor, the guy whose job and oath he swore went against everything they just did. "Gary?"

"I'm good." He rubbed his shoulder "Bastards shot my partner. Can't let that stand." Then he pointed a finger at the other three and became serious. "Every time I deal with you guys I get hurt. This sucks!" His face then broke into a wide grin. "You guys play rough. But damn, you play to win. I like that."

The three men laughed and patted Trainor on the back. "C'mon, Gary, admit it, you like this stuff."

Kaderri gently put his arm around Trainor's shoulder. "Gary, I told you I'd get you back for your wedding!"

Trainor's face beamed then it broke into a wide toothy smile. "Guys, I've been involved in more life and death situations with you than I have ever been with the two police forces I served. I would be honored if you and your wives, or girlfriend," he nodded towards Wolff, "would come to my wedding."

"I'm there," Wolff said first and gave a thumbs up.

"I'll see what I can do," Hughes said. "Thanks."

"Count on me and Sara." Kaderri then clapped his hands. "I got cigars! Who's going to get breakfast and alcohol?"

CHAPTER TWENTY-SEVEN

Monday, November 24, Scotia, New York

The jet plane landed just after ten in the morning at the Schenectady County Airport. The overnight flight piloted by Rusty Doyle and Steve Blackwell went smoothly and Kaderri promised them a bonus, which they refused. They said the short time in Moscow that Kaderri had paid for was a good enough bonus for them.

After Doyle and Blackwell went back into their office, the group gathered for one final time before they headed in their own direction. Wolff was the first to speak. "Jesse's staying with me tonight and heading back to North Carolina tomorrow. We're going out to get drunk, you guys want to join us?"

"Nah," Trainor shook his head. "You guys are dangerous. I'll wind up getting hurt again." Everyone laughed. "I'm going home to my bride-to-be. Can I take a rain check?"

Wolff offered his hand. "Anytime, Gary, anytime. I'm glad you came along."

"Me, too," Hughes said and shook Trainor's hand. "Take care of yourself, Gary. I'll see what I can do about your wedding."

"Great. It'll mean a lot if you can make it." He turned to Kaderri and shook his hand. "Marc, you delivered on everything as promised. I'm sure I'll see you downtown."

Kaderri nodded. "I'm sure."

Without another word, Trainor turned and walked to his car, leaving the three members of SFOD A-524. Men who considered him family.

"Sure you don't want to join us?" Hughes asked with a shrug.

A big part of Kaderri wanted to but he reluctantly declined. "I better get back to Sara and the kids. She's probably worried sick."

"I hear ya. Listen, Boss, thanks for help in my neck of the woods," Hughes said. "Thanks for putting all this together. If you didn't figure this out, Borushko may have succeeded. I am forever grateful."

"Ditto on that one, Bear Hunter," Wolff agreed and tapped Kaderri's arm. "I'll make sure the rest of the team knows what happened."

"Stop. Enough." Kaderri wasn't good at taking compliments. For him, it was just the right thing to do. He was looking out for his men as he always did and always would.

The handshakes immediately turned into heartfelt hugs. "See you soon, Boss." Hughes clapped his friend's and commander's back one more time.

"Talk soon." Wolff and Hughes then turned and headed for the car.

"Hey!" Kaderri called after them, "if you guys need anything, call."

Gary Trainor had spent the entire ride back from the airport thinking about what he just did, the comment Wolff made about him liking it and what he was going to tell Amanda and Joanne. Dealing with Joanne would be easy. He would tell her nothing since she wasn't involved in any aspect of the operation. What she didn't know wouldn't hurt her and he didn't want to put her in between the proverbial rock and a hard place. On the flip side, she was his partner and she had every right to know that her partner had gone to all lengths to protect and back her up. He finally decided to cross that bridge if and when he got there.

Dealing with Amanda was completely different. She knew he was going overseas with Kaderri and Wolff to do some unpleasant business. Because of the Black Warrior incident, she knew of their history and the reason why he sought out their help to take the racist militants down. Honesty, he thought. He would have to be honest with her. He was just scared that she wouldn't be there when he got home, despite the assurances she gave before he left.

Nervously, Trainor pulled into the garage and was instantly relieved when he saw her car in the other stall. "Thank, God," he exhaled. He pressed the button too close the garage door and immediately the kitchen door flew open.

Amanda stood there wearing sweats with tears flowing down her cheeks and her hands covering her nose and mouth.

Trainor felt his heart flutter as he got out. The second he stepped past the door, Amanda leapt into his arms and wrapped herself tightly around him. "Oh, Gary!" she shook in his arms. "I'm so happy you are home!" She sobbed and sniffed and hugged him even tighter.

The hugging caused a stab of pain in his shoulder. "Hey, honey," he whispered in her ear and held her almost as tight as she held him. "I love you." He used his hip to close the door and carried her up the stairs into the kitchen. "Can I put you down?" He didn't want to and hoped she would say no.

"No." She gripped him tighter.

"Ok, how about a kiss?"

Before he could finish, her lips locked onto his. She had to cut the kiss short because of her stuffed nose. She finally lowered herself down, wiped her tear strewn cheeks and asked, "Are you ok?"

"Yeah, got a little scratch, that's all."

Her eyes went wide and she looked him up and down, searching for evidence of the injury. "You're hurt?"

Trainor didn't want to tell her at this moment that he was shot again. That would wait for later. "Hey," he deflected her thoughts, "the good guys won."

She leapt back into his arms on the news. "That's great! Tonight we have to celebrate your homecoming!" She held on to both his hands. "Shall we go out to eat or do you want me to cook?"

Trainor became overwhelmed by her outpouring of love and affection. At that moment he knew she was there to stay. It reaffirmed what he always knew, Amanda was the woman he wanted to spend the rest of his life with. "Amanda, before I decide on that there's two things."

"Sure, honey. What are they?" She wiped the joyful tears from her cheeks.

"First, I invited six more people to the wedding, is that going to be a problem?"

"The guys you were just with? No problem at all."

"Second, can we suspend the no nookie rule?"

Amanda's face was so bright it could light up a city. "That's a no brainer. We'll suspend it immediately." As she pulled him towards the living room, he quickly read the note on the counter that said for him to call Paul McKnight about a possible job.

Marcus Kaderri called the house to give Sara a heads up that he was on his way home but the answering machine picked up and he didn't want to leave a message. He thought about calling her cell phone but not knowing where she was he knew she would drop everything to get home. That could get her, the kids or someone in her way, hurt.

When he pulled into the garage, he was glad to see all the vehicles they owned were parked in their spots. Quietly he walked into the kitchen and didn't see or hear anybody. He turned into the den to put his luggage down and some of his gear away. When he turned back towards the door to bring his dirty clothes to the laundry room, Sara was standing there, tears in her eyes, arms folded across her chest and biting her bottom lip.

Kaderri's heart leapt into his throat and he dropped the bag. "Hey, babe." He held out his arms for her. "I'm home. Just like I promised."

Sara briskly walked straight into them and wrapped her arms around his broad chest. "I knew you would."

He held onto her tight, sniffed her hair and felt her love flow into him. For him, that was the greatest feeling in the world. The love of his life wrapped within his arms. "Love you, babe."

She squeezed him tighter. "I love you too." Sara pulled her head back and looked up into his eyes. She personally knew the men that went along with her husband on his journey. They risked their lives for her in the past and she was concerned about their well being. "How's everybody?"

Kaderri smiled. "We all came back ok." He took her face in his hands and looked deeply into her eyes. "The threat has been taken care of."

"Daddy!" Sean yelled from the door and sprinted towards him. Right behind him was Sam.

Kaderri crouched down to catch them both in his outstretched arms. One at a time they slammed into him and he effortlessly scooped them up. He brought each one to the side of his neck and kissed them on their heads. He moved so Sara could get into a group hug and she wrapped her arms around the entire family This, he thought, was the greatest feeling in the world and there was nothing that was ever going to keep him from it.

Made in the USA
Columbia, SC
05 May 2022